This Island, This Life

David Sahatdjian

In loving memory of my mother and father

"Take off the mask. *Off,* I said."
—Anonymous

Chapter 1

I will sleep the sleep of the just, Johan thinks, as he dozes off, having consumed his brown bag lunch of hummus, pita bread, and a juicy navel orange. Such a delicious snooze it is, leaning back in his state-of-the-art orthopedic desk chair, so powerful and deep that when he is awakened, it is almost as if in stages that he comes to, full consciousness not entirely certain.

"Are you here, Johan? Are you among the living?" The hand shaking his shoulder. The teasing voice. The sour face of that HR woman, Jeanine Juddster. Standing with her a woman of considerable girth.

"How may I help you? Is my assistance being requested?" he says, still groggy and struggling for his bearings. "In need of some edits? Has your series comma gone missing?"

"Sleeping on the job is not a good way to make an impression on your new boss, Johan," Jeanine Juddster says.

"I am on full alert for the action that is required of me. I am here to get the job done."

"Exactly," Jeanine says. Turning, she says, "Lurleen Lulabella, I would like you to meet Johan Manootdjian, senior editor in the publishing department. Well, one of them, anyway."

The woman's face is flushed. Beads of sweat have appeared above her upper lip and her smile is too intense for the occasion. Johan notes the ballooning black skirt that falls to her ankles and those flat shoes her weight compels her to wear.

"Well, that name of yours. You must be some kind of foreigner," says Lurleen. *Fur*eigner. The first syllable sounding like an animal's pelt.

Lots of people stumble over his last name. He has only to remember back to the first day of grade school, and how he would hear laughter from the other kids as the teacher paused in going down the roster and visibly struggled with his name. How easily Billy Baines had sailed through, and Johnny Jones, and Jill Johnson, and all the rest.

Lurleen's Southern accent suggests she may be suffering a kind of culture shock in multicultural New York City. And he might have made some concession to the reality of the country in which he was born by shortening his name instead of holding onto his father's Old World identity. As for her weight, there are many "large ladies" at the org, as his previous boss, Miss Carmelli (never Ms.) noted. Never mind that. She is some visitation from his past, with the musty smell of the church of his childhood upon her. Some disturbing resemblance to his mother there.

Before he can respond, and as if she is thinking along with him, she says, "Are we having a come to Jesus moment here?" Lurleen spreads her legs, leans back, and simply lets rip. What words can a person apply to such a sound? Unbridled? Freight train loud? An image comes to him of a trumpet player blasting notes from his instrument skyward. Laughter that shakes the entire department, the force of it like a detonation sufficient to rattle windows. In its volume and in its depth, it is laughter that is making a statement: *I am a force of nature that can sweep over you at any time. I am the flood no walls can stop. I am here and I am powerful and no matter what you throw at me, I will trump it all with this triumphant, mocking sound.*

Even Jeanine Juddster looks startled and finds herself staring at Lurleen Lulabella with newfound curiosity, as if trying to figure out who the org has brought in as its most recent hire.

"Well, yes," Jeanine says, which is enough to release an aftershock of laughter.

A woman peers in at Johan some minutes later, after the two have gone.

"Are we having fun?" Fiona Beasley asks. The timing of her rhetorical question and her raised eyebrows leave no doubt as to the identity of "we."

"Seems like someone was having a lot of fun," he says.

"Let's hope that she can write and edit better than she dresses," Fiona says.

While Fiona is formidably intelligent—she has the kind of mind that allows her to do her own taxes effortlessly—and has a grasp of the organization few others possess, she is not herself a good editor, which are the skills you might hope for in someone employed in her capacity. She is responsible for the org newsletter, and when she leaves, she may be remembered as the editor of an unread monthly, a description, Johan realizes, that could easily apply to all of them who labor in the publications department. But then, what is an editor if not someone who places a premium on hiding, a person who, despite his protestations that everything in him screams for recognition, at depth, where such decisions are made, chooses to go faceless in the world. Someone who positions the front of the cereal box to face the wall and does the same with all the products in his apartment. A person who, as he wanders the streets of New York City, looks up at the buildings and imagines himself concealed in their remotest spaces.

Besides, no great value should be or is placed on those who can spell and on good terms with the rules of grammar. Of this Johan is quite sure. Generally, they are the skills of those who cannot master anything else. Sad cases of arrested development who cannot grow beyond those junior high school years. The kid who could get *nauseous* right in Miss Thornbill's seventh grade spelling bee but later struggled to solve a quadratic equation and approached the biology lab with horror—such was he.

"I see you got your ears lowered."

"Yes," he says.

"Looks nice," she says.

"Thank you."

Fiona lives alone with her cat. She rushes home after work to watch *Law and Order,* stopping on the way at the salad bar of the Korean deli in Astoria, Queens. She is locked in a longstanding battle with her landlord, who wants to evict her from her rent-controlled apartment. Johan suspects she is socking away a lot of money. She is invested in the market and has a financial adviser, a professional counselor he doesn't associate with people in their salary range.

Occasionally, they have clashed, and he has heard of her battles with others. She can be nice, as now, with her engaging smile, and she can be ferocious. It is the latter that gives him the sense of a thwarted sexual drive informing those bursts of fury. He only knows her as a woman alone, seeking to be perfect for the org, but surely there have been lovers. In her mid-fifties now, she retains her youthful figure: long, thin, beautiful legs and, when she wears a tight blouse or sweater, breasts that his eyes cannot resist.

I see you got your ears lowered. He hears her words as an invitation. It is the excited way she speaks them. She is a woman who misses, even longs for, the human touch. He understands. It is something he misses as well. But in spite of how well she takes care of herself, there are other things he notices as well— the skin pallor and her imperfect teeth and those gaping nostrils. And, yes, her temperament.

"You never know what the cat will drag in," Fiona says.

"You certainly don't," Johan agrees.

"Our new savior."

He hears the heavy org cynicism in Fiona's voice, that for the first six months Lurleen Lulabella will be part of the solution; thereafter, she will be part of the problem.

Fiona leaves. There is nothing more to say, certainly not about their new boss. Like himself, Fiona Beasley is a longtime member of the org. In fact she has been here longer than any other member of the department.

His is a cubicle you can pretty much cover in five or six steps. When people stop by they often note how neat his desk is. He is not one for having papers strewn about or piled high. Disarray makes him unhappy, and worse. It causes a kind of discomfort that won't let him rest. If into chaos he was born, it is from chaos he must emerge; clutter must be dispensed with so he can approach the tasks before him one at a time and give to each the full attention, care, and even love that it warrants with a mind at ease in the knowledge that the order he seeks within has its correspondence in the material world. He now knows no other way to live than to strive to do the things in front of him and to be where his feet are.

Chapter 2

"I want to know only one thing. Are you listening, people?" Lurleen Lulabella has called the staff into the resource room, where they are now seated around the conference table. She sits at the head of it, her small, chafed hands resting on the polished wood.

"We're listening. At least I am," says Mary Terezzi, one of the several senior editors in the department.

"We're all ears," Blanche Givenchy says, cupping hers.

"You, Blanche, with the ears, go to the newsprint on the easel," Lurleen commands.

And so Blanche does.

"Now write the following: F as in Frank, U as in universal, N as in nutty."

Blanche writes the letters with a black magic marker.

"Fun. F-U-N. That's what I want us to be about. If you're not having fun here in this department, then there's the door. And if you are, then welcome aboard. And do any of you care to tell us why fun is the essential element in the health of a department? How about you, Johan? You look like you haven't had a good laugh in years. Would it crack your face to even smile?"

"I don't know. It's been a while, as you say."

"That is the starting point for reclamation. *I don't know.* On that basis are lives salvaged and rebuilt. Now I will leave our shattered friend Johan to recompose himself and move on. How about you, Fiona? Can we put you at the service of doing something more than making faces at me? You have a look of institutional weariness about you that we are going to change so it shines with a fervor for the mission."

"Excuse me?" Fiona says, visibly seeking to process all that Lurleen has hit her with.

"Now you look affronted, but that don't move me none, as we say down home in Mobile. Don't nobody be messing with Alabama. The Crimson Tide's coming for you and at you. Now Fiona, we need to galvanize you into action. Roll, Tide, roll."

In fact, Fiona does look affronted, as if she were a model of dignity whose face had been treated to a mudpie.

"I don't know what to say," she says, the trace of haughtiness in her voice supported by an attitude of rigid superiority as she straightens her spine.

"Well, think of something. We're expecting bright ideas from you."

"I don't normally associate fun with the workplace. It's not a day at the beach, after all. It's a place to get work done," Fiona goes on.

But Lurleen has moved on, leaving Fiona's rebuttal out there to die unacknowledged. "Since you are all having such a hard time, I will tell you. Blanche, back to the drawing board. Got your magic marker ready?"

"Yep."

"All right. After 'Fun' write an equal sign and then this: O as in only, N as in Nancy, E as in Edwina. Now what do we have?"

"Fun = One?" Blanche says.

"*Yes.* Fun = One. Can someone tell me why?"

"For myself, I would be more comfortable with Fun in the Sun = One. But I think I know what you mean. The team that plays together stays together. Is that what you are getting at?" Johan says.

"You are, fundamentally, a dull man, Johan, but I will call you my shining star for now."

Then it is for the others to witness what Jeanine Juddster and Fiona Beasley and Johan already have, the laugh-a-thon that follows, bringing tears to Lurleen's eyes, until her shuddering body comes to rest and she can finally speak.

"Do not mess with the belle of Birmingham. Let me say that again." And she does.

His shock at Lurleen's resemblance to his mother and her confrontational style aside, Johan in those first few months seems to flourish in her regime. As much as he had come to love and respect Miss Carmelli, she had imposed some hardships on the staff. Had weeks not gone by with no work to speak of? It wasn't that projects hadn't been coming into the department. It was simply that work was Miss Carmelli's sustenance more than food. Her plate was piled high, while her staff often suffered through times of meager fare. Lurleen, on the other hand, heaps large portions on his plate, and these added responsibilities are in noticeable contrast with those lean years under Miss Carmelli when, in order to protect himself, he had learned to cultivate an attitude of indifference. What had it mattered if his desk was empty? He was really a writer anyway. Why not be grateful for the opportunity to give time to his creative pursuits? But along with that line of thinking, there had been sadness, an image coming to him of his father, who spoke five languages, standing in a suit and tie and wingtip shoes behind a gleaming silver cash register in a midtown restaurant earning less than some of the customers paid for their dinner and drinks. Had he, Johan, not overdressed for his job as well, buying suits and spiffy sports jackets and ties that would add a splash of color so he could spend a day sitting in a cubicle whiling away the hours? Had he not imagined the horror should his now ex-wife, Isabel, witness his sinecure: the numerous trips to the cafeteria for tea, reading the dictionary, dozing off in his swivel chair? There can be no question about it. The projects that now come to him provide a surprising sense of nourishment. For the first time, he feels he has a real job that requires effort.

But this matter of Lurleen's laughter is a mysterious thing. To Johan's ears, it can seem like an expression of unfettered wildness. Alone in the universe, and with only God as her mate, she is the incarnation of a new, hard to define, spirit at loose in the land. It might be the man in from the wilderness in a lumberjack shirt standing at the bottom of the escalator in Grand Central Station handing out religious tracts to rush-hour commuters, an Ozarks incongruity in the belly of Gotham with his wild gray hair and untended to face and bad backwoods teeth. Or maybe it is those Westerns enjoying a revival on TV, in which coarse white men punch each other in the mouth in barroom brawls and shoot each other, like those lead-slingers when Johan was a child in the nineteen fifties and early nineteen sixties gorging on *Gunsmoke* and *Paladin* and *Rawhide*. Some attempt to turn back the clock going on?

Chapter 3

Isabel,

The streets of New York City are generally longer on the east-west axis than north-south. Do you suppose it was intentional? That last side street I walk between the Avenue of the Americas and Fifth Avenue to reach the org is surely one of the longest, and while I mean to commit all the shops to memory, as I have those on my childhood block, the necessary power of retention is not there. It may be that the street has a sadness to it that even the morning sun so glorious in its ascent cannot lift from the mind's perception of perpetual shadow. The sidewalk is of cramped, ungenerous width, and leaves one impatient with those ahead, the dog-in-the-manger types who, having seized the lead, then sadistically dawdle for no other purpose than to hold you back. It is an unfortunate fact that one of the disfiguring wounds of childhood still persists, my mother calling me away from the TV set to run an errand, not only depriving me of the remainder of *Gunsmoke* or *Paladin* or *Hawaii-Five-O* (do you remember Kookie, Kookie, lend me your comb?) or Peter Gunn (what crazy-making theme music, that, how it made you want to jump up and run in ten different directions at once) but, having placed me under her command, further disrupting my evening by taking her sweet time in writing out the items on a torn piece of brown bag paper. It was here that the chant "You're stalling me, quit stalling me," had its genesis, a display of foot-stomping fury that would elicit only a chuckle from her and a reaction that lives on today in me should I encounter a slow-moving bozo on our pedestrian pathways.

Isabel, I mention my mother apropos our new leader, Lurleen Lulabella, who reeks of Jesus and the old rugged cross and the Blood of the Lamb and all the rest. Another minute with her and she would have been singing "Blessed Assurance" and speaking in tongues. She would fit in, I am sure, at that tabernacle where I spent so much of my first thirteen years with my mother. We will see.

Chapter 4

He is in a hotel room in Buffalo, New York. He needs the time away from the mass of recovering alcoholics who have converged on this city and taken over the hotel for a weekend of conferences and panel discussions and meetings and more meetings. It is all good, but he has a private self as well he has to nurture. Yes, RoR—Rooms of Recovery—has saved his life. A miracle has occurred. He will not die a sot's death, one day at a time. Nearby he hears the whistle of trains, a mournful but comforting sound, calling him to the adventure of faraway places.

When he phones home for messages, there is a beep, beep on his answering machine. Yes, a fish is on the line. Two, in fact. He can hope that at least one call is from a beautiful woman; there have been a number he has expressed a so far unreciprocated interest in. But the first is a telemarketer expressing some surprise that Johan hasn't yet responded to the great debt consolidation offer he has previously made. It is the voice of the great American huckster seeking to use whatever resources available short of mugging or burglary to tap into a person's wallet. A caller singularly predatory in his intent.

The other comes as a surprise. "Hello, Johan. It's me, Luke. Your brother. Me and Kelly and the kids are back in New York. I thought I'd give you a call…"

Your brother.

"Things are bad down there. We've got this nice trailer home, but there are no jobs. You know what I mean? Service industry stuff. Wal-Mart. The 7-11."

Luke is talking about central Florida, where he has been with his wife Kelly and their two kids since…since when? Since their mother died. Before their mother died, actually. Johan couldn't get hold of him. No one could.

"Well, it's good you're back. We've missed you." *We.* It sounds better than *I* somehow, less intimate, though what *we*? His sisters, Hannah and Leah. The two who are still alive.

"Yeah, I figured I'd come up here and get a good-paying job. You know I got my college degree. Right?"

"That's great." How should he know what his brother got or didn't get since he dropped off the map years ago?

"Magna cum laude I graduated. Some of my professors said I wrote the best papers they ever read."

Something in his voice. Anger. Old anger. The same voice Johan heard all those years ago down at the old St. George Hotel in Brooklyn, where Hannah had taken them swimming after Friday Bible school. "The world's largest indoor swimming pool," the hotel had claimed. Cannon-balling off the high diving board. Johan stayed in the chlorinated water till his lips turned blue and his body was covered with goose bumps. Luke poking his head in the shower stall where Johan had retreated under a stream of water. Luke saying, "You're all skin and bones. I could break you in half with one hand tied behind my back. And mine is twice the size of yours." That tone. As if Johan has something that Luke wants only he can't say what it is.

"I'm glad for you." Johan doesn't ask how, with two kids and Kelly's disability, Luke was able to go through four years of college. It's not his business.

"Are you still working at that women's place."

"It's not a women's place."

"What's it called again?"

"GoAN. Girls of America Now."

"It must be psychological or something. All those women in our family. You need to be around men more. Too much female energy weakens you."

"It's OK. They treat me well."

"How's your wife? What's her name again?"

"Isabel."

"Things good between you?"

"We're doing fine. We're close."

"What do you mean, you're close? That's how husbands and wives are supposed to be."

"We're not husband and wife. We're friends."

"Friends?"

"We got a divorce."

"That's too bad. She had real quality. I can spot those things in a woman right away."

Even after all these years how quickly things revert to form. His brother crowding him, pushing in, going where he doesn't belong. But Johan doesn't say to him, You're back a day and already you're weighing in on my job, my marriage? Where do you get the right? He says, "I'll see you soon. Bring the kids."

"Yeah. I'll do that. I'll show you what a real family looks like," Luke says.

Isabel,

I didn't ask for this, but just because I didn't doesn't mean I will run from it. I am not my brother's keeper but maybe I can help. Still, if this is a homecoming, then why is it I am not rejoicing? There is a weight my brother brings with him, a rolling mass of unmanageability that threatens to crush me. Forever it has been this way, and now it is back again. Oh, Isabel, that I have you in my life as my shining star and can come to you for understanding.

Here in this hotel the halls are exploding with gratitude and a spirit of oneness. The lame walk, the blind see, and the drunks are sober. I need refuge from this bliss. Sometimes I need refuge from everything. Do you understand? Oh, I need not ask. I need not.

Chapter 5

The kids are pencil-thin, attractive, but Luke has to be a hundred pounds overweight, the Pillsbury dough boy in middle age. Astonishingly, he shows not the least self-consciousness about his condition and the children seem not to notice either. He's come back here to die, Johan thinks. What else can he think that a fifty-four-year-old man should let himself go so badly? Does Luke not know that trim is in if he is interested at all in longevity? The dire warnings of health professionals about obesity and high cholesterol have half the city lapping Manhattan in jogging suits and eating nonfat yogurt. But then, Luke hasn't been living in health-conscious Manhattan. Luke has been sitting in a baking-hot trailer down in central Florida.

With dismay Johan watches as Luke lowers himself into an armchair, a process that is carried out in slow, deliberate stages, like a man lowering himself into a challengingly hot bath.

Although his oldest sister, Hannah, lives little more than a mile north of Johan, he hasn't invited her. Nor has he suggested that Leah, his youngest sister, come down from Westchester, where she is living with her family. They can make their own plans. His sisters have had years of bonding with each other. Now is an opportunity for him to connect, or reconnect, with his brother.

Johan is not a great host. He has not cooked a meal or baked a cake. All he has for them are nuts and popcorn and fruit juice he has bought on sale at OrganicOnly. They are in July now, and the sun is pouring through the western-exposure windows, showing the plant-enlivened apartment in the most flattering light. Katie and James stare at him a lot. Their looks are friendly, curious. That is something to hold onto.

Apart from his weight, there is something else about his brother. It is his demeanor. He is not as he was on the phone. There is a sense of vacancy, of being only half there, and a strange equilibrium. Johan sees something of himself as he had once been in that dark, messy stretch of years when he relied on tranquilizers and speed as well as alcohol to face the world.

On the far west side of Manhattan, with the Hudson River and the palisades of New Jersey just beyond, is Riverside Park, a narrow refuge of trees and grass and beautifully laid out footpaths. It is a park that called to Johan and Luke when they were young. It is there they went to explore the railroad tracks that ran through the tunnel set below the park's surface.

The sun is kind; it does not scorch them with brutal July heat. Slow afoot, Luke shows no awareness that they are moving along at a crawl. Joggers and cyclists in bright Spandex zip past, young people with firm, trim bodies and blue-chip degrees and high-paying jobs. In the clear light Luke's fallen face and sallow skin and gray hair serve as an unwelcome mirror that only a sibling can provide. Could Johan possibly look to others as Luke does to him? Has he been fooling himself as to his own appearance? After all, Luke isn't ten years older than Johan but only two.

As they approach the river, they pass, to their left, a semicircular window with vertical bars in the high stone wall, beyond which is the railroad tunnel. Some years ago there had been a sprawling freight yard down below Seventy-second Street. A residential development now occupies much of that waterfront space, and the Amtrak trains that roar through the tunnel carry passengers, not cargo. The past tugs at him. The tunnel is the place of hiding from all that he does not understand and fears, a state of mind as much or even more than a physical space. It is a place where isolation can be king and power can be real and tangible, the felt power of a train briefly illuminating the darkness it has entered as it rumbles past. The tunnel is for men whose fathers have been absent from their lives. He wants to be there, alone and hidden. He does not want this complexity he has entered into in the bright light of day.

The city is experiencing a growth spurt. The blight of the previous decade has been erased. You do not see whitewash on the windows of stores that have gone belly up. The real estate market is no longer falling through the floor. A spit shine is on the city and the formerly desolate area of the rotunda above the boat basin offers a small example of the entrepreneurial overdrive now current. On its tiled surface dining tables and a bar have been set up, and the strong smell of charcoal-burned meat fills the air.

James and Katie have good appetites. They order hamburgers and french fries and shakes. They are still at an age when they can eat with impunity. Not so with Johan, which is why he orders a veggie burger.

Is it an act of faith and courage to eat at a restaurant or café, particularly one such as this, located at the river's edge, or folly fueled by sheer denial? Johan has seen the water rats of New York City along the banks of the Hudson, rats as big as cats. Who is to say that, come nightfall, these filthy creatures do not gorge on the leftovers of the fare now being served? And are there not hygiene-challenged humans about? Look at the waiter. Just look at him, a creature with rings through his ears and a bigger one through his nose and God knows where else and his crazy gelled hair shaped like a rhino's tusk and his ghostly white flesh and red eyes and deranged senses. He has probably been on a cocaine and alcohol run for days and now, here he is staggering around with trays of food and drink trying to rein in his delirium. Can fastidiousness prevail in an environment such as this? These are not dedicated young restaurant professionals. These are from the I-am-going-to be-famous-someday tribe, the slash brigade of waiters/actors, cooks/poets, etc.

Should he not have lifted a finger to prepare something for his brother and the kids back at the apartment beyond the tray of assorted nuts he had set out? Johan thinks of the kitchen stove and the oven he has never turned on. It is not fit for use until it has been given a cleaning, but he cannot bear the thought of applying elbow grease to someone else's years old grime.

He seldom has company, let alone entertains. He has grown used to living alone and being alone. Some years back, during a marital separation, Johan had briefly seen a woman who lived in a rented house in Westchester. He remembers that it was a rental because the woman made such an issue of the fact that she was not the homeowner she had been before her divorce (*"He left. He just left."*) The copper cookware that hung in the kitchen was covered with dust, and on the counter were a stack of napkins with the name of the fast-food giant Wendy's on them. The image of her sitting alone night after night with a greasy bag of burgers was somehow repellent and antithetical in Johan's mind to forming the ties that bind. To be appalled by his own humanity is a problem that he recognizes, and yet he seems powerless at times to do anything about it.

"So. It must be a big adjustment for you, moving to a new state and having to start at a new school in the fall," Johan says to James, who has ravenously devoured his burger and is now scooping out the last of the coleslaw from the small wax container. James is tall and gangly, as his father had been, and has the same acne problem that had caused Luke such grief as a teenager. Johan remembers those green bottles of Phisohex, and the milky-white lotion they contained with which Luke, to no avail, washed his face three times a day.

Luke speaks for his son. "James hates it up here. All his friends are down in Florida."

"Come on, Dad. I didn't say I hate it. I just…"

"He has a girlfriend down there. He misses her. I know how that is."

Johan knows how that is, too. Like the time back when Luke was in tenth grade and Johan woke to see him sprawled and moaning on the floor of their room, a cap-less and emptied aspirin bottle nearby. Such was the power of Nancy Becker manifesting in his life. Luke had discovered her back in ninth grade. He had seen her potential and claimed her for his own and when she didn't want him a year later, he didn't want his own life. There on the floor with his Elvis hair. Their father thought it just another stunt and resented the disturbance of his quiet time in the dining room with their mother, who was beside herself. "Are you crazy, you foolish boy?" she cried, while kneeling over Luke, before dispatching Johan to call for an ambulance. Luke lived through women as their father lived through women and as Johan had learned to live through women.

The force field of women. The power of women. The thing you don't have in yourself to be with them in the right way that makes you go to the trains and devote the days of your life to watching them rumble past, at least in your mind.

Luke got back with Nancy Becker after his failed attempt to take his life. His need for her was too strong and all-encompassing. He and Nancy Becker would come down to this same area of the park. There was no outdoor café back then. Untainted by commerce, it was just the small plaza with the fountain and the arcade and the view of the marina and the expensive yachts. Luke associated this period of his life with the song "Blue Moon," as sung by the Marcels, and what it was to have a love of one's own and then lose that love and be left with ceaseless longing and regret that turned the moon blue in all its phases.

"How about you, Katie? Are you liking it up here in New York?" Johan sees himself as he imagines Katie does, a clumsy, overeager older man stiffly trying to connect with the younger generation and failing miserably.

"It's all right. There was nothing great going on down there. Not for me, anyway. And it was hot, real hot." Her voice husky, passionate. It has love and caring in it. She puts stuff into her words. Her mind is alive.

A trailer, somewhere in central Florida. It sounds desolate and dull, a place for those with hard-scrabble lives.

"There are people with college degrees pumping gas. That's why we're up here." Luke isn't looking at Johan when he repeats what he said on the phone. It is as if he is addressing himself to the air or the universe. And yet Johan feels what his brother has just said is tinged with reproach. Johan has things.

"That must be rough." Johan hears himself trying to sound empathetic.

"We got by," Luke says.

Johan doesn't so much communicate with Luke as bounce off him. Is he on some sort of mood regulator drug? So low-key, so subdued, that medication seems a plausible explanation.

Those boats down in the marina. He doesn't envy people who live on the water. You pay out a lot of money for a yacht and then the thing owns you. An encumbrance. That's what it is. Like marriage and family life, maybe. And you're restricted in your movements. You have to think about every step you take. A real logistical operation.

Johan turns to James. "Are you into sports? How about hoops?" James is tall and thin. It seems reasonable to think he might like basketball.

"James is a computer whiz. He's a complete genius. He knows programming and everything. He taught himself, too. That's where he spends all his free time," Luke says.

"Is that true?" Johan asks James.

"I do OK with the computer. It's what really interests me. I'm not too much for team sports." He has the voice of modesty, as an instinctive counterweight to his father's boastfulness.

"How about you, Katie? What do you like?"

"I really want to be an actress. That's all I think about." She has the voice. Johan expects Luke to testify to her ability, as he had about James, but he doesn't. Luke's silence doesn't mean a whole lot, except that while Katie might be the apple of his eye, it is somehow plain that Luke is invested in his son scholastically.

The sun is toward the palisades when the waiter, with a trembling hand, sets down the check. A noticeable silence falls as Johan removes a credit card from his wallet. He senses the children's eyes upon him and then the blue plastic card he places on top of the check, as if some moment of truth has arrived. Right there, on the table, is what he has and his brother doesn't have. For some reason he feels the silence most from Katie. Is he reading something into her emotions, or does she seem ashamed? In any case, Johan has his own feelings to deal with, feelings of fear and anger and sadness, triggered by his concern, not new, that Luke has returned to New York City to leave him with all that he has wrought.

He walks with them out of the park and watches as they slowly descend into the subway, imagining their long ride back to the Bronx and the different trains they will have to catch. Though he waits, they don't turn back to wave.

He returns to the park, drawn to the river's edge. There, on the horizon, over on the New Jersey side, a smog-induced sunset of brilliant purple and orange. Lovers out for a stroll. Parents with their young children. The river exerting its natural sedative power. Then he walks some more. Soon he comes to the railroad tunnel they had earlier passed. He rests his face against the bars and imagines himself on the other side, in the tunnel itself, as if, in that moment, seeking the darkness like a drunk seeks a drink, some oblivion agent that his mind is not providing. Something violating, shocking, unbearably cruel, about that scene at the river café. Putting down that plastic on the table like that, his brother emasculated in front of his own children. Not right. Not right at all. He should die for having caused such an event to happen. But the feeling doesn't hold. This is no place for him to be. Beyond those bars is a place of sterility and crushing loneliness. Seeing, for the moment anyway, that the past is not so much a place to go into, as if one could, but to emerge from.

Chapter 6

He wanders the floor. Women mostly. The occasional male. Faces turned to the computer screen. An electronic hearth, as powerfully transfixing as logs burning in a fireplace. The other departments on the floor, most of them, are areas of activity he gives little thought to. There is something called Interactive, so au courant it doesn't even require a noun for its identity, and to which he attributes the intent, threatening to his mind, of migrating everything from print to cyberspace. Technicians really, space explorers unafraid to break the mold and going on and on about platforms and whatever. He has a sense it is a crew that regards him as an antediluvian print editor. But even in that electronic world literacy is required, he tries to reassure himself, and so maybe the future holds a place for him as well as these cutting-edge souls. And there is something called Communications, which 'interfaces" with the org's internal and external audience by way of a blizzard of media releases and media blasts and some such. And there is Audiovisuals and something called Brand Marketing, a team working diligently to replace the image the general public has of GoAN as a passé org. He feels a rush of judgment as he strolls past. *Propaganda blather bunch, dedicated to the proposition that a falsehood can replace the truth.* He hears this harshness within himself and sighs, seeking a necessary correction. How hard it is to truly belong and to align oneself with the purpose of the org. This contrariness. This inward pull toward less than full cooperation. Is it ego or an instinct for survival?

As he loops the floor he comes to Graphics, the one department on the floor with which he has a strong affinity through the magic of their Macs. He sends the designers Word files and they return him flowed pages. And it is an affinity that is increased by the presence of Gwen Mazely, who leaves her desk and walks with him down the hall, saying in an urgent whisper, "I need to talk with you. Do you have a minute?"

"Sure I do," he says. Both of them look reflexively into Lurleen's corner office as they pass by. Seated at her catty-corner desk, she is ready to meet their glances with an unsmiling stare, as if she had been expecting this unwelcome alliance.

"Lurleen frightens me," Gwen says, continuing to whisper. They are in his cubicle now, and she has pulled her chair close to his. His eyes are drawn to the red barrette in her brown hair and the red bracelet she wears on one thin wrist, as they are to the assortment of rings—even one on her wedding finger--as if to confuse those, like him, who are helpless in her presence as to her status.

"Frightens you?" Johan says, experiencing tightness in his chest, several months of a working relationship with her having given rise in him to the foolish notion that someday there might develop a mutual interest.

"She's critical of the cover designs for the last two resources. She wants revisions that are uncalled for, as I see it."

"And what do you say to her?"

"I try to explain my decisions. I mention complementary colors and the like. But—"

"But what?"

"I think she has a plan."

"A plan?" He is whispering now too.

"Whatever it is, I'm afraid I'm not in it."

"Well, let's see what happens," Johan says, trying to put a face on things.

"Unfortunately, I see exactly what is happening," Gwen replies, resignation in her voice.

The hours pass, and Johan is ready to leave, having stayed well beyond his normal departure time of 6 p.m. At the far end of the hall, a light burns, and Lurleen stands, in its soft glow, her coat over her arm, like an actor spotlighted on the stage. Against his will he is drawn toward her.

"Are you working late?"

"I have some business to attend to," she says firmly, her laugh-prone nature well in check.

Over the top of the bullpen divider he peers, and there is Gwen, leaning into the computer screen as her hands manipulate the keyboard.

"You need to finish up quickly," Lurleen says, addressing herself to Gwen.

"Trying," she says, a hint of annoyance in her one-word reply.

"Is there something I can help with?" Johan asks.

"No. You have yourself a good night now," Lurleen says, dismissing him as much with her emphatic tone as with her words.

There is something ruthlessly intimidating about Lurleen, and predatory. She has cornered her quarry and wants now to finish her off in privacy. He feels her focused fury, even as he slips past her toward Gwen, saying, "How you doing in here?"

"I just learned this is my last day."

But Lurleen interrupts. "Johan, I must ask you not to distract her. She has been instructed to clean up her files. Human Resources has a policy firmly in place that I must see her to the door. She cannot leave unescorted."

"I'll escort her out. I'm in no great rush. It will give me a chance to say goodbye. She is a friend of mine."

Visibly angry, Lurleen steps away.

"She thinks I'm going to make off with the company's property. Like I'm going to walk out the door with a laptop under my skirt."

"When did all this happen?"

"Two hours ago. She called me into her office and told me my services would no longer be needed."

"Did she give you a reason?"

"She said the organization would be going in a different direction."

Gwen is a long-term temp, one of a number the org has come to rely upon. Such an arrangement spares the org the expense of offering the worker a benefits package, including health coverage, and often has the consequence of creating an expectation in the temp that the org will someday "marry" her or him. Additionally, the presence of such a worker can create a subtle tension between the temp and full-time staff. The temp feels envy of the staff person's security, such as it is, while the staff person feels insecurity in sensing that the temp wants her or his job. Johan sees them as petitioners in unsettling numbers flocking to the palace gate. They are a reminder to him that outside those gates life can be hard.

Not that such feelings come into play with Gwen. She is a graphic artist, not a word person. No rivalry there. All he feels about her now is a frenzy of desire: to touch her face, to kiss her lips, to hold her slender body against his.

"A different direction? Gee. What could that be? From bad to worse?"

"Yep," Gwen says, shutting down her machine. As she bends down for her bag, her tight blouse rises up and he sees the wide wing-like tip of a tattoo above the glorious butt her skirt conceals. The tramp stamp, he has heard it harshly called.

"Can I help? Here, let me carry that," he says. The small box contains her philodendron, some books, other personal belongings.

As the elevator lowers toward the main floor, he says, "Well, look, maybe we can stay in touch," even as he feels the moment getting away from him, the spell of intimacy wrought by a shared office life dissolving now that it is over. His words, neutral and bland as they may appear, still lay bare his interest.

"Sure. Shoot me an e-mail."

The door opens, and she speeds forward over the faux marble floors. He struggles to keep up, her box in his hands, unable to tell her that he doesn't have her personal e-mail address. Beyond the bank of elevators, she turns left. The lights have been turned low. A young man with impossibly short hair and that facial stubble the young favor is standing by the concierge desk, on the other side of which the sleepy night attendant sits. The young man is electric in a ribbed short sleeve body-clinging shirt worn outside the equally tight designer jeans in vogue with his generation. Some sort of statement it is that they are out there, unadorned, unencumbered, in collar-less shirts. Gwen rushes into his arms. Some preposterously long squeeze.

"This box yours, babe?" the young man says, eyeing the small load Johan has been carting after they have eased apart. That terse, monosyllabic conversation they affect. Anal in their dispositions, with some complex code of interaction that keeps them together and him apart.

"Yeah."

"All set. We're out of here," he says, relieving Johan of the box without bothering to address him and heading with Gwen toward the exit on the south side of the building. Halfway there Gwen turns and holds up her hand and raises and lowers her fingers several times. Her goodbye wave, accompanied by a little smile that says, Sorry, so sorry I couldn't save you from your life, you deluded old fool.

Dear God,
Is it in the normal order of things for the cleaver to strike bone with authority? I have seen butcher blocks. In my childhood there was one at which Manny the butcher in his white apron wielded just such an instrument in separating the pork chops one from the other.

I too have been struck with authority, cleaved clean of her. I ask for your circle of love and feel it coming, a peace entering me following this separation that has been wrought. I have been brought back to my true place. Oh, God, you are that place, that home, and have always been had I the capacity to listen. Teach me to love, dear God. Just teach me to love. Let me seek to approach the truth by putting a name to things. I resent Gwen. I feel she made a fool of me. I feel she played me, to use the odious word spoken by psychopaths and those heirs of Jacob who champion cunning and wiliness, as if they were virtues. This affects my pride and my self-esteem. My part? I go where I don't belong across generational lines. I am irresistibly attracted to the young. My mistake was in misinterpreting Gwen's connection with me. Only your providence, I am afraid, can save me from such further humiliations. But you must not think that I hate the young or even envy them. In a real sense, it is a great relief, beyond the initial pain, to have Gwen close the door on me so firmly in running into the arms of her young Mr. Studley. It is a reminder to me that I am entering a different phase of my life in which I can no longer live in the domain of the body but must, if I am not to lose everything, cultivate the life of the spirit. An attitude of detachment is called for that I am not always capable of, but I will be content with a small measure of progress and accepting of these seeming setbacks. I will pray for Gwen and her trim beau that they have love and joy and peace and happiness and all good things. And dear God, I will do it more than once. Walls built with the mortar of judgment must come down. Only your love can dissolve them. We are all one, I hear you saying. Oh, there is work to do to have the memory of you fully restored but I am on the path.

Chapter 7

He is not entirely without ambition in the job world. Or if he is, there were some at the org who nudged him toward higher ground, saying he owed it to himself to apply for the director's position when it fell vacant. And the more he thought about it, the more the idea grew on him. Galvanized into action, he updated his résumé and sent it, along with copies of his previous three performance reviews, to Jeanine Juddster.

A sense about Ms. Juddster, based on numerous small exchanges through the years, is that a tendency toward unfriendliness is part of her makeup. And there is that startling and preposterous plaque displayed prominently on her desk: "God Does Not Make Junk." Johan is all in favor of affirmations, and draws on them himself to get through the day ("In this moment I have everything I need. In this moment I am being taken care of. In this moment I simply am.") but is Ms. Juddster thinking clearly in confronting job applicants with such a blunt and yet ambiguous pronouncement? After all, who ever claimed that God did make junk? Or is there a qualifying, if unspoken, addendum: "God Does Not Make Junk, But You Sure Could Fool Me, Given the Number of Chuckleheads Who Enter My Office." And Johan does have reason to believe the latter might be more in line with Ms. Juddster's thinking when she says, holding his résumé with two fingers as if it were an exceedingly smelly fish, "Why are you even bothering? You're not qualified. You're simply not qualified. You need executive experience for this position. You need business experience," putting a few z's into the b-word for emphasis. The full weight of institutional weariness and cynicism with which she lands on him is an affront that leaves him momentarily speechless, until he can find the presence of mind to say, "Please don't speak to me this way."

"Speak to you in what way? I'm simply laying out the facts and trying to save you and the organization some time. That's all." But the smile as she speaks her wounding words suggests time management is not her only consideration and that she is someone for whom inducing pain is a supreme pleasure. "Look, you want an interview? I'll get you an interview. How's that?" Ms. Juddster continues, as if he is a whiny child who has taxed her to her very limit.

"I look forward to it. Thank you," he says.

He is not a young man. He has come to the org at age thirty-seven, and now it is many years later. The velvet prison, some call the eight floors the org owns in this recently built office tower. He has traded challenge for security. He has coasted. These things he understands, as he also understands that it is an org with an inferiority complex, no matter how much preening it does with its position statement, "The premier leadership experience in the world for girls." Essentially, it is an org that says, "If you're desperate enough to come to us in the first place, that is all the proof we need of your worthlessness."

The vice president of marketing, Selena Crackner, interviews him some days later. She is a woman big in size and big in gifts. Her financial acumen has brought her to the top of the merchandising department, which has temporary responsibility for the Publications Department on the ever-shifting org bubble chart. She is a woman he knows only enough to say hello to in passing. There are people he shouldn't come too close to, and she is one of them. And yet he is kind and respectful in his attitude toward her. He finds his voice to say a few things about the department he has been a part of for all those years and how it might better meet the challenges of the future. Selena listens attentively as part of the perfunctory exercise, thanks him for his "thoughtfulness," and the following week Lurleen Lulabella is standing at the entrance to his cubicle.

Jeanine Juddster is not done with him.

"Johan, I would like you to meet Margo Breeder Fullsley, the new director of Graphics. Johan is one of the editors."

"Pleased to meet you," Margo says.

"Welcome aboard," Johan says. Margo's carefully made up face breaks into a friendly smile. A woman as well groomed as Lurleen is unkempt. Like Lurleen, a large and middle-aged woman.

"Johan has been in that cubicle forever. He's a man who knows his place. Don't you, Johan?" Jeanine says.

"So you say," he replies.

"Well, nice to meet you," Margo says, sensing friction, and they move on.

If Jeanine Juddster has her slogan, "God does not make junk," he has one that he can utilize, too, "What other people think of me is none of my business," however long it may take to kick in.

As the days pass, Johan sees Lurleen's logic in hounding Gwen from the office in favor of Margo Breeder-Fullsley. Her tread is soon easily recognizable, a padding sound of her floppy shoes on the carpeted floors as she slowly makes her way to Lurleen's office. And there is that baby-voiced patter. "Knock, knock. Do you have time for itty-bitty me?" Lurleen has brought on board a lackey she can completely trust and dominate, and is well within her rights to choose her own staff, though such obsequiousness is painful to witness.

And Fiona Beasley and Blanche Givenchy notice too, as does Mary Terezzi, the other senior editors.

"Lurleen is a complete embarrassment. She will be a wrecking ball on this department, I fear," Fiona says.

"Why do you say so?" Johan asks.

"Why? She has no publishing experience and keeps on her desk a big book on bookmaking and design to try to familiarize herself with the production process. From what I can gather, she has a background in marketing. And that toady she brought in."

"I agree. It's like hiring a fire captain to head the police department," Blanche says, in her pleasingly husky voice. She has been loved by many men, and is eager for the love of more. Blanche is a woman of unusual ability, the only truly top-flight editor in the department, by Johan's reckoning. But she is also burdened with a manic-depressive illness and the medications that have become a way of life for her have dulled some of her natural vivacity and sharpness.

Of all of them, Blanche is the one he most has a feeling of love for, or if not love, at least care and concern. She is something of a female hound, using and disposing of lovers. In spite of this voraciousness, the consuming mode in which she lives her life, a flame of purity burns within her, a standard of excellence she applies to her work, obsessively wrestling and torturing manuscripts into shape. Mad scrawls and query tags on every page. This relentless drive for perfection is what Miss Carmelli recognized. She saw a kindred soul.

Johan sees the sun when he sees Blanche Givenchy, even if it is a waning sun.

"We'll just have to wait and see. Lurleen has the power," Mary Terezzi says. Johan hears a note of chastisement in her realistic appraisal, as if she might be saying, "Get a grip, people. Get a grip." Johan feels a manic surge of his own, some delirium mounting, a need to relate events to what he knows from times gone by.

"Yes," he says. "Mary is right. Power. And no one to run against her. Does anyone remember that campaign ditty? 'Whistle while you work. Stevenson's a jerk. Eisenhower's got the power. Whistle while you work.'"

"Johan, are you on something?" Blanche Givenchy asks.

"Only herbal tea. It doesn't take me up and it doesn't take me down." Words do arrive in his consciousness that do not always fit the occasion.

Fiona goes on. "Lurleen may suffer from a touch of paranoia. She let Gwen Mazely go because Gwen spoke with Gladys, the receptionist on this floor. Gladys is outgoing. She talks to everyone. Lurleen doesn't want any of us in Publications or Graphics discussing what goes on in the department with others in the building."

"Weird," Blanche says.

"Let's see how this thing develops and if there is a storyline here," Mary Terezzi says.

"The storyline is already here," Fiona says.

Johan talks to Gladys Goswald all the time. Rather, he communicates in passing with Gladys, who has the strange power to make him perform. Her smile beams through him as she says, "Well, good morning, Johan. How are we doing today? Are we doing just fine?"

"Fine and more than fine, Gladys. We are sailing along smooth and strong. Right dandy are we today."

"That's good, Johan. That's so good," Gladys says, her laughter following him past the reception desk.

Whatever the subtext is he doesn't quite know, and seeks out Blanche for some understanding. "Tell me what you make of it," Johan says. "I'd really like to hear. What is this strange power Gladys has to compel me to do a glide along the dreary stretches of the eleventh floor, as if I were Fred Astaire dancing to her very sound?"

"Oh, it may just be some kind of mating call. It may be she is calling you into her kitchen," Blanche says.

"No. That can't be. It's some form of cool jazz, a way of skating on a complex and possibly dangerous surface. She is from the South. She knows the ways of white folks."

Blanche stares at him. Her eyes have the film of dullness that afflicts those on certain medications.

"You and I have a history," Blanche says, seeking to give their conversation a new direction.

"Yes," he says.

"We have to see where it will lead us."

"Yes." Thinking, it won't be into any kitchen.

Restless, he goes down the hall and seeks out Mary Terezzi. "Can you sing me America's theme song?"

"What would that be?"

"'Why Must I Be a Teenager in Love.' Dion and the Belmonts."

"That's everyone's theme song?"

"In Peter Pan America it is."

"And I would know it?"

"You are Brooklyn-born, even if now you live in Queens. You have the right stuff for this song. Of this I am sure."

Mary Terezzi is obliging. She gives her hair a flip and in a sweet, fragile voice sings about each night asking the stars above why it is she must be a teenager in love.

"Yes. Oh yes," he says, leaving Mary Terezzi and the song right where he wants them, on some dark Brooklyn street circa 1959.

Chapter 8

"Children, children. We are one with each other but apart from the rest. We must gird for battle. We must deal with the dawdlers. We must eradicate the institutional mentality and for it substitute the for-profit spirit that is the engine of success. The time of torpor is over."

Call it Lurleen's mission statement or call it her need to speechify, but she can do more than talk. The changes in Graphics are followed by a change in Publications. The temporary nameplate identifies the new face as Nanette Nobling, a woman with an air of confidence and self-possession. It is for Johan to extend himself, as she makes no overtures. More significantly, Lurleen doesn't introduce Nanette to him or the rest of the staff either. This breach of protocol adds to his sense that she is here on a hostile mission, or at least one hostile to his interests.   He can smell a rival, and perhaps it is to Nanette's credit that she is cool and no friendlier than the situation warrants. Where is it written that the executioner should be amicable toward her or his intended victim?

Though he may affect a cavalier attitude toward the org at times, it is no small matter when he sees someone with the org he has worked with in the past now heading for Nanette's cubicle instead.

"What's up with this? I thought I'd be working with you. I asked specifically to work with you in fact," Rita O'Rourke, a program specialist, whispers, entering his cube after seeing that Nanette has stepped away. Rita laments that she has been directed to this new person. The projects are the org's flagship publications, handbooks for girls and guides for leaders that the org will depend on for a significant portion of its income stream.

"I've been put out to pasture. What can I say?"

"Come on, Johan. You're a good editor."

A graduate of Dartmouth College, Rita O'Rourke is a talented writer who expresses herself effortlessly on paper. She is also a long distance runner entered in marathons all up and down the East Coast, and can be expected to be seen wrapped in a silver foil cape after completing the one in New York City in November.

"I'm so sorry to have kept you waiting. Come into my office," Nanette says, on her return. Rita gives Johan a sad, what-can-she-do look before following after Nanette.

As if he is right there with them in the adjoining cubicle, he hears every word. "I think we have to move this forward…we need to strengthen the opening…we are looking for a little more verve in the language on this particular page…I tried to restructure this chapter somewhat. Thought we would lead with this activity rather than the one about nature trails…"

He has work of his own to do, the little jobs that come to him: reviewing and editing a proposal written by the property management folks upstairs, a data analysis report by the marketing people, a media release the communications director has asked him to work on. He turns to those tasks, telling himself that humility is a desirable quality, and that he has a long way to go before he gets there, but that this incident can help him along the path. Anyway, what does it have to do with him if Lurleen Lulabella wants to bring in someone new and give her the choice assignments? He has been a little man before, and he can be a little man again, living day by day in the recognition that he is completely expendable.

Some hours later, approaching Lurleen's office, he braces himself, as a laugh-a-thon is going on. Unfortunately, there is no alternate route. He heads past without looking in, but Lurleen has positioned her desk so that, when she is seated, she can see the human traffic passing by. "Hey, there, Johan, come on in. We want to have a word with you."

"Just one?" he says, going no farther than the door and seeing that Margo Breeder-Fullsley and Nanette are occupying the only other chairs. His response triggers another laugh storm from Lurleen, who does seem to know how to give herself a good time.

Emboldened by the company of her new staff members, she says, "Johan is too much, just too much. Did I tell you that when HR brought me down to meet the Publications team, we came to Johan's cubicle and there he was asleep in his chair? Oh, Lordy." And she is off once again on another jag. "Jeanine had to shake him by the shoulder. He came to looking like he didn't know where he was." There are tears in her eyes as she tells the story. "We've got a big job turning around this ship of state, let me tell you. We've got to get you revved up for the mission. Wouldn't you say so, old Johan?"

"Oh, I'm revved up all right, but I'm not sure it's about the mission," Johan says.

Now some serious laugh blasts are coming from Lurleen. Her eyes are tearing. She's in a state. When she calms down sufficient to speak, she says, "We're going to get you with the program, old Johan. That's what we're going to do."

"Thank you." For some reason no peals of laughter follow him down the hallway. Perhaps it is that he has stepped over the line into mockery. Alone in the elevator as it plunges toward the main floor, he leans his head against one of its walls. "Oh, God," he says. "Oh, God."

The next day Lurleen calls him into her office.

"I thought it would be good if we had an old-fashioned sit-down."

"What's so old-fashioned about a sit-down? A sit-down is a sit-down."

"I like it when you are on your toes, doing your editorial thing. What do you call it, querying and striking?"

Johan looked at her blankly.

"Well, never mind. I've called you in because I want to get you up and running. You see, Johan, we need everything we write to be forward-looking and positive. That long face of yours suggests you're a negative type, and that is not very American. It's not what we're looking for. Have you ever heard the song about accenting the positive and eliminating the negative?"

It would not do to tell her the word is *accentuating*. He has enough to worry about with his own blunders.

"Here is the thing. I want us to be proactive. Let's not say, 'In the month of February many program activities were delivered by all the councils.' Let's say instead, 'In February the councils delivered many program activities.' I don't ever again want to see passivity and defeatism lying there on the page. That's why I'm here, so I can impart to all of you a vision for the future. Do you share my vision?"

"You want us to use the active tense in all our copy?" Johan says, trying to stay out of her vision thing.

"Strength. Vigor. Vigilance. That is my motto. Do you share my excitement over this significant change? Do you share with me the goal of turning around the ship of state? Are you one with me that in the beginning there was the word?"

"Which question would you like me to answer first?"

Lurleen Lulabella throws back her head and lets rip .

Isabel,

We are in a presidential election year, and it does occur to me that an ill wind is blowing throughout the land. I was in Norway a while back when I read in the *International Herald Tribune* that the vile Kenneth Starr delivered his impeachment tome to the United

States Congress. There was in me a sense of helpless outrage. Naïve as it may be to apply such a word to politics, the document and the systematic harassment of Clinton seemed to me to be an act of stunning unkindness, not only to him but to the country as a whole. The essence of the drive to oust Bill Clinton from the White House for his peccadillo was the Right's conviction that they had a permanent claim to the Oval Office and were justified in removing the interloper by any means necessary. Those same people are driving the Bush candidacy, you can be sure. As you may recall, I have an intimate relationship with the Republican Party. The presidency is a matter I have had my mind on since childhood. I was born looking up, as all children are: at my parents, at God, at that man in the Oval Office. If anarchy was not to be upon the land, it would be necessary for the Republicans to remain in charge. So was I led to believe by all the powers, seen and unseen, who worked to influence my mind. But that time is long ago. The letter of commendation I received from Dwight David Eisenhower for helping him defeat Adlai Stevenson has long since been lost, and I have moved beyond the ranting of Pastor Horvath at the Pentecostal tabernacle, who branded John F. Kennedy the antichrist. Something is afoot in this country. There are those who do not mean us well. And now Lurleen Lulabella is here in New York City and at the org. My question to you is this: Is our little department a microcosm of something that is playing out on the national stage, a force diabolical, and am I being called upon to engage in the unfolding drama so as to affect its outcome?

Chapter 9

Luke and his family are living far up in the Bronx, a long ride on the number 6 train. They had arrived back in the city without first having secured an apartment, Luke evidently thinking that things would somehow work out. Sharon, the niece of Luke's wife Kelly, has given them the upper floor of the two family home. Without her, they might have wound up in a shelter. Luke has no job and Kelly is unable to work. She has a severe disability owing to a brain aneurysm. Kelly's monthly disability check keeps the family afloat. It unsettles Johan to think about his brother and the precarious circumstances in which he and his family live. It also angers him. Since they were quite young, Johan has been inclined to worry for his older brother. But the children fill him with hope. They are bright and attractive. And so Johan calls to ask if he might have them for an afternoon that weekend.

"Can I trust you with them? It's a responsibility. You've never been a parent."

"Hey."

"A biological parent, I mean. You're not a breeder."

"Stop with this stuff."

"Just kidding around with you. You've always been a little too sensitive, you know. A little too much clinging to mommy."

"Right. Of course."

"That's why you work at that girls' organization. You need to be with men more."

"I'm with men enough."

"You see. There you go. Being sensitive again when all I'm doing is kidding with you."

Luke moving beyond monosyllables and terseness and Johan wishing he had remained there.

Johan arranges a date with Katie and James for a Saturday afternoon in July. He is not in competition with his brother for their love; it is, rather, his love he wishes to win through his interaction with them. But it is also this: while Johan claims no prophetic powers, for many years he has sensed that his brother would multiply upon the earth and then go away before his time.

In dressing for the occasion, it occurs to Johan that he has put on the same clothes that James and Katie had probably seen him in the last time—a green and white checked "tablecloth" shirt, white chinos, running shoes, and a blue blazer with a torn lining. This lack of variation would only be a depressing repetition. As he dresses so he lives and eats: narrowness of style and experience and palate. Meditation. Some writing. A bit of housecleaning. Perhaps a walk in the park if the weather is good. Perhaps a visit to one of the city museums on the pass that got him in free and then a trip to OrganicOnly for dinner items and some provisions for the next day. Katie and James. They are his variation, his reprieve from the sameness of his Saturdays.

On the way out the door to meet them he checks his wallet. Money. It is always a consideration. Around the corner, on Amsterdam Avenue, old men sit outside the bodega on folding chairs. There is the clacking of dominos as they set them down on the table. Johan gives a wide berth to a leashed and sour-looking pit bull with a studded collar around its thick neck. A more pacific scene, the menacing dog notwithstanding, than the old days, when some crackhead would wave a machete at the morning sky, scaring even the police.

Observant Jews stream from a synagogue as he walks east along Eighty-sixth Street, banked by tall, well-maintained apartment buildings. The men wear ties and white shirts and dark suits. Some in those big hats. The women and girls in black dresses. Traditions to bind as well as to liberate them. Johan feels admiration but also a touch of envy for their embrace of tradition and their rootedness in their own history. So many milling about that he has to step out into the street to get past. A sense of being displaced in more ways than one by their disciplined orthodoxy. Remembering Krishnamurti about the championing of ethnicity being insufferable, or was it William Buckley? A statement that wouldn't apply here. On the corner of Columbus Avenue, a big and welcoming Starbucks, laptop users behind the dark windows oblivious to the sun in its blaze of glory.

It is a day for walking, even with the suddenly darkening sky. He cuts cross-town through the park rather than take the bus now speeding through the transverse on its eastward route. One of those jumbo tandem buses with the accordion coupling. On the sweep of lawn inside the park's entrance, a father lobs underhand tosses of a whiffle ball to his young son, who crouches with his plastic bat cocked. Riveted, Johan takes a seat at the end of a bench, a bat and a ball still having the power to bring him to full attention. When the boy misses the first two pitches, Johan grows anxious. Something in him screaming for contact. The boy doesn't disappoint, sending the third pitch on a line past his father's reach, and now Johan can go on his way.

Joggers are doing their laps around the reservoir, but not in such numbers that he would impede them on the running path. Some carry portable CDs, the music streaming through their headsets driving them forward. Others have small portable radios strapped to their upper arms. In clinging Spandex and looser, less confining shorts they run. For the most part they are young, some with the names of their colleges or universities on their T-shirts or shorts. If Johan's generation was lemmings to the sea, as the *Times* editorialized, this generation is hell-bent on self-preservation, placing a premium on education and fitness and getting ahead. The heavy and the plain he turns from, while the beautiful hold him in a merciless thrall, like the tall, thin blonde in the powder blue T-shirt and black shorts cruising past him on her long, tan legs as the goddess she must know she is, her ponytail swishing.

Down a slope of tangled growth a bridle path parallels the jogging path. The private vehicles of cops are parked by the far side of it. Beyond is a low-slung brick building with a tiled roof and bars on its windows, part of a police compound. Several hours he spent in this compound one summer day in his sixteenth year. His friend Sean's older brother had been driving an unregistered car. Sean given to violence, sometimes directed against him. To touch on those years was to touch on failure—the low board score in math, the clear dawning that he was not among the chosen.

A bridge, perhaps as old as the park itself, spans the bridle path below. The bridge is a gathering place for the joggers. Buoyed by a sense of their own accomplishment in lapping the reservoir, some more than a few times, they can now unwind with long stretches, the railing serving as a support for their legs. Their bodies glisten with sweat. The blond jogger is among them, bent forward with both hands around the ankle of her raised and straightened left leg. She looks neither right nor left, but keeps her attention on the task at hand. After holding the position for a couple of minutes, she does the same with the other leg.

She turns and spots Johan and instantly looks angry, hateful. What is it about the eyes that they can record in an instant everything there is a need to know? Johan had assumed she is part of a group, or has a boyfriend waiting behind the next tree, but on completing her ritual, she walks off alone, crossing the road closed to weekend traffic and heading toward Fifth Avenue down the path at the north end of the Metropolitan Museum. In spite of the withering stare she has cast him, he follows behind. The thing has a momentum of its own. Isn't that, after all, the function of a woman, to ultimately scorn, humiliate, dismiss the man? Isn't that what the two genders exist for?

As he catches up with her, she visibly flinches. Seeing the tension he has caused, he hands her his card, but she makes no effort to take it. "I probably have no business even speaking to you from across generational lines. I am a lifelong New Yorker. It is here that I will live and die…" he begins, expecting he doesn't know what, a slap to the face perhaps. Instead she begins to laugh. It causes her to buckle and bend at the waist. Is that what the expression "You crack me up" is supposed to convey?

"Is something funny?" Her extreme response seems to beg the question.

Slowly she finds her bearings and wipes the laugh tears from her face.

"Nothing. Nothing is funny," she snaps, all traces of amusement now having vanished. His hand still holds the proffered card, which she snatches and sticks in the elastic band of her running shorts, as close to her he is ever to get, he is sure.

Above the crack of thunder and a great flash of lightning. "If you don't care to share my umbrella, can I give it to you? It's a three dollar street deal."

"You've given me enough," she says, leaving it to him to interpret her words.

Within a minute the downpour begins. Looking back, he sees that she has adopted a slow pace, as if to mock the elements and their drenching power. She is surely among the chosen, with parents who love her and whom she easily calls mom and dad. There is an older brother and a younger sister with whom she will remain on good terms for the rest of her life. She has excellent board scores and a Seven Sisters college to burnish her résumé. There are friends, and many of them. There is no room for the likes of him, and why should there be? The authoritative crack of thunder and a great flash of lightning prod him back into motion. He raises his three-dollar umbrella for protection as the downpour begins and hurries toward the exit.

On a clear summer day Fifth Avenue is orderly: the stands of trees are neatly trimmed, the buildings have the shine of wealth, the museums along this strip of culture—from the circular and modern Guggenheim to the stately Met— show their enduring strength, and the young children in the playground are sparkling little emblems of their parents' prosperity. But on this Saturday an assaulting rain strikes the streets and sidewalks like an unending hail of silver bullets. The rain does not have to be an unpleasant visitor, not for someone with an umbrella. But that is not the scene Johan witnesses. Staring in dismay at the drenched foursome, huddled under a tree with their hair plastered to their scalps, he focuses on his drenched brother and hears his naked cry, saying, *yes I have come here to die, yes I am defenseless, see and feel the weight that I am here to place upon you.* It isn't simply that the sight of them standing so passively makes clear their inability to cope with everyday life. Again, it is that Luke looks so old. Does every mirror lie to me? Johan can only wonder. Has he too been ravaged by time, as his brother has?

"You didn't bring umbrellas?" he asks, unable to keep a tone of reproach out of his voice. "We don't *have* umbrellas," Katie says, more as a retort than a response.

"We don't mind the rain. It's hot. The sun will dry us off," Luke says. "Kelly and I are going to take a walk in the park and eventually wind up down at Times Square. Have ourselves a couple of hot dogs and maybe see a movie. Right, Kelly?"

"I'm sorry we're burdening you, Johan," Kelly says. She speaks fast, her words a blur. "But Katie fainted just as she was getting on the bus, and so we had to ride in with her."

"Ma—"

"Sorry. You know how kids are. Everything's big for them."

"Ma, please."

The jogger passes them there on Museum Mile, takes in the scene at a glance and turns away. At least she hasn't pulled his card from her waistband and torn it into pieces and dropped them at his feet. Probably tossed it already.

Saturday night. You can't hide from the reality of your life on this particular night. The pain of your aloneness has a way of finding you. Couples holding hands, college girls with their studleys walking arm in arm all along Broadway or sitting in restaurants with linen-covered tablecloths and having intimate conversations, the promise of sex at the bottom of the menu. How exposed this one night of the week leaves him feeling, the world seeing his isolation and the sheer poverty of his life that he has no one in it. Like he is in a trap he can't get out of.

And yet some newness has come into his day. Katie and James provided it, even though the afternoon got off to a rocky start. *Spiderman,* an early dinner at a popular eatery nearby, where James and Katie again devoured jumbo hamburgers and equally huge portions of French fries. Johan grew more comfortable with the long silences. Didn't try to make small talk. Just let the two of them be. And then he took them over to Third Avenue, where they caught the express bus back to the Bronx. Sure, they just flew onto the bus without giving him a hug, but what is that? Kids have their own world.

Saturday night always surprises him with the intensity of the longing it can still summon. During the day he is all right, as if protected by the light. But after leaving James and Katie he is alone with nowhere to go. Time to get off the streets so he will not be conspicuous in that aloneness.

At OrganicOnly, his organic foods resource, a man is standing at the salad bar. He picks at the offerings as if he is creating a work of art, not a thrown-together dinner. He has steel wool hair and his worn jeans are baggy in the seat.

"Am I in your way?" The man holds a full load of dripping hijiki in metal tongs and deposits the load in a carton. Sam, a neighbor from the floor below.

"Take your time," Johan says.

"You're sure you're not in a hurry?"

"No."

"I see you rushing around during the week, so I'm surprised you're not rushing around on a Saturday night, too. Guess you want to relax after a hard week, huh?"

"Right. Something like that," Johan says.

"How old are you anyway? I'd guess we're about the same age, right?"

"I don't know. Maybe."

"What do you mean, maybe? You don't know? I'm fifty-four. I'd say you look the same."

"That sounds about right."

"What do you mean, about right? What? Your age is some sort of state secret? Let me tell you. The reason guys our age don't like to reveal their age is that they're afraid they're not going to get any young pussy. We're hoping to fool all the young pussy out there that we're younger than we are. Am I right?" A screw loose in Sam, Johan suspects.

"I don't know if you're right," Johan says, looking around and fearing others will hear Sam's crudeness and associate him with it.

"Let me tell you. Unless you're rich or famous, you're not getting any young pussy. All you're getting is X-rated movies for the rest of your life. If you're lucky, they won't find you dead of a stroke on your bed in the act of masturbating to *Debbie Does Dallas* on your TV screen. You know what I mean? You may want to keep your porn stash at a minimum. Like every year, as you get older, thin out your inventory. You don't want people to find you with all that stuff. It's bad for your reputation, even if you are dead."

"Jesus," Johan says.

"Don't be telling me about Jesus. I'm a Jew. Get yourself a dog. They're good companions. You come home, they lick your face. Their love is unconditional. They don't give you any crap."

Au contraire, they give you a lot of crap, at least Sam's pit bull surely does, a dog that is always trying to get into Johan's groceries when Johan sets them down in the elevator. He refuses to pet or even acknowledge the dog, and Sam surely takes his resistance personally. Missy. "Come on, Missy. Come on, girl. Take your time." A dog that lies down on the elevator floor. Still, Johan is afraid of the obese and low energy canine, afraid it will summon enough initiative to remove a calf muscle with one chomp of its powerful jaws. Jesus, to encounter not some beautiful woman at the salad bar with whom he could maybe strike up a conversation, but his troublemaker neighbor whom everyone shuns.

"I'm afraid a dog is out. I have allergies."

"That's too bad. Me, I'm allergic to people. You don't have that allergy, too, do you?"

"No. I don't think so," Johan says.

"You're in trouble if you do. No dogs. No people. Could go crazy in your head."

"Thank you, but I don't plan on that," Johan says.

Sam is a reminder of everything he is and doesn't want to be. He brings a bad name to singleness, dashing, for the moment, the bright promise of aloneness in New York City that Elizabeth Hardwick characterized, in her novel *Sleepless Nights,* as being "married to possibility."

For the next few minutes Johan wanders the aisles, fuming at the human obstacle to the reduced price fare he has been counting on, sensing that Sam will simply not budge if he stands there with him. With the coast finally clear, he loads up on broccoli and shredded carrots and chickpeas and garbanzo beans, seeking out produce that doesn't look picked over too much.

Levan, the new doorman, is on night duty. Handsome, like Cary Grant, a Georgian—the republic of Georgia— Cary Grant. That good-looking. Brilliant, too, but with his youth snatched from him. Twenty years in a labor camp for political activity at the university. His dream of being a scientist quashed. "No complaints," Levan says, when Johan asks how he is. Always the same answer. He has sealed himself off from his pain, a strategy for his own survival.

"Armenians smart people. Good people," Levan says, having made note of Johan's last name. He has brought his nationalism with him from the old country. Johan has been at pains to explain that he is only Armenian on his father's side, his mother having been Swedish. A WASP, he would joke—a white Armenian Swedish Protestant—but Levan might not understand.

In spite of Johan's demurral, Levan grabs the bag of groceries and is obliged to set Johan straight. "I the doorman, you the tenant," he says firmly, as they head for the elevator. Other tenants expect Levan to tote their suitcases or their groceries to the elevator. Nothing in their emotional makeup mitigates against their proper use of Levan. But Levan knows Johan is not the others. He knows it very well. As if Levan can imbue Johan with the manliness he exudes. Even the doorman needing to set him straight.

Johan is anxious to get upstairs before Sam returns, having seen enough of him for the day. A couple has entered the lobby and Levan holds the door for them. The woman he doesn't know, but the cleavage and the long thin legs and the pertness and the Broadway all-stars varsity jacket and the saucy popping of her bubblegum suggest she is a woman with sexpot ways. The man a tenant Johan doesn't know by name whom he assigns an ingrained selfishness and a predatory pathology that works with women. Not a young man. Not young like the woman, not with those crow's feet and the graying hair. *He doesn't care about them. He holds them in contempt. That is the secret of his magnetism.* Why is it that, at his most depleted, Johan always has to run into someone like this, who can, with his big, bold, and camera-like stare, see right into the heart of his pain, as this man whose name he doesn't know is doing now? Then it is the woman's turn to work him over. "I'm so excited about this new gig," she says, flashing teeth of radiant whiteness and allowing a glimpse of her alluring tongue and placing her hand on the man's ass as a hint of the intimacy to come. We are all connected—by pleasure, by pain—Johan thinks, as the woman turns a predictably mocking eye upon him, thinking, *Lover boy has what you can only dream about.* She sees what she needs to see, the look of injury that he isn't getting what he wants, namely, her feathery touch strategically placed on his human contact-deprived flesh.

That night he listens for a while to Garrison Keillor on *Prairie Home Companion* while eating his salad right out of the carton on the kitchen table. Some Guy Noir, private eye, skit. A bunch of droll horse crap. Credit the guy with something. A vision. That voice coming at you like a heavy fog, the way it envelops you. Just something Johan has to get through, that ache of longing. Remembering the jogger with the swishing ponytail. Remembering Gwen Mazely. Remembering.

After dinner he totals up his expenditures for the day, from movie tickets and the diner to tickets for the express bus to the half-price salad from OrganicOnly. He records the amount on an index card below those for the preceding days of the month. He has been budgeting for years, ever since Isabel divorced him. Keeping a record of his spending is a way of maintaining control, a way of keeping the street at bay.

Returning to *War and Peace,* which he has borrowed from the library, he follows the lives of Prince Andrei and Pierre. Something comforting about escaping back into the past. The meticulous realism of Tolstoy. His panoramic vision. His understanding never at the expense of objectivity. At 11:20 pm, he begins to feel the call of the TV. Reading is good. It's what he's supposed to do. But the TV screen is what he wants. In order to have it, he must first earn it. At 11:25 pm he closes the book and heads to his bedroom. Even though it is several minutes before *Saturday Night Live* comes on, he would rather be early than late. It is like a party he can't bear to miss. If he can't be young, at least he can be among those who are, sort of. That opening with those quick takes of the young stars out there partying to a background of upbeat music. Praying that the host will be a woman, and that she will be young and gorgeous, so he can fall in love one more time before he falls asleep. But when a young male with gelled hair emerges to take center stage, his disappointment is enough to cause him to turn off the set.

He has an exercise mat from his days with Isabel. He has long since given up on the Royal Canadian Air Force exercises that had been a staple of his day, which the mat had been useful for—the sit-ups and pushups he no longer does, including that preposterous one where you raise up and clap your hands together and then reposition them to break your fall. No thank you. Who needs a Marine Corps chest anyway. Too many people walking about with far too many muscles than they need. But it is a perfectly good mat, and like so many of the possessions from that time—whether it is a clunky sofa, a worn-out carving board, stained dish towels or placemats— he is reluctant to part with it. The mat is something he must not discard, and beyond that in his thinking he does not need to go.

He takes the lightweight piece of nylon-covered foam from the walk-in closet, draws the curtains in the living room, lights a small candle, and turns off all the lights. Then he sets the mat on the floor by the front door and lies down on it. That is all right to do. It is, after all, his apartment, and he is free to feel not only safe but the thrill of adventure in knowing he is lying in a place in the apartment he has not lain in before and no one is there to see him. No one no one no one.

It has been a hard day. Nothing about it has been easy. Certainly not the jogger. What did she mean laughing at him like that? Every advantage is with the young that they can be so heedless of the longings of the not-so-young. Then there had been the shock of seeing his rain-soaked and hapless brother and his family, all of them drenched. And James and Katie had been aloof. Had they been feeling guilty in leaving their parents to go off with him? Or maybe it is simply the way teenagers are, terse and guarded, as if the crazy adults all around them would try to hinder or even snatch their lives before they have hardly begun. So very hard to enter on a teenager's wavelength. He is sure he had looked foolish in the attempt. *Are you looking forward to school? What are you reading this summer?*

As he lies there on the mat, he becomes aware of some Saturday night hubbub next door. The elevator is arriving with some frequency. Though it is late, party voices. The gaiety, the sociability, does not elicit in him a wave of envy. Rather, it draws him further into the treasured sense of safety he is seeking, as if now he is finally situated in a place where he can realize a fantasy from childhood, that magical hiding place he had envisioned, as he lay in the top tier of the bunk bed he shared with Luke in their second floor room looking out on Broadway, a hiding place high up on the wall in the living room, a slot just for him where he could remain detected by no one, not his marauding older sisters, not his temperamental father, none of them. A place just for him, away from all danger. The virtue of solitude. Somehow it had been established in his childhood. Just too many people in too small a space. Just too much clutter and chaos. Just too much pain and emotional disturbance and sadness.

He falls off to sleep, curled in the fetal position, his cheek resting on his boxer shorts and the teddy bear Isabel gifted him with clutched to his chest. He began relying on these comfort items after his separation from Isabel. All he knows is that he cannot close his eyes for the night without them as companions. Later, he will get up and go to his bed, but for now it is simply too delicious to be in such hidden proximity to life, to all that going on beyond his door.

Chapter 10

Isabel lives over the bridge—the George Washington Bridge—in Teaneck, New Jersey. After a grace period of some years in which he could do little wrong, he was seen by Isabel as doing everything wrong, and eventually there came a time when she asked him to leave. And so it was that his worst fear, that he would lose the paradise he had entered, became a reality, and he found himself living in an East Side sublet. On waking in the morning he would have a brief reprieve before the full consciousness of his situation came to him, and he would ask, in anguish, "Why me, God?" And, of course, the answer he received was, "Why not you, Johan? Why not you?" and so it was a question he stopped asking.

Johan once heard a man refer to New Jersey as the "stupid state." Something in the man's tone as much as the words he spoke made Johan laugh, though Johan had no real idea what the man might have meant, for how can you characterize an entire state as stupid, and one that claims a renowned Ivy League university? And more recently, some study, according to a radio reporter, concluded that New Jersey has the most sleep-deprived population in the nation. A state that renders its residents chronically fatigued as well as stupid? And yet Johan too can adopt the attitude of the superior New Yorker, as when he says, "Oh, those people. They think fine dining is subsisting on Wonder Bread." The fact is that Johan is a Manhattan provincial and New Jersey represents a world he does not really care to know, some undesirable outer ring, like the other four boroughs of New York City. They are, at best, the nether reaches of the balcony, where the dead in life have been consigned, while Manhattan is front row center, or the stage itself. To be in Manhattan is to feel the eyes of the nation and the world upon you. It is to know you are within the gates, pearly or otherwise.

And yet, whatever smug attitudes he has adopted about this state across the Hudson River, no such superciliousness is to be found in him regarding Isabel, now a resident of the prosperous township of Teaneck, just a fast drive to midtown Manhattan.

Not every Sunday do they get together, but every other Sunday, and seldom during the day but in the evening. And though it might sound peculiar for a divorced man to say, given that he is talking about meeting with his ex-wife, somehow it has evolved in Johan's mind that Sunday evening is the ideal time for them to meet, a kind of family day with no heat of sex attaching to it, as with a Saturday night.

She is already seated at the restaurant and facing the entrance when he arrives. Her short, black hair is still wet from her bath, and she is wearing a new gray top with her black dress slacks. She frets that her hair is thinning. Her appearance is something Johan notices and doesn't notice, as befits a situation calling for a position of neutrality. If once they had been physically intimate, that is no more.

Happy is an inadequate word to describe how he feels on seeing her. She is his centering point, his past and present and future. She is the place he comes home to. It is as if the emotional infrastructure he possesses is built to sustain and grow the love he feels for her. And while there is longevity in her family—her father is now a nonagenarian and her mother is not far behind—he can sometimes shudder, life being the perishable thing that it is, at the grief that may await should she pass on before him. That his history, his heart, should be tied to impermanence.

"I saw them yesterday. Luke and Kelly and James and Katie. I was hoping to see only James and Katie, but they showed up, too," he says. As always, he comes to her with a need to talk about the things of his life.

"What was the plan? That you would see the children alone?" She speaks softly. A friend once said she has a voice that makes men melt, and it's true.

"Yeah. But she fainted as they were putting her on the express bus."

"She fainted?"

"Maybe it was psychological. Maybe she just hadn't eaten. Who knows? So they came in, too. I really wish they hadn't."

"Why?"

"I met them over on Fifth Avenue, and by the time I arrived, there was a heavy downpour, and there were the four of them under a tree without an umbrella among them and totally soaked."

"Why didn't they have umbrellas? I guess they forgot. They probably hadn't checked the weather forecast."

"You don't understand. I asked them the same question. They don't have umbrellas."

"Everybody has umbrellas."

"Not them. That's my point. They don't have anything."

"That's silly. Everybody has something," Isabel says.

"They pretty much live hand-to-mouth."

"But doesn't Luke have a job? Don't they have any savings?"

"People in my family don't always have jobs. They don't always have lives," he says, picking up the menu in a futile attempt to hide his annoyance. But it is more than annoyance. The word *job* freezes him. There is shame that he has even suggested to her the lamentable state of his brother's finances. "But how do they live if he isn't working?"

It's in the nature of smart people to ask questions. Their curiosity drives them forward into areas that duller people don't know to go. And Isabel is nothing if not smart.

"They have their ways of getting by."

Isabel knows his emotional nature. People who have lived together as man and wife for a number of years inevitably do, and the fact of separation and divorce does not diminish that knowledge, particularly when the two maintain an emotional bond enhanced by frequent contact. And Johan knows that she knows. If he has learned anything from past excesses, it is to not go too far down that road so ruinous to him in the past of resentment that builds on itself. "I'm sorry," he says. "I just found myself unsettled. You have to try to understand. There's no stability in my family. My older siblings are like a giant building collapsing on me. To see my brother and his family standing there in the rain was my worst fear coming true, that he is out on his feet and has come back here to die. He's strange. It's like I don't know him. He says unsettling, even vile things."

"What kinds of vile things?"

"Just things. He takes jabs at me for working at GoAN. Says I'm dominated by women. Just assumes the right to criticize me in this patronizing way."

"I'm sorry you have to deal with bad behavior. It can't be easy."

Isabel is gracious. She always is. A reasonable and courteous manner is part of Johan's ongoing amend to her, a kind of loving and supportive detachment. They are not so very different in that, through the years, they have learned to read others for their anger while seeking ways to deflect it. It is unfortunate that, as part of the dynamic of their marriage, it was *his* anger she had to read and so often, quite futilely, try to deflect. But that was then, and a new day has dawned for them, though the wound is still deep in her from his mistreatment, the bouts of anger by which he ruled the home, the cosmic joke being that the man he least wanted to be like—his father—he had become in both his marriages.

Taku is one of the great restaurants of New York City because of the high quality of its cuisine. It occupies a small space on Amsterdam Avenue, a corridor of the city that resists as much as any the conspicuous upscale trend for some years now. What does it mean to see along Broadway restaurants with entrees that start at thirty dollars or Godiva Chocolates or a Coach store or a Victoria's Secret half a block in length? Or for realty companies to offer one-bedroom coops for mega thousands and more and banners to be spread along block-long buildings proclaiming: "LUXURY CONDOS STARTING AT ONLY $1 MILLION? It means only that wealth, an insidious onslaught of heartless gentrification, is spreading everywhere. And so Taku, with its small back-less chairs that you somehow don't fall out of and nicked wooden tables is a simple, unpretentious sanctuary from the more upscale commercial enterprises now appearing, and one can always expect to receive deference and a desire to help from the amiable wait staff.

Isabel has ordered two appetizers, a burdock root salad and spring rolls. Johan's request is for a serving of salmon with sesame ginger sauce and yams, the root vegetable of the day. As Isabel well knows, his mood picks up when he has begun to eat. He is not necessarily a squalling baby when hungry, but his irritability level is definitely higher. With food as his pacifier, he begins to talk more equably about Luke.

"I've probably told you, but he's big as a house. And he has no exercise regimen. It was an adventure for him to get up out of a chair," Johan says.

"What about Kelly? How is she doing?"

"The way a woman is who doesn't know if she's coming or going or whether it's even worth it to try to figure such a thing out," he says.

"What's that supposed to mean?"

"Kelly has one gear. She's always in motion. She's always trying to get on top of something she can't get on top of."

"Well, I guess she has a lot to get on top of," Isabel says.

"This is true. The woman is nothing if not frazzled."

"Didn't we visit them once? Somewhere in Brooklyn?"

"We did." Luke and Kelly lived on a desolate street in a rough section of Brooklyn. The quality of life had fallen as the middle class left; drug trafficking and drive-by shootings became commonplace. There came the day when their own building was shot up, which Luke took as unwarranted retribution for some imagined offense taken by one of the neighborhood dealers. Johan and Isabel found him completely soused in the meagerly furnished apartment playing old Elvis Presley records while Kelly tended to James, then an infant in a crib.

"Poor Kelly. What a hard life."

"Yes," Johan says coolly, seeking to hide the flash of irritation that her words have triggered. Not a yes of agreement but simply a receipt for her words, sympathy being fuel for self-pity as he sees it.

How he speaks determines how he feels. If Johan says things are bad, he creates that reality of hard times in his mind. Such is the power of words. And yet, he is aware that the discipline he would hold others to he himself falls short of. It is his way of promoting guilt in her. Because if he has it bad, he is also saying she has it good. And he knows, if he knows anything, that he is not supposed to go down that road, but deprivation is the theme of his life.

Let it be understood that Isabel has been hearing such concerns and complaints from Johan about his family from the beginning. It is nothing new for either of them to seek refuge from their families in each other, to offer comfort when the wolf appears to be at the door or when that giant wind is blowing that promises to knock down and destroy all that they have built up in their fragile world.

Johan finds the gray, fatty strip of his salmon inedible. Though it is no great offering, she loves it. He peels it from the back of the cut like an adhesive strip and deposits it on her plate. It is for Johan to know that Isabel cannot satisfy her appetite through the order she places. Food in abundance that comes to her through her own expressed desire is impermissible. Such a bounty would summon feelings too complicated to discuss. But it is another matter for her to help Johan out so that good food needn't go to waste. Is it excessive to call this a ritual of love?

Their waiter, a smiling young Tibetan man named Daivika, brings the check while Isabel is in the ladies' room. "Did you and your wife enjoy the meal?" he asks. He has been one of the regular waiters at Taku for at least a year.

"It was excellent," Johan says. Though the waiter's misunderstanding of his relationship to Isabel causes some discomfort, Johan offers no correction. Why go to the trouble? Maybe the waiter needs to feel he and Isabel are man and wife. Maybe he would be severely disappointed to find out otherwise. Maybe something would even shatter in the waiter should he be made aware of the true status of his two long-time customers.

When Isabel returns to the table, he tells her of the waiter's assumption. It is a risky thing to do. The words "marriage and "wife" and "husband" and related terms do not sit well with Isabel. She is not enamored of the American family, or any family. She has her reasons.

She laughs nervously. "Don't worry about it." They both agree no clarification is required. And there they let the matter drop.

And then comes the high point, the dessert. Tonight it is raspberry tofu pie, drowned in almond soy cream. One piece of pie, two forks, and the lion's share to him, as Isabel tires easily of the taste. Oh heaven.

They split the bill down the middle, at Isabel's insistence. The thing is that her share is generally less than his, as it is on this night. Her offer seems to place a moral decision on him—is he to acquiesce or is he to call honesty into play and not allow her to pay more than is due? It is for him to live in the world with his conscience as it is constructed, and so he returns to her the few extra dollars she had laid out on the table.

It is rare for them to extend their evenings much beyond dinner at the restaurant. Oh, sometimes, if it is still light, they will take a short walk, or visit the Barnes and Noble down on Eighty-second Street and Broadway. Or now and then they will meet at a museum before dinner. Although Johan's apartment is only two blocks away, their meetings have come to be restricted to the public places. Whether she feels the threat of a private environment as much as he does he cannot say, but from where he stands, the threat is real, and for many reasons they must not go where they have formerly been. For many, many reasons.

As they walk toward her car, which she has parked on Riverside Drive, he looks up at a lighted apartment window over a canopied entrance to a building on West End Avenue. The light is warm, and shows off a neat, homey living room with shelves filled with books. It is the sort of apartment a couple might be living in, a couple comfortable with each other's ways and secure in the knowledge that they are growing old together. A pain he recognizes as a longing for permanence comes over him.

The car is waiting for Isabel, a cheery, apple-green two-door Toyota. Even its license plates New Jersey cannot get right, Johan thinks, staring at the drab yellow rectangle of tin attached to the back of her car. They kiss on the cheek and he watches as she gets in and pulls the door closed with authority. As she turns the ignition key and the headlights come on, he makes the motion he always makes, moving his right hand from the top of his left shoulder diagonally down across his chest. She draws down the safety belt against her, and as she drives off, he can be at ease in the knowledge that she is buckled up and secure.

It is early—4:30 a.m.—and first light has not broken through. In the kitchen he sits at the table writing in a mottled composition book about his evening with Isabel. If discomfort and downright shame are attached to the word "job," as Isabel has used it—*Luke has a job, right?*— there is a reason. These strong emotions are a testimony to something, and what else could it be than his fear?

Johan has never told Isabel that Luke was as dependent on Kelly's monthly disability check as Kelly herself was, and that those checks, along with unpaid loans, provided him with the means to attend college full-time as a man in his forties with two young kids and a wife with a severe disability. Not only did Luke not have a job at the time he passed away. He was without a job for all the years that he and Kelly had been married. This he feels he must conceal from Isabel, as her opinion of him means a great deal, and any displeasure she directs his way is experienced as a tear on his very soul. Is it not understandable that he would wish to withhold from her this information lest she draw a conclusion about one brother based on the other brother's pathway through life?

He will say only this for now. Isabel is a woman who comes from a family of great means. When he entered her life his financial resources, as they are now, were far less than hers. But as for work, can anyone fairly compare him with his brother when he has been employed for all but several months out of the last twenty plus years? He doesn't know who or what troubles him more, his brother for this life of his he has to hide from Isabel, or Isabel, for the wounds around money that are still there waiting to reopen from their marriage that ended in divorce.

Miss Linsley, her name was. The world was in her and she was in the world. A singer, or aspiring to be one. He would hear her at night going through her vocal exercises as he lay in bed. Whether she ranged from high to low or vice versa he cannot say. The technicalities of music have never been his concern; distinctions between contralto and mezzo soprano his mind is dull to. But a boy doesn't need a musical vocabulary to recognize a voice singing from a place of freedom. He would picture her on the other side of the wall in a black evening gown. Often his mother would pound the wall with her shoe, demanding silence in the adjoining apartment. Only when her demand was met and the lovely voice of Miss Linsley was stilled would his mother come to him and together they would recite the "Now I lay me down to sleep" prayer, his ardor for Miss Linsley in temporary abeyance owing to the sweep of emotion that the prayer, as well as his mother's voice—so very different from the one she exercised on Miss Linsley—summoned in him. Please, please understand that this infatuation was not for Miss Linsley herself, but for the independence she embodied, a world removed from the chaos around him. Someday he too would be on the other side of the wall. Someday he too would occupy a space such as hers. Neatness and order, not clutter and disharmony, would reign, in an apartment where music, not angry shouts, filled the air and where he could be unencumbered.

Can a man in middle age, living alone after a divorce in a one-bedroom apartment on the top floor of a prewar West Side building, say he has realized his childhood dream? The next morning, after a sleep that generally comes so easily to him, he experiences profound gratitude that the nightmare he has awoken from is only that. He does not have to live in a state of pain and regret beyond description. He has not given up his rent-stabilized apartment in a doorman building to live with Isabel in a ramshackle house in Riverside Park that is open to the elements and characterized by the irreversible disorder of rooms rife with clutter.

A close call. That is the feeling the dream summons in him. The way you might feel when, distracted by the workings of your own mind, you step off the curb and come within a hair of being mashed by a car tearing along at lethal speed. You are grateful for the reprieve but shaken by the realization that the blind spot which placed you in harm's way in the first place will inevitably recur, and that no amount of vigilance can prevent this.

Chapter 11

That week, Sam nowhere in sight, he does meet someone at the salad bar in OrganicOnly. Says to her, "Do you have time for a quick cup of coffee at the Starbucks on the next block?" Says this when his mind, for the moment, has been far from the prospect of a woman in his life. And she says, "Yes, sure. Let's do that."

Buys her a double hazelnut caffe latte grande. Such terminology. For himself an herbal tea.

"What kind?" the woman who takes his order asks.

"The calm tea, please," he says.

"What size?"

"Medium." Doesn't know a venti from a grande. Can't keep any of that straight.

"One or two tea bags?"

"Just one, please."

Wanting her to hurry, so the woman he has just met doesn't change her mind.

"What kind of work do you do? Are you a doctor? You look like a doctor," the woman says.

"No. Actually, I'm an editor."

"An editor? What kind of editor?"

"A print editor. I work on manuscripts. Turn them into books. That sort of thing. And I do some writing on the side."

"What publisher are you with?"

"Well, not exactly a publisher, although I used to be with a book publisher."

"What does that mean, not exactly a publisher?"

"I work for an organization."

"What kind of organization?"

"A not-for-profit organization."

"Which one?"

"GoAN."

"GoAN?'

"It's a complex organization with a big quasi-corporate structure and--"

"Are you Jewish?"

"No. Did you assume I was?"

"I am sorry. This has been a mistake. If you will excuse me, I must go."

"You must go? Why?"

"I am Jewish. People misunderstand because of my blond hair."

"Jewish women don't have blond hair?"

"You are a very nice man. This I can see. But really. Goodbye."

Takes her double hazelnut whatever with her.

All he wants is to return home for a reset, so he can shed his work clothes and give his hands a good scrubbing to free them of the grime of the city before unpacking his groceries and sitting down to dinner. And he is almost there, the elevator door half-closed, when a hand intrudes, the electric eye now prompting the door to reopen. Lover boy and his belle enter and can barely keep their hands off each other. Again she blows a big pink bubble that she pops all over her pert, pretty face before sucking the gum back in. How much younger she is than the gray-haired man with his hand resting casually on the small of her back. The man thick-necked, with those imperious gray eyes that say to the world what's mine is mine and what's yours is mine, that radiate his will right into you in an obliterating, plundering foray. Saying to Johan, his words passing those ungenerous sliver lips, "Are you a young lover, too?"

And Johan saying in that moment, "How young do I have to be?" Not liking this man. Not liking him at all.

The woman saying, "Come on, honey." Pulling him out the door.

People with their smallness, their unkindness. The more they get the more hateful they become.

Isabel,
A person can be perceived by others as the most arrogant soul on this earth, but if that person can recognize his or her limitation before God, then who can justify such a judgment? What a blessing it is that pain now has value, compelling us to turn to him who has all power. And he is there. He is always there, opening a space for us to expand into. Or maybe it is God who expands into us. It does not matter. Oh, Isabel, there are the words we say by rote, and then there are the words that stop being words so there is only the silence into which we have entered, and the world is far away and we are receiving strength and hope.

It is nothing to weep over, this experience with the woman in Starbucks this evening. I know the blandness of my makeup. I understand what some, perhaps most, women are seeking—the bigger brain, the bigger portfolio. Such women need to know they will be taken care of, so this stranger's questions, while jarring, were necessary in meeting her goal, a man of means to share her life and her bed. It may be a sign of the times that there is an increase in orthodoxy among the Jews on the West Side. That is my impression. We are all looking for what we think we need or want. The heart is selective. Meanwhile, the city is full of laptop lonely hearts sitting in Starbucks. Let us both tend to the spirit, Isabel. Let us do that. In this moment we have everything we need. In this moment we are being taken care of. In this moment we are, we are.

From the subway station at Times Square to his place of work on Fifth Avenue is about a six-block walk. Everywhere old commercial buildings enduring the metal embrace of rickety scaffolds thrown up by underpaid and poorly trained laborers, crews careless with their hammers and wrenches, some perhaps in a hung-over state. There is a new ethos in the land. Corners are being cut. Regulations loosened. Hear Johan say, I will not walk in shadow on a sunlit day. I will assess where it is my feet can safely go. I will pick and choose those streets, hard as it may be, where the risk of a fractured skull from a plunging tool or of being crushed under the weight of a collapsing scaffold will not be my fate.

People racing, in harness to the morning imperative of the work week. Mammon must be served. Work as homage for food and clothing and shelter, whether the dashing souls are in silk suits or the enduring brown of the UPS truck driver. Oh, life manifesting energy and drive on the streets of Manhattan.

The esoteric mantra 433.33 establishes itself in his mind as he heads down Seventh Avenue. "Four three three point three three." Over and over he repeats this figure, the amount of his allocation from each semimonthly paycheck into the 401(k) that will leave him less than destitute in the years to come, or so it is his prayer that such a thing should be. The sound of the figure is delicious in his mind. Equally delicious is that no one can even suspect, as he walks along so unassumingly, that he is inching closer and closer to the finish line, and so cannot snatch his future freedom from him.

As he does every weekday morning, Johan passes a corner bank where, some years before, he had what he calls his epiphany, in a time when he and Isabel were separated but not yet divorced. In that phase of their relationship, he had access to the money of the marriage, and once a week or so would withdraw cash. Isabel had a great many investments, and her accountant had set up a system in which dividends from those assets would flow into the account. The amount would range on any given day from forty thousand to sixty thousand dollars. On those days when the green phosphors on the screen would present a low balance, a feeling of dread would come over him. Poverty was looming, not only for himself, but also for Isabel. The evidence that his world was crumbling right there before him. At the other extreme, with the figures high, the sun was shining even on the bleakest day. And so it was remarkable that one day, as he inserted the credit card she had obtained for him years before and punched in his PIN, he saw his financial tie to Isabel for what it was. The money of the marriage was not so much protecting him from the street as insulating him from life. In that moment he saw himself as a man wearing a hugely padded down vest on a warm day. And while he did not shed the vest then and there, the awareness that precedes action had come.

As he waits in the lobby for the elevator, it is apparent that the org, once a sleepy backwater, is attracting a different kind of worker. Slender young women, who exercise regularly and eat carefully, are moving in. The plumper, older staff are seemingly being, well, thinned out, although the recent arrival of his boss Lurleen bucks the trend. Who these new women are in their flashy clothes he can't, in most cases, say. However unsettling change is, can it be altogether bad that a number of the new people are attractive? Still, the org is not yet Media of America, the rather glitzy and very *for profit* company whose staff use the facing bank of elevators. MOA's women are uniformly hot and their men are cool. They look to Johan like America's chosen, while the workforce of GoAN, himself included, at least in years past, resembled a mixed bag, as you would expect to find in a New York City subway car.

Two men are standing outside his cubicle. One is attempting the difficult task of unfurling a tape measure with a blueprint in hand. The other is doing walkie-talkie squawk talk. Static pours from his hand-held device before he ends his communication. So many the modes of communication; so little to say.

"Are we good here, Joe?"

"We're good," the man with the blueprint says. Large men with loud voices, the kind of men who know how to build things and whose waists are banded with tool belts. Men who speak in a language honed to a practical essence. A thrill Johan can hardly describe comes over him. They have come to expand his cubicle and give him one of those horseshoe-shaped desks that the org managers get to sit at. How happy he feels that he is being recognized for his contributions in this way.

Soon Lurleen approaches, her long skirt stopping just short of her thick ankles and the sneakers she must wear, her weight being too much for heels to bear. Johan doesn't want to gush, but still, the wellsprings of gratitude have been tapped, and he should really acknowledge his boss's gift. But she keeps her eyes on the men. If they ignore him, they bend toward her like flowers toward the sun. The sense of exclusion summons darker emotions, which intensify when she leads the men into her office and out of earshot. Smarting at the snub, he is reawakened to the exclusion he has experienced over the years at the org, women pulling rank and treating him like a boy not needed at a table of the grownups, or talking among themselves as if he weren't even present. Well, it is for him to comfort himself with the image of a renovated and expanded cubicle.

Johan has no sooner logged on to his computer than he hears a tearing sound behind him. He turns to see Lonnie, the maintenance man, holding the Velcro-backed nameplate he has pulled from the outer wall of Johan's cubicle.

"Hey," Johan says. "What are you doing?"

"Doing my job is what I'm doing," Lonnie says, his voice full of the South from where he has come. As Lonnie employs his spirit level to ensure that the new nameplate is straight, Johan stands behind him. Unless the org has given him an alias and scheduled him for a sex change operation, it isn't his. "Nanette Nobling," the nameplate reads.

"Are we feeling displaced?"

Alan Neverby is staring at Johan, his full moon face radiating amusement. He is middle age white but could be mistaken for a roly-poly buddha, like those mammoth statuary figures Johan is drawn to in the Asian art section at the Met. Men of detachment who had been meditating in the back of caves for centuries to achieve their bliss. But Alan Neverby doesn't do caves, and the only bliss he knows comes from the pharmacological treasure he has access to through his lover's connections.

"Never mind the 'we' stuff. What is going on here?" Johan says, not caring that he is addressing himself rudely to Lurleen's administrative assistant.

"Nanette has been upgraded, and Lurleen has given her your cubicle, as befits someone of her new station. If you will follow me, I will show you where you will now be sitting." He leads Johan to a lonely outpost, windowless, with tighter dimensions than his co-opted space.

"She wants me to sit here?" Johan asks, in the grip of his own astonishment. He can't bring himself to speak her name.

"Lurleen has a master plan for the well-being of all her staff. First and foremost in her mind is that they be situated properly," the odious one says, Johan hearing all too clearly his mastery of Lurleen Speak.

"Go away."

"Having a bit of a bad attitude day, are we?"

The weekly staff meeting is scheduled for that morning. Johan considers staying away. He will disappear on the woman, and in that way register his disgust. But wouldn't that be just what she wants? He doesn't know what to do, and so he sits in meditation trying to get his bearings. Yes, right there, with the risk that someone might enter and see him with his back straight in his chair and his hands gently touching and his eyes closed, though he counts on his sense of hearing to tell him that someone is approaching. You do what you have to do to reach that still point, to come to that place of understanding that maya is at play once more, as she always is. Slowly the inner chaos begins to diminish. He comes in touch with the fear that the eviction has unleashed in him. If Lurleen can displace him from his cubicle, maybe she can also displace him from the org itself. Once more he sees her as this implacable force sweeping over the org, with the same aura of inevitability as the Republicans are projecting in their drive to consolidate power in the country as a whole. Sensible questions arise in his mind. Why hadn't he been given notice? Why was he not being offered a more appropriate space? The realization surfaces that maybe he has certain rights and isn't simply a piece of furniture to be moved about at her whim.

Lurleen enters. She has brought no papers with her, just herself. "I want to start this meeting, if I may, with a now familiar equation: Fun = One. Let's begin with our friend Johan. How high is your Fun = One quotient today? Are you feeling the magic?"

"How high does it need to be?"

"High enough so we can see a smile on your face every once in a while."

"Face police. Calling all face police," Johan calls out. "Arrest immediately the sour and the dour. Behind bars with them all."

The staff laugh nervously. They are not with him. They are not against him. They are on the sidelines.

Lurleen continues, as if he hasn't even spoken. "Because frankly, anyone who isn't interested in creating such an environment maybe shouldn't be here."

"Why not focus on how people do their jobs rather than whether we are walking around with big smiles on our faces?" Johan says, adopting a more sensible tone. Because there is something sinister and bullying behind that fun format. There are those annoying creatures who suddenly appear and say, "Smile. You look like you just lost your best friend." Some kind of judgment is going on when people lay that kind of imperative on you. People who want to distance themselves from their pain. Yes, the face police, ready to place you under arrest for a frown or a sad look. They appear when you least expect it and disappear so suddenly you don't have a chance to respond, not that you could anyway, because you are rendered so stunned and immobilized and temporarily ashamed by their effrontery, as if you truly have done something wrong, truly have committed an offense that requires censure.

"Because we want all our staff to be happy. And we want to create an environment in which new staff can feel welcome and happy as well. That is why the workmen are here reconfiguring your former office space."

"Reconfiguring? This is a dislocation of a long-term staff member from his office with no prior notice or discussion to a smaller, more cramped, and windowless space." This is not good, to be talking this way in a meeting chaired by his boss.

"It is very unfair to the staff to create this unpleasant disruption of the meeting. I am only sorry for all of you that you have to witness this."

"What's unfair is what you are doing."

"What's unfair about meeting the needs of the department and the organization?" Lurleen says, coolly. "We all need to align ourselves with progress and become agents of change. The status quo has simply got to go. Fun = One, Johan. Fun = One."

He returns to his new and windowless cubicle feeling very much out of control. It is not his way to fight as he just did. Not for some time has he done that. Why can't he be more like Fiona Beasley or diplomatic Mary Terezzi? Why does he have to do things that only increase his fear and sense of isolation?

Separation is painful. Isn't connection what everyone longs for? But he is in a new territory. Sometimes you can't simply be meek and detached. The bitch. The big fat bitch. Sticking him in this windowless shit hole.

"How could you?" Lurleen asks, standing at the entrance to his cubicle.

"How could I what?"

"Don't pretend you don't know. What is wrong with you? Everyone is quite upset."

"Everyone?" Is the woman going the route of cowards in seeking safety in numbers?

"We were counting on you being a team player."

"Has someone moved you out of your spacious office into a tiny windowless box? If you want a team, start with courtesy and respect to staff members about sensitive issues such as office space."

"You will be getting a wonderful space. A plan is in place for all my staff to have window offices."

"Your use of the word 'plan' and the future tense are very reassuring."

"There is no satisfying you. You are a completely ungrateful person."

"On the contrary, I am grateful for the things a person should be grateful for."

Having come to the limit of her words, Lurleen turns and walks away. Or perhaps it is the tears Johan saw welling in her eyes that have caused her to leave. A devastating form of manipulation. Women of every description, with their instant waterworks. It's cruel. It's cheating. It leaves him on the ropes, emotionally speaking. Plunges him back into childhood. That ritual he and his mother would enact, she calling him by the name of one or a number of his siblings—"Luke, I mean Leah, I mean Hannah, I mean Naomi"— before getting it right and he storming off to his room, where he would lie in bed listening for her footsteps and awaiting the chance to spurn the evening meal she was forced to bring to him since he wouldn't come to the dinner table. Turn her away once, turn her away twice, turn her away a third time until she would cry and cry, his heart fit to burst that he had done such a cruel thing to Mommy, who tried so hard and had such children as he, all of them treating her like dirt beneath their shoes.

Oh yes, the past as prologue to the future.

On a Post-It attached to his computer he stares at the number "24" without comprehension before remembering that it is supposed to serve as a reminder to postpone angry outbursts, spoken or written, for a day. The despair he feels is not simply that he has done this awful thing but that he is destined to do something similar all over again, given his inability to practice restraint. All his conviction in his own rightness fades. He made a mistake. A great and crushing weight descends upon him. It occurs to him that by operating in a hysterical mode at the meeting, he will now bring on that which he most feared, release from the org.

And then an idea comes to him in a flash as a way of dissolving this burden of guilt. A true eureka moment. Yes. He will apologize to everyone in the department via e-mail. The note will have a comic touch to lighten the mood. With one stroke he can be free of the department's collective displeasure.

> My apologies to one and all for my poorly considered outburst at our staff meeting this morning. As punishment for my ingratitude, and justifiably so, Lurleen has consigned me to the coat closet as my new office space, where I am to work standing up and in the dark.

Johan hits the send button and voila, a departmental distribution of his mea culpa, including to Lurleen. The power of words. Used the wrong way, they can condemn you to pain. And yet, with the right touch and spoken in the proper spirit, they can truly liberate.

Within minutes Lurleen is back in his cubicle space. No tears are welling in her eyes this round. "That is a complete lie. I said no such thing. How could you send such an e-mail to the entire staff?"

"I was trying to apologize for what I said in the meeting, since you told me I had offended the staff."

Her mouth a thin red line. He is looking at someone who doesn't like him and she is looking at someone who doesn't like her back.

"You will pay for this. There are laws that protect against libel."

"Libel?"

"You have held me up to public ridicule with your vicious note."

He hasn't seated himself in Jeanine Juddster's office before she says to him, "You'll need to make it snappy. I've got important org business to attend to. Some prize recruits. You wouldn't believe their credentials. A lot of people lining up to see me."

In a soft and reasonable voice, he presents the situation as it has developed.

"Never mind the narrative. Is that the e-mail?"

He is holding a printout of the note. "Yes," he says.

"Give it to me and save the rest of it for your novel. All you types are writing one. You'd probably hang yourself if you didn't have that. Not that anyone will want to read it, not even the friends you probably don't have. Still, if it does get published, just remember: you put me in your book and I just might sue you. And if I don't do that, I might just hunt you down. Don't look so worried. I was just joking."

She is either a slow reader or else she is giving each word her full and deliberate attention. The notes she was taking as he gave her the background are a reminder that these human resources people, in addition to their listening skills, have teeth. They keep files. The org is not as benign as it might want to appear. People here one day and gone the next. Some means in place to get rid of you fast.

"What are you, a comedian? Want to be the star of your own show on Broadway?"

"I wanted to rectify a difficult situation with a bit of levity. I meant no harm."

"Look. You're not an old man but you're getting there. I checked your file before you came up here. You've been with this outfit for more than a year and a day. I found you snoozing in your chair when I brought Lurleen around to meet you. You're tired. You want a park bench to sit on. Try not to make any trouble for the next few years. You'll get to leave with your little pension and you'll have the sort of life someone with your abilities can have. But don't be tearing down people who have a bigger endowment than you. You understand what I'm saying?"

"Not exactly. I believe you may be misunderstanding my intent here."

"Look. Mind your p's and q's. The org is ramping up. Small people like you often have secretly contrarian ways. We need you to get with the program."

"I don't know…"

"Of course you don't know. Two weeks. Give everything two weeks."

"Two weeks?"

"Didn't you hear what I just said? Now, before you leave, I want you to look at my sign."

"Your sign?"

"The one you're always laughing about in your mind. Now read it out loud to me."

"But…"

"Read it."

"God does not make junk."

"Good. Now let that be your thought for the day."

Isabel,

It may not be cause for weeping in the general population, but Blanche Givenchy and Mary Terezzi have heard from her own lips the sometime sadness of Lurleen Lulabella. It seems that she confided to them, when she could put aside her dopey Fun= One equation long enough, that life is not always a cabaret for her. One cold and rainy Thanksgiving Day, she stood with others lining the sidewalk ten and fifteen deep to see Snoopy and Goofy and all the other Disney critters blown up as giant balloon figures. All alone she was, with only her umbrella for company, a child in an adult's body, come to embrace the magic of America with unadulterated joy, and to be part of a community of good feeling. And what happened, Isabel? A man knocked her umbrella from her grip. Clearly, the man saw what he had done, but he did not see fit to pick up the umbrella and place it back in Lurleen's hand. There the umbrella lay on the wet pavement as Lurleen stood at the back of the throng—cold and wet and miserable, a solitary woman well into middle age among young mothers and fathers with kids on their shoulders screaming "There's Mickey, there's Mickey." I find such a story unbearable, Isabel, and hardly know where to go to hide from its effect on me. I must find a way to bring healing to this problematic relationship while at the same time remembering that she is an agent of worrisome darkness. Nothing makes sense other than to observe our feelings while not allowing them to preclude us from taking the necessary action. After all, it may be that Napoleonic, outsized ambition is driving her. Is there not every sign that she is not shy about fighting a four-front war, sending her sans-culottes streaming into org turf that flies the flag of its own autonomy. It may be that One = Under My Thumb more than fun. I will keep you posted, from my personal observation post.

Chapter 12

As he waits for the elevator, he notices, not for the first time, that the small square panel above the door with the directional arrows is slightly askew. Someone working in haste or not too handy with a spirit level. The panel is a reminder that he is out of alignment as well.

The elevator takes him to the top floor, where, fittingly, the CEO and her staff have their offices. Through the glass doors he passes, after touching his ID to the security pad. There is a library-like hush throughout, and the wood-paneled walls give the floor an aura of formality different from the other seven the org owns. On a marble base stands a bronze bust of the org's founder, Minerva Rowe, as a reminder that GoAN has a history, and a long one. And as if to remind the staff of the purpose of its existence, the corridors are lined with blown-up color photos of young girls, all of them smiling. Johan resists looking at the photos, though he can't say why. There is some kind of excess here. Some misuse of the young as confections for the old and gray. He doesn't quite know.

Everything about the org feels oppressive to him as he heads for his appointment. Why should he have to spend his days here instead of home on his own writing projects? He reminds himself that he has more than enough time. It is only fear that he doesn't have a handle on the project he has been assigned and that he will never be able to put it together, like those blocks on IQ tests that used to distress him. Editing is like that scene in a Hemingway story. The young man is staring into the brook. He stares and stares and sees nothing. Only after a while does he actually see the trout there at the bottom. Staring. You have to stare at the copy. And then you have to go away and come back and stare again. It's only then that you begin to see. And it's then that you say wow, yes, and your fear transforms into energy and you are engaged and confident.

Isabel,

There is too much escaping in this world. Only yesterday, I saw on TV an advertisement that said so much about our embrace of mechanization. Four burly men are carrying the coffin of a friend or family member up the steep steps of a church. Suddenly, they look at each other and, as if on a signal, drop the coffin and race back down, the abandoned coffin sliding in the same direction. Cut to a scene of these same four men roaring through the snowy woods on snowmobiles. Are they drunk? Are they cruising for a bruising? Will they smash into a tree in their manic effort to frolic? Such escapism goes on all the time, and none of us are immune to it. Beyond being a facilitator of our own comfort, what is technology but an attempt to deny the reality of death, the very impermanence of our lives?

He has called ahead to alert Marie Crain as to his imminent arrival. A reminder is not something he would normally give, once an appointment is made, but Marie is well beyond the normal retirement age, a GoAN lifer, and not as sharp as she once was. He wants to avoid arriving at her office door to find her in a game of online solitaire. The screen has the transfixing power of a campfire and generates its own kind of warmth, real or imagined. Lonely, atomized souls, and yet connected by this addictive magical invention. To be on the safe side, he heralds his arrival by calling out to her as he approaches, and there she is, swiveling in her chair to face the door and going through the charade of sorting through a batch of papers that clutter her desk.

"Whatcha got for me there, Johan?"

He has a lot. Too much, he fears. A governance and management tome. Strategic planning. Tactical planning. The role of the CEO. The role of the board of directors. Staffing designs. Fiduciary responsibility. Stewardship. Performance review and appraisal. Graphs. Charts. The kind of stuff he has been working on with her for years.

Marie is hard to work with. Copy is missing that she can't find, no matter how many piles of paper she goes through. Things like this happen when you are seventy-five, when you have been in the workforce long enough to earn a sizable pension. Marie was in military service for a bunch of years before entering civilian life, so she has a government pension to look forward to as well.

"Maybe Pensiva would know?" Johan asks, Pensiva Gwalt being a senior vice president.

"Oh, she doesn't know a damn thing," Marie says, reinforcing her contempt with a quick dismissive forearm gesture in the direction of Pensiva's corner office. The words and the gesture are a bit shocking. He realizes, in that moment, and not for the first time, that there is a definite hierarchy in the org, and that he is a kind of servant, his purpose being to make others look good. He helps prepares the meal, but he doesn't sit at the table. There are power struggles, likes and dislikes, here in the upper echelon that he doesn't get to see. Consciously or unconsciously, he has bought into this hierarchy, and made of these people parental figures he is duty-bound to try to please. It is like a child suddenly hearing one parent speak harshly of another.

An image comes to him of Tony Manero, in *Saturday Night Fever*, bopping along a Brooklyn street in his mod outfit, presenting the image of a young man who is going places. And yet the cool of

Tony's disco look is offset by the empty paint bucket that he totes, and which he is returning to the hardware store where he holds down a dead-end job. Some people work for the man; others work for the wo-man.

And if he continues with this thought pattern, he knows he will soon be asking himself questions like what has he done with his life that he placed himself in an org where he can't move up and where he can never be more than a boy among these women and wonder further about the nature of the will and whether it is possible that some advance in life not on the basis of talent alone but through intense and forceful communication of their intent that amounts to an unspoken yet entirely coercive demand. Is it possible that people are in these offices simply because they fully expect to be?

The view outside Marie's window is urban-spectacular, achingly beautiful: tarred rooftops and those squat, cedar-shingled water towers with beanie tops reminding him that there is life beyond the sealed windows of this building where he spends so many days and hours of his week.

"Well, I'll have to get back to you about that, Johan. What else do you have for me?"

"Just a few things," Johan says, hardly knowing himself. Query tags, notes written on small pieces of colored paper, are attached to the many manuscript pages. He points out instances of inconsistency, makes suggestions for cutting repetitious passages, and proposes that one entire section be moved forward. They may want to think about an introduction and creating an appendix. Maybe the abundance of forms and charts would be better placed at the back of the book. Cross-references can be added, so the reader can easily find them if he or she chooses. In this way, the narrative has a chance to flow without so much interruption.

Marie is acquiescent. He senses that she is eager for him to take the lead. A former mover and shaker in the organization, she comes here so she doesn't have to sit alone in her apartment and to take her mind off the regular dialysis treatments she must endure. She comes here because she has no one out there except a brother who lives across the continent. She comes here to play her games of solitaire and to shuffle into the cafeteria five minutes past noon so she can be fed.

"I'm so glad you're on this project," Marie says, and briefly places her hand over his, as if she senses his sympathetic accord with her. "How far back do we go? A long time, right?

"A few presidents have come and gone," he says. Their first project had been a monograph for councils about governance: the role of the president, the CEO, and the board. Reading between the lines, it was really about how to keep the contending factions from killing each other out there in council land. She had not let him change very much in the text of the monograph. "Don't get rambunctious," she had said, taking his wrist, in that moment telling him something about who she was—that she had fixed ideas—and the org he was now working for. A workhorse she had been, the kind who used to say, "Whatcha working on these days, Johan?" and never mind with the "How are you?" stuff.

Well, maybe it's all right. Maybe it's life and let him take refuge in gratitude for all he has been given.

"Most people come out of the closet. They don't go into it." Blanche Givenchy has come to visit him in his new digs. She wears a mustard-yellow top with her brown skirt. She is still clothes-conscious and has a genius for assembling a low budget wardrobe.

"Hah," Johan says, grateful for her company. No one else has been by to see him since the dustup. He has been feeling kind of shunned.

"There's hardly enough space for two chairs," she says, seating herself in one. "But at least she gave you a walk-in closet. How many people have those in Manhattan? Well, I guess it's just a case of the cream rising to the top. Some folks get the corner office. Some get the corner closet."

Johan laughs. "What's that old advertising jingle about a title on the door rating a Bigelow on the floor?"

She looks at him as if he has lapsed into Swahili. "What's a Bigelow?"

"Some kind of office carpeting, as I recall," he says. The late fifties? The early sixties? Actors dressed up as doctors promoting cigarettes. Alka Seltzer. Plop plop. Fizz fizz. Oh what a relief it is. Janitor in a Drum. The Colgate protective shield. Maybe they had different commercials out there in Kansas, where Blanche is from.

"Are you trying to get fired?" She has leaned toward him. Her voice is hushed, soft.

"No, I'm trying to stay," he says, seeing no need to alter the volume at which he is speaking. "But I think I see where you are going. Lurleen is no one to fool around with."

Blanche laughs loudly. She is a woman with big emotions, a woman who would be vocal and passionate in bed. She is also as close to a female hound as he has ever seen.

"Are you fooling around with someone now?" she asks.

"I have some friends." A true enough statement. Blanche is a friend, if he chooses to consider her one. Keep it general. Keep it vague.

Some years ago Blanche wrote a book of tips for men on how to make themselves more attractive to women: effective pickup lines and conversational gambits, ways to dress, and good grooming, including removal of unwanted ear and nose hairs. Men are, or were, Blanche's passion. There has been an endless succession of relationships but never marriage, an institution completely antithetical to romance, in her opinion. Many of the men she has been involved with remain her friends after the sexual fever has died out.

And Blanche needs friends. There had been a hip injury as a child, and the botched surgery left her with a weakened joint that gives her constant pain and affects her mobility. She has long lists of men she can call to run errands, do repair work on her apartment, lend her money, and comfort her when the meds don't seem to be working and her fear is taking her to a very dark place. Not that any crisis could ever shake Blanche's faith in modern medicine and pharmaceuticals. God is a foolish concept for foolish people. The mind is all a person has, as Blanche sees it, and yet her mind is a torture chamber in which she lives without a still point.

Sooner or later it comes down to that with Blanche Givenchy. She can appear to be out of it owing to her pain, physical or psychic, but her sensors are always on. Something about her, her sexual capacity, fascinates him. She is not a Manhattan ditherer, a woman who gives the appearance of an interest in sex with none of the follow-through. Blanche, he senses, would be responsive to the slightest touch and ready to go. And yet Johan finds an attraction to her is lacking. She takes good care of herself and dresses well and has a pretty face, but she has also let it be known that her breasts are not quite her own, having been surgically enhanced. There is no way for him to move forward with Blanche in the sexual arena with the knowledge of her synthetic parts.

"Women friends?" she says.

Only once have they been alone together outside of the office, and that was for lunch sometime after Isabel and he had married. Because she is a cynic about the institution, men who wear wedding bands are not off limits to Blanche. In fact, their precertification and limited availability make them a draw. At the restaurant Johan was unhappy to hear Isabel's name from her lips. He felt encroached upon, as if the wolf was at the door. It wasn't that Blanche was too strong for marriage, he saw in that instant; it was more that she was unequipped for it. And what she couldn't have, she was not averse to trying to destroy. She suggested he come visit her at her newly decorated apartment. She had redone her bedroom. She wondered if it would be to his taste. In such a way had she spoken at their lunch. And in speaking this way, he had seen her selfishness. It was there, in the shape of her mouth, which somehow suggested avaricious cruelty.

"A few," he says.

And so his instinct to keep his distance from Blanche has proved to be correct. But then came the day he could never have imagined, when Isabel and he separated and some years after that, to his horror, the marriage was dissolved and so he was now free in the same way that Blanche, through the choices she had made, was chronically free. Other women were no longer off-limits. He would meet someone and come to Blanche with questions or anxieties. He sought to use her as a wise consultant in a way that he could not use Rita O'Rourke, who had no real hands-on experience with men. Could a man go out with a woman twenty years younger? Should he go out with a woman he wasn't overwhelmingly attracted to? With questions such as these was he also keeping Blanche's interest in him alive. If he was available for other women, why should she not think that he was available for her as well?

"Come on. Tell me about your newest flame."

A feeling of shame comes over him. He sees himself as a complete impostor in regard to women. He is somewhere back in childhood, naked and surrounded by his mocking older sisters, hearing the message he has been hearing his whole life: *You, a man? Now there's something to make me laugh.*

"All is quiet on that front, I can assure you." What more can he say?

And so Blanche returns to office matters. "You need to be careful with Lurleen. She's dangerous. She's hounding me about deadlines all the time. I've become a nervous wreck. I can hardly think."

And in fact her hands shake and there is a slight quiver in her face. And those eyes. Deep-set. They used to sparkle. Now they show a pharmaceutical dullness. Some light has gone out in Blanche. Something instructive and disturbing here for him as to what the mind can do when it turns on you. Blanche Givenchy is a computer without a firewall; her antivirus program has been disabled and disturbing stuff keeps popping up on her screen.

"She can't do anything to you as long as you do your job," Johan says. "If you're really concerned, document everything. When projects come in, your progress with them, etc. That way you have a written record."

"But the woman has a plan. My sense is that she works from an unfriendly and aggrandizing format," Blanche says.

"No doubt about it. But sometimes bullies overreach. Look at Napoleon."

"I guess."

"Look, what can happen? With all due respect, there are people in this org who can't walk and chew gum at the same time, so why would the org dispense with its best editor? You're fabulous at what you do."

"Oh, come on, Johan."

"No, really. Anyway, Lurleen needs editors. She wouldn't know an em dash from a cheese Danish. And her e-mails are unbelievable. Homonyms are just an interesting irrelevance to her. So what if she writes "there, t-h-e-r-e," when she really means "t-h-e-i-r"? It's not her fault if grammarians want to nitpick and fuss over the difference between the adverb and the plural possessive. If the words sound the same when you speak them, then you should be able to use them interchangeably in written copy." Lurleen's lapses make him feel competent and safe and secure, if only for the moment. His sense of himself as an editor depends on being right, on correcting, on being the ultimate arbiter. It is why he reads and rereads the *Chicago Manual of Style* and *Words into Type* and *The Careful Writer,* by Carl Bernstein. It gives him an edge not only on Lurleen but the entire building to know when to use "compose" and when to use "comprise," or the correct placement of the adverb "only" in a sentence. But there is also that small voice within him that says he and the rest of the staff are getting it wrong. It is a voice that suggests to him his pettiness. After all, there is something commendable about Lurleen that she can fire off her hastily written messages. They reveal a woman who has larger concerns than typos and grammatical lapses. Her opinion of herself rests on something more than *The Chicago Manual of Style* or the dictionary. She is not afraid to be herself—wise enough to play the fool and fool enough to be wise. It is this voice that whispers to him that Lurleen is big not merely in body but in spirit as well.

Miss Carmelli was good to Blanche. She had her shortcomings, mainly resistance to delegating, but she was also protective of her staff and loyal, particularly toward Blanche, whose extreme talent was matched by the extreme vulnerability induced by her overheating mind. But they are in a new time, and Lurleen is a reflection of that change.

Maybe it is all just org conversation, the kind that is going on in thousands of offices across the city and the country even as he speaks. The boss conversation. The boss has done this and the boss has done that and the boss will try to do God knows what. Talk driven by fear and the need to gossip and bitch.

"Johan, she's dangerous. Look what she did to Gwen."

"I need to remember that."

"What are you on anyway? Horse tranquilizers? You're always so calm."

Johan laughs. "I haven't been so very calm at some of our meetings."

"You're very kind."

He is taken aback by the seeming non sequitur. A stillness follows, some unbearable and unwanted intimacy. The embarrassment. The something. "Tell Lurleen," he manages to say.

The slow padding of feet can be heard out in the corridor as Margo Fuller-Breedsley chugs past. "Knock knock? Do you have a minute for little old me or should I come back?" That baby voice and that deep complicity with Lurleen, as if they are one. And yes, Lurleen has time for her. Almost always Lurleen has time for Margo Fuller-Breedsley. And within a minute there is that uproarious laughter in Lurleen's office. Not that their laughter blends. You really couldn't say so. If Lurleen's laughter is like a powerful river, Margo's has a harsher sound, not exactly mean, but grating, like that of a porcupine devouring a piece of wood in the dark of night. The two of them sitting together and consolidating power. Oh, there are meetings with staff, but really, it is just the two of them.

"The ass licker. She can't go to the ladies' room without first asking Lurleen's permission," Blanche says.

Isabel,

In the time before Lurleen Lulabella there was a week when Blanche Givenchy went missing, but during her absence made her presence felt via the telephone. "Holy crud. Jumping Jehoshophat. Snakes are curled up on the kitchen table and cows sit in the trees. The woman is nothing if not possessed and order is not so much as a fleeting hope on this day," we heard Miss Carmelli exclaim as she flew from her corner cube. It seems that Blanche Givenchy, over the telephone, had some provocative things to say to her boss. "How are you, my little Lucifer? Whose milk have you poisoned today and how many are the babies whose blood you have drunk?" The bottom line is that Blanche Givenchy was coming from an angle of vision that left her apprehensive of a mother's love. And, of course, I had heard this some years before when I had watched Sarah, my first wife, in the throes of a breakdown, literally refuse a glass of milk her mother offered, paranoia having come to afflict her as well. Oh, Isabel, women too close to their fathers and not close enough to their mothers. Men with the opposite alignment, so that, at some point, you have a picture of emotional deformity as common, and maybe that is either the beginning of wisdom or terror, or both.

Miss Carmelli, having strange powers, performed a miracle of metamorphosis and flew about the tenth floor as a giant black insect, her eyes magnified into omniscient orbs and her wings generated a buzz of energy that expressed a kinetic soul with their whirring action. Such displays of her puissance placed us in a state of temporarily cowering disbelief. We are not speaking here of a fruit fly or a mite but of a creature sleek and agile with its proboscis dangling.

But if I say all this, I must ultimately assert that Miss Carmelli formed the ties that bind.

We saw those ties in the devotion she was to manifest toward Blanche Givenchy. Miss Carmelli did not enter into a state of high dudgeon. She did not vow to smite Blanche for her apostasy. Nor did she seek termination of the ailing one. She did not go down the dinky road of punitiveness. Miss Carmelli loved the free spirit she saw in Blanche as much as she did Blanche's lapidary editing. Blanche Givenchy was her prized and gifted and wayward child, summoning from the depths of her being great love and compassion.

Miss Carmelli, Fiona Beasley, Mary Terezzi, and I went calling on Blanche Givenchy. By this time Fiona and Blanche had become best buds. It had become a daily ritual for Blanche to brief Fiona about all her woman-on-the-town doings, her louche nights with the roués along First Avenue. It provided Fiona with vicarious pleasure to receive such reports of urban randiness, for even back then Fiona had the shut-down look of a woman who wanted little more than to go home and turn on *The Brady Bunch* or whatever prime time fare was being offered.

Mary Terezzi at the time had a look of teenage peeve, as if someone had just delivered a stinging slap to her face. She was living apart from her husband. The word "party" from her lips came out hot and scorching, with razors along all its edges. Partying here, partying there. Once or twice, she even suggested we might like to party, but I felt no physical pull toward her. I liked Mary Terezzi as a friend. There was something about the sound of her voice. It was soft and full of caring. She had street corner harmonics in her Brooklyn-born self. That she would so readily position herself next to me as we approached Blanche's building suggested that she knew me, recognized me as a kindred New York City soul, though our boroughs of operation had been different. I had the sense that we could have frequented the same bars a decade before in the searching seventies.

We found Blanche sitting in an upholstered chair, her legs splayed and her eyes fixed on us. Not a basilisk's eye, but not a friendly one either, as if we were a source of amusement. A man with gray hair and a nervous smile stood by her.

"Ken, get these lovely creatures a drink, will you, and pour one for me while you are at it," she said, as if he were at her command.

"Just water for me," Fiona said.

"What's the matter? Afraid of growing some hair on your balls?' Blanche said. Turning to me, she said, "Maybe you could use some hair on your balls. It's for sure you've got too much on your head."

Miss Carmelli, tiny and frail, the half-smile on her face registering her unease, didn't know whether to stay or flee. A wild woman letting it all hang out was not her thing. Miss Carmelli was alone in the world; she connected to it through a high level of service to the org. If her sister was a Dominican nun, Miss Carmelli was a secular nun. She was out to do good.

Isabel, I wondered at the ability of Miss Carmelli to absorb the shock of Blanche's assaulting rudeness, and whether she wasn't seething under her outward appearance of tolerance and compassion. Some of us like a crisis, as it's an occasion to escape from our own humdrum lives, and some of that may have been operating in Miss Carmelli. But having rushed down to rescue Blanche Givenchy, there was now nothing for her to do but stare at her troubled staff member as she bore into us with her eerie, witchy glare.

Blanche's friend Ken reassured us that everything was under control and that both he and Blanche had been in touch with her doctor. Because there is a tyranny that the sick can seek to exert on the supposed well, I felt some relief on leaving.

Evidently, these were episodic occurrences with Blanche, and within a week she was back at the org and unapologetic, as though nothing out of the ordinary had happened.

And now there is another who comes calling.

"I need to have a word with you. Do you have a minute? I can come back if you are busy." There is no irony in Hank Farquist's voice, even if he has caught Johan dozing in his chair. Hank has a certain tact that allows him to see without saying.

"Come in," Johan says, and watches as Hank, a very large man, seats himself.

"It's only this," Hank says, turning down the volume on his normally booming voice. "I like Fiona. I really do. She has some very good qualities. And I don't mind that she gives me tedious proofreading assignments, but I find it strange that even when I do find typos or grammatical errors, she inevitably stets every last one of my corrections. She seems to have a core of impenetrable conceit that does not allow her to see she is capable of making mistakes. Or maybe she just relishes the power of being the ultimate arbiter. The result is that she is constantly producing a newsletter full of errors. How can such a thing be?"

"Maybe no one reads it?" Johan says, causing them both to laugh.

"Well yes, that is a possibility," Hank Farquist says. It is not in his nature to go down such a road. He is a builder, not a denigrator, a man of great energy and ability who has been led to the org in his later years by an unfortunate happening some years ago. In his late fifties, he had an irreparable falling out with his long-time partner and their flourishing production company was dissolved. And so, at age sixty, when he expected to be feathering his nest, he found himself struggling to achieve mastery over an array of software so he could hire himself out as a word processing temp.

"To be honest, this department seems to me to be cuckoo land sometimes. If Fiona is a terrible editor, then Lurleen is even worse. I have the sense that she is trying to learn as she goes. Have you ever considered that you should be sitting there in Lurleen's office? You know more than she does."

"The org has made its decision as to who should head the department," Johan says.

"I've worked in many offices and seen many things happen—workers who you hardly paid any attention to suddenly getting the boss's job. Underlings promoted to directors. It could happen here, if you made the right moves." A guileful look has come over Hank's pale face.

"You may want to keep copies of your marked copy for comparison with the printed issues," Johan says, seeking to bring the conversation back to where it started.

"Yes, I have been doing that. It is insulting. I have a strong résumé. I am a member of Mensa, and yet she treats me as if I am a doltish child."

In another time, with his powerful physique and huge hands, Hank would have been tilling the soil of the Midwest, like his forebears.

"Yes, you have stepped onto Maggie's farm. No doubt about it," Johan says.

"Excuse me?"

"Not that Fiona is sixty-eight and claiming to be twenty-four."

"Are we talking about the same thing?"

"'Maggie's Farm.' An early song by Bob Dylan. He is easier to quote from than Shakespeare. 'Maggie's farm' is any condition in which tyranny reigns and where the flag of freedom is yet to fly, and it is this intolerable condition that must not be allowed to continue. I will work on it from my end. Rest assured that this will be the case."

"Well, thank you," Hank Farquist says, with tentativeness in his voice, for he is not of the popular culture that Johan has referenced. Hank Farquist lives in the world of opera and classical music. It is at the Met that he can be found, in the cheap seats, when his budget allows, weeping at the lustrous sound of some world-famous coloratura singing some sad, sad aria that wrings his very soul.

Isabel,

Weeping. There should be a daily time set aside nationwide for the shedding of tears on every street and in every building, over the things we, as human beings, do to each other. When we deviate from love, cruelty asserts its reign. Now have I been called to action, that tyranny be banished from the earth and the flag of freedom fly once more. The cause of Blanche Givenchy I may not be able to easily advocate for but this matter of Hank Farquist may not be one to take lying down. It is a crime to hold a good man (or woman) down. That is all I mean to say. We are not on this earth to use each other as pawns in our power games, those of us who are not Stalin or Mao or Pol Pot. I will not have Fiona Beasley asserting cruel hegemony over Hank Farquist, even if she is only avenging herself on him for some ancient wrong done her. But tell me this: how is it, if I am so bad, that some come to me for good?

Chapter 13

A trumpet sounds. And then this, from the org herald: "Make way for the leadership team. Make way." All throughout the org its clarion call can be heard.

At the head of the procession is Jane Fallows, the org CEO. A luminous American star: summa cum laude graduate of Stanford University, Rhodes Scholar, highest-ranking female officer in the United States Air Force. This is no dowdy bureaucrat risen through the ranks of GoAN, no feeble not-for-profit type who can't distinguish between a bottom line and a goal line. This is a high-achieving woman from the real world who can get the job done.

Tall, erect, slender, resolute, and *forward-looking,* those are words Johan applies to Jane Fallows as she stands before the assembled in her GoAN adult uniform—a light blue dress and red ascot—and holds up her fisted right hand, an org sign for quiet that brings a hush to the spacious meeting room. *Duty. Mission. Service. Purpose. Inclusivity.* These words ring like gongs in her speech. A movement for all girls, wherever they might be. A pledge that the org will reach wider still, that the girls of today will be the leaders of tomorrow. A shared vision will mean communities and country bound by the ties of a common purpose.

A brief PowerPoint display accompanies her speech. Extrapolation of essence from long-winded sentences into bullet points. Economy applied to language as well as money.

- Service—to community, to country, to each other.
- Effective communication of org message equals dramatic upsurge in girl and adult membership.
- Who we are and what we stand for.
- Together we will meet the needs of today *and* tomorrow.

From another world has Jane Fallows come to New York City. But not for her the analyst's couch yip-yapping about Mommy and Daddy and Sissy Poo. Nor does she get next to hip-hop clothes and tattoos and pierced ears and studded noses. No flag-burner, no dope-smoking, levitate-the-Pentagon chanting, freak flag flying, grooving to the Grateful Dead hippie would she have ever been. Jane Fallows is a true believer, a patriot, a woman of conviction with the clarity of mind and strength to buck generational currents, even those with the force of a tidal wave.

And yes, make way for the rest of the leadership team. Stand back, every last one of you, stand back. Coming through.

Make way for Jeanine McQuaid, senior vice president of Council Services. She has the physical strength of a man and the perseverance of a pioneer. A woman who, in another lifetime, helped settle the Wild West and wrestled longhorns to the hard earth in her leather chaps. A woman who held the reins while riding on the buckboard of a Conestoga wagon and busted sod and felled trees and rustled up some grub and played the harmonica before the old campfire. Hear her sing "Kumbaya, My Lord" on org retreats. Hear her, I say.

Make way for Maeve Muldoon, senior vice president of Program Resources. Her department a small empire and showing no sign of contraction. Maeve Muldoon gets the job done; she delivers the goods. Fiftyish and stylish, her teeth expensively white. Catholic. Cold cathedral walls. The Atlantic Ocean in January, gray and forbidding. A whiff of incense and the catechism attaching. Maeve at age ten in her schoolgirl jumper at the Our Lady of Perpetual Sorrow Parochial School in Woodside, Queens, the nuns and the brothers working overtime to create restraints in her against unbridled sexuality. But how to reconcile that chill with her fire. In another time, woman or no woman, she would have been one of the Gaelic horde, riding bareback and bare-ass into battle.

But if you know nothing else, Maeve Muldoon would have you know this, because it is written large on her face or wherever such assumptions get posted so the inner eye is made aware of them: Maeve Muldoon's's husband is a real man with a real job, high up the corporate ladder at CBS News. A man playing in the Big Show. Power lunches, Lear jets, a monthly expense report a block long. But the same cannot be said of Johan Manootdjian and never will. As pride is written on the face of Maeve about her husband, so too is something written about Johan Manootdjian on her face, for he reads it each time he encounters her. And if he doesn't read it, he feels it or hears it, somewhere deep in his being. It is simply this: *You cannot be a man and work at the org. It is scientifically impossible, and I, Maeve Muldoon, know science, as does my husband, which is another reason why he is a man and you are not. You do not and never have known science. You do not have so much as a passing acquaintance with science. When you were assigned to a project of mine, it became clear that you did not know the phases of the moon, did not know the old gibbous phase from the new crescent phase. At that point was it established in my mind that I was with my inferior. It was a moment of recognition for both of us and a moment of deserving shame for you as well.*

Yes, do make way for the Leadership Team. Do make way for the senior vice presidents who head up Information and Technology and Finance Services and Corporate Administration and Planning and National Properties and Human Resources, women like Francine Polanka and Hermione Gourd and Alison Grinkley and Fedora McIlway and Pensiva Gwalt.

Make way for women who see you without seeing you.

Jane Fallows continues. Like her hair, every word in place. *The power of girls together…advocates of change while adhering to tradition…spirit of cooperation and collaboration…….let us all pitch in and build this barn together… neighbors joining to create glorious renewal…the launch of a national campaign to brand the GoAN name into the consciousness of every adult and girl in this country. A strong brand that will define who we are and make our vision a living reality that GoAN is where girls grow great. We are not different things. We are one thing. We are the future of girls. We are girls!*

It is hard to say if these women who make up the Leadership Team will be galvanized into heroic action by the speech of Jane Fallows. More likely it's just that happy morning buzz permeating the assembly room before the day exerts its gravitational pull into the depressive state they all fall victim to by the afternoon. Maybe the only thing anyone really believes in at the org is lunch.

Johan struggles to fend off a narcoleptic snooze by wetting his fingertips and touching the skin just below his eyes, a driving tip he learned so he wouldn't fall asleep at the wheel while negotiating the tight curves on the Taconic and the Saw Mill Parkways back in the long ago when Isabel and he were still together and they were returning from their country place. Ahead of him sits Lurleen, several rows back from the Leadership Team, as befits her lesser status. If body language means anything, she seems deeply moved by the words of Jane Fallows. She holds her hands together just under her chin in smiling admiration, as if a fervent prayer is now coming true. She has met a woman with whom she can have an alignment of purpose.

Johan has heard it before: the speeches that seek to stir but offer instead strained rhetoric, the ambitious agenda whose goals will never be met, the new crusade that is the old crusade repackaged. Other CEOs, bursting with enthusiasm, have appeared on the scene only to leave a few years later with the status quo maintaining itself. It may be an org that is short on substance and not a little boastful, like those sports fans shouting into the camera, "We're number one. We're number one." Very American, very insecure, under the preening stance.

Jane Fallows saying, *Think out of the box. Step out of that box and step out of it now. Out with hidebound traditionalism and "We do things this way because we have always done things this way." Toss your hierarchies out the window and pull down the vertical so horizontal rules the day because we are all in this together. There is no top and there is no bottom.*

The presentation is a welcome distraction from cubicle life. His calendar is accessible to everyone online, and essentially it is empty. He comes in, sits in a chair, and goes home. So why not be happy to sit in the assembly room among the crowd with nothing expected of him and sunlight pouring in through the big windows that look out on Fifth Avenue? But the same thing that makes him happy also can depress him, if he thinks about it. It is the sense that none of what has been said has anything to do with him. Jane Fallows has been talking at him and not to him. He is invisible to her. Her words are all that matter to her. And something else. A feeling of shame has come over him. It has been with him ever since Jane Fallows entered the room. It is everything for him to stay in his seat and not flee. He has a few questions for Jane Fallows. *What do you, Ms. overachieving former high-ranking military officer, really think of us, this motley crew who stares back at you? Do you suppose we don't know that we're not good enough for you, as the shabby apartment I grew up in was not good enough for those friends of mine who happened to see it? Do you think I do not know that just as Billy Baines and Johnny Jones walked into my family's apartment one day in my long ago childhood and saw what they saw sufficient to tell others at the school that I lived in a pigsty that you are not seeing the same thing here in the org? Can you really believe I don't know that?*

But these are not questions to ask of a CEO, and certainly not in a forum such as this. It is for Johan to know his place and to fit in and to be of service delivered with an attitude of detachment. It is for him to please the women of the org, as it has been his dictate to please women his entire life. And it is for him to be invisible in the eyes of these women of the org as he goes about this service and to know that he has no context but the context of invisibility.

One further word about the leadership team. They are not necessarily a team. They do not always hang out together. Some of them don't hang out at all. Some don't even talk to certain others among them. This one has done this and that one has done that. Their eyes can narrow and flash with sparks of anger at the mention of each other. There can be grievances small or profound. But they do come together at meetings. They do strategize and execute. They do abound in brainstorming and the executive stance.

Isabel,

Today dinosaurs ruled the land once again. The plain of battle on which they met was our own Publications Department. Maeve Muldoon arrived, her face flushed with Irish fire. "I will have your job. Do you understand? I will have you out of here." This she said to Lurleen's face. Because Lurleen has trespassed. She has encroached on Maeve Muldoon's turf with her strategy to move the department out of its customary service mode into a more proactive stance. Maeve Muldoon will not tolerate encroachments on her domain. It is only this. Lurleen has been dispatching Nanette Nobling into foreign lands. Nanette has been taking on the Program folks. She is not showing the deference that was a hallmark of my approach. In the aftermath of this tempest, Lurleen called a meeting, at which she said the code of complicity with inertia is being broken. It is cause for rejoicing that the enemy has shown her face, Lurleen says. We must expect more such rearguard actions in the future, as revolution is not an easy task, Lurleen also says. What is this world, Isabel, where the impostor adopts such revolutionary rhetoric?

Lurleen suffers from grandiosity as big as her laughter. She has a notion that we can become a rival of Simon & Schuster and other titans of the publishing industry. Thus, she is not seeking to fit herself into the org but to shape the org according to her dictates, a perilous and vainglorious venture, given the fact that GoAN is an institution in the best and worst sense of the word, with pushback inevitable. A willful ignorance pervades the org about the publishing process—for example, the gestation period from manuscript to bound book—that no amount of "education" can overcome. During Miss Carmelli's tenure, we were known as a service unit, and service is definitely the key word. We will have no end of trouble if we try to place ourselves on anything but that basis vis a vis the org, I am afraid. Servants do not sit at the head of the table. Lastly, it is important to recognize when repression masquerades as liberation. Essentially, Lurleen Lulabella is a force for darkness, not light, no matter how much jibber-jabber she spouts about fun and how many laugh-ins she inflicts on us. Her values are those of a time past. She has no real place in a progressive environment. Just the other day she was heard to say that she would allow no teenage daughter of hers to read *Cosmopolitan*. *Cosmopolitan*, mind you.

"We never see you anymore, Johan. Have you been disappeared? Dropped from a helicopter into the Atlantic never to be seen again?" the woman stands outside an empty conference room.

"Just one of those cubicle guys restricted to quarters," Johan replies.

Ellen Deutsch is no cubicle guy. Not with a corner office and a promotion every year, driven by her professional cachet, a PhD in psychology, and a long list of books on children that she has authored or co-authored. She is Maeve Muldoon's right-hand person.

`"Come chat with me. What is going on down there in your department?" And so they sit at the long conference table.

"The truth is that I don't quite know, but it feels progressively unfriendly, like some kind of hostile takeover. The natural progression is to move up in an organization, but if space means anything, I seem to be going in the other direction." He stops himself, suddenly aware that he is speaking only about himself. "Sorry. That's just some personal stuff. She kicked me out of my cubicle and stuck me in this tiny space. Now we have this new person sitting where I did. Nanette Nobling, who Lurleen says has great editorial expertise in the area of children's literature." Johan has a long history with the Program Department. He has always gotten on well with Ellen.

"Yes, I've met Nanette. She's taken it upon herself to rewrite all our resources."

Ellen's words, along with Maeve Muldoon's confrontation with Lurleen, have boosted his confidence that he is not simply an uncooperative troublemaker with an outdated notion about how to relate to the rest of the org.

"She has managed to alienate our entire department."

"So I hear. She has some grandiose notion of what our department should be. From her point of view, the organization is really about books, but my understanding has always been that our main product is direct services to girls, and so the Program Department will always be the prime mover and Publications serves an ancillary function. You are content experts in the area of children's development and so you write these resources that we shepherd through the publishing process. Lurleen has been encouraging staff to be proactive, to use her word. Beyond that, she has a plan to place some manuscripts under contract with outside writers. It is like Lurleen has launched a war on many fronts, seeking to overrun not only the Program Department but Purchasing and Marketing as well, in an attempt to bring them under her power. She's like some hostile, endlessly subversive, and implacable foe. I have suggested to her that this is an institution and if she steps on toes, there will be retaliation." He has said too much, he senses, and in doing so, has given Ellen Deustch everything she wanted by asserting the primacy of Program and portraying Lurleen as an aggressive expansionist. But isn't that his purpose? He is afraid of Ellen Deutsch. It's that PhD. It's something she said years ago that she might not even remember. Something about her reason for leaving the university tenure track position she held was that her students weren't bright enough. Some mediocre institution, is how she spoke of it. In dismissing the university and its mentally dull students, she was dismissing him. That intellectual wound, passed on from his mother, he believes. Enough to paralyze him at times.

"She's stepping on toes, all right, and the whole building knows it," Ellen says.

"I asked her a while back why I was no longer working on Program projects. She said she had other tasks for me. She also said that Program had requested a new editor to work with." Johan remembers the conversation as a typical Lurleen tactic. Make it seem like he was standing alone. But the matter is risky to bring up, as suppose what Lurleen said was true?

"Don't trust Lurleen to tell the truth. The woman lies. It may not even be lying, in her mind. She may, in fact, believe what she says. It may be a clinical problem."

Ellen had actually proposed to Johan that he apply for the director of Publishing position when it fell vacant. But Johan senses that she had her own expansionist format and that she saw him as amiable, docile, afraid. In all likelihood she has sensed her innate superiority and ability to make him serve Program purposes.

Ultimately it is just another org blather session, even if it is with a Program powerhouse such as Ellen Deutsch. The problem, Johan senses, is that Lurleen's opponents are destined to lose. They don't know who they are up against, or maybe they do know and can't fully admit it to themselves. Lurleen is like a cartoon character others can squash, compact, trash, defenestrate, eviscerate, disintegrate, and in other ways dispose of only to find that she is back bigger than ever. She draws hatred, vituperation, scorn, etc., from them as a leech draws blood from a river wader. She thrives on their judgments and their outrage. They are elements as nutritive to her as food and drink. Opposition only causes her to bear down harder. She knows, as they know, that she will outlast them, for she exists in a category beyond any they can place her in.

Anyway, whatever happened to taking care of his side of the street and keeping the focus on himself? Whatever happened to suspending judgment?

Ancillary. Later, he must turn his face to the wall that he spoke such a word when a simpler one would have sufficed. Trying to rise to Ellen Deutsch's level on the basis of a single word. As if she didn't know. As if everyone doesn't know.

He has left the org behind to walk west among the lunch hour crowd in Herald Square, drawn past Macy's and the banal obscenity of Madison Square Garden, standing on the ruins of majestic and long-gone Pennsylvania Station. Beyond Seventh Avenue, the grip of commerce eases. Before him, on Eighth Avenue, stands the behemoth General Post Office, with its granite walls of mailman gray.

The round, stained-glass window of the old church has been breached in several places, either the target of rock throwers or simply the victim of age and neglect. A patchwork of plastic has been added to keep out the rain. Gone is the neon sign in the shape of a large cross that once glowed a beckoning red in the night, but the signboard offers welcome assurance that the church is still functioning: Sunday school and the Sunday afternoon service and Friday Bible School. And the pastor's name, Benjamin Horvath, spelled out in white movable letters.

A woman, old and bent, emerges and holds open the door.

"Are you looking for something?" she says. Her face shows suspicion. It is the face of one whose fears have grown with her years.

"I can't say," he is about to say, but what sort of unnecessarily vague mystery is that to involve her with? "My family used to worship here. I was in the neighborhood, and so I thought to stop by."

She stares down at his loafers, as if they might offer a clue whether he is predatory and dangerous. Satisfied, she says, "Come in," and stands aside.

The winding stairs creak as he mounts them. Even as a child the staircase seemed small and confining, and now, decades later, he must bend from the waist and lower his head. How did the congregation get in and out? he wonders, until he remembers the wide set of stairs outside leading up to the nave. He pauses at the landing and stares at the three sets of padded swinging doors through which the majority of the congregation would enter to fill the pews for the Sunday afternoon service.

He has no idea why he has come. He believes it may have been the water towers he saw that morning from the top floor of the org, putting him on the painful trail of something lost, or about to be lost, of childhood forsaken. He came because it is only here, in this desolate space, that he can be with his family, and his life, as it was in the beginning.

He climbs another equally tight set of twisting stairs to the balcony. He goes where his mother would go. It was not her way to sit below, or in the center of the balcony and facing Pastor Horvath at the pulpit, but to the side, where she would stare down at him in profile, as if it would be too much to take the full force of him head on.

The full congregation is gone, and with it vibrancy, leaving only a dark and declining structure: torn carpeting and peeling paint, and, in place of ripped out pews, those white plastic lawn chairs and a few metal folding ones.

He hears his mother rise in a delirium of sound, that stream of unintelligible syllables. Recalls the tears on her face and the fear he felt during her spells. He sees Pastor Horvath as he lowers Luke into the now dry baptismal font and remembers his silent scream, "Don't do it. Don't do it, Luke. Don't let them take you. Just don't do it," then watches in horror as Luke emerges with his wet hair plastered to his forehead. So many things he told Luke. Not to antagonize their father and suffer his blows. Not to marry his pregnant teenage girlfriend. The younger brother playing the older brother. Something like that. But what choice did he have? He saw what he saw.

As he is leaving, he is presented with a strange and shocking sight. Can it be? There, below, sitting alone in a pew near the transept, is Lurleen, her head bent in prayer.

The sun is still out when he leaves, but the mournful sound of the "The Old Rugged Cross" is loud in his ears. The emblem of suffering and shame…for a world of lost sinners was slain…till my trophies at last I lay down." A song sung at the pace his mother slowly walked up and down that long block.

Chapter 14

It is years earlier. In a long corridor leading to a suite of offices is a gunmetal-gray desk. The suite is located on the floor below the adult trade division, where Johan Manootdjian only months before worked for a senior editor named Milton Marg. It is as if Johan has been dropped from above into a hole from which he cannot find his way out, and in which there are long stretches of silence and inactivity. Though the adult trade division of Pentacle Books is only a short walk up the spiral staircase or a quick ride on the elevator, he stays away. He feels that he has been led to a place of deep seclusion that has severed him from the previous thread of his life.

There is a woman on the floor above. Her name is Doris Kleno. The personnel director for Pentacle Books, she is a woman on the downside of her beauty but still with the power to attract. It is, quite simply, that cleavage, those mesmerizing breasts. A woman who takes the liberty of expressing herself crudely has put it this way: "If the woman tips the scale at one hundred pounds, trust me, ninety-five of them are in her chest."

He had been with Mr. Marg for over a year. Wasn't age thirty too old to be an editorial assistant? He cried the day he reached that watershed year: a washout as a son, as a husband, as a would-be writer. All he has is the job, and what is that, to be at the beck and call of Mr. Marg every day? Others in his position are already advancing. Jeanine Ribaldi down the hall has gone off to join a literary agency, and Phil Leiter is now at Doubleday as an assistant editor. He doesn't know how to make these connections. No one is calling him to go anywhere. No one but Doris Kleno, the personnel director.

Since arriving at the company, a force field has kept him away from the other editorial assistants in the adult trade division. He was intimidated by their elite college backgrounds and the fact that they were younger. Around them he felt this paralyzing insecurity. He was afraid of their laughter, afraid he would say something foolish and be held up to ridicule. They are like those kids from Claremont, the private high school he attended years ago, intellectually gifted and from upper middle class homes. At Claremont he managed to go through all four of those school years without allowing the other students to know where he lived. Such was the power of shame in his life. It has not been so different at Pentacle Books. Go through the day with as little interaction with others as possible.

"Are you crazy? Don't you care about your life?" Emmy Eastley, one of these young editorial assistants in the adult trade division, said to him in amazement, having heard from him Doris Kleno's proposal that he enter the world of children's books. "Don't you know you'll get typecast and never get out?" How did she know such a thing? Was it because she had gone to Wellesley? Was it because she had an unerring instinct for the top and strategies in place for getting there?

It was as if she was saying, You only just got here. You only just joined us. Don't disappear now. Don't do it. Don't go, Johan. Don't go.

But he did go. Down the spiral staircase he went. Why? Because he had to. Because Doris Kleno told him to and he didn't know what else to do. Because he was married and because he would be given an office and so wouldn't have to sit outside Mr. Marg's office in plain sight of everyone.

All he wanted was to be left alone. He didn't care about options. If anything, the thought of having to make a choice summoned anger in him. That Wellesley girl. So full of herself, so confident, so unfettered, so able to chart an upward course.

He did not know at the time how committed to memory the floor above would be. Rhona Glock had arrived as the new editor in chief. She was the energy and devotion he was not. She was power personified, someone to steer clear of. She had arrived from Simon and Schuster to turn Pentacle Books around. She lived somewhere in Scarsdale and was married to the head of a Park Avenue legal firm and they owned a boat and somehow had three children. Rhona Glock had eyes that saw through Johan Manootdjian and so he tried to stay out of her sight.

There was Irene Schleff, the rights director, in the next office down. Young and unmarried, she carried the affliction of her anger in her pretty face. She was looking for someone to love. She said with her eyes that it could be Johan. She was Jewish and powerful, but she was wounded. She could not go forward like Rhona Glock. She could not have the babies. She paralyzed Johan with fear. He was good at all times in her midst.

There was Myra Fleischman and Laurie Newman and roly-poly Allan Jergens and Clyde Maillor (who knew how to do and close the deal) and Harran Ryder, who went to Yale and was said to be psychotic, and Phil O'Reilly and Pam Gooden and Ed Chase. They were there and all the others were there.

He thought his new position would give him an office but there is no office. There is only mortuary stillness in the infrequently traveled corridor where he sits. He is told that the person who previously sat at this desk hanged himself. He has a distinct memory of seeing an older man with a haggard face and wearing a rumpled suit at that same desk.

A young man with deeply black skin saunters past, then pauses. Though it is winter, he is wearing luminous red hot pants and a sleeveless top and black lace-up boots. On his arm he carries a fur coat.

"A gift from my honey bunch. You should get yourself one. Get you some love, too, while the getting's good," the young man says.

Normally, he does not so much as acknowledge Johan with a look or a word. His flesh is ample and yet he is not fat. A round man with saucers for eyes and a permanent smile, as if happiness is his birthright. Johan does not keep a log of his appearances, but at least once a week he makes his jubilant entrance.

Johan's boss is a luminary in the world of children's books. His name is Augustine O'Clair. He has a high forehead and a receding pile of white hair. He occupies a corner office at the far end of the suite, sitting behind a desk piled with papers, which he shows no inclination to tend to. Several times a day he passes by Johan's desk with a large coffee mug and returns with a refill. How pale he is. How old he looks. How fallen and solemn his face.

How can you be a luminary when there is no light? Augustine O'Clair looks like a man who has lost all hope. A walking cadaver, with deadness in his eyes and that pallid complexion.

Johan has this idea, from the jacket copy of his books, that Mr. O'Clair lives quietly with his wife and daughter on the East Side of Manhattan. He imagines him in his book-lined study in a velvet robe, and a faithful golden retriever lying beside his slipper-clad feet. Johan assumes he is a man in whom the fire of passion has been banked, so he can maintain without distraction the life of the mind.

Johan does not know that Mr. O'Clair lives estranged from his wife in the Murray Hill Hotel, a seedy refuge for transients, drug addicts, women of the night, the criminally insane, and welfare dependents in a neighborhood that has fallen from grace. He does not know that Derrick, the hot pants messenger, is in fact his lover. He does not know that within a few weeks Mr. O'Clair, grossly addicted to cocaine and bourbon, will be found dead on the mildewed carpet in his room by a hotel maid.

At the lunch hour Johan walks through the ornate lobby of marble and gold leaf in the direction of Madison Avenue. Suddenly he stops short and experiences a wave of terror at the sight of Mr. Marg ahead of him in his full-length wool coat. Like the other men and women of power at Pentacle Books, Mr. Marg is off to lunch with an agent or an author. Is it the Oak Room at the Plaza or will it be Twenty-One? No matter. The deal will get done. Royalties. Rights. Sub-rights. Options. Johan does not fully appreciate yet what he will come to find out. The world is about connection. The world is about relationship. It is about being able to do the deal. Mr. Marg knows how to use people and allow them to use him when it is in his interest. He has an understanding and acceptance of the world that precludes judgment. What is, is. He sees the big picture and can break the mold. All Johan can do, from his place of hiding, is see that the sentences are grammatically correct, and sometimes he cannot even do that.

Johan hangs back, dawdling at the concession stand while outside on the avenue Mr. Marg shoots his arm out to command a cab. Thinking, I am in another world now. I have fallen back into childhood. We are strangers to each other. What have I done?

Thinking, Mr. Marg goes to the Oak Room. I go to McDonalds.

Channeled between tall buildings, a biting wind from off the river blasts him as he reaches the corner. Into B. Altman he ducks, the arctic cold having shot through his pea jacket and settled into his bones. Wood-paneled walls, the scent of perfume, the ding ding of gentle bells. He is not there in the department store to buy. There is no money to buy. He is there to live. He is just walking so he will not go crazy, so he will not be a pane of glass shattering into thousands of shards never to be put back together again. Please, dear God, hold me. He is not a man who prays. Prayer is his father saying an endless grace and dissolving into tears as the food grows cold. Prayer is the tool of the impractical and the weak. Is this what it means to be newly sober? You turn to God rather than to the bottle?

Some blocks away, on a side street east of Park Avenue, he sees, through a barred window of a brownstone, into a small, dark room filled with people seated in folding chairs, and descends a few steps to join them. Sitting at a right angle to the gray-haired speaker, he listens as she tells her story in a matronly voice. Shaker Heights. Wealthy parents. Father socially prominent. Debutante ball and a Radcliffe education and marriage to the Harvard quarterback. Five beautiful children. But she never felt good enough. Some lingering insecurity from childhood. Drinking helped to ease her anxiety while her husband was away on frequent business trips. The scotch made her glow. Made the room glow. Had to rely more and more on maids and nannies to tend to the children's needs as the drinking progressed. And then there was the trip her husband didn't return from. Someone else, a younger woman on his office staff, had entered his life. "I just felt so left." The words torn from her and penetrating Johan's heart.

He stares out the dirty window to the street. He can see people's legs and nothing more as they move past. Isabel. He had her in his life but now another man has taken her away. She too, like the speaker's husband, has left. A gnawing pain. He is here, hidden away in some musty basement, just as at Pentacle Books he is hidden away in the children's books suite. He has lost. He has been defeated.

Things coming undone. Hadn't even been able to send out Christmas cards. The drinking in the way of everything so he picked up the phone and left a message for his therapist, **Dr.** Reiner. "I'm going to put a bullet in your brain." A crazy, unkind thing, to threaten a man who kept him out of a mental institution when he cracked up three years before as the result of a daily regimen of speed and alcohol. "You don't need a new typewriter. You need a new life." So Dr. Reiner said the next day, after Johan offered the lame excuse that he had been upset because he was unable to afford the second-hand machine in a store window.

He attends another meeting on a Saturday night in a church basement down near Waverly Place, in Greenwich Village. Yes, it is only a mile or so from Isabel's apartment. Yes, he could go there, but no, he can't. Not with things as they are. Not with him as he is. He is close but he is very far.

Seated in the back row and clutching a copy of the *New Yorker* magazine, he listens as a fifty-year-old man shares about his fall from grace. Lost his Westchester home. His lovely wife. His beautiful children. His position with a prestigious firm. His descent to short-order cook and the abandoned building in New York City where he passed a hard winter rather than surrender to the men's shelters he feared. The bottle gangs he drank with. Now he is building his life back slowly. Rents a room in Astoria, Queens. Part-time work as a proofreader.

The man has gone on further with his drinking, but the identification is there. Hadn't Johan too suffered blackouts? Was he too not missing work because he was too hung over and sick from the previous night's excesses?

Afterward a powerfully built man in jeans and a work shirt introduces himself. He says some members of the group are going to a local coffee shop. Would Johan care to join them? Johan senses the man is gay and immediately places a sexual meaning on the invitation, assuming that it is simply a prelude to the man asking him back to his apartment. He declines Claude's offer, but leaves the meeting happy to feel desired.

And then there is another lunch hour meeting, near his place of work. It is led by a young and attractive woman. He goes up to her afterward and introduces himself. Would she give him her phone number so he could perhaps call her? "Why not get his phone number?" she says, not unkindly, pointing to a straight-arrow sort of man in a business suit. He feels, rebuffed, humiliated.

A memory comes to him. He is quite young, a child, and walking along Broadway with his sister Leah. Coming toward them is a woman from the building where they live. He extends an open hand, palm up, toward her. "Could you give us a dollar? We're orphans," he tells the woman. She responds with a smile and a quarter. Did it start there?

At still another meeting a sobriety enthusiast throws her arms around him and smooches him on the cheek. Her name is Love, and she is one of a number who have formed the hug and kiss brigade in the church basements of New York City. Love locusts, feeling if only temporarily, their oneness with the universe. He sees it, the monstrousness of his rage, the desire (not acted upon) to to push her back, to say to her and to the women of America and every woman who was ever born, I have had enough of your power and dominion. I am here to be free of you.

And to hear a woman who was counting down to her wedding day say, in another church basement, that she picked up a drink after several years of sobriety because her fiancé broke the engagement. Dependency his own Achilles' heel, he understood. No one must have that kind of power over him anymore. No one.

His workday over, he steps from the building and makes a beeline for the candy store just across the street. Big jars of candy beckon. A bag of Swedish fish in hand, he enters the subway at rush hour. Bodies are pressed against him, and yet the crowd is no deterrent to stuffing his mouth with the chewy sweets. One after another he devours, until the bag is empty. A man stares at him in amazement and disgust. "Eat. Have a malted or a candy bar. It lessens the craving for alcohol," people in the meetings say. The train arrives at Union Square, and then Astor Place. He feels no need to bolt upstairs to the wines and spirits supermarket for the big bottles of hearty burgundy.

In the Bowery loft Sarah and he can see their breath. That is what happens when you move into a loft one sweltering summer day seeing only the vast space and the layout and fail to notice, until winter arrives, that the building lacks a boiler and the only defense against the debilitating cold are two space heaters suspended a foot below the ceiling. Even tilted at a downward angle the air blown out by the heaters quickly rises to warm the floor of their neighbor in the garret above. Their bodies are padded with several layers of clothes as they sleep and wool caps cover their heads. The hiss of a radiator is his dream.

A devastating fire on lower Broadway, near Bleecker Street, has burned away virtually everything but the girders and masonry from an eight-story building. Huge stalactites of jagged ice hang from the skeletal structure, making for a terrifying sight against the gray sky. Surely there were victims. And surely Sarah and he will also be incinerated when their ancient little building goes up in flames like kindling. The gas heaters will explode as they sleep and dental records will be needed to identify them.

One evening, as he sits in the living area of their loft, the front door is rattled, a sound inexplicable except as the brazen attempt of a murderer to enter and dispense with him with cold efficiency, a knife with a serrated edge his weapon of choice. The murderer has come calling. His name is Boldness. The time for talking is long since over. Nearby, Sarah is working away in her studio with a focused look on her medication-thickened face. Not even the murderer at the door can distract her from the easel and the brushstrokes she applies to the canvas. Dark, dreamlike landscapes. Distorted figures. Those who are out there and lost she embraces. Ensor. Soutine. Johan tries to call to her, but it is like those childhood dreams in which, even with the advantage of distance from his nemesis, he could neither cry out nor run, his feet fixed to the spot by terror as the annihilating figure streaked closer and closer. He has no voice. He has no power.

Beyond a view onto the Bowery through those ugly silver gates that mar so many windows. The eyesore that security requires. He and Sarah are shut in and *they, they,* those others, are shut out., and have been since a second story artist entered through one of the two windows a few years back. The drifter had jumped up and knocked the weighted fire escape ladder off its hook so it would swing down and he could ascend. A man in need of his daily bread.

Sarah startled from her nap. She threw a plate and he fled only to come back a second time.

And where were you, Johan Manootdjian? Where were you?

At Jones Beach, images of bodies, not Sarah's, in my red-light district head.

When he finds his voice and approaches the demarcation line between the living area and her studio, a worn expanse of pale green carpeting that no amount of vacuuming can restore to its original luster, and asks her to corroborate the violent rattling of the door, the bold attempt at entry, she remains engaged, as if he is not there.

"Did you hear it?" he says a second time,

Finally she looks up, if only briefly. Her eyes are small, smaller than they used to appear when she bothered with mascara and eyeliner and the like. And they have gone beyond reproach and accusation and settled into hardness.

When he presses her a third time, she says this: "Can't you leave me alone? Can't you? How many times have I asked you? Is it a thousand? Two thousand? Just try not to come in here when I am working."

She does not say, "Open that door and open it now. Take his knife, baby. Take it in your ass and take it in your chest. Take it in your eye so it comes out the back of your head. Take it like the man you never have been. Get your just deserts, bastard."

They had bought the loft fixtures from a lawyer turned painter who was moving to a bigger space in SoHo. "Look," he had said. "We'll have a party. Your friends and mine. What do you say?" And of course there was no party, as there were no friends, at least of Johan's, only Sarah and him. Maybe the man had no friends either, but somehow Johan doubted that. He had left wife and kids and career to pursue his calling. And he had left behind in the loft a steamy letter from a woman, obviously his lover.

He withdraws into his study, a walled-in space of sheet rock nailed to the columns that support the loft bed. In this small space is a desk, a set of shelves on which he keeps his manuscripts spread out, and a manual Smith-Corona portable typewriter. To one side of the typewriter, in that other life, would be a joint and on the other a mug full of blackberry-flavored brandy. From the synergism of the grass and the alcohol, perhaps he could hope for magical prose, sentences of Henry James-like length and quality. Without such intoxicating and stoning influences, there was no possibility of expressing anything worthwhile on paper. Now, without the buffer of alcohol and reefer, he has nothing, only a brazen would-be murderer seeking to dispatch him from his barren life.

In the stillness, he hears the swish, swish, of his virtually shut-in wife as she cleans her brush in a jar of turpentine. How dare she have ambition? How dare she want to live and thrive? How dare she outstrip him? How dare she win?

Now the would-be murderer is inside the door. Now it is he who is the would-be murderer.

Isabel,
What I am saying is that things happened too fast. I wasn't ready to stop drinking. It was like having the blanket pulled off me on a freezing cold night.

"I'm pregnant," she says.
"You're what?"
"Pregnant.'"
"How?'"
"How else?" she says.
What else do you remember, Johan? Yes, you, Johan Manootdjian.
"I am still with Mr. Marg. It is before I have fallen into the children's books department with the arrested ones, the ones with wounds that only allow them to pretend at adulthood. I discuss the matter with Dr. Reiner. I guess you could call it a discussion. I feel, I don't know what I feel, that things are out of control. Not only

am I having an affair with a woman but now she is pregnant. There is something painful here. I don't know how to describe it. Sarah makes fun of pregnant women. She refers to them as cows. No great love for children coming from her. But Isabel is different. She has already had a child, beautiful Mia. And now she talks of having this child by me. But then it is something else. I don't know. Once again pastel chairs. Once again Muzak in the waiting room. I wonder, yes I wonder, what it would be for this amazing woman to have our baby. But how can such a thing be achieved, given our circumstance? As I escort her home from the facility (is that the word?) all I can think of is her pain. She can hardly stand and doubles up as I try to hail a cab. What have I done to this beautiful woman? What scar have I placed on her? What wretched experience have I put her through? The pain, her pain, travels through me in waves. I want to protect her. I want to love her. But Dr. Reiner is there. Somewhere he is there. He does not let me drown in my own feeling. He throws me a line. 'She made a choice.' It is cold water in the face. He is the father I later threatened to kill.

The thing is…never mind.

The table is made of oak and lightly varnished. It has a busy structure underneath and leaves at either end. A gate-leg table, the antiques store owner over on Hudson Street called it. That would be several years back, when the side effects of the Haldol were acute and he had to get out of the cramped apartment where they were living on East Sixth Street, the walls closing in on him; his very skin oppressive. He was only taking the medication because there had been the knives. He had seen them plunging into Sarah's chest, the grisly images produced by the diet pills he took and the booze he drank and the feelings he didn't talk about or even know he had. Crying on the street without any understanding why this might be so.

Behind him a water heater, cylindrical, white, vertical. Walls painted a strong purple and something called a lofa bed of a similar color, a long cylinder coiled like a giant turd as a substitute for a sofa, one of the fixtures the previous occupant left behind—a man who came to art late in life, and with a big wallet, shedding his career and his wife and family for a new direction and a younger woman. Two windows facing west and looking out on a courtyard they have no access to, but which will place you in a state of meditative calm as, for long stretches of the day, it exists in peaceful shadow under the branches of a honey locust tree. You can see down to a battered fence of weathered wood, the earth partially freed from a crumbling layer of paving. You can see the progress of ruin, a patient struggle waged by nature against artifact.

The sun, when it finds you from the other side of the Hudson River, will be gentle, even in summer. It is tired by now, and ready to duck down over the horizon in a haze of smog-induced beauty that pollutants can produce.

He wants to tell you about the table because he sits here many hours of the day, thinking about what he will do or trying not to think at all. The table is clear. It must remain so. Order must always maintain itself.

Sarah receives a monthly check. Her parents lead a life of self-indulgence, she reasons, and are the cause of her many problems; it is only right that they be responsible for her therapy bills and living expenses.

She gets up when she can, long after Johan is gone, and struggles into her day. The daily shopping expedition at the A & P across town on LaGuardia Place gets her moving and helps her mood. They eat poor. Pasta and tomato sauce out of a jar. Salads of iceberg lettuce and those tasteless supermarket tomatoes. Shopping, cooking, cleaning—it is the service she can provide.

Because the bathroom, a narrow space with a toilet at one end and a shower stall at the other, lacks a sink, they use the one in the kitchen area for purposes beyond washing dishes. It is where he shaves, staring at himself in the mirror above the faucets, and where Sarah applies her makeup on those occasions when she still wears any.

"I hear you masturbating in there, skinny dick. Don't think I don't. I hear everything you think but don't say. I hear all those thoughts you're having about her." It is her morning song. She has seen through the closed door and through the wall. She has seen that Isabel is a living, breathing presence in his mind.

"I'm sorry…I'm sorry." He leaves a trail of apologies as he goes toward the door that morning. He will make it up to her. He really will. He will buy her a new press, a better, sturdier kind than the one she now has. It will be the very same kind that Isabel uses. He will pay for it on a layaway plan, since no credit card is available to them. Twenty dollars a week. In no time she'll be up and running with the best tools.

They have made no structural changes to the loft. They don't know how. They just live there, she painting and making her prints and he doing some writing when he can. Things—canvases, prints, manuscripts—pile up, but neither gallery nor publishing doors open. Only his mind opens. Suddenly, while seated at the table, he is defenseless against the truth. A sense of his own insanity comes over him and he begins to cry over his treatment of his in-laws. There is no way to justify his conduct or the attitude he has harbored toward them. He places a piece of paper in the typewriter and addresses himself to Sarah's father. He cites all the kind and generous things he and Sarah's mother did for him: bailing him out of jail when he was twenty-one, their endless hospitality, their financial loans. *How long are we going to have to take care of you, Johan? How long? The sting of her mother's words in his ears.*

He is not attacked by this truth. It is just there. Things he couldn't see when he drank he can see now. The bottle is not his friend; the Van Dines are not his enemy.

What is God if he is not vision?

He mails the letter. He has to. There is a burning need to say it: I'm sorry. I'm sorry.

Her name is Olivia Davies. She is the new director of the department. She has come to Pentacle by way of Scholastic Books, where she was a senior editor. She whisks past Johan's desk wearing a navy blue pea jacket, as if she has the will to ward off winter blasts by the heat of her own temper and the indomitable nature of her will. An early warning sign of danger, he will come to know, is when her cheeks puff up and her eyes narrow. If she can claim her temper as an asset, she can do the same with her plainness. She wears it with a defiant pride. Small eyes, sliver lips. A face that allows her to dispense with any attempts at charm. Intelligence, toughness, shrewdness, and wit are her calling cards. She is not Ferdinand O'Clair. She has written no books. She is not ruled by dissipation. Her love lights do not shine for a boom box lover or perhaps any lover.

Olivia Davies is wrath itself, Johan fears. He is nobody she would have hired. She has surely seen him as he is, a tall, skinny man who sits at a virtually empty desk for the entire day. He has been given refuge from the cold. The alternative is the street, where he will die. No one else will hire him. This is his lifeline.

There is a sales conference that winter at the nearby Union League Club, to which the president of Pentacle Books, Mr. Felton, has ties. It is one of those old money clubs with oil paintings of financial titans—railroad barons, oil barons, men in vested suits with big mustaches and pocket watches—hanging from its oak-paneled walls, a place permeated with reserve, as if it has bent to the character of its founders and their heirs. America's past lingers here. The ghosts of old men with shriveled calves seated in wingback chairs can be felt. More visible are the grownups, of course, the editors of adult books, including Mr. Marg, whose suspenders are today emerald green and whose tie is a bold cobalt blue and whose eyes sparkle with mirth and power through the lenses of large white plastic frames. Mr. Marg defies age. He defies time. He growls it into nonexistence with his fervor for life as he pitches his spring list, including a new novel by an old author and a mega-book by a rising Hollywood star. His audience is the jaded sales force, men and women inured to the road and bad food. Men and women of the Ramada Inn and Holiday Inn who journey near and far to move Pentacle's titles.

Representing the children's books department, in addition to Olivia, are Charles Nigel and Claire Eastland. Charles is a wonder, with a master's degree in art history from Yale University. Some days he arrives in a preppie blue blazer and charcoal gray slacks. Other days he appears in well-tailored suits. And then there is his casual attire: jeans and a white Oxford shirt under a crew neck sweater. Early thirties, close-cut hair prematurely graying, wire-frame glasses. A deep, refined voice. He is masterful at all he does. Johan leafs through his edited manuscripts with shock and amazement. The intelligent, perceptive queries, the bold substantive editing, the easy way he has with everyone that comes from being sure of his ability.

Charles Nigel's lover calls Johan when Charles's line is busy. His bitchy voice. "Is Charles there?" he says, wearily drawing out every word, as if to put Johan on guard that this is a caller with nails should there be even the hint of an attitude in his response. A caller who lives for provocation, whereas Charles Nigel is genial.

Johan thinking, I don't want to compete with Charles Nigel. I must not compete with him, not simply because I would lose, but because my life depends on not competing with him. Johan thinking another thought: Charles Nigel is my brother as my brother could not be, and even if he isn't, I must make him so. I must have somewhere to turn. Oh God, oh God.

And there is the art director, Deana Matthews, but formerly Deana Zeromskis. A woman with the power to change her name and her life. By some coincidence, she was married to a boarding school classmate of Charles Nigel who went on to become a physician and from whom she is now divorced and learning what it is to be a single parent of two young children. Already Johan knows things about Charles and Deana. He knows, for example, that she favors Charles greatly over Olivia, for Deana is a real woman responsive to a man's touch, and Olivia, as Deana sees her, is the other, that children's books other, a woman who sleeps alone and has always slept alone and who favors cats over people.

Deana is full of opinion, of judgment. She has read *The Painted Word*, by Tom Wolfe. Armed with his exposé of the art world, she denounces those frauds who are driven to abstraction because they cannot draw or paint real life figures. She sees them with their fake intelligence and fake talent because she knows the difference between fakery and talent. Deana Matthews knows the real thing, and Charles Nigel is the real thing. "He should be the director of this department, not Olivia," She says. And if that is not enough, she also says: "He could be an art director as well as an editor. He has that kind of ability."

Deana's words pierce him like a sword, for that is Johan's affliction, to interpret, to personalize. In elevating Charles, she has lowered him. As if she has read Johan's mind, she says, puzzled, "You are so humble," when he comes to her office with an armful of mechanicals with overlays of a picture book Olivia has approved for the printer.

"Yes?" he says, unable to say more. He hears the word as an accusation. What is it with people that they take the liberty of assessing him?

"Don't you have any ambition? Any drive? Don't you want to do something with your life?"

Leaving him speechless.

Now they are at the Union League Club, and Olivia is presenting their books, and Charles Nigel is also talking about their books, as is Claire Eastland. It is not possible for Johan to comprehend how they can stand before this large gathering and speak in such a way and endure the visible indifference of the sales reps, who know small potatoes when they see them. He does not belong in this world. He never has. He must find a room where he can sit alone and have his insignificance reduced.

Because he has told Dr. Reiner the utter truth, which is that he is incapable of being in the same room with others without some chemical equalizer and will have to run and hide forever if such pharmaceutical aid is not dispensed, Dr. Reiner has written out a scrip for Haldol and Artane. Not that he is psychotic. Sarah's father, Mr. Van Dine, may say so because Johan suffered an auditory hallucination the night he imagined that Sarah had been abducted by a monster, but Dr. Reiner knows better. Dr. Reiner knows who Johan is and what he is. He knows that Johan is a narcissistic fool who has made a hash of his life and that he is incapable of coping.

Johan runs to the pharmacy on the corner of Eighth Street and Second Avenue, where old Mr. Minskoff pecks at the typewriter keys to fill out the prescription label and becomes Johan's best friend, his very best friend. While waiting, Johan stares back out at the street through the glass-paneled door and makes eye contact with a man who looks like he has been sleeping under bridges and on sidewalk grates, a man wearing rags and with matted hair and street grime absorbed deep in his skin. Through the rattled door he comes, lumbering like Frankenstein, his stench the kind that can empty subway cars—a smell of caked shit and dried piss and sweat and all other ingredients for overwhelming B.O.—preceding his arrival. He has seen Johan's paralysis. Like a dog he has smelled his fear. Instantly and without a word he begins kicking Johan on the shins with his heavy boots. Though he is a big man, the winter elements have sapped his strength. The kicks are almost feathery.

It is for the pharmacist, liver-spotted, frail, approaching threescore and ten, to intercede for Johan with his newfound friend. "Get out of here immediately or I will call the police," he commands, and though Mr. Minskoff comes only to the giant's chest, Johan's assailant turns and does as he is told, without a word being spoken.

Some years later a man will say to Johan, "Fear is a form of prayer" and Johan will know what he knew all along, that he drew the down-and-out man to him, as if his eyes were suction cups. And the man will say other things: "What we are running from is what we are running toward" and "the goal is continuous prayer" and "The truth without love is an attack." And Johan will listen, and try to apply these words to the workings of his runaway mind.

Is Haldol the agent? Is Artane the counter-agent? He cannot keep it straight. So much depends on remembering and yet he forgets.

He lives in the back and forth of the subway, the screech and the roar and all the noises mechanical things make in this city of engines turned on so their power can manifest. Above the ground, below ground. It does not matter. Do not give your life to them by wandering into their path.

He has been tasked with sending galley proofs to an author. It is not type. It is just proof that type exists. Then there will be something called repro that proves even more that the type exists, or maybe it is the type itself. It is all beyond him, as the difference between a lithograph and an etching is beyond him, or what on earth intaglio really is.

It is not working. He cannot pull the facts together fast enough. He cannot marshal them as his line of defense. To calm down he sits at his student desk in his study. He has another desk, too, a ship captain's desk of blond pine wood he bought at an antique shop some years ago. It is there in reserve, another surface on which he can write. It is good to have options, or does he mean to say choices?

A coffee table book on caves lies open on the desk. The glossy pages are crowded with tiny text. English spellings abound: "colour" for "color," "theatre" for "theater." He is trying to hold in his mind the difference between a stalactite and a stalagmite. The mnemonic trick is working—""c" for ceiling and "g" for ground. One tiny piece of the body armor he will need is now in place. More additions will come. Yes, I can do this, he thinks. I can stay at my desk and read. And no sooner does he have the thought than he goes to the lofa bed and lies down. It is not for him to wear things out. Everything must be saved, lest he become an overwrought engine that goes to pieces all by itself.

A lofa bed for a loafer man. Hah hah hah.

In the morning he wakes early and reads the production guide *Pocket Pal,* grappling with letterpress and offset and other printing techniques, duotones and halftones and the four-color process, quads and quoins and kerning. He is fortified not merely with fact but that second cup of instant coffee and that extra smoke so he can be supplied with both caffeine and nicotine. Oh, the combinations of life. He cannot get enough. He wants their power in every cell. He wants to kiss someone given the morning joy he is experiencing.

He enters the Bleecker Street station to find men sleeping on flattened cardboard boxes. There are patches of wet darkness on the platform where they have relieved themselves in the night. An early bird among them has been roused from slumber and staggers toward Johan as an express roars past on a downtown track. The man's face, blistered by the cold, has been grooved, perhaps with a box cutter or broken glass; his nose is mottled and bulbous. He comes to Johan with his hand open to receive. He is looking for his morning love. He is looking for his warmth in winter. He is looking for his Forget All This. Johan does not taunt or mock him. He does not make some little looking for the hair of the dog that bit you joke. He *sees* him, sees the man's need, his absolute necessity. He sees who the man is behind the grime.

"Can you spare a quarter, buddy?" the man says.

Johan will do him better. He reaches for his wallet and extracts two dollar bills.

"Thank you, buddy." The man's voice does not go with his appearance. A soft voice, that of a human being.

Johan remembers fantasies in the last year of his drinking—the flatbed railway car on which he sat, pecking away at the keys of his Olivetti portable, or the crummy hotel with the bare lightbulb in which he ate ravioli out of a can.

He turns away, feeling sickened by his own attempt at goodness.

It is the rush hour, and in the subway car he notices, beyond the attractive woman who has become the one millionth love of his life, an advertisement for Transit Authority token booth operators. The salary is more than he currently makes. He imagines himself in one of those booths, riders slipping their bills and coins through the small opening in the bulletproof window in exchange for tokens to drop in the turnstile slots. Given his level of anxiety, the job has enormous appeal: security and a level of responsibility that won't overwhelm him. After all, how much math do you need to exchange money for tokens? And there is also the comfort of repetitive action and protection from extended interactions with the riders. Accessible to the public and yet protected from the public.

At work he has his mug of coffee where he can keep an eye on it, right there on his desk. His mother's milk. To be without is to incur anxiety. And he really needs it that morning, and lots of it, for Charles Nigel has asked him, in that caressing, deep voice of his, to send galley proofs, with a cover letter, to an author. Then Charles goes and does something. He places a stopwatch on him. Johan can hear its relentless ticking. He cannot think hearing the movement of the second hand. He is losing the race against the clock. And then Charles comes right back and says he has a second set of proofs for another author. Charles's voice and the ticking have triggered some contraction in Johan's skin. It is pulling too tight. He must loosen it so he can breathe. It may be only a matter of stepping away from his desk and going to the bathroom, which is spacious and has those cool tiles on which he can lie down. He runs down the hallway. But his mind has lied. The bathroom offers no relief. It gives him nothing but a space in which to feel more torment.

He bolts, coatless, out of the office, nearly colliding with Olivia, who has managed to jump back and now stares with astonishment as he disappears into the elevator. Through the lobby Johan zips. See Johan run between speeding cars and dodge the oncoming bus. See him descend, two steps at a time, into the subway station some blocks from the office. Mercifully he has a token ready for the turnstile slot, but when he approaches the platform's edge and peers back up the tunnel, there is only the emptiness and stillness of a weekday morning past the morning rush hour. There is no time to waste. If the local lacks the common decency to run on the tracks that have been laid down for it, then he must utilize those tracks himself. At that moment of resolve comes the roar of a downtown express. Parallel with the cars of the rushing train he runs along the platform, then jumps to the tracks and enters the darkness of the tunnel. He is not five yards into it before he trips and sprawls on the gravel and ties between the rails.

As he struggles up he turns and sees behind him that the local has arrived and in fact is just leaving the station. The train's lights have found him. There is the protracted blast of its horn as he staggers into a scalloped recess in the wall. With hands over his ears he lets out a scream drowned by the train's roar and sees the blue flash of electricity from the train's interaction with the third rail. He is short of breath and wheezing like an asthmatic. He hears the thump thump in his chest. Until he tried to run, he had no idea how out of shape he was.

The train has stopped. He can see the lights in the car above shining so bright in the contrasting darkness of the tunnel and a woman staring as if from a dimension he is apart from. He must go. He must get help. He must not let the train people find him. Not when there is such an affliction to his skin.

The platform is not so far away, and there is a ladder to assist him onto it. He runs past the three last cars still in the station. Their doors are closed. Nothing has changed. He is still in the tortured state. If anything, it has grown worse. But now he has a plan, a plan born in the depths of necessity, and driven by it he mounts the steep stairs. His plan will work where nothing else could. It has to.

On the corner of Thirty-fourth and Park Avenue, below a tall and regal apartment building, stands a pharmacy. He will enter an orderly world where he will find another Old World Jew in a lab coat who is a master of pharmaceutical magic like Mr. Minskoff down on St. Mark's Place. And the pharmacist, Mr. Ginsburg, will find him, Johan Manootdjian, bursting through the door in clothes streaked with dirt and his hand outstretched, pleading with the good man to give him one, just one Artane, so his skin can be returned to normal.

Mr. Ginsburg could humiliate him. He could demand that he leave the pharmacy. But quietly he receives Johan's plea and returns with that one solitary pill in his open hand for Johan to take. Mr. Ginsburg has taken pity on him. For this, as the pill begins to work its magic, dispelling the web of torture that gripped him tighter and tighter, Johan can only say thank you, thank you, with tears in his eyes as he backs out the door.

"I love you. I really do," he says, crying, his relief so immense, to the staring Mr. Ginsburg, who turns away. To be a Jew is to be holy. To be a Jew is to walk the earth and partake of its fullness. It is to retreat to a temple on Saturday for the power tradition can bestow.

In the men's room at work he can do nothing about the creosote stains on his shirt and pants from his fall. Olivia sees his dishevelment and looks away. She has England in her bones, the Magna Carta and the right to privacy. She comes from the land of private gardens, overgrown and lush.

He thinks back to the panhandling bum he encountered in the Bleecker Street station that morning. He drinks the now cold coffee, then goes to get some more. Then he sits and sits and sits in the peace that he has found.

Claire Eastland can do no wrong in Olivia's eyes, nor can she in Johan's. She is tall and thin, with long brown hair that falls freely to the small of her back when she allows it to, for there are days when she wears it constrained in a braid that hangs straight down like a long, thick rope. Her waist is small and her hips round and her legs slender and shapely in a way that makes him quiver. No hair style or apparel, no changing look, can mute her power.

Claire Eastland comes to them from Harcourt Brace Jovanovich, a mouthful, where she was an editor in their children's books department. Johan has learned further that she is a graduate of Vassar College. The thing, of course, he wants to know is if she is deeply in love and, even if she is, whether she has a predilection for wandering ways. This is the state of mind he finds himself in with his depleted resources and idle days. Olivia rules with her anger but Claire has him bow down to her with her beauty and her brains.

In the aftermath of the sales conference, Olivia arranges a departmental luncheon at a nearby Japanese restaurant to formally and belatedly welcome Claire, who, because of the urgency of the situation, has had to hit the ground running, Olivia says. As the cork is popped on a bottle of champagne and the bubbly foams out its mouth, Claire turns to Johan with a stricken look and surprises him by whispering in a voice of desperation, "I can't drink. I'm an alcoholic."

"Just order Perrier. No one will notice," he says quietly. He too has experienced that same fear of being found out as an alcoholic for refusing a drink.

And she does just that. When a toast is proposed, both she and he raise their glasses of mineral water with a twist of lemon.

Her revelation has moved them closer in his mind. They now can stand on common ground. Such intensity of emotion her confession has elicited in him. Such an unbearable desire for more. But how? He must find a way. He must.

Though he is normally out the door at 5 p.m., on this day he hangs back as first Charles Nigel and then Olivia and Lorna Simpkins, the department secretary, leave.

"All work, no play?" Charles says, in ironic counterpoint to the fact of his bare desk.

"Oh, he's so good. So organized," Olivia says, sending shivers of fear through Johan in anticipation of the time when she will see he is not so very good, the time when she will break him with the crushing weight of her anger.

But Lorna is within earshot. "Are you so good, Johan?"

She is young, adrift, with big, laughing eyes when sadness does not overcome her, and her overbite puts him in mind of Eleanor Roosevelt. Teeth are not meant to be so much on display.

Lorna comes from wealth; thus, she never contemplates it. It is just there, a given. A father who owns half the real estate in Manhattan. A free apartment. A free life.

Already she is on Olivia's radar screen. Olivia has detected the smell of sex on her. Always that smell is on Lorna. She arrives to work wearing the same clothes as the night before. It is her boyfriend. He is a rocker in the downtown clubs. She is game, and goes where he leads. She has an appetite for her own demise. There is richness in her life that she must squander.

A laugh and a smile, so knowing of who he is, accompany her query.

"How good do I have to be?" Johan says.

"Well, I don't know, Johan. I just don't know. Maybe we should explore that."

Johan sees her attractiveness, the ample cleavage his eyes go magnetically toward, noting the swell of her breasts under her tight mustard yellow sweater. And those full lips and that aura of lazy sensuality and those glittering, mischievous eyes. But it would only be a matter of time before she became disparaging, before she ran him down. Wasn't it only last week that Charles Nigel asked her to type a letter, and she said, "Why not give it to Johan? He just sits there in the hallway day after day." Disrespecting him. Laughing at him. Telling the truth about him. So much shame. So very much shame breaking over him, like a powerful and flattening wave.

A liberty. That's what it was. She took a liberty with him. She had disregarded his title and placed him at her level. She made him into a child, a goof-off just like her. She got his pride involved. And now she is taunting him again, just drooling on him with her contempt.

He has hurt himself by entering the world of children's books, he fears. There is a feeling of painful compression, as if his size thirteen foot has been jammed into a size ten shoe. But that's not it either. It is a feeling of being back in elementary school, with all its associations of early social failure and classroom dullness. He was not a reader as a child. He had no involvement with books. The streets had been his books. Do they not know that? What is this manufacture of innocence that they collaborate in? Picture books? He will give them picture books. He will give them knife fights and drunken brawls and men lacking the restraint to keep their hands off children.

Claire Eastland. Not a discordant note in her name, the syllables breaking her way. It feels crazy to approach a woman of her pedigree based on one blurted confession, but he has no choice. This is his moment. If not now, never. Humiliation is preferable to the pain that would result from cowardly walking out the door. Love is paramount and must be bowed down to and obeyed wherever it is found, and Claire Eastland has become the object of that love. When the bell rings, you must answer it. He is in the wake of a marriage. He must go where there is light and energy.

It is not as if Claire Eastland is waiting for him. She sits inside her tiny office profile to the door, her back ballerina-straight as her fingers fly over the keyboard of the taupe state-of-the-art IBM Selectric III, equipped with a correcting key she will seldom need. A typewriter a perk reserved for elite staff. She turns toward Johan and appraises him while her fingers continue to hit the keys. Though she sometimes wears contacts, this is her day for specs, which do not detract at all from her appearance. In fact, the designer quality of the red frames and the clear, tinted lenses enhance her appeal. What is sexier than a cerebral as well as beautiful woman with the hidden wantonness of the town librarian?

"Are you OK?" she asks, her hands now off the keyboard.

The protective space that Johan has felt himself in, which has mitigated the sense that what he is proposing to say will be ruinous, suddenly has disappeared, like a warm spot in the ocean that quickly vanishes. He stumbles forward.

"You see, if I can go back to what you said to me at lunch, well, the thing is, I'm one too."

"You're one what?" she says, not sharply or evasively, but as if to be faithful to her ordered mind, she must hold him to a standard of clarity.

"I have the same problem you told me you have," he says. When she says nothing, he goes on. "It's been a month since I last drank. I've been getting some help. I go to these RoR meetings."

She suddenly bristles. "Oh, I know about those meetings."

"You do?"

"Sure I do. They all lie."

"They lie?"

"You heard me. They're liars. Every last one of them. Don't you see? They aren't sober. They only *say* they're sober. They're *lying*."

"Lying?" He can only foolishly repeat her last word. "What about me? Am I lying?"

"You tell me," she says.

"No. Not lying. Not at all. Not me."

"An honest man is hard to find," she says, and, to signal that the conversation is over, goes back to her typing.

An orderly guides a gurney down the hall and pauses at the nurses' station. An old woman rests on it, her body shriveled. Briefly his eyes make contact with hers before the orderly pushes the gurney forward, lets it go, and repeats the pattern, as if he is a kid in a supermarket aisle playing with a shopping cart.

"Can I help you?" The nurse cradles the phone receiver between her neck and shoulder.

"I'm looking for the detox ward."

"Anyone in particular?"

"My brother. Luke Manootdjian."

She turns to a clipboard. "Down the hall and through the swinging doors."

His brother stands alone, grinning, as if he is in his living room rather than the drunk ward of a major metropolitan hospital. Other patients, also robed, wander about.

"I brought you these," Johan says, handing Luke a pack of Marlboros.

"Veni, vidi, vici," Luke reads on the pack as he removes the cellophane. " I came. I saw. I conquered. You thought I didn't know that, but I did. There are a lot of things I know. Like how to get a woman just by making eye contact. You know how to do that?"

Johan ignores his brother's provocation. The fluorescent lighting is unflattering. It highlights Luke's acne-cratered face. He was found passed out drunk on a street in Queens. A truck driver came within a foot or two of running him over. Cops. The ambulance. And now the detox ward. "He's out of control," Kelly had said.

"Hey, Gene. Hey, Sally. Come over here. I've got smokes for you." The two do as Luke tells them, and soon there are others who are recipients of his largesse.

"Why don't you just give away the whole pack?" Johan says, when Luke's friends have dispersed again.

"They're friends of mine. We're tight. That's the thing about you. You don't know how to make friends the way I do. You're too alone. Too much in your own head."

"If you say so." What is this tie of blood you cannot outgrow but that makes your get-togethers little more than perfunctory?

"I've got this thing beat, man. My counselors say I'm the best of all the patients in the ward. They say they're banking on me to get sober and stay sober. They see how smart I am. They really do, man. They believe in me because they see how much I know."

"Don't know so much,"

"What's that mean?" Luke is no longer smiling. He knows when Johan is being critical of him. He has a long history with Johan's admonishments.

"I mean only that this thing is tricky."

"What thing? What are you talking about?"

"The thing that put you here."

"I know that. You think I don't know that?"

But he doesn't know. No one who talks like his brother knows anything. His brother jabbering at him like the Big Stupid he is. All intelligence and no brains, just as Joseph Heller wrote of a character in *Catch-22.*

He is somewhere in Queens. An industrial area. Warehouses. Noisy, belching trucks. He catches a Manhattan-bound train and stands inside the unheated car. Soon he is staring across the main concourse in Grand Central Station at the arrivals and departure board. Poughkeepsie. Right there on the chattering black and white board he sees the name, and more than once. A train goes there along the banks of the Hudson River. Claire Eastland rides that train in either direction. Claire Eastland knows the allure of the Hudson River and what it means to go north out of New York City. And she knows what it is to live in a city like Poughkeepsie that is hardly a city but something else he can't even identify except it makes his heart pound with an excitement and longing he cannot stand.

Luke was an obligation, but Claire Eastland is a need.

She is standing this very minute in a spare, pristine one-bedroom apartment with low ceilings somewhere in that city. There is no clutter. There is no filth. There is freedom from all that is not functional and pleasing to the eye. And there is a car. She is a woman who needs wheels to get her where she needs to go.

She has told him about Poughkeepsie and the preposterous two-hour commute that she somehow endures. She has opened a door for him to enter. You must always walk through a door a woman has opened. You must always see what is inside. You must simply go there. That is what it means to be alive.

Poughkeepsie information knows exactly who Claire Eastland is and gives him the telephone number he needs. Even over the announcements on the public address system he hears the digits and writes them down so he can have them forever. And yet there is the possibility of complete humiliation should things go badly, that is, should she not have the darker side beneath that tightly controlled persona she lapsed from with her panicky admission and reject his interest in her in a cold and disapproving way.

But he must have his new life. He must be reckless in pursuit of it. He dials that number. The phone rings and rings as he focuses on the arrivals and departures board. He remembers Cary Grant and Eve Marie Saint in *North by Northwest,* and their love affair that starts on the New York Central out of that same terminal. The magnetic north. The magnetic Claire Eastland, with her long legs and smart Seven Sisters ways. A woman who could help him, who could lead him out of the life he has made and in which he cannot stay.

The ringing goes on and on. Claire Eastland is not there. She has found another place to be on a Saturday afternoon.

And so he catches a train that afternoon, the train he is always catching. The number 6 train making all local stops: Thirty-third Street, Twenty-eighth Street, Twenty-third Street, Union Square, Astor Place, Bleecker Street.

And isn't the truth a simple thing? Isn't it simply what it hasn't been for him to even contemplate, that Claire Eastland has found someone to be with, as one of her caliber would have to find someone to be with? Would it be possible that a woman of her worth wouldn't have been claimed, ruthlessly and instantly, so she would never be compelled to know what it is to be alone? And is there any way for him to confirm this obvious truth other than for her to tell him?

"I'm living with a man. You must tell no one. No one. He's famous. At least in our children's books world he is famous. Olivia must not find out. Do you hear me?"

They have gone for lunch, just the two of them. Her idea. Her invitation.

"Yes," he says. He has not told her about the telephone call and how the phone rang and rang in the Poughkeepsie silence, and how he thought, he really thought, that she would be up there in the north country waiting for him and how they could have a life without the complexity of anyone or anything, just him and her in her modern apartment.

"Yes what?" she says.

"Yes, I heard you," he says. "You have nothing to be afraid of. Isn't your personal life just that?"

"Not in the real world, I'm afraid," she says, without elaborating.

Though he does not want to press the matter and irritate her, he remains curious. "People do live together. It's nothing to be ashamed of."

"I'm not ashamed. But the fact is that he is recently separated from his wife."

"I see," Johan says, when all he really sees is that she has a need for secrets. It is not for him to say that men separate from their wives in the real world. It would only make her angry. He can take some comfort in the fact that she confides in him.

"A glass of white wine," she says, to the white-jacketed waiter.

"And for you, sir?" He orders a Perrier with a twist of lime, as he is learning to do.

"Are you sure you won't join me?" she says, when the waiter returns. The wine is chilled; there is cold sweat on the glass. It has a sweet bouquet, like those Rhine wines he would buy on sale toward the end of his drinking. Not that he ever bothered to drink them chilled.

"No, but thank you," he says, raising his glass of Perrier self-protectively in a toast. "To health," he hears himself saying.

So with Olivia and the rest of the staff she is in a panic about drinking, but with him it is nothing to order a glass of wine and then two others.

Returning to the office she takes his hand briefly. "I get very friendly when I drink," she says. He has a thought of steering her into a doorway on the side street and kissing her right then and there, but there is no doorway. There is just a midtown sidewalk crowded with people.

"Can you give us an overview, Johan, so we are not mired so deeply in the particulars of your story?"

"I was in bondage to Claire Eastland. As I have mentioned, she had the name and she had the pedigree. But I was also in the process of getting sober, and there was the fidelity factor at play in this new life. I had done grievous wrong to Sarah. She was war-wounded. She had the shrapnel of my alcoholism impacted in her psyche. I had to love her in a correct and exacting way. Things of weight and terrible substance were falling out of the sky. They took the shape of oil drums which struck the ground with terrific force, missing me by feet if not by inches. I had to call on the power of Dr. Reiner to assist me. He was not negligible in his capacity for insight. He said the weight of my past was raining down and seeking to crush me. What I am saying is that strictures and structures came with being sober. I was not free to do the wild thing with impunity. So maybe something cautionary was entering the picture, no matter how spellbound I was with the elite status of Claire Eastland.

Sarah was sick. The depth of her illness only God could possibly fathom, though her psychiatrist, Dr. Frodkey, did his best. My sense of guilt was exacerbated by her condition. I couldn't help but worry that her dysfunction was entirely my fault, grandiose as such a notion might sound."

He stops off at the deli at the corner of One Hundred Fifteenth Street and Broadway. An expanded space and a different name than when he was here at age fourteen with his neighborhood friend Jerry Jones-Nobleonian and bought, for the first time, a six-pack of beer. Bart's, it's called now. Three checkout lines, where there used to be only one. And there Bart is, a thicker and grayer Bart than Johan remembers, with hair cut neat and short, as he has always worn it. A man in bondage to the store he owns.

"Is that you, Johan?" his mother says, and opens the door before he can answer. She is not one to live behind a triple-locked door.

"Am I waking you?"

"It is four in the afternoon. I sleep at night, not during the day."

"Of course," he says.

She has a mole above her upper lip, from which a hair has sprouted. Her scalp is now showing through her thinning hair.

"I brought some things. Cheese. Some fruit. I thought maybe you would like something."

"I will get some plates," she says.

The apartment needs a fresh coat of paint and some new furniture and a little more care. There are water stains on one wall. As a child he would flee into the streets. The rooms were not hospitable. Too much dirt and clutter.

"Something has happened," he says.

"What has happened? Tell me. I won't breathe a word. It is not Sarah, is it? She has not taken ill?"

"Nothing like that. I have stopped drinking. I go to some meetings and…"

"Do you know that my mother had me go out in the snow and find my father and smash his bottles against the rocks? You do know that, don't you?"

"Yes," Johan says, noting how her description doesn't change, from year to year. Always she is being asked to go out. Always she is being asked to smash the bottles against the rocks. Traumatic recall and repetition, this condition of her father's and all that it brought to pass.

"But did you also know that I never so much as took a drop of alcohol because I was so afraid of developing a craving for it?"

"No. That I didn't know." He remembers his mother's Biblical admonition about alcohol: "Wine is a mocker, strong drink is raging." And those times when his older sisters might bring home a bottle of wine for some festive occasion. "Oh come on, Mother, for God's sake stop being such a saint and have a glass with us. It won't kill you," he recalls the oldest, Hannah, saying, right there in the living room where they are now sitting. He remembers too his terror that his mother might reach out for that glass of wine in response to Hannah's goading and that whatever change resulted would not be good.

He tells her about Rooms of Recovery. She does not look happy. He has seen that look before, when he was a child and she led him into the bedroom and slowly coaxed him into opening his fist, in which he had held two quarters. "Have you been in my bag?" she said back then. And though his denial came initially strong, she had been able to bend him to her will insofar as confession. But then she had pushed on. She had tried to seal him into goodness so he could have no life of his own. She had dared to say, "Will you promise me never to do this again?" It was then that he smiled and smiled and smiled, so that the fear came into her eyes, the same fear that he was seeing now, that whether bad or good, he would live to be beyond her control.

Things are not good at work that winter. An accumulation of snow on a drain-poor and shoddily constructed warehouse in Parsippany, New Jersey, causes the roof to fall in and destroys the company's entire inventory of books. Even the best minds can do little more than worry and fret as an emergency planning meeting is called. Johan, for all the time he has spent in publishing, hardly knows a backorder from a backhoe. His world is smaller than that of dollars and cents. He is restricted to sentences and is just trying to stay faithful to his sobriety and to the pain of longing he has fallen into for Claire Eastland. What is this fuss about books? Why can't they just make more of them?

He has *Pocket Pal* to read and the *Chicago Manual of Style* and the dictionary is becoming his friend. He alternates his daily reading of a page between "m," right there in the middle, and "a," the alpha of all things. That way he can make progress that will seem faster even if it isn't. Because if he knows the words, he has the cover for the things he doesn't have and he can get on with his life properly dressed.

Some days he occupies the province of the normal, having gotten his combinations right with the Haldol and the Artane. As a precaution, he takes to carrying pen and paper at all times, so on those rare occasions when Olivia will do something more than shoot a puzzled glance his way while transiting the area of his desk and actually require his services, he can record her words so they will stay in his possession sufficient that he can act on her commands. To be in her presence is no easy thing. Her words hit him like bits of glass. He wonders at a world ruled by a temperament such as hers, so angry and controlling. Still, there is no question but that she knows her figures and that agility of mind is the true source of her strength. Art director Deana Matthews can question her right to be at the head of the department, but Johan sees that Olivia has the right stuff.

In the morning, on his knees, he cries and says to God that he doesn't know if he wants this marriage and would God please direct him what to do in his own good time. Because his mind is a hamster wheel. Only God can cease the around and around loop his thinking is prone to.

His face has a surprise for him. It seems to be getting a makeover from within. In the public bathroom, in the lonely part of the floor where children's books is sequestered, as if in stepchild status to the rest of the company, he stares at himself in the mirror over the sink. No fairy tale rhyme comes to him, no mirror mirror on the wall stuff. He is perplexed to see an expression of sincerity whereas, at the end of his drinking, there had been a sort of smirk to suggest that he was a man of two worlds and two minds, having read but forgotten or was uncaring that in the book of James a man of two minds is said to be unstable in all his ways. It is an expression he would have rejected and even reviled only months before as that of someone who drinks milk and parks himself in a church pew on Sunday mornings. It is the face of a simpleton, a doofus, and yet it is his face, the one that is emerging from the core of his being.

Once more he stares in wonder and amazement and surrender to the strange process of being, God forbid the term, born again.

"I will be going for lunch. I can flee many things, but not my own hunger," he says that workday.

"Very good," Olivia says.

"I want to tell you so you won't think I have gone missing, should you need me."

"Yes. Thank you," she says, called back from the manuscript she had returned to.

He leaves wondering if she would make the same response should he tell her he was planning to roller-skate up Madison Avenue; he is of a mind to think that she will give her blessing to anything he proposes so long as he doesn't continue to stand in her office.

Zum Zum's is his very favorite, along with McDonald's. It serves bratwurst and knockwurst and delicious potato salad on metal plates, and the staff are all Fräulein friendly in keeping with the chain's German ownership. The restaurant is located in the art deco recesses of the Empire State Building lobby only a short two blocks away. While sitting at the counter and waiting for his order he looks up at the clock. Ten a.m. Can that be right? Clocks have been known to be wrong, and so he asks Rosie, the counter woman, to confirm the accuracy of the Zum Zum clock, as she is wearing a watch and he isn't. And Rosie does, and makes it worse by informing him that the wall clock is actually ten minutes fast.

"Are you OK? Because you have a portentous look on your sad face," Rosie says.

Johan knows she is well meaning and that she is only being Rosie. She is not the face police who want to arrest him because he is not perpetually smiling.

"I think I'm going to get through this, Rosie," Johan says.

"You'll get through it even better when I bring you your bratwurst. And it's coming right up," Rosie says, and Johan is sure she is right. Though he feels chagrined and deflated and can only wonder what Olivia must be thinking, he tries to put his mind to the bratwurst on the metal plate before him at the counter and does devour it, then has himself a cup of coffee so he can smoke a cigarette that actually tastes good before hurrying back to his empty desk.

"I am sorry. I miscalculated my watch," he says on his return, having found Olivia steadfast over her manuscript and her pencil active on its pages.

"What is that you say?" She looks perplexed.

"I left my post for lunch when the time for it had not come. The clock deceived me. I will look askance at it from now on."

"Well, you are back now, so all is well."

"Yes. I am where you can find me."

"Very good," she says.

And if he is suspect in Olivia's eyes, it is only a matter of time before Claire Eastland will see him as he is. She has given him a proofreading assignment, and evidently he did not do well, for now she says, "Things get by you," and drops the proofs on his desk. She does not dawdle. She does not need to. In fact it would be against her nature to stay, for excellence calls to excellence, and as he doesn't have any, what business of hers could it be to linger with the likes of him?

Johan stares at page after page containing her elegant markings. Typos. Spacing problems he had missed. Bad word breaks. Widows. It is a painful blow to see that perfection is her domain and he can't live there. She has found the window into who he is. She has seen the lack of quality substance that a woman needs to discern to want to get next to a man. He has wanted to believe that their problematic relationship with alcohol is the only common ground they need.

And Claire Eastland's insight doesn't end with the page proofs. She sees something more when he is called to be among her and Charles and Olivia to review the mechanics of a book for young readers on sources of energy. The absence of a science aptitude is the pain he is feeling as he stands in the midst of their individual and collective intelligence. He does not know about coal and oil and the energy of the sun, and the illustration of a refining plant shows an apparatus that is beyond his comprehension. Because science is for men and he is not a man. He feels like he is back in a grade school classroom and being singled out for his doltish ways. Nothing he is feeling in that moment is lost on Claire Eastland. "What is wrong with you? Are you OK?" He hears the impatience in her tone. He knows when a question contains its own answer.

Her words a kind of reproach that his feelings should be so written on his face. And she hadn't even asked so no one else would hear. Had he traded on her vulnerability when she had made that confession about being unable to drink safely? Did he repeat her question so everyone else could be onto her business? He isn't liking Claire Eastland. He isn't liking her at all. He has been a fool—what else?—to have thought they could meaningfully connect.

That very day does Charles Nigel come to him and let it be known that he is leaving. Not the earth but Pentacle Books. Someone better wants Charles, someone with more publishing might and a ring of light around his name. Charles will have a bigger office and more money. Nothing but progress is in his future.

Charles Nigel does not toot his own horn. He doesn't need to. The art director Deana Matthews (yes, formerly Deana Zeromskis but now shed of the sound of foreignness) confirms his worth. "He's too good for this place," she says, and though she does not name names, it is for Johan to know that Deana is flying in the face of Olivia with her words.

But now Charles, so reserved, so moving on with the business of life, lets his wisdom show. Surprising, because the personal is not his nature. He does not have the dullness for sincerity. And yet here he is being nothing but sincere when he says, "You might want to consider leaving yourself. You've got two career women here now. That might not be so easy."

Like a flock of pigeons suddenly flying up into the air with a loud clatter of beating wings are Charles's words. The bold clarity of Charles's mind has revealed itself to Johan in a new and startling way. But does Charles not know that he, Johan, can only go where he has been assigned? And the anger and the self-pity. Does Charles not know no one will ever come calling for him, Johan Manootdjian? Does Charles not know?

(Yes, he has taken back his name. Yes he very much has. He has dropped the name Hedberg into the past so he can be reunited with his personal Calvary, the surname his father imposed on him. Because regardless of the truncation measures that Mr. Marg would lay on him as an expediency factor for his survival and ultimate triumph, he cannot be a chameleon. He must have a logical progression out of what he was into who he is now. He must be a part of his father because of his father he was born and he has committed enough betrayal and must commit no more.)

But then Claire Eastland does come calling, not that day but the next, as if in sleep Johan's face came to her as a direction she needed to go when she awoke. She just appears at his desk, from which any clutter has been eliminated so he can be safe in the knowledge that things are under control and nothing is being asked of him that he isn't performing. And if his face bears any remnant of the wound her commentary of the day before inflicted, she is not seeing it sufficient to lay a squawk on him for sulking. She is getting tickets for a baseball game up at Yankee Stadium. The Red Sox are coming to town. Would he like to go, just him and her?

Where there was humiliation, there is now elation. She has invited him to have sex with him. They can find a motel next to the stadium. Maybe after the third inning. Maybe. Just him and her, Claire Eastland, butt naked but for her Yankees cap.

He hasn't forsaken the meetings. They call to him. A bedrock all their own. The lost have now been found. The woman in the straitjacket who now is free. The man who had started out in Kansas but wound up in Paris after a night on the town. The woman of the night who now holds a job and keeps regular hours. The financial expert who wrote bad checks but who now can part his hair in the middle with pride. There is no fulminating pastor from his childhood, saying you should or you had better, no one to tell him the fires of hell burn hotter than gasoline and in perpetuity. There is only this welcoming love. Come in. Have some coffee. Take a seat.

Nor has he forsaken Sarah. He doesn't return to her drunk and raving in the wee hours of the morning. He comes home to her now right after work and they sit down over quiet and humble dinners. There are no big bottles of wine on the counter that he will steadily drain in the course of the night. He is just there. He tells her about his day. He complains about his boss Olivia and gives her the news about Charles. About Claire he says nothing.

So many improvements are necessary. They need a new stereo system, one that actually works rather than the dysfunctional components her family has passed on to them. Things. They just need things. A coat for him and a new one without a torn lining for her.

They walk over to SoHo. Those long cobblestone streets, loft buildings full of artists pursuing their vision. They pass the bars where he would drink: Funelli's, on Prince, with the old Italian bartender who now speaks through a voice box because of throat cancer, and the Spring Street Bar down on West Broadway where, in the soft lighting, he would start with beer and go on to scotch and end the night with cognac. They end up at the Broome Street Café, another former drinking haunt, down near Houston Street. The menu written out on a blackboard in pastel colors. The same pretty waitress with the puffy lips and the short skirt, she the star of the Broome Street Café if nowhere else, her eyes bleary and her skin pasty from all that boozing and cocaine. Drunks hanging out in the light of day. It is what couples do on a Sunday morning. They go out for breakfast or brunch. They stroll.

And then, halfway through his omelet, he sees her through the narrow casement window. Isabel. There on the corner, with her poodle. A woman with her dog. Her slim figure, her being, rivets his eye. She is not alone. Her husband, Philip, and another man, his lover possibly, are to either side of her. The men wear baggy jeans and boots with thick heels. How ugly denim can be.

"Are you seeing something? Are you seeing *someone?* A ghost from the past?" An unpleasant smile she shows him.

It is not over. Nothing is over. Only drinking.

Making love is not easy. She has gained weight. All those medications. She is dead to him. She just lies there. It feels like necrophilia.

She cries about her hair. She will lose it and be bald, totally bald, she is sure. The texture has changed. It looks stiff and straw-like now, and there is less of it. Too many chemicals? Those birth control pills she has been taking since age sixteen, and now all those pharmaceuticals prescribed by Dr. Frodkey? Older age has come early for her. She is not ready.

One night he dreams that her nightmare has come true. There she is, sitting up in bed with a head bald as an egg. He can't share his dream with her. No man can do that to his wife. Her crisis causes him to think of his own hair. What would he do if his scalp was exposed? How could he possibly live with the humiliation of his flat head out there for everyone to see? Surely would he have to leave New York if not the planet.

That etching press. He has been making progress. Every pay period he gives the store where the press is sold something on the layaway plan. He feels his own goodness break over him like a wave. Oh, there is so much he wants to make right. So much. If only the time could go faster so he could be there already.

One night she bursts into tears, right there at the dinner table. What is it? he asks. Has he done something? But she cannot speak. As the minutes go by, the pasta begins to grow cold. When she settles down, he finds himself as startled by what she says as by her weeping. No, it isn't her hair. He is being too good to her. She doesn't deserve such goodness, she says. He wonders what on earth she could mean. What is she seeing that she could say such a thing? He hasn't showered her with gifts. He hasn't given her anything.

He isn't drinking. That is changing everything. He doesn't know how, but it is. It is like he is in an elevator going up and she is in an elevator going nowhere, or maybe down. Why should this be? He is a criminal. He has damaged her. "You are a tornado through my life…you don't deserve to live with anyone…I can't sleep in the same bed with you, you stink so bad." Words she has spoken to him sometime in the past.

But she is trying. She really is. Trying not to be imprisoned by her mind. Dr. Frodkey structures her. He tells her he lives with his wife in a a suburban house full of state of the art appliances. He tells her stories about how once, back in another chapter of his life, he could only communicate with the dead. Why else would he have become a pathologist? But then the blackness dropped away and now he is seeing in vivid colors. Seeing Dr. Frodkey helps her. Dr. Frodkey is hope. She can feel loved and special. He tells her she has value. Not in those words. He doesn't speak that way. But something he does invigorates her. He tells her to apply for a job, and she is receptive. Dr. Frodkey she can believe and respond to.

Forgiveness is not a concept that enters her mind. There can be none for her mother for casting her as her shadow, or of her father for not loving her as he once did. Because if he still loved her, her life would not have gone the way that it has.

She takes a job at Gimbel's East up on Eighty-sixth Street. It is a store with no future but the owner has opened it anyway. She stands behind a glass case containing men's shirts, working with Black girls from Harlem who show her a cold manner as they crack their gum. Their unkindness is entrenched. They see a white girl who is down and they are going to keep her down, though how down can whiteness ever be in a white world? Someone has to be punished for what life is dealing them. Why not her white face?

"What you be sayin'?" "Don't know nothin' 'bout that." In that way do they talk to her, with frost and rebuff in their clear, strong voices speaking in the tongue of contraction.

There are a couple of gay men, and they are friendly in her presence. Whatever their wounds, they have no need to retaliate against her. They are free with their warmth and consideration. Theirs is an arsenal of love, not spite and enmity.

The cycle of exclusion wears on Sarah, but she hangs on. Dr. Frodkey gives his full support.

Sarah has a layaway plan of her own. She has her eye on a thin Seiko watch for Johan so he will know what time it is.

Sarah's struggle is not lost on Johan. He has a loving heart when it comes to her, even if he cannot stay faithful to her in his mind and with his body, and even if his tongue sometimes ignites and sets the loft on fire with his attacking fury, burning Sarah and all the contents therein. He sees what he has done to her. He has a mind's eye with which to see, a mind's eye undiminished by time so it can observe the wreckage, Sarah standing outside the Prado in Madrid having to wear long sleeves in the heat of summer because of the bruises to her arms inflicted in one of their fights. He knows what the word *abusive* means, whether by hand or tongue. He knows the indictment of him that has to be issued. All that he knows, as he knows what the words *restitution* and *amend* and *make right* mean.

Johan has not forgotten the Yankees game. It is not every day that a woman of excellence, such as Claire Eastland surely is, comes strolling into his life. But as the days since her invitation pass, he sees something more than Claire lying naked on a motel room bed with only that Yankees cap as an aphrodisiacal delight. He sees the fact that he is married to Sarah and that maybe there is no right way to do a wrong thing without the benefit of alcohol to ease his mind. A strange thing is happening. He cannot hold it together to go down that road. As if the words come from someplace not his own, he finds himself saying to Claire, "What about if my wife Sarah comes along? Would that be all right?"

"Fine and dandy," Claire says, and if that isn't enough, "No prob."

He retreats to the public bathroom, where he leans his forehead against the cool tiles. Several times he allows himself to lift his head away before bringing it back, but gently. If his action is temperate, his emotions are not. He prays for unconsciousness, for the immediate cessation of himself as a sensate being. If he had tried, he couldn't have hurt himself more than by declining Claire's gift. He has gone and thrown it away, and for what? What? A woman he no longer wants to be with, an….No. no. He castigates himself for thinking such things. This is Sarah. This is his wife.

On a raw spring evening Johan sits with Sarah in the reserved seats along the first base side of the field. The chalk lines have been laid down, the pristine white bases have been set out, and the groundskeepers are now hosing down the infield, turning the base path dirt a dark brown. A rich green carpet of grass covers the outfield, and past the monuments in Death Valley, as centerfield has come to be called, the huge scoreboard is lit up brightly against the increasing darkness. Beyond the confines of the spacious ballpark stands the Bronx County Courthouse, an edifice erected in a more orderly time than the borough has recently been experiencing, given the arson that has gutted sections of it.

He takes it as a hopeful sign as he glances frequently at the entrance ramp below that while the stands steadily fill, the two seats next to him and Sarah remain empty. Perhaps Claire and her beau will not show. Perhaps Claire will have come to her senses, and, feeling the same discomfort if not dread as Johan, forego the abominable evening. But his optimism is short-lived, for soon there she is, mounting the stairs slowly with a haggard and considerably older man who, once seated, tries hard not to sound as brittle as he looks. "Come on, Guidry, blow it by him. Take that sucker," he shouts, making his direct address to Ron Guidry, aka Louisiana Lightning, out there on the mound as Jim Rice, powerfully built and in the cleanup slot the *red handkerchief of Black defiance hanging from his back pocket, saying everything he can't say,* waves a menacing stick. And that is the way it goes. All his vocal efforts are directed at the field and to brief communications with Claire. He understands, as does Johan, that this pairing is not going to work.

There is that line from Dylan about the woman being an artist and not going where she doesn't belong. Johan is no artist and is always going where he doesn't belong.

So yes, there is the discomfort of awkward communication for three hours, but there is also the game, so exquisite in its slow unfolding. Guidry coming out of his windup on his bent left knee to fire blazing southpaw heat past the BoSox batters in their soft gray uniforms with red lettering and trim. Does anyone have the grace of the BoSox's Fred Lynn patrolling centerfield or that sweet left-handed swing out of an open stance. And there is Reggie Jackson supplying pinstripe power (yes, he is a prima donna, yes, he is afflicted with affectation with that raising of his fingers to his mouth to wet them, but he has to advertise himself because he sees that it is built into every white fan in the stands and the whole world to forget him as soon as they can, no matter what he does, for the crime of not being white and Mickey Mantle or Black like Willie Mays).

As a child he would beg his mother for the money to buy a cheap ticket and a couple of hot dogs and sit alone high up in the grandstand staring down at The Mick. You could not take your eyes off him, whether in centerfield or at the plate in that coiled stance, as if a nimbus of light attached to him. And there was Maris, of course, with those beautiful arms and that beautiful lefty stroke, and Skowron and Richardson and Boyer and Ellie Howard, the token Black. It is different now. Back then there was pure joy and wonder. Now, now he feels the burden of his life, of things undone. Sitting there feels like some sort of wasteful escape.

Perhaps Claire and her friend have taken the words of Sydney Greenstreet in *The Maltese Falcon* to heart about fast goodbyes being the best goodbyes, for they flee down the stairs and to the exit ramp before the players have left the field. On the long subway ride home, it is for Sarah, with the powers of discernment she possesses, to say: "Are you in love with her? Is that why you brought me, to hide your love behind some social pretense, the way you did when you took me to that party last year and we wound up in that woman's bed?" Sarah referring back to the fiasco in Isabel's apartment.

And Johan responds, imagining Claire and her beau in car flight out of the ruins of the Bronx, "Why not ask me if I love the wind or vapors we cannot see?"

"Shut up and answer my question."

"Don't take me down that road." But he has heard her. He sees where her mind's eye has gone.

It is possible that Johan loves Charles Nigel, not with a love that has a sexual content to it, but as he would a wise older brother, as Luke had trouble being. And so when Charles Nigel vacates the premises, and Deana Matthews, the graphics director, is driven by her loss to wailing, "He was the best, he was the very best," Johan can only concur.

But then, something he could never have imagined occurs. Olivia comes to stand in Johan's face, not with the asperity of her manner showing but with a smile of genuine appreciation. She had assigned him to write jacket copy for one of their books and is pleased to report that it is much better than the copy Charles Nigel had been producing. Johan truly does not understand how such a thing could be. Olivia is a graduate of Oxford University (the real one, in England, in case there are any others), so she surely is possessed of a critical faculty. Can she not see the high specific density of Charles Nigel's prose and the lightweight substance of Johan's own meager offering? Can she not see that there is no meat on the bones of Johan's words? If he is initially puzzled, the answer is not long in coming. He discerns envy and malice and manipulation behind the blandishment she has offered. Olivia, he comes to understand, has to drive Charles Nigel down so she can live because she can place no man, no matter how manifest his talents, above her. But because she has nothing to fear from the likes of Johan, she can easily dispense her praise. Still, her words do mean something. They are a ray of hope. In any case, he will need to remain vigilant. The smile from her he has earned today may be replaced by a wrathful visage tomorrow, should he displease her. She has claimed ownership of him with that smile. He must be for her whatever it is she wants him to be.

A design studio is one thing, but for his wife to stand on her feet all day selling men's shirts in a floundering department store does not seem right. He can't place her in such a context without pain bordering on horror. There may be a better way. Johan sees the saccharine quality of the illustrations in the picture books Pentacle publishes, pages filled with cuddly animals and doe-eyed children. He sees that stars are being born every minute on the basis of little merit and how people position themselves in the world for advancement, how they have all their papers in order so they can proceed. He sees how they let nothing hold them back and impose their will on the world sufficient to establish themselves and consolidate their positions.

If his thinking is insane and bitter, it is nevertheless his thinking.

He will show Olivia Sarah's worth. After all, Sarah has an affinity with childhood. She has experienced those years richly, having been read to when she was a child. She could present a quality of truth that children need to see. If he cannot come forward with his own work, at least he can do that with hers. Maybe Olivia will give her a contract and free her from the men's shirts department.

Olivia does not laugh in his face. No one should underestimate the integrity Olivia possesses. She is England born. The Brits have given the world the Magna Carta. What more needs to be said about the democratic impulse and the invidious scourge, by comparison, of all those who thought the rule of law was they themselves (Are you listening, crazy Lenin and deluded Trotsky and paranoid Stalin?). That democratic impulse is in her bones. She knows how to see fairly, and with love as her guide, even with her flintiness showing.

Still, Olivia has assumed responsibility for a department. She has accountability to the bottom line. Beyond that, she does not go to the dark places in her soul. She does not seek out James Ensor and Chaim Soutine or the horrors that Goya reported on. She has a disposition toward balance. Her heart is in childhood but it is not in blackness. What she sees in Sarah's monoprints disturb her. There is no quality of light, only souls on the extremes with bared teeth, the damned glaring back at her with fire-filled eyes or faces malignly radiant with demented smiles.

It is not enough that Olivia is there. Deana Matthews, art director on a mission, and Claire Eastland are also present for the review of Sarah's portfolio of black and white prints. Together they form a battery of diplomats from the world of civilization meeting up with a representative of a more primal scene—disembodied heads peering out from the darkness with faces of lewdness and laughing torment. Under the fluorescent lights, the prints look peculiar to them. Sarah does not know from the world of light in which they stand. Johan sees the discomfort, the forced smiles, on the faces of Olivia and Deana and Claire and hears their struggle to say something positive. "Interesting. Very bold. Quite original."

"If we have a manuscript that requires this kind of visual treatment, we will be in touch. Thank you so much for showing us your work," Olivia says, signaling that the review has come to an end.

There are no repercussions. Sarah does not enter a state of emotional turmoil. She has a guiding light, some inner balance where her work is concerned. She will go where she has to go and allow them to go where they must. All she will say is this:

"Are you fucking that woman Claire? Are you *fucking* her?"

Luke's boozy voice comes through the line. Sarah answers and listens as Luke speaks from a knowing place, giving her insight into her personality when he can offer nothing about his own. He does what some men in hateful bondage do; he elevates her even as he seeks to debase her. He is a sick man when he drinks.

When Johan gets on the line, his brother's corrupting manner is quickly felt.

"You weren't so bad," Luke says.

"What do you mean?"

"Your drinking. It wasn't so bad."

"Do you remember that time a car backed up and knocked you down and you had pain in your knee?"

"What about it?"

"Do you remember what you said to the doctor?"

"No. What did I say?"

"You said 'How bad is it?'"

"So?"

"So he said, 'How bad does it have to be?'"

"Why are you starting on me, man?"

"I'm not starting on you. I'm saying how bad does my drinking have to be before I stop? And how bad does your drinking have to be before you stop?"

"There you go with your shit again. I don't have a problem with alcohol. I was just going through some stuff with Kelly. That's all it was. I don't need any of those meetings. And you don't either. You need to relax and have some fun. You know what I mean?"

On the other end of the line Johan hears the rattling of ice cubes in a glass, as ice cubes used to rattle in his glass when he was on the phone with Luke.

It is all right. No need to get world bodies involved. No need to take his outrage to the United Nations and offer a public denunciation of his wayward brother.

Jesse is a longtime friend of Johan's. They go back to a time when they were young and at the City College of New York and to the General Post Office at Thirty-third and Eighth, where they both worked the evening shift from six to ten pm, sorting mail into the box scheme of the fifty states. They go back to the time when Jesse was Whitmanesque holy, massive in body and cosmic in mind, like a psychedelic prophet out of the Old Testament with that big beard and that open, Semitic face that saw everything with Buddha breath calm, even if pharmaceutically induced. They go back to the time when Jesse came down the aisle of the P.O. in the jeans and blue work shirt that were the staple of his dress and placed himself before Johan and without a word slowly opened his hand to reveal in the palm of it a pink, heart-shaped pill, a love offering that required no words. And so Johan took the pill and placed it in his mouth and he felt good, he felt very very good, he felt limits fall down dead at his feet and walls dissolve. He felt the expansion of his life sufficient to make him weep. And so he lay his head on Jesse's shoulder and said he had found the older brother he had always been looking for.

The restaurant is called McFinn's. It is a dark place with colorful bottles behind the bar. Some come to drink their lunches. Others, like Johan and Jesse, are there to eat. Jesse is a manager with CorpNow, a corporate annual reports company. He shows up in his farmer's overalls, making a mockery of office attire. His beard is full and his long brown hair is pulled tight into a ponytail.

"Madeleine's asthma drives me crazy. She drives me crazy. It's not her fault. I just find myself thinking I can't sleep with this woman anymore. I just can't. But somehow I do. Mostly I just drop Quaaludes and watch the tube."

Though it is at least a year since he saw her, Johan remembers Madeleine. With marriage should come motherhood. Beyond her job, that is her ambition.

"How are things with you?" Jesse asks.

"I'm OK, for now. I'm grateful to have a job, even if it doesn't always feel substantial. It feels like I have come in from the cold. And I'm going to those meetings and not drinking."

"Well, here's to warmth," Jesse says, lifting his glass of Coke. Jesse is not a drinker. For him it is dry goods all the way.

Johan hears defensiveness in Jesse's tone. Does he have anger of which he will not speak and issues he cannot explore? Is he finding it harder to put himself above the rest with the mind that he's been given? Johan feels, horrible as it sounds, that he has been moved to stable ground that does not require Jesse anymore. How uncomfortable to feel you are leaving someone even as you are sitting with him.

Oh, Johan, that is what happens when a drunk is rendered sober. Sight that was not yours is now yours. Places you could not inhabit you now are in. Tracks your train could not run on it now rushes over. Some you were close to are now farther away. It is what it is, and if you are shocked you keep it to yourself.

Isabel does not become a memory in this time. Claire Eastland does not remove her from Johan's internal sight. You cannot consign a light that is glowing incandescent to utter darkness, as if its filament has burned out. There is no filament here. His light is not a bulb but a flame of permanence with no need to prove its reality.

Isabel is not with him but she is within him. He never entertains the possibility that she does not love him anymore. It had never been a consideration as to whether she loved him in the first place. He has incorporated her so the light of her is in him. And if it is strange that a woman who has spurned him for another man should have this effect, he does not think it so.

Sarah sees that this is so as well. She had seen Claire there at the baseball game and at the portfolio review, but she had really seen Isabel, and so it is of Isabel and not Claire that she says, when she is given to say such a thing, "You were going to call me by her name. Admit it. You almost called me by her name." And whether Johan has Isabel's name on the tip of his tongue or not at that very moment is not the point. Sarah is simply putting him on notice that the light is visible to her as well.

But what does such a light do? It makes Johan happy. It gives him a sense of hope. It manufactures joy and power in his psyche that he could have found a woman of the caliber of Isabel with the dimensions he has been seeking and could lie down with her and do the things he has done with her so that the bed itself was singing.

One Sunday, in the Arts section of the *New York Times,* he sees her name. There it is. She will be having a show. At her young age. A one-person exhibit in SoHo, the new art mecca. A gallery on West Broadway. The announcement lifts from the newspaper and stabs him. She is winning and he is losing. She is out there in the world of glitter and he is sitting in church basements trying to stay sober. How painful that the world should call to her and not to him. It is so very simple. If the world wants her, then she could not possibly want him. Failure is a requirement of love. Failure keeps you isolated, while success brings new possibilities. New men. Powerful men. Men against whom he cannot possibly stand a chance. Well, he will stay away. Isn't that what smart people do? Isn't that what Bob Dylan's artist did, the one who never went where she didn't belong? But would that be right? He owes it to her to show up. What kind of man is it who can't bear the success of his ex-lover? Is he the type such as Claggart that Melville portrayed in *Billy Budd,* the one infected with envy, a defect men are loath to admit to, so shameful do they find it? And yet a person can have his initial reaction. That isn't the sum total of who he is.

"Tell us, in your own words, what happened, Johan."

"I remember a man. He was full of his own power. He stood in the gallery in award-winning silence and struck me as a fiend for acquisition. Everything about him said he knew how to win and that he had won. He was across the finish line though he was only starting out. I had come there on a weekday morning, when many are trapped in their office routines. But this man wasn't. He was not sitting at a desk of prosaic gray working for a scold named Olivia. He had the power of his own mind. I heard a truck outside and thought of my childhood and how in my sickbed I would sit up and drink ginger ale and listen to the traffic down below. The gallery space was narrow

and rectangular. It had no room for extravagance. Isabel's paintings held up well. You couldn't stand before them without amazement. One in particular told the story of my life. It showed a woman looking in a window. Or maybe she was on the inside looking out. Delicate cross-hatchings abounded. Hundreds of tiny lines. The painting said this was an artist steeped in the old and the new as it grabbed hold of my heart. There was a living, breathing presence in that painting, a woman I had seen as a child."

"Go on."

"When I was very young there was this mythical creature, a girl of stunning dark-haired beauty whose father owned the hosiery shop on Broadway around the corner from where I lived. I had no reason to love her except that she filled her clothes so well and bore the word feminine *on every part of her being. Her father never neglected his purpose. He was in that store every morning. He knew that women will always have a need for stockings, and because he was driven to be a part of their world, he supplied them with the delicates they sought. What is that to go through your day taking thin boxes from a shelf and unfolding the tissue to expose the silk stockings underneath, then to take those stockings carefully from their bed of tissue and hold them gently for the customer's inspection? Are we not speaking of a world of exquisite boudoir intimacy here?"*

"Where are you going with this, please?"

"Somehow the younger daughter, who had not received the gift of physical beauty, found herself in my parents' apartment one afternoon and washed my hair in a sink with rust stains in the bathroom off my parents' bedroom."

"And what does this have to do with Isabel?"

"You see, my entire life has been spent with women who have not been gifted with physical beauty in the degree that Isabel possesses it. Isabel is the hosiery shop owner's beautiful daughter. I had finally found the girl's equal in Isabel."

"Can you tell us something more?"

"*Maybe it's not so much that I was in love with Isabel as that I wanted to be Isabel. All my life I have wanted to be chosen. All my life I have wanted to be cared for and catered to, to be told I was special and to believe I was special, to have the sort of gifts that would cause people to seek me out. Children know immediately who has it and who doesn't. They quickly perceive the hierarchy and where they are on the grid. It is possible that all my life I wanted to be a little girl, an adorable little girl. Think of the power a beautiful girl has. She does not have to occupy herself with pursuit. She can rest assured that she is loved, doubly so if she has intellectual and artistic gifts on the order that Isabel possesses. All my life I have been this mad dog throwing myself at people, saying love me love me love me. And they don't love me. They don't love me because they see I don't love myself. Self-love has been taken away from me or I never possessed it. Or even if I did, it was not enough for people to stop and take notice and say, 'This is a man worth knowing.'*"

"What else?"

"*If you are born a Jew, you are born in possession of yourself and your identity. The whole world is anti-Semitic, and none more so than so-called friends of Jews. Because the existence of the Jew— his tradition, his industry, his self-reliance, his status as chosen, his insistence on maximizing his potential and enjoying life to the fullest—is a reproach to the non-Jew. At some point the most virulently afflicted succumb to hatred that can, of course, reach diabolical proportions. No one on the face of the earth is so hated as the Jew, and why? Because the light of truth is in the Jew, and many there are who cannot bear that light.*"

"So these things were on your mind when you went to see her show?"

"*Yes, I felt that she had won and I had lost. And yet I survived on a fool's hope that one day I too could have my own identity, but of course that hasn't proven to be so. The world continues to say no to me, no and no and no. And like a fool, I say to myself, yes but next time it will be different.*

"But you haven't spoken of the gallery owner, or at least not much."

"Why speak of conquest? Why speak of cooptation? You know and I know the world is ruled by men (and women) who can not only put things together but then go outward with the product of their industry. You would not expect a man of Quinlane's aptitudes to be outside that mold. He was not the type whose thoughts short-circuited themselves, the kind who wrote a poem that made his heart sing only to stash it in a drawer never to be seen again because his heart had turned against it, because the revulsion with his identity extended to a revulsion with the things of his creation, so nothing could ever be good enough until and unless everyone said it was, and even that was not enough. These self-defeating tendencies did not imprison Quinlane. At the same time, he was a man who sold things, a purveyor, and the price he paid was that he was involved with possession at the expense of creation. A merchant, a marker-upper."

"This is what you have to tell me?"

"God, if indeed you are God, you made me as I am. It is not for me to reach the terrain of excellence without assistance."

Sarah, of course, had a family. Most people do. Her father was in her image as he was in hers. They had the same blond hair and same manner of nonnegotiable apartness from the world. But Peter had served in World War II. As a bombardier, he had been involved in campaigns over Germany. "They were all guilty. Guilty as hell," Peter said. He knew what it was to be in harm's way. On the bombing runs he sat, as did his crew mates, on his helmet, fearing anal penetration by flak from the ack-ack guns below.

Peter had not wanted to be a war hero. He had only wanted to continue his history studies at Rutgers College, in New Brunswick, New Jersey, and paint and draw. He was Dutch and so of sturdy stock. His ancestors were yeoman farmers. He sought to reach them with the penetration that only history could allow. History was the preservation of time through the facts one could assemble about time. It was the channeling of heart and mind into a vision of what had gone before so a continuum could be established and you could see the ground you stood on had layers underneath.

His father had worked with his hands. He was a plumber. He knew how to cut pipe and join pipe. He knew how to make water flow without spilling a drop. The family did not starve in the course of the Depression, but Peter knew what it was to get through a day with only a candy bar and a carrot.

When Peter met Lydia, Sarah's mother, he met salvation. Every woman is a potential savior. What Lydia did was to rescue herself by rescuing him from his own tendencies. She threw pebbles up at the window of the room Peter had rented in a yellow house in Cambridge, Massachusetts, where he had gone to study on the GI Bill following the war. She threw those pebbles with a powerful will. She had him come down, down, to where she stood on the ground. Lydia was muscular in her desires. She had an appetite for food and flesh. She would not be denied. There had been a husband during her Radcliffe years while the war was still on, but he was as gone as last week's mashed potatoes.

If Peter came from working class stability, Lydia came from domestic ruin. What does it mean that your father kills himself on a country road or that your mother goes on an iron lung or that you are left with a dowager grandmother and a dipsomaniac uncle for structure and support? Her uncle's name was Ned and he was of the sodomite kingdom when what had been asked of him was that he be a man of the West Point mold. He could not live in the world that had been constructed for him, and so he dwelt in the bottle and among the woodland trees under which he frequently passed out.

Without her parents the wind rushed in at Lydia from all directions. Ned proved to be no buffer. He fell down when the wind blew. He disappeared for days. He once took her to Europe and abandoned her on a Paris street corner.

Lydia knew about disappearance. What she needed to learn about was permanence. She needed someone who could stay and never went.

She also needed someone on whom she could bestow her bounty, for she had inherited much in a material way with her parents long gone.

"Why do you talk of people in such a distanced way, Johan? Why are you not on the ground with them?"

Do not seek to impede the progress of my words. As rivers flow to the sea…

Peter was blond and bronzed in all seasons and wore a bomber jacket from his service days. He had the relaxed and even dazed manner of someone who has seen what it is to live when others around you are summoned to die. But he had not fought the battle of the bed despite the powerful apparatus that Lydia had discerned him to possess, and when he finally stood naked with his prowess revealed Lydia almost fainted from the delirium the sight of it engendered, but she revived quickly enough to say to him that he must be with her forever. A woman living in need of the absolute, for dead certain certainty. Because, in addition to high energy and resolve, ennui had held her in its grip. Because without a father or mother she had no center and lacked a direction home. Because she did not exist for her own accomplishment but to love and be loved.

Because a shoe had been found in her refrigerator by Peter.

Because the apartment she shared was in further disarray.

Because she had begun to frequent the bars, *not knowing what else to do.*

On the other hand Peter was allied with purpose and industry and resolve. He lived for the intellectualization of personal hurt, an animus against the world as it was. He saw a culture that would not accept him with the tendencies he was showing. If he fell in love, it was not with women but with men. There were those of his own sex who bowed down to his blond hair and lean physique and penis stature.

So there was reason for Lydia to be with Peter and for Peter to be with Lydia. He was saving her from a life in the bars and she was saving him from the love that was wise to not speak its name, not in the time that they were living.

It was a necessity of Johan's mind to think of them.

This much Johan knew. Peter betrayed her, but not with an immoral act. He betrayed her with his nature, which was to stand up to the world by not participating in it. He had had his time of participation, dropping bombs from great heights. And if he did withdraw, it was because she gave him the resources to do so. Because the ground she stood on was the ground of money, and when they tied the knot, when he crossed the finish line into her earthly paradise, when she said, you will not have to live with lack anymore, you will not have to go through your day with only a candy bar and a carrot, he was only doing as an American male of his meager means and his disposition could.

But the comfortable life that Lydia's inheritance provided could not remove the wound of his own limitation. And Peter was wounded. If he was excellent with the coordinates of a map to qualify as a bombardier, he did not have the wherewithal to fly the plane itself and it was deficiency on that order that caused Harvard University to smell the distinct scent of the wrong percentile on him sufficient to bar the door to his further academic progress. Harvard University said to Peter that he would have to go away, that his blood did not bleed crimson and that his step did not create the correct echo in the quad as reasons to reject his application for admission to its doctoral program. If he wanted to stay in Cambridge for a cup of coffee, that was fine, but he would have to go and sit in the local Hayes Bickford's.

When a man feels lacking, brought to that place by an institution with a civil yet stinging tongue, he must fall back on character. That is a rule that God has made. Peter was turned back upon himself by this defeat. He had to find the private places within himself that he could go. He was reinforced in his notion that the world did not want him and he did not want the world. He felt the fires in his mind smoldering at this banishment. He could smell the smoke of his own fury. And yet he was Dutch, and so he kept a level gaze. He went to Minnesota, where the snows of winter ruled even in spring, and a whiteness was cast on the land even as a leaden grayness covered the skies. There was a solidity to the Nordic stock he found in this state, where he had come with the encouragement of a visiting professor whose course he had taken at Harvard. At the university the winter wind barked its pleasure at his presence, and he signaled his acceptance with an exhale of smoke from the Tareyton cigarettes he embraced *regardless of the state he found himself in.* Peter was beautiful and Peter was dying, but death is the domain of the historian. It is his fertile ground of frolic. He goes there to breathe the breath of life into the deceased, knowing there are many who are dead in life. Fact, embedded in a narrative, inhabits the realm of eternity. Fact is God and has always been God, and he who has the most facts is the most that God can be. So Peter would have told you, though in a more elegant manner, with metaphysics hanging from every sentence.

"Why do you talk of a man you knew, who showed you kindness, in such a way?"

"Am I not a historian myself? Do I not have to say the things I think and feel? And do I not have to report on those I have deceased?"

Lydia was not invisible in this time. Her inheritance was Peter's sheltering sky. He went to her with all the things he felt a need to express and she became big with their progeny. The family that was created became his bed, Sarah said.

Lydia never went as far as her volatile daughter. Lydia was not a creature of the extremes. She did not denounce. She did not offer verdicts. She did not hold forth as Peter was to do, pouring his theories about things American into her ear. Lydia never said of Peter that he had made of their family his bed in which to lie. She did not allow herself to even think such a thing. But she did have a sadness and a pain that Peter had not sallied forth, that he could not see the world as a place of adventure rather than a sphere to retreat from. Books were not a steppingstone, a preparation; for Peter they were an end in themselves.

A degree that took others four or five years to acquire engaged Peter for well over a decade. In this time he was not always in the quiet places of his mind. Six months he spent abroad, studying with a master of American history who could only be found in Salzburg, Austria. If he had left his children behind, he could also know they were in good hands, for he saw that he had married a woman with earth mother capacity.

In the Austrian Alps Peter fell in love. The man was not in his image. Dieter had a mind that had moved beyond what his country had wrought, a mind full of determination to live in the aesthetic places. Not only was Dieter German but he was also strong, some saying the two went very much together. He had a maleness component that did not require women as anything more than friends and he had the sharp-edged instincts of the reality-based man to pay his own way. Dieter was not of the world, but he truly was in it, sufficient that he could stand up and teach and be paid for what he had to say.

Peter saw in Dieter the way he could have gone if only he hadn't been Peter. He returned stateside to the soft folds of what he knew, with Lydia's billowing warmth there to greet him. By now they were living in New York City, where excellence was everywhere on display. Peter had not been able to see the city from where he lived growing up in south Jersey, but his eye had been upon it all the same, given that its origins had been within the Dutch experience.

Their life was lived on Riverside Drive in a magical apartment with room upon room looking out on the Hudson River. The river had sedative qualities and a subtly monitoring nature. It could keep an eye on him and he on it. Beyond the river he could see the sun setting on the horizon. Imagine that, he thought, in an idle moment (there were many), the sun setting in New Jersey, where everything had begun.

The river pointed north as well as south. It had more than a saltwater estuary as its goal. And it could not be violated forever. Somewhere there was a pristine source, way up in the mountain tributaries, debouching into it hundreds of miles away.

North beckoned and the area slightly to the west of the river beckoned. Lydia had her birthplace to return to. Her dowager grandmother had passed on, as had her alcoholic uncle. The house was rundown, the lawn was wildly overgrown, and weeds were sprouting in the flowerbeds. On a weekend outing Lydia showed Peter where she had begun. They drove up the Palisades and onto Route 87, exiting at Kingston, then pushed west on Route 28 through towns like Mt. Tremper and Shady and Phoenicia and Allaben. The Catskills spoke to him as they drove. The trees spoke to him. He heard their whispering words, as if the history of the region was meant for his ears only.

Foxtail. Queen Anne's lace. Quack grass but also hemlock trees rising shapely from the earth.

A gray and dour sky that mirrored his own state of mind at times. A history of poverty and beauty. The extension of Appalachia.

The earth itself had been given to him. Hundreds upon hundreds of acres. His bower of bliss was nature. He longed to lie down on coniferous duff. He said as much and acted on that desire.

A marriage is a partnership. Lydia supplied the property. Peter supplied himself. It was a lot. He had a caliber of sturdiness she could not match. Her father had left this life when she was a child. She knew what the valley of depression looked like, as anyone who stores shoes in her refrigerator does. Peter was not her dipsomaniac uncle Ned. He kept his drinking under wraps. There was the tall glass of beer with lunch and an old fashioned or two before dinner, but of liquor nothing more. Peter had a twin brother. This was also a fact of his life, and it meant that his brother was alive while he was alive and that his life would stay current with Peter's life so long as he drew breath, but if Peter was the sun, then Ben could only be the shadow. Because this brother Ben lived alone in a trailer and had wounds where people do not have flesh. He was a contagion of negativity and unceasing lewdness and the bottle was his constant and only companion. He had been there at the wedding, a baleful drunken presence. And now he had situated himself on the other side of the mountain in a trailer park for the hardscrabble sort who populated the region. Well, that was all right. He was who he was. Peter had compartments in his mind where he could place him, *make historical sense of the phenomenon of a twin.*

We're talking now about the 1950s, a time of emerging strength. A victor will always feel his oats and drive a big car. Peter had conquered the Germans and in conquering them had conquered Europe, and now he had conquered Lydia too. He saw that she was helpless without him as he was helpless without her. Lacking Peter, she would have continued the trend of her Cambridge days, that inexorable pull of the bars. The entanglements brought on by alcohol-fueled desire would have diminished her, left her a corpse or a floozy by age thirty. She saw the tendency toward complete surrender to debauchery there within her. Seeds of dissipation were definitely waiting to be lubricated.

Johan was alive by now. Consciousness of the world had come into him in the year 1947. By the 1950s it was not enough for Patti Page to sing "How Much Is That Doggy in the Window?" His sister Leah had to have one. Johan was not one to contemplate the mysteries of a sister at a young age, but only to have one and several others as well. And to eat Drake's Cakes and Hostess Twinkies and Mars Bars and Snickers Bars and Goldberg's Peanut Chews and Good n' Plenty and Sugar Daddies and Tootsie Rolls and follow them with Mission soda, grape being his very favorite.

Peter was not aware of the Come to Jesus camp on the other side of the mountain, owned and operated by the angry Ukrainian Chernenko, who was given to sputtering rages and fulminating sermons in a makeshift tabernacle with crude pine board benches. Peter did not know this rotund pepper pot of a man with an orange toupee that slid loose on his head as he performed the baptismal rite on his young flock in the rocky creek under the bridge just off Route 9A. Pastor Chernenko was in that long line of evangelical preachers who had to look good while sounding crazy. Peter had not the same renouncing ways as Chernenko, who condemned the world with the adverbial form of the word, but Peter was in a retirement mode of his own by now, clearing land and sprucing up the house with a fresh coat of paint and finding new uses for the outlying structures, including the barn which he converted into a guest house. It filled him with purpose to make this land his own.

And Johan couldn't have known, though it would have meant so much to have known, that while Pastor Chernenko was spanking his Bible, slapping its gilt pages so very good and exhorting the children in the tabernacle to accept that they had the filth of sin upon them and to come to the prayer altar to be washed in the blood of the lamb so they could be rendered white as snow, that on the other side of the mountain lawns were being cultivated and shrubs were being planted and rhododendron were spreading over the patio trellis, that drinks were being served and beauty was on display in the form of the frolicking Van Dine children and talk of art and politics and literature was riding forth on the 1950s air. No, Johan could not have known about Peter or about Lydia (or about Sarah, his true salvation) and yet he had to know about them because they were American and they would not be able to know about him because he was not yet American and maybe never would be American in a way that would render him whole and visible in their sight. Because it was one thing to be American and another to want to be American.

The point is only this: If Johan in the year 1967 arrived at age nineteen as a plague of locusts on Peter's well-kept land, if he drank up all the Van Dine whiskey and swallowed all of Peter's sleeping pills and abused his daughter Sarah there on the property and carried himself in a sullen and truculent manner, if he lived in his sense of separation and differentness and held fast to the sense of abiding deprivation that told him the Van Dines had everything and he had nothing, if self-pity and rage seeped from every pore as he created a hostile nationhood of himself alone, that was all from a self-perpetuating past from which he was struggling to free himself.

Since first laying eyes on him, Peter grasped what was happening. He saw the lunatic in his midst. He saw Johan as a young man of no consequence trying to give himself meaning, a pathetically oedipal insect seeking to emulate and overtake the master. Sarah belonged to him, Peter. She was flesh of his flesh. She was the product of his loins. It was in the natural order of things that she would return to her source. Johan was but some temporary aberration, an affliction on his land and on his family.

Peter heard the clack clack of the typewriter keys. What was not to hear? The renovated barn, where Johan was situated, was adjacent to Peter's studio. What Peter saw was the sad folly of a would-be man trying to cure himself with the illness of his own mind.

"It's time to leave here, Johan. Yes, it's time. I won't say you can't come back. I would never say such a thing. But for now we must go."

Chapter 15

Isabel,

On election night, I stopped in at Popover, on Eighty-Sixth and Amsterdam, where I ordered a veggie burger, which I smothered in ketchup, practically emptying the tomato-shaped plastic dispenser. There is nothing like ketchup to drown out the taste of suspect food. Popover is not a vegetarian restaurant. Veggie burgers are not their specialty. We cannot know what level of care they apply to a minor offering such as this. There are matters of both personal and restaurant hygiene to consider. Overall, the place has a sad, worn feel to it. A fresh coat of paint for the walls and some new carpeting to replace the old and moldy one would be welcome. And the staff do not, by and large, have a professional manner. I was polite to the waiter, and frankly rather frightened of her. I may have said thank you one time too many. I can get that way, afraid of hurting others as well as of being hurt. I didn't want to make too many demands, lest she get angry. We don't always know what goes through a servant's mind, and waiters can be seen in such a light. Of course, I am a servant, too. I serve the powers that be at the org, and try to be as perfect for them as I can. Perhaps, more than anything, my excessive politeness reveals an underlying attitude of superiority, a lack of respect for the vocation she has chosen or been led to. Perhaps this politeness is an apology for having more than her. Enough thinking about a woman I will possibly never see again. My mother was once a serving woman, for a wealthy Park Avenue couple. But I may have already told you that.

There was rejoicing in my heart that night when Florida lit up blue on the electoral map. Light was once more on the land, that blue possessing the purity of a cloudless sky in summer with the smell of freshly cut grass in the air. All that pain from the impeachment process, all that unkindness directed at the Clintons, was about to be assuaged. And when I say unkindness, I mean just that. Is there another word for the treatment they received? There I was in Copenhagen the year before reading in the *International Herald* about the Starr Report, that pornographic tome. Election madness goes back a long time with me, Isabel, as it does with all of us. We are, all of us of our age, chasing those floats with the blaring Sousa marches and the red, white, and blue bunting with the smell of vinyl records in our noses and Bing Crosby singing "White Christmas" in our ears. These are not presidents. They are gods. They are our deepest hopes and aspirations, as well as our worst fears. Yes, we must demonize one candidate while lionizing the other. Yes, we must remain spellbound by the TV, waiting for commercial breaks to sprint to the bathroom or the kitchen, so as not to miss a second of the election coverage. And when yellow, or undecided, gave way to blue, such sounds I made, Isabel. Such whoops of joy, my fist punching the air. And such shouts, like "Take that, Lurleen Lulabella. How's that for your mo-fo'ing right-wing agenda?" I was hardly able to wait for the next day, when I could strut into the office. But it was not to be, Isabel, as you know. It wasn't enough that they took away the election; they gave us, in its place, the aura of their own inevitability, the dreadful sense that they would always find a way to win.

"We have a president-elect who has come to Jesus, and now it is for you to do the same. The last days are fast approaching. The rapture is nigh. Are you listening, old Johan? Are you really listening?"

"Eh?" Johan says, cupping his ear, in no mood for Lurleen's post-election rap but curious and concerned about her new religious tack.

"Don't worry, old Johan. I saw you in the church. I saw you there seeking. I saw your need, your come to Jesus need. You and I are going to be 'one equals fun' before all this is through."

And then, what else, but the booming laugh.

If it was, for Lurleen, a day for triumphant laughter and misery for Johan about the election result and dwelling on Lurleen's somewhat spooky religious aspect, the following spring brought sorrow and heartbreak over a familial circumstance.

"This is hard… I'm sorry to have to tell you in this way." He hears the words of someone caught up in the drama of the situation she is about to present. His brother collapsing down in Florida. The closest hospital not close enough. The attempt to rush him by helicopter to the nearest medical center, miles and miles away. The woman—Sharon—has the knowledge that we all have when someone close to us dies. For a period of time we will be stepping out of our ordinary routines. There will be a reprieve from our solitary lives, our daily worries, our concerns. Now will be the time of grief and sorrow and shared remembrance. The drama of death will bring temporary closeness. All distinctions, all differences, canceled out by the one great fact and its ineluctable call.

Johan hears deference, kindness, an eagerness to please in Sharon's voice as she rushes her words, explaining that Kelly, his brother's wife, is too shaken to come to the phone. It is understood that she, Sharon, is stepping in to hold things together.

"Thank you. Yes. Thank you. It is good of you to call. I need…well, yes, I will be back in touch shortly." He doesn't want to overextend Sharon. He doesn't want to try her patience. Death is not a ground of unity forever. There are differences, antagonisms, under the surface that time and exposure to each other will inevitably bring into play. She belongs to the rough world, the world that he is no longer a part of. She belongs to the Bronx. This is who he is. This is what he lives with. *Leave me alone.*

Minutes pass before it occurs to him that it is unseemly to remain at his desk when such an event has come to pass. The stirrings of anger come over him that he would even think of carrying on with his workday.

Death. It is some sort of private space. Like a drop of a powerful dye in a glass of water, its effect has spread quickly through him, coloring everything. He is no stranger to this change. He has been there before. He will walk with it now.

In another time Johan would have stepped into his boss's office down the hall certain of his rights to bereavement leave owing to the death of an immediate family member, as those rights are clearly stated in the personnel policies manual. But this inimical regime dictates that prudence be practiced and that he bypass Lurleen for a visit with the human resources folks.

Though for a man such as Johan, twice divorced and living alone and over fifty, human touch has become less frequent occurrence, the need for understanding and acceptance from others remains strong. But is this what is meant when people say, "Don't go to the hardware store expecting to find doughnuts?" he can't help but wonder, as he seeks out Jeanine Juddster.

"Well, that's too bad, Johan. Loss is bad, but there is no death. You have to hold onto that. This whole world is an illusion. Trust me, I know. I've lost two brothers and two sisters. God bless them, but they were all pains in the ass who never did right by me. Still, I forgive them. My whole life is about attitude adjustment, as yours should be."

"About my bereavement leave."

"Don't worry about it. You're covered. No one will miss you. Give yourself a good time. You need more of a carpe diem mentality. You thought I didn't know any foreign words, didn't you, but I read the dictionary, too."

"Thank you." He got up and moved quickly toward the door. "Hey—"

"Yes?" Johan turned.

Jeanine Juddster points to her sign. "Remember, Johan. Remember."

Johan points two fingers back at her, as he has seen some actor do, some all-the-rage hand gesture that makes him feel cheap and not in keeping with the sadness of the occasion.

Lurleen has set up her office so she is facing the door when he enters, and her computer is at an angle so no one can see the screen.

"How do you like my new office décor?" she says.

"I like it," he says, even if he doesn't.

"I got a little tired of them there snoops, if you know what I mean. I don't need nobody in my business," she says, going down home on him.

"Snoops?" he says. She has taken her penchant for secrecy so far as to lock her office door at night, and even when she is called away for an hour or less to attend the innumerable meetings that go on at the org.

"You heard me, varmint. Snoops. You all hate me."

"I don't hate you." And he doesn't. He has never hated her. It is more that he fears her.

"Yes you do. All of you."

"All?"

"Every last one of you."

"You are making me feel very bad with what you say."

"You should feel bad."

"Have I done something to make you say such a thing?"

"You are always doing something. Even when I cannot put my finger on it, you are doing something."

"What I am doing is maintaining my life."

"Johan, you are a fine, upstanding citizen. Let's leave it right there. Now what are you doing standing here in my office?"

"I will need a short leave of absence. My brother has passed away. I just found out less than an hour ago." A wave of anger passes through him. He doesn't want to admit loss to Lurleen. She is not the right audience, any more than that creature Jeanine Juddster, and he does not fail to note the expression of false sympathy she struggles to manufacture. And is it possible that this facial contrivance is a cover for the smile she sought to repress as her instantaneous response?

"I'm so sorry to hear that. Well, you take care of yourself." Her voice so clear. A voice meant to echo through canyons. She has already moved on from this conversation and is simply eager to return to the e-mail correspondence and her daily machinations.

"I'm allowed five bereavement days, but I'll probably only take three. And I'll check my messages," he hears himself say.

"Give yourself the time you need." The phone begins to ring. "I need to get that," she says.

As he pushes through the revolving door, there is Allan Neverby amid the other smokers outside the building. Johan's legs feel lost in the Lands' End four seasons wool pants. His short-sleeved shirt could use some touch-up ironing and the cheap pair of oxblood loafers he bought on sale at Macy's do not provide enough support for comfortable walking. Suddenly he sees himself as someone else might, a ludicrously self-important person with an unchallenging job, the kind of man who goes about in this day of business-casual in a cheap suit and tie carrying a knapsack that has nothing in it but the daily newspaper and perhaps his lunch. This feeling of expendability grows in him. A perception stabs at him like a dagger. *My whole childhood a desperate desire to see myself as important in my mother's eyes. My life the slow progression of understanding that I wasn't.*

On the corner of Fifth Avenue, a vendor sells those nitrite-loaded hot dogs boiled in filthy water. It amazes Johan that people still devour them, as one man is doing now, the whole carcinogenic feast gone in three bites. He shudders seeing the man involved in a mop-up operation, licking his dirty fingers that only a moment ago were touching U.S. currency, which has been God knows where. An endless procession of tourists file up and down the avenue, with their cameras and guidebooks and their "I Love New York" T-shirts and unfettered enthusiasm for this city in which he was born and raised. A tourist. That is what he is when he goes abroad. He cannot fool himself that he is any different from these sidewalk gawkers freed from the strictures of their daily lives to roam this metropolis. They have either been or are on their way to the Empire State Building, that secular mecca only several blocks away. Numbers of them have already done what he has never done, actually been to the observation floor just below the giant needle.

A throng gawks at the Lord and Taylor window displays that feature those mannequins of tall, fashion-model thin women clothed in summer dresses. Johan steps into the street to skirt the crowd, feeling outside the world of fashion as he feels outside of so much, including the seasons. There is nothing to mark them, no beach house, no country retreat. There is the world of work and subways and concrete. He has come to an age when the bigger world seems out of reach, including women, at least the younger ones who render him utterly helpless when in the presence of their beauty.

He turns west at Fortieth Street, at the south end of the New York Public Library, and into Bryant Park, a workday refuge, even in winter, from the vertical towers of glass and concrete and the commercial buzz of the area. And it is the kind of day in early May you want to take advantage of, one that reminds Johan of his childhood in this city when he would wake early and roam the streets and parks until dark.

The sky is cloudless and should be a spirits-lifting blue. The sun smiles at disfigurement. The sun smiles at torture and disfigurement. It smiles at unwarranted incarcerations and defenestration. It smiles at the blood pouring out of a child's open wound. The sun has its smiling way and the power to cleanse through burning.

Johan doesn't know anything about the sun—or the moon or the stars. He is here, on this earth. Sort of.

He has been to this same park earlier in the day, where he was one of many occupying those little folding chairs and enjoying the calm engendered by the rich green lawn and the plane trees around its perimeter. Now the men and women, many of them young and in office attire, who had been wolfing down their takeout lunches of poisoned food in Styrofoam cartons and chatting on their cell phones, have fled back into the office buildings that had disgorged them for their one hour—the sleek and concave Grace building to the north or the American Radiator Building to the south or any of the towers in the bustling area near Times Square. The chairs are mostly empty, and discarded papers and other litter speck the emerald green lawn. And with them has gone the noontime energy. The scattered few who remain—the elderly, the tourists, those homeless who live out of their plastic bags—sit in the quiet spaces of the afternoon on the gravel path.

As the sun shines its westerly light on the Beaux-Arts rear of the New York Public Library, he imagines an afternoon in the reading room of the block-long institution, and a feeling of claustrophobic gloom comes over him. The main library seems like an antique, a space-eating relic of another age whose contents might one day be easily accessible on a small disk. Is the reading room still there, and those lamps with shades of green glass? Are book requests still sent by pneumatic tube down to the stacks? *Books are good enough in their own way, but they are a mighty bloodless substitute for life.* He has nothing in his memory bank regarding Robert Louis Stevenson, not the slightest memory of *Treasure Island* or *Kidnapped.* But this quote from R. L. he remembers. This he holds onto.

The sun feels warm and welcome on his skin, after the meat locker chill of the org. At his age, off-putting whiteness is a permanent condition; no amount of exposure to the sun can eliminate this distressing pallor for long in his melanin-deprived skin. *Male, pale, over fifty and stale.* Still, it does his body good to place himself outdoors and absorb all that vitamin D from the sun. It is not for him to fear its toxic rays when he is out so little in it, though he is aware that when the temperature climbs and that same sun is scorching, prolonged exposure can be a torment. Something has changed, for sure. That hole in the ozone. Only fools and children get wantonly dark on the beaches anymore.

At a table near a refreshment kiosk on the other side of the park he sees a woman. Though some distance separates them, he discerns beauty in her slender frame and her posture, something in the way she leans back and crosses her thin legs.   His feet lead him one step after another along the cinder path in her direction; he has no seeming power to resist. In a spasm of self-consciousness, he looks quickly around before making his final approach.

"Excuse me?" Not the greatest of opening lines, but the woman is engrossed in her book so what can he do? She gazes up from her paperback, with its embossed cover and ungenerous margins. Up close, he sees that she has a carapace of hardness. She is a woman who sits at the mirror applying foundation, blush, eye shadow, mascara, and perhaps a powder dustup before venturing out into the world. Artifice. Warfare. A woman's world is deep, mysterious. They have holes you fall into and sometimes never come out of. And yet they need their weapons to deal with louts on the loose.

As if it were a taped message, he delivers his nervous pitch, an audition doomed to failure before he even launches into it. "Hi. My name is Johan. I work in the area. I'm an editor and also a writer. My company is just a couple of blocks away. Can I join you?"

She holds him in her line of sight with clear and steady eyes. "If you are prepared to meet my boyfriend Rocco as well," she says.

Boyfriend alone would be enough cause for fear, but *Rocco* elicits in him terror he is unable to hide, a horror of being pummeled by some outraged lover with power abs and gelled locks and an Italian stallion disposition.

"I understand. I'm so sorry to have intruded," he says.

And if the words *moral leper* and *pervert* and *loser* and even *aged sex offender* are now assailing him and he feels the judgment eyes of the whole city cast in his direction and hears its one voice declaring,

"Shame shame double shame everybody knows your name," it is not something new, not a place he hasn't been before. As he walks west, restraining himself from a panicky trot or an outright gallop along the new Forty-second Street—shimmering glass towers risen where porn theaters once stood— he hears an amplified voice, loud and commanding, say, from somewhere nearby, "Hey, you, yeah you." Johan cringes as he turns, trying to prepare for the punch to the face that will surely come as just and deserved punishment, but there is no irate, thick-necked boyfriend, only a cop in a squad car barking an order for the driver of a van stalled in the bus stop to move it.

Slowly releasing from the burden of shame, he stands in the middle car of the number 2 uptown express struggling for an expression of bland innocence. As the train roars forward, he thinks, Where does a man go given the reality of death but toward life, and what is life in America but a young woman of beauty?

That afternoon he rents a video at a local store. He knows just what he wants, having read about it in *The New Yorker*. And if something is OK with *The New Yorker*, then how can it not be all right with him? Because quality counts. That understanding has been with him since he was a child, and his mother sent him to the neighborhood Gristede's for Crosse and Blackwell jam, and only Crosse and Blackwell jam. Is that not what it comes down to, *brand name goods?*

Though he has some qualms, given the news he has received about his brother, he slides the cassette into the VCR and lies back on his bed. The performers truly are impressive, so large and out there in their emotions. He marvels at their courage, or have they learned some trick to master their fear of the audience sitting as their collective judge, the kind of lesson he wishes he could learn.

His bedroom is a crowded space: a large desk dominated by a computer and printer; a cross-country ski machine to keep him in some semblance of fitness (no, it has not become an expensive coatrack, as a cardiologist predicted some years ago); filing cabinets and bookshelves. And a queen-size bed, though for some years now he has slept alone.

There was a woman. Her name was Maura. And while it is true that they often spent weekends in this bed or hers, it is also true that within a year of their involvement she had begun to pull away. Given that he was approaching fifty at the time and she was shy of forty, her biological clock, so she said, became an issue. She was in need of a man to marry, she said, someone to father the baby she wished to have and with an income that could sustain a family. Johan was not the one. Never mind that, to his knowledge, she remains unmarried and childless. Never mind any of that.

At some point the performance of the standup comedians featured in the video grows tiresome. The jokes seem coarser, the laughter more forced. Everything about the event now strikes him as excessive—the oversize theater, the flashy clothes, the glamour pusses so eager to show off their camera-ready big smiles and flash their expensive white teeth. As darkness falls, he realizes he has reached the outer limits of escape, that he has been using death to take a holiday from his life and must now begin his return.

He is a Manhattan provincial, a lifelong New Yorker, a villager in a city of eight million, living alone in this one-bedroom apartment on the city's West Side with his plants the only other living presence within these walls—a struggling ficus, a flourishing spathiphyllum, the hardy philodendron whose leaves hang down from the glass bookcase in the living room like a girl's wild tresses. There is stillness and order, and the path is always clear from the bedroom to the kitchen, where he now sits at the table in the predawn darkness with his spine straight and his eyes closed and his hands gently touching.

In the hour that he gives to this practice the fear and despair fall away and the light of love gradually spreads through him. He has come home to himself. He knows what it is he has to do.

That morning he picks up the phone. Thinking, when we do life, we do life, and when we do death we do death. Surrender to it, he tells himself, while waiting for her to answer.

"Hello?" Kelly's sleep-clouded voice.

"It's me, Johan."

"Oh, Johan. Hi, hello. Sharon told me she spoke to you. I guess I was kind of a wreck yesterday. A lot going on. Sorry you had to get the news like that. How are you? Everything all right?" Some agitation sparking her fast words. She is uncomfortable. She is where she is.

"I thought I would come over."

"Come over? When?"

"Today. This morning."

"Sure. You can do that. It's a big day."

Yes. A big day.

That morning, while waiting for the elevator, he stares at his neighbors' apartment door, as cluttered with decals and drawings and uplifting quotes as a community bulletin board. *Violence in America is a descending spiral—Martin Luther King, Jr.....Protect a woman's right to choose....Save the Amazon rainforest.* The Flessers represent what some would say is the reflexive liberalism of the Upper West Side, as if liberalism has now been quarantined on this narrow strip of the island. The Flessers align themselves with the angels on issues ranging from civil liberties to gun control to conservation of the earth's resources.

The door is slightly ajar, a circumstance that amazes Johan, who himself cannot go to bed without twice checking that both his front and rear doors are locked. From inside comes the powerful voice of Marty Flesser. "I'm leaving now, honey," he shouts. Though Johan has tried to brace himself for his neighbor's appearance, he feels his equanimity dissipate as Marty steps out onto the landing. After the briefest of acknowledgments, they stand awkwardly, waiting for the elevator to reach them. With rocks and trees I do fine, but people, people? He remembers hearing a man say.

"How's it going?" Marty finally says. That penetrating voice rippling through Johan. They have stepped into the elevator, beautiful if unreliable, with its walls of baked green enamel.

"I'm doing OK," Johan says. It is all he can come up with.

A fit man with a spreading bald spot at the top of his head, Marty is famous as both a singer and an actor, including a lead role on a prime time TV series in which he plays a wise-cracking detective with the NYPD. The consummate family man, he lives with his wife Riva, herself a singer and actor as well as a writer, and their two prep school teenage children, a son and daughter. Johan has seen them for years without setting foot in their A-line apartment, which he is told has four bedrooms and three bathrooms. Nice work, rent control, if you can luck into it. Nor have they set foot in his rent-stabilized apartment. They are famous and Johan is not. They are Jewish and Johan is not. They are a family of four and Johan is a divorced man living alone. After all, with fame come requirements. Because they leave their door open does not mean you are free to walk in. He is grateful to the Flessers for the stability they provide, the *New York Times* reassuringly on their welcome mat each morning. Their home is not roiled with violence. They do not threaten. They do not steal. They are full of light and love and energy and their heart is in the right place. They cannot be faulted for who they are, for the innumerable parties they throw with guests spilling out onto the landing or the interviews they give or the recordings they make or the films and plays in which they star or the recognition that follows them along the city streets, no matter how casually they are dressed, as Marty is now in his baggy, wrinkled khakis and T-shirt. They are blessedly rich and they are productive and brimming with a sense of community.

And yet, as Marty says, "Have a good day" before spurting on ahead of him through the spacious marble lobby, a memory from childhood comes to Johan of knocking the yarmulke off a boy's head as the boy escorted his two younger brothers down the block just two miles north of where he lives now. All three of the boys dressed in suits. It must have been a Saturday. Probably they had been coming from temple. A stupid, bigoted, and cowardly thing to do, sensing as he had that the boy would not retaliate. Memories of his mother saying of the Jews, "They have such ambition. Look at all they have done." Memories too of that heavily Jewish private school, not so far away, that he attended. Four years of high school, going through each grade with that idiotic and amiable smile on his face and hiding from his classmates, not being able to tell them where he lived for fear they would learn things he didn't want them to know, couldn't let them know, about his family. You hideout man, you, the same hiding as when you were a boy, going through life showing people nothing but your permanent cipher status. Because Marty Flesser summons in him what he so desperately wants to forget—how very much he wants to be un-hidden. Say it, Johan, say it: Famous, famous, famous. Famous doesn't have to be the lonely and lunging soul in Bryant Park; instead, women will instantly recognize and flock to him, beg him for his company. Famous doesn't have to walk alone, as he is always walking alone. And the Marty Flessers of the world see this envy, this longing. They see what they spark in the hapless ones like Johan Manootdjian, who even on New Year's Eve is by himself with his little bags of groceries and his pathetic cassette from the video store. And the crueler ones, the ones unlike Marty, they smile in recognition of your envy and resentment. Because you can't hide envy. You can't hide resentment. They seep from your pores. They are in your tone of voice, your body language.

On Broadway Marty Flesser turns north, with Johan trailing farther and farther behind. He has come to understand the expression "He's lost a step or two," said of athletes past their prime. Short of breaking into a run, he has no way of catching up with fast-track Marty. That is all right. The rush is over. There's nothing to catch up to, as he follows with his eyes Marty crossing Broadway and entering a fitness center. At ground level is a supermarket, while on the floor above are mostly young people in colorful shorts and T-shirts working up an aerobic sweat on treadmills and exercise bikes and trying to burn off the few pounds they gained eating the food from below the night before. A funny sight, if you care to think it so. A *New Yorker* cartoon, maybe.

At Ninety-third Street, outside a Starbucks, a man steps into his path. Wearing a worn gray suit and tie, he looks like one of those bland Jehovah's Witnesses who hand out *The Watchtower* and *Awake!* in public places. But though he has the demeanor in his fallen face of someone innately peaceful, his words are provocative. "What are you going to do about racism?" he says.

"Racism?" Johan asks, repeating the word slowly.

"Yes: What are *you* going to do about racism?"

This is not a question Johan knows how to answer or wishes to answer, at least in a forum such as this, with a challenging stranger staring at him. But the man is blocking his path and demanding an answer.

"Let it begin with you, and let it begin with me." Johan surprises himself with his emphatic tone.

"What?"

Johan's answer shows no sign of having mollified the man. If anything, he seems put out now that the element of surprise has been taken away from him.

"You monitor your heart for what it holds and I will do the same with my own," Johan replies.

The man continues his hard stare before turning away. "What are you going to do about racism?" Johan hears him say, having found someone else to query. Relieved to be free of the man, he descends into the subway.

Isabel,

Have I told you that the station was extended southward from Ninety-sixth Street? That would have been the late 1950s. Previously, there had been a local stop at Ninety-first Street, but at street level that has vanished without a trace, the beautiful wrought-iron and glass kiosk gone as all of them are, though underground the station platform remains, a dark and ghostly sight, garbage-strewn and the walls covered with graffiti. I have grown older in this city and have seen its changing face within the street grid that remains intact. With so much history around me, I often see it without seeing, walking through my past with no consciousness of anything but the present. After all, Isabel, a mind can try to create significance where there is none. What can I hope to wrest from the fact that I once attended a Sunday service at the Lutheran church on the corner of Ninety-third Street at the urging of my childhood friend Jerry Jones-Nobleonian, or that I spent several of my happiest years back then at a private school just up the block that now serves as a co-op apartment building, or that Johnny's Pizza across the street, which offered the chewiest and thickly cheese-topped slices in New York, is now gone? It really is best to keep walking in time with the time that is ours and to render ourselves insensible to fruitless dwelling on time past in this city where I was born and would choose to die.

But understand this. The city has changed, coincident with the arrival of a Republican mayor, a virtual oxymoron in this Democratic town. And despite the cries of segments of the populace at the new mayor's abrasive style and the harshness of some of his policies, he has brought order and a sense of security where there had been little. The criminal element, so conspicuous on our streets and in the soaring statistics on rape and murder and theft, has declined. Still, let me say emphatically that I have never pulled the Republican lever in my life. And the question remains: what price have we paid for the security we have received? Where are the homeless who were once legion on our streets, plastic bags bulging with their life's possessions? Why are they no longer conspicuous in our sight? And what is the meaning of an unleashed police force such as the one I saw on display after the election of Rudy Giuliani—police officers in jackboots and leather jackets lounging on their Harleys, a squadron of white, thick-bodied men projecting an attitude that a new time had come, that they had been unfettered from the yoke of a Democratic regime featuring a Black mayor and a Black chief of police portrayed in the media as more sensitive to the issue of police brutality than to the very real victims of crime, and who had turned away from the pleas of one mostly Brooklyn Jewish community as Black youths marauded through their streets?

A further question. What is the fractured state and what is unity as its opposite? That I can answer from my own understanding. It is the silver rails gleaming from repetitive use so the rust of neglect can never attach to them. It is operational signal lights in the tunnel, blue and red and green and amber. It is the long straightaway from Ninety-sixth to One Hundred Tenth Street and the Central Park North station looming on the periphery of Harlem. The fractured state is where I could not go and unity is where I now can go free of trepidation along this straightaway on the Number Two. My progress is in increments over long stretches of time. As I stare out the window of the front car at the tracks in front of me, rejoicing at the wonder of what a tunnel is and at the miracle of mechanization that allows its mysteries to be explored in this onrushing way, I am aware that flanking this train are two sets of rails laid out on gradients that rise far above, one for northbound and the other for southbound trains with the numerals 1 and 9 showing forth, these being the trains of my childhood, taking me to and from the destinations I could not break from along the secure stretch I could tolerate, while the Number 2 northbound was an adventure into deep foreboding of what a knife in the darkness could do and of vengeful actions behind a baleful stare. Believe me when I say I am thinking only this: that I am going where formerly I could not. Something is happening here to make these moments holy.

When order establishes itself, sooner or later it will be embraced. Mayor Giuliani was counting on time being on his side and on the understanding from the populace that he would keep certain elements in check so they did not turmoil our minds and batter our bodies. He was no Don Corleone, speaking in a raspy whisper.

Rather was he a crime buster extraordinaire, one who went to great lengths to put the Corleones and Joey Bag of Doughnuts and Tony "Fat Tony" Salerno out of commission for the near and long term. Mayor Giuliani had no interest in glorifying the Cosa Nostra but solely in eradicating it. And if he could stand up to them, then he could also, to some voters' way of thinking, stand up to felonious elements contributing heavily to the rising crime rate.

Mayor Giuliani was Italian but also a native New Yorker, and a mythology was current in the time when I was a fearful child growing up in Morningside Heights in the 1950s: it was that the Italians of New York City were the only ethnic group the Blacks in this same city feared. The Italians fought back and then they fought some more and possessed a vengeance streak of their own in their combustible mentalities.

All this being said, there is still a truth that needs telling, without which the picture will not be complete and fairness and justice will not reign in the land: When I was alone in the voting booth, I pulled the lever for Mayor Dinkins, Dawdling Dinkins as the then challenger Rudolf Giuliani dismissively called him. But a further truth needs telling as well: I was voting for Mayor Dinkins with the knowledge that his time was past and that if it wasn't past, it should be. I was voting for Mayor Dinkins even as I accepted that I would not be sorry if he lost.

One last thing. To be a Republican is to be returned to an antecedent life. It is to be a boy growing up in New York City with immigrant parents who reflexively vote for the Grand Old Party. It is to have a mother who believes that Abraham Lincoln was the most handsome man to ever live. It is to scan my father's *New York Times* during election campaigns and be overcome with fear that the Democrats will win a plurality of the governorships and that the ship of state will be undermined by anarchist forces. It is to have the same fear of the Democratic tide back then that I now have of the Republican onslaught. And so I say to you this, Mr. Street Level Inquisitor: Now is the time for spiritual development come, when

Black is white and white is Black and opposites are seen to attract and dissolve and reappear in the other's clothing. What is the face of racism and what is the driver of it? Ask me then what is this fear of the lurking unknown, of the wild and predatory tiger in the night? It is the mind informed by Salvador Agron, the Cape Man, casually stabbing to death two boys in a Manhattan playground in Hell's Kitchen on August 25, 1959. It is playfully tossing a snowball in the direction of Winston, a Black boy from the welfare hotel down the block, and standing frozen as Winston picks up a board and crosses the street and offers a hard smack to the face with it. It is whites on the beach at Coney Island beating a Black man unconscious for daring to put down a towel on the sands they felt they owned. It is the witnessed horror of preadolescent Black boys shot dead by an undercover cop after they asked him for his money. It is fear sectioning you off from one part of the city after another as the escalating accounts of street crime cause an unreasoning terror in your separating mind. Let safety show its face so unity can abound is the platform on which I declare my candidacy.

Johan surfaces from the subway at 125th Street and Lenox Avenue, a wide boulevard running north-south through the center of Harlem. On one corner a ubiquitous Starbucks and farther down the block a Burger King, where patrons munch on beef and fries and down sugary drinks under bright lights. He heads east in the direction of the Metro-North elevated platform traversing the street and an environment of decay, buildings with boarded up windows waiting for the developer or the bulldozer or both. A man in a white robe and fez stands at a table display of incense with a pungent scent. Another sells flawed goods on a blanket spread out on the sidewalk: a toaster lacking a cord, a vacuum cleaner minus the hose. Young men with do rags on their heads walking four abreast forcing him to clear a path. It is a quiet weekday morning in May, and he is in Harlem as it can be in that time and he feels quietly delirious under the blessed sun. Oh life that I would hold so tight, I would spend an eternity trying to capture you.

May I tell you one thing more, my morning interrogator? May I? The human heart—any human heart—can be vile and treacherous and murderous in its intent. It is when we own the corruption in our heart and acknowledge our darkness that the light can enter. Without this admission, our tendencies are too much for us. Pull down thy vanity; pull down thy self-deception.

Boarded-up windows on desolate streets and from a corner eatery, its windows steamed, the stench of grease; inside men are devouring large portions of ribs slathered with barbecue sauce. Above and in the distance a sleek caravan of metal commuter cars glides through the 125th Street station on its northbound route. A snaggletoothed rapper slouches down the street in ballooning jeans and a T-shirt he wears like a dress, the Lord of Crazy that he is, drunk on the rapid-fire words he spits out and hooked by the temporary relief and sense of power they give him. *I know who you are, you who are electric in my heart with your desperate poetry.*

If he were to continue his trek to the end of the island, he would come to a scene of rampaging cars ripping along the East River Drive and of ramps and a graceless bridge spanning the fouled waters of the river, in the middle of which sits Ward's Island. He could ask the small island to speak its name and tell its history. He could say to his sister Naomi, "You who have been gone so long, step forward now. Cross those murky waters. Walk upon them in your hospital gown and tell us the names of those who would abuse you at this psychiatric facility called Manhattan State, would hit you and then hit you some more. And then tell us that we who heard your cry from beyond the walls where you had been sequestered did not come, did not break the bones of your abusers in both their faces and their bodies so they could not torment you with threats of violence and hard slaps and kicks even after you had given them all in the way of money and cigarettes that you had. Tell us what it was like to be a lamb among the wolves in the general population, patients who lived in dread of the fist to the face and staff who placed carnality before professionalism. Tell us how much you wanted to live and were denied that chance by our indifference. Tell us that Johan Manootdjian was the one who received your call but came not. Tell us that he heard the hymn 'Rescue the Perishing' over and over in his childhood and yet did not apply its words to you on the particular day you called and had the misfortune of getting him on the line. Tell us how he informed his mother and your husband Chuck and then forsook you for the pleasures of the night. And you, Johan Manootdjian, you tell us too. Give us your lamentation sound here in the middle of Harlem."

"I will," Johan says. "I will tell you that from the time I was born she was both light and affliction to my mind, and that if I have said there was no need for histrionics about her demise and lashed out at those who would shed tears of falseness, there were reasons, for is it not true that I must call death what it is, the return of order where none had been, so far as my family is concerned? Is it in the natural order of things for those of the neighborhood to say in jest of this sister of mine on the suicide ledge eight flights up, 'Is it a bird? Is it a plane? No, no. Wait a bloody minute. Is that the Manootdjian woman way up there?' For were there not many who joined the shame shame double shame everybody knows your name chorus, who knew me as a blood tie as I turned the corner of Broadway and saw her way above, my legs trembling as a murmur of recognition came from the crowd. Should I tell you that I knew the names of institutions—Bellevue and Manhattan State and Rockland State— as I knew the names of baseball teams?

Johan descends into another subway station, down one level and then another into its depth. On the crowded platform he hears the words "Jesus! Jesus!" and then "Jesus! Jesus! Jesus!" shouted in a raspy voice. Something frightening, hysterical, about the sound, as if it carries the threat of anarchic violence. Among all the people of color in the subterranean space the man's whiteness stands out. A testifier. A modern-day Isaiah. "Lesbians are filth. Women who leave their husbands are filth. Husbands who leave their wives are filth. God is watching, God is watching. Only Jesus can make you clean. Only Jesus Jesus Jesus can clean your filth."

Jesus as detergent. A bar of soap. The deep sudsing action of Jesus.

Finally Johan spots him, a small man in a flannel shirt buttoned at the top. A jug-eared, pasty-faced white man with a fifties buzz cut. He stands in front of the newsstand shouting his message of the other world, the world of spirit rather than the world of flesh. Behind him at the newsstand an Indian man, from the subcontinent, sells his newspapers and magazines and candies and sodas. A man with God in his genes, no doubt, but calmer about it.

What is this so human need to lecture, to fulminate, to orate, to threaten? Who is this loud little man trying to shout over the roar of the trains? Does he ever say he doesn't know? Does he ever just talk to anyone? Does he ever just cry? Does he now or has he ever had the love of a good woman? Does he eat nourishing food? Does he carry anything about with him but his own terror and confusion and God of punishment?

Johan sees in the man the face of white anger. It is that which disturbs him. From poverty stricken and backward regions he and others are streaming in, with their bad teeth, their poor nutrition, their Bibles. They have something for the overeducated, overanalyzed types in New York City. If they cannot visit God's wrath on the populace, they will visit their own.

The train arrives and takes Johan away from the preacher and the newsstand and into the South Bronx. Brook Avenue. Cypress Avenue. Pastoral names attached to rundown stations with missing tiles and littered platforms streaked with urine. Hunts Point, a major food terminal. Then the train breaks free of the tunnel and moves along the el. A scarred landscape. Neglected and abandoned housing stock and ugly gates in the apartment windows of those buildings still suitable for habitation. A borough rendered hideous by the expressway mania of Robert Moses, tandem trailers rampaging along roadways set down through bulldozed neighborhoods where children once played and neighbors sat on stoops and chatted on summer nights, and brought close to its final ruin by the arsonist's torching of one block after another in the 1970s.

At Buhre Avenue he steps off the train, one stop from the end of the line at Pelham Bay Park. The feeling of depression that has accompanied him on this part of the journey, the perception that he was witnessing a part of the city that had lost its former luster, begins to lift. The commercial strip below the el—the restaurants and the Korean grocery with its bright array of flowers, the copy shop, the dry cleaner's, the supermarket—provides a sense of community and hope that there is life beyond the island of Manhattan. Maybe I could live here myself when skyrocketing prices drive me from the West Side. Maybe here is where I could grow old and die. He has begun to think that way.

Things that have been down coming back. People, too. Revival. Redemption.

He turns right on Park View Lane, a long, tree-lined block of attached two-story homes and narrow, buckling sidewalks where tree roots are pushing up against the concrete slabs. Several kids are out on the street, one of them in an oversized New York Rangers' top, whacking a puck with their hockey sticks. Not many people of color here. Cops and firemen. Men and women with parochial school backgrounds trying to preserve something they feel is threatened, some vision of the past when the borough was theirs. An atmosphere of fear and repressed anger, people sitting alone behind triple-locked doors.

Katie stands at the top of the narrow stairs of the two-family home staring down at him. She has grown tall and pencil thin. When he hands her the teddy bear he has brought along, she clutches it to her chest, so Johan has to give both her and the teddy a hug.

"Thank you so much, Uncle Johan," she says, placing a prolonged stress on the word "so," as the young now do. A feeling of embarrassment—call it shame—comes over him. It isn't the gift itself but the word *uncle*. What can he offer himself by way of explanation? A poor image of himself as a man, as he had held a poor image of his father during his childhood and adolescence? He wants to tell her to simply call him Johan. *Uncle.* It defines him as a blood relation. It brings him *into* family, when there is something in him that needs to stand apart.

From another room Kelly arrives. Luke's widow. A word that spreads its bleakness everywhere. From obligation more than instinct he gives her a hug as well. Her body has a middle age thickness and feels hard and unyielding, as if she is saying she does not like to be touched, does not understand touch, has gone beyond the place where touch has any meaning for her. Right away, she starts firing questions at him. He doesn't have time to answer one before another arrives. "How was your trip? Did you have any problems? People say there are incidents on that subway line all the time. Can I get you something to eat? What would you like? Tell me. Tell me. Can you believe it? Just like that he's gone?" Her speech is speeded up. It always is, like an old 33 rpm record playing at 78 rpm.

They have the entire second floor of a two-story house. Nothing about the apartment has their stamp on it, not the sofa or the dining table or even the paintings on the wall, Hallmark-like depictions of nature scenes. Sharon, Kelly's niece, who called Johan the previous day, got them the place fully furnished two years before when they first arrived from Florida with just a few suitcases and a couple of boxes. Luke had packed up the van with no real plan, not having realized the city had changed. Rents were considerably higher. Realtors had quick access to credit ratings. They were just about broke and driving around in circles when Sharon stepped up.

James calls frequently that afternoon with updates. He had dropped out of the depressing and dangerous public high school and fled back to Florida and the trailer rather than try to hack it in the Bronx. James was right there in the trailer when his father slumped to the floor. Luke had made the twenty-four hour Greyhound bus trip from New York City to see his son and renovate the trailer. The arrival of the medics, then the helicopter, when it was understood that too much travel time was involved in trying to get him to a hospital by ambulance. Luke's weight a problem as they tried to load him onto the chopper.

Johan does a lot of sitting over the next couple of hours. Somehow it seems like the right and only thing to do, as if he is following some universal tradition, like the Jews with shiva, of just being together when someone has passed on. Kelly brings out fruits and pies. Every few minutes, or so it seems, she is asking if he wants something to eat. "How about a sandwich? How about something to drink?" He finds himself having to fend her off and considers it his good fortune that she has all these calls to distract her. Periodically she excuses herself to go out back to cop a smoke. She is thoughtful that way.

"Ma, poor Uncle Johan doesn't want to eat. Can't you see that?" Katie says, coming to Johan's aid. That big, warm voice. It seems meant for an audience larger than her mother and Johan. And her big eyes, eyes that take in everything.

"Everyone's hungry. Everyone needs to eat. Keeps your strength up," Kelly says, punctuating her assertion with a hollow laugh.

And to oblige her, he reaches for a piece of cantaloupe on the cantilevered table while passing on the cold cuts and the apple crumb pie. About the dessert he is ready to explain to her that he needs to avoid sugar for health reasons, but he doesn't want to start a whole thing about his diet. It would only give them reason to dislike him, though, of course, their dislike of him is inevitable, as everyone sooner or later must come to dislike him for the simple reason that he is only partially present. There is a part of him that stands back and observes. The episodes and incidents that make up his life are just material for the book he is always writing. He can never be fully genuine because he is so often committing experience. Yes, he is there to give, but he is also there to take away, and so, in his heart of hearts, he feels like a thief. What will they say when they see themselves in the pages of my book? What will they say? Such thoughts as these enter his mind.

The feeding thing. It is what Kelly has done for Luke and to Luke. Bringing him the store-bought pies from the PriceRite down on the avenue. Buying sale items. Buying with coupons. Kelly knows how to make a dollar go far, or as far as it can these days.

As she moves about, Luther remembers her years ago walking up Broadway on the Upper West Side. Heaviness and the trauma that molds her face into a mask of fear are ahead of her. Kelly Doherty is in her teens and thin and pretty, with a figure that makes men as well as boys turn their heads. Her lips are full and her curly black hair is cut androgynously short. There is excitement in your blood when you see Kelly Doherty back then. She is walking at a fast clip and looking straight ahead—there is no time for sideways glances. She possesses a quality of womanliness that elevates her above the other girls in the neighborhood, and the world has begun to notice her, too. Since she was a baby, there have been modeling assignments, and now she is beginning to perform as a singer. She is said to be bold; the Catholic strictures cannot hold her in place. She has a manager who is said to be more than that. This is in the time before her first husband, Richie.

She and Richie are young. They are in love. Richie has his own business as an electrician. He is making good money, but he is a gambler and his reckless lifestyle is taking them down. Huge debt, the loan sharks threatening to break his legs and worse, and yes, the drugs and drinking that lead to derangement and fuel the abuse and the beatings. She can't take anymore. All she wants is to care for her child and be able to pay her bills. But when the abuse increases, she is forced to get an order of protection.

At which point Luke moves in with her. Johan tells him not to. Johan tells him he has entered a house on fire. But he is always that way about his brother, warning him, cautioning him to hit the brakes or at least go slow. Her son, Brian, is five years old at the time. A slender kid with big eyes. Like a deer. It is in this context that Richie calls. He wants to talk. That's all. He's feeling bad, all ripped up inside. His life is in a thousand pieces and he needs to put it back together again. Sure, he knows he has done her wrong, but he loves her. He really, really does. He sees the mistakes he's made. Is he asking for so much to see her and the boy? He wouldn't take up much of their time. And they could meet in a safe place. What was safer than the zoo in Central Park? All those people around. They'd meet and watch the sea lions slip in and out of the water. "Come on," he says. "Trust me, baby. Trust me. I just want to see you and Brian. That's all. I just need to see my family. I just need to try to make things up to you." And so, she goes to him because she has to go to him. It's always that way with Richie. She goes even though Luke tells her not to go, ignoring the bad feeling he says he has about such a meeting. She disregards Luke just as Luke disregarded Johan and went to her. The world is a disregarding place. It is about not listening and as a result going into the places that are not safe for you, and it will always be that way until you learn to listen to that voice within that frees you from the hot spots of insanity by disappearing them from your consciousness. And not even that will make you safe, though you will think it does.

And so Kelly goes to Richie not as if she has accepted her fate or from willfulness so much as from obligation. A man-child has been crying. She must comfort him. She goes to understand what cannot be understood, the state of her life and how she has gotten there. And she sees Richie, and Richie sees her, and Brian see Richie and Richie sees him, and Brian stands close and protective of his mother while the carousel whirls in the distance with the horses going up and down and it is to the sound of a waltz and all the soothing feelings it is designed to summon that Richie, who has fallen from grace into the place of darkness where only death offers the prospect of the union and harmony he is seeking, pulls out the pistol and shoots the boy and shoots Kelly and then administers a shot to himself so he can join them where they all are now going so the merry-go-round of the world can no longer be in play. Kelly wounded. The boy wounded. The father dead.

An aneurysm. A bullet in the brain that causes her synapses to misfire, her speech to speed up, her thoughts to scatter into random bits without the thread of connection. She had been agile in her mind as well as beautiful. Now she has a face that you recoil from, given the anger and the hurt and the injury impacted in it. You have to go past that face. You have to go back to what she had been and is now still trying to be. Then you can see her quality and you can love her.

"I have something for you. I want you to see the goods. He was your brother. You need to see the goods, don't you think?" Kelly says, placing a single sheet of paper on the table. Luke's résumé contains the college degree he had earned six years before and a couple of jobs he had held prior to that. It is a single page that contains nothing of his life. It is as if she is saying, "You see, there, there, right there in black and white is all he hasn't done." It is a reminder of all Johan himself hasn't done as well, a reminder of what it truly means to be a Manootdjian.

"Very nice," Johan says, feeling the stares of both Kelly and Katie.

"You should try on your brother's pants. Would you like that?"

"Mom," Katie says.

"Mom what? A man needs clothes. That's what brothers are for."

"I don't think Uncle Johan came here for Daddy's pants," Katie says, humorous exasperation in her voice.

Some feeling of being nourished, of being taken in. Some glimmer of rediscovered understanding of what family is. The warmth of it. He knows the public places of New York City. He sits in parks and occasionally eats in restaurants and walks the streets. He is a man who lives outside the buildings of New York City, unless they are his own and his place of work. He is not a man who is invited, nor does he invite.

The hours pass comfortably before he hears footsteps on the stairs. He feels the tension and fear in him rise as every step comes closer. And when the knock follows and Katie unlocks the door and says, "Hi, Aunt Leah" and "Hi, Aunt Hannah," in her big, friendly voice, the contraction only continues within him, as if the presence of these two large women who now cross the threshold poses an annihilating threat.

Leah, the younger of the two, has big hellos for Kelly and Katie. "Very nice. It has lots of potential," she says of the apartment, perhaps forgetting that they have been in the apartment for two years.

Compatibilities develop in any family, and certainly that is so among the Manootdjians. Johan's had been with Luke, who had come into this world two years before him. One brother and four sisters, three of them considerably older, Hannah being the first-born and seventeen years ahead of Johan.

"Here. Sit," he says, after greeting each of his sisters with a kiss.

"Johan's being a gentleman, Hannah. What's gotten into him, do you suppose?"

"Johan's always a gentleman," Hannah says.

"That's more than I remember," Leah says, ready to go down memory lane at an instant with her stories of misdeeds real and imagined.

"Leave Johan alone. It's a trying time." Hannah says, as she opens a bottle of wine. "Here. Have a glass of Burgundy. It will do your blood good," Hannah says.

"No thank you," Johan says.

"What's the problem?"

"No problem. It just doesn't agree with me."

"What's not to agree with?"

"It's just Johan trying to be different," Leah says.

He moves to the sofa. It must say something about his relations with these two sisters who have arrived that he now wants to go. It would only be a matter of time before Leah manages to marginalize him anyway. Yes, they kiss, as a brother and sister should, but it feels false. Something about Luke's reappearance has worked to worsen their relationship. The fact that Johan has been sitting there for the past few hours in the smug knowledge that he has arrived first says something. He sees, not for the first time, that for the past couple of years he has taken secret pleasure in spending more time than Hannah or Leah with Luke's children.

Marbles, Katie's tortoiseshell cat, rubs up against him, but when he reaches down and tries to pat her, she darts away.

"I guess I scared her," Johan says.

Katie laughs. Her resilience is a good thing to see. "It's nothing personal. She freaks out sometimes. It runs in the family."

Against the far wall is a computer in that standard beige color. It has all the elements—a keyboard and a monitor and a tower—but it is disassembled. "Does it work?"

"Oh, no. That's James's old computer. He gave it to me after it broke. My dad got a new one for him when we were still down in Florida. James is a real geek. The computer is not my thing." She speaks only when prompted, as if engaged in some urgent piece of required communication with a grownup that has to be gotten out of the way so she can return to her own thoughts.

Katie's dismissal of computers concerns him. Sitting in front of a screen is what her generation does. Won't she fall behind? Has Luke encouraged her indifference. Has he been holding her back so James could advance? Maybe not such a crazy notion. Had Luke not suffered a gross sense of intellectual inferiority in relation to the women in their family? Wasn't that what his enrollment in college later in life—in his forties—was about? Was he not trying to catch up and prove himself? Maybe Luke had not wanted life, and women, to beat James in the way that he had been beaten. Maybe maybe maybe. And what does any of it have to do with him anyway? Johan asks himself.

In the brief time that Johan chats with Katie the pain that started with Leah's arrival hasn't left. He feels himself holding onto Katie for protection from Leah and to prove that he isn't alone. Danger danger danger. The lights are flashing in his mind. As if she senses his misuse of her, Katie drifts back over to the table.

Nothing is going on and yet everything is going on. A family that needs death to bring them together, and even then, they are only partially there with each other.

"What kind of medical service is it that they can't get a heart attack victim to the hospital in time? It's not for me to tell you your business, Kelly, but we should think of suing. No one should be treated with such neglect, no one, don't you agree? And if they do want to treat you that way, then they should be made to pay and pay." Hannah's loud, aggrieved voice. For his oldest sister the lawsuit is an old friend, a way of getting back at *they* and *them,* those not always identified forces that have conspired to cheat her of her due in life. Like the time in the long ago she tripped over a box outside Isaac's Hardware down the block and fell to the pavement and demanded an ambulance. All the family heard about for the next month was the lawyer she had retained and the apartment of her own she would move into and the color TV she would purchase and the trip to sunny Greece she would take and the dark men she would meet when the judge ruled in her favor.

Talking that kind of stuff to a woman who has just lost her husband, and in front of her thirteen-year-old daughter. And the pronoun *we* as well, as in "We should think of suing."

Kelly saying, "We don't know what the future holds. Only that it is today. Have some more pie, anyone?"

Kelly stays busy. Neither Hannah nor Leah offer assistance. They fill the air with their loud, dominating voices.

Marvin, Leah's husband, arrives separately with their daughter Gretchen, only a year older than Katie. Johan holds onto him as long as he can, before he is inevitably pulled into Leah's orbit, as Gretchen already has been.

"How was the drive? Did you have a hard time getting here?"

"No. It was OK. MapQuest makes driving pretty simple," he says, in his slow and thoughtful way.

Johan is grateful for his brother-in-law's gentle presence. Quiet and sweetly broken by life, Marvin is a good husband and father and provider. He works for a large research firm where he is well compensated for his prodigious math skills.

"It's been a while since I've been behind the wheel of a car," Johan says.

"There's no need for a car in New York City."

"Do you ever miss the city?"

"I miss not having the same variety in movies up where we are," Marvin says.

"Seen any good flicks recently?" Flicks. Does anyone use that word anymore?

Several evenings each week Marvin finds celluloid sanctuary in some suburban Cineplex. While others consume giant bags of Twizzlers and those enormous tubs of popcorn and drink those vats of soda served at the concession stand, he sits fully focused on the screen without so much as a Milk Dud to pop in his mouth. Oh, maybe there is an item he purchases for his eating pleasure, a box of Good n' Plenty or a Clark Bar, but he is truly there for the sense of joyous solitude the dark can bring. It feeds him to be there, unencumbered, full of the childlike wonder still visible in his middle-aged and bearded face.

"I saw four movies last week. Two dramas, a comedy, and a spy thriller. They were all great. I'm hoping that I can go again tonight," he says, looking at his watch. "If not, I'll have to make up for it by going tomorrow, which is my usual night for staying home."

The movie theater is an arena where he weeps and laughs but never judges, never administers the good, bad or indifferent rating critics by their temperaments and the dictates of their jobs render. Johan has never heard him say, "This one is a dog" or "Forget about that one." And yet he is not amiable beyond belief. His head is crowned with the poison thorns of resentment. Long into the night after the movie credits have played he remembers slights from years gone by or even decades past, a torment that threatens to explode his skull and that leaves him drained as dawn seeps through the bedroom curtains.

Marvin tends toward the silence, and when he speaks, does so softly. The volume turned way too loud in that Coop City apartment in the Bronx where he grew up with a raging father.

Isolated men. Broken men. Johan thinks of his own wounds, and how through the years they recede only to resurface. Leah, younger by a year, has pursued and passed him and has had the upper hand ever since: her *summa cum laude* B.A. and PhD in Comparative Literature from Yale University, and now her tenured professorship at SUNY Purchase. You would think he could adopt the posture of an admiring older brother and be happy for her successes—her stable marriage and solid academic career. But all he has ever felt is fear and discomfort when she has walked into a room, except for when they were young and before she came to feel like a shadow on his life.

They all are old now, except for his nieces. He doesn't enjoy the same comfortable connection with Leah's daughter, Gretchen, as he does with Katie. As his relationship with Leah goes, so goes his relationship with his pretty young niece. That is just the way it is. He tells himself that he should remember Gretchen's birthday with a card if not a gift. And he should reach out to Leah more. But it all seems too much for him, some complex emotional equation he cannot begin to solve. There is no place for him in Gretchen's life. She is following her mother's achieving path. She is not standing on the foundations of ruin that will forever be Katie's inheritance. Gretchen is part of the world of success that Leah has embraced. She is on the fast track, with her prep school enrollment and perfect report cards and the high IQ her mother proudly reports her to possess.

I have won and you have lost.

Where is his brother? Where is his father? Where is anyone to protect him from these women?

Marbles has leapt onto the table, near where Leah is sitting. "Marbles? That's the name of your cat? Why did you give her a name like that?" Leah asks.

"Because sometimes she tears around like she's lost her marbles," Katie says.

When Marbles shows an interest in her apple crumb cake, Leah tries to shoo her away. Marbles reacts by raking her forearm.

"Did you see that? Your cat attacked me. She attacked me for no reason."

"She didn't attack you, Aunt Leah. She just responds to moving things by instinct," Katie says earnestly, wondering how her aunt could so misunderstand Marbles' attention.

"No, I'm sorry, but that was an attack. You saw it, didn't you, Gretchen?"

"I don't know, Mom." Gretchen smiles, fearfully.

"You should get rid of that cat. That cat is dangerous," Leah goes on.

"I should get rid of my cat for something she didn't do?" The smile has faded from Katie's face; her tone is one of astonishment.

"Never mind," Leah replies. Coldness has come into her voice.

The table is crowded. All are around it by now. Even Marvin has shoehorned himself in between Leah and Hannah, Johan sees, as he moves toward the door.

"Leaving already?" Hannah calls out. She has aged well, her skin still smooth, even if she is far too heavy. She is playing with him, as a cat plays with a wounded mouse. She holds the power now, the power of numbers but also of knowledge. And what can that knowledge be but the advantage that comes with her years. She was with him in that crowded apartment when he was a baby and she was seventeen. She has seen him naked, with all that means. It is a smile that says he cannot hide from her, now or ever. She will always know his dimensions.

Even Kelly seems won over by his sisters. "Yeah, Johan, why don't you stick around?"

"What's the matter? Got someplace better to go?" Hannah adds.

He stands by the door feeling paralyzed.

"Why doesn't everybody just leave Uncle Johan alone? He's been here a long time."

It takes Katie to come to his rescue. He is grateful to her and at the same time his sense of shame and humiliation grows that she has to come to his defense.

"Thank you, Katie." He comforts himself that it takes a certain courage to be the first to leave a family gathering. After all, the others will linger and he can only imagine what they might say.

Kelly and Katie get up from the table. He appreciates that. He gives them both hugs and tells them he will be back the next day.

"Bye, Uncle Johan," Katie calls, as he hits the bottom step.

Uncle Johan. He doesn't recoil at the words, hearing them now.

The soft daylight saving time light of a gentle spring day is fading as he stands on the platform at Buhre Avenue staring north at the sloping rails. Railroad tracks never fade. Railroad tracks are strong and defined and eternal. They are silver threads over the horizon to God. They are a reminder of Luke back in their childhood room with their "027" Texas Special twin engine diesel and the layout Luke built as Johan looked on. What longing does an airport runway or a steady stream of highway traffic create in a man's soul? Where is the romance in such venues? What solace could be found in such sterility? Railroad tracks are an expression of a man's anger. They are where he goes when family has become a closed circle he can't access or won't access. They are a man's way of saying he needs only the thing in front of him. To be married to the railroad tracks is to be married to the journey, wherever it might lead.

He suddenly feels old, at the place where things will no longer change, except for the worse. He is no longer a divorced man who will sometime soon meet the next woman. He is now a divorced man established in his pattern of aloneness.

There is a vibration in the old elevated structure as the train bears down. It will remove him from this environment of urban decay and familial disharmony that combine to leave him feeling that disaster is nigh. So he thinks as the train closes in on the station and causes the platform to shake.

Father,
I have read somewhere that all memory of you is dependent on forgiveness, as only forgiveness can remove the barriers to love. There are events that antedate my time that had a shaping influence on Hannah. No, I cannot know what it meant to be the firstborn in a family such as mine, and to have borne the brunt of parental dictate and undue attention. And so you are asking me to put myself in Hannah's shoes and to move further from that time when she appeared in raiment all of black in my mind. My only crime against Hannah is the crime of judgment, and that has eased. I see now that she was constitutionally incapable of leaving home. I see more clearly my own shortcomings, and so can try to forgive her for hers. And it is in so doing that I can see her in a brighter light.

Inside PriceRite shoppers cruise the brightly lit aisles, throwing into their carts and baskets corrupted packs of poultry and beef and chemically treated fruits and vegetables. Standing outside Johan imagines soft rock playing, songs focus group-tested for their ability to separate shoppers from their money, and commodities he has long since abandoned, remembering a childhood and adolescence of sodium-rich Campbell's soups and Oscar Mayer bologna and Chef Boyardee Ravioli eaten cold right out of the can, and the long-abandoned sugar heaven of diabetes-inducing Kellogg's Frosted Flakes (not to mention Post Toasties, which were always suspect in his mind—something about the very sound of the name), ReddiWhip, Drake's Devil Dogs, and Hostess Twinkies, washed down with vats of Seven-Up, Coca-Cola, and the more invigorating Pepsi, with its taste that could not be beat. The products of agribusiness have a home here so the might of America can remain just that. Except for the aluminum foil and plastic wrap and toilet bowl cleanser he sometimes seeks out in its wide aisles, he takes his business elsewhere now.

Once upon a time there was no supermarket or high-rise luxury tower on this West Side site. Once upon a time there was the New Yorker Theater, with its jutting marquee and its name spelled in jumbo-sized lowercase letters. Once upon a time…

Not that the patrons of PriceRite are uniformly ashen, potbellied, and prematurely aged. Women with golden tans and teeth that flash white and their tanned and trim studleys are to be seen entering its brightly lit premises. Women who can pick up the telephone when it rings, women who do not sleep alone but with their virile mates, women with children on their hip, women unafraid to bite into life even as it bites into them. These are very much among the patrons of PriceRite.

Still, OrganicOnly, the health food store on the opposite corner, just past the seafood restaurant and the small, narrow shop of Sammy the Sturgeon King, is the place for him. It puts a song in the heart of every patron, as do the dusty-skinned Bangladeshis behind the counter— bright, cheerful, no attitude of surliness as they bag your groceries. Sheikh. Mohammed. Quamrul. Shamsur. Ahmed. Zaimul. Bobita. Such names as these you hear in this store which has the vibration of their spiritually centered souls presiding over it. No atmosphere of corporate sterility here.

Though it must be said that the patrons of OrganicOnly do not appear uniformly healthy any more than those of PriceRite all look ill or malnourished. OrganicOnly does attract its share of the anorexic and the reticent, those wounded and conflicted and unable to heed the call of life in a way that draws them out of their solitary existences. And yet, good food is good food, and ruinous fare is just that. Best to accept that the earth itself is poisoned, or that the air in New York City stings your eyes with its toxicity and is the equivalent of two packs of smokes a day. There are antioxidants at the vitamin counter to protect Johan's lungs from the greed-induced folly of humankind and foods to maintain his other vital organs. Says Johan: "Bring on the bulgur wheat and rolled oats. Bring on the burdock root. Sing to me of low-fat granola and your products from the kingdom of soy. Let me redeem myself for the ginger ale I drank at Kelly's place. Let me overcome the harmful effects to my system of eating fruit sprayed with pesticide."

His relief at being back on home turf vanishes at the sight of his neighbor Sam bent over the salad bar once again. Does the man live here?

Johan reminds himself that Sam is his teacher. He is the mirror Johan must look into and accept what he sees, if he is to dissolve duality, even though what he wants to dissolve is Sam himself, if only from OrganicOnly.

Finally, Sam shifts, creating a space for Johan to approach the salad bar.

"Were you waiting? Sam asks, turning his fallen face on Johan.

"Life is a wait," Johan says, not wanting to give Sam the satisfaction he suspects he is seeking.

"Life is a wait? In what sense?"

"Give it some thought."

Sam, if he weren't a tortured, lonely soul, might be a Talmudic scholar. Johan now senses his response has been a mistake. Sam is easily capable of countering his glibness.

"My thought is that you might be looking to dialogue with me. Because if you are, I'm all ears. I'm sensing some underlying problem."

"No. No problem tonight," Johan says, with forced lightness, as he assembles his salad. On a bed of spinach leaves he places a large quantity of shredded carrots, six florets of the fresher-looking broccoli, and a couple of serving spoonfuls of chickpeas, then gives the whole thing a dousing of balsamic vinegar while avoiding any of the oils. With self-conscious quickness he makes his selections, the better to show his contempt for Sam's fusspot ways.

Sam is blocking his path as he turns to go. "In a rush?"

"Sort of," Johan says.

"Where are you rushing to? Why don't you give that some thought, and we can continue the discussion tomorrow?"

"I'll think about it," Johan says,

"Because you really don't know where you're rushing to, do you? From now on, I'm going to call you Rush. How would you like that?"

"Mr. Rush might be better."

"All right. Mr. Rush. Let me tell you something. You're going to need me before this is all over."

"When what is all over?"

"Come see me and I'll tell you. And in the meantime, get a dog. You're going to need one."

"Thank you for the advice."

eulogy, n. "a laudatory speech or written tribute. Great praise or commendation." What he writes is an assessment and not even that. What he writes is a grabbing hold of Luke so he will not disappear. What he writes is maybe in anger at all that has befallen him and the family with the idea of giving a hard slap to those who would dare to try to put a face on things.

Not good. Not bad. Just a statement of where he is at that particular time. Does he know it will cause trouble? There is reason to believe he does.

Whether it is emotional fallout from Luke's death or simply proximity to his own family, each morning he must adhere to his ritual of journal entries and meditation and prayer to dissolve the dark cloud that seeks to settle over him. He reminds himself that his illness, so to speak, would have him focus on his body— the paleness of his skin; that stupidly sincere face he must see in the mirror as he shaves; those same dull clothes, the Eddie Bauer casual slacks and sale-bought shirts that lack color and fail to provide attractive definition; the fact that no woman gives him a second look on the street. The fault-finding, if he indulges it, can be endless. What's up, in the jargon of the young, that a man his age doesn't even own a car, let alone his own apartment? And those piles of failed novels, stories, poems. Why is he even alive? Why should a person of such plainness and limitation be allowed to walk the earth? What is the point of this daily repetition, of showering and riding the same subway he has taken for his entire life? How long must he be here, anyway?

You have never left home, Johan. You have never lived. Your life has been as wasted as your brother's. This too he hears.

Oh, God, let the reign of lies and distortion cease. If you made me as I am, then I must be as I am. Let me feel the light of your love.

Seeking that happy glow, better than any drug or drink.

And so he can leave his apartment with his heart in sync with the morning sun and appreciation for the perceived truth that Kelly and Katie are giving him far more than he is giving them. They have provided him with a place to go.

And there is added motivation, of course. If his difficult sisters drove him away the other night, let them be put on notice that he is coming back and will always be coming back.

"Uncle Johan, you were here when Leah said I should get rid of Marbles. Just like that she said it. And just because Marbles swiped at her after Leah tried to shoo her off the table." Katie's voice is full of astonishment and outrage. She stands before him seeking his understanding, her face an open wound where it has been struck and lacerated by Leah's insensitivity. Leah, who could get in her car with her family and go back to her suburban home telling Katie, who had just lost her father, to get rid of a pet she held dear. And yet, even in that moment, Johan wonders whether, sooner or later, Leah will not bend Katie to her will.

"Well, she probably didn't mean it,"

"She did too mean it," Katie says right back. "I asked her why I should get rid of Marbles just because she jumped on the table and hissed, and Aunt Leah said she couldn't like any pet that threatened her. That's not right, is it, Uncle Johan?"

"No, I can't say that it is. But it's your apartment and your cat, so you don't have to give what she said any more attention than it deserves," Johan says. Kelly chimes in. "Your sisters can be something else. Luke told me all about them. I come from a big family, but my brothers and sisters aren't like that. We pull for each other."

It comforts Johan that Kelly has a cruelty detector. Luke must have installed it in her. Like many injured souls, Luke lived in the past: the hand Hannah had raised to him repeatedly, and the sins of the two others, Naomi and Rachel, who no longer walked the earth. And of course their father, whose violence was physical, not verbal, earning him entry in the Oppressor's Hall of Fame, with the whip-like sting of his hand once he had been made to get up.

Kelly's and Katie's confirming words have reawakened in him something big, something he can go near but not fully grasp. Always he has been the one to leave, to stand outside, as if born to be alone. The two of them, Hannah and Leah, coming in and taking over. Just taking over.

Though of course, there is another side of the story, theirs of him. His selfishness. His disdain.

James checks in frequently from Florida. The paramedics had called for a helicopter to whisk Luke to a hospital. Not the paramedics' fault, as Johan saw it, that they were living in a shit-hole state on which the Republicans were taking enormous dumps, stripping every county of needed services and making you think they had done you a favor. They had discovered people didn't mind being shit on so long as the shat upon believed it was for their own good, that being shat on made you a man, that having no pension made you a man, that having a job that paid two dollars an hour made you a man, that bad teeth and bad health made you a man, that needing no one and nothing made you a man. The paramedics told Luke he was going to make it, and as the copter lifted off they got the defibrillator on him, trying to shock his heart back into a normal rhythm, and Luke was still among them on the gurney in emergency care when his heart stopped and he went away.

It's nothing Johan wants to hear, imagining the medics racing against death. Who ever wins that race? All this would have and should have. Just shut the door on all that stuff and say Luke's time has come and now he is gone.

"I'm not ready to die. I don't want to die." Luke's last words, from James's own mouth to Kelly.

Luke had boarded a Trailways bus down at the Port Authority on Forty-second Street with a big bag of Kelly's supermarket food. No plane or train. Couldn't afford either. He set off proud of James for showing such independence and for not being average in his mind—for not applying docility to circumstances that went against his grain. James was simply correcting the error of having been ripped from his friends down South and deposited in an anarchic school in which, in spite of a police presence, sullen teenage hoods with practiced baleful stares menaced and intimidated him and made him a target for their smiling rage. Luke saw that James gave no undue power to the lockstep of educational progression. He had knowledge that went beyond books and the classrooms. Luke went to him because his son had a claim upon his heart with the angry need that he expressed to make the trailer more habitable after the neglect it had seen since they had come north. Luke was heeding his son's call, as any real father would, and as Luke's own father hadn't, when Luke had called to him.

The light of understanding has been turned on. Johan sees that while he has a credit card, Luke had a family.

"I know you're there, so pick up the phone." Leah's voice is on the answering machine. He is a screener, but why shouldn't he be? There are would-be violators at loose in the land. Is no value to be placed on peace of mind and the privacy of one's domicile? Only now his hand reaches for the plain black Princess phone, in obedience to Leah's command that he connect with her. Her tone of imperious omniscience has him rattled.

"I was just coming in the door. I've been up in the Bronx visiting with Kelly and Katie." A true enough statement.

"You know they don't even have enough money for the funeral. You know that, don't you?"

"Why wouldn't I know that?" Johan says.

"You haven't brought the matter up, and a funeral doesn't pay for itself." She has her crossness going for her. The time has come for her to put him in the small place.

"I was talking with Kelly about the possibility of cremation. Evidently, that was Luke's wish, even if he left behind no will that put this in writing."

"My brother is not going to be cremated."

"Doesn't his wife have something to say about that?"

"Kelly, as you may have noticed, is not well."

"Not well by whose standards?"

"Is it that you have no money put aside? You do have some sort of a job, don't you?"

"What exactly are you asking me?"

"If you can contribute two thousand dollars toward the funeral. I've already discussed the matter with Sharon. She can make arrangements with a local funeral home."

"Well, sure, I can contribute."

As you may have noticed. Some sort of job. His whole being feels polluted. He wanders into the bedroom, where on the top of a bookshelf sits a framed photograph of Leah and Marvin. Gretchen is but a toddler perched on her father's shoulders. She is like a trophy held aloft. All three of them are smiling. Johan never looks at the photograph with full happiness. Rather, it evinces a wince whenever he notices it. But to remove it would be what? A violation of what a brother is supposed to be? Bad enough you absent yourself from their lives, Mr. Johan, as some kind of protest. Bad enough you can't share the same physical space. Now you can't even endure her photo? And so it remains, year after year, as a kind of reminder of a goal, that until he is at perfect ease with her he is failing and there is work to do.

There were three of them in that childhood room overlooking Broadway: Luke in the bottom bunk, Johan above, and Leah in a cot. It stayed that way until Johan was eight or nine, when Leah was given her own room. Until the last couple of years of high school she was there but not there, in the way that a younger sister perhaps can be to an older brother. And maybe that is her wound. In Leah's eyes, he was their mother's favorite. "You don't know how painful that is for me to have to accept," she said, a while back. It's true his mother, born and raised on a farm near Stockholm, called him "Svenska pojka," or Swedish boy, because his hair was blond and he was more in his mother's image than that of his father. But how can Leah know such a thing?

All his photos of his mother are somewhere in the back of the closet. Too disturbing, too smothering, to hang on the wall. The same with his father. Armenian by birth, he survived the genocide in Turkey during WW I. A drifter. A traumatized soul, his race decimated and scattered. *They doused the girls with kerosene and used their braided hair as wicks.* Marseilles. Nice. Paris. Some classes at the Sorbonne. Immigration to America in steerage. A few years living on the outskirts of Boston among Armenian exiles and working in a shoe factory, before he came down to New York City and met Johan's mother in Central Park, of all places. A man who walked and walked. A man always alone. Even in photos, surrounded by people, he was alone. Saying, "I don't know what would have happened to me if I hadn't met your mother. I just don't know." Saying, in ruling the household with his hand, "Don't make me get up. I have no idea what I might do." Saying, in the middle of a conversation, *"Do you know we lost everything? Everything?"* Those rugs he hung on the wall and his pockets full of matchbooks from Jack Dempsey's restaurant, where he worked as a cashier.

But if Leah has a wound, Johan has his own. He remembers those times when Leah would call on her father's power, and even seemed to delight in having such an annihilating force at her beck and call, as when she shouted out, from their bedroom, "Daddy, Daddy, Johan is bothering me. Daddy, please come and make him stop." And of course he did come from the bedroom he shared with their mother, and he did threaten to deal with Johan if Johan kept mistreating his sister. And Johan did get to witness the expression of sly satisfaction that came over Leah's face as she saw the terror on his own. Emotionally speaking, she had made their father hers. She had found the power, accessed the power, and aligned it against Johan.

He is aware that any guilty verdict he wishes the court of world opinion to return against Leah will not help him personally, and that what he says and thinks about her is incomplete and not fully on the mark, simply hashed and rehashed material that suffers from the flaw of a limited perspective. It is Mommy gave him this and Daddy didn't give him that. Must he live and die here? Must he buttonhole every other person on the island of Manhattan and explain why he is the oedipally driven man-child he still is? Is there nothing more? Is there no real transcendence?

At age twenty-nine, he came in the care of a psychotherapist, Dr. Reiner, whose face now appears in his mind. Johan sees his red hair and neatly trimmed beard and recalls his soft, sometimes inaudible manner of speaking. He imagines Dr. Reiner, not his father, entering that same childhood room and saying, "So what's going on with you two, anyway? What's the problem here?" He imagines Dr. Reiner tending to his wound by rendering him visible. Dr. Reiner *recognizes* him. Maybe, Johan thinks, there is a child in many of us screaming, "It's not fair. It's not fair," a child seeking the receptive ear of a grownup, who will say, "OK, let's take a look at that. Let's hear what you have to say."

Across from him a wicked pretty girl with deep-set eyes that sparkle, her thin legs sheathed in tight white slacks. She sips through a straw from a large container of soda and eats a glazed doughnut, retracting her lips so only her stain-free teeth touch the carbohydrate and sugar-loaded goodie. A girl who will develop the sweet blood. Infection. Gangrene. Amputation. When the train screeches its way to the next station, she flings the carton with a backward motion of her arm through the closing doors and onto the platform, then carefully brushes her blue blouse and pants free of any crumbs.

In the middle of the car high-school-age kids talking loud, as they do when they are young and rowdy, talking not necessarily for themselves and each other but for a wider audience, sucking Johan into their nonstop sound in some complex interaction that tests the limits of his tolerance. So intruding, so canceling of his own thought patterns is their verbal barrage. Is the carpet of sound laid down designed to make him feel as dominated by them as they perhaps do by the culture as a whole? Sensing a challenge to come out of his pose of bland neutrality and to tell them to shut the hell up so they can have an excuse to go to work on him.

He has begun to feel the workings of peristalsis, and now the train has stalled in the tunnel. The coming scenario an obvious and humiliating one—the gang of four and Ms. Fastidious witnessing Whitey poop his expensive suit pants in a crowded New York City subway car. On his tenth repetition of the Serenity Prayer, the train once again begins to move.

Aboveground boarded-up buildings awaiting the demolition crew. A mangy dog trotting past a partially uprooted fire hydrant that tilts toward the street like a junkie in a serious nod. A man leisurely urinating against the side of a stripped van. Farther down, a lot piled high with abandoned cars and refrigerators and other metallic refuse. A KFC grease pit for the already obese to get another fill of croak food. A cluster of kids with time bomb personalities doing the homey thing in front of it, wearing unfriendly, broad-billed baseball caps that engulf their heads to their eyes and those oversize jeans hanging halfway down their butts, leaving their boxers exposed. Their boxers. Their bods. Their goods. Hip hop rap a whap, a barrage of remorseless staccato boom box sound. The hard heart as the way to go. The pulsing bass whacks the spring air, driving the word torrent up his spinal cord and into his brain, causing his insides to yield so he finds himself walking to the wick-wack beat wanting to spout his own crazy shit and feeling the rush of empowerment the powerless can find in the spoken word. This surging poetry of the desperate, a step beyond graffiti, beyond funk-a-dunk dress. Taking a hammer to form, to function. Thinking, as long as they're rapping they won't be capping. The word their only currency. Poetry, street or otherwise, a means of survival.

In the middle of this endgame scene stands Amato's Funeral Home with its tattered red awning. No one will be embalming him and lowering his chemicals-saturated body into the earth, Johan thinks, looking to the bright sun in the blue sky as a positive counterpoint to this scarred urban tableau. In this moment all he wants for himself is to die with his affairs in order and his ashes scattered in a strong ocean breeze.

Under the awning stand his two nephews. One fills him with fear, the other with love.

"My moms be telling me you be acting bad toward her." The words are spoken lazily, on the low end of the arc toward violence. The smiling impudence. The affectation of ghetto patter by this hulking man child with a fullback's thighs. The timing.

"Are you threatening me? Is that what you're doing, Rick? Do you want to go back where you came from? Have your mother visit you upstate, the way it used to be?" He stares hard at Rick. Takes in the pills- and pot-induced film of deadness over his nephew's eyes.

"Did I say I was threatening you? Did I say I wanted to go anywhere? Did I say anything about my mother visiting me?" Only now the smile is off Rick's face, a face more boyish than his forty-three years. His malign brain has to factor in the NYPD and the courts and revocation of his probation and the state correctional system, specifically Dannemora, whence he came.

Johan gives James a hug and, his arm around his shoulder, moves him away.

"Man, what was that about?" James is equal to him in height. A gangly mass. All arms and legs, as the saying goes. He wears a long-sleeve paisley shirt that doesn't quite reach his wrists, and his jeans do not cover his ankle bones.

If he knew more about family pathology, Johan might be able to say. "He has issues." Before James can reply, Johan says, "How are you?"

"Me? I'm all right." It's not the kind of question James asks himself. He's not that sort of kid.

"You've had a rough few days."

"It wasn't fun," James says. He is private. He must get that from his mother. Everyone in the Manootdjian family is only too eager to tell you their trials and tribulations. He himself is as bad as the rest of them. A Manootdjian can be ravaged by the worst illness and the rest of the sorry bunch will go on and on about their own afflictions, as if none of them got enough love when they were kids.

"No, these things aren't," Johan says, his thoughts returning to Rick.

Inside the funeral home tired carpets, a dying rubber plant, a glimpse into a small office where the business of death is calculated by the director himself, attired in a thin black suit and a wrinkled white shirt. Who works on corpses? Who makes a living injecting them with embalming fluid? Who smears lipstick on the deceased and lays them out in their finery? Who holds onto what isn't even there?

And then a stuffy room where the viewing is being held. His eyes travel past the rows of metal folding chairs to the front of the room and the open casket. Leah wanted a body? Leah has got a body. There, at the front of the room, in the raised open casket. Johan stands back. Not for him to go near that lifeless shell of his brother. Not for him to touch this approximation of life without the life.

Kelly introduces him to Hope, her oldest sister, shrunken and sixty and pale from the indoor life. A woman who, from what he has heard, gets through her days and nights with her booze and her smokes and the tube glowing in the dark. Hope has the financials for a slow drunken march toward death, neighborhood properties she owns and rents out. Her husband is gone of liver cancer and she has Sharon, her daughter, to take care of business. A woman not used to being out in the daylight hours and with no plans to make such appearances a regular occurrence.

And Sharon's husband is there, too, to support Sharon and Kelly and all of them. A cop, of all things. Built low to the ground. A real man. Such mismatching, death bringing together strangers who will remain strangers, never to see each other again after they disperse.

Kelly, in frantic mode, introduces him to Eileen, her other sister. Leathery and alert, smoke seeping from her pores. A woman who needs to nail things down tight and fly about with the speed and alertness of a bird. Johan thinking, It is trying her patience to be here. Any moment now she will explode. What can I do to prevent it? Anger is everywhere. It is not my job to monitor and mollify.

No high school friends of Luke. No bonds of love that defy the ravages of time. No testimonials from north, south, east, or west. No voice from his past saying, "I remember the time…"

No organ. No music. No eulogies but Johan's own, and that not so much a eulogy as just words on paper, a chronicle of stuff. A reticence expressed before he begins, signaling what? Leah's mocking smile says it: *We knew you'd have something to say.*

I'm grateful to Kelly and her children and all her relations that we could have this time with them. I think it is what I will remember most, sitting with everyone for a few afternoons in Kelly's apartment and beginning the process of coming to terms with Luke's passing. The death of a loved one is an unfolding. It places us in a different relationship to life. It's a quiet time that has its own rhythm. We lose the fear of death when we lose the sense of the finiteness of life itself. The dead, so called, are with us, and we are with them. There is a continuum that a focus on the body seeks to obscure. That is my sense of things.

Luke was Luke. He wanted life and he wanted the things of life. He was a fan of the big event, the hurricane that would finally topple the radio store sign swinging wildly from its support below the window of our childhood room; the blizzard that would paralyze the city. As a child he could not contain his awe of nature's power. But it was not only nature. Luke loved the things of this world. With a boy's enthusiasm he built model train layouts that dominated our room. He loved trains the way he would later love cars and motorcycles and boats and all the good things of life. And it was for Luke, driven by curiosity, to know how things worked, to disassemble and then reassemble, to hook up train transformers and fix the flatted out bike tire. It was for him to be able to do.

Luke was not contained by caution. He did not allow fear to say to him, you can go here but not there. He swam not to the end of the lifelines in the Coney Island summers of our childhood, but toward the horizon of the gray Atlantic, not heeding my fear as I stood on the shore that the ocean would claim him but listening instead only to the beckoning blasts of the lifeguard's whistle and megaphoned voice.

Luke was on the ground—rooted to the earth. He took the bottom bunk, while I slept above him. A strategic mistake, by my reckoning, as his lower position placed him in easier reach of our father's hand. But for Luke, some touch was better than no touch at all; he saw my father's treatment as a poor but acceptable substitute for love. There was the time he was beaten, for no apparent reason, by two older boys, outside our building. I could wonder if there was a connection, if the matrix from which he was sprung had made him receptive to such abuse.

Luke cultivated the look. The Elvis look. The pompadour. The garrison belts. The Wildroot, the short-sleeved shirts. The sleeves given an extra flip to show off teenage bicep. Every week a new paisley shirt from Morris Brothers, the discount store on Ninety-ninth Street. The chinos with the buckle in the back. The belted buckle meant you were going steady. Unbuckled meant you were free. He drove my mother crazy with his peacock show.

He liked the things our religion called "worldly." He liked girls. He liked dancing. The Madison, the Lindy Hop, the Stroll, the Hand Jive. Luke liked the wild nights calling, and I truly liked him for it.

There were our nightly walks through Riverside Park. He would talk of the apartment he would someday have away from the tensions in the crowded apartment where we lived. A clean place, a place he could be comfortable in. Success for him, as for me, meant getting away from where we grew up, and the fear that somehow we wouldn't, that we would be trapped. The night. The dark. The temporary release that walking gave us. My relationship with Luke became the model for all my relationships with my own gender, invariably seeking out the slightly older, more experienced male to whom I could turn.

He believed the lie of his own unworthiness. A long and tortured relationship with a girl in high school. The girl, her family, the time he spent with them, their beautiful apartment. Her brains. Her potential. The great college she would go off to. What about you, Luke? Where were you? What about your potential? What about your college, Luke, as if life was nothing more for you than to be a witness to your girlfriend's show?

The time she left him and he swallowed a bottle of aspirin and had to be rushed to the hospital. That was Luke, too, set up to believe that when the woman left there was nothing left of him. The same thing our father believed.

Too much Mommy, not enough Daddy. It was dangerous to be a male in our family. You said it succinctly, Luke. The women had our mother; we had Daddy. Not to blame; simply to assess.

At age nineteen he was arrested for attempted auto theft in Albany, New York. He and a friend under eighteen had put in gear a car sitting in a driveway and then walked away. The minor was released and Luke was placed in a jail cell awaiting trial. He was there for weeks and had to fight to protect himself. Our father sent a minister, not bail money, not himself. It was so like Luke to be arrested for stealing when he wasn't capable of stealing. It was so like Luke to be punished so severely for doing something so small.

For a time you didn't get away, Luke. The building pulled you back.

He moved to what we called the penthouse, a shed on the roof of our family's building. To pay for his lodging, he did custodial work. He mopped the landings. He painted rooms. He sat night duty in the lobby. Drinking helped him in this period to deal with the reality that he was settling back into the building rather than moving out. The Coast Guard notified him. He had aced their test. The highest percentile. Why wouldn't he ace their test? He could take a motorcycle apart and put it back together blindfolded. But the arrest for alleged auto theft came to light. No Coast Guard. No career. Just the building and a mop to swab the landings. And the wine. Always the wine.

Drinking separates people. It separated me from my brother. By the early 1980s he had left the building. The few times we talked there was a barrier between us. Then there were those years in which he was absent from our lives and impossible to reach. Our mother passed away and he wasn't present for the funeral. It was great news when he put down the bottle and began to reclaim his life, when he could begin to be more present for his family and to realize his potential, to undertake the things like education that he had run from.

A few years back I traveled through the Southwest. One day I was sitting alone in a diner in Moab, a town in southern Utah. I felt like a modern-day nomad, that I had lost touch with my roots and was somehow adrift. It occurred to me that family was more important than I had been willing to admit, and I determined to have at least a bit more contact with my own. I wonder if the same thing hadn't been happening with Luke. I wonder if his decision to return to New York City wasn't, among other things, a desire to come home, to heal the strange separation that had gone on for so many years. Whatever his reason, I'm grateful that he did return and share himself in the way he could before he left us, that he didn't pass away in some far-off state without this chance for contact.

There was something different about you, Luke, on your return. You were sober. You were peaceful. You were living within yourself. You had matured. Still, sometimes I could feel frustration. I felt you weren't giving enough. But that wasn't true. Your giving had gone elsewhere. You were sober, yes, but you were now a family man as well. Your sobriety was your success. Your family was your success. Your communication was with your children and your wife. That was where it was supposed to go. Your success was that you had made the transition from son and brother to father and husband. I thank you for your time with us, Luke.

While reading, Johan felt strong, as empowered by his own words as the rappers he heard on the way to the funeral parlor. But now, in the immediate aftermath, he fears that wisdom, the intuitive knowledge of what to say and when to say it, has once again eluded him. There is a feeling that he has transgressed, misused the forum. A statement he heard a while back comes to mind: The truth without love is an attack. He feels himself in free fall, with no one to brake it.

And if he needs any confirmation of this feeling, the eye contact he makes with Leah and Hannah should suffice. Eyes that communicate their displeasure are what they show him. Eyes that say, You will pay for this. We'll get you for this.

Now, even when he goes toward people—toward James and Katie and Kelly—they seem to be moving away. He senses that if he were to try to embrace one of the mourners, his hostage would only push him away.

You must live with this now, he tells himself. You must. Show some dignity. Accept the blow.

A young man jumps up and rushes to the front of the room. A young man with the eyes of a fawn. "Luke was fun," he virtually cries out. "He'd get us in the car and we'd all just take off for the hills. You never knew where the hell you were going to wind up with him. It was always an adventure." His smile widens at the recollections his words seem to trigger. As he expands, Johan seems to contract. He is the rebuttal witness eclipsing Johan's tarnished star.

The young man has a name. It is Brian. He is her son from the marriage to Richie, the one wounded by the bullet from Richie's gun that afternoon at the zoo.

Afterward Hannah and Leah claim Brian for their own. They gather around and thank him loudly. He is good Brian, as Johan is bad Johan. That is all there is in this world, good and bad, guilt and innocence. "Your stepfather was a great raconteur. He was so funny," he overhears Leah say to Brian. Yes, the deceased as a barrel of laughs, a source of endless amusement. Keep it positive. Keep it *American.*

As the mourners file past, Brian moves close to the coffin, but goes reeling back. "Man, death is death, I guess. I won't do that again," he says, gagging at the whiff of chemically treated rot he has received after kneeling and sniffing the corpse.

Soon the small motorcade leaves the wreckage of the Bronx behind, the bad-ass boys and girls with their bad-ass sound, for tree-lined boulevards and the reassuring spectacle of well-kept houses and tidy lawns. There is something about motion that can lift a spirit. Twenty minutes from the funeral home, they find themselves on a manicured hill that slopes downward to the Hudson River, and there it is that staff from Rosemont Gardens, using canvas straps, expertly lower the closed wooden casket into the hole they have dug with the aid of a backhoe. Katie and James toss in flowers as Johan stares at a commuter train racing past on tracks running parallel to the river. The sight of the train lights him up, changes him, imbues his life with newfound meaning. He is there with the train. It is taking him away with it, far far away into the never ending promise of childhood. Around bends and through deep mountain passes he travels with it in the night and in the bright light of day.

The train. Was it in 1955 that Lionel manufactured the magnificent New York Central twin diesel in the "O" gauge series, the engines painted a corporate gray with white markings and that heartbreaking red decal on the engine's nose? And did the New York Central not rule the very rails he is now staring down at? He is taken back to that childhood room once again and memories of the Lionel catalog, their real Bible. Was it not a source of torture to him that he and Luke had chosen the inferior Texas Special? No majesty there, in that dinky red and white engine and its B unit. The thrall that objects could subject him to.

The train. It will keep Luke company in the long hours of the night and through the boredom of the day. It will give him something to look forward to. The sound of it approaching and passing will keep him alive in his death, so-called.

Isabel,

I rode the rails of the words I wrote to a lonely destination, where even the wind whispers that I did wrong without any real intention of doing right. I wanted them to know that I know. But what do I know? That Luke had a hard time of it growing up, as we all did in our way? When will I embrace the courage of silence? Betrayal is my middle name, Isabel. I have defied the code of omertà that applies to all families, not only Sicilians. I am a petty thief, snatching up pieces of other people's experiences for my own exploitative purposes. I steal from my family's lives as I once stole from my mother's pocketbook, and the posses are riding hard to serve up their unforgiving justice.

In his dream, the empty glass lying tipped over on the living room rug puts him on terrifying alert that his security has been breached. Instantly he looks up to see a man disappearing out the back door. Leaving him what? Crushed, totally crushed. Everything out of control. Nowhere can safety be found. The violation will happen over and over again. Not even all the lights turned on can save him. The dream will recur. A man. Always a man. And solitary. And fleeing. Never confrontational. Just stealthily invasive. Waiting for you to realize he has come and timing it so you can only glimpse his departure.

There is a spirit world that is now pressing in on him. Something, someone, wants to make contact. Woken by his dream, he has turned on all the lights and, after checking the locks, from the kitchen stares back at the bedroom, fearful that that someone will materialize right before his eyes.

"Father, is that you? Father, have you come for me? What do you want? That you are not at rest? That I misjudged our relationship and misrepresented your contributions to my life?"

The air pregnant with possibility.

Chapter 16

A large ficus tree in a clay pot has been set down on his desk. The leaves richly green. A red bow around it and a card that says, "From Lurleen and the staff." Oh, life that dares to assault him with something nice so that the burden of gratitude has now been placed upon him. His mind shouting, "Hit me with a stick. Beat me with a bat. But don't give me your kindness so I have to be responsible to you, have to die for you, have to do whatever it is you want me to do."

And Lurleen is no help. When he enters her office to thank her, she says, "You all hate me, every last one of you."

"I don't hate you. I don't see it that way at all," Johan says.

"And what way do you see it?" she challenges.

"What I would say is that I *oppose* you, when necessary, like a political party that sets up in Congress as the loyal opposition. And if I should oppose you, it is only in the exercise of my loyalty to the organization. We must have checks and balances against the imperious urge, wouldn't you say? Are there not hearts out there blackened by their own self-will and their thrusting drive for hegemony?"

"Oh, you are just a totally preposterous man. I am glad you are back, but if you would please just go away. I will keep you in my prayers that the day will come when you have a come to Jesus moment."

He stares at the calendar push-pinned to the wall above his desk, noting the date and reminding himself that the month is now slightly past its midpoint. In two more weeks he will be able to place a mental X through it. One month will be down, never to come again—finis, kaput, terminally deceased. And while it is true that he will have to go through the same process of eliminating the year day by day and month by month the following year and the year after that to claim a full pension, doesn't the likelihood increase that the company will keep him on the closer he gets to the finish line? Would that not only be a matter of company principle but also an act of prudence, given the possibility of legal action should the full reward for his loyalty to the org be denied him so close to his retirement? Because he wants to be able to sit in peace out there in the park amid the kids with their high energy shrieking as they play, their patient nannies looking on, or maybe watching a softball game from behind the batting cage. He wants it to be nice, like when he was a child on those long, leisurely summer days.

He reminds himself that the emotional tempest with Lurleen is like being on a ship in a storm-tossed sea, but that the vessel is sturdy and balanced and the crew experienced, that the elements will subside and the next morning or the next hour the sun will be shining and land will be in view. And yet, as with those old movies in which the progress of time is visually depicted by the months flying off a calendar, he longs for some means to speed up the process so safety can assuredly be his and the threat of financial insecurity will never visit him again.

That morning he is listening to his messages on the speaker phone when a woman enters his cubicle.

"Not here. You're not making that racket in my space. You're not going to be my neighbor if that is the case. Do you understand me?"

"Hi, neighbor," he says. "How did you get into the next cubicle?"

"Lurleen wants me here for strategic reasons, if you have to know. So do you promise not to do that again?" The woman is in a terrible rage, her face ablaze.

"Do what?" Johan says.

"Go Speakerphone on me again. That's what. I have work to do. Business to attend to. Got it?"

Alice Piccoli tends to the reprints, handling corrections and trafficking proofs with the local printers the org uses. Baggy jeans she wears. And that old and faded denim work shirt.

"Yes, of course I've got it. Thank you, Alice," he says. Speakerphone is loud, and, for privacy reasons and out of consideration for others, he doesn't normally use that feature, and wouldn't have this time, but he was trying to open a package of rice cakes. Well, he will be more careful.

The morning is half gone and he has not yet had his tea break. It is a situation he cannot allow to continue. If he is Mr. Cubicle Guy, he is also Mr. Cup Man, just someone born with drink ware in his hand. Whether hot or cold, there must be liquid by his desk or he simply cannot live. Finally has the brightness of day arrived, he feels, as he enters the cafeteria relishing the thought of that first sip of HeavenBrew, an ersatz coffee made of barley, chicory root, roasted carob, cinnamon, allspice, and other ingredients. A satisfying taste that does not leave you wired for sound at day's end, as ten cups of real deal crank will. This tea he savors is his by way of the one and only OrganicOnly. Boxes of it he keeps in his cubicle so he will never be without. The men in suits who rule this cafeteria, those who come once a week with their attaché cases and their calculators, do not share the mindset of the holistic crowd but sink their teeth deeply into the fatty meats of this world and reward and refresh their unclean mouths with one nicotine hit after another.

He pays Esmerelda ten cents for two Styrofoam cups, the other being for the spring water he must drink in sufficient quantity to remain fully hydrated. It is then for him to make the critical decision: whether to use the water from the urn for his delicious tea and run the risk of also ingesting toxic metals and chemicals that turn his bathtub chlorine green or draw on the bottled water from the fountain and nuke it in the microwave, thus subjecting himself to potentially harmful levels of radiation. He does not want impurities in his body. He does not want his body defiled. He wants to be able to sing a song of strength and health. Though it is time-consuming ("a watched microwave never boils") he opts for the bottled water drawn from a pristine spring in Maine and takes the gamble that no harmful level of radiation will do him in at a later date.

A word, if he may, about Esmerelda. He is always exceedingly polite with her. She is from somewhere in Central America. He asked her once and has now forgotten whether she gave Honduras or El Salvador as her country of origin. She comes with full maternal instincts that she showers on her young daughter, who sometimes spends the day with her. There is a world of understanding in the pools of Esmerelda's big dark eyes. He feels she sees him with warmth. He has established a relationship with her based on simple politeness, and never wants a harsh word to come between them. He feels they see kindness in each other, if he may say such a thing, but he also worries that the familiarity of this morning routine will erode their present amiability and that her sunny face will inevitably turn surly with the frequency of his visits. What he is saying is that he is *conscious* of Esmerelda and that he is in a sphere of goodness that is unbearable for the pressure that it brings.

The cafeteria, with its chartreuse walls and utilitarian décor, is subsidized by the org as a gift to its employees. No six dollars here for a ham and cheese on rye, hold the mayo. No big bucks for a roast beef on roll. Staff receive quality fare at reasonable prices. And such sandwich-board stuff says nothing about the hot delights the chef Ernesto serves up each workday at the lunch hour, the pot roast au pommes and Cajun chicken and tortilla platters and hearty lasagnas. Lunch offerings with a theme. But first things first. The grill is still open for breakfast so staff can order their eggs and bacon and wicked-looking sausages. They can do a bagel with cream cheese (toasted sesame seed is Johan's personal favorite) or look for morning sustenance in any of a myriad of breakfast cereals. And on a bed of ice on the buffet counter will every morning be found the visual delight of a fruit bowl resplendent with color for those with pounds to lose or pounds they wish to not put on at all and low-fat cottage cheese to make it absolutely clear that they are serious in their intent.

In truth Johan says no to Ernesto's fare most days. Yes, he will have the occasional toasted sesame seed bagel *easy very easy with the cream cheese.* Yes, he will risk perdition by once a month indulging in a ham and provolone, heavy on the mustard, and two of your most delicious slices of pickle and just a small portion of your chips if you would. But then he will respond in the days and weeks that follow with a regimen that holds to a simple piece of pita bread to tide him over between the high-fiber cereal he eats at home for breakfast and the lunch he consumes at his work desk, which will be the highest quality hummus from OrganicOnly and an orange from OrganicOnly to give his taste buds something to smile about. And of course he will have his daily apple (also OrganicOnly) when and if the mid-afternoon hunger pangs come. And let him say here that, out of consideration for his office co-workers, when that time comes he will remove himself from his cubicle and sit in the emptied out cafeteria, Ernesto and his staff long gone and all foods put away, and bite into this apple and know that health-inducing pectin and colon-friendly fiber are now entering his system. For nothing is more ruinous to office harmony than the sound of a staffer noisily crunching a golden delicious or a Cortland, or his all-time favorite, the heavenly Macintosh, or any of the shining varieties God delivers on this threatened but still-fecund planet.

But a darker truth about this cafeteria is that he sees the lack of fastidiousness among the staff. He sees Bed-Stuy Lamar in his kitchen whites in the bathroom and can't fail to notice that he runs a little water over his hands after coming from the stall rather than scour them clean with soap and hot water. He sees the single knife he uses to cut both meats and breads.

Lamar is Black Black with his baseball cap turned back and his low-slung baggy jeans. He is tall and lean and style itself. His presence dominates the room. There is Lamar electric on the dance floor at the annual Christmas party, Lamar dancing without dancing, no movement of his feet but just his hips. And there is Lamar now, behind the counter, as the white men of management, the men from Queens in their thin suits and polyester ties and their patches of mustache arrive and take a table on which they spread out their papers. Lamar sees what he sees. He sees the parochial schools they come from. He sees the heavy hands of their fathers. He sees their white anger and the bars they frequent at night to soothe that anger, the scotches on the rocks at their favorite watering holes. He sees their *Daily News*'s and their *New York Posts* and their divorces. He hears the hard voices of their police and firemen fathers, sees the bruised knuckles the punches of these fathers to their sons' young and defiant faces have caused, and knows they could be living in that white enclave in the Bronx where Kelly and Luke now are, as well as Howard Beach, Queens, or the areas of Long Island that they can afford. And, of course, he sees their judgment of Lamar that he is not one of their own. And yes, that they think they are superior to Lamar because they wear those suits and carry those attaché cases.

Lamar. Lamar is working for the man, Johan thinks.

Where has Lamar come from? Has he come from drugs and armed robbery and prison? Is he one attitude from busting loose again? Is his life a crying shame of squandered potential because he is Black? And then Johan thinks, who am I to even think about Lamar? If Lamar is the captive of the man, I am the captive of the wo-man, as I have always been the captive of the wo-man.

Whether it attaches to Esmerelda or Lamar or the men of management with their so-white faces and their mustaches, he is afraid of anger, and aware that niceness and a self-conscious air of innocence *I have done nothing, nothing* are his only defense from a beating.

My wiring is of a certain kind, he says. I see the things I see and feel the things I feel.

And if his cup of tea puts him in a state of mind to sing of Heaven, it makes him happy in a way he can hardly express to now see Rita O'Rourke seated alone, her head down as she fills the pages of a legal pad with words endlessly flowing from her nimble mind through her ballpoint pen. Oh, that he has her, and she has him, for the brief time that they can be together. The cafeteria has become her second office. She is there virtually every morning, and he suspects it is loneliness that drives her from her cubicle on the sixteenth floor to occupy the chair she now is in. All kinds of promise is held by the day ahead, even for those who chronically sleep alone, and so it is with Rita and himself.

She sits facing the entrance, the position of one who is living in the possibility that today is the day when it, *it,* comes along, just as, at the end of the day, one returns, alone, to that same hope that the mailbox will contain something more personal than a bill or that the blinking light on the answering machine will hold on the tape the voice of that someone special.

Women don't like it when you are too demonstrably happy to see them. Somewhere down the road they will hurt you for that spontaneity; they have no choice. Don't ever, ever crowd a woman. Don't ever impose on her. Don't do such a thing. Isabel taught him that. And so he has to mute his response to Rita as he joins her table.

"Tell me about your weekend. Have any fabulous adventures on the subway? Meet anyone on the grocery line?" Her voice carries the high spirits of one who has known a Saturday night alone and who is now buoyed by the contact she is finding.

"No adventures. Not one."

"Come *on,*" she says, as if she could order one out of him.

Her line of conversation is not without cause. It has become his way to tell her about the women he has met underground or in OrganicOnly or on the street. He has wanted her to know that he is a player, even if, after a time, she has come to see, as he has, that there is always something to abort the process of engagement.

"Actually, I had family matters to see to. My brother died suddenly."

"No. I'm so sorry. How? Why?" Rita gasps. It is a sincere gasp, Rita being one who values family.

"A heart attack, more than likely," Johan says, really not wanting to go down the road of cause. Death is death. Let the body go. Don't fuss over the particulars. He can't help but wonder, in a flash thought, if this inattention to detail is the reason why he is such a failure in the world. His life is a rush for something else, the open space, not the room crowded with boxes of records piled to the ceiling.

"Oh, poor you."

"Not really. I expected him to die. I really did."

"Why would you expect that?"

"He didn't take care of himself."

"Your week must have been very difficult."

"Well, I had a nice dinner with Isabel this weekend. We had a good time."

"Your voice always changes when you speak about her. Maybe you two will get together again."

"We are together, in our way," he says simply.

"But maybe you'll live together."

"Not necessary." Twelve years ago he didn't know he could be happy with Isabel just as things are. He would have told you cohabitation was a requirement for happiness. Now the thought is not particularly welcome, not as Rita expresses it. A feeling of being trapped comes over him to even consider such a development. Rita has gone further than he wants her to.

"I haven't seen you for a while. Were you on vacation?"

"I wish. I was on the road for a couple of weeks," she says, her voice full of weary acceptance.

"What were you doing?"

"Visiting councils. Talking about the new program materials that will be coming."

"How's your running buddy friend?" The current man in her life is married. She jogs with him now and then.

"Actually, we were out for a run this weekend."

"Yes?"

"He's a hard person to figure out."

"Maybe he wants female companionship other than his wife."

"I would never do that," Rita says, as if it is understood what *that* is. "We went to a bar afterward. He says he likes talking to me." The story always ends in a bar, whether it is the jogger or someone else.

Briefly, Johan went out with an Englishwoman, who remarked that dating in New York City was something of a con. To paraphrase Oscar Wilde, she said with some bitterness, it was the unavailable in full pursuit of the even more unavailable, and none of it was to be taken seriously.

"Do you see this jogger every weekend?"

"Oh, no, Only when he calls me. Anyway, next weekend I'm going with my dad to Washington, D.C."

"What's in Washington, D.C.?"

"The museums. The Mall. Lots."

The song "My Heart Belongs to Daddy" was written for her. The thought is not a kind one, but it is nevertheless true. She is always doing things with her father—concerts, the opera, museums. He is her date, and she is his little girl and the family's little girl. There is a reason Rita and he are sitting together, Johan figures. On the developmental curve, they can only progress so far. He wants to shake Rita and tell her to go to bed with the jogger, married or otherwise, that she is too young to be always sleeping alone, and that in the years to come the passage of time will only accelerate. Carpe diem, he wants to scream. Carpe diem.

Suddenly, in sitting with Rita, he sees the future trajectory of his life. The passion has fled and the waiting has spread, like a vast ocean encircling the tiny island of his life. He sees himself as living in memory of what was as the phone continues not to ring. He imagines himself sitting not in a workplace cafeteria but a senior center.

She limps as she goes to the urn for another cup of coffee and winces as she returns.

"Did you hurt yourself?"

"It's nothing. Just my knee."

"Just your knee?" She speaks as if the problem were a broken fingernail.

"Well, yeah, my doctor wants me to give up running for at least a month. He says I'm in danger of serious injury. He just doesn't get it. I have to run."

It would incur Rita's displeasure to ask why she has to run, and so he refrains. She runs on sprained ankles and broken toes and muscle pulls and tender knees. A couple of ibuprofen and she is into action. The New York City marathon, the Boston marathon, marathons out west. Running clubs. She is a heavy woman who has become thinner through jogging. The weight loss and runner's high are powerful incentives. Why is it that a heavy woman who has become thin is just that to him? There is something unnatural about such a willed transformation.

He offers sensible words about listening to her body, but she is not of a mind to respond affirmatively.

"Tell me about your job. Is it getting any better?"

"She leaves me alone, but I am afraid she is now exceeding wroth for my irksome ways. What can I say?"

He might say more but Rita makes a slight nodding motion with her head to warn him that they have company. He falls silent as Lurleen walks past.

"Hello, Rita. How are you?"

"Oh, I'm fine, Lurleen How are you?"

"Just fine for a Monday," Lurleen says.

Lurleen stands at the cash register chatting with Esmerelda. "How are you today, Esmerelda? Things going well?" It is what the lonely, like himself, do, talk to people who are virtually strangers. Esmerelda assures her everything is fine in her world and Lurleen says, "That's good to hear," as if she means it. One of those conversations meant for listening ears and watching eyes, to show that she has friends, too. Because Lurleen can't like it too much that he is sitting all cozy with Rita, from Program, a department that has caused her so much trouble. Lurleen carries out her midmorning snack, a blueberry muffin and a can of Coke. She eats with impunity: KFC chicken and Big Macs and Domino's Pizza. Her faith in corporate America is almost religious, and it is an act of devotion to eat its fare.

"Lurleen has a thing about staff communicating with the outside world. She thinks we're talking about her." Although Lurleen and he are fairly close in age, he suspects, he feels like a kid gossiping with his teenage buddy in the school cafeteria as the principal enters.

"God, the woman sounds out of control. But how do you know that?"

Johan looks at his watch. Twenty minutes have passed. His life at work may be one long break, but it is still not a good idea to be so conspicuously idle with all that is going on, as he fears Lurleen may have the clock on him now. "Later," he says.

He does no work that morning but reads a page—one page only—from the dictionary. He has gotten to C, cataplexy to catechism. And he reads two pages of the *Chicago Manual of Style,* fortifying himself about names and terms, and feeling that he has a leg up now that is confirmed for him once again that the article "the," before the name of an institution, company, or organization is lowercased in text copy. Oh, to be armed with rightness. Oh, to have the last word.

At 11:45 that morning, he hears in the adjoining cubicle the unmistakable sound of someone rooting around in what sounds like a paper bag. In a process that he will come to know too well, he next hears the crinkling of aluminum foil. It is Alice Piccoli unwrapping her homemade sandwich. Other items are then unwrapped, perhaps raw vegetables she has cut up for consumption on the job. For the next twenty minutes he has the privilege of listening to Alice Piccoli masticate loudly her lunch and gulp a beverage from what he guesses is a mug by the dull thud it makes when she returns the vessel to the surface of her desk. The sound of her chewing and drinking and every sound associated with her lunch operation puts him in a state of full emotional disturbance. Perhaps the worst is when she gets on the phone. Is it her husband she speaks with in a barely audible voice, her throat clogged with food?

All his life he has had a keen sensitivity to mouth sounds. There was a time in his life when he was driven to take action, either to speak out forcefully against them or even, as a dire extreme, to go against them with his fists. Luke himself was a prime example of the offending mouth, Johan recalls, and so it was necessary for Luke to feel his younger brother's wrath when they were children. There was a sound Luke made, a *wet* sound, perhaps the kind a person makes when his lips part and his mouth opens, leaving Johan no choice but to punch him in the face because it was a sound of mockery and triumph over him, a sound impossible to tolerate when it comes with such a message.

There is another noise coming from Alice Piccoli's cubicle, not a human sound but that of a small fan whirring madly. It has been turned on simultaneous with her finger punching numbers on the telephone touch pad. The fan is going to make her personal conversation that much more difficult to hear but also, Johan will come to know, it is on because she is at that period in her life when hot flashes afflict her. And yet, the suffering of a menopausal woman will not invite compassion in Johan, or if it does, it will be mitigated by other things he will come to find objectionable about her. Take the matter of the thermostat, which she prefers the maintenance people to adjust to cool for their particular area. He can live with the discomfort of unwelcome coolness, but he will and must at the same time take note that on the sly, and in her schmoozing way, she arranges with Vito, the maintenance man, to regulate the temperature to her liking without so much as consulting him.

He will come to say of Alice Piccoli that she is a *smooth operator* and that her laughter is full of corrosives showing a hateful soul. He will come to say of Alice Piccoli, *She doesn't care about a goddamn person on this planet but herself.*

And he will come to know it is about money that Alice Piccoli and her husband speak, and only about money, and that the thrust of their conversation is basically about how to get more and more of it so they can be safe.

And he will assail Alice Piccoli in his mind as well for her grotesque habit of hanging her tongue out of her fish-shaped mouth in the middle of a conversation, as if she is seeking to inflict permanent damage on his senses. So astonishingly gross is her habit that it will make him shield his eyes.

The bill of indictment does not end there. Is it frugality or pathological miserliness that drives her to every catered farewell event at the org? Is it not clear, members of the grand jury, that she streaks from her cubicle not to wish the retirees well but for free food? How many times must we see her fly into the cafeteria on Fridays near the end of the day to scoop into a big bag bagels, pastries, slices of pie, etc., that have been set out as freebies before calling her what she is, the Vulture?

Hear Johan. Hear him now say, Oh life, oh people, what are you but a mirror held up to me? Do you think I lack all understanding? Do you think for one minute I do not grasp the street adage "If you can spot it, you've got it." In burying the hatchet of judgment deep in the head of Alice Piccoli, do you imagine I for one minute don't recognize that I am maiming myself? Alice Piccoli, c'est moi. Am I not the same self-obsessed, security-driven wretch as this woman in the next cubicle? Given that office life is primarily about a paycheck, can we suppose it has another function—to rage and rage at others even as we slowly surrender our sense of duality?

Johan stands up and looks out over the top of his cubicle and encounters Hank Farquist staring back at him from his own space with small, unfriendly eyes. No words of greeting can cover up what they each have glimpsed. Their eyes, Johan is sure, tell a simple story. Hank wants his job and Johan is afraid he will get it.

Swine. Treachery Incarnate. Archduke of Duplicity. Scheme Queen. Foul and pestilent plague upon my humanity. Through cogent argument, has Johan not pleaded Hank Farquist's case for liberation from the oppressive rule of Fiona Beasley, telling Lurleen that he was too good to be left under the thumb of fusspot Fiona? No man should be Fiona's office slave. Is it not reasonable to feel disgust with Hank Farquist, given all Johan has done to help him leave behind his temp status and become a full-time editor?

Hank's voice is loud. A stage voice, someone calls it. The space beyond Johan's little cubicle seems to be all Hank's on this day. His booming voice, the loud, somewhat hysterical laugh that erupts from him, the high-volume bonhomie, even the constant jiggling of the coins he keeps in his pocket as he races past, all testify to his emerging power.

I will kill this aggrandizing graybeard.

Life is a spiral. Things occur and recur. Someone knowledgeable about baseball history and the 1962 National League pennant race in particular might understand. Not that anyone would have said Hank looked like the San Francisco Giants' Baby Bull, Orlando Cepeda, or Willie "Stretch" McCovey or Juan "Five Varieties of Fastball" Marichal, nor would anyone have said of Johan that he was the Los Angeles Dodgers' fleet Maury Wills or slugging Tommy Davis or greyhound Willie D. patrolling centerfield. But if they knew anything about that season and the place those Dodgers occupied in his adolescent heart, they would have seen the fear that grew and grew in him as the season moved into September and the Giants, behind the pitching of Jack Sanford, kept winning and winning. They would also have known that his identification with the Dodgers was matched by the attachment a slightly older boy named Sean had for the Giants, and that the nightmare conclusion of the season was not only that the Giants had overtaken the Dodgers but that, in some way, Sean had overtaken him as well. They would have seen that the paradigm operating in that season was essentially the same one operating now, with Hank, once such a long shot, now breathing down his neck. They would have been able to gauge that the situation for Johan, from an emotional standpoint, was comparable to that in those dreams of childhood in which he would spot a man quite far away. The man clearly represented danger, and yet fear would immobilize Johan, causing him to remain rooted to the spot and helpless to keep his pursuer from closing the distance between them with mercurial speed.

And then it is noon and time for his twenty-minute period of meditation, whatever the dictates of that particular hour might be. He can adjust the time forward or backward, but he must have that time, as he must have it at 5 p.m. or thereabouts. It is his step-away time. It is calling on the aid of the infinite to alter the perspective that Alice Piccoli is loathsome in the extreme and in need of summary banishment from the planet, and for Hank to be banished with her. But is his assignment in life truly to see himself as one with hideous Alice Piccoli and the plotting Hank Farquist? Can he not deal them both a death blow? Can he not cancel any and all who violate him in their various and sundry ways? What mercy can the infinite be offering that it asks him to see Alice Piccoli as his sister and Hank Farquist as his brother? Is it not a lunatic impediment to perverse and hate-drenched joy to have to connect with the odious ones?

There is no cause for concern. While his short period of meditation has created a slight shift, he is not approaching the gates of oneness that afternoon. Such a possibility is eliminated when the Lord on High of Duplicity, Hank Farquist, calls on Alice Piccoli in her cubicle and ten minutes of gleeful, excited whispering ensue.

"You did? That's incredible. Incredible," says Alice, choking on her food as she laughs. It is a sign of the times, of course, that Hank goes directly to her, not him, with his good fortune, whatever it might be.

Is it his imagination, or does he hear Alice Piccoli say, "You're good enough to be a senior editor here. Just keep pushing." Does he not hear their cabal establish itself more deeply? Is it possible that if we are afraid of people there is often good reason? If he feels that Alice Piccoli has a poisoned soul full of hidden malice not simply toward him but toward the world, then is there not the probability that this is so? And yet, even if there are people on this planet who wish us no good, what are we to do with a truth such as that? What indeed, but to bless all our fears and return them to the universe as love, as all his spiritual readings tell him to do?

And who is Alice Piccoli really, with her gray hair and her bad teeth and her hideous tongue? Alice Piccoli is his sister Leah, and Johan can tell you why. Reader, listen now to a story Johan feels he must tell.

It happened in the long ago, in the building the org formerly owned and occupied on Third Avenue. It was in that building of tinted glass and steel and in that time that he saw, actually saw, Alice Piccoli hovering by a wall in the maze of cubicles on their crowded floor. At the time she was a woman you could see without seeing: plain, self-effacing, and silent as to her intentions, a woman quite used to her invisible status and somewhat older than Johan and others in the department, and of whom you would be led to say, *This is a woman I have no need to care about or think about other than to say the occasional hello.*

He didn't know that Alice Piccoli was an orphan and had the jeering manner that can develop from such an experience. He didn't know the deep sense of deprivation that informed her personality. To Alice Piccoli's credit, she doesn't wear it on her sleeve that her parents were killed in a car accident when she was very young or that she spent years as a ward of the state before being placed in a foster home. She is not one to fly the flag of victimization.

Alice Piccoli has gratitude for the things of this earth that have come to her. She knows where she has been. She knows what the word *mollycoddle* means and she knows further that the word doesn't apply to her. If a piece of bread is out there, you snatch it and you eat it before the others do, like the pigeons pecking for their morsels in nearby Bryant Park. Alice Piccoli knows what hunger means. She has meditated on the word *reality* and defined it as want and more want and the endless pursuit of the freedom from want. Alice Piccoli is a driven woman. Do not stand in her way. Do not ever stand in her way. She is saving for the future. She is saving for her life.

Alice Piccoli, at the time he saw her hovering by the cubicle wall, was simply biding her time, the way that people of her kind do. There was something she could taste here, and her slack mouth was salivating for it.

Have you ever heard the odious expression *a bigger slice of the pie?* Alice Piccoli has. Alice Piccoli doesn't know what the word *renunciation* means.

And of course Leah, in the long ago, was biding her time too, the way that people of her kind do, siblings born last in a large family and who feel they have been neglected and slighted and received less than others. A strategy for life is just that, and both Alice Piccoli and Leah have one.

Because for many of those growing-up years Leah was also invisible to his sight. Oh, he saw the things she did to him. He saw her calculating strategy. To this day he knows she deprived him of his father's love, that when he and she squabbled, she would call in their father's artillery fire. Has he not already noted that she would say, "Daddy, Daddy, Johan smacked me. He smacked me"? *Smack.* A word forever set apart in the English language and reserved for her use. And when their father had done his deed, when he had entered the room she and Johan shared, and dealt with Johan, unquestioningly taking her side and for, as he put it, *aggravating* him—is that not something to note and remember, particularly as she sealed the incident in Johan's memory with the gloating smile that came over her face? Is it not safe to say that she would have been thrilled if, indeed, their father had exterminated him on the spot?

How pitifully deforming are the wounds of childhood that a grown man should revisit them in this way. But life truly is a spiral. We come back to *the scene of the crime* from a higher perspective. Still, no matter what new light may be shed on ancient conflicts, it would not be wise for him to bet the house that Leah and he will ever be truly friends. Too much may have gone on for such a bridge to have been built. Enmity may be a safeguard against an unbearable, and dare he say it, unnatural intimacy.

One thing he does know, from the vantage point of time, is how needy he was for his mother's love and for her attention, for they were one and the same, and how tiresome and irritating this need must have been for both Luke and Leah. It was imperative that his mother *see* him. Without recognition there could be only death. And with the attention of his mother as the prize, is it any wonder that he should provide Leah with another opportunity to present him as darkness itself, as on a day in childhood when his mother arranged for Luke and Leah and him to be photographed? Leah will tell you, if she hasn't already, that while the three of them were posed for the photographer's camera, he suddenly and treacherously nudged her off the end of the bench, causing her to fall, in her Sunday finery, to the floor. And if he has no memory of such an incident, that is of no importance, for she does. And when an older brother has been treacherous, when he has systematically tried to render his younger sister insignificant if not invisible, then retaliation is in order and entirely justified, would you not say, and would you not say further that the retaliation should be ongoing and fierce and ceaseless? Is it not the basis for a life's work?

Is it not for all the women of the world to take their revenge on him for trying to hold them back? And is it not for him to accept their blows and their taunts as they find ways to surpass this man who was not born to succeed except in his own mind? For just as Leah surged ahead, so too has Alice Piccoli. The woman who was once invisible now requires that he see her. No longer is she in whispering mode, except when in the throes of intrigue with coin-jingling Hank Farquist or on a sotto voce phone binge with hubby. Long gone is the time of hovering by the cubicle wall. The time has come for Alice Piccoli to raise her voice, and raise it loud.

The past. You go rushing into it with expectation. Why is it you find no one there when you arrive?

Chapter 17

He walks and walks. Says hello to the streets and to his fellow pedestrians. Says hello to Bryant Park and to the new and sanitized Times Square and all the vertical glass and steel boxes that have shot up. Cold and gleaming corporate power everywhere. Says hello to the tall cranes and to Radio City Music Hall, the sight of the huge old marquee triggering a thought of his father, as if he can see him now crossing Sixth Avenue in his wool overcoat and fedora. His father a walker too, and to the ghost of him he gives a big hello as well. He says hello to the Summit Hotel and to the taxis lined up for fares. He says to the cab drivers, with the pain of remembrance, I was one of you once. I too waited outside that hotel. I was there and now I am here, on the other side of the street. He walks with the faith that it will give him something, give him the peace of mind that he is seeking. Always that, the still point, the place of equanimity.

By Fifty-fifth Street he is impatient for the concrete to end. Like a diver with bursting lungs struggling to the surface, he is frantic to reach the refuge of Central Park. When he enters it at its south end, marked by an equestrian statue of some South American liberator high up on a pedestal, a feeling of peace, of having entered a sanctuary, comes over him. It is something to savor, the effect of the trees and grass and footpaths. On a bench he sits for a while.

People come and go. The young. The old. It is all right. It has always been all right. Whatever *it* is.

And then he follows the arc of the path toward the West Side. For a brief while he stands, transfixed, watching a batter step to the plate on a distant ball field. Two company softball teams. Women as well as men. They will go out together afterward. Drink. Make love. Whatever they do. The men performing for these women. What is all the dawdling about? Why can't the pitcher just pitch? And then, when he does get going with his underhand delivery, why can't the batter connect? Smack the bejesus out of that ball. Send a rope down the left-field line already. After witnessing a weak groundout he is moving again. The Tavern on the Green. He was there. With someone, but he can't remember. Ordered overpriced and runny scrambled eggs. That he recalls. The years indistinguishable. No markers. No major events. How long will this go on? Not forever.

And yet the machinations at the org, the infighting, seek to intrude. Bring it back to the breath, Johan. Bring it back. God is. I am. God is. I am. In this moment I have everything I need. In this moment I am being held.

The RoR meeting has its share of one-time mountebanks, felons, arsonists, hit men, women of the night as well as those of sterling character and high achievement. Some of them his best friends, even if he doesn't know the last names of most of the or what they do with their lives besides sit in these folding chairs. He is home. He is where he has wanted to be all day. Work is what we do on our way to a meeting. Build your day around a meeting. Never place anything ahead of your recovery. SLIP = Sobriety Loses Its Purpose. You can't keep it unless you give it away. First things first. HALT (Don't get too hungry, angry, lonely, or tired). Easy Does It (meaning let Easy do it), Let Go and Let God. One Day at a Time. You can't get drunk if you don't pick up the first drink. EGO = Easing God Out. The problem is alcoholism; everything else is a situation. You don't have to be alone anymore. Progress, not perfection. Meeting-makers make it. It's alcoholism, not alcohol-*wasm*.

There is no love like the love of one drunk for another. The most flawed human being on the planet can still experience that love, someone shares. That Big Book has more uses than to prop up a microphone, someone else shares, referring to the thick hardcover book on the speaker's table. The basic text of the recovery program. "Judge it. Mock it. Try to rewrite it with the deranged contents of your puny mind. The bottom line is that the book has saved the lives of countless thousands and millions since it was first published in 1939. We are the children of the author's white light experience. The man was on fire with God when he wrote that text. Others had to rein him in, get him to write about the experience of drinking. All drunks can agree on drinking. Not the same with the God thing. And that third chapter, 'More about Alcoholism.' It describes beautifully our mental state before we take that first drink, why Jim pours milk into a glass of scotch. Why? Because we're nuts. That's why."

It is all happy talk, the talk of those out of their isolation and into a sense of oneness. Minds join; bodies separate. Bring the body and the mind will follow.

Another: "Because by this time in the evening I would have been well on my way to getting blotto, sozzled, snockered."

Maybe fifty people. Maybe more. A mixed bag. There's Conor from Hell's Kitchen ("which of youse is going out for coffee afterwards?") and Professor Phil ("I'm working on a biography of Machiavelli. Flying to Florence tomorrow to do research.").

That whole thing of going out for coffee something he hasn't quite mastered. He stands outside the meeting place afterward. Even after all these years he feels alone. Conspicuously alone. People sense it. Stay away. Find other small groups to attach themselves to. Like it was in high school. He was OK in the classroom, but when he left the school, he stepped into a void. No invitations to parties. No dates with the girls in his class. None of that. Couldn't risk the possibility of having people see how his family lived. This feels like a second chance to connect, that these are the people he avoided back then. One day he will. Connect, that is. Or maybe not.

Hard to leave. He feels all eyes on him as he turns and walks off down the long block toward Broadway. Feels that his social failure is there for everyone to witness and that he is admitting defeat. But that is just a feeling. They're like clouds scudding across the sky. Once again discovers his breath. His heart opens to the evening in New York City, to Papaya King on the corner of Seventy-second and Broadway. People eating the filet mignon of hot dogs while standing up. Pickle relish. Sauerkraut. Onions. All that poisonously good stuff. The subway kiosk, newly remodeled, in the middle of Broadway, and the second one across the street. The rat-infested coffee shop on Amsterdam Avenue; innocents sitting at booths chowing down on burgers and *egg salad sandwiches* and *London broil*. No matter. Sees the blue Fairway Market sign, where the price-aware go, and where he does too when OrganicOnly threatens to be a budget buster. Feels his happiness and his pain coexistent.

Alex was the first. His face bore a crescent scar from the knife wound a trucker inflicted in a bar brawl somewhere out West. The face of a scowling cat, full of fire. The film *Gandhi* was playing. It evidently made a great impression on him, for in a state of excitement he phoned Johan from the street and said, "I'm feeling so spiritual after seeing that movie I know I can drink." And drink he did. When he next called, his voice and manner were different. Johan heard the roar of active alcoholism coming through the line. He heard his fire and never heard from him again.

Then there was Freddy. No, he hadn't read the basic text. It was so good, he was sure, that he was afraid he might wear it out. But a book was not an ice cream cone. It wasn't perishable. Perhaps he might even consider reading it more than once so he could see things he hadn't the first time around. So Luther suggested. But Freddy went silent. A shock of recognition went through Johan, as if I were seeing some aspect of himself, that thing in him that won't or can't get started in this life. That part of him that holds back, intent on saving. All those pencils in his drawer. Those reams of paper. A selective hoarder.

And Ben, a systems analyst, who had Johan over to his apartment and, in a state of great agitation, pointed to a framed print of a Thomas Cole landscape on the living room wall. He had an impulse to move the print somewhere else in the apartment, but the prospect was causing him great anxiety, as the change would mean a break with the existing order. "Order is everything to me. Everything," Ben said, with great emotion. Johan understood only too well. A life spent in fear of breaking the mold.

And Marco, a man with a violent streak. He called twice a day for several months, until the day came when he said, "My disease doesn't want me to speak with you." Those his last words to Johan before the phone went dead. And so he can wonder where he is, too.

Many were missing. Donny the shoplifter and Drago the assassin for hire and Pooli, who used to sell himself on Forty-second Street. And Manfred, too, with his upper middle class affect, and to whom Johan said, about carrying a switchblade, that he might wish to consider that people far crazier and more desperate and with nothing to lose, in their estimation, were wandering the streets, and that unless he was willing to go all the way with that weapon, maybe he would be wise to dispose of it.

Yes, there was this dynamo on which he drew that caused his heart to open and sing. And what did any of it mean if he lacked people to share with? And so he was grateful that the men of New York City continued to call him, at all hours of the day and night. Like Mandy in the Bronx, sufficiently frightened by his financial circumstance that he contemplates a plunge from the George Washington Bridge. "How's that for an IRA?" Mandy says, seeking a laugh. Or there is Palmer, who has been toying with the idea of taking up with a woman other than his wife. And just last night Johan spoke with Desmond, who has grown frustrated that he is not yet rich and famous. Has he mentioned Harley, a rich man's son who struggles to stay off the sauce and out of the crack house, and for whom prostitutes are his only connection to love? Has he told you of the desolation alleys from which they have emerged and that seek to pull them back? Has he told you that love is connection and that they are in his life so he can tell them what *he* needs to hear?

Chapter 18

Fatigued by the mundane and in a state of hopelessness insofar as establishing physical intimacy with a woman—a man imagines the door has permanently closed on such possibility and that he must maintain himself in solitude on the streets of New York City and elsewhere, buy his groceries and feed his face and sleep with his teddy bear and live in the aloneness of one uneventful holiday after another. Such a man, if he is to survive in peace, must recognize the finite life of the flesh and experience the song of his own Self. He must be in love with the voice for God and the joy-inducing center within him. And then he must feel once again the pull of illusion, the pitiful yet prayerful reaching out that is our deepest instinct. He wasn't misrepresenting the truth to Rita O'Rourke. Now and then he does meet someone on a grocery store line or on the streets of Manhattan, or even below street level.

The intimate confines of a subway car as the train speeds and screeches its way through the network of tunnels is a prime opportunity for meaningful eye contact. On leaving work the next evening, he finds himself seated on the Number 1 (train number this and train number that when years ago there was the West Side local and the BMT and the IND) opposite a woman who lapses from the protective strategy an attractive woman generally maintains of averting her eyes even as she senses the gaze of men upon her in such an enclosed space. Seeing through to his heart's desire, she does not look away.

Every cell of his being is focused on this woman now. He has been lifted free of the dreary round into a realm of possibility that brings him intensely alive.

Before all things, pray, the voice within him says, and so he does, asking that he be composed and centered when he approaches this latest manifestation of Maya.

He sees it as a positive sign that they both get off at Eighty-sixth Street. They have the neighborhood in common. He moves slowly with the crowd as it pushes toward the exit stairway, trying not to lose sight of her and at the same time not be caught staring, should she turn and look back suddenly and perceive him as a stalker. At the corner of Broadway, in front of a cavernous Banana Republic store, he calls out to her. It's a risky business to approach a woman in New York City, where the safety factor is paramount. Will she bolt? Will she tell him to leave her alone in a voice loud enough to draw the attention of passersby? Or will she simply tell him she already has a boyfriend and his name is Rocco?

"Hi, my name is Johan? I'm from the neighborhood? I'm an editor and a writer? I know it's New York City and all that, but I was wondering if I gave you my card, we could meet for coffee or drinks?"

A Southerner he knew some years ago spoke his sentences in the form of questions, and now he is doing the same. The interrogative a kind of hook that he hopes will hold her more than a simple period. All he wants is that she not blow him off quickly, an expression the young are now using, as if you were little more than a speck of lint on their blouses.

She responds with a question of her own. "Do you always approach women in this way?" His balloon has been deftly punctured. A woman doesn't have to send him on his way. A cold tone of voice, a harsh response—these will do the trick.

"I don't go to bars. I'm not on any party circuit. I don't do online dating. What is a man to do but say hello to a woman who looks interesting?"

"I have one more question for you. Are you on drugs?"

"They are not part of my daily regimen. But why do you ask?"

"Because you seem so calm."

"There are other ways to achieve calmness," he manages to say, while fumbling in his wallet for his business card, with all its lack of professional cachet, to offer her. The card has proven to be a dicey part of any such introduction, as even in these liberated times women tend to rate men in terms of what they do, and what does it mean to be an editor for a not-for-profit org? Will she take his card and read it and say, "Is this a joke? Are you serious? I would go out with a man who works for Girls of America Now?" and then laugh in his face, as a woman once did.

"No, please. Don't hand me your card," she says, now that he has finally found one. She has eyes that invite you in and lips that are full and teeth that are white. She has the luminous quality of those blessed with beauty.

"I see," he says, deflated.

"You see what?"

"To be honest, I see that you are unavailable."

Another train has pulled into the station below. Another crowd is surging up the stairs from the platform. Maybe he could blend into their midst and disappear.

"Your card won't do it for me. I'll never call you. If you ever want to see me again, it will be for you to pick up the phone."

And so he jots down her number, as the evening rush hour crowd moves past. The directness of her words communicate her serious nature. He is a lucky man, he senses, as he returns his small notebook to his inside jacket pocket. Several times he pats it on his way home, checking that it has not disappeared.

A man needs a break from death and family and the machinations of a boss. That weekend, over a light lunch, he sits with her at the same outdoor café where he had sat with Luke and his kids a couple of years back. His fastidiousness sensors are active again. Are the chef and the wait staff all addicts rendered unhygienic by excesses of the night before? Are river rats having first dibs on the food? Is the grill properly scrubbed at night or is it coated with months-old grease? He skips over the bacteria-laden meats on the menu and settles, as he did previously, on the safety of a veggie burger, though even this he cannot be sure of, for who can truly know what the malefactors have done to the tofu and wheat germ and rolled oats, and whether or not those same river rats have been bathing in the tahini and the tamari? And so he makes a special and urgent request that ketchup be brought with the meal to drown out even the hint of an unwelcome taste.

Camila shows no such qualms. With boldness as her guide, she asks for a burger with fully burnt flesh showing on an open bun— never mind the protective cover of bread or lettuce or tomato or onion or other alimentary doodads. Begone with such distractions from the true carnivore's delight. And when it comes, she also forgoes the ketchup for the full flavor of the meat. He will only say of her choice that it is noted.

Johan averts his eyes from the workings of Camila's mouth (mercifully unable to see his own) and only when her devouring deed is done (the horror, the horror) can he engage her in full conversation, noting with some relief that she has chosen a glass of iced tea to begin washing away some of the impurity that she has ingested. Nothing is as cleansing as the action of a liquid, be it hot or cold, on the foulness of corrupted food. A liquid, if applied in sufficient quantities and followed up with thorough dental hygiene, will do much to restore us to the desired state.

His initial impression is correct. Pretty enough that he should be drawn to her on the subway, though with the sun angling in from the west, lines that he couldn't glimpse in a duller light are appearing on her face.

That she is a clinical psychologist who administers IQ tests to high school students makes her formidable in his mind. Her interview is polite but skillful. What kind of work does he do? Are his parents alive? Where did he grow up? What schools has he attended? However, he tells himself there is no need to feel daunted. She wants to believe. She wants the facts to align with her feeling for him. No woman can possibly want you if you want her too much, and after the eating episode he has witnessed he doesn't want her so very much. This lack of desire—or call it reservation—she has to sense. It only propels her forward. And what of his interests? Does he go away weekends?

He tells her of the *New Yorker* cartoon pinned to his bulletin board at home. An unkempt old man sits in a barely furnished room. The caption reads, "During the week I'm downstairs. On weekends I'm upstairs." The cartoon, as he presents it, draws a reluctant laugh. It is a moment of liberating honesty. He will not be playing the image game. He will not be its sad captive. No, she will not be spending weekends in the Hamptons with him, and no, they will not be dressing in nautical whites and navigating coastal waterways on his fifty-foot yacht currently moored at the marina down below. More likely they will be riding the hot and foul-aired subway, where they had met, to movies and restaurants that fit his "cheap but good" motto.

That afternoon, emerging from the lower level of Riverside Park, they come to the Soldiers' and Sailors' Monument. Several kids are skateboarding aggressively around the sullied limestone cylinder, trying to negotiate the steps with their boards. Angry, cerebral kids at play not in nature but on asphalt and concrete. He hates the loud, spanking sound of those boards. What is that to try to land with a strip of board on a step? He fears broken ankles and fractured skulls. Are the kids trying to make everyone bear witness to their inevitable pain?

Camila keeps to her agenda. Because they have left the café does not mean that she has finished with her interview. "So where were you during the war?" she asks.

They have taken a seat on a bench not far from two cannons positioned to fire out toward the river.

"Which war would that be?" he says.

With the memorial in full view she says, "The Vietnam War. Were you in the military?"

Stricken by her question, he follows the path of a southbound bus as it moves slowly along the flat stretch of road. He has been plunged into a lake of shame. The attempt to classify him. The underlying question is whether he is a real man prepared to take a bullet. Somehow he finds his way back to shore by drawing on the power of honesty, or partial honesty. No, the military did not want him, he tells her. His lottery number had come up in the early seventies, and he found himself down at the Whitehall Street induction center in lower Manhattan, where he was disqualified on physical grounds, having failed the height/weight ratio. Too many drugs and too little food had left him with too few pounds spread out on his tall frame.

The physical inadequacy is easier to admit to than being both amused and chagrined by the intelligence test, which in his vague memory consisted of line drawings of mechanical images. Can he tell a clinical psychologist who doubtless prides herself on her intelligence that he may have failed this test as well, or risk being seen as cowardly if he also discloses that he came to the military induction center armed with a note saying he was psychologically unfit for military service from the psychoanalyst he was then seeing?

The skateboarders are still at it, skinny kids in baggy pants and oversized T-shirts down to their thighs and baseball caps worn backward. They are only a few years younger than he had been when a photographer asked Sarah and him in the spring of 1968 if they would pose with the memorial in the background. Sarah had long, curly blond hair and he had a white man's Afro, and so you could assume the photographers had sought to juxtapose antiwar youth against a memorial dedicated to those who had served and died in service to their country. This story he could tell Camila, as he could tell her that Sarah's family lived in the tall apartment building that gracefully followed the curve of the drive and that her father had been a scholar of American history and her mother a Radcliffe graduate. He could tell her about the burning obsession he had for Sarah and the fear he lived in that she would leave him. He could tell her how the family took him in and how, in a sense, he spurned his own family. He could tell her so many things, but it isn't for her to know, not then, if ever.

But what is really not for her to know is that the photo appeared in the *New York Times*. More accurately, the photo with Sarah in it appeared. Having told Camila that he wasn't good war material, it doesn't seem necessary to tell her that he had been cropped out of a photograph because he isn't photogenic either.

It is a road he has been down too many times, the Sarah road, the life that is gone now road, the road for which he has only to press a button to activate the prerecorded message. And what can it bring him? What?

But while he withholds some things, there is the need to reveal others, and thus keep himself at the center of his own life. What is a confessional nature but a need to share one's life, to pour forth a torrent of experience into the ear of another?

And so, on their second date, he meets Camila at a West Side café. No high-priced entrees. Just salads and soups and quiche and desserts. And a little off the beaten track on the self-congratulatory West Side. Small marble-top tables and pretty young waiters wearing white blouses and short black skirts and black tights. A step up from the riverside café where they met the other week. His concern about fastidiousness in abeyance.

Another concern diminished too, at least for the time being. His fear that he is being disloyal to Isabel by seeing Camila or by seeing any woman. An old fear that fills him with dread and takes him back, way way back, into the terrain of Mommy Land, and which, even adult in years, he cannot fully escape. A fear that says, no, I must be good, I must be loyal, I must do nothing to hurt Isabel. A concern that doesn't let him see that *Isabel asked him to leave. Isabel filed for divorce.* A fear that takes him, yes, back to childhood, that overwhelming impulse while headed to grade school to rush home and be with Mommy because she needed him, she always needed him, and she was at home right that very minute crying, so sad that she could die. Not seeing, as a child, that she sent him away, sent him off to school as in summers she would send him off to those Bible camps in the Catskills.

Do you want to talk about those camps, Johan? Do you want to do that? Do you want to say what they were like, the cars idling outside the tabernacle on west Thirty-third Street and the men who drove those cars with the windows rolled down and their left elbows resting on the door frame, the way that real men drove their cars? Do you want to resurrect that past, go back to that time you stood on the front porch of the dilapidated cabin feeling that monstrous anxiety, that desperation to get back to Mommy, who needed you more than words could possibly express? Do you want to tell about the calculations in your child's mind, how you thought six more years to high school graduation and then four more of college and then law school so you could save Mommy from all the evil being inflicted on her by the building owner before the terror wiped the construct away, simply vanished it into nothingness, and you saw that you wouldn't make it, you couldn't make it, that time would run out before you could come to Mommy's rescue? Saw in that moment that time could never work for you, could only be a source of torment, because there would never be enough of it. Never.

Tell her everything, Johan. Everything. Tell her about Pastor Chernenko and his altar call on those cool mountain nights in the tabernacle, children leaving the pews to kneel on the dirt floor. Tell her how fat and sweaty he was, and about the orange rug he wore on his head, and the time he nearly twisted your ear off for throwing rocks. Tell her about the fiery pit and the gnashing of teeth. Tell her how the time came when the children no longer flocked to the altar to fall on their knees and cry out to Jesus their sinfulness, but how instead they ran out of the tabernacle and down the hill into the waiting meadow and fell on each other, boys on girls, the fire for each other now more than the fire for God, and how the counselors beat the bushes for them, shouting dire warnings of the perdition to come.

No. Despite his confessional nature, he doesn't tell her everything.

Camila goes for the ham omelette. He orders a spinach quiche and a cup of mushroom barley soup, his very favorite. A combo special. It says so right there on the laminated menu. It's all right. He can deal with the cholesterol. He'll hit the hummus hard for the next two weeks. The pale walls like scabby skin, dark and embossed in places, and what are those nets hanging from the ceiling? Is this by design or a sign of neglect?

"There's something I should tell you," he begins. Should? There is no should, only choice. The waiter having taken their order, Camila won't bolt and run. Even if the waiter hadn't, she wouldn't, he somehow knows. He's made it to the second round, passed that battery of questions. He doesn't quite know why he needs to tell her what it's on his mind to say. Maybe because his life without mentioning it isn't much? He can't imagine she would be very interested in the writing he does. What is that to be in your mid-fifties with only a handful of published stories? Maybe it's to push her away?

"What would that be?"

"Nothing too dark. It's not like I'm an ax murderer or a deadbeat dad or practice poor dental hygiene. It's simply this. In my twenties I became increasingly reliant on alcohol. I couldn't stop. I had to seek help. And I did. And so I've been sober for a number of years."

She does not throw up her hands and say, "Whoa, whoa. Please do not wave your stump in front of me so early on." Nor does she analyze him as to why he should be telling her something so personal. "Congratulations. Do you still go to meetings?" she says, signaling that she understands.

He feels a swell of pride. The ego has been involved here, he now sees. She has picked up on his need for approval. "Yes," he says.

In response she surprises him with an intimacy of her own. Several years before she had been diagnosed with breast cancer. A malignant tumor was removed.

"I'm sorry," he says. His sister Hannah had breast cancer many years ago. A shiver runs through him as Camila presents this chapter of her medical history. Horror aside, the self-centered thought occurs that she has made herself available to him because her illness had limited her options.

"I'm all right now. My doctor has given me a clean bill of health," she adds, thinking along with him.

That evening, he sits at the opposite end of the sofa from her in the sunken living room of her apartment—spacious, a bit messy—in a wonderful Art Deco building just off Columbus Avenue. A large magnet on the side of her stereo catches his eye. "Stop Whinging!" it says. Illness has made her a stoic.

It is like talking across a great divide. That is fine with him. She not only looks older but also heavier. It's those white, loose-fitting slacks and the white blouse. They don't become her. How did he get here? The answer is simple. She invited him. It must have been those secrets they shared. Somehow they sped up the process. First emotional intimacy, then the other. But he doesn't want the other. Not now. Not ever. Not with her. Can he just run out the door?

Camila pats the sectional next to her and says, "Come closer." Though he accepts her invitation, elation is entirely missing. Grotesque thoughts fuel his terror. *Suppose she picks her nose? Suppose she does worse?*

But he does as she asks.

"This is a nice apartment. The sunken living room. The steps and the wrought iron handrails. It makes my heart ache. Really. It does. Takes me back to sixth grade and Lonnie Reisman. A friend of mine, sort of. We bonded on the basis of sports. Before that we had no connection. He had me over to his apartment for a seder. Candles on the table. Never been to anything like that before or since. Somewhere on the Grand Concourse. It was called the Champs Elysee of New York City back then. Wide boulevards. I would like to see the Bronx be viable again. I read somewhere that it has 'good bones,' a developed transportation grid. I root for things that are down to come back, like Bobby Bonds and Bill Walton. They were athletes with great careers who suffered injuries. I can't tell you how much of my energy and devotion I gave to them even when the press wrote them off. I guess it's kind of sad. Says something about me that I probably need to look at." He worries that she sees his babble is meant to fend her off. Whatever, she is OK with the silence that follows his word burst. There is a time for talk and a time for no talk. There is the silence fraught with meaning, the silence to which words deliver us, the silence that speaks more eloquently and profoundly than words ever could. There is the silence that says I am a human being and I have need of you and you have need of me and we are going to try this thing together now, we are going to step into the void and explore the mystery and see what happens. This is the silence of life and creation and union that we all are waiting for. She is a psychologist, after all. But that is not the case with this silence.

"I should go," he says.

"Why?"

"I can't explain."

She moves toward the door and holds it open. En route he makes a decision to kiss her. It is something he can and must do, now that he is on the way out. On the street he spits several times between parked cars and anxiously rushes home to wash out his mouth.

He doesn't know. He doesn't know.

Camila has a friend who is performing in a play. Would Johan like to go with her that Saturday? He would love to, he says. And why not? It is for him to go forward, having initiated contact with this woman. And a play. A play. The woman is inviting him into her life. He is being received. He can do it. He really can. So what if he spit, shocking even himself? He can overcome that. Besides, doesn't he want to do something more than stand at the salad bar at OrganicOnly on a Saturday night, vying with contentious Sam for the leftovers?

But as Saturday approaches, resistance builds. On the eve of the third, and what he senses to be the advanced intimacy date, he picks up the phone to cancel, and is grateful to get her answering machine. Something unforeseen has come up, he says. He cannot tell her that it is his phobia, which requires him to run toward women only to run from them and from the body and all its repellent potential for decay and disintegration. The horror of the human condition cannot be covered over by lipstick and mascara or fishnet stockings and garter belts or slinky summer dresses. The horror of the body is yellowed teeth and sagging flesh. It is cellulite and the visibility of veins and watery eyes. It is everything the Buddha saw in the palace that night—drooling courtesans writhing in their sleep, their faces contorted—that drove him to his sitting posture under the Bodhi tree. Slowly, inevitably, irreversibly, the awareness of our creaturely nature has been growing in him.

And though no one can think well of him for saying this— after all, we are talking about a woman who had a major medical procedure—if he is to be honest, it is not an unhappy thought to be the one rejecting and not rejected, to say no when the other has said yes, to end, if at least temporarily, the losing streak that has seen women send him away when he wanted, or said he wanted, for them to say yes, come on in.

Sometimes I wonder who it is I am addressing. Is it you, Mother. Is it you, Father? Or is it some vaster audience, some anonymous gathering of the elite to whom I am appealing and to whom I have been appealing my entire life? And what exactly do I want from you? Am I seeking your acceptance? Have I made a blood offering of my family so you will see I am not one of them and you will have me? Am I seeking from you a refuge from my low birth and my low numbers? Have I been ruthless in sacrificing those whom I should love for you whom I don't even know? What accounts for my mockery? What accounts for my jaundice? Why can I not be one with those whom I report on? Why can I not stop reporting on them in the first place? What do they owe me? Is this some kind of salvage operation? What would happen to me if I fell silent, if, just as I don't take the first drink, I didn't write the first word?

—Journal entry of Johan Manootdjian

Chapter 19

It is 1982. Another century. Another lifetime. Imagine, if you will, a drafty loft on the Bowery in New York City, just a few steps from Houston Street, where in the numbing cold of winter homeless drunks lie frozen on the metal grates they sleep on while others huddle around oil drum fires fed by garbage and scraps of wood and extort drivers stopped at the intersection by threatening to smear their windshields with filthy rags. Imagine now a woman holding in her right hand a carving knife in the kitchen area of the loft. And then observe, in a corner, where he is boxed in near the water heater, a tall young man afraid to move lest the woman intercept and impale him on the stainless steel blade. It is a domestic scene that ends on mortuary slabs at the city morgue every day. Further, it is a scene that has been brought on by the violence of the man's mouth. It is not nice to call the woman to whom you are married a bum. It is not wise. And where has kindness and decency fled that such a word gets used in the first place? This, after all, is Sarah, mythical Sarah, whom the man had obsessed over, making his true major in college not literature but her, and kept close through endless phone calls and sudden visits to Boston, where she had been living the life of an art student. Only Sarah is thirty-two now, not eighteen, and the years have not been kind to her. She has gained weight. She has grown pear-shaped, her finely chiseled face is now puffy, and her once glorious blond hair is straw-like and thinning to the point where scalp shines through. The medications for her schizophrenia have also taken a toll, dulling her affect. The prospect of the brilliant career predicted for her when she was on fire with her own feminism and ambition has also faded. Even so, in this moment she has come alive; rage dominates her livid face and her voice is clear and strong. "Where do you want it, Mr. Skinny Dick? Up your skinny ass? In your gut?"

Broken glasses and plates litter the floor. She has virtually emptied the dish rack at him before escalating to the knife. For years now she has been absorbing his tirades and living in terror of them. He says things that no man should say, and he says them more than once. A man who causes a woman to cover her ears as he speaks is not a good man.

In later years he will tell people a story. He will present as one of the small wonders of his life the time a month before this incident with the knife when he was walking home from work and experienced an epiphany on Twenty-third Street, at the south end of Madison Square Park, not far from the Flatiron Building in downtown Manhattan. The word *epiphany* itself he will stay away from when he speaks. He will use the word *awareness* or *sudden awareness* in its place, as *epiphany* may be received as pompous or at least inflated to any careful listener. But nonetheless, the word will be the descriptor he attaches in his mind to the experience, for in that moment he realizes that his marriage with Sarah Van Dine is over. In a state of quiet wonder he sees that he has been *released* from the marriage.

The progress of his life has meaning for him. He must note the markers and make others aware of them as well. He must.

Sarah Van Dine has a fate, just as he, Johan Manootdjian, has a fate, and he must let go of her if he is to live, regardless of her emotional fragility. It does not matter that she has become wildly ruminative, as when the counterman at the Second Avenue deli charges $3.50 for the half pound of ham she has purchased and she returns to the loft weeping that the counterman should be so cruel as to place a value of $3.50 on her and not the cold cuts. He learns that he must not go down the road of sorrow and ache and endless restitution, that he cannot save Sarah Van Dine, who is now a virtual shut-in in the ramshackle loft where they have been living. He cannot live with a woman who cannot be out in the world, a woman who cannot grow. He cannot be a nurse. He does not have the character, the will, the stamina, for such a life. Nor can he be the sole provider. It is shameful, shameful, that he lacks the staying power, but so it is.

Though really, it is Sarah Van Dine who leaves, moving in with a man down in Brooklyn who wears a ponytail and the same jeans for a month at a time. His name is Bart and he curated a show in which she participated, thus laying a basis for connection. Johan is not shattered that she would leave him for another. He is, more than anything, relieved somewhat of his guilt that she has someone to be with and now he can go to the one he has come to truly love, the one who has been a beacon of light in his consciousness though they have been apart for some years.

In this period when Sarah has gone off with Bart from Brooklyn and Johan still remains in the loft, he begins to see Isabel. Initially he approaches women at work and is somewhat amazed when they rebuff him. He cannot understand. Were they not his for the asking? And then it is women beyond the work world who say no. He reaches but there is an invisible yet firm divider that he butts up against between him and these women who show no interest. Fear, anger, bewilderment take hold. Old feelings begin to surface, feelings that go back to childhood. Names like Billy Bruce and Johnny Joe come to him, boys who have the imperiousness that comes with last names that could serve as first names. And girls like Jill Johnson and Laura Langley, they too come to mind. Pretty names, American names, names that stay within the realm of their American prettiness. Women who thrive on excluding more than including. He, Johan, knows it is madness to go down this paranoid road. He knows it is an indulgence of his self-pity to believe that he is being shunned by women in his current life as he was shunned by grade school classmates from the parties organized for them by their parents. But a part of him rejoices at being an outcast and lives in those memories of girls and boys talking among themselves in school about birthday parties and other activities he had no knowledge of. He knows the awareness of social failure started early for him.

Isabel,
I had read a book when I was a child. Started to. Said, I can read. I can read. Seated in a wicker chair in the living room. An organ grinder and his little monkey. And a wall of red brick, with the branches of a tree overhanging it.

My heart was singing. Mott Street. Mulberry. The fabled red brick wall around the church in Little Italy. Like the wall I had read about in that children's book. Do you know what you did to me? Do you know how taken over I had become? Do you know what the consolidation forces were in me that dictated I not go forward without going back? There was something I needed for you to see, my newfound goodness. I wanted to build on it. You had light around you, and the ability to strike boldly if gently out into the world and smile engagingly at what it had to offer. No one would ever leave you permanently lonely, as I was doing to Sarah—moving on, after all, was your abiding strength.

SoHo is brightly colored cast-iron facades of buildings on the cobblestone streets, buildings kinetic with artistic enterprise. Painters and sculptors occupy these vast lofts that once housed garment factories. Johan has some clear memory of having visited this area, perhaps this very block, back in childhood, of his aunt dispatching him in a cab on a bright summer day from the Upper West Side to pick up an order of bathroom tiles. He remembers the small but surprisingly heavy boxes and the workers grunting as they emerged from under a metal awning and loaded them into the back of the cab.

As he rings the downstairs buzzer of one such sky-blue building, he feels his earlier confidence slipping away. This is no ordinary person he is calling on but someone who can negotiate for herself in the world. This is also a woman who can have babies.

Five flights of wooden stairs, all with metal guards to protect against wear. Long, steep flights that cause even a young person to pause before going on. Each of the lofts Johan passes has its own story. Juwan, a drummer and the owner of the building, lives in the first loft with his wife Jodi and their two girls, Bareek and Ashilane. African names for his girls, or names that have the sound of Africa, for he is Black and his wife Betty is white but the stamp of authentic Blackness must be upon the girls, or something must be upon them that will make them his and not white America's that he is and he isn't a part of. Juwan, who will have words with him one night, when Johan protests against the racket from the restaurant below. Juwan, who will use bluntness in getting to the heart of the matter and put him in his place. The loft is not his, Johan's. The loft belongs to Isabel. Juwan speaking to Johan as if he is an interloper. More gently will Dr. Tobin, some years later, suggest that Johan has a way of going where he doesn't quite belong.

But that is in the future—the future that has not yet happened. He is there and he is meeting with Isabel in a loft that is vast and blindingly white. White walls, white floorboards, white ceilings, even a white dining table throughout the incredible expanse of space. It is early afternoon. Mia is still at school. A vestibule and then a kitchen area and then a living room and there is a bed, exposed, and beyond the bed there is, in the farthest part of the loft, looking out on the street, Isabel's studio with her paints, her brushes, her turpentine, her frames. She has gone away from painting, at least for now. Ever since her one-person show she has not been able to return to canvas. She has begun to work in wood—reliefs and carved figures. There is also a figure in clay she is modeling. The little wood figures are startling. Men, women, children, animals painted in bright greens and reds and yellows. *I have seen these figures before. They are buried in my mother's Swedish past.*

Johan feels uneasy. This woman is too much. Too strong, too powerful, too intelligent, too successful. What can he offer someone such as herself? He feels the demon of competitiveness stirring in him. It threatens to freeze his face and make her a rival. He is done for if she sees his real nature. In that moment he feels he has nothing, nothing. He doesn't have her education (how does the City College of New York stand up against the Ivy League colleges that begged for her). And what recognition has ever come to him, with his myriad of rejection slips versus her numerous one-person and group shows? In that moment he sees the gap between fantasy and reality. She doesn't need him. He has no place in her life. She too will turn out to be part of that wall of rejection he has been experiencing since Sarah left. She has moved on. She was moving on even when they were seeing each other in that last disastrous year of his drinking. Did she not take up with another man just so she could get him to stay away. Johan a man alone with no real prospects. A low-paying publishing job that is not even a real job. A rundown loft that he can't quite afford on his own salary. He feels the nip of that depression that came over him in the supermarket the week before, standing in line with his modest provisions for the night—his peanut butter and pasta and jar of tomato sauce. A depression that laid him low for days. Like being at the bottom of a deep well. Life going on somewhere far above and no ability to resurface and join it. And why bother anyway? Everything truly was over. No one cared. No one had ever cared. He had been like some big, sloppy dog leaping all over everyone. And if he hadn't, no one would have gone near him. It was that simple. The phone simply too heavy to pick up. The phone going days without ringing.

And then his mother, of all people, calling, and bringing him out of it. Life was about connection. He saw it, in that instant. People were as necessary as food and water. He could actually feel himself expanding as if he were a deflated balloon and air was now being pumped into it.

He could leave. He could walk out the door. That would work. No, it would never work. It would destroy him. Those few other women have been simply a distraction from this, the main event of his life.

"How is your back? Has it gotten better?" she says on this day that he has waited for, an endless stretch of time spent extricating himself from Sarah so he could be here. She is smoking a cigarette in that stylish way, her thin arm raised and the Camel held between her index and middle finger. She is not afraid of the bite of tobacco. If there is an incongruity, a delicate woman smoking an unfiltered cigarette, she embraces it.

The accident had occurred two years before. The West Village. The screech of brakes. Johan thrown from his bike to the pavement, where he landed on his hands and knees, gravel driven into his palms. Unable to move from that position. The driver still at the wheel, staring straight ahead impassively, as if nothing going on had anything to do with him, or maybe there was a look of grievance or at least annoyance on his face that he had to be inconvenienced in this way. What right did this white boy have to be there in front of him with his damn bicycle? When would white boys learn to get the hell out of the goddamn way and stop trying to hold the Black man back, the way they had been doing for centuries now to the point that they didn't even see what they were doing, they just went and did it? And there was Sarah screaming at the driver, "You ran him down on purpose. I saw it." And the pain. Finally, the ambulance, somehow getting him onto a stretcher, Sarah riding in the back with him, crying, and Johan feeling a strange peace, as if his life had been taken out of his hands and there was nothing to do anymore but be taken care of, if it came to that. A feeling of guilt. If he hadn't exactly willed the accident, he was secretly glad because now the pressure of work would be off and the pressure at home as well. Injury had a way of simplifying your life, reducing it to one essential, survival.

The emergency room a scene of failed suicides, men and women knifed and shot, hit and run victims. His crumpled bike has been chained to the fence outside the hospital. He is wheeled into the X-ray room on a gurney. Johan is on his back with his knees up. The technician wants him to slide forward but Johan says he can't move. The technician just stands there, impassive. Like the driver of the car, he is Black. He wears the same expression as the man behind the wheel, only maybe it is worse. Johan feels a silent hatred coming from the man. *Motherfucking Whitey is down. Now he be the one begging, moaning. Go fucking die, Whitey. Die and die and die.* Finally the technician breaks his silence.

"I don't have all day. Get yourself on that X-ray table."

"But I can't."

The technician lowering his glaring face toward Johan's. "Then I guess you can't have an X-ray, can you?" he hisses.

Johan doesn't say the obvious, that the man is supposed to be there to help him. There is no point to that. The gurney is level with the table, but even so he is afraid of falling off and injuring himself further. The pain is severe as he moves, as if he has been bludgeoned in his lower back and something is broken.

Within a half hour he is back in the emergency room and being told by a doctor to get up and go home. The X-ray shows nothing. Johan protests but, with the help of Sarah, makes it to a cab.

He is sober by now. Really sober. Six months without a drink or any mood-changing chemical. He has left the hospital with a prescription. He doesn't want to give in. And yet his back feels like it is on fire. After a couple of hours he tells Sarah to please take a cab to the all-night pharmacy and fill the prescription. And yes, the medication works. It really does. The pill performs its magic.

In the morning a call comes from the hospital. Johan is not to move. An ambulance will be coming for him shortly. There is no further explanation. And so the ambulance attendants arrive and lower him from the loft bed on a stretcher and whisk him back to the hospital. He doesn't mind. He is now on vacation from his life. The X-ray had been misread. Fractures have been found on his spine. He will be admitted after all. Good.

None of it matters in the least, except to Johan. His personal history is all he has. Every scrap, every incident, every nuance of thought is important, because if he doesn't pay attention to himself, then who would, and without attention paid a person disappears, a person dies, a person stays at the bottom of that hole into which his depression has plunged him. A person has to have hope. A person has to have light. And the past, strange to say, is his hope. If he can only hold onto it so he can mine what is there, if he can only place it in the order it needs to be in, if he can only create a mold into which to pour his life, then he would have it for eternity.

What he sees is that he has willed the accident to happen. The callous driver of the car, the hostile lab technician, the incompetent—or worse—emergency room doctor, they are simply creatures he has compelled into existence. When you bicycle with abandon through the streets of Manhattan, when the ego takes over and you convince yourself that you are a match for the buses and trucks tearing up Madison Avenue by virtue of your agility, trouble inevitably awaits.

There had been a transit strike, and so, of necessity, he had begun riding his bike to work. Images that make him shudder come of being sandwiched between giant buses and trucks tearing past on Madison Avenue. He remembers the insane cockiness that motion engendered in him that he could dance among these behemoths. One pothole, one deflection to the right or the left, and he could have been crushed. *And would that have been such a bad thing? Would it?*

And yet none of it does matter. It is all the stuff of a sad life. What is it to be a man in his early thirties working as an editor in the children's books department of a publishing company and to have as a boss a controlling Brit with a harsh tongue? What is it to be editing books in a genre he has no feel for and for a boss who throws him scraps? What is it to stare into store windows at typewriters, thinking if only he had a Smith-Corona electric typewriter or an IBM Selectric III typewriter, or an older model typewriter, or a typewriter of a different color, or several typewriters, or a typewriter with pica type or maybe it should be elite type? His life is one fixation after another on the things that do not matter because he cannot give shape to his pain in any sort of way that will matter. He cannot express the longings of his heart. He has the aspiration to do so but not the gift. His whole life is about learning to live with the things he does have because he can never have the things he wants to have. It is for Isabel to have the things she wants, to place herself squarely behind her art and say, This is who I am, this is what I do, and for her art to be seen. It is for Sarah, poor afflicted Sarah, to do the same. But he, Johan Manootdjian, cannot do this because he is ashamed. He is not good enough. He will never be good enough. He will have to live his life in the key of envy and ceaseless longing. He will have to live his life in hapless service to the women he hides behind.

He has compression fractures in his lumbar spine and severe muscle trauma. And yet, no surgery is indicated. Rather, the specialist, Dr. Amortequeza, is recommending bed rest over the next several weeks. And so he lies there, day after day, and groans when the nurses come and push him to shift position so he won't develop bed sores. Young women in white, tough and dominating. Catholic in their dispositions, their sensuality tainted and made hysterical by the strictures of their religion. Pissed off women who can only give way to libidinal promptings with a few shots in them.

The windows are open for the hot summer air and the rain that splatters the sills during violent thunderstorms. Won't someone introduce an element of darkness and be rid of this unpleasant light? Such thoughts as these arise in his listlessness. And along with that the sweet drug-induced lethargy, the secret joy of being off the hook for the time being with Sarah and with work.

The art director, a Belgian woman named Beth Shockley, comes to visit. She is blond and effusive. She has the face and the dimpled chin of a female Kirk Douglas. She will fly around the planet alone while expressing a desire for a mate. She has left Brussels. She has left her boyfriend of some years whose school papers she used to dutifully type and her place of birth for ambition and expansion and a city where she can be left alone. Because truthfully, she is too strong for men and doesn't need them. Her relationship is with the universe. There are some like that. So yes, he remembers Beth Shockley for the sisterly way she was with him and knows now that she recognized something in him as he did in her, whatever that might be.

Though what Johan remembers most about the hospital stay is calling Isabel from his hospital bed, her phone number committed to memory though it is two years since they have spoken. He experiences a mix of fear and relief hearing the operator's voice in a recorded message: *This number is no longer in service.* The good thing is that Isabel has moved away and is out of his life, though of course that is the bad thing as well. But then the operator is offering him a new number with the same area code. The door has not closed. And so he calls her. He will offer his injury. That is a reason to be in touch. It will somehow leap him over the hurdle of his hurt that she drove him away by taking up with someone else. The new phone listing must mean that she is gone by now from that West Village building with the paint peeling and curling on the façade where he would visit her in those last *Blue Velvet* days and nights of his drinking.

It is four years before the accident and Johan Manootdjian, at age twenty-eight, is a hackie doing ten-hour shifts behind the wheel of a big, boxy Checker cab. Every bump in the road registers in his spine. He drives mainly through the streets of Manhattan, though there are the occasional forays into the outback of Queens and

Brooklyn. He is at the height of his narcissism, with his long, curly hair and tall, slender body, and the penetrating stare he applies to every pretty woman on the street. "Bedroom eyes," Sarah's mother says he has, though she applies the term derisively. He is good about not drinking while he is driving, unless it is dark and the passenger is an attractive woman who is willing to see past his hackie status and head with him to a bar. The result of such an engagement can be problematic. One drink inevitably leads to another for Johan, and whether frantic lovemaking ensues in some dark, secluded part of the city or not, he will ultimately stagger about fully drunk and be a while in finding his cab. There will follow the spectacle, as he turns off Sixth Avenue, of the night manager halfway down the long side street anxiously awaiting the return of the drunks from their shifts. The manager gestures wildly when he spots Johan finally turning the corner. An urban cowboy, driving the strays back toward the herd.

On one such day that summer, he is turned away at the depot, as no cab is available for him in the afternoon shapeup. And so, disappointed, he totes his hackie paraphernalia—cigar box, hack license, portable radio— back down to Greenwich Village in his backpack, where on the corner of Sixth Avenue near the Jefferson Market on a Saturday afternoon he runs into an acquaintance, Augusta, who writes poetry to rock and roll music and lives off a small trust fund that should be more and would be more if not for the machinations of her wicked stepmother, she tells him and everyone. She badgers Johan to come over and meet her beautiful friends in their gorgeous townhouse.

"Come on. Just come on," Augusta says. They met at a writing class at the New School some years before and would head to the Cedar Tavern on University Place and drink afterward. Though he is quite uncomfortable, Johan walks west with her. He hears from her mouth words like "marvelous," "brilliant," "extraordinary." And yes, the word "exquisite" is in there, too, in describing these artists and their work. And the words "gallery shows" and "successful" are spoken as well. This is nuts. I am a goddamn taxi driver, he tells himself, and this crazy woman wants me to meet the beautiful people just so I can serve as a cover for her aloneness?

He could run away, of course, just bolt down Greenwich Avenue and avoid the disaster that is looming, but her hyperbolic description of the couple provokes curiosity as well as fear, and anyway, he seemingly has no power to resist.

Indeed a townhouse in the West Village. Indeed beauty sufficient that, seeing Isabel, he sees nothing else. She possesses him. She intoxicates him in every cell of his being. She is everything he is not. She is beauty, yes. She is intelligent beauty. Yes. She is big dark eyes that sparkle. Eyes of someone he has known. Yes. Eyes of his perished sister Naomi. Those full lips and big eyes, so dark and full of laughter and life, a life that speaks of sexuality and art and the wild edges on which she can walk.

She listens. She seems to receive him. And she serves him drinks. Gin and tonics. Perfect for a summer afternoon. What does he do? She asks. He tells her the truth. He drives a cab. He would like to be something else, but he is afraid of the mainstream work world. How do people situate themselves in offices? You need elaborate credentials and he doesn't have them. He doesn't say to her that at the same time he feels too good for such a life.

"What's wrong with driving a cab? It sounds wonderful."

Has he said there was something wrong with driving a cab? Evidently, Isabel thinks so.

Philip, her husband, insists that Augusta and Johan join them for dinner. He won't hear otherwise. He is short and compact, with red hair and a florid face. Augusta says no, she has to run.

"Then your friend will join us. He has no choice."

Philip is right. Johan has no real choice, not because of Philip's autocratic will, but because of Isabel. He has been given a reprieve from leaving her.

On the way Philip takes a sidestep into the bizarre, borrowing an eggplant from a sidewalk vegetable stand and placing it against his fly. A crazy, impulsive, startling gesture that he directs toward

Johan. No words. Just the image and his eyes on Johan for his shocked reaction. The hugeness of it. A graphic statement of the supremacy of Philip's sexual endowment? An act of bold aggression against Johan's fragile psyche? Who is this prankster married to beautiful Isabel?

And then on to Pierre's, a restaurant down on Prince Street in SoHo with a pricey menu and a wine list. The waiter recites specials with names of dishes Johan has never heard of and that his mind can't retain: steak au poivre, duck confit, Hudson Valley magret. Soft music and soft lights. A linen tablecloth and linen napkins. Seated by the window, Johan stares out at the harsh streets. Isabel has granted him a reprieve from them as well. Already there is before Isabel and after Isabel.

"I want to die," Isabel says, out of nowhere. Not to him but to Philip does she express this wish. The statement is startling, disturbing, but at the same time reassuring. There is some suffering in this world of wealth and success.

"If you do, I'll have to kill myself as well," Philip replies. Can the phoniness level of such a reply begin to be measured? Johan wonders, in amazement.

No elaboration follows. She has made her statement and Philip has made his and that is that. Maybe Philip isn't being phony. Maybe he is simply being fey in asserting her death would inevitably be followed by his. Hearing the exchange, Johan has the sense that Isabel and Philip have had a similar kind of exchange before and that it serves some purpose in their lives. And he would never ascribe a particle of phoniness to her words, which he has received as genuine. Even as she sits at the table, he can sense there is some pull on her from the other realm.

Philip may be done with talk of death but he is not done with Johan. Again he shows his ability to surprise, only now it is with words, not images. "I think our friend here has pimples on his ass," he says to Isabel. He carefully assesses Johan's face for the damage he has done. Yes, he has broken through with the surprise attack, just as he had with the eggplant. Johan's sense of insult is buried beneath the shame he feels that Philip may have exposed a truth about him. Because if what Philip has said is true, then the attack is somehow deserved. Johan is rendered speechless. He can only offer a pathetic and pained laugh to go with a weak smile. Secure in his triumph, Philip leaves the table and takes a seat at the bar with the owner.

Johan tells her of his attempts to write.

"So what do you write?" Isabel asks.

"Just stuff," he says. But he is still back there with Philip's remark. "Does he always say things like that?"

"Always," she laughs, and so he has to laugh too, while wondering if Philip is not in some way Isabel's weapon.

"Why do you want to die?"

"Why does anyone want to live?"

"I can think of many reasons."

"Can you give me one?"

"Well, to find out what's going to happen tomorrow." He doesn't mention Isabel's daughter back there with the nanny.

"I know what's going to happen tomorrow. That's not very compelling. How do you manage to drive a cab and also write?" she says, moving him away from her now.

"Well, I don't exactly do them together." They both laugh.

"And your girlfriend is a writer?"

"Actually, she's a naturally gifted writer, but she's a painter."

"That's wonderful. How would you describe her work?"

"Well, a lot of self-portraits. She's working with canvas sculptures, too." He feels the vacuous quality of his words. Nothing. She's working on nothing, just as I am working on nothing. We are only pretending to work because we lack the courage to accept that we are lost. He doesn't say this, does not go down the denigration road. Anyway, it's not Sarah who is lost so far as any artistic vision is concerned. It is he.

I want to spend the rest of my life in a darkened room with you feeling the warmth of my own specialness reflected back to me through you. I want to kiss those lips. I want…I want.

"I guess I should leave," he says. But he stays.

Not then but later, much later, he will tell her about the St. George Hotel down on Clark Street, in Brooklyn, He will tell her how his oldest sister Hannah would take him there on Friday evenings. He will tell her all about Hannah and the things she did and didn't do, but related specifically to the experience at Pierre's Restaurant he will tell her that, when his lips began to turn blue and his skin developed goosebumps from overexposure to the chlorinated water in this pool, he would head for the steam room, where he would sit on a wet wooden bench in the mist with the men old and young and *be unable to return to the water from which he had come.* He will tell Isabel that on the night he met her *the steam bath was to the pool what she was to the rest of his life.*

Maybe he will tell her.

At some point she grows tired of him. It is by now he has had three drinks since Philip went to the bar, where he remains. Johan can't say how he knows her mood has changed; he just does. It is the sudden shadow of impatience darkening the smile that has been a constant. Inwardly he responds with terror, for Isabel has reminded him that all power is with her, and that power is the power of dismissal. She has built him up and she can tear him down. He is all hers to do with as she will, and what she now wills is that he go away so she can get back to her life.

No, he can contribute nothing to the bill, she says. Philip and she said they would take him to dinner. By the way, she says, she is assigned manuscripts to read and review by a publisher. Maybe he would like to do the same. He should call her if he is interested. On the inside of a matchbook she writes her name and number. The letters sing. The numbers sing. Each is distinctive. A calligraphic hand she has. Visions can be built on this, he thinks, noting by comparison his own poor penmanship and the inner chaos it reveals.

And alcohol. What will he tell her of that? Will he tell her that somewhere on the long walk east along a desolate stretch of Bleecker Street, he stops off in a liquor store and buys a pint of scotch and continues his journey? At the end of the street is the misnamed Palace Hotel, as it is obviously a flophouse, but Johan is not headed for any flophouse. He hangs a right on the boulevard and heads toward his building, halfway down the block. At home he will do some real drinking because the thirst is so strongly in him. Yes, he will tell her, as he will tell her some years later about driving back from Wellesley, Massachusetts, and how, along the way, the road signs begin to say Cape Cod, not New Haven, so that he realizes he has made a wrong turn and that it is a simple thing to turn the car around and get back on course. But not so with the drinking life, he will say. The drinking life offers a road that is free of potholes and without the nuisance of toll booths and traffic jams. It is a road parallel to the main highway and yet distinctly apart, and on which he can speed along alone and unhindered. On this road there are no signs, or if there are, they are covered up. The only signs he can read are those held by sexily dressed women reading "Pleasure pit five miles ahead. Keep going." This he will tell her too.

For six months thereafter he drives a cab. He will continue with these daily shifts until the ache of loneliness, the divide the Plexiglas places between him and the passenger, is too much. At JFK one night he reaches his limit, in a parking lot that serves as a giant urinal for cabbies to relieve themselves, one after another of them converting their cabs into a makeshift stall by standing behind the open driver's side door hosing down the asphalt below with their piss. While waiting for a rumored flight from the Caribbean and a juicy fare back to the city (what kind of flight plan would that be to deposit passengers at the airport at one in the morning?) it suddenly surfaces from deep within him, the sense that doors are going to close unless he acts, and acts soon. There had been an exchange back at the depot some weeks before. A surfer type with long blond hair and bronzed skin had told an old-timer with a customized seat pad that he was only doing the driving gig for a short while. The sweaty old guy with a kerchief around his neck and a lifetime of cafeteria fare in his bulging gut removed the cheroot from his mouth and said, "Kid, I said the same thing—twenty-five years ago." The mind could fool you. It was a deceiver. Life could fool you. You thought you were great if only anyone knew it and yet you wound up pissing in the parking lot at JFK and carrying a cigar box with coins and dollar bills into public bathrooms. There is suddenly terror at the prospect of missing the party, whatever that party is, of permanent exclusion and poverty. He has pushed up against something, some core of pride and sense of self-worth and dignity. He is not laughing anymore. Yes, he wants something better for himself.

Besides, it is dangerous. Some Black kids jump in his cab outside Madison Square Garden and direct him up to Harlem, where he gets caught in a melee between the cops and the community people— bottles, bricks, nightsticks. Bodies slammed against gated storefronts. One of the kids, surly, saying to him, "What you looking at, Whitey?" A miracle they didn't beat his head in or feed him a bullet. And then another time on some Harlem side street blocked off at both ends by dealers, his Checker used as the site of a drug bazaar.

And it is the ache of loneliness as suddenly you realize you are invisible, that people aren't really seeing you as an interesting young man who drives a cab but simply as a hackie.

So at age twenty-eight he starts another life. Dressed in corduroy slacks and cheap, colorful shirts from the bin of a discount clothier on Canal Street, he shows up at 250 Madison Avenue as a temp for Pentacle Books, a trade publisher. He negotiates no big deals. He offers no contracts with specialty clauses. He does not cause the coffers of the company to swell or participate in high-powered executive meetings. He sits alone in an empty office typing labels on a massive Olympia electric typewriter. Well dressed men and women pass by his open door. His happiness is beyond words that he has been freed from the wheel of the cab to be here with them. He has come in from the cold. No more entering restaurants with his cigar box full of dollar bills and change fearful of being stopped before he can avail himself of the restroom. He is not unfit to be among people, or if he is, he can apologize his way through the day so that he can stay. And stay he does.

Somewhere on the road of life he lost his way. He remembers that as a child he held jobs—delivery boy for the local florist and grocery and dry cleaners. Work thrilled him. It gave him a feeling of happiness and accomplishment and purpose, though he sees, looking back, the taint of self-righteousness and perfectionism that accompanied it. Something about pleasing his mother and proving that he was better than his troubled older sister Naomi. But in his college years he made a wrong turn. Maybe it was there. He maneuvered his way into the renting office of the building his family managed and devised a scheme for embezzling money. Some idea that his mother had kept his father out of the business but she wouldn't keep him out. Some idea about claiming his patrimony. Some crazy force that drew him back. The venture lasted five years, in which he amassed considerable stolen funds and paid the fixture fee on the loft in Chinatown into which he and Sarah moved. They were years in which he began to fancy himself as a writer and in which his drinking became daily. In that period he let go of his law school dream, unable to show up for even the orientation to the school that had admitted him. If once upon a time he had dreamed of basketball stardom he now imagined himself as a great author. Success required that he write novels, and to write novels he needed time. The function of the money that he had stolen was to give him that time. But the novels didn't get written, or they got written badly. He wrote increasingly when he was drunk or high, his days frittered away in distraction and dissipation. He had grabbed for a life—Sarah, the writing thing, the money—that hadn't brought him any great happiness. He had given himself all the time he needed to be miserable. In stark moments, when the rationalizations fell away, he saw things as they were, saw, that is, that he was corrupt in the areas of work and love. There was no work. What was it to show up for a couple of hours each day in the renting office of the family business and leave with a pocketful of bills? Was that a life he could share about with others?

"Join us. Just join us," a psychoanalyst had said to him some years before. Join the human race, she had meant. But he hadn't known how, and he still didn't, but at least now, with this little publishing job, he had a reason to get up in the morning and a place to go. And within a couple of months he was offered a full-time position as an editorial assistant to a senior editor in the adult trade division, a man named Bill Marg. And though a feeling of shame attached that, at age twenty-eight, he should hold a job kids just out of college normally took, still he had a desk to sit at outside his boss's office and he wasn't driving a cab all hours of the night. And the job had some responsibility that went with it. It wasn't all just answering the phone for his boss or typing his letters. There was some actual editorial work for him to do. He was asked to edit several manuscripts as well and in a couple of instances wrote jacket copy for books under contract.

A feeling of pride took hold. He had not been living well. In fact, there were elements of his life that had been insane. As the months passed he shuddered remembering those long evenings behind the wheel of the cab. He had a beachhead on respectability now. He was working for a well-known publishing company right there on Madison Avenue. Sure, the salary was low, but the work was meaningful and there was always the hope of advancement.

Of course, he couldn't give himself to the job too much. It was important to remember that he was really a writer and he eventually had more important things to do than to spend his time advancing the work, most of it inferior, of others. Because though he could feel like the lowest of the low and in a percentile that left him without a prayer of meaningful accomplishment, at other times he walked the streets feeling like the prophet armed and dangerous. He wasn't going to wind up like others in the company he saw virtually sleeping with their manuscripts. The dream of greatness remained alive, even if a humble pose had been forced upon him.

And yes, there was a humiliation or two, starting with his name, but these things were to be expected when you walked the earth with the name Manootdjian and had the affect that he showed. Mr. Marg himself was the son of immigrants. Through his parents he was close to the experience of being newly arrived to these shores. A lesson he had learned was that you could shave your name as well as your face. And the thing was that you only had to shave your name once. Having done so, you had no reason to fear it would ever grow back to its original length. The deed was done. *Fait accompli.*

Mr. Marg called Johan into his office to discuss the matter. He didn't say Johan couldn't have the job unless he consented to a name change. He simply pointed out that a name such as Manootdjian might hold Johan back in the world of publishing or in any industry, for that matter. America is about simplicity, Mr. Marg pointed out. Americans don't like to be confronted with spelling challenges. It makes them angry and they retaliate in subtle ways. They form judgments. Problems arise, Mr. Marg said.

As befit his status, Mr. Marg had a spacious corner office. The shelves were crammed with best-selling books he had published. He was on a first-name basis with all the leading literary agents in New York City. He was said to be a publishing legend.

Mr. Marg was generous with him. He shared his own humble origins as the son of Russian immigrants, and how he had started as a clerk in the mailroom of a publishing house back in Chicago. His own surname had been Margovich, and as a young man he decided to Americanize it so the flavor of ethnicity would be removed. The change helped him enormously. It gave him the confidence that he could move about in the world without the baggage of the past. Mr. Marg only wanted the same freedom for Johan.

All Johan could do was nod his head in the presence of such a powerful man sitting at his large desk in his executive chair.

"Good. Then we have a deal," Mr. Marg said.

Johan had been instructed by Mr. Marg in the steps to take to effect the name change. He had been so nervous during the discussion that he couldn't be sure he had heard right, but he didn't dare double-check, for fear that he might incur Mr. Marg's wrath, for there was talk about Mr. Marg's temper, particularly after a long business lunch during which a few martinis had been part of the meal. Something about circulating a memo to the publishing staff. Well, the first thing was to write the memo.

To: All Staff Members
From: Johan Hedberg (formerly Johan Manootdjian)
Re: Name Change

This is to inform you that, after lengthy discussion with Mr. Marg, we have decided, in order to facilitate my entry into the publishing world and make the burden on everyone lighter—the bearer of the name and its receiver—to give my name an alteration that will accomplish a long sought after personal goal of simplicity. I will, effective immediately, and for entirely pragmatic reasons, replace my paternal surname with that of my mother. Words cannot express the freedom I now feel to walk among you in this more presentable fashion. Though many of you have hardly had the chance to know me as Johan Manootdjian, please, in all further communications, address me as Johan Hedberg.

Then it was only for Johan to photocopy the memo and leave it in the in-boxes on the desks of the other editorial assistants for their bosses. He saw to the task right away and returned to his desk so he could continue with his work. So far as he was concerned, the problem had been resolved and he could now move on.

In his short time with the company, Johan had noticed a number of young, attractive women on the floor. Whereas he sat at a gray metal desk outside Mr. Marg's office, they had offices of their own, offices with doors they could close so even in this world of business in which they had found themselves, they could, if they chose, have a modicum of privacy. Ambitious young women, women who dressed well and for whom their work was a source of seemingly great pleasure. Women whose names he was beginning to know: Midge Millicent and Caddie Calistra and Sophie Swaghart. Names that caught your attention and stayed in your memory bank. And there was the sexual smolder that their carefully applied makeup couldn't hide. But mostly women with luminous minds focused on their own advancement, that being their right as their beauty was their right and the good life and the friends with which they were blessed was their right.

It was these women who came to him, singly and in pairs, copies of his memo in their hands. And it was these women who said to him, as if in unison, "Surely this is some sort of joke. You can't be serious." Women calling to him from their place of power and yet setting aside that power to talk to him as if he were a friend. And he was touched and thrilled that they would give him this attention, but he was also frightened and inevitably covertly hostile, because once a thing was done it should be seen as done.

No, he was not joking, he told these women. Mr. Marg and he had decided on a course of action regarding his name. More than that he didn't care to say. The presence of these women was unsettling. What did they want from him? Why couldn't they just accept what the memo stated? What business of theirs should it be if he wanted to change his name?

"What's the matter with that man?" Midge Millicent said. "Does he think we can't spell?"

She nodded in the direction of his boss's office. Her question suggested less than reverence for Mr. Marg. In fact, those few words told Johan everything he needed to know about the attitude of the up and coming young women in the company toward Mr. Marg. They saw him as a conceited and arrogant patriarch. Indeed, Johan had overheard these judgments rendered about Mr. Marg. Evidently, they considered Mr. Marg an impediment to their own progress. The irony of his position became apparent. He, who had been trained by Sarah in anti-patriarchal warfare and the unending battle against the *fucking pricks,* he who had contorted himself beyond the warp that his own severely oedipal tendencies had inflicted on him, was now, for all practical purposes, an agent of the patriarch. He was, for better or worse, Mr. Marg's boy. And yet here they were, these ambitious women saying, in effect, "You cannot be a part of us unless you are apart from him." Johan sensed the closeness they shared with each other that they would never share with him. They were women of the world, and he was not of the world they circulated in.

As the months passed Johan became more acclimated to his environment. For the most part, Mr. Marg seemed happy with his performance. Toward the other editorial assistants Johan was polite and friendly, but also reserved; a sense of his own station in life kept him apart, for his peers had the cachet of Ivy League educations and thus the firepower to destroy him instantly.

"Stay sober," Mr. Marg would say to him, on departing the office some evenings. Johan did not read into the unusual farewell. He simply assumed Mr. Marg said goodbye to everyone in similar fashion. It never occurred to him that Mr. Marg might suspect he was on the bottle every night. And why should Mr. Marg suspect such a thing? A toothbrush was a useful tool. A little toothpaste applied to the bristles in the morning and a good brushing and the smell of booze after a night of drinking was eliminated from his breath. So he believed.

He now brought alcohol home rather than heading for the bars. Was it not cheaper and more convenient to drink at the loft rather than run up a hefty tab while perched on a barstool? When he left work there would be this debate of sorts whether he should get off the subway at Astor Place and go to the wines and spirits supermarket or stay on until Bleecker Street, his home stop, thus ensuring a night free of drinking. He didn't see that the decision was not his to make and that he had no power to resist the supermarket. He didn't understand that by five p.m. his body was beginning to crave a drink. Or if he did understand his need for alcohol, it was a fact he could not explore.

What he did see was that there were certain experiences he must in future avoid, such as the evening concert at Carnegie Hall Sarah persuaded him to attend with her girlfriend from work. While the female vocalist was compelling, by eight p.m. his every thought was of the drink he needed, and at intermission he fled, with the single-minded goal of getting back to the loft as quickly as possible with a bottle in hand. When the subway stopped between stations, he had the notion to jump on the tracks and run through the dark tunnel to the next station and up to the street where he could flag a cab so he could drink in the way that he needed to. Only the train lurching into motion that minute saved him from acting on his desperation.

However, there were still those occasional evenings, though infrequent, when he would head for a bar after leaving work rather than go directly home. One such was Home Base on St. Mark's Place, a dark and smoke-filled space where one-time hippies who had in their youth disdained alcohol for more mind-expanding substances now passed the time downing boilermakers. His goal was a simple one: release from the consciousness of his failure as a writer and all concerns about the day and hope for the appearance of a beautiful woman who would want him for an hour or two before he headed home.

Despite the emotional dependency, he had reservations about his relationship with Sarah. It was only weakness and fear that had led him to live with her in the first place. So he could sometimes think. At Sarah's family's country place, he meant to speak frankly with her about separating, having decided a woman entirely out of his reach at work might be more suitable. He had been nipping at the bottle all day, and that evening hit it harder to summon the courage to say the things he needed to say. Instead he found himself reaching for a rifle and heading out for the front porch. He remembered loading and reloading the rifle several times with .30-.30 cartridges, pointing the barrel toward the sky, and firing. The rest of the night was lost to him. In the morning he came to on the bathroom floor. He could recall being out on the porch and the rifle blasts and nothing more. Sarah's parents gave him a wide berth. Their silence and the anger and concern in their faces spoke for them. It didn't surprise Johan. People of all shapes and sizes and at all socioeconomic levels suffered from the affliction of unkindness, its most loathsome manifestation being to ostracize a man when he was down. It was in the nature of people to be small and vicious. They had no choice but to band together and attack those such as himself who were kind and gentle.

Or there was the time Sarah invited a guest for dinner, the former boyfriend of her girlfriend Molly. The dinner was nothing Johan looked forward to, and he postponed his arrival, instead meeting up at a SoHo bar with a woman he had been to bed with, a woman he would never be close with in the way he once was but whom he reached out to now and then in his desperation. She was a woman with a big brain, a woman who sometimes said disturbing things to him, as she did that evening. "You're an alcoholic,' she said, without accusation, her words accompanied by a smile, when he ordered his third scotch and water. Seeing that she hurt him, she sought to qualify her statement. "A budding alcoholic." Still, the shame was severe, as if he needed a crutch to get through life or was a grown man who still lived with his mother.

He would have gone home with her. He wanted to, but she had made other plans.

Labeling him as an alcoholic had slowed his drinking that evening, but now, on leaving her, he found another bar, rougher than the chic SoHo establishment they had left. Here there were no women, just boozehound men drinking from quart bottles of beer dripping with cold sweat served to them by a bartender with a scarred face. He downed several scotches within a short time before proceeding on his way.

Sarah and their guest were seated at the dining table when he arrived home. The sight of them together brought a surge of anger. He opened the refrigerator door and threw some of the content onto the floor. He remembered nothing after that until he was woken by a terrifying phone call. What? Sarah had been kidnapped? She was being held where? In what hotel? Sarah clearly not in the loft. Their guest not in the loft. All he knew was that time was not on his side, and he must struggle to remember the name of the hotel where she was being held. He had the name, then he lost the name. Had it again, then lost it again. Couldn't understand why it kept slipping away from him, and then it got farther still before he could even write it down. A panicked call to Sarah's parents at their country home, where they had gone for the week. *Do you know your daughter is dead? Do you know?* Shouting those words to her father and hanging up before her father could respond. That set the record straight somehow. Now he was free to go out and get some beer. That was all he wanted and needed. Some beer from the all-night bodega down on Second Avenue so he would not have to think. The streets of the city quiet, even the ambulance parked just outside the loft building brought to that place of quiet, its lights and engine off and none of that wailing sound so much in its nature to make.

He sat at the dining table drinking the tallboys. Budweiser had this creamy taste. And he had five more of them in the fridge. And then he had another six-pack of tallboys, the more metallic-tasting Miller, for reinforcement. Oh yes, he had set something in motion now. No doubt about that. People knew where he lived now. He had given them the message loud and clear. And wasn't that more than the kidnapper had done with his sketchy information delivered with his confusing call? And wasn't finding him, Johan Manootdjian, the least they could do? Didn't they owe him that much? Wasn't it about time somebody put aside all that stuff that he wasn't good enough to be found so he could be found? Wasn't it about time somebody came to him rather than him having to go to them?

He had done nothing, nothing. He had just screamed out the truth about a situation too horrible to contemplate. For God's sake, his girlfriend had been abducted. What was he supposed to do, keep it to himself?

Only later did he understand what it might mean for parents to be woken in the middle of the night with the hysterical message that their daughter was dead or what it might be for those same parents to drive a long distance in the dark trying not to believe the worst. And only later did he understand the significance of the ambulance outside, that someone had called ahead to New York City that help might be needed at the Bowery loft where he and Sarah lived.

In the moment that Sarah's parents arrived sometime before dawn with a friend of the family and the Emergency Medical Services Team, he understood nothing. All he saw was people crowding into the loft. All he felt was embarrassment that they should find him drunk and with empty beer cans all around. And to have them, or anyone, in his living place, judging him, looking down on him, the way they did, the way that everyone did. Had him dead to rights and put him in the shame space, the way those classmates had done back in grade school, sticking their heads inside the door of Johan's family's apartment and then spreading the word throughout the school that Johan lived in a pigsty. Oh, there were other things to notice, of course, like their penchant for insensitivity manifesting in an unwillingness to listen and accept the reality of the horror that had been inflicted on him by the phone caller in the night, the one who woke him and said that Sarah was his hostage. Every last one of them turning a deaf ear to what had really, really happened, and how terrifying it had been for him to feel completely helpless in terms of trying to save Sarah.

Sarah's father saying, in a state of fury, "You are psychotic, completely psychotic," as Johan clung to the story of the kidnapper's phone call in the night and continued to ponder why such malevolence should exist on the planet. "One more time. One more time," said Sarah's father, a civilized man driven to wagging a threatening finger in Johan's face.

And Sarah's mother. She was not to be outdone. And so he remembered her words, too. And wasn't it just her way to pack them with such overwrought exasperation, saying, "How long will we have to take care of you? How long, Johan? How long?"

Shortly after they arrived, Sarah's sister Claire telephoned to say that she had gone to their parents' West Side apartment and found Sarah was safe. Sarah had informed her sister *not even having the decency to inform him,* that she had fled there and, knowing Johan's ways, placed pillows over the phone to muffle the calling that was sure to follow.

But that didn't mean the kidnapper didn't exist. That didn't mean any such thing at all.

In a condition of sleeplessness and terror did he show up for work that morning, knowing he must do the bidding of Mr. Marg if he was to have any life at all, because by this time the job had become powerful in his consciousness as a beachhead on respectability. It was the thing that could keep him from the street below.

He needed an ally, or at least a sympathetic ear. Jesus, didn't he deserve that? Maybe Mabel Gowalt, another editorial assistant—the only assistant on the floor older than him—would care to listen. Why not take a chance and ask her? And for whatever reason this woman, unglamorous in her thick glasses and drab attire and haggard face, was more than willing. And so, having talked to virtually no one on the floor in personal terms, he now poured out his tale of the night before to Mabel Gowalt, there in the back of the cavernous Lucky Garden Chinese restaurant just down the block from Pentacle Books. Mabel Gowalt nursed her one drink while Johan kept the waiter busy with scotches on the rocks. Yes, he was tired, exhausted really, and running on adrenaline, but it was 5:30 p.m., by which time every day the thirst was upon him. Did Mabel not think it unjust that Sarah's parents should direct such cruel words at him when he was in a state of complete terror over the fate of his girlfriend, given the call from the fiend on that dark night? And was it not an understandable source of anguish that Sarah's family should now be advocating that she stay with them until she could find a suitable alternative to what they perceived to be his drunken and psychotic brand of lunacy? Mabel Gowalt listened and nodded. She gave him the ear he was looking for and counseled that he just give the matter a little time before helping him into a cab.

It offended Johan that the driver should pull up not in front of the loft but diagonally across the street at the Palace Hotel and that he should associate him with sots who had lost everything but the rags on their alcohol-ravaged bodies and for whom this flophouse was their only alternative to the street. Drunk or not, he felt a chill pass through him that the hackie, whether by design or mistake, had deposited him there.

Sarah stayed with her parents for three weeks before returning to the loft. Within a month, there was another incident. At a party they attended, he met a woman receptive to being led into a dark and unused room and receptive to being kissed and having her dress unzipped and her bra unclasped. What was it to have the encumbrance of a girlfriend, that restraint should be imposed on him at the very moment he had found the pleasure he wanted to live in for the rest of his life, that a search party of the supremely just and moral should find him with this woman, actually turn on the light, and confront him with the unwelcome truth that Sarah was worried and looking all over for him? What was it to be interrupted in this way before pleasure could be fully had? Why could he not live in a whorehouse with an endless supply of liquor? Why could he not run drunk and naked through the streets of Manhattan for the rest of his days?

It was one story, and one story only, the progression of drinking and the veil of illusion he couldn't pierce though Johan saw it only through its discrete parts that he hoped to thread together in a narrative so he could say, Don't you see, don't you see? It has only been grist for the literary mill." *She had a perfect bottom, perfect teeth. I needed her to make my life complete. She had made a mysterious appearance in New York City from the great state of Vermont and opened her mouth when I kissed her and gave me her tongue. Some kind of gloss she had on her lips. She was willing, pliable. There was nothing she would not do. A woman who let me touch her after only two minutes of conversation. Do you know the treasure that was denied me by this interruption? Do you not know that I lost the thing I was looking for right after finding it? Do you know what it is to seek your salvation through a woman only to see it disappear? Have you ever, ever, contemplated the anguish of loss? How often can such a creature be expected to come into your life?*

But also hear his penance for having abandoned Sarah. *I am nothing but a horseshit desperado. I should be beaten with a stick.* Hear that he bashed himself in the head repeatedly with a Campbell's soup can or that Sarah escorted him to the emergency room, on her therapist's suggestion, or that he took off his shirt in an act of narcissism for the female doctor, who determined his blood alcohol level was sufficiently high for admission to the hospital's detox ward, or that he left in the wee hours of the morning before the paperwork could be completed for his admission? Or that, penniless, he walked home desperate for a drink and, seeing that Sarah had fled once more, knocked in panic on the door of the upstairs neighbor, whom he knew to be a caterer, and begged him for a bottle of wine and when he received two, could have fallen at the provider's feet and kissed them for his celestial benevolence before taking those bottles downstairs so he could restructure his internal environment and prepare for another day?

Who was anyone to limit his desire? Was he not of his generation, a child of the sixties, when dating did not exist and you simply fell on the floor and *did it?* And did he not, in the next few months, develop a growing interest in a young woman named Jennifer Sayles, a fellow editorial assistant, who skipped rope outside her boss's office during the lunch hour? Was she not thin in the way that Sarah wasn't? Did she not have the curvy hips and tight round bottom that he was seeking? Was she not dark where Sarah was light? Did she not have mysteries in need of exploration? Was she not destined for glittering middle-class success on the basis of her Ivy League degree? Were not he and she and other editorial assistants given a freebie to a screening of a movie that the company had a tie-in with? And did Johan not show up at that Broadway theater on a rainy afternoon with the anticipation surging through him of seeing the movie with her—*her*—as they had agreed? And did she not have in tow another editorial assistant with the stamp of Ivy League success on him as well? And did Johan's eyes not meet theirs as they approached the theater *holding hands* before he could get away? And did they both not see through to his crushed state even as he sat with them seeking desperately to pretend that nothing was amiss in his world? And did he not go home that evening muttering *fool, fool, foolish fool?*

And yet, miraculously, did not the dream of Jennifer Sayles revive some weeks later when he called her during a weeklong binge of drunkenness, Sarah still gone, and heard her say, in a voice lusciously hot with her own breath, "Do you want to come over and fuck me?" And did she not give him the address where this fucking could take place? And did he not whoop and holler in joy and downright euphoria standing in front of the bathroom mirror seeking to scrape away the beard that had grown over the last three days on his pale and haggard face? Did the sun not shine brighter than ever following this invitdtion he had been given? And did he not find himself at a red door within sight of Grand Central Terminal and did not a woman three times the weight of Jennifer Sayles and twice her age and with gold front teeth not answer the door? And did not the woman beckon him into the darkness that awaited? And did he not recoil and run stricken with horror back to the loft from which he had come, where he could turn to his one reliable friend, the bottle? Did these things not happen in the days of Johan Manootdjian, born to be on this earth but without a sound grasp of how?

All these things came to pass for Johan Manootdjian, who had not come to his mother's Jesus but instead was lost in the folds of his own billowing desire. And you can also say that on the days Mr. Marg wore pink suspenders he departed from the office with the words "Stay sober" for Johan Manootdjian as he did on the days when he departed with belted pants, for on all days of the week was Johan drinking without so much as a thought that others knew.

What is the goal of a narrative of this kind? Is it to revel in the inevitable by situating oneself in the worn groove of progressive drunkenness? Who are you, Johan Manootdjian, child of darkness, you whose only master is the guilt you serve by accumulating more? Do you want to tell us every last bad thing you have done as a shield from truly knowing you? How long will you ward off intimacy with your chronicle of shame? How long will you spurn the love that is yours in this very instant?

What is that you say? You are not finished? There is more? You need to tell us about the sense of desperation that led you to marry Sarah and all the things that followed? Understand that you rely on narrative the way you once relied on alcohol. The next drink will set you right, the next turn in the story will do the trick. And so you go on and on with what you no longer believe in because you feel you have no choice, because what is that to just sit on a garbage can and emit peaceful vibes or stare lovingly at the trees in your wanderings through the park? The fact is that the world is pouring in on you at a faster and faster rate. Time is accelerating. One thing happens and then another and you feel you have lost control, that you cannot contain the flow of events, that there is no net to throw over experience and pull it tight. All you can do is bear witness. You cannot put your life between the covers of a book and call it complete. The blood and pain, the aspiration that comes from breathing, seeps out of the pages and runs loose once more. Things break down and no repairman is at hand. Your defenses are collapsing, Johan Manootdjian. You are standing more and more in the face of love. You are striving for connection but barriers persist.

Proceed if you must.

A turning point came when Johan decided to marry, when, that is, he decided to dig a deeper hole as a way of getting out of the one he was in. He loved Sarah. She was a true love, but she was not a love he could grow old with. She was a love of his youth that he had needed to leave there but couldn't leave there. The marriage took place at City Hall in a sterile room with a clerk standing in for a priest. In attendance were Sarah's parents and Johan's mother. It was a shrunken affair that spoke to the poverty of their lives. No friends. No dancing. And, to Sarah's mother's amazement, no ring.

Frankly, it had not occurred to Johan that there would be the need for a ring. Johan did not know about rings. He did not know about ritual. He had never been to a wedding. No one had asked him. *Your sister Leah hadn't asked you, Johan? Your sister Leah hadn't? Your friend Efram hadn't asked you?* He had been introduced into no social structure that would generate such an event. All he knew were the bars of Manhattan, where sots imbibed and, if the attraction was there, fell on the floor and fucked. A life with strangers meeting in the half-dark.

Johan's mother was seventy-four. She had met Sarah but not her family. Johan had seen to that. He had placed her in the shame closet along with the rest of the family. He was afraid she would not reflect well on him. He had left his own for the Van Dines, only he hadn't left at all. She was a part of him and he was a part of her. It was just that way, but the love he felt for her could not fully express itself. There were obstacles he had no resources to remove.

Johan, tell us the things you remember, in your own words.

"I went to Pentacle Books that morning to prove my devotion to my job. Mr. Marg had given me line-editing responsibility for a manuscript under contract. Something called *Don't Let Your Spouse Drop the Atom Bomb of Guilt on Your Sorry Head If You're Inclined to Take It on the Lam,* by Dr. Carmelo Quint. The book was a practical guide to getting out of an unhappy marriage, and I could have taken the content as a sign, especially when Mr. Marg said to me, 'You don't have to do this,' meaning, you don't have to go and get married, this being the only instance of him giving me personal advice, aside from what he shared with me about my surname. Mr. Marg had powers of clairvoyance, but a death march is a death march, and so, by midday I was at City Hall ready to tie the knot with this bulky manuscript in my backpack. I thought it revealing that Sarah showed up with alcohol on her breath. It seemed to me a sign that she as well was experiencing some conflict about this step into matrimony. A young politician hurried past. I recognized him, for he had become a prominent figure in the life of the city, his photo being frequently in the newspapers. He was handsome in a dark, slightly Neanderthal way, his eyes set back in his head and his forehead bulging. In this institutional setting of government clerks and other minions of the bureaucratic apparatus, he strode through the marble halls like a prince, empowered by wealth and position. His eyes met Sarah's and smiles signaling intimate compatibility were exchanged. In that moment he was her art school lover, Lane, her genius boyfriend, the Jewish prince. He was a reminder to me that whatever picture my ego presented of our relationship, I was not Sarah's first choice but someone she had settled for when she couldn't have the god she had left behind in Boston.

"It was not easy for Sarah to surrender her freedom. She had been born to live alone, she often said, in that time when we were young. Maybe my crime was not listening to her when she said in her art school days that she could never cohabit with a man. Maybe my crime was to have gone where I did not belong. Maybe that has been my crime throughout my life. Maybe I was born to be alone and simply good, in keeping with my mother's dictate. By good I mean amiable and kind and apart, the sort of person who even when young sits on a park bench and feeds the pigeons and does not heed the call of passion.

"'The world has nothing that I want,' my mother would say when I was a child. Maybe her perspective should have been mine.

"My bigger crime and also my sadness is this pervasive shame about myself and, by extension, those who make up my family. With Sarah I had been as much in love with what she represented as who she was. All that culture, all that wealth, all those ancestors going back generations. My life was about escape—escape from my family into the other.

"As I recall, we crowded into a booth at some dark and expensive Italian restaurant, with my elderly mother and Sarah's still relatively young parents. How my in-laws must have loathed me. What had I given them but grief, after all, starting that summer in 1967 when I stayed at their Catskill estate and Sarah's father threatened to throw me off the property for my sullen manner and abuse of his daughter. Had they not bailed me out of jail when I had been arrested on the unfounded charge of felony possession of narcotics? Had they not loaned me their car and sums of money? Had they not offered me endless hospitality? And how had I repaid them but to do them dirty with sniping and terrifying phone calls in the night? I saw none of this. A drunk can't afford to see the problems he is causing. He can only be sensitive to his own pain.

"'She is a woman of great character. You can see it in her face.' These were words Sarah's father spoke of my mother some days after meeting her in that restaurant. They came from the quiet place within him as a statement of his own humanity. In speaking those words he conferred respectability on my mother. He showed me what I had, in my deepest self, known. Can anything be more shameful than to have to be told who your mother is in order to override the negating devices of your own mind?

"Strangely, Sarah was not nearly as deflated by the marriage as I was. She did not enter the realm of the frantic in seeking to escape from it. Sarah had the capacity to sink into her own life, to be in the place where she was. She had the ballast of her artistic integrity to keep her afloat and on an even keel.

"By contrast I returned to the loft as a resident of the land of death. Marriage hadn't compromised me; it had eradicated me. The ritual of legal union had failed as a solution. I needed something more than it could possibly provide. If I had been promiscuous when we had simply lived together, the urge to meet other women was in overdrive now that we had entered the matrimonial state.

"Sarah had a capacity for genuine friendship, the ability to let people in and take a sincere interest in them. Along with a moral compass, it was another quality that distinguished her from me. As a result, she retained friends from earlier days. Molly, whom she had met back in high school, was one. Herself an artist, Molly worked by day as a graphic designer for an internationally known furniture company and arranged for Sarah to come in and do paste-ups and mechanicals. It was there that Sarah met Audrey Eastbrook, a few years younger than her and also an artist. In fact, they had both gone to the Boston Museum School. Audrey had beauty but she was running on empty. She lacked the self that governed Sarah's life, the grounding element of work that returned Sarah to her studio each day, no matter how tired or beset emotionally she might be. People had gotten too close to Audrey. They had overrun her garden. She didn't know how to keep men out.

Audrey was in the middle of a marital separation when Sarah met her. All I saw was the way Audrey filled her jeans and the barrette in her brown hair, which precluded any possibility of a real break from the advances of men, who were rendered captive by the package she presented.

"I may have told you that this was not a period in my life when I understood the word *restraint*. My life was predicated on the pleasure principle. And though the language of possession is sad and diametrically opposed to love in relation to another human being, the fact remains that I had to have Audrey, who gave signs of being not unwilling. She had taken the measure of Sarah and found herself lacking. She saw the artistic vigilance. She saw the darkness Sarah operated in and was unable to go there herself. She was not in the world of art for the long run. She did not have the necessary wound or perhaps the talent. The kinder thing to say is that she had too much beauty and a natural way around men and a need for them. She was not in opposition to partnership and even stewardship of her life. The parameters of normalcy were surrounding her. She was not a woman meant to sleep alone but to love men and life above all else.

"We met on a dark street in the west seventies. Grass was the instrument of my seduction. I told Audrey I had a contact and could get some good stuff for her cheap—Acapulco Gold or Panama Red or whatever the name of it was. It was all just herb to me, but the cover of a promise of something material was required for the rendezvous to happen. I remember the Museum of Natural History being closed for the night. The birds and animals in their dioramas had their place and I had mine under the watchful eye of the turreted towers looking down on Columbus Avenue. I remember oriental rugs staring out from the windows of closed shops and the streetlights reflected in the wet slickness of the black roads after a rainfall and a feeling of quietude, as if Audrey and I were there and the world had gone away.

"I took her for dinner and drinks. Complicity governed our meeting, that is, Audrey knew the consequences should Sarah find out. She was not assuming my presence with her was the generous act of a monogamous spouse, and when I suggested we return to her place to sample the goods, she did not say, 'Would the evening be complete without that?' but 'Sure,' a prompt reply more potent sexually for its blunt, game brevity.

"Audrey lived on One Hundred First Street between Broadway and West End Avenue. Everything in New York City is between something or other, of course, but this location had particular significance. One, it brought to mind a vanished bookstore that had featured a white castle with crenellated towers, the sight of which, in the window, would drive me wild with longing when I was a child. For weeks and months it remained an object beyond my ability to have, owing to its cost, and I don't know if it ever came to be in my possession. But that it should be there, in that window, and for sale when the store principally sold books, is beyond my ability to express. And then there was the sweet smell of pastries, a constant as I stood at the bookstore window, but where on earth could it have come from?

"Perhaps, more importantly, the building, and in fact, the apartment, in which Audrey lived was the same one where I would visit my childhood friend Jerry Jones-Nobleonian years before, and if he seems out of place in this narrative, I must emphasize that period as formative. It seemed incredible that his parents and sister and he could share such a small space, and yet they did. Back then there were what were called 'welfare hotels' on many blocks of the Upper West Side, and Jerry's family had moved out of one such hotel down the block to be in this seemingly safer building. And yet violence followed them. Outright mayhem seemed frequent. Skulls cracked with baseball bats, gouged flesh, shrieks and groans, wailing ambulances and police cars. The dead or seriously wounded removed. Sometimes, back then, New York City seemed like a chorus of pain; dread could live in your bones if you saw enough of it.

"Jerry had a younger sister, Carmen. Even now I see myself as a child offering her my hand and proceeding along the path of exploration we never took. It was a different time in the life of the city, but inevitability showed its hand. Carmen grew up to become a prostitute and Jerry was found dead in a Bowery flophouse with gangrene in both legs.

"If you ask me about Jerry's mother, I will tell you she was an Estonian woman who had not been spared the ravages and destruction and utter scarcity of war. My strongest memories are of her standing transfixed before some Broadway store window staring at the display of merchandise and of the Planter's peanut wrappers she saved in a box for redemption for some gift of yesteryear. America had come calling on Europe, and Jerry's father, a Black G.I., had been part of that force. She is gone, as is Jerry's father, who made his living driving a cab following his wartime service. He had goodness in his bones and muted outrage at being a held-back Black man in the late 1950s.

"I could tell you that I did not love them enough at the time when loving was required, but what would be the point? I was a child lacking an understanding of what it meant to be a Negro, as African Americans were then called, in New York City or elsewhere.

"Whatever, I was still here after Jerry and Carmen and their parents were gone and feeling blessed with the discovery that new life had come to me in the form of Audrey. In this apartment of my childhood friend she offered me mad scribbles on drawing paper as testimony to her artistic accomplishment. The kind of girl I should have been with, I thought, in my deluded state, a girl more within the range of the normal, with none of the heavy emotional baggage that Sarah carried. A girl whom I could kiss, such intimacy rarely being part of my life with Sarah. But she stopped me on this night as I fumbled with her jeans. She was having her period. It wasn't a good time. No consideration on my part of her mental state or that danger might lurk, that her irate husband might appear at the door in a mayhem state of mind. No considerations of that kind at all.

"My desire for Audrey did not abate. Had I not kissed her? Had she not allowed that intimacy willingly and with enthusiasm? Was I not to believe that her loveliness could and would, under the right circumstances, be available to me? She had a last name, Eastbrook, that had the bounty of America in its sound. She had the goods. The jeans and black top she wore that night were holy. Her panties, red and which I only glimpsed, were worthy of a shrine.

"Some years before a prophet had shown up at the SoHo Bar. Truth was available if I would only pierce the veil of illusion, he said. I was ready to be dismissive, given the excess he was manifesting with his language. He told me from the vantage point of his assumed authority that while I thought I was drawn to the warm lights of the bar by women arrayed in their nocturnal finery and signaling their desire with made-up faces to the plaintive sound from the jukebox of Freddy Fender singing "Before the Next Teardrop Falls," it was truly the bottles on the shelf behind the bar that had the summoning power night after night to make a deadly claim on my being, and that I was drawn to them by the promise they could provide what God could not. He told me further that an abiding sense of inadequacy had led me to do battle with God the Father, that I was compelled to seek to slay him once and for all for the crime of having delivered me into this world with such limited gifts, that in short my life would be one sustained humiliation because while I had the desire for greatness I lacked the wherewithal for achieving it. He promised me that there would come a day when I would step over naked and beautiful women to get to the bottle and that, only on the unlikely chance of intervention by extreme Providence would I be spared the oblivion plunge and enter the realm of spirit and access the one who has all power to magnify me beyond the contracted state and render me defenseless against the simple truth that priceless gifts were my birthright and that, conditional on my relinquishment of the arena of fruitless striving, they would be revealed to me.

"That night I wound up not with God but in a deserted parking lot down by the Hudson River with a woman from the bar and made love with her in the back of an empty bread truck. She questioned me beforehand about the urgency of such carnal need, but I could only answer by having that desire speak for itself.

"And now, many years later, building on that desire to once again unzip Audrey's jeans and move the evening past its aborted conclusion of the week before, I positioned myself in an X-rated movie theater on One Hundredth Street and Broadway, a theater that had once shown Hollywood feature films but since had succumbed to the inevitability of porn ('Sex is at the bottom of everything, everything,' a voice from my past saying). And it was on the second floor of the theater that I now set up a vigil, having positioned myself at a window from which I stared out over the top of the marquee to One Hundred First Street and Broadway praying for a glimpse of Audrey so I could importune her for an opportunity to experience the oneness I was seeking. You might say she was my one last best hope for salvation, and because this longing had a life of its own that would not leave me, I had to try to see this thing to its conclusion.

"For companionship and fortification I had a pint bottle of blackberry-flavored brandy to keep my hope alive that with her period over, Audrey would want me in a fuller way. We wait for women, we wait on women, we do so until we do not have to go to them anymore and can instead inhabit the space of oneness that can only come from dying to the dream that has held us in its thrall.

"In the bathroom were men loitering over stained urinals, libidos revved by images on the dirt-flecked screen of copulation and fellatio. Women OK with having it done to them by the men with big things. As if the whole point of these films was to prove to myself that women could be willing partners. As if it was something I couldn't know, even from my own experience, that women had sexual appetites as well. Grotesque, that word *appetite,* in relation to sex. This is not the time to tell you of my worship of the giant dong, the horse cock of Johnny Holmes. And yet, why not? I could say to you my capacity for humiliation would approach its limit were I to confess to another inadequacy, not merely of mind but of body, and ask you this: what choice has a person but to flee to the bottle or to God when his overriding thought is that his own average endowment is simply another wound? Must we pretend we don't know the answer? Must we forever live in the lie of the body that is perishing even as we speak and that can never be anything but perishable.

"The world of pornography was not new to me. Have I told you about my mother, and the circumstances of my growing-up years, and of the magazines I would find her turning the pages of in the rooms she cleaned for men in the building where we lived? Have I mentioned how she would stare at the spreads and quickly hide the magazines away when I arrived? Sex as something illicit. Evidence of it to be shoved under pillows, under mattresses, under the beds in those rooms she let herself into with her master key. Later the magazines I stole from the luncheonette around the corner, slipping them into the centerfold of the *Daily News* and praying that Iggy, with those faded blue concentration camp numbers on his wrist, wouldn't catch and humiliate me and that I could just place a nickel on the counter and be off. And then, in my early twenties, when X-rated films began appearing in movie theaters, the overpowering impulse to visit those theaters once the thought entered my consciousness.

"Pornography. It was fitting that it should take me to a seedy theater, where I was alone among other lost souls, just as I was growing more and more alone with the bottle and drinking in the dark. I had gone on a separating journey from Sarah with sex, some years before placing a weekly ad in the *Village Voice* in which I described myself as a bisexual male seeking bisexual women. Good God, the letters and photos that poured in from all over the country to the post office box I had rented. What was such a thing about except some internal corrosion, aided by the daily diet pills and the considerable consumption of alcohol? What was setting up a life with Sarah that allowed me to cruise the bars at night, looking for any adventure that might come along? And my probing conversations with Sarah, seeking to ask without directly doing so if she were amenable to group sex and the swapping craze that had spread throughout the country? Those moments of truth when I saw, through a gesture or look or perhaps something she said, that such a thing was beyond her realm of comprehension and completely outside her moral universe, sent a chill through me because I was left briefly defenseless against the truth of just how sick I had become. I would see once again that she lived in one realm of existence—sane, normal, productive—while I was somewhere in the lower regions, trying to pretend that derangement was in fact health. Not only was her relationship to alcohol different from mine ("In my family people don't drink like that," she said matter-of-factly after one week of living together when she caught me cracking the seal on a bottle of scotch, knowing as she did I had no intention of sharing the contents) but that she didn't think like me either. And so I could only feel relief that I had been able to refrain from asking whether she wanted to step into that world of the unfettered libido among the living dead.

"The disappointment I felt on returning home that night without meeting up with Audrey would be hard to exaggerate. The stale sameness of my life seemed suffocating. My whole being cried out for variety and change. At the same time it occurred to me that new levels of insanity had been reached. I had fooled around with Sarah's girlfriend the week before, and now was returning home feeling thwarted that I couldn't do so again.

"Sarah was her usual model of artistic endeavor. As I walked in the door I heard the rattle of her brush against the can of turpentine before dabbing at the palette. A feeling of anger, driven by competitiveness, came over me. Her industry was a reminder that I had lost my way with my own work. In my little studio space were piles of manuscripts, the sight of which completely dismayed me. They represented repetition, sloppiness, stupidity, complete lack of structure, failure failure failure. The same material gone over and over in these separate manuscripts testimony to the reality that I was as promiscuous in my work as I was in my life, always going with momentary impulses, being pulled here and being pulled there by these whims. I loathed myself for not being able to bring projects to completion and envied those who could.

"In that moment of need for something to rescue me from myself and my life, I happened to see, on the bulletin board in my studio, a phone number written in pencil on a scrap of paper. No name, just the phone number, and yet I knew the name that attached to it, knew that the number stood alone not simply to avoid Sarah's curiosity but because there was zero risk of forgetting the woman who would be on the other end of the line, it being a given somehow that she was forever in my consciousness.

"I opened my desk drawer. There, at the bottom, buried under rubber bands and index cards and pens and pencils and old postcards and all manner of whatnot was the matchbook in which Isabel had written her name and number in her elegant hand. I kissed the matchbook cover, then pressed it against my forehead and sat there with my eyes closed.

"Some minutes passed before I reached for the phone. The radio was on in Sarah's studio. Surely she wouldn't hear me over the Bach cantata playing on the FM station. Though I told myself I must be mad to be contacting a married woman on a Saturday night, particularly someone of Isabel's stature—a courage born of desperation drove me forward. Yes, surely this was an idea whose time had come. After the second ring her velvet voice came through the line.

"It's me, Johan? From a couple of years ago?"

"I haven't forgotten. You're the writer."

I glanced into the studio and was reassured to see Sarah facing the easel with her back to me. "Sort of. I've been working on a story. Some magazine almost accepted it. Now I'm trying to revise it."

"I'd love to see it. Would you like to come over?"

"*Love. Like.* Was I drunker than I imagined? Was I hallucinating again, as I had been when I had showed up at the door of the prostitute a year before near Grand Central Terminal, expecting to find that rope-jumping editorial assistant from Pentacle Books? No, I was mildly but not insanely drunk. A door had opened. It was for me to walk through it or remain trapped forever.

"If you ask me how I could come and go so freely, I will tell you that self-righteous anger manifested in me on a frequent basis. As a child did I not often hear my mother say, 'I am not afraid of a little dirt' and 'Those women in their rooms with their leisurely lives. I work. Why can't they?' I heard these words she spoke about some of the tenants in the building that she and my aunt managed. I tell you that I heard them to be reminded of the power that words can have. And so, if judgment was part of her emotional makeup, in spite of her Christian bearings, was it not likely that I too should be infected with my own self-righteousness and someday come to use Sarah's financial resources against her, and in fact batter her with drunken complaints about having to show up for a job five days a week while she could devote most of her time to her art, her freelance design work requiring only a day or two every other week? Did she not owe me for all my hard work and sacrifice? Should I not be free to come and go as I needed to? Do not laugh at me for telling the truth, dear God. Do not ever do that. The consequences could be very, very severe.

"So when I said to Sarah that I wanted to visit the bookstore up at St. Mark's Place, she simply said fine. We are talking now about a woman who had suffered a serious breakdown and now survived on a daily regimen of psychiatric medications. This was a woman who could ruminate wildly. That a woman with her mental frailties should have given herself in marriage to a philanderer. More than once she had voiced her concern that people at the design studio were whispering about her behind her back. She had the sense that there were things they weren't telling her, and that Audrey was behaving strangely toward her.

"The wounds I inflicted on her were serious, or maybe her condition was predetermined and my conduct had done nothing or little to bring on her break. Maybe sleeping with her younger sister Lenore after Sarah had confided her fear of her to me is not a hanging crime and can be attributed to raging teenage hormones, as was my failed attempt to do the same with her older sister Claire. A woman was a door. Sooner or later you had to try to enter.

"Over the previous year or two, since taking that publishing job, a routine had established itself: show up for work, head for the liquor store afterward, go home, get drunk and pass out. The wild nights calling were fewer and farther between. Why drink in bars anymore when I drank too much and too fast and the prospects of meeting someone were slight? Why not just spend the night at home with the bottle? Alcohol had truly become an anesthetic. I was drinking now to turn off my mind and my feelings to the fact that I had lost my way and was a failure in most departments of my life, including writing, the one that mattered most. Basically, I was drinking for oblivion. The only difference between me and those unfortunates covered in filth on the rough streets of the Bowery, those with their hands out trying to scrape up enough for another pint of Thunderbird, was that I had a roof over my head, a job, and a wife. But living with Sarah could not entirely ease the loneliness. Sitting night after night at the dining table by the water heater, I would stare out the window at the honey locust tree in the backyard and watch the day slip into darkness. It was as if there was a party somewhere nearby, but my legs had grown too heavy to walk out and join it. There would be a pang of longing to connect and a sudden fear that I would sit alone for the rest of my life filling and refilling a glass. Life had gone in one direction and I had gone in another, or not gone anywhere at all. And then I would think, well, who wants that party anyway? I would drink such thoughts off my mind, as I would my failed manuscripts and my failed life.

"Often now I would combine alcohol and sleeping pills, not lethal barbiturates but over-the-counter sleep aids that I would wash down with the cheap sweet wine I poured into my glass from the half-gallon bottles purchased at the wines and spirits supermarket. The combination of barbiturates and alcohol would temporarily brighten my spirits. Empowered to mingle once again, I would fly across the street to the punk rock club where coiffed and pencil-thin musicians held center stage and the pot-bellied owner, a pasty-faced older man, walked about with a construction hat on his bald head. There I would impose myself with effusive chatter on kids obviously younger than I was who would quickly move away. These ventures into the nocturnal world beyond the loft would be short-lived. Within a half hour I would return home and crash into bed. The sole exception was the night a rocker with spiky, bleached blond hair took an interest in me sufficient that she walked me out of the midnight madness of the bar and deep into the East Village. Without her escort and safe haven I might have simply collapsed on the street, for the next morning I woke fully clothed and flat on my back on the floor of her railroad apartment with extreme cottonmouth and a brutal hangover.

"Oh, there was other lunacy of this kind, such as the time I imposed myself on a woman who showed only a modicum of interest in me at the same club and tore back across the street to the loft fully intent on grabbing some manuscripts off the shelf to impress upon her my worth only to have the sleep potion do its work before I could return.

"And yet, here I was, a man who depended entirely on an environment of soft lights and pretty bottles and loud music for what socializing I was able to do with complete strangers, only now I had a personal invitation to enter the home of someone of quality. Suddenly, I had an in.

"Although Isabel had given me the address, it didn't occur to me that it was a new one. I simply expected to find her living in the same townhouse elegance with a maid at her disposal. But if her residence had stayed the same in my mind, somehow her marital status hadn't. It was somehow understood that she was alone and that there would be no Philip there ready to pull his squash stunt or sting me with a calculated insult.

"Nothing is as powerful as being received by a beautiful woman, and that is what Isabel did for me on that night. Yes, there was surprise and even disappointment to see that the Perry Street address in that warren of West Village streets was not the privately owned building where I had first met her but a neglected edifice with paint peeling from the façade and rotted sashes. That being said, when I rang the buzzer and mounted the creaky stairs of the walkup and entered the apartment she now rented, a fever of sexual excitement obliterated any concern for what appeared to be her lesser circumstances. Only two hours before I had been in a seedy movie theater conducting a fruitless vigil for a young woman who had left me behind. Now I was with a woman who far surpassed her. The change in my fortunes amazed me.

"The apartment was a scene of clutter, books and magazines and papers scattered everywhere, as if control of her life somewhat eluded her. And yet there was nothing shabby about the place. A texture to her life was manifest in the piles of books and the sheet music atop the grand piano she had somehow fit into the space. Even more, it was the artwork all about, such as the painting on the mantelpiece: in reds and blues, a woman, distorted, staring timidly out a window. The painting had a quality of solitude to it. Yes, the painting was hers, she said, when I asked. This was no Audrey doing a poor imitation of Jackson Pollock with her mad dribbles on canvas.

"Not only was the townhouse gone but Philip had moved in with a male lover. There was no reproach or hurt in her voice as she told me. I imagined him to have the perfect life, from his point of view: a wife who would not divorce him no matter what he did and financial security through her ample resources. If a judgment formed in my mind, it was the result of not understanding that he was the the sort of man Isabel was looking for, a man who would not press in on her.

"From my stacks of failed manuscripts I had brought along the story. I had drawn from my childhood and the religious camp in the Catskills where I had been shipped for several summers, a camp owned and operated by Pentecostals fired up for God and endlessly sermonizing about his terrible wrath. The story was about prayer calls and speaking in tongues and the blossoming of preadolescent sexuality amid all this religious fervor. It was a story that had written me and in which I was emotionally invested, as it also captured the unbearable longing I would experience for my mother when I was away from her and how that homesickness fell away when we children fled the crude tabernacle and the fiery sermon one night and flocked to the meadow where we fell down upon each other, boys on girls, to experience what heaven in the here and now could be, and never mind the hereafter.

"In that long ago time girls like Sarah or Isabel were entirely beyond my station in life. Is it not an irony of sorts that on the other side of the mountain, away from those Ukrainian men and the peasant-like women who cooked and laundered and did the chores, there should be the Van Dine estate, a liberal paradise beyond my imagining when I first set foot on it? And does it not say something about the nature of life that Sarah, who once had been my Botticelli angel, now seemed more and more a weight on my existence, and that artistically brilliant Isabel should be the focus of my obsession? Would it surprise you that I reached out, with all the desperation of a drowning man, for her on that night?

"Isabel hadn't placed the second page of my story under the first before I touched her on the shoulder, then took her by the hand and led her into the bedroom. Her only protest was that first she should bathe, but there was no time for that, as there was no time for her to finish the story.

There had been other women. But because they came into my life in the dark of night and were gone before the light of day, none of them posed a threat to my relationship with Sarah. They existed as expressions of my anger at Sarah, the hurts I had received from Sarah, or simply my own unbridled hedonism when I was drinking. But Isabel was trouble, if you could apply the word "trouble" to a beautiful woman who allowed you into her bed.

"Beyond that force field of carnality that enveloped me, a quality of light had penetrated. More accurately, the light of Isabel had been in me ever since we had met, and now it had simply grown brighter through sharing her bed. Returning home that night, I could look with almost drunken pity at the scene along MacDougal and Bleecker Streets, midnight pleasure seekers pouring in and out of the noisy bars and cafés. I knew what it was to be such a searcher, and yet, for me, no more searching was required. I had found who I was looking for.

"When I called her from work the following Monday, she said, 'I loved your story.' Was anything more needed for the hook to be fully in than for an alcoholic man failing in his marriage and his work to be accepted creatively as well as physically by a beautiful and accomplished woman?

"An added sense of empowerment was derived from my job at the publishing company, ludicrous as that may sound, given that I was a thirty-year-old Steady Freddy office worker sitting at a desk eight hours a day and making under ten thousand dollars a year. But Isabel spoke in the language of excess in regard to my job. Words like "wonderful" and "fascinating" came from her mouth in regard to my employment. Her natural high spirits sent her into that zone.

"A pattern developed. At five p.m. I would leave work and take the D train downtown and bound upstairs, my progress halted only briefly by the spectacle of the run and gun athletes racing up and down the asphalt basketball court opposite the Waverly Theater in the warm spring weather.

"It was the dinner hour, and the smell of cooking came from the small kitchen. Isabel had a child to feed, little Mia toddling about the living room when I entered. In this atmosphere of mother-daughter intimacy I would sit and drink one vodka and orange juice after another. Generally at home I was content to get slowly bombed on a half-gallon of wine backed up by a six-pack of beer. But the screwdrivers were extraordinary, and I would virtually suction the glass empty.

"It was clear to me from the start that she was a good and attentive mother, and in my own way I was touched to watch her cut Mia's food into bite-size bits and feed her slowly. For an hour or two

I would just get steadily drunker as she attended to her daughter's needs.

"I became uncharacteristically sure of myself, and why wouldn't I, since Isabel offered no resistance. Did I ever hear her say, 'I will not have you in my house draining my vodka bottle and then tossing me into bed. I will not have you distracting me from the attention I need to give to my daughter. I will not subject her or me to your lunatic and drunken company'? No. What I heard her say was, 'I'm so glad you called. That was wonderful last night.'

"You can say I was deluded in believing another woman could rescue me from my unhappiness, and you would be right to a certain degree, but the fact remains that I had made a mistake in trying to build a life with Sarah. I had done so partly to appease her, that is, because I didn't have the courage to say no when the man of her dreams no longer wanted her and she came back to me many years before.

"I did not hide from Isabel that Sarah and I were still living together. It was not a matter concern for her. Though lonely, Isabel tolerated her husband living with a male lover for the simple reason that she needed the breathing space other men hadn't been able to give her; it was nothing less than a complete necessity.

A mysterious affliction had come over Sarah, I explained. It was as if a button in me had only to be pressed and the following prerecorded message began to play: Sarah had a severe breakdown in the first year of our living together in the Chinatown loft. Was it a developmental problem? Was it something in her brain chemistry? No one has the definitive answer. All we can tell you is that she has not been the same ever since, making her collapse an event of heartbreaking proportions, in that she has legendary abilities. Time and again have I beseeched Dr. Frodkey, Sarah's psychiatrist, to make her better, but his only remedy is the pharmacological solution of Mellaril and the like.

"The question, of course, is what on earth was Isabel to do with such information, given that I spoke of Sarah with such intensity and respect? 'Poor Sarah. Oh, how awful.' Such was her general response. She went where my words took her, to the sorrow gulch, where all a person can do is weep over what was and what is. What I heard was compassion with a sardonic ring to it, a slight mockery of the horror I was presenting her with. What I heard was Isabel calling me to her, to the living presence she was, for all these historical romps ever did was lead me to her bed, for which I was on fire.

"You have to understand what it means to be thin and beautiful and female in America, the way the fabric accommodates the curve of her body and paralyzes a man with desire so he can think of nothing else or eyes her graceful movements so each and every one is meaningful, from the holding of a cigarette between the index and the middle finger or the slow and lithesome manner in which she crosses a room, or the silkiness of her voice."When you are lingering in bed with another woman and the understanding is present that you will be back, then you are in the process of creating something more than nebulous relationship. Was it not enough that Sarah was hearing whispers at the design studio to intensify her anxiety? Now I was bringing something more tangible into the loft, having, as I did, the scent of Isabel upon me and the power of her effect on my spirit. This was not Audrey of the diminishing return, Audrey who had vanished after first contact. This was Isabel with the staying power of one who has experienced deeply the loneliness of a Saturday night.

"As it was, the innuendo at the design studio finally drove Sarah away. She simply could not abide the assailing thoughts she was having. She cried bitterly at this defeat. She didn't want to be a shut-in, but the voices in her head had become too strong to silence. She had to get out or go crazy.

"I was disappointed if not crushed. I was, as I have said, making very little as an editorial assistant. Publishing was still seen as a bluestocking industry, staffed with upper class women who screwed up the books by not depositing their paychecks. But noblesse oblige was not an operating factor in my presence at the company, not with rent to be paid and the prospect of the street looming. And so we did what we always did, or what Sarah did. She turned to her parents. You can be sure they were not thrilled to have their twenty-six-year-old daughter requesting that they underwrite not only her expensive therapy but also provide for daily living expenses.

"A word here about her parents. While Peter had written several books and a number of scholarly articles, he had never shown his face before a classroom, as Sarah's mother hoped he would. He was complicated in his arguments against teaching as a profession for himself, but the bottom line was that the family was forced to depend solely on the inheritance Sarah's mother had received. Perhaps since Peter had been unable to enter the workplace, Sarah's parents felt they had no choice but to send her a monthly check. Still, Sarah's expenses were an emotional if not financial burden for them. I had no way to think about any of these matters except to drink, and that is what I did.

"The erratic pattern of my nights continued. No longer could Sarah count on me coming home to our simple dinners, after which she would return to her studio for an evening of more work while I drained the bottles of wine I had brought in with me. The truth was I was no more present those evenings when I sat with her than when I failed to come home. And on those evenings that I was not home my sustained absence was viscerally felt by her. A woman knows when she has been abandoned, as does a man. I would return soused and hours late and seek to bum's rush her suspicion out the door with hysterical and horseshit messaging: 'The company is in crisis…firefights have broken out left and right…Even as I speak is Mr. Marg holed up in his office fighting for his life…an emergency situation of the most serious nature has developed…please, please don't press me for details in this, my darkest hour.' Following such babble I would climb the ladder and pass out in the loft bed.

"We aren't born to bear up under the burden of such lies. We aren't born to take farm-fresh eggs from the refrigerator and gently lob them against the wall, one after another, as a cruel ploy to completely undo the one we are supposed to love so she cannot even begin her line of inquiry to gain a fuller account of our doings.

"The light of my mother's love that had become the light of Sarah's love had now become the light of Isabel's love, and if you say a light is a light and love is love, you will be mistaken, for Sarah knew which light was hers and which wasn't. The full disclosure option did not apply where Sarah was concerned. Yes, I had rampaged through her life, but it was not for me to add to her pain with brutal honesty. Such was my specious reasoning.

"Augusta, the woman who had introduced me to Isabel, was throwing a party. The main event was to be Augusta writing a poem to 'Maggie,' as sung by Rod Stewart. Augusta had written her best poems to the songs of Rod Stewart, she said. Rod Stewart captured the energy and vision of her generation, she said. Rod Stewart prompted words and images to flow from her pen, she said. I tried to stay out of the matter of Augusta's poetry. After all, I was floundering in my own failure gulch. The thing is that Augusta deserves some mention, for she was a type. When I say type, I mean that she was waiting. Her mother had died, and a stepmother had come along to occupy her father's time, a worrisome development in the mind of Augusta, for this was a classically wicked stepmother with an agenda of consolidation of all the family's considerable assets into her sphere of control. Augusta suspected that this stepmother was poisoning the mind of her father against her so Augusta wouldn't ever see a dime of her inheritance. Already, she had managed to reduce the flow of trust fund money into Augusta's account. This stepmother had her insidious ways and was, to use Augusta's words, 'simply appalling.'

"The legions of the lost are found where they are. They are present and accounted for in all precincts of this earth. Like had found like, those with special claims flocking to their brethren. As to a cathedral, those blessed only with feebleness had retreated to the realm of art. I exempt Sarah and Isabel here with their high dedication to their work.

"There is no need to tell you every detail of that party. It is ground I have gone over before. The Foxwellings were there, and the Geedermeisters, and the Swalebirches and the Cummings-Bodkins, both Hale and Heletha. Luminaries of lunacy from both the East and West Side showed their idiotic faces. They came in capes and slinky dresses and pants many sizes too big and held forth as if their lives were grander than they were. The truth is that I didn't have an eye or a mind for most of them.

"It takes shallowness to know shallowness, as it takes entitlement to know entitlement. Augusta was too painful for me to contemplate soberly, with her speech full of hyperbole and her proneness to flattery. You were great because she saw herself as great, except when she didn't.

"And so the guests gathered, and we, Sarah and I, were among them. Augusta invited Isabel as well, her presence at the party given our secret liaison adding high-risk excitement. Perhaps the secret might have maintained itself, but I had badgered Sarah to stop off with me en route for just one at the White Horse Tavern over on Hudson Street. A true paddy boy, all in black and with a thick brogue, was working the stick behind the bar, and the scotch he served was smooth going down my throat. It was for Sarah to pull me away after the fourth.

"I remember Isabel standing against a wall masking her fear with a smile as I introduced her to Sarah. Vaguely do I recall chatting with a woman and suggesting that we go up to the roof and get naked under the full moon and her slowly backing away from me. Unanticipated was the sight of a red-haired hound attaching himself to Isabel and the mounting anxiety the thought of her leaving with him unleashed in me. How cruel if I should lose Isabel right before my eyes. Driven by my thirst and also by fear, I took up where I had left off at the White Horse.

Much of the remainder of the evening was a blur. Yes, the song "Maggie" came on, and yes, Augusta began to compose at her typewriter, but if the muse had truly visited her on that evening I could not say, for even as her fingers pounded the keys to the sound of Rod Stewart's raspy voice, I was bound down the stairs with not only Sarah but Isabel. I do recall skipping along the street holding their hands, but there all memory leaves me until the morning, when I awoke in familiar surroundings not my own with Sarah beside me. Her words had a blunt force. 'Bastard. You went like a homing pigeon for her bed. You complete bastard.'

"What is this thing called love that drove me into Isabel's bed and that required Sarah to lie alongside me, fully clothed, as Isabel herself lay through the night on her living room sofa? Where was the lunacy commission that it did not arrange for my detention on the spot? Was this my way of telling Sarah without telling her what I had been about and where I hoped to go?

"On that morning I made no attempts at denial. I merely stared in despair at the radiator in the corner of the room with a certain longing for the innocence of inanimate objects. Hearing the sweet patter of baby Mia in the living room, I sensed the jig was truly up, for when I emerged she declared brightly, 'Momma, Johan. Johan.'"

"Sarah, naturally, reported the chaos to Dr. Frodkey. He said I should come with Sarah to her next session. The office was well appointed with framed degrees on the wall and a view looking out on Fifth Avenue and Central Park. He was a bull of a man, with a fullback's thighs. Clearly, in the years she had been seeing him as a patient, he had taken a shine to Sarah, for when he turned to me, it was with no great regard. I can only assume he had been receiving a weekly briefing about my behavior. And so it was a rough fifty-minute hour. Basically, he set aside the understanding mode of the therapist and went after me with a prosecutor's zeal, pressing me to come clean, that is, to confess that Isabel and I had been a party to coitus. After a time I could no longer deny him the pleasure of confirming the judgment he had formed, and when I acknowledged Sarah's suspicion to be true, she burst into tears, saying, 'You have no idea how much I have loved you.' Seeing her weep as she did, he was moved to say to me, 'You should get down on your hands and knees and beg her forgiveness. And yet you display not one sign of contrition. Not one sign.'

"He was right, of course. Dr. Frodkey's consternated manner had elicited defiance in me, and I had likewise steeled myself against Sarah's emotional display, as if my life depended on not succumbing to guilt. I had nothing to say about my alleged cruelty. The good doctor had moved me not one step closer to contrition, for how can you apologize for love of a woman, warped as it might be, and even if she, Isabel, wasn't my wife? I was not a brave man. That should be obvious. But I did have the quality of endurance, living through, as I did, one humiliation after another. Everyone has an innate desire for consolidation, for oneness. No one chooses to be pulled apart. The thing I had to recognize was the force and the brutality of love in its carnal manifestation, moving me slowly and painfully out of one place and into another. The installation was to take years, of course, cohabitation with Isabel being five years in the future.

"The disapproval of Dr. Frodkey was insufficient to make me toe the line. Several days passed in which my impulse to run to Isabel was held in check, but then the emotional fallout from the calamity began to lessen. Sarah hadn't died. She was still working away in her studio, having relinquished all claims the outside world sought to make on her. And I hadn't died either. Fear is a powerful agent. Now it was not only thoughts of pleasure that began to turn my thoughts more and more to Isabel but also fear that I might lose her if I did not act. The face of the red-haired satyr was right there in my consciousness as a torment. There was no escaping from the awareness of his lecherous intent. I had to get to Isabel first. I had to solidify my standing with her. The scales were quickly and dangerously tipping. My fear of losing Isabel soon outweighed any further harm I might cause Sarah. And so, after this brief lull, I resumed my cross-town runs.

"When I arrived at her door, Isabel had company. But the imperiousness of my urge for her, fueled by the courage I gained from having consumed a half-gallon of wine, caused me to do the

Stanley Kowalski thing, leading her into the bedroom after ordering the man to leave. Fearful of confrontations with men as I am, I must have sensed her guest was gentle and would not oppose me with a brutal physical action that would leave me bleeding and senseless.

"But after a few such forays, another shift occurred. Dr. Frodkey's censorious words and the toll of my lying and cheating caught up with me. Coming to one morning from my blotto state of the night before, I realized that this affair, for lack of a better word, could not go on. The alcohol could no longer numb the pain my betrayal of Sarah was causing. Somehow I made the decision that I would have to let go of Isabel; otherwise I simply might not survive. There was no protest on her part when I called her from a phone booth down the block. She too recognized the necessity to terminate the involvement. I had to accept that things were as they were. I felt sadness but also relief.

"A week or so later I was down at the Hong Fat restaurant on Bayard Street in Chinatown ordering takeout, General Tso's chicken for Sarah and moo goo gai pan for myself. We're talking here about early Saturday afternoon, not the evening or the midnight hour or beyond, when forces for my demise gather strength and urge me forward. The sun was out and the streets were packed with shoppers drawn to the sidewalk markets: all manner of fish on beds of ice and a bright array of produce. You had the sense of community and industry. There was safety on these bustling streets, some mammoth intelligence free of the clamoring Western ego. I couldn't really say why certain places are holy, but Chinatown was one of them for me.

Actually, I was back in childhood, with imperturbable Charlie Chan in his white suit in a world not quite my own solving the mystery of the day with the assistance of his ineffectual but well-meaning son. It was a world in which some degree of tranquil order could reign. I was safe from myself and from the world I lived in with the peerless one. Charlie Chan was the room I could go to where no one could find me. Do you understand? Do you?

"Suddenly, on what had been a peaceful afternoon, a thought, not quite slight enough to ignore, came to me. Was it possible? No. Absurd. Such a thing could never have happened. No way. How could it have? But if it didn't, how was it that the afternoon had come without a morning to precede it? As I stared into the open kitchen of Hong Fat and watched the white-clad chefs among their big pots and skillets, the twinge of doubt grew.

"The restaurant had a pay phone in the entranceway, the availability of which I took as a sign of its readiness to relieve me of the distress my mind was manufacturing. As if she had been waiting for my call, Isabel picked up the receiver on the first ring. All I wanted from her was one simple word. That was all. Would it be too much to ask that she just say no, as in 'No, of course you weren't over here earlier today. What a silly notion.' But she had no such word or words of comfort for me. In a voice noticeable for its absence of warmth, I heard her say, 'Yes, you were here, and do not ever come in such a state again.'

"I did not ask Isabel what I had done. I was afraid to know. I walked back slowly along the Bowery, holding fast to the takeout bag. The boulevard had its usual mix of human misery and industry, bums trying to scrounge up money for another taste in front of restaurant supply stores and other small businesses. Along the way I passed the Salvation Army residence below Houston Street. Some men were milling about outside, sobered up men of middle age with time on their hands. You somehow knew they didn't have much more than the clothes they wore and the cigarettes they smoked and the rooms they had been given. Men without women. I shuddered seeing them and moved on.

"There had been blackouts before, but this one seemed of a different order. It was the fact that my visit to Isabel must have occurred sometime in the morning, not after dark, that most devastated me. Had I gotten up during the night and begun to drink? Or had I been drinking straight through the night and showed up at her door after daylight? I couldn't remember a thing. For the first time, I was truly afraid of what I might do while in such a state. Weren't there stories of men rotting in prison cells for horrendous crimes they had committed while soused? Didn't I have a measure of recklessness and bad judgment, if not real violence, in me, given the gun incident of the year before? How crushing to realize I was completely out of control, at least when I drank, and that it was a given I would drink again.

"Have you ever run into a tree or a lamppost at full speed while looking away? Have you known the pain of such a thing? On my next visit to Isabel—it did come, oh yes it did—a few days later, when I was *feeling better,* I rang and rang her downstairs bell. Though the light was on in her window, there came no response. Still, I can report that no frustration of a high order took me over. The rumination mill did not have the chance to go into full operation before I heard that buzzer release the front door lock so I could climb the stairs to paradise.

Have you ever been met at the door by a lover in a silk camisole, her exquisitely wrought knees and calves and bare feet on display? Have you ever met her looking so kissable? Has the very sight of your beloved summoned levels of desire you didn't know were possible? I thought in my delirium that we were in deeper sync than ever, that having anticipated my arrival, she had simply prepared for bedroom ways. But she did not receive me into her apartment, let alone her bed. 'I have company,' she said. If there was feminine softness in her appearance, her words had blunt force. She had quickly checked my aggression; she saw my fear, and saw too the look of hurt and shock when, in answer to my question as to whom she might be entertaining, the red-haired man emerged and stood bare-chested behind her to provide the silent answer on his own. Have you ever seen a satyr's face? Have you ever seen it tinged with red and his hair and beard on fire? Do you know what it means to have him slobbering on your beloved's flesh? Do you want me to say I smote him with my fists or my words? Do you want me to say that I resorted to the arsenal of primal man?

"The truth is as you know it already, of course. I did nothing but reel back into the street from which I had come. If fear is a negative form of prayer and your fear comes true, then what is there to do but take flight? Isabel knew exactly what she was doing when she took up with the red-haired beast. She knew with the coldness of an executioner that she had killed my mad streaking to her door so very dead. She knew that it was one thing for me to triumph over a husband who had left her but another to deal with a sex machine at the height of his lewdness.

"The end came that holiday season in December 1978. Soreness gripped me. I couldn't get it together to buy gifts for Sarah and my family. Never mind that I was showing up to work in wrinkled shirts with dirty collars as drinking interfered with my ability to do laundry. Never mind that the whole quality of my life had been impaired. It was the fact that I had done no holiday shopping or even sent any Christmas cards. A measure of control was important to me, and yet I saw that I had none, and this awareness led to intense anger.

"In this time clothes or material possessions, in general, held no great interest for me. More and more the bottle seemed to take care of my needs. There was one great exception. I would stare in store windows at typewriters on display the way another man might spend time in automobile showrooms gazing at the newest models. For some reason my spirits would brighten if I saw an old Olivetti 32 portable with the distinctive square keys and sleek green metal body or an even older black portable L. C. Smith machine. The sight of these machines brought me to a fever pitch. They were what I needed to make my life all right and more than all right. I suppose, in a way, they were like all those bottles I had drained in the course of years. I imbued them with magical properties, believing they could do something for me that I could not do for myself.

"We are talking of a time that is no more, of course, when the IBM Selectric, with its many golf ball elements, was state-of-the-art office equipment available to only the chosen few in most offices. Even then, before the widespread advent of the computer, the burden of my attachment to the past was on me, a weight that would not easily allow me to move forward into the bright light of the current day.

"There was this one store on my way to work. As I came to it, an almost unbearable pain of longing would grip me and only intensify as I stood staring into the store window, a longing unmitigated by the awareness that it was incommensurate with the happiness any purchase of another typewriter would bring. And though I did not weep or tremble so even the unfocused eye would see, yet the inward response was acute. Beyond this world of forms and discrete parts there is the one who, when we find him or her or it and plug into the dynamo where all power is to be found, dispels the affliction, that ceaseless hunger for the object that cannot satisfy and never could satisfy. But I did not know you then. I had no understanding of you then. As I had shunned my father, so was it necessary to shun you, who could only be in his image.

"In that store window was a Smith-Corona electric typewriter, the Secretarial Coronamatic. In two-tone brown, it showed itself as the model of attractive and efficient design. And was it ever my good fortune that I could step inside the store and type away on the machine on display. How clear the letters appeared on the page. How error-free my typing as my fingers struck the big keys. But I could not take the plunge. Questions of a disturbing kind had to be answered. How would the machine fit in with the two manual typewriters I already owned? Was I supposed to spurn them for this newer purchase? Wouldn't that be highly unethical and conspicuously wasteful, given the fact that they still had a substantial amount of writing life in them? And if their needs had to be satisfied lest they feel wounded by neglect, wouldn't it look odd to type part of a manuscript on one machine and another part on a second and even third? And suppose Smith-Corona went bust? What would I do for new replacement parts or new cartridges? In this way, by making myself a slave to absolute certainty into eternity, did I hold myself back. My whole life a kind of dithering dance.

"It happened that this particular store was owned by a young Asian man with a capacity for insight. At first he was nervously solicitous as I typed at the display model while standing up. Could he help me? Did I know that the store was having a special sale? But he was not oppressive in his bid for my business. When I told him that I was still *simply looking,* he withdrew graciously. *How can you buy a typewriter when you haven't even bought your wife a wedding ring?* Lost to the bottle, lost to an obsession for typewriters, lost to myself.

"My days came to feel incomplete unless I visited the store on my way to work. And so I would stare at my beloved Smith-Corona Coronamatic and imagine that I was alone and away from this world I did not truly know how to be a part of, and then I would find it was not enough to just stand and gaze through the window but that I had to go in and actually be able to touch it, and yet I also sensed that such frequent appearances would perhaps not sit well with the owner, given the powers of perception I ascribed to him. And, to be honest, I was a collaborator, an aid to his perception, because before he even saw me as I saw myself, that is, saw me as enfeebled and incapable of doing, saw me in the totality of my sickness, I saw myself in this light. Because the man was able to do one thing I could not do and have trouble with to this day: he could discard what was not useful to him and move on. Sorrow and loss were not part of his nature. There was nothing for him to get back to. Information was there at his disposal as to who was in his store and he shuddered with disgust *and knew to move on to those who were serious in their intent.* In that moment you can be very sure that he reflected my illness back to me.

"I haven't told you of the times I sequestered myself in unused offices at Pentacle Books and tapped away on typewriters that caught my fancy there as well; how, that is, I did not stay faithful to the Smith-Corona Coronamatic but fell in love with a full-size electric office machine made by Olympia or the Royal and Remington models and other such machines. And even though the perceptive eye of the typewriter store man was not upon me in the office setting, my feeling at the time was that these were stolen moments when my illness was on full display for those who cared to see.

"How to make things fit. How to organize an unorganized life. How to keep things together that had always been separate. How to assemble the parts. How to secure eternity from a manufactured good.

"Dr. Reiner, my therapist, had it all: Yale, medical school, military service, the burdens as well as the joy of fatherhood, head of a large hospital department, a growing psychotherapy practice. He saw the smallness of my own life. I had come to him three years before in the throes of a crisis. For two years prior to that I had been relying on diet pills during the day and drinking at night. *All this explanation. What purpose does it serve?* A kind of madness came over me, obsessive fantasies in which, to my horror, I saw a knife plunging into Sarah's chest or into my own. The pills and the alcohol had rendered me out of touch with myself. No grief when my father died or when the bloated corpse of my sister Naomi was found floating in the East River by a police patrol boat. Dr. Reiner was there for me. Is that not the hideous expression now in vogue, as spoken by those who are there for no one, not even themselves?

"At first Dr. Reiner had believed in me as a writer, but after a while he saw that I was going nowhere. You can tell when a person loses faith in you and is no longer invested in your sense of yourself as being special. He gave me the support with which I could find *gainful employment,* for I was approaching financial destitution by the time I arrived at his office door.

"And so, that holiday season, probably weeks after having been abandoned by Isabel, I called Dr. Reiner and left that brutal message about firing a bullet into his brain on his answering machine. I then hung up and drank my wine. A feeling of peace came over me. I was not alone in the universe. Someone—Dr. Reiner—would now be coming. Attention would have to be paid to the one he no longer loved.

"If I have never told you this before, as a child I was expelled from grammar school, and even if it explains nothing, I feel obliged to present this incident. We are always doing that, aren't we, seeking to shed light on the present by referencing the past? What is this proprietary attachment to all that has gone before, as if we have accumulated some vast treasure that is to be examined at length? My whole life has been driven by this need to discuss my past. I cannot have a conversation without it coming up. Even in childhood I believed I had a story, if only a story informed by self-pity over what I perceived to be my deprived circumstances in life.

"I was in the sixth grade at an Episcopal school, which my brother Luke and my youngest sister Leah also attended. It was housed in a former mansion on Riverside Drive, a gloomy building neglected for years before being renovated. But expansion is the way of the world. Everyone has an idea on how to grow, and the Reverend Mother *her face I could not see apart from the habit that framed it* was no different. In any case, I stepped into the boys' bathroom on the second floor one afternoon in early spring. My schoolmates Billy Bruce and Johnny Joe stood inside as if awaiting me, and just so you know that I had found myself in the realm of the truly American. These were boys with agile minds and respectable Riverside Drive homes and with fathers who walked with one hand in the pants pocket of their suits, as was the corporate style back then. *Punish them with your disdain, Johan. And punish yourself even more.* I had seen their homes and been astonished by the color-coordinated furnishings and plush carpeting and complicated window dressings. All we had, by comparison, was linoleum laid down in the living room and a bed for a sofa and the chaos of clutter everywhere. *'If only I had the time we would have such a beautiful home' So my mother spoke. Did you know my mother? Did you ever see her walk the face of the earth?* We had a Manootdjian home, a home that befit our name and which I was ashamed to allow Billy Bruce and

Johnny Joe to enter. But my mother *I know you knew her. I know it* was not infected with this same shame; she had her protection in you from it. *When did she come to you? Was it when I was not looking?* And so when Billy Bruce and Johnny Joe came knocking at my door one school day morning as the tandem force they sought to be, my mother was there and responded in the way that you would have her respond, that is, as if she had no secrets to conceal. And why would she? She was not invested in the material world. She did not see the smallness of the hearts of my so-called friends and the machinery of judgment with which they were equipped. She did not see their contracted states or the malice in their smiles as, with their heads inside the door, they assessed the territory where I lived sufficient to confirm that they were exalted above me by virtue of their domiciles.

"You know what happened next. Having seen the squalor of my home relative to theirs, that day Johnny Joe and Billy Bruce noised it about the school that Johan Manootdjian lived in a *pigsty,* a word some of the other kids were to taunt me with. So that, already at that age, I was put in my place and learned what I have continued to learn ever since, that there exist a class of people I do not belong with. You it is who knows the savagery of self-judgment, how exquisitely delicious it has been for my whole life to feel cast aside *so I can bathe myself in the pity that no one else will provide me with.* Oh, I could make forays into their world, but it was understood that I lacked both the social standing or the requisite abilities to interact on an equal footing. I accepted, in the way that people should, that defeat is final. Too much is made of upward mobility in this country. If you are a dog, you should stay a dog. If you are stupid and you come from a shabby home, then let the verdict stand as to who you are. Go into the defeat posture and spend your days there. A person must accept his *station* in life. All my life have I been aware of this station in life to which I was assigned by birth and congenital limitation. Exhortations to the contrary will do a person no good. Do not make noise about your failure. Do not pretend it could have been otherwise. Just accept it, Johan Manootdjian. So I have told myself since childhood. It is painful to see this contrary state of non-acceptance so rife in the land. It is imperative that we recognize our superiors. Because without such acceptance, a person tends to cast blame and live his life in the envy key, and then trouble of a violent nature is bound to result.

"I offer the above to you not as a definitive and final statement of belief but as an example of the contracted cast of mind that would have us accept that we are lackluster stars invisible to the rest of a shunning universe. Without you that is the state of mind I must live in. My soul doth magnify the Lord, but truly it is you who magnifies me, providing the intelligence needed for my daily bread. And it is you I could not find back then but only your *faux opposite*, this thing called fear.

"My encounter with Johnny Joe and Billy Bruce was my encounter with society at large. Their presence shocked me. Opening the door and seeing them in the boys' bathroom, I recognized immediately that I could not step forward without an annihilation of extraordinary proportions taking place. The smiles of unspoken complicity that showed on their faces were arrived at without so much as a glance at each other. They were in perfect accord that someone beneath them was in their midst to sport with as they would. On both their faces was written large the word they would use as a descriptor of my family's apartment and surely another equally devastating as to the totality of my mind and being.

"With such a formidable alliance before me, I had no choice but to deflect attention in the only way I knew how. I *acted out,* as we say today. Though it was a cool spring day, the window was open halfway, and rolls of toilet paper were stacked on a nearby table. Down below I saw the nuns in their black robes and the white interiors of their habits walking double file like school kids and living in the embrace of their own goodness. It can seem that way with some religions, can it not, the faithful driven by dread to practice the sad rituals of perfection-seeking children.

"When I tossed the rolls, it was not with any idea of rebelling, though many were the Saturdays when, in compliance with the punitive norms of the nuns, I would show up for the janitorial duties my three weekly demerits warranted. Yes, dear God, I had heard the words 'more elbow grease' and 'You missed a spot over there' from the hovering nuns and yet, to my conscious mind, regarded them not as adversaries but saw them simply as *frozen white in the face of you and devoid of the blood that makes for human warmth.* I was not so much going against the nuns as symbols of authority with these objects for the anuses of the *young and old;* rather, I was seeking to protect myself from the merciless gaze of Johnny Joe and Billy Bruce, suggesting a state of high knowingness as to who I truly was. I did not mean for treachery to be in play. I did not even mean to bounce the rolls off their habits, to go upside their heads, forcing them to look up in stupefied wonder at what *God in his wrath was inflicting on them now.*

"Let me not say a single word more about the incident, except to note the following: intention is not always a conscious activity of the mind. The nuns came, a flock of them, and sequestered me in a room where, alone, I stared out another window, this one with a view down to the main staircase below and Riverside Park beyond and the Hudson River beyond that. When my time in the room dragged on, I had the sense of something about to happen, though I had no idea what. Then I looked and saw that those steps, which had been empty of people, were now being climbed by my mother. Slowly, given her age—she would have been fifty-four at the time —she made her way to the top. She wore a man's shoe and rubber support stockings for her varicose veins. She had ailments of which she would not speak and burdens that were large, and her slow step spoke of her careworn ways.

"The Reverend Mother, the headmistress, it was who had called my mother to the school. In a private meeting she explained the incident that had occurred. It could not be permissible for any student to hurl objects at the nuns, even a soft object such as a roll of toilet paper that could do no real physical harm, the Reverend Mother said. And it wasn't an isolated incident but part of a progression that marked my unfitness for that particular school. Hadn't I been a disciplinary problem all along, throwing pieces of chalk at classmates and the nuns themselves during classes? And hadn't I, on school outings, instigated my school chums to run free of our teachers? And hadn't there been that incident back in third grade when I surprised poor Jill Johnson with the unwelcome kiss I planted on her cheek, a girl whom I dared not so much as say a word to? Were these not instances of an impulsive unruliness which, if not checked, would lead to significant trouble some day? And it wasn't as if redeeming factors were to be found in my scholastic performance. Was I not bringing up the rear of every class, whether it was math or Latin or French or the simplicities of plain English? Had I not failed completely to comprehend the mysterious *pi* or hic haec hoc or the plusque parfait? And so, having laid out these and other facts, the Reverend Mother resolved that it was time for this chapter of my life to come to an end.

"With some sadness my mother must have heard these words from the Reverend Mother *her liver-spotted hands her unsmiling face the nightmare vision of what she might look like with her headdress removed.* I was supposed to be my mother's shining star. Was it not for me to make up for all the pain and suffering and intense disappointment my older siblings had brought to her life? Was I not to make up for my very much older sister Rachel, who had pushed her backward into the Christmas tree when all Mother sought to do was welcome her daughter home from college with open arms? Was I not to make up for my oldest sister, Hannah, who, though now in her late twenties, had never left home? And what about Naomi, my middle sister, and the suicide watch that had to be applied for her life to be ongoing? And must we speak of my older brother Luke, and the failure path he wandered? In any case, here I was, at age eleven, establishing a failure path of my own.

"The truth is that an oppression existed beyond the ability of my mind to put words to. Perhaps the assaulting action that I took was not simply to distract Billy Bruce and Johnny Joe but to secure a degree of clarity in my life so order could begin to provide some meaning to my days. The fact was that I had lost the ability to see. Day after day it was women dominating me, scolding me, judging me. Who were these creatures who covered their bodies in black to protect the whiteness of their souls? Who were these women for whom I had to be perfect and for whom I could not ever be perfect? What choice did I have but to remove myself from an environment in which I could not win and in which I was never supposed to win in the first place?

"I don't know anything, dear God. In my more lucid moments I understand this. I know only that beyond the mind, beyond the intellect, there is you, and that I sit in silence for periods of the day seeking to effect that contact. And then, of course, lacking sufficient mental discipline, I come back to this, the past. Was it you who made me this way, or did I do it to myself?

"And so my mother led me away by the hand down those same steps I had watched her slowly mount. We walked quietly the few blocks to the building where my family lived. My mother was a busy woman. It was not an easy thing for her to leave her work. We can discuss her job and the ramifications of it another time, but for now let me simply say that she did not scold me or hurl the word 'expulsion' in my face.

"The point here is that, as the toilet paper I hurled those many years ago in childhood was a cry for help, so too was the insane message I left for Dr. Reiner on his answering machine many years later. A prayer can be made anywhere, whether in a former mansion housing an Episcopal school or in a Bowery loft. Dr. Reiner was fully understanding of the power of prayer. He understood that he was being importuned. He did not call the riot police or the National Guard when he heard my threat. Instead he simply used his strong powers of inquiry to arrive at a truth he already knew. 'What was that message you left me the other day all about?' he asked. 'I was upset. I couldn't get it together to buy Christmas cards,' I replied. 'I got your Christmas card,' he said. And so I said, not believing my words even as I spoke them, 'I saw a typewriter in a store window and was upset because I didn't have the money to buy it.' And not even the Smith-Corona Coronamatic but an old L. C. Smith portable. All the nights I could have spent with that machine in perfect happiness—admiring it, stroking it, talking to it. 'You don't need a new typewriter. You need a new life.' That is what Dr. Reiner replied on that day.

"I didn't know that Dr. Reiner's words would bring me close to you, dear God. I didn't know that by threatening to kill a surrogate father I would find a real one. I didn't know."

Chapter 20

A windowless room. The resource room, they call it. A long conference table. Lurleen at the head of it. Hank Farquist to her right.

"Hi there, Johan. Have you been in hiding? Haven't seen you all day." Lurleen says.

Johan does not say that he saw her, right there in the assembly, sitting as close to the front as protocol would permit so she could place herself in the eye of the powerful. Why cause any more trouble? "Cubicle guys are always in hiding," he says.

Lurleen throws her head back and laughs uproariously, proving once again that laughter is part of her makeup and her resilience. Johan tries to imagine himself enjoying the sun out in Bryant Park on a glorious spring day. This will not be a good meeting. Lurleen is too confident. She is up to something.

Fiona Beasley has the look of a woman who has just been slapped or grossly affronted, like military brass captured by a rude enemy. She's not been the same since Miss Carmelli left. It is common knowledge that Miss Carmelli is the standard of excellence by which Fiona judges everyone else, and so, everyone else comes up short. And maybe she is right. Well, she can afford to look any way she wants. She is halfway out the door, and with a sizable nest egg too as a result of all the money she has socked away thanks to her rent control apartment. A woman who must have been stunning when she was young. But that attitude of haughty superiority. Johan suspects that she is one of the org dinosaurs whom Whitney McNair, the change master, has targeted, the kind of woman who is stuck in the "good old days" mentality. A woman with a big brain who has been reduced to getting up and getting to work and going home with salad from the buffet of a Korean deli and escaping into prime time TV. "She has an incredible knowledge of art, but you would never know it. There is some part of her that is dead, just dead," Ms. Carmelli once remarked about her personal factotum, who made a point of starting each workday by sitting in Ms. Carmelli's office to maintain her most favored status with the boss.

He thinks of those water towers he saw on the nearby rooftops the other week and the freedom he is afraid to claim. Office life. In the faces of time-ravaged souls like Fiona Beasley and Alice Piccoli with her drop-down tongue he gets to see his own slow progression off this mortal coil. *Male pale over fifty and stale.*

And Mary Terezzi is there, with her look of teenage peeve. And Blanche Givenchy, who keeps to herself.

"You were all witness to the extraordinary attack by Maeve Muldoon. I'm so sorry that you have to be exposed to such hostility. At the same time we must consider these attacks in their proper light. They are a clear sign of our progress and that the status quo is threatened. And as we have heard time and time again, the status quo can no longer be tolerated. It is time for the Publishing Department to assume its rightful place in the life of the organization, and I am here to ensure that we realize our full potential. So I want to thank all of you who stand with me in this struggle." Lurleen places her hand on Hank's shoulder. "And I don't have to tell you that this man, this man, has the team spirit that I am looking for. For all the contributions he has made, he will be moving from his current space to an office with a view. Are there are any questions or comments?"

The word "comments" rings loud in Johan's ears, as if Lurleen is saying, How do you like this apple, Mr. Big Mouth?

"I have one. Way to go, Hank," Alice Piccoli pipes up.

It is a busy afternoon for Hank as he trundles office materials into his new space, his keys and the coins he keeps in his pocket jangling as he shuttles back and forth past Johan's cubicle. From down the hall can be heard expressions of surprise and approval as visitors find him in his new workspace.

"Man, what did you do to rate this?" one such visitor remarks.

"Just lucky, I guess," Hank replies with a laugh.

The following morning, in the twelfth floor training room, Sally Mintner, pointer stick in hand, takes the staff through the electronic editing feature of the new Windows program, including tracking and reviewing. Sally is the young and rising star of Info and Tech. She is free and loose at the front of the room, a natural performer. She is like a big ray of sunshine, a golden daffodil.

Johan thinking, Sally Mintner is what America should be all about. A sense of unbounded joy surges through him in the presence of her manifest excellence. No sour attitude. No mediocrity. No muddled sentences. Just clarity and conviction in her strong, sweet voice.

A swivel head she has turned him into: the luster of her hair, the cheery spring combo of her tight white slacks and oversize yellow top.

Unlike technophobic Miss Carmelli and Blanche Givenchy, Lurleen once again has affirmed her embrace of the future. She would relieve the staff of the colored pencils with which, through the years, they have been marking manuscripts, for this more expeditious way of working on documents. But while the future may enthrall Lurleen, Sally Mintner clearly doesn't. No huge laughter pours forth from her now. Looking sweaty and uncomfortable, she sits in the first row, glaring with those small, hard eyes at wondrous, golden-skinned Sally. Perturbed Lurleen may be, but silent she isn't.

"Now suppose two people want to work on the same document, only they want to be able to tell who has made what changes?" Sally asks.

Lurleen's hand shoots up. No sense of herself as the director of the department. Lurleen the star pupil, eager to outshine her staff. "Very simple. The feature will automatically assign one color to one editor and another color to another editor. Or you can choose your own by going to the drop-down window."

"Very good, Lurleen," Sally says. Does he hear a trace of mockery in her voice, as if she has just recognized the teacher's pet in middle age?

But then there are other questions, and while Lurleen's hand flies up with the same eagerness to impress, Sally chooses to recognize others: Fiona Beasley, who responds as if the question is an affront to her intelligence; Mary Terezzi, who answers with cool precision; and Johan, whose delight at being recognized by Sally he does not try to hide, sensing, as he does, that it will cause the flame of jealousy to burn that much brighter in his temporarily subdued boss.

And so Lurleen calls another meeting. "It isn't really fair to the organization for instructors to be so ineffective. She gave me the impression that she wasn't really trying. We need people here at the org who embrace its mission and sense of purpose."

"She was carrying on like a performer, not an instructor. A real prima donna, and not such a donna at that," Alice Piccoli concurs.

"Well, she is young. We have to hope that she will learn." Lurleen sighs, as if to convey a charitable understanding of the folly of youth.

"She's a wonderful instructor," Johan hears himself saying. "The organization is lucky to have talented people like Sally."

It shouldn't be a crime to be attractive as well as intelligent. Lurleen is trying, in her sly way, to turn the group against Sally.

"This isn't Hollywood. This is a workplace. She wants to be a performer, let her strut her stuff on Broadway," Alice replies.

"Well, if Johan says so, then it must be so," Lurleen says, offering sarcasm in place of laughter.

There had been some open conflict with his previous boss, Miss Carmelli, but then he would often eventually offer an apology, not always because he had been wrong but because he couldn't handle the stress of legitimate disagreement. The apologies had come because the truth was too hard to bear: in some way, his employment with the org fostered the same kind of passive dependency as the men in his family—his father and Luke and himself—had shown. Let Mommy run the show. Let Mommy take care of everything. What did it matter if Miss Carmelli didn't consult him about cover designs for projects in his care or called meetings with sponsors about his projects to which he was not invited? What did it matter if his work life didn't add up to more than little copyediting assignments here and there? Why fight for more responsibility when he wasn't capable of handling it?

But he has come to a place with Lurleen where apology is somehow not the answer. It is a surprising and satisfying development that he doesn't always buckle when there is discord. He had thought, with the little he knew about his new way of life, that it was about acquiescence and acceptance. It hadn't occurred to him that the path might also require standing his ground. No amount of apology is going to erase the substantial differences he has with Lurleen, even as she exerts her influence, through a system of rewards and punishments, to induce others to toe her line.

Maybe he can use that sense of isolation within the department to grow stronger. Maybe he can further learn how to comfort himself. Maybe, in some way, the point of his workplace experience is to break free of the tyranny of other's expectations of him. Maybe he doesn't have to die if he doesn't please Mommy.

So what if the dynamic has changed. So what if vast forces are arrayed and aligned throughout the country to consolidate power and that Lurleen, in the microcosm of the org, is an agent of that plan. So what if Alice Piccoli and Hank Farquist, erstwhile underlings, are even now whispering gleefully in the next cubicle. Must he unleash liquidation forces so he can survive or is it not about time that he embrace the concept of dignity and strength?

Isabel,

Hank Farquist has my number. I am only all right with others so long as I am on top. When they assert themselves or win, I have no choice but to run away. Have I told you of that time back in childhood down on a baseball diamond in Riverside Park? Yes, there was, just beyond, the West Side Highway on which the cars of New York City were heading north and south, and just beyond that was the Hudson River, biding its time before rising and breaking from its pacific state. But let me not digress with cars or rivers or the hard, pebbly surface of the diamond itself, with the outfield grass worn away. Though my memory of the event is hazy, there was a baseball game in progress. Either I was called out at first or my team was losing or the perception of some other intolerable occurrence was ruling my consciousness. And so I walked off the field. I left, just as, some years later, I quit the high school varsity basketball team at halftime, simply hung back in the locker room as the rest of the team returned to the court, got dressed without showering, and disappeared, not because we were losing but because I was no longer the star, having been eclipsed by my rival and supposed best friend. I was in protest against the world, Isabel. That is the truth of it. I was rendered small with vindictiveness at a God who would put me here on this earth with so little—a flat head and a body bordering on emaciation, and born into a family that lacked the necessities for distinction. But that was then. Do I look like I am running now? Do you see me taking ball and glove and going home? Or rather, do you see me saying, Come on, Mr. Mensa Head, Mr. Chow Down, stuffing your pasty face with jumbo bags of Goober's from the Ninety-Nine Cents Store. Isabel, I am walking through some serious fear here. What, after all, can Hank do to me?

Is he, despite all his intelligence, the better editor? Clearly, Hank doesn't think so, judging from the obsequious way he still seeks me out about some copyediting matter or another. And whatever his natural gifts and his size, what is he but an old man? Does he not have the unmodulated voice of an ancient? Is a Post-It note not attached to his office phone with the admonition "Shh!!!" as a reminder that perhaps it isn't a good thing for the entire staff to overhear him in personal conversation? And he misses things he might not have five years before. Typos appear in his copy, perhaps as the result of failing eyesight. And is he not known to doze during the day even more than me? Is he, in fact, not often heard snoring in his chair? What, when I stand back, is Hank but a hurt, frightened, and angry man looking to slip into retirement, a man who feels cheated that fortune has not been kinder to him?

Imagine it this way. A cold, rainy weekend afternoon in some year past. That is the point, is it not? All the years now past. All the years but a blur, one indistinguishable from another. I am walking north on the east side of Broadway, the wet concrete heartless, the honey locust trees on Broadway heartless, the leaden clouds heartless. Thus am I walking north when a burly man steps out of the photocopy shop and runs into me, knocking me backward and almost off my feet from the force of the collision.

"Hello, Johan," the man, unrecognizable to me, says in a voice less than friendly, pointedly offering no acknowledgment, let alone apology, for the fact that he has just plowed into me. And is it not true that this failure of recognition is owing not merely to the watchman's cap pulled tightly over his head but also to the look of brimming hatred and envy so clearly communicated in his malign smile, so out of keeping with the amiable, obliging nature the man showed back at the office. All elements of our malignity must sooner or later be drawn forth, like iron filings to a magnet. They must be definitely gathered and collected.

"Hank?" For what could I offer to this being of implacable enmity but a tentative identification?

"Happy to see me, Johan?"

Though it was only a moment in time, the incident must remain in my consciousness as an example of the peril we face in walking upon this earth. There are those with smiling faces who do not wish us well, those who would take what it is that we possess, as if it is their birthright.

"So how are you?" I said, seeking to maintain an attitude of courtesy in the face of his unfriendly vibe, as primo peeve was he displaying.

"Great. Just great. No job. The landlord at my door. Bills piling up. Sending out over thirty résumés a day and getting no responses." He had been let go by Miss Carmelli the year before, having been with us as a temp, when she no longer had need of his services. Perhaps the brutal cold was reminding him of the harshness of a life without shelter, but my heart hardened rather than opened to him, owing to his hostile manner.

Isabel, you may remember the Santa Barbara zoo on that trip we took to California following our wedding. We may make nice with animals all we want, but concerning those with a carnivorous bent, it is best that we understand their essential nature. Specifically, I refer to the Bengal tiger that rushed the bars as I stood with my back turned to the cage. Its roar traveled from my toes up through my spine and the top of my head. That was the true meaning of the zoo visit. But was it also the true meaning of my encounter with Hank Farquist, who stood there confronting me in his creaseless pants? Or was the true meaning what he said without saying: "If I am your brother, why is it you did not see that the org kept me on? My life is your fault, and will always be your fault"?

PS

It occurs to me, Isabel, that if we are not to fall into the ranks of the hopelessly virtuous, that is, the truly delusional, then we must take to heart the rebuke of Baudelaire—hypocrite lecteur, mon semblable, mon frère. Yes, Hank carries the rage of a Bengal tiger, but I harbor my own. Hank has had his chance in life. Why does Mr. Mensa Man have to ruin mine just because he has made a mess of his own? I have paid the price of working for an org that confers no social prestige whatsoever. I learned my place in life early on. Now here is Mr. Filthy One. If he were to plunge down an elevator shaft, it would be no cause for lamentation in me. If his heart were to burst his chest on Broadway, would I do more than cover his corpse with yesterday's discarded newspaper?

Isabel, here is a short list for success that I will try to embrace:

1. Accept my workspace. Recognize that it is not the isolation ward Hank finds himself in.

2. Weather the emotional storm. Within a couple of weeks the outbursts of surprise by visitors to Hank's new office will fade, and Hank will realize that the peripheral space he occupies is akin to being put out to pasture. It will just be a more private place for him to do his afternoon snoozing after a morning of high volubility and bonhomie.

3. Turn my attention to the calendar pinned to the wall of the cubicle. Never mind waiting for a whole month to put an X through it. Each passing day I can mark with the faintest touch of the tip of a pencil, this while looking away so someone spying might assume the mark is just a bit of carelessness, bringing me one step closer to the security that, progressively, is becoming the only thing I desire. And the beauty is that no one will know my plan, for if they did, surely it would be taken away, like so much already has been.

The org has these dark windows you can see out of but can't see into, like the windows of some cars and trucks or the sunglasses worn by stars and thugs and celebrity wannabes. There is no sinister intent. The org just wants its privacy. You don't have to be knowing its business every second of the day. You only have to know what it tells you. Sometimes people want to think business that isn't their business is their business. They want to make trouble. Why? Because they have nothing better to do. They like to pull down and tarnish. Some people you just have to watch out for. Or sometimes you have to hurt them so bad that they are driven to cry with pain even worse than listening to Paul Anka sing "I'm Just a Lonely Boy" on a Saturday night somewhere in the lost past.

Blanche Givenchy has pulled her chair up close and has her hand on Johan's wrist, as she has whisper words for him, words not to be overheard, words that she means to have staying power. Her words have tiny points, the better to stick. "A word of caution, now that you're right next door to Alice. Be very wary of her. She's treacherous, and that's something you should know."

Blanche looks vulnerable. Her hands tremble. Is her future the paper slippers and the gown and endless shuffling through some brightly lit ward? Maybe there will be a walker. This is what it is to grow older. It is to fade from the light, for your skin to turn pale as your eyes scream their terror at the oncoming abyss.

"Treacherous?"

"She's Lurleen's eyes and ears."

"She's a snitch? How do you know that?" He is whispering now, too.

"Because Lurleen has found out things she couldn't have come to on her own, things I said on the phone that Alice must have overheard when her cubicle adjoined mine. Now it's only a matter of time before Lurleen drives me out of here."

"But why would she want to drive you out of here?"

"She doesn't understand that the editorial process is process, sometimes tediously so. She has a marketing, not an editorial, background. It's sort of like placing a police chief at the head of the fire department. And Alice is perfectly compatible with her because Alice is an editor in title only. She has absolutely no standards. Her mantra is 'I could care less' when it comes to the quality of our publications."

Within a few weeks Blanche Givenchy is no more than a memory to those in the org who have worked with her. She is shown the door for having failed to adapt to Lurleen's regime. Technically, this is not so. In one weak moment, driven by her anxieties and the pressures she has been experiencing, she offers her resignation to Jeanine Juddster, in Human Resources.

"Just remember, Honey, you are not junk," Jeanine Juddster says, as Blanche signs the necessary forms. "Just remember that God has a plan." There is no other attempt to comfort Blanche or help her through the pressures she has been feeling. There will be no counsel that she postpone her decision for a week or two.

"Who?" Blanche says.

"You heard me."

When Blanche Givenchy the next day sees her situation at the org in another light and tries to withdraw her resignation, Human Resources refuses her request. Surely they would if Lurleen stepped in and went to bat for Blanche, but this Lurleen will not do. In ways large and small will Lurleen serve as an instrument of change in the org. She is sending a message to staff that they are disposable, all of them. Any illusion of a safety net, she is saying, is just that. Hear her words and hear them now, for she is the voice out of the wilderness and now here in the Big Apple: *America does not offer protections. America throws you out on the street and leaves you unsheltered in the rain. You get what you deserve in America. If you are poor, it is your fault. America knows this is true, and I know it is true, and God knows it is true.*

And Lurleen says further: *I am the org and the org is me. I am America and America is me. I am Wal-Mart and KFC and Burger King. I am a strip mall come to Gotham. And trust me when I say I love God but none of you.*

Blanche is not Lurleen's office star, as she had been in the eyes of Miss Carmelli. A virtual technophobe, Blanche finds the simplest computer function a challenge. There are days when she comes completely undone, fearing that she has permanently lost a file. And some days she arrives late and leaves early. And then there is the day that she doesn't come in at all. Lurleen has no interest in cutting Blanche the same slack as Miss Carmelli. "She could go right to the top. She could be at Knopf or Random House. The girl is a genius. A genius. She finds things nobody else can possibly see," Miss Carmelli said. Though there is moral outrage at Lurleen's treatment of Blanche and her indifference to the standard of editorial excellence she represents, Johan is relieved that he too hasn't been shown the door.

As he passes Lurleen's office that evening, where she sits with Margo Breeder-Fullsley, Lurleen calls out, "Going out on a hot date tonight, Johan?" The usual roar of laughter follows.

It is complicated. That is what he wants to say. That is what her laughter says.

Isabel,
The wild surges of anger and revulsion I am prone to here in this office are a challenge, but I am here for just that—emotional healing, an easing of the sense of separation—as much or more than to earn my daily bread. I am not at GoAN through some flaw in my psychological makeup that precludes me from playing in a bigger arena, but for karmic reasons. I have an amend to make to the women of the world, and what better place to do so than in an org dominated by women that places itself at the service of girls. And it comforts me to believe that my progress is ongoing.

But now, it is not scheming Lurleen Lulabella or loathsome Alice Piccoli or flatulent Hank Farquist or controlling Fiona Beasley he must discover his oneness with, but Melvin Kleiner, Lurleen's new hire. Nanette Nobling, Lurleen's previous addition to the team, has quit. A phenomenon this Melvin Kleiner is. A short man with a sturdy build, he doesn't so much walk as strut, his chest out and his head back. And yet, more than Melvin's bantam rooster bearing is the effortless speed with which he moves, the curious impression he gives of being borne along slightly off the ground, as if some unseen force has taken charge and is physically transporting him.

So much work to do. Such a long journey it can seem. What is to love about a man who occupies one of the prestigious cubes? What is to love about a man with a clearly bigger and better brain than his, given his degrees from Brown University and Harvard? What is not to fear about a man with that strange, empowered walk, as if he, like Lurleen, is a force of inevitability upon the land?

How small and shrunken he feels. What can a focus on the breath do about such threatening conditions? What are these dark clouds that have gathered not only over the country but, in microcosm, the department? Why is it becoming night even in daylight?

Isabel,

For what is God but a power that can be harnessed to formats evil as well as benign? Are we not seeing it at large in the land? And are duplicity and guile not its calling cards? Lurleen may have her god, but in the realm of office life her deity has a Machiavellian dimension. Can you tell me this is not so? The woman simply cannot be defeated. She has no love life, she has no social life, and that lack has flung her and her corpulence into the arms of God, and from this relationship born of desperation she receives her daily bread, the gift of renewal each morning brings. Ideas pour into her. She has a source of power, too, and it tells her that her weight must be applied.

Lurleen has directed the staff to put together a style guide for the department as well as for distribution to the entire org.

"And I have placed Melvin at the head the committee so the language of the org can move forward with the times and not have the dust of the past all upon it. We are changing it up, folks. We are changing it up."

Johan hears names—Fiona Beasley, Hank Farquist, Mary Terezzi, and another new hire, Rhoda Bahr—but not his own.

Alice Piccoli comes to him later. "Feeling a little alone, are we? Not experiencing that loving feeling?"

"What do you want?"

"I just want you to know that what happened to Blanche can happen to you, Mr. Big Shot. How does it feel to be brought down? How does it feel not to have your edits respected?"

"My edits respected?" Johan begins to laugh.

"That's right. Your edits. Your edits aren't going anyplace."

"And where would my edits go?"

"To the style guide committee, if they were good enough. But they're not good enough. Your edits smell. In fact, they stink."

"How about your edits, Alice? Do your edits smell. In fact, do they stink?"

"Edits are not my thing. I do business. I do the moolah. That's what real people do."

"What else do real people do?"

"They do this." And with that, she shows him her tongue once more, just letting the whole grotesque thing hang out.

"Oh, Jesus," he says, shielding his eyes.

If it is a blow to his pride that he is not a part of the committee as well as further proof of his doghouse status, still, along with his hurt and anger, there is also relief. The other members will see that he knows less about matters of style than someone with his years with the org might be expected to know. He remembers the careful notes Blanche Givenchy compiled and how he often went to her with copyediting questions. He suddenly realizes that if he were to leave this day, he would have nothing to pass on but twenty years of weightlessness.

Hank Farquist's booming voice travels to him from afar. "Shouldn't Johan be a part of this? He's been here so long. He might be able to make a valuable contribution."

Johan doesn't have to get out of his chair to know that Hank is standing at the door to Lurleen's office. So it has come to this? Mr. Pass Gas is now his intermediary with the boss?

"Of course he should be a part of it. Johan always has a valuable contribution to make, even about things he knows nothing about." Like toxic sewage does Lurleen's laughter flow out of her office.

As he stares at the calendar, he feels crazy, just crazy.

The resource room is small and crowded. Too many chairs, too many boxes filled with org materials that will never find an audience. And some daffy chart that Lurleen insisted on posting on the bulletin board to show visitors how busy the department is. Melvin sits at the head of the conference table. His wide mouth designed to bite into life shows him as a man used to taking charge with his aggressive and confident manner. And derisive, too, to Lurleen's delight. He holds up several org publications, which he has taken from the floor-to-ceiling shelves.

"These resources go on and on, making the same point over and over."

This is going to be hard, very hard, Johan senses, as Melvin mocks the publications.

"Melvin's right. There is repetition within the book and duplication of information from one book to the next as well." So says Rhoda Bahr, another new hire.

"We tell the reader what we are going to say, we say it, and then we tell the reader what we have said. This is the org way. It makes for a kind of thoroughness. In this way we cover our bases and penetrate the consciousness of the reader," Johan says, his voice trembling with fear and anger. It is inevitable that, with the years, he has come, to a degree that can surprise him, to have an identification with the org. The cutting, dismissive remarks of Melvin and Rhoda wound him. In denigrating the org, they are denigrating him and Blanche Givenchy and Miss Carmelli. He wants to tell Melvin and Rhoda that they are poisoned by conceit, the same conceit that operates in all the new hires, including Lurleen Lulabella, saying that everything the org has done prior to their arrival is somehow worthless.

"We are looking to be on the cutting edge. We can't do that with this approach," Rhoda Bahr says.

"Don't you understand that in five years the so-called cutting-edge materials that the department is now committed to producing will look as dated as the publications you are now dismissing?"

"Our patriarch has spoken," Melvin says. The room seems to favor Melvin, if the laughter that erupts is any indication.

"What's with the title?" Johan asks, smarting from the rudeness.

"I'm not talking about your age. I'm talking about your longevity with the organization. Twenty years is an amazingly long time to be in one job."

"I'll say," Rhoda says, causing another eruption of laughter.

That perpetual smile on her face as she rakes you with her long nails. Her teeth the only thing youthful about her, so synthetically white and protuberant.

"It's a privilege to be in the same room with you. You must have this incredible knowledge. You'll be a great help to our committee, I'm sure." So Melvin says.

"No one who puts me on a pedestal means me any good," he says, finally recovering, and now it is for Melvin to flinch, for a look of insecurity to chase his mocking grin.

"Why are the names of all the officers in capital letters? President, Chief Executive Officer, Secretary, Treasurer. First and Second Vice President." Rhoda Bahr reads from a list of org names and terms. Why can't we simply lowercase them?" she asks.

"Good question," Hank chimes in.

"I agree, " Mary Terezzi says.

Rhoda is observant. She is smart. "We've always capitalized the titles of national headquarters officers," Johan says, trying not to sound defensive.

"And so we have to continue? Isn't this the kind of thinking we're trying to get away from?" Rhoda says.

Why can't they just leave things alone? Johan asks himself. They attack publications from years gone by. They attack him for his longevity, insinuating that he is a freak and that he should just go away. They want to put their hands on everything.

"We capitalize the titles of national officers and lowercase the titles of council officers. It avoids confusion as to which officers we are talking about, those from national headquarters or those from the councils." The others in the room are watching him now. He feels isolated and on the verge of losing. He didn't want this kind of conflict. He didn't want it at all. How does such a small matter come to have such an emotional charge?

"Is that to suggest that somehow national staff are more important than council staff?" Like a needle Rhoda Bahr's question penetrates.

"I don't believe that is the intent at all. It's simply the way the style evolved."

"Sounds like rigid thinking," Rhoda says.

The discussion might have gone no further, but then Melvin speaks up.

"Reserving capitalization for one set of officers is a blatant example of elitism. Let's take these people down a peg or two," he says.

"You sound like Leon Trotsky," Johan blurts.

"And you sound like Joseph Stalin. No icepicks, please."

"We're not here to take them or anyone else down a peg or two," Johan says, They can see him as the patriarch and protector of the old order if they wish, but he is frightened and offended by this raging insurgency that wants to come in and smash things up and knock people down. He is desirous of quelling it. When had he become identified with the org in this way? When had he begun to care?

Hank Farquist has a mind that notes conflict. Seeing the impasse that has been reached with Rhoda and Melvin on one side and Johan on the other, he is ready with his solution. "Since Johan feels so strongly about this matter and you and Rhoda have strong feelings as well, why not put your cases in writing and send them to Lurleen to adjudicate?"

"Sure. Let's do that," Melvin says, adopting the posture of the reasonable.

The idea of Lurleen as arbiter is hateful and fear-inspiring to Johan. It places him in direct competition with Melvin and Rhoda. And surely Hank has to know that given even the smallest opportunity to stick it to him, Lurleen would do exactly that. Anyway, Hank himself has said that editing is not her strong suit. What is this but another instance of Hank's sly and clever treachery?

"No," Johan says, and then quickly reverses himself, having seen his blunder. The committee will vote then and there if he doesn't agree to have Lurleen adjudicate, and he will experience the humiliation of being on the losing side. *I'll go to Mommy with my argument and Melvin and Rhoda will go to Mommy with their argument. Like squabbling little children will we go to Mommy.*

"Of course you and Rhoda will probably lose. After all, Johan is always right." A smile on Hank's face as he speaks.

"Is that true, Johan? Are you always right?" Melvin asks.

"Maybe the real question is whether you are ever wrong," Johan replies.

It is painful to see himself as he is in relation to others. So fearful of being overtaken and dislodged. So needing to protect an image of competency. And yet he isn't the only one creating an undercurrent of animosity and tension on the committee that makes a mockery of org buzzwords like cooperation and collaboration. He feels alone. He feels like mean and uncaring people have arrived, people who just want to sweep him away.

Something is going on. Something just isn't right, and it is important that he push back.

Within an hour there is an e-mail from Melvin to Lurleen and a cc to him and the rest of the department in which Melvin lays out his cogent argument for lowercasing the titles of the org.'s leadership team:

> "A number of us on the committee feel strongly that an egalitarian, nonhierarchical, model would be exemplified by a lowercase style for our officers rather than separate them from the rest of us with capitals…

As Johan reads the e-mail, a feeling that he is not long for the org comes over him. Why fight to hold on when so clearly he is being driven out by people who are smarter and more capable than he is? He stares at the sunlight on the department store across the street and then up at the verdigris on the building's parapet. There is a world out there. He shifts and stares at the calendar pinned to his bulletin board. If he could only have the courage to let go and leave.

He places a piece of paper in front of him on his desk to create the impression that he is busy and positions himself in his chair so his back is to the entrance to the cubicle. With his spine straight and his eyes closed he tries to focus on his breath. In this twenty-minute period the phone rings twice and he hears the ping of several e-mail messages newly arrived. But as he leaves the world to itself, a sense of hope comes to him. He won't have to be pushed into the sea. His cause is not, inevitably, a losing one. An effective response to Melvin's e-mail is right in front of him, over the signature of their National President (not national president) herself, a letter that includes all the corporate titles, with capitalization preserved. And is it not important, in the third year of the org's triennium, to preserve the established order, given the fact that the policy-making convention will take place in a few months and any style change would require the agreement of the officers and not some unilateral action on the part of the Publications Department? Further, would it not be advisable, given the fact that some of those convention materials have already been printed with the established style in place, to continue with the established order rather than deviate from it now? Lastly, does the *Chicago Manual of Style* itself not support his argument? Does it not say that an *experienced* (italics his) editor knows hard-and-fast rules cannot always be applied in the matter of capitalization?

Of such stuff are rebuttal e-mails made. Oh heart that is so easily wounded, that takes refuge in rocks and trees and the silent spaces of your own aloneness and finds such friction in the company of people, you are finding your way here. So the song of himself goes in that holy moment. Johan does not run. He does not hide his head. He does not take his marbles and go home.

And when, thereafter, he encounters Melvin in the men's room and sees the look of peeve on his nemesis's face (*experienced* would be the word that zinged Melvin, Johan suspects), his sense of hope rises that maybe the tide is turning and the force of inevitability Melvin presents himself as is diminishing. Perhaps Johan has more staying power than his fear wants him to believe. Perhaps he can't be so easily swept aside on a tide of insurgency after all.

And then more compelling evidence comes from Lurleen herself, who doesn't flatten him but instead offers thanks for his "thoughtful" note, and what can that be but a signal that Melvin and Rhoda perhaps aren't going to have their way.

And what further evidence does he need that office alliances really are temporary in nature than the appearance of Hank Farquist at the entrance to his cubicle? What can it mean that he has not made his daily beeline, coins and keys jingling in his pockets, for the perpetually consuming tinfoil lady herself, the vulturine Alice Piccoli, but instead stops at Johan's cubicle? Not that Johan meets him with open arms. Yes, falling-outs are inevitable when people are thrown together in work situations of this kind. Yes, insecurities come into play. Yes, people want what they see other people getting. But all that being said, cool but correct is the order of the day.

"Lurleen has me working on a staffing design booklet. I thought you might like to see this," Hank says, in an attempt at a whisper. He hands Johan the document, open to a page with the departmental grid. All the staff positions are in boxes, with lines connecting them to other boxes above or below or on the same line. Johan doesn't want to touch the document let alone look at it. The suspicion grows in him that it is not meant to put his mind at rest. When Johan is slow in focusing, Hank directs him with his thick index finger to the area of the page he wants Johan to see. There it is, in black and white. Alice Piccoli and Melvin Kleiner and Rhoda Bahr are higher on the grid than him, while he is paired with Hank. The hierarchy, laid out so clearly, stings. What is more troublesome is that Hank has felt the need to bring it to his attention. Instinct tells him to shun both the messenger and the message.

"Keep the faith," he says breezily, as he returns the booklet to Hank. He then turns back to his computer to signal that the visit is over.

But the visit isn't over, not in his mind. The offering, it is clear, has not been benign. Rather, it feels like Hank has dangled poisoned bait in front of him, more harmful than the giant bags of candy and cookies he buys each week at the ninety-nine cents store down the block and sets out for the staff to munch on. Can he not pray that Hank understand that he is dismissing not only the diagram but Hank himself for his odious, troublemaking ways? Can he in that moment offer not a benign prayer but a prayer of malediction—not for love and joy and peace and happiness and all good things for Hank but one that Hank drop dead on the spot for the crime of trying to place them in the same boat?

And yet, if this is where office life has brought Johan Manootdjian, his fear and his smallness and his antipathy on full display, see him now at the end of the day, not in his cube in that same warren of offices, amid his plants and colored pencils and stacks of papers. See him at home kneeling by his bed in all the darkness that he can summon. Hear him as he says, reviewing where his day has left him, "What is this life that I should have to see myself as I am? And where can I turn but to you when there is no one else?"

Chapter 21

Claire Eastland was gone from Pentacle Books, her last day made memorable by her bad temper standing at the copier, which was balking her efforts to tie up loose ends and flee the scene. She, like Charles Nigel, had followed her star elsewhere, in this case relocation to the West Coast. Did I miss her? Yes. My heart howled at her departure with that decrepit old man. Beauty had left and the scold, Olivia, remained. It was all very strange. I didn't belong there and yet I did belong there. Uncomfortable as it was to admit, some part of me identified with Olivia. She was like me in ways I could hardly express. There was something here for me to learn if I was to survive.

And so an awkward but manageable working relationship developed. Perhaps Olivia found it useful to keep me on. She gave me Claire's title without really giving me Claire's responsibilities or, I suspected, Claire's salary. Claire, after all, had been an acquiring editor, and there was no reason to believe that Olivia would choose to hand over that authority to me as well. And why should she? I had no expertise in children's books and no abiding interest in the genre. A picture book was not a special event, as it was for Olivia. I had come to the department sufficiently unread in the literature to even be familiar with Eeyore. Claire's departure freed Olivia to consolidate power. The list she shaped would be entirely hers, with only minimal input from me. Projects she had inherited that she had a special distaste for she would hand over, like some preposterous tale of the sea or a dull book for intermediate school readers on the anatomy of the ear. If I felt ashamed to be a grown man with such small responsibilities— basically a title and little more—it was for me to nevertheless be grateful, as I understood that neither Olivia nor anyone else would ever have hired me on the basis of my résumé.

Something noteworthy occurred when I would step into Olivia's office. She would lose her voice. Not always, but often. There she would be, seated in her chair, her lips moving and her hands gesturing, but nothing emerged in the way of sound, as if she was pantomiming the act of speech. My thought was to fetch her a glass of water, and yet, as I backed toward the door her voice returned. Like a radio broadcast that is suddenly interrupted by technical difficulty and then resumes at the point to which it would normally have arrived, so too would she come back on the air, and if I had no idea as to what she had "spoken" before, I had no choice but to be obliged to act as if I had heard every word. I mean, what is a person to do in such a situation?

If it had happened only once, there would be nothing to remark upon, but as my entry and her loss of speech repeated itself at least ten times, there is no conclusion to be drawn other than that my presence in her office had an emotionally devastating effect. And since I was a male, what was I to conclude but that my gender more than anything might be contributing to this phenomenon? I remembered Charles Nigel's out-of-character advice that I might find a more suitable work environment than to position myself under a career woman such as Olivia.

A person should never go where he does not belong. Was it possible I had done just that? If so, I felt I had no way out. Evidently, I was a man whose only strategy in life was to keep writing and perhaps become published sufficient to leave my job, which more and more seemed a pipe dream.

The net effect of what I interpreted as Olivia's subconscious antipathy toward me was a desire to keep as low a profile as possible and adopt an unthreatening posture. Because I was a tall man and Olivia was quite small, I would try to minimize the height difference by stooping in her presence. On one occasion I elicited her disapproval for rolling up my sleeves in her presence. Whether she considered this action too personal and thus bad manners or found something objectionable about my bare forearms I couldn't say, but the cockatrice's glare she applied to them let me know that any adjustment of my clothing would be done out of her sight in future.

Whatever acceptance of my situation I tried to bring myself to, there was also anger. I felt controlled, held back, emasculated, and sought for ways to assert my independence. If Olivia had a weakness, it was a lack of confidence when it came to public speaking, especially when, at sales conference, she had to face the jaded Pentacle sales force—mainly men habituated to hotels and motels and the boozing and whoring that come with life on the road. The terror that had gripped me at that first sales conference following my attempt to get sober had left me. There was no longer the need to cower under the table. I found myself speaking easily to the salesforce and connecting with them. If anything, I drew strength from Olivia's evident uptightness in front of this crew. She could rule her little domain, but in this bigger sphere she appeared small and tentative and lost. The gathered were witness to the fear behind her ill temper. The difference in our presentations was striking: I was as loose and humorous as she was nervous and grindingly serious. Whatever she may have been thinking, Olivia offered me a gracious smile.

But when the same triumph occurred a second time, at our next annual sales conference, her puffed cheeks told a different story. She noted with displeasure, as if she had an insurrectionist in her midst, the extemporaneous nature of my presentations, and put a procedure in place that would have me submit to her any future presentations in writing along with the requirement of an oral pledge to follow the script. It was, of course, her right to expect subordination from a member of her staff, but I also reserved the right to resist. What was that anyway, people going through life with their wretched strategies for controlling other people?

Was it not enough that I had to be bent down and held back in that little department? Why would I not want to appear before this salesforce at my full height and not as some cowed cur on Olivia's leash?

But if I sought ways to break free, I nevertheless admired her dedication and intelligence. She was a professional devoted to a genre she loved and she was in it for the long run. Some mornings I would see her in her office checking the status of her stocks in the financial section of the *New York Times*; she had made peace with the fact that she would have to take care of herself, as no one else would. And it wasn't lost on me that she was down to earth and disliked pretense of any kind.

When I thought I knew her, she would surprise me. One morning I was startled to see her with a copy of Richard Yates's *Eleven Kinds of Loneliness* and was further startled when she said she had read it more than once and would read anything he wrote, for in my mind she had been apart from concerns of an adult writer such as he, so focused on sadness and loneliness.

She lived alone and so avoided the scenes of messy domestic discord that were part of my daily life. She wasn't burdened with a spouse she wasn't sure she wanted. While Sarah and I were home fighting, she was out at the opera or at a concert. She had something to teach me about making my way in the world. Working with others can sometimes do that. It can infuse you with a respect and even a quiet love for them. It can enter you before you are aware of its arrival.

None of the above stopped me from performing my shenanigans. In compliance with her new requirement, I showed her my written presentation for the next sales conference, which she returned to me with heavy revisions. A week later, I stood before the sales crew with neither the original nor the revision in hand. Instead I held forth with a lavish appreciation of *The Story of Your Heart* (husband and wife team of Abner and Agnes Finchwaite, illustrations by Mary Goodwine) and *Tales of the Robber Baron and Little Pip* (author Belinda Biddersly, illustrations by Faith Sweetlove). In the course of my oration I asserted that it would take a dunce not to see that both books should leap out of their library-bound status and marketed to the chains and independent bookstores as extremely viable candidates for all the national bestseller lists.

Daggers flew from Olivia's eyes. When she saw I was still standing and that she could not slay me with her arsenal of fury, she resorted to words that would not come. Right there, in the hotel auditorium, for everyone to witness, from the president to the most jaundiced member of the sales team, was the spectacle of Olivia, her eyes bulging and her cheeks puffed, miming speech. Seeking to stoke her fire just a tad more, I removed my jacket and slowly, with calculated ostentation, rolled up one sleeve, and then the other, sending her deeper into her state of apoplexy.

Love takes many forms, dear reader. Suffice it to say that it does not always seem to appear in its finest light. That said, there can be no question but that Olivia, in her own way, had drunk of love potion number nine, even if, for a time, it manifested as sheer hatred. No, I was not let go. No summary termination of me as an employee of Pentacle Books followed. Beyond this brief piece of speculation I will not go.

But Diane Matthews, the art director, was gone. She had the cold eye for realistic appraisal. She knew that the primary talent had fled the department and felt the atmosphere of repression. Also, she had remarried. She had found a real man who could make the bedsprings sing and do the deal in the halls of business, a man who could get planes to fly and stop at his command.

So yes, there was no Charles Nigel or Claire Eastland and now there was no Diane Matthews. They had moved on, in the way that people who can move on do. But I could not move on because I had no place to go and nothing anybody could possibly want, given that my résumé lacked luster. ("Keeps his desk clean and orderly and his pencils sharpened. Hire him now or you'll be sorry.") No, it was better to show up at this office day after day and sit at a virtually empty desk, sometimes going almost an entire morning and afternoon without a passing conversation. And even if I did not earn a big salary, I could tell myself it was a respectable job. I was working with words, after all.

And then it changed, and it changed just like that. Olivia came to me and said the department was being disbanded. She would lose her title as director but be allowed to stay on as a senior editor with another children's books imprint within the company. But I could not stay. I was not wanted anymore. "You got screwed," she said, referring to the fact that I was two weeks short of being vested in the company's pension plan.

Her words did not mean so much to me then. It seemed right and proper that I should be let go, given the meager level of my contribution to the company. What was that, after all, to sit idle eight hours a day drinking coffee and at the lunch hour Monday through Friday have a sandwich and a container of soup from the deli down the block? What was it to gather at the elevators for a fire drill and realize I had no one to talk to as others huddled together, a circumstance offered as compelling evidence once more of the poverty of my social skills? I was not launching any books of note. I was not bringing in sales. The company was simply doing for me what I couldn't do for myself.

(I too was to learn what it is to be alone, to be among people in this city of eight million and yet not be with them, and would seek to fill my night with an event so I could have a change of pace from the solitude of my apartment. One evening I attended a concert at Carnegie Hall. The performer is lost to me now, along with her evening's repertoire and the sound of her voice. But I do recall the Broadway bus that I afterward set foot in and saw, at a glance, while pretending not to, Olivia seated toward the front. And I do recall she participated in the charade as I backed off the bus and to my freedom, so overwhelmed with fear was I to share the same space on the short ride uptown with this former boss of mine. The years had brought an increased measure of respect for her, but the incongruity of our relationship had also only grown with the passage of time in such a way that flight was not a consideration but a necessity.)

Father,

An accounting of my life with Isabel will be difficult, I see. I am with her now in spirit if not in body, and what is a body after all, as one gets older but a thing more and more in need of repair as it slowly runs down. From the highest perspective love never dies, and the light of love still burns bright within me regarding her. However, it can feel like a betrayal of trust to make a record of one's personal life. Is there not a punishment for such a thing awaiting me, as punishment awaits me for committing parents and family to paper as well? And will that punishment not come in the afterlife, where I will have to pay for such a grievous wrong? What kind of man is it who cannot live his life without seeking to report on it? May I hear from you about this?

Isabel read my novella "Broken Resolutions." I had shown her an artifact of my emotional reality and she had been taken with it. In expressing her liking for the novella, I became not the young man who had shown up at the door of her townhouse with a cigar box full of change and my laminated hack license. For a night at least, I did not have to fear that I did not belong in her company.

Love, at that point of my life, was cohabitation and physical intimacy. It was in the natural order of things that we should want to be together. Isabel was accommodating. She took me in. She said she was so happy I was in her life.

The loft took up an entire floor of a cast iron building on Crosby Street. Being just below the roof, it had a skylight through which an intruder had entered some years before. Isabel had happened upon him as he was burgling the place. Though lust drove him toward her, he did Isabel no physical violence, a miracle attributable only to the fact that she fainted in his terrifying presence. When she came to, he was gone. In the aftermath she purchased a shotgun and took to sleeping with it under her bed. She was determined never to be in that place of powerlessness again. Being the artist that she was, she couldn't resist carving the stock and enlivening it with paint.

Love was sharing and creating a space for myself in the loft. To that end I cleared away the clutter in the loft bed, including a rug that had been partially eaten by moths. There were many such pockets of disorder into which I hoped to bring order and sparkle. There was the mop I would use to clean the white-painted floorboards, section by section, every two weeks, and the brown sofa I would try to vacuum free of cat hairs.

"In five minutes he can make an area of the loft look entirely different. He's amazing," Those were words Isabel spoke of me to a friend, and more than once.

The day came when her parents were to know their daughter was living with a man who was not her husband. Inevitably, I would have to meet them. But how could such a thing be? Her stepfather was a physics professor, recently retired. Her mother was an anthropologist with many books to her name. Where could I hide when they shone their light of inspection on me?

In this time Isabel said, "My stepfather is not who you think he is." Her statement was not emphatic. The air did not ring with her words. Nor was anything more forthcoming when I asked her what she meant.

"Just that," Isabel said softly.

In this time there was a man. His name was Nathan Sbar. A bald head and a satyr's gleam he presented to your eye. Like many of his kind, he was on the lookout for excellence, and when he saw it in Isabel he made it a point to be her friend. And yet, despite his lasciviousness, he never approached Isabel with overt carnality. He did, however, reveal a patriarchal claim on her when, after meeting me, he shouted his disapproval. "What will your father have to say about this?" Such were his reproachful words to Isabel about the fact of our cohabitation. Nathan Sbar did not know enough to say stepfather. I will say nothing more about him now or maybe ever.

The day came when Isabel brought me to meet her parents at their penthouse apartment overlooking Central Park. Her mother gushed to Isabel, "He's handsome," even though I wasn't. Her stepfather received me favorably as well. Both were relieved that she was out of her marriage to Philip. With her former husband as the only basis for comparison in their eyes, I could initially do no wrong.

The living room was vast. The colors were warm, but the room felt cold and not quite lived in. Their life was in the kitchen and their separate bedrooms and the den, where they served, as hors d'oeuvres, thin, delicious slices of salmon on crackers and pitted green olives.from Zabar's. The room was wrapped around with books, mostly hardbound, on shelves from floor to ceiling, and featured a display of shells under glass on the coffee table.

From the start I felt more comfortable with her stepfather than her mother, as Iris had a capacity for judgment that frightened me. She was intellectually gifted, possessed of real ability in the hard sciences as well as literature. She even had musical talent, having won a scholarship to Juilliard for her violin virtuosity.

There was an embarrassing moment in that first visit when Iris asked about my family. I told her that my father had died but that my mother was still among the living.

"Do you come from a large family?" she asked.

"Yes," I said.

"How many siblings?"

"Well, I have a brother and three sisters." I did not mention that one of my sisters had died.

"And what does your brother do?"

"He is involved with real estate," I said. It was true, in its way. He lived in an apartment or maybe a house. That was being involved with real estate.

"And what about your sisters?"

"My youngest sister is a university professor."

"And where does she teach?"

"She teaches comparative literature at Purchase."

Iris stared at me as if puzzled. "What is Purchase?"

"It's where students learn how to purchase things to facilitate their blending into our consumer society."

"Bizarre. And where does comparative literature fit into all this facilitating?"

"Well, yes, they read Charles Dickens even as they learn and build on their purchasing skills. I once took an acting class and the teacher said you can't learn to swim the English Channel by reading Proust, but clearly there are some in this world who are ignoring or challenging his assertion."

"Astonishing. And what about the other two?"

"One is a legal secretary and the other is a religious thinker."

"A religious thinker?"

"Yes. She thinks a lot about God," I said.

"Well, what exactly does she think about God?"

"That he exists. She is awaiting the arrival of his son. She believes that he will come as a thief in the night, as the Bible says."

"And does she write and publish articles and books on this subject?"

"Rachel has arrived at a place where books are more or less immaterial to her," I said. "That wasn't always the case. As a child I remember staring in amazement at the sea of books the floor of her room had become."

"Books are immaterial?"

"The progression of her mind has been in the direction of the one book—the good book, as it is sometimes called."

"The Bible?"

"Yes, the Bible. The King James Version."

"Amazing."

"It's where her life has come to. She wasn't always that way. You might say she was positively worldly, to use a pejorative we would hear in the church in which I was raised applied to those who were too much in the embrace of this realm. And Rachel was very much such a person in those years. She applied henna to her hair, shaped it in a formidable and unfriendly duck's ass, wore those dark I-can-see-you-but-you-can't-see-me glasses, and drank to excess and yet, when my father died suddenly of a stroke, she seemed to change on a dime. She was no longer wild and drunk; she now adopted a sober demeanor and had indeed been rendered sober; she has not touched alcohol since. You might say her drinking was a form of rebellion and my father's death took away the thing she had been rebelling against. Perhaps she was seeking a kind of redemption, like Prince Hal in *Henry IV, part one,* who no longer wants to be seen as a wastrel but would rather, like Hotspur, be seen as the theme of honor's tongue."

A silence ensued in which I became aware of Max's fixed gaze. He seemed to be summoning extraordinary powers of perception with which to fit me into his frame of comprehension. His expression was neither friendly nor unfriendly but simply focused.

In the aftermath of our visit with Isabel's parents, I had a severe reaction. Outwardly I was OK, but inwardly I was stricken, simply horrified by my performance. Shame engulfed me that I had exposed my family to these accomplished people in this way. And it wasn't even my family. It was that I had exposed myself and dared to presume that they could have an interest in someone such as me. Once again I was seeing myself through the imagined eyes of others, people who were my betters, people who would put the laughing thing on me, just laugh and laugh that I would even dare to show up in their midst. A man is supposed to have some protection against such feelings, but they poured in on me intensely, so that all I could do was utter nonsense syllables as a way of blocking them until the shame fever could run its course.

Some days later Max requested that I meet him for lunch in midtown Manhattan. And so I stepped off the street and to the other side of a heavy door into the exclusive Century Club, where I was greeted by an elderly Black man in a tuxedo, who directed me to sign the guest book before I proceeded up the marble staircase to the floor above. On the walls were paintings of men of power and prominence. I entered the spacious and ornate dining room and assumed my place at a linen-covered table, where Max was already seated.

There had been Peter and Lydia, and now there was Max and Iris, and I will tell you that, on my way to meet Max, Peter's face flooded my consciousness and I started to cry right there in the concourse in Grand Central Station. I cried because of all the hurt and judgment I had inflicted on Peter without any show of real goodness. I felt like I had just spurned and rejected him and Lydia and Sarah. What kind of cold and heartless creature walked out on one life with one family to start another with a second? Peter, who had studied history, was now part of my history, and as soon as a part of your life becomes history, you can revisit it but you cannot stay.

Isabel spoke of her stepfather as if he was a terror, but she was referring me back to a different time and place, when she was a child and he was at the height of his powers. The man I sat across from, who wrote out our order with the fountain pen he held in his shaking, liver-spotted hand, was not an academic dynamo but a retiree weakened by age and infirmity and whose calendar was now empty. Time had defanged him. The relationships that had been established through his work life had not survived the transition. He was not needed anymore. The waves of his hand and the nods he exchanged in that exclusive, wood-paneled dining room with men from his professional life were the only vestiges of contact that remained. They existed for each other only in passing. It was that I was seeing as I sat with my shrunken future father-in-law in his expensive and now ill-fitting silk suit, the insubstantiality and impermanence of power and prestige. And despite all his talk of his own ambition and the drive that had enabled him to rise to the top in his field, the sense I had was that I was sitting across the table from an exquisitely lonely old man.

If much of what we talked about was soon lost to me, one thing remained, a simple sentence that seemed to come from nowhere. "I approve of your regime," he said, after handing the waiter our order. "Regime." A strange word to apply to a marriage, if that was his reference, and yet one that came to make sense in the light of events to follow.

My separation from Sarah had one worrisome aspect: I lived in fear that some disaster would befall her. She was unquestionably ill, and I would find myself suddenly in terror of the consequences of having allowed a vulnerable and disoriented woman-child to step out into the world on her own. Blood on the walls, a gruesome bathtub scene involving slit wrists, the onetime love of my life lying with a blood-soaked blanket over her corpse on some New York City sidewalk following her plunge from the roof of a tall building. At such times I would have to remind myself that I had not allowed anything and that a breaking point has been reached when you verbally assault your wife and she empties the dish rack at you and then corners you with a carving knife. And yet, though she had been provoked to threaten me, that seemed meaningless next to the threat of suicide; I was in far more fear of her taking her own life than I had ever been of her taking mine.

Someone might well ask, as Isabel did, why Sarah had been displaced from the loft while I remained in a space designed for an artist. My answer was that she had chosen to leave. It wasn't for me to say, at the beginning of a new (or resumed) courtship that Sarah's departure had something to do with my self-righteous anger. Would it be to my advantage to tell Isabel how, since my days as an editorial assistant with Mr. Marg, I would talk with some frequency, even compulsively, about my job, not only with Sarah but also with her parents as a way of letting them know that I worked and implicitly drawing attention to the fact that they didn't. Such a focus had, in retrospect, an obnoxious if not odious aspect to it. Prompted by my hysteria and woeful insecurity, I might go on about the trials and tribulations of dealing with a boss like Mr. Marg or Olivia, but I was also seeing to it that they knew I was participating in life in a way that they weren't. On a level below full consciousness, I was perhaps rebuking them for their wealth and the free time that it brought.

A further review, if I may. A kind of normalcy, if you can say such a thing, had been achieved in our lives prior to the breakup. The accumulation of sober days and months had turned into two and a half years. I had bought Sarah that quality press on the layaway plan. I had not once come home drunk and torn the house apart. We had taken our walks around the neighborhood. We had eaten peaceful breakfasts at the Binibon down on Fourth Street and Second Avenue and gone for dinner at Phoebe's on the Bowery. I had discussed with Sarah the cruel regime of Olivia and she had been supportive of me. But none of that mattered against the fact that my love had gone elsewhere.

"I know something that will get you out of here," Sarah said to me during one of our exchanges, for she herself was not without weapons. I did not ask what she meant. Her tone and her crafty smile told me where she was going, that she was angled for descent into commentary on an anatomical feature of mine related to size. Her threat was effective. She could see I was undone and unwilling to challenge her to say more. It was a master stroke.

It was in August that Sarah left the loft to stay with her curator friend Bart—he of the ponytail and the forever unwashed jeans— in Brooklyn. And where was I? I was in the country with my in-laws.

Oh life that is not so much strange as preposterous. Are explanations necessary? Can things not just be as they are?

One afternoon, while staying with Sarah's parents, Peter and I walked a long trail. He wore hiking boots and shorts. I wore sneakers and jeans. Though I had thought it diplomatic to follow behind, I found myself in the lead because of his slow pace. The trail took us to an overlook and a deep drop down a rocky gorge. The twitter of birds in the trees and sudden, startling sounds came from the bush. Peter paused to light a cigarette and take in the view.

"I'm a failure as a father," he said with some bitterness.

"But look at all you've done. You raised a family,"I said, frightened by the bluntness of his statement.

"Don't ever have children." The sun high overhead in a sky of breathtaking blue could not mitigate the fact that he was a man in the gray sorrow of his life.

In the evening I would go to Rooms of Recovery meetings in Woodstock and Saugerties. At one such meeting I shared that my marriage had survived my drinking but it didn't appear that it could survive my recovery. A perturbed young man then shared. The veins in his neck bulged as he declared his love for his wife and his loyalty to her. He was not going to abandon her now that he was sober. Was that what I was doing, simply discarding Sarah now that I was getting on my feet?

In the car that I had borrowed from the Van Dines I listened to Bruce Springsteen sing "Born to Run." It served as a narcotic, a high I never wanted to come down from, like listening to the Youngbloods sing "Come Together Now" on some country road in another Van Dine vehicle many years before as a couple of speed pills ate away at my brain. And then the thought followed that thousands, millions of Americans, were experiencing the same thing in the privacy of their own cars or homes or wherever.

In Woodstock I met a thickset woman while browsing in a bookstore on Tinker Street. The prospect of capitalizing on my freedom by being with someone new was exciting. We made tentative plans, but then they fell through. The idea of her proved better than the reality.

An old friend of the Van Dines, a writer, was coming to visit. Lydia asked me to be present for his arrival. "The two of you could talk shop. He might even be able to help you."

This was not good. I knew when disaster was nigh, when foreboding driven by comparison was so strong within me that no basis for communication was possible. I had seen the man on TV with his his drooping mustache and mirthful expression chatting about his latest book. Worse, the man had a son with the suffix "Jr." who had positioned himself to rise high in the eyes of the world if the college he attended—Swarthmore—was any indicator. And didn't it, in truth, have to be? I heard the isolation ward calling. I knew where it stood, just across the lawn, in the guest house with the many mullioned windows.

My thinking went like this: The Van Dines were more a friend of the guest's than the guest was of theirs, as he was in the world and they were not. In all likelihood, the guest really looked down on the Van Dines but was too polite to say so, and even if his manner suggested as much, they were probably too painfully needy of people in their lives to notice. He was only coming because they had coaxed him into doing so. With all this going on, how could I possibly fit in? Would shame not be the prevailing spirit at this gathering? Would attention not be drawn to the distinct difference between the guest on the one hand and Peter and Lydia and me on the other?

There was only one thing to do: steal into the renovated guest house and lie low for the night with the lights off and not dare to show my face until the wooden boards of the bridge were made to rumble as the guest's car passed back over it.

And was that not the story of my life, a life missed because of fear and shame, a life of staying alone in a room while next door others gathered? What is it to have a mind that keeps you apart?

A fiction, uncorrected by me, maintained itself during my stay with the Van Dines. It was that Sarah had initiated the breakup. The day that we were to travel to camp to spend my two weeks' vacation with the Van Dines, it was left for me to tell Lydia that there'd been a flareup between Sarah and me the night before and so we wouldn't be coming. Sarah had already packed a bag and headed down to Brooklyn, But for some reason Lydia insisted that I still catch the bus at Port Authority and stick to the plan. Possibly she had some notion that Sarah would follow a day or two later. All Lydia knew from me was that Sarah was staying with a friend, whose gender I didn't reveal. Lydia was in frequent phone contact with Sarah, who revealed to her some days later that she was staying with this chap Bart. Lydia would give me updates, trying to instill in me hope that Sarah would come to her senses. Lydia could not imagine the darkness that came over me in hearing her words. They carried the threat of possible removal from the sunlight of freedom, where I had now found myself, and a return to marital gloom.

It was another perfect blue-sky day, the kind you cannot take for granted in the Catskills, when Lydia and Peter drove me to the end of the hollow road. If they knew I would never be returning, they did not let on. The bus arrived shortly, and as it came to a stop on the shoulder of the road and pulled away with me on it, I can't say that I myself knew I would never again see the whole strange, beautiful world they had allowed me to enter all those years before.

The firefights Sarah had progressively engaged in with her parents and the endless rumination her mind caught her up in as to what they were doing to her and not doing for her had grown tiresome. Over time she had been displaced by Claire as the center of attention in the family, a situation she found impossible to accept. "Maybe she has a developmental problem," Dr. Reiner had said. And maybe she did. Maybe if you can't take care of yourself, maybe if you can't fully go out on your own in the world, you have to turn back on your parents. In this way she would make them pay. The full burden of responsibility for her would be with them.

I thought I had moved beyond my family, when in fact I had married my older sisters. My limited exposure to the work world and my sobriety had changed me. I loved my mother, as I always had, and was in horror of the judgments I had made about my father. I saw no profit in spending my days vilifying either one of them.

Predictably, Sarah's affair with Bart soon ended, Bart having an appetite for sex but little capacity for relationship. Faced that fall with the prospect of finding a place of her own after staying with him at his Brooklyn apartment, she headed up to camp, her parents having returned to the city. An antique vase, her father's camera, an elegant old lamp—one by one, items of value throughout the house began to appear in a local pawn shop so she could meet her living expenses.

Though we were physically separated now, the imminent threat of disaster, a phone call in the night, kept me on edge. I sensed what others, including her parents and her doctor, evidently did not: she could perish by her own hand. I said as much to Isabel, who had her doubts, as she did regarding the permanence of my separation from Sarah. My fear was that suicide would be Sarah's final blow.

It nearly happened, whether by accident or intent. While heavily medicated, Sarah fell asleep at the wheel of the family jeep, causing it to fly off the state road she was racing along. The jeep was totaled, but miraculously, she escaped death or serious injury, as did the several shoppers who scattered as the jeep sped toward them and slammed into a roadside store.

Beside herself, Lydia called me at Pentacle Books and inquired whether Sarah was still covered by my insurance policy. She was understandably rattled. If there was no coverage, the family stood to be ruined, given the charges Sarah was running up at the psychiatric facility down in Kingston, where she had been committed after a brief investigation. A tirade ensued. Lydia had no more noblesse oblige left in her. She ranted that she had a husband who had never brought in a cent and a daughter in his image who was going to leave them destitute. She, Lydia, had been bilked long enough by the parasites of the world. Thousands and thousands of dollars paid out to a Fifth Avenue shrink so she, Sarah, could go and flirt with her married doctor and sit in judgment of Lydia and Peter, and now an expensive mental institution.

At first I had to restrain myself from laughing, that helpless kind of laughter which would have revealed the sometimes antagonistic nature of my relationship with Lydia and the possibility of my own baseness. How did it feel now that her cocoon was in jeopardy? How did it feel to feel as I did much of the time? She was used to her leisurely ways, to her long naps in the afternoon, to her journal writing, to her twice-weekly sessions with the Jungian she had been seeing for years. She was tired and she was disgusted. First her husband did a flop by not going out into the world as she had expected him to, and now the daughter who was most strongly in his image, the daughter she had least rapport with, had become their albatross.

I did not want Lydia's way of life to be threatened. You should not think that I did. It would have pained me greatly if she and Peter came to financial ruin. I had a love for the Van Dines that I could not always express, and an understanding of all they had given me. And if the only thing that seemed to matter during Lydia's rant was that I was relatively safe and secure, given that I held a job, in the aftermath I saw with great shame how sadly deficient as a husband I had been to have so little sense of responsibility for another human being. Lydia's spirits were higher some weeks later when she called to tell me that my insurance had fully covered Sarah's stay in the psychiatric facility.

Sarah came to be fully in her parents' care. They had the means to buy an apartment for her in Brooklyn Heights and provided her with a monthly allowance. When we were young she had insisted she was born to live alone, but I had laughed in suggesting that maybe she was mistaken. I hadn't known to take her at her word. And so I interrupted the natural path of her life. I had coaxed her into an arrangement that was not suitable for her. But now the error had been corrected. Now she could be as she was evidently meant to be and true to herself.

I sold the loft fixtures to an artist couple eager to move in. They were young and stupid. I recognized the rush to impermanent happiness in their faces. They were members of the slash brigade, as was I, he a dancer/construction worker and she an artist/waitress. Half the money I received I gave to Sarah. It was the least I could do.

I then hired a lawyer, Mabel Muldoon, to initiate divorce proceedings. Not having a lawyer of her own, Sarah met with mine. Ms. Muldoon worked out of her apartment down on Carmine Street. The walls were of exposed brick, a feature I associated with Greenwich Village. As grounds for divorce there had to be a cause, she said. From the list she presented, I chose abusiveness. I didn't like the word as it applied to me or the fact that it would appear for all time in a legal document. The word triggered feelings of shame but also anger and hurt that all my years with Sarah, in which I could at times be genuinely kind and loving and supportive, should be so tersely summarized.

If it is not for me now to present a comprehensive list all the things I ever did to her, allow me to offer a partial one:

- Slept with her younger sister Lenore, of whom Sarah was deathly afraid owing to Lenore's social prowess and other strong attributes.
- Tried to sleep with her older sister Claire, and only didn't because Claire rebuffed me.
- Likewise slept with some of her girlfriends and tried to sleep with others.
- On more than one occasion, was verbally abusive to her to the point that she had to cover her ears.
- On a trip to Europe when we were still in college, physically struck and restrained her in the course of a tussle, so that in the summer sun of Spain she had to wear a long-sleeved shirt to cover her bruises.

Is it necessary to tell you why I did these things? Would it not be enough to say they happened?

Sarah arrived wearing boots and a full-length coat, though the weather was mild. I looked and then looked a second time. Were those small wads of tissue paper in her ears? I sought to ignore them, but was unable to stay silent. And so I said to her, "Sarah, what is it? Do you have an earache?"

"Do I look like I have an earache? You don't have to deal with the fucking pricks, the ones whispering about me all the time, down there in the subway and up here on the streets and even when I have the door shut against them. Yes, my ears ache."

Behind us, in a playground, were some kids scampering around in the innocence of their years. Jesus, the ways life could go wrong. "What are they whispering?" I said, trying to conceal my disbelief with an expression of concern.

"They are whispering all the things the world has ever wanted to say to me. That I am no good, that I should die, that I stole my father from my mother when I never wanted him in the first place."

"And do you answer them?"

"I answer them with my silence. The truth is that I don't only hear with my ears. I hear with my eyes as well, and so long as I have these eyes I will be hearing."

"Then why wear the tissues?"

"To show that I'm on to them. That is why."

Isabel's name did not come up, though by this time Sarah knew we were living together. My sense was that she did not want to go down that road. Evidently, she had enough in her life now, her disability notwithstanding, that she didn't have to. She had gotten what she wanted all along, the full return to her dependent status.

I walked with her to the subway station on West Fourth and Sixth Avenue and watched as she disappeared down the steps. She was still wearing those tissues in her ears. A pickup basketball game was in progress on the asphalt court nearby. Grateful for the diversion, I stood on the other side of the metal fence as the African American men slashed and powered their way to the basket or launched jump shots. I hung around long enough for the emotional overload from my afternoon with Sarah and the divorce lawyer began to leave me. In my long ago past basketball had been a theater of action for me as well. Then it had been Sarah. Now it was Isabel. I headed down to SoHo to meet up with her.

I was out of work for four months after being laid off by Pentacle Books. In that period I stood in line to file for unemployment insurance and went through the motions of finding another job, primarily registering with a few agencies that specialized in publishing. Clearly, I was not a hot commodity, as they never called me with leads. In all fairness, who would want an editor of children's books with very little knowledge about children's books and even less interest in them? None of the jobs listed in the *Times* classifieds appeared to have my name on them. Even after embellishing it, my résumé was thin. Now and then I sent it out, but my days were not spent pounding the pavement looking for work.

By this time I had set up a little office for myself on the unused loft bed, but while Isabel could go through the day carving her animal figures, I was done at the typewriter after an hour or two. The arrangement wasn't the best, as I was literally on top of her, given that her studio was directly below. Evidently I lacked the necessary energy and drive to be a stay-at-home writer. My mind drifted, the way it always did after sitting at the typewriter for a while. I had this desperate urge to write—my life was unbearable without this activity—but once I sat down and actually began, a little progress was sufficient to provide a reprieve from self-hatred. A feeling of peace and contentment came over me once I had received my fix for the day, as if writing was some sort of release, like masturbation.

No, it was better for me to fit my writing (how I hated that term; I could as easily have been saying "my sickness") around a job, which I could fall back on as an excuse for not producing work of better quality. If you lacked determination and talent, what did that leave you with but writing as an exercise in self-therapy? It was a means for me to feel good about myself, like washing the dishes or making the bed, and did not require endless amounts of time or effort.

It wasn't as if I had a wide circle of friends who might call me with possible leads or help open doors. Apart from Isabel I really had no one. A couple of months into this period of idleness, an ad appeared in the *New York Times* for an editor with experience in children's books. There it was in black and white. *I found my job through the* New York Times. How many times had I seen that ad in the subways and on the streets of New York City in years gone by? And now the thought occurred to me that I might be able to say the same thing.

There was a fair amount of urgency insofar as seeking employment in that my funds were running low, which was cause for anxiety, but beyond that, Isabel's ex-husband, Philip, had taken advantage of her financially, and I didn't want to be seen in the same light.

At the time Girls of America Now owned and occupied an entire ten-story building, a blue-tinted glass and steel structure far over on the East Side. The flag of America and the blue and white org flag fluttered in the spring breeze.

(I had taken to wearing glasses with an orange frame. They did not go with my skin or my hair or anything else about my person. But I wore them anyway, for the feeling of individuality that they provided. It is possible, dear God, that I owe them to my publishing father, Mr. Marg, who, as you may recall, would arrive at the office in loud suspenders and colorful watchbands and other accessories that would catch the eye.)

"Suppose you are at a cocktail party and someone asks where you work? How would you handle such a question?" my interviewer, Ms. Anita Dariano, asked. She had a face Connie Francis might have owned in middle age, long after she had outgrown her Mouseketeer outfit.

I would simply and proudly say that I worked for Girls of America Now, I told her. Not that her query was a foolish one. Over the years people have posed just that question to me. And my truthful response has been met, variously, by looks of incomprehension, confusion, disappointment, and such. As I have mentioned, one woman put her laughing thing on me and asked if I were joking as she read the name of my employer on the business card I had handed her. Clearly, serving as an editor for Girls of America Now does not carry the same cachet as holding the same title in the employ of Simon and Schuster or Farrar Straus and Giroux. But it is also true that many in the for-profit sector have fallen on hard times, while I remain a vested member of an organization which, if I hold on, will provide me with a substantial pension. In addition, there are copy-editing and production skills I have had to develop, skills I did not bring with me from book publishing, should anyone wish to think, as I did, that the org is simply a sleepy backwater.

To my surprise, Ms. Dariano seemed impressed with my educational background, treating the fact that I had a flimsy master's degree from a mediocre college with noticeable respect. "With your qualifications, why aren't you teaching?" she asked. I told her it had never been my intention to become a teacher, which was true, and that publishing allowed me to work with words in a way that I found very satisfying, which was sort of true.

Ms. Dariano appeared nervous and even intimidated as the interview continued. "How will you feel about working with people whose strong suit is not the written word, people who may have trouble expressing themselves on paper?" I told her I would take them as they were and work with them to achieve the desired result. While I had responded truthfully, what I hadn't said was how moved, almost to tears, I was by her question, because it placed me in the position of being kind and generous with the vulnerabilities of others. What she was really asking, to my amazed ears, with this and her previous question was not whether I was good enough for the org but whether the org was good enough for me.

A week later I was called back for a second interview. Ms. Dariano led me to a conference room. Within a minute or two a diminutive woman with a shy smile entered, whom Ms. Dariano introduced as Miss Carmelli, before withdrawing. The two of us sat across from each other at the long conference table, on which I had placed a small stack of children's books that I had edited and written jacket copy for. Miss Carmelli's big and sparkling eyes, set in such a narrow face, gave her the appearance of a creature from the insect family.

Strangely, Miss. Carmelli showed no curiosity about these books or my life at Pentacle. Instead she talked in a raspy voice about the heavy workload soon to descend on the Publications Department she headed and the lack of support she had been receiving from the organization. Her voice rose. She became visibly agitated. Lack of understanding was a major problem she faced as a publishing professional in an organization whose primary focus was not on books but on services to girls. No one upstairs really understood the pressure she was under. The higher-ups simply did not grasp what went into putting a book together. A bunch of dolts were drawing fat paychecks for doing nothing but sitting on their cans and reading the *New York Times* behind closed doors. They simply handed you a document and expected that magically it would appear printed and bound the next week.

"There are people here who just think it's about fun and games in the old schoolyard. A day at the beach is what this place is for them. There are people in America making a lot of money who don't know what it is to work. All they want to do is sit in meetings and discuss big ideas and be too big for their britches. For crying out loud, they should show respect to the people who are getting the job done and bringing home the bacon. Give me a break, ladies. Give me a break."

Miss Carmelli was talking to someone. I just didn't know if it was to me. Still, something must have gone right, because the next day I received a phone call from Ms. Dariano in which she told me to report for work the following week.

My years at Pentacle Books had given me an identity. Through association I had derived a sense of being among the elect the way a butler might come to believe he is a cut above the rest through his service relationship to a wealthy and distinguished family. Every man has the right to claim he is better than the next, and then spend the rest of his life finding out he isn't.

At Pentacle there had been offices and secretaries, or editorial assistants. sitting outside them at those battleship gray metal desks. But here at the org, the elevator opened and I stepped out, accompanied by Ms. Dariano, onto a floor covered with raspberry-colored carpeting, a huge space filled with a maze of beige cubicles, each with a nameplate to identify the occupant. Harsh fluorescent lighting shone down from the ceiling fixtures onto the scene of sequestration below.

Ms. Dariano led me to the other end of the floor and turned me over to Miss Carmelli, who occupied not a corner office but a corner cubicle, more spacious than most of the others. Miss Carmelli then led me to a tiny cubicle with my nameplate already on it before introducing me to the rest of the Publications staff.

A much younger Fiona Beasley was already on the scene and very much dug in as the eyes and ears of Miss Carmelli. I was led to this understanding by a duo of women in the department, Felicia Marcos and Karen Raven.

"So what do you think of the Snorkster?" Felicia said to me that morning, setting upon me in an aggressive manner. She was a rotund woman afflicted with a strong tendency toward confrontation and a knack for assigning nicknames to people.

"The who?"

"Snorky. Miss Carmelli."

"She seems very nice."

"You hear that, Karen? He says Snork sounds nice."

"What are you doing, grilling the poor guy? He just got here," Karen said.

"I'm a writer who is trained to look for the story. That's what I'm doing."

"Oh, right, I forgot," Karen said, shooting me an is-this-woman-to-be-believed look.

"What about the Toad? Have you met the Toad yet?"

"She's talking about Fiona Beasley, Snorky's confidante," Karen said.

"Fiona's a complete toad. All day long she kisses the Snorkster's ass. What kind of name is that, Manootdjian? You look like a Jew, but that's no Jewish name," Felicia said, reading my name off the nameplate.

"Felicia, what's wrong with you, anyway?" Karen said.

They were a pair. I suspected this was an act they had been refining for some time.

"Let the man speak. I'm a writer, and writers need to get to the bottom of things."

"It's an Armenian name," I said.

"All right, there you go. Important information. So does your father hang rugs on the wall? Do you hate the Turks? Black people in this country haven't forgotten what white folks did to them and still be doing. We will never forget. We know a thing or two about hatred and how it can color you, no pun intended. You're not a racist, are you?" Felicia was the child of a Filipino father and a Black mother, I was to learn, and powerfully identified with Black people and all people of color.

"Felicia, you really need to stop this," Karen said, an admonition I could sense she had given before in response to Felicia's excesses and that would, Karen had to know, only goad Felicia to say more. The impression formed of two women somewhat young for their age, which I guessed to be their mid-thirties, about the same as mine.

"No more than you, I wouldn't think."

"Did you hear that, Karen? He called a woman of color a racist."

"Don't mind her," Karen said. "She hasn't had her breakfast."

It was to be a job with a lot of down time, as I learned in those first few weeks. Miss Carmelli—it was not for me to call her Snorky—asked that I familiarize myself with the department's publishing history and the org culture by reading through its many publications. There were, of course, handbooks for girls, with camping activities and outdoor education, but the org also published resources for the numerous regional councils it chartered on topics from fundraising to property management to governance. Girls of America Now had a lot going on, as befit a national org that owned an entire building in midtown Manhattan, flew its own flag alongside that of the red, white, and blue, and employed a workforce of four hundred fifty people.

How lucky. I had landed a sinecure that would require little more than for me to languish in my cubicle—sort of an office away from home in which to do my own work. I became intensely happy with my good fortune and altogether, a peculiar sense began to grow in me that I was right where I was supposed to be.

There had been a woman named Miss Nickles—Miss Nelly Nickles—who lived in the same building as my family when I was a child. She was old and frail and solitary, and when Leah and I went to visit with her, Miss Nickles would reach into a large mayonnaise jar filled with pennies and count out ten for each of us. Somehow, in my mind, she became linked with Miss Carmelli. They weren't the same, but they were the same in their petiteness and shy smiles.

Miss Carmelli engendered in me a sense that I had come home to my childhood, in the same way that I had come home to my childhood through Isabel, who had her own antecedent in that building where I had grown up. On school day mornings my mother would say, "You with your long legs, go to Miss Kindelberger with this," and hand me a plate of pancakes with lingonberries sprinkled with sugar. On the floor above, I would find elderly Miss Kindelberger already at her easel in a room that smelled of oil paints and turpentine, and it was with her that my mind linked Isabel, as if in Miss Kindelberger I had both the past that I shared with her and the future I would have with Isabel, the two of us growing old together, one day at a time.

After sitting in my cubicle for a couple of weeks, Miss Carmelli called me into her office to say she had an important assignment. I was to proofread a text that had come down from the office of the National Board of Directors. The task did, if I am to be honest, seem like an inconvenience, as it pulled me away from my writing. I went through the material quickly and returned the document to Miss Carmelli, as instructed.

With the assignment behind me, I returned to a story I was working on, but I was not engaged with it for ten minutes before Miss Carmelli came to me. A look of severity had replaced her smile, and she spoke in a tone of amazed indignation. "Holy crud. There is one mistake after another in this copy," she said in a loud voice, placing the text before me on my desk. Her marks, in green ink, were all over the pages. Spacing and alignment problems, as well as typos. She let me absorb the proof of my incompetence before hitting me with the coup de grace. "If I had known you were going to do this kind of work, I never would have hired you." She then turned and left me to myself.

We are talking here of Miss Carmelli, a woman with formidable powers, not someone simply shy and diffident but at times peculiarly vociferous, thinking back to the interview. This was a woman who, I was to find out, was a master of organization and detail, and the possessor of superb skills not only in writing and editing but the heavy work of book production and design. She was also blessed with a simple grasp of the concept of service. Her day in the office started early and ended late, a schedule which did not prevent her from availing herself of the cultural events of the city. She held season tickets at the Met and often took in concerts at Carnegie Hall as well as Broadway shows. Miss Carmelli was a devout Catholic but she was not renunciatory. Her curiosity drove her to buy books by the cartload at Barnes and Noble. A seasoned traveler, she had visited many of the great cities of the world.

Yes, Miss Carmelli's words stung. It was Claire Eastland all over again. Of all people, I sought out Olivia. What a strange thing to sit with my ex-boss over lunch and tell her about my new one. To go to a scold to be cured of the lash of a scold. Now that our work relationship had fallen away, there was only the possibility of friendship, but the gap between us was too great, I could see, for our contact with each other to continue. I took from her what I could in the reassurance that I had been a good worker and gave her, in return, the admission that I was an alcoholic who had found a solution for the problem. Clearly, she grew distressed at this revelation; my fear was that I had made a great mistake, as if one suddenly confesses to be an ax murderer. And so I was surprised when she proceeded to confide in me her concern about her niece's increasing reliance on alcohol. But I pushed matters a little too far in telling her of my newfound relationship with God. Please understand: I was addressing myself to a private person, an Englishwoman of considerable reserve. Regarding this second disclosure, she could only offer me her silence.

I was at the org for only several weeks when Miss Carmelli organized a staff outing to a design and production company in South Jersey. We gathered at Penn Station for the train ride, at our own expense, down to Philadelphia's 30th Street Station. The outing summoned the feeling of intoxication that can accompany even a modest trip, and on pulling into the station in Philadelphia, there was the beauty of the main concourse, with its decorated ceiling and marble floor, which triggered a sad awareness of what the senseless destruction of the original Pennsylvania Station had cost my own city.

A thing of consequence happened as we waited for the company representative to take us by van on the last leg of our trip. I wandered off across the concourse in the direction of a phone booth, a sudden impulse to call Isabel having come over me. In that moment you could say I felt torn between two masters—the woman I lived with and who had my heart and the woman, Miss Carmelli, for whom I worked. Amid the hundreds of scurrying travelers, I felt the burning sensation of her eyes on my back as I approached the phone booth, the thought occurring that I was not only conspicuously betraying her but in some way *showing her up*. By my action I was saying, "You may think you're important with this little outing, and you may have supervisory power over me, but I have things you can only dream about."

You must understand that I have spent a lifetime setting myself apart. It is not a tendency that ends quickly.

And yet, even in this worrisome spotlight, real or imagined, I was happy to briefly connect with Isabel.

The company was situated in an industrial park in downtrodden Camden, New Jersey. The reality of decline was everywhere: mounds of uncollected garbage, abandoned buildings, idle men hanging about on broken sidewalks at 10 a.m. The park, with its patch of grass and newly planted trees and sparkling structures, stood as a pocket of order amid the encircling blight. (In this time whitewashed store windows and "for rent" signs were ubiquitous in New York City.)

We were given a tour of the facility: designers and typesetters at the controls of state-of-the-art equipment that summoned a dread I could trace to grade school, a sinking sense back then that I would never master the complexities of long division and thus be left behind now manifesting as a fear that the future held no place for those like me, built as I was for smaller things—paper, pencils, erasers—than the consoles that lined the walls of the workrooms.

Lunch was served in a windowless room. Miss Carmelli sat alone at the far end of the conference table, virtually hidden behind a stack of proofs, which she busied herself checking as the rest of us ate. It occurred to me that the material in front of her was the true staple of her diet, the thing that made her big and strong beyond her size. It also struck me that she was afraid of us. In that moment a feeling of sadness came over me and my heart opened to her.

Since putting down the drink and attending RoR meetings, I had been buoyed by a sense of hope, but now that hope seemed to have vanished one evening as I returned home while still with Sarah. It was as if I had butted up against a ceiling and had no more room for growth. Horizons must be unlimited for an alcoholic to survive; the world must truly be one of infinite possibility, whether drunk or sober. And so I phoned my mentor, as he had answers no one else on the planet had the seeming ability to provide.

Zed was no one to take lightly. I had glimpsed his storehouse of anger. For that reason, as well as the disparity in our ages—he was twenty years my senior—my manner toward him was deferential. Love was current as well. I had stood naked before this man and he had accepted me. I had told him every vile thing I had done, every instance of harm, small and large, that I had inflicted on other human beings. I had shared my envy, my lust, my humiliations, my inadequacies, as I saw them. I had sat there in the studio of his ramshackle Scarsdale home ("We rent," he had chuckled, conveying that it was the ultimate putdown of home dwellers in that upscale community) for two afternoons on back-to-back weekends and the experience changed me in ways that are hard to express. For one thing, I felt part of the universe and a measure of compassion for the boy and young man I had been. I saw how lost I had become in the course of my drinking life. I saw, in addition, that I had done the very best I could and that I had always been all right. I hadn't needed to be more than I was; I hadn't needed to go to better schools, just as I didn't need more intelligence than what I possessed.

"Sit with your spine straight and your eyes closed. Focus on your breath—breathing in, breathing out. When your thoughts stray, bring them back to your breath. Do this for five minutes." With that he hung up the phone.

Years before, as a teenager, my focus had been drawn , if only briefly, to my breath, and the peace such focus could bring. But I drifted away from this discovery, and so the world had me and the world was all I had and no relief was to be found except for the comfort I could find in the bottle.

I sat at the same oak table where, for some years, I would drink myself to sleep, relieved that Zed had not required me to seat myself on the floor and adopt the lotus position, as my body lacked the suppleness for such a posture. The simple exercise was transformative. In those five minutes I found a place that I could go, and it was not to the drink or the drug or the woman or the job or any other external facet of my life. I could go inside. I could sit and do nothing but focus my mind on my breath, as I had done years before, and the soreness that had afflicted me vanished. Now, though I could hear Sarah in her studio, as I had heard the sounds of Broadway those years ago as I lay in my childhood room, I had arrived in a space of peace, and hope and light were mine once more.

The source of the power I was seeking was not outside me; it lay within. And what was that power but one that enabled me to think and act and feel as I couldn't without it. In this way was a thirst for booze replaced with a hunger for the power of the universe.

As I gradually expanded my sitting time, from five to ten to fifteen to twenty minutes, the sense of your presence grew, to the point where, as I walked the streets, I was filled with an inner glow such as I had never known. In such a state did I arrive at a bookstore up on St. Mark's Place in the East Village and saw a clerk with the still watchfulness of an owl as he sat perched on his stool. I saw Carl Jung on a shelf shouting for my attention and Sigmund Freud on the shelf below clamoring likewise. I saw the confines of the place in which I stood and could not stay. It was a habitation too small for where you had taken me. I spoke with prostitutes and hooligans and blotto bums on the depraved streets. I called out to suicide candidates in seedy hotels to share their names and asked the wind to shed its invisibility. The structure of innocence revealed itself to me. It was there in plain sight to see.

I said many things and did many things and yet I did nothing but be with you on harsh streets amid the undocumented histories of the fallen.

And yet, at some point, I said please stop. The ecstasy, odd to say, was wearing me out.

As the months passed, the intense effect of the powerful dynamo I had plugged into diminished and a low-grade happiness and quiet sense of purpose took its place.

The point was that, having found this interior space, I had to return to it regularly, if that irritability wasn't to find me again, as once I would return to the drink, but with the difference that freedom, not enslavement, was the result.

And then there was that Saturday morning, as you will remember, when, list in hand, I rushed out the door without the morning meditation to which I had now grown accustomed. There wasn't time. Too many errands to run. Trash and broken bottles littered the sidewalk. A bum was sleeping off a drunk on the pavement. I pushed on, but as I made the purchases my list required of me, no happiness resulted. Rather did the soreness mount and mount, my mind becoming a torment and life in broad daylight a horror: the overweight woman caught in the act of stuffing her face with a street vendor's hot dog; the wail of an ambulance coming for a man who lay unconscious and bleeding in the street, having been struck by a cab. Everywhere scenes of pain under an indifferent sky of leaden gray. The problem was the eye I was seeing with. That eye had to change, and only sitting, I sensed, would allow that perceptual shift to occur. It was a mistake I was not to make again, I want you to know.

Isabel had friends who were a cut above anything I could ever hope to be, friends who had gone to exclusive schools and now, in their thirties, were making their mark in the world. It was not that I wanted to leave the room when they were present; it was only that I felt I had to leave the room. I was a dull light in comparison with shining stars like Frank McGwire, a rising young painter with his Yale MFA and movie star looks. And how was I to hold my own with

Maude Swain, Isabel's friend from childhood, who too had gone to Yale and now was a rising defense attorney with a Park Avenue law firm? Numbers would appear in my consciousness, numbers far lower than theirs. I was sure they could see those numbers, as if they had been summoned onto my forehead to glow in neon, and that I had forced myself into a league I was not qualified for. They were there bearing witness to the contraction taking place in their midst, the shriveling of my God self into the paltry dimensions of my default being. And in those moments I saw the naïve foolishness of my belief that a life in God predicated on oneness and a de-emphasis on the intellect could equalize me with others. The separate worlds of winners and losers had a way of enduring.

And yet I did not hate high numbers because to have hated high numbers would have meant hating Isabel, who had scintillating numbers and as a result was a beacon drawing people from far and wide to the brilliance of her light. Up all five flights they would trudge just for the opportunity to sit with her, and if they had to endure the gaunt and serious-looking man who was her new companion, that was simply a price they were willing to pay.

If Isabel had a family, I had a family of my own. Leah at this time was living in the city. Her spacious Riverside Drive apartment signified her status, as did the doctorate she had received. She was by now married to Marvin, a man seeking refuge from his pain through the habitual use of marijuana but who functioned in the real world sufficient to get the job done. They were a married couple whose daughter Gretchen had yet to be born.

Leah took a liking to Isabel. If I had the fear of them becoming too close, I kept it to myself, though you must know the fear of women bonding and leaving me behind was there. It was in my bones that such a thing could happen.

And I was at a juncture in my life that I had to go to Leah with an acknowledgment of my crimes against her humanity. I had to tell her every last thing I had done to her in betraying what a brother, *an older brother,* is supposed to be. I had to confess that back in high school I had in one instance hidden her school books in fear that otherwise she would someday catch up to and surpass me. I had to tell her that I had failed to show up for her wedding or her graduate school commencement because of my own smallness. I had to acknowledge that I had been afraid of her. If I was to move beyond the dinky dimensions that my secrecy had imposed, I had to come clean.

Because if you are a brother to my sister Leah, and a brother to other sisters of mine, you will find reason to apologize in the course of your lifetime. You will come to know the penitent as a role assigned to you.

If I did these things, if I went to Leah as a way of effecting change in our relationship, I stopped short of telling her that she had stolen my father's love or that she had sought to eradicate me from the premises of this earth through her thoughts and actions. It was not my business to say these things, but I did say as much to Isabel, who became my confidante as well as my lover, as Sarah had once upon a time filled those same roles.

And I told Isabel about Hannah and how she had been a towering figure of darkness in my life and how her hand had been an instrument of pain and humiliation, and of the tongue she had placed between thick lips as she smacked and smacked when I was a child, and of the words she had spoken, "You just leave these fresh brats with me. I'll take care of them," as my mother was about to leave the apartment for a rare Sunday evening at church with my father. Yes, I told Isabel these things, as I had to tell her, seeking desperately for the ally who would keep me safe from Hannah even at the age I had come to. For unto Hannah a son, Rick, had been born when I was age ten, a son she had taken unto herself in the privacy of the room my mother had assigned her in the building where we lived and where she could visit on him the smacks she had inflicted on me and that our father had inflicted on her. I told Isabel what it was to be a boy with nothing in front of him but his massive mother and a father not even on the horizon, Hannah having placed his identity in the category of a state secret.

Isabel,
I had to tell you these things. I was into this family born and took them where I went. But I withheld from you my fear that they would degrade or take you from me. Who were *they*? Who else but my sisters and even my brother. We were a family without boundaries. There was no territorial integrity. I understand what you might think. Why is Johan talking about boundaries and territory? Is he a piece of property? But when you have been overrun in the past and your father has been stolen from you, then you will have a high degree of suspicion, for you will recognize that escaping from such beings is your true life's purpose.

I will not say you were my identity, but you did represent the thing of value in my life. To be honest, I had the promise of a finish line looming through the marriage, and so could not, without some trepidation, enter into the potential realm of destruction that an environment occupied by my family of origin represents. Do not underestimate my powers of understanding and awareness. Yes, I was born a Virgo for a reason, to exercise the critical faculty that would allow me to see the mistakes that had been made by those in the family who went before me and, in discerning those mistakes, perhaps escape my older siblings' fate.

Let me go to the heart of the matter. Hannah had made her son Rick the instrument of her will. This happens when a boy is taken unto a woman and can see only the woman so wherever he turns there is the flesh of the woman before his eyes and in his mind. He is her this and he is her that, but he is never himself alone. The proprietary clamp will never be removed. He can go on to high school, he can go away to college, he can have a girlfriend or two, but sooner or later he must return to that room he grew up in with his mother. I am my mother and my mother is me, the boy says, as he throws the perfect spiral pass half the length of the football field into the outstretched arms of the receiver. Always his mother is calling to him. Her silent whistle is everywhere.

You say to me, why must you be so harsh? Why must your vigilance be so soaring? Why are your words so dire? Why can you not see them as two human beings?

And I say to you this. When a young man of imposing physical dimensions, who has been known to punch men in the face for no reason, can be said to be the instrument of his mother's will, and when that mother still has the smacking hands that she employed when I was young, then a primal fear is awakened that requires me to be on high alert.

I am aware of the problem of separation, Isabel. Do not think for a moment that I am not. I see the ways in which I held myself apart from my family and spent my life trying to prove I was different, only to find that I was an apple fallen from the same tree. And yet, if it is a spiritual truth that darkness can be mitigated by love, there is no given schedule for the light's arrival. A person does not casually place himself in harm's way when dysfunction and derangement are abounding.

I looked forward to seeing Leah and Marvin. The wound I had experienced at her advancement in life was healing and I was beginning to approximate the proper relationship of an older brother to a younger sister, though I had a ways to go. Simply know that by this time it had become my way to pray for love and tolerance and patience and understanding of all those in my life. And if I could not come by equality with Leah on my own, you, Isabel, were now on the scene to give me a compensatory boost that would allow me to be more presentable than I could otherwise be.

In our courtship, if it can be called such a thing, you once called me from a party given by your Texan friend Abilene South. I was still in the Bowery loft, Sarah having left by then. You said a profoundly creepy man was following you from room to room. You meant me no harm with your words. It was not for you to know or be concerned that your call summoned in me such distress or the nature of my wound and how flooded with terror I instantly became on hearing your telephone report. My mind convinced me that he would have his way with you, if not there at the party, then at your place. He would escort you home and simply win you over. In the cool night air of SoHo you would see him in another light. You would find his humanity. You would let him into your garden, as you had the satyr in that last year of my drinking. It is not for a man to show jealousy or fear around you in regard to another man. This will not serve him well. You will have to hurt such a man, and hurt him very badly. You will have to punish him to the end of his days with dismissal from your life. It was for me to know this disposition instinctively about you toward the weak, the needy, the clinging, and the savage blow that you would ultimately deliver. And yet my terror would not abate. I could not read, I could not think, I could not eat. I remained locked that night in obsessive misery. Now I had a rival who saw you as I did, a goddess supreme.. How strange and yet necessary that pain should be the catalyst in driving those in relationship to have no choice but to find God.

My own pain grew worse when, in desperation, I called your number some hours later. As you may recall, when you answered I barked at you for having scared me half to death, and in response, you expressed amazement that I would be undone by such a character. The dread the prospect of losing you to this man had summoned in me was nothing in comparison with the horror I lived with for the duration of the night, knowing you had seen a facet of my being I so wished to keep hidden, namely, my woeful insecurity and the fear it spawned.

Leah's apartment, as you yourself noted, was typical for a prewar West Side building, with its high-ceilinged rooms. In the living room, which had a set of French doors, a computer sat precariously on a typewriter stand. The room had an oriental rug, somewhat worn, and a number of plants, but what caught my eye were the framed doctorates of Marvin and Leah hung at eye level side by side on the wall. Leah had turned a room meant for socialization into her office. I took in the doctorates at a glance. By averting my eyes I was hoping to neutralize Leah's power and not take the salt right into the wound.

It is possible that Leah had designs on you and wished to claim you for herself. At that Christmas dinner several years before at my mother's apartment, where we had our row, it was not lost on me that she had pulled family members from the room, including Hannah and her son, saying to them both, *"Get away from this devil. Get away from him,"* in that way positioning herself as a creature of goodness and me as a visitor from the underworld. This ostracizing tendency has been going on a long time. Leah had given herself certain rights. She had in some way made Rick hers as she had made Hannah hers as well. A connection had been assumed by Leah that allowed her to utter this kind of directive. And given the fact that in my early years she had appropriated our father, my fear that her power would extend over you seemed not unreasonable.

I could see my mother's effect on you. You were receptive to her love. And you even expressed a worrisome liking for Hannah. What trouble could come from such a nexus I could not bear to contemplate. But really, if many people were present, there was only one, and his name was Danger. That is no way to speak of one's nephew, of course. Love and the bonds of blood should abide in every family. Still, Rick was a hound, he was on an invisible leash of ample length to roam where he would in that big apartment. Isabel, you had the power to draw him, but unlike Hannah, you had no power to control him. She, and only she, held the leash. The animal had found his prey.

When I later remarked on Rick's inappropriate attention to you, you acknowledged your discomfort. "I was unable to get rid of him," you said. Feigned or otherwise, the attention you showed this nephew of mine only increased your power over him. He was starved, starved, for the attentions of someone such as you. Rick was a young man who had no possibilities on his own.

By comparison, one had only to look at Marvin. He was able to marry, and one day soon, his daughter Gretchen would enter this world. Marvin could chat with you, but there was no cause to doubt his intentions, as he had a moral core that Rick seemed to lack. Marvin was not infected with narcissism that would dash him on the rocks of life.

The real problem, of course, was that Rick was me and I was Rick to an excruciating degree. Watching him trail after you from room to room was only to watch myself at my predatory worst, wrapped hopelessly around women, as if I had no destination home without them.

And then something utterly shattering happened, not there at Leah's but the following week. You have moved on from that event, Isabel, and yet it needs recalling. Quite simply, Rick was arrested for the crime of rape.

We all want to be somebody in this life, even the most self-denying. We all seek a measure of recognition and even glory. Rick's dream was to be a star quarterback for a great university. And in fact he was accepted to an excellent college, where he was gaining attention for his performance on the gridiron. But the student body council did not take kindly to what it considered unprovoked assaults on its students, and so Rick found himself expelled when he was entirely unapologetic for causing serious injury to a fellow student with several punches to the face. He returned to live with Hannah, and an alternative dream developed. He would trade in his shoulder pads for dancer's tights. Perhaps he was seeking to develop a gentler side of his nature. He met a young woman in one of his dance classes. They went out for dinner one evening in the week following Leah's party. He then returned with her to her apartment on the pretext of having forgotten his bag. Or maybe he didn't mean to leave his bag behind. But once in her apartment, he told her he wasn't going anywhere, and she wasn't either. He said he would have to hurt her if she tried to scream. He smoked some dope and then forced her to have sex. When he had to relieve himself, he brought her into the bathroom and held her down as he sat on the toilet. When, some hours later, he fell asleep in her bed, she fled out the door, and ran in only an oversize T-shirt into the street and called 911 from a public pay phone. This was a little after 4 a.m. Things proceeded from there, of course. The apparatus of the state entered the picture, and Rick became grist for its legal mill.

The defense Rick made was no defense at all, as the deft prosecutor pointed out. Rick just happened to be there in Denise's apartment. He had no idea how she had incurred so many bruises or what would possess her to run half-naked from her own place in the dark of night and phone the police. From his standpoint they had been enjoying a pleasant evening of consensual sex. The term *forcible compulsion* was spoken by the judge and the definition read more than once.

As you know, Isabel, a direct appeal was made by Hannah for a contribution to Rick's legal defense. As you also know, I declined to come forward with even a nominal sum of money. This refusal was a mistake on my part. It was for me to stand by Rick and see that he received adequate legal counsel, regardless of his stonewalling manner. At the same time you must understand the fear behind this decision. To my mind, Denise could just as easily have been you. If the circumstances had proven right, Rick would have been holding you down in that bathroom while he relieved himself. His arrest for the rape of Denise was not out of line with my own projection as to where he was headed. My heart was with the prosecution. I wanted him stopped.

Rick was dismissive of the charge. "There's something wrong with that girl. I go and give her good sex and what does she do? She drops a dime on me." If there was any regret, it was only that he hadn't been a better judge of character. "I guess I just didn't know, man. I just didn't know. Man, did she have me fooled." He, not Denise, was the victim.

Hannah herself was entirely supportive of her son. She was his mother, after all. As the legal machinery moved on and the trial began, she became engrossed with the courtroom drama, not missing a day. The trial filled a void in her life. Her conversation grew full of wild rumination about the motive of the prosecution in going to such great length to harass her son. To question in the slightest her son's innocence was to unleash her sizable wrath, as my mother, for one, found out.

The adamancy of their position led me to see Hannah and her son as one. They had in common mental vaults in which to seal from consciousness unpleasant truths. She could not bring herself to ask what part he might have in these difficulties. Because to raise questions about him would be to raise questions about herself. Hannah was practiced in the art of concealment. It is not for nothing that she glorified the Mafia for their embrace of *omertà*.

Isabel, the contribution of money to Rick's legal defense constituted, in my mind, an endorsement of the criminal direction of his life. My failure to write a check was a reaction, not a response, to the history of pain and terror that Hannah had inflicted, which might grow worse unless she were somehow parted from her weapon, that is, unless Rick was convicted. I should tell you that I did actually approach Rick about the circumstance of his arrest. I did not confront him. I did not demand an explanation. Rather, I simply inquired whether he might have had a part in his own troubles. But there was nothing in it for him to go down such a road, he said, an expression of slyness accompanying his words.

Inevitably, the judicial wrecking ball came in on his life as he had known it, parting him from his freedom with a five-year sentence, which he served in a maximum security prison up near the Canadian border. When the verdict was read and the judge remanded him for sentencing, the composure he had been maintaining throughout the courtroom drama fell away. A hysteria-driven howl tore from him, and several court officers were needed to lead him away, but not before Rick shot me a look that said, "I'll be back. I'll remember you," turning a basilisk's eye upon me.

What can anyone really make of eye communication, Isabel? Is it truly so nakedly expressive? What was I to make of Hannah turning to stare back at me, at some earlier phase of the proceeding when, conceivably, she allowed herself to believe that Rick's poorly prepared attorney was mounting a credible defense? All the ill will in her being seemed to gather in her dark eyes and radiate their toxic effect into my being in that one moment of unspoken communication.

You must understand, Isabel. Do you see those pit bulls with such muscular bodies and locking jaws on the street? You know that whatever their natural dispositions, their handlers can breed them for harm. Many of these owners show a disposition toward violence on their truculent faces. But others have this pacific appearance, and yet you can be sure they too have a score to settle—with the universe, with God, with whomever or whatever placed them here on this earth in the wretched condition they find themselves. And so they have no choice but to poison the environment with the skillful use of proxies. And poison it they do. By secret signals that defy detection, they launch their canines on the most savage attacks— the German shepherd that suddenly lunges and tears off a man's face or the Rottweiler that devours a baby in the infant's carriage or the Doberman that snacks on the calf of a runner who had been streaking through Central Park and now writhes in agonizing pain on the jogging path. What do the three owners of these treacherous canines have in common in the examples given, Isabel? Yes, of course, they all protest their complete innocence or place the onus on the victim. The leash just happened to slip from their hand. They were distracted and looking the other way when the nanny passed by with the baby carriage. But why did the baby have food around its mouth? Did the runner have to wear such brief and brightly colored shorts? In such ways do they seek to provide cover for their wills of pure evil, and it is only the most intense and relentless line of inquiry that can summon the concealed beast lurking in them.

You know where I am going with this, Isabel. You definitely know. Rick was Hannah's pet. He had no self of his own. He was forced to spend his life in Hannah's dark places. She made him hers, and only hers, forever. And now, moving forward in time, past his prison term, they live together in my mother's apartment. Everyone else is gone, but they remain. That is just the way it is. From the very beginning was he fully claimed as her own.

We had a City Hall wedding. What can be plainer than that, a man and woman standing before a civil service worker in an unadorned room of the Municipal Building in lower Manhattan? We were in agreement that simplicity was preferable to the ordeal of a big production. You had been down the aisle before and so felt no need to call attention to this second betrothal. Now, with hindsight, it may be safe to say that there was a less obvious reason for your interest in a low-key ceremony. The marriage was never a joyous prospect in your eyes, if the gold wedding band you chose meant anything. Quite thick, it symbolized, you later said, the slavery into which you had entered.

Maude, your friend from childhood, was present. She had learned that day of her hire by a prestigious law firm. This was a woman who wanted the things of the world and who was practicing the art of acquiring them in a skillful and methodical way. Though she often professed a desire for "a man," as she put it, and it was probably a great desire in some part of her being, could it not also be said that ambition was her true and constant mate?

Maude was our only witness, and so it is for me to be grateful that she had come. Still, her Ivy League credentials, certifying her brilliance, served as an oppressive weight and increased my self-consciousness as I quickly succumbed to a tendency that has been with me through the years of seeing myself through the eyes of others. It should be all right to be ordinary in this life and to not have attended the finest schools. But I felt, standing in the sterility of the room where the civil service official led us through our marriage vows, and later, sitting at the West Broadway café where we had all gone, that Maude perceived in the depths of her being that you had married someone who lacked your luster and your intelligence. Undone by the weight of her gaze, all I could seem to offer was amiability as a deterrent to any kind of attack, though as a strategy it was doomed to failure. When you are not real, when you do not present a genuine person, then you forfeit credibility and are dismissible.

(It is years later and I am on the Number 9 subway, bound up the West Side of Manhattan. Toward the front of the car I sit when I notice Maude seated with a man I do not know. Though it is my prayer that she will not see me, she does, and it is as if we are frozen in place. There is an understanding that we are strangers who were brought together by you and now we are apart again. All the comparative data are laid out that compel us to be apart— intelligence, schools attended, the works. A ride more terrifying than being in the same subway car with a bunch of thugs. Oh, Isabel, the dream of being really real has not died in me. I must come forth. I must.)

To be honest, Isabel, I didn't feel our new life could begin until we were alone. Maude saw I couldn't extend myself any further than I had. And yet she was a light breeze in June next to the ordeal that was coming. Your parents, with the enterprise they could muster at their advanced ages, sought to enhance the plain matrimonial occasion we had opted for with a reception that same evening at the Cosmopolitan Club here on the East Side of Manhattan. Waiters in tuxedos navigated the creaky floors and worn rugs of the room with trays of hors d'oeuvres. A setting with a tinge of the past on it.

I had an amend to make to my mother, Isabel. You know I did. As I entered my teenage years I had distanced myself from her in public. I didn't want my friends to see I had a parent approaching sixty who wore sturdy shoes that belonged on the foot of a man as well as those beige rubber support stockings for her varicose veins.

You see the problem, don't you? Hidden, hidden, hidden. The shadow of shame cast over every person in my life except for you.

But I had been rendered sober and now had the chance to correct the errors of the past, to walk down the street with my mother, so to speak, she whom I had denied more than once.

Isabel, you wore a dress of many colors. Were you a female Joseph? As for myself, I wore a gray suit of tropical wool. The choice of color was an odd one for a wedding, but it was my one suit. The thought had come as to what kind of man it is who does not possess a single suit. And where else would one go but to Brooks Brothers for the quality I was seeking? The salesperson assured me that even on the hottest days my suit would breathe. We are talking Brooks Brothers now, on Madison Avenue, in the heart of Manhattan, where madras and seersucker and argyle socks and the bowtie still flourish. It was here that a tailor of great renown was assigned to take my exact measurements.

Isabel, my mother showed up strong. She did not cower in her bed or fret about where she stood in regard to education and achievement. My mother was activated in the things of the Lord and lived in the realm of the spirit. She did not turn your mother into an intimidating intellectual force whom she had to bow down to or flee from. My mother was eighty-one when she made her appearance at the Cosmopolitan Club. By this time the outside world was but a blur in her mind. She had her preparations underway for leaving this earth. When your mother spoke of all the parts of the world she had seen, my mother could only stare and say, "Oh my. Is that so?" And so your mother had nothing she could do with my mother but to sit with her. It was not in your mother's nature to forego a discussion of Michelangelo or Fra Lippo Lippi or Caravaggio or the scientific vision of Leonardo or the drunken poems of Li Po composed under a full moon. My mother had been reduced to the place of her own contentment and in that place had been magnified. Because she walked with God and talked with God she could face people. She did not have to hang back with only rocks and trees and other inanimate objects. And the replay mechanism was missing from her mind that would have her review in agony what she had said or not said.

There were others who came, and they too must be named, as they are with me wherever I go. There was my sister Hannah, who needed to bear witness to her own pain. I have a long history with her, having been born to an awareness of her deprivation, and received advance information in regard to it while still in the womb. It was the song she sang to an indifferent universe. Hannah came alone, that is, without her son, who was now in a cell out at Riker's Island following his arrest. She trumpeted notes of misery into my ear, deafening me for the duration to everything but her travail. "You of all people should understand my son and help him." And there it was, Isabel. There it was. I was obligated not only to Hannah but to he whom she had brought into the world. The burden of her weight was too much for me. It always had been. I could only meet her pain with silence, as what were words in a circumstance like that?

Those present were real world power players making an impact in all fields of endeavor. There was Calliope Juttingham, world-class violinist. There was Sidmantha Smeld, award-winning author. There was Sylvester Barricado, U.S. Supreme Court petitioner extraordinaire, whose powers of legal logic had divested the justices of their robes and left them standing naked on more than one occasion. And there was Abel Plenty, who could make the purse strings of commerce sing with the deals that he could do.

Hannah had drawn their attention with her outburst. Possibly they saw it as a breach of civility, so inappropriate to the occasion would it have seemed to them, their social graces being at the high level they were. Surely they felt for her, but at the same time would have perceived that she was not suitably calibrated for their circle. But no *odar* Armenian, no quasi Armenian, really is, is she (or he)? Hannah, by her lights, had the right to impose her bad mood not only in a family setting but wherever she was, and no one was going to deny her that right. No one is as unrestrained and self-indulgent as a Manootdjian. Alienation was her defense against intimacy, and having ruptured the social contract, she was under no obligation to repair it. In fact, it was in her interest that it stay broken, the payoff being, in her mind, an enormous dividend of self-pity and self-righteous anger. I talk as one who knows. Some of us do find a painful pleasure in seeing from the point of view of what others have and they don't. And that, of course, is what Hannah was finding that night of the reception. I had you and all you represented and all her son Rick had was a cell and the prospect of many years of imprisonment ahead of him.

What is that expression, Isabel? It is no skin off my nose? Rick's misery was skin off my nose, deny it though I might. As I have said, to look at Rick was to look at myself, or an aspect of myself that horrified me—narcissistic, needy of women, frighteningly impulsive. Had I not had episodes with women about which I was not proud, even if not in the degree to which Rick had taken things? Hannah had linked the two of us, and she had reasons, I suppose. But there was one major difference between her son and me. I could tell the truth, and Rick was deficient in that regard, and so was she.

It is a grave problem in America that finds the unmatched being brought together. Not everyone is suitable for the company of everyone else. We are not interchangeable on this physical plane. All this upward mobility. Possibly we should return to the idea of one's station in life rather than strive to be what we can never be, with the result that we have to envy others because they succeed where we have failed. The quality of your family and their friends was astonishing. Their success was no mystery. They were blessed with intelligence and my family wasn't. Your family and their friends had brains and my family had God.

So it goes in life. So it goes.

To root it to the concrete to the extent that I can, let me note that Maude's parents were present at the reception. Her father was laden with own discontent. On his face it was written that he was *only* a physician. He inspected bodies for a living, Isabel. He did not live in the realm of art but in the corporeal. He had no literary leanings to speak of and suffered from the same relationship to your parents as Maude did to you, that is, from a position of looking up. Had I not seen this before among the Van Dines, who also had among them the star worshipers secretly rooting for them to fail? The pecking order never ends, and one chafes against his own standing in life. But what kind of man, would you say, notices such things? What kind of man indeed? When Maude's father saw me, he saw himself, which gave him no basis for hope, as when I see Rick, the light inside goes out and darkness reigns. No one can bear the dismal reality mirrored in the faces of others with whom they have negative identification. No one. From such a perception must we flee.

And what other meaning can God have but to allow the premises of our own minds to receive glimmers of his so we can relinquish the contracted state and rest in the embrace of the eternal?

As you will remember, Isabel, we flew off the next day for San Francisco, a city which neither one of us had ever visited. Ours had been no June wedding. It had taken place in the harshness of a New York City December, and so the warmth of the West Coast beckoned. California was definitely the land of milk and honey, a state bathed in the aura of a golden light. And if we anticipated that Frisco might be cold and raw, well, we would definitely be following the sun in heading south along the Pacific Coast Highway to Los Angeles.

I had brought along a biography of Theodore Roosevelt, significant for its weight but also for its sterling scholarship. I learned much about TR's thirst for knowledge and his boundless energy and his affinity with nature. He was good company for me on this trip. It was my thinking that he might possibly add some weight to my mind if not my bones.

The plane ride, of course, was a torment. Do you know the danger you summoned with your laughing manner? Do you suppose Thanatos doesn't frown on such disregard of his lurking presence? I made up for your insouciance with vigilance that I can only describe as soaring. What made the experience of air travel all the more perilous was the simple fact that the craft was a DC-7, a plane that had ushered numerous passengers into eternity after lulling them into the false belief that the safety of terra firma was imminent. And so I focused hard on keeping us aloft, from takeoff to landing, never allowing myself the mistake of unfounded confidence.

Do you know how many have gone to their deaths in just such a fashion, laughing and gay and then, the next moment, terror-struck and seconds after that mortally injured. Punishment will always find those who are not vigilant, or who slyly bring on that which they fear by pretending they didn't know that danger was lurking, as the woman crushed by the speeding bus along with the child whose hand she held. I did nothing. I did nothing, such a woman would dare to say, when you and I, gentlemen and gentlewomen of the jury, know far different, know, that is, that she was, with vicious slyness, purposely looking the other way while stepping off the curb.

Who talks like this, Isabel? Who? I will tell you who. A person who believes, beneath his superficial affect of love, in a punishing God saying to the human race, "You're in pain? Tough bananas, baby. It's all your fault." Only a man in the grip of his own cruel perfectionism can speak in such a fashion.

In Frisco I locked onto a trio of elderly and dour folk as they were exiting a Catholic church into the gray day outside. The man, with two women on his arm, looked at me with eyes full of hate, his jowls flapping in an affirmation of his distaste. He had a puss the face police wouldn't touch. Not one from that wretched yet so American crew would ever inquire as to why he wasn't smiling or seek to place him under house arrest until he did. He was not a man who would countenance such inquiries, and would be sure to hurt you very bad should you even try to play that way. There is no use asking why a Buster Keaton face such as this is in the world. It is there because it has willed itself into creation, saying to one and all, You will take me as I am and never lay your intrusive commentary upon me. Your face police will not approach me.

But I approached this man, Isabel. I most emphatically did. I captured his mug with my camera and he assessed me coldly for it. Believe me when I say he did. When you shoot a man, you shoot a man. There are no two ways about it.

A photograph will engender a kind of pain like no other. You will enter a museum and walk past the Rembrandts and the Monets to stare endlessly at photos of a Whelan's drugstore in New York City, circa 1944, or a lonely street in the Murray Hill section of the same city in 1946, and you will say why could I not be there? Why must I be here where I am with this longing so strong to get back to what I possibly never knew? Or you will say, Was I there and simply don't remember? Isabel, a photograph will call you to the past and seek to make it present forevermore. With a single-lens reflex camera you will find yourself seeking to stop time altogether, and an appetite for more and more images will grow and grow. And yet, you cannot keep up with the world with technology alone. The forms are too discrete. Nothing stays in place in this world; it is just a madhouse of change. I didn't know that I would have to relinquish the camera to find what I was looking for, the thing beyond which nothing more is needed, if only I have the faith to believe that this is so.

I could not tell you our exact itinerary. I do know we had Christmas in Carmel, as per your plan. Of the gifts we gave to Mia on that holy day I have no recollection, or of those I gave to you or possibly received. But we did our duty. We showed our love. As to where those gifts are today, I have no idea. A flea market in Abilene, Kansas? A median strip in Denver, Colorado? We mustn't concern ourselves with such thoughts, Isabel; they are not good for the mind.

The trip had its moments of great pleasure and happiness, but there were also times of sad self-awareness, as when I placed my rigidity on full display in insisting that Mia sleep in an adjoining room and remaining adamant even when her cries of anguished protest could be heard from the other side of the hotel wall. What adult gets in a test of wills with a child who cannot bear to be separated from her mother in a strange city? Where was the voice of love and reason fled to that I should have come to such a mental and emotional pass? Let it be said, however, that this very voice did ultimately come shining through to send my folly on its way and dissolve the wall that separated Mia from you so that two together and one apart could now be all three in the same room, with Mia sleeping on a cot furnished by the hotel.

So maybe the question is this: what is the point of going on, Johan Manootdjian, about Hannah's abuse, when you display a similar bent in your own right?

Bernhard Goetz was in the news at this time. His forebears had been eliminated in the ovens of Nazi Germany and by other means. He himself had the experience of assault, having been dealt some savage blows by the ruffians of New York City. And now it was that rowdy young men with faces full of laughing anger came to prey upon him in the subway. They created a commotion of sound among themselves, seeking to dominate the car with their noise and ominous presence. Isabel, they were talking not so much to each other but a wider audience, drawing you into their party of sound with some complex interaction that tested the limits of your tolerance. So intruding, so canceling of your own thought patterns was their interplay as to leave you wondering if it was the chatter of desperate and yet smiling hatred, designed to make you feel as dominated by them as they perhaps did by the culture of whiteness all around them, and of course challenging you to come out of your white pose of bland neutrality. Isabel, they did not see Bernhard Goetz in the way he saw himself. They had no contact with his feelings or whether he even had any, as he himself had no contact with theirs. They did not speak the language of violence directly. They did not say, Give us your money or we will ensure that you are done with this earth and this earth will be done with you. They merely played with him as a prelude to the attack he believed was to come. Bernhard Goetz did not believe they placed a value on his life and so he placed none on theirs. He fired not once but many times, bullet after bullet, so that the injuries were numerous and severe.

Do I have any idea what it is to be Black in this society that these young men should stand over Bernhard Goetz in this way? And what do I know of Bernhard Goetz and the horrors his ancestors endured, and the fear that lived in his bones except to say that his fear was fear that I had myself experienced.

Isabel, let me be honest. Once I rode the shuttle that connects Times Square with Grand Central Station. The subway car I rode in had its share of passengers, but the aisles were unobstructed. When the doors closed for the two-minute ride, two young boys commanded our attention. "Yo! Listen up. We be doing the thing for you," one of them announced. They got their boom box sound going, harsh yet hypnotic rap with a pounding bass, which they accompanied with quasi-martial art dance moves along the aisle. I was disturbed, Isabel. That is the truth. I wanted them to go away. With those doo rags upon their heads and their aggressive manner, they made me uneasy. And when one of them did backflips through the moving car, I grew terrified that he would break his spine.

And then it occurred to me, Isabel. I had been like those disenfranchised kids. From morning till night I too had ridden the subways of New York City as a child, with my friend Jerry Jones-Nobleonian from the SRO down the block. But I had no act to perform, no gift to give the grownups around me. And no hat to pass afterward for contributions. Instead of dancing to the beat, Joey and I would purchase stink bombs at Times Square novelty stores and place the capsules on empty subway seats. Oh, the laughter that we would try to suppress when unsuspecting passengers sat on those seats and the broken capsules released that rotten eggs stench of the foulest fart.

If I had any concern at all about this trip, Isabel, apart from the plane travel, it was that I would meet my fate at the hands of a death-dealing male in Los Angeles, our final destination. I had to set all my vigilance sensors to high to safely reach our car in the basement garage of the Best Western Hotel where we stayed. It was touch and go in that endless and forlorn space through which we walked in search of our vehicle. Was I unwittingly crying out for my executioner to appear and lay me out with you and young Mia as witnesses to my demise? Can you not easily imagine his cold, impassive eyes, as if he had been born with the sole purpose of killing and more killing? And can you not understand his psychology, how killing takes on a life of its own, the very act placing you in another zone of existence? When you slay a human being, the need to unleash your power on another victim will sooner or later call out for more such action again and again. Call it a hunger, call it a thirst, but it is real and numerous on this earth are those afflicted with such a compulsion.

Though the navigation through this desolate underground garage was terrifying, we prevailed with our lives nonetheless. As I have noted, the failure to remain vigilant brings ruin to many. Too often people go to their perishing with a false sense of shock at the circumstance that has befallen them as they lie in their own blood, when in fact they brought on the very thing itself. Such is the perversity of human nature to seek out the very thing we insist on pretending to deplore.

Where does such pathetic severity come from, Isabel? What is it to be so wantonly disregarding of empathy? Am I not really saying to the unfortunate with severed limbs lying on the train track to which he has fallen, "You got what you deserved, old chum. Heads up next time. Heads up"?

But do not dismiss me. Do not. I am seeing the things I need to see and saying the things I need to say. And along the way I am coming to understand that the journey is about becoming not God but a human being.

Isabel, there are three other noteworthy events from this trip. One, a Bengal tiger, rapacious in the extreme, rushed the bars at the Santa Barbara Zoo and gave a roar that traveled from my toes through my spine and up through the top of my head. This tiger was letting me know the nature and extent of its power and that the universe is ruthless in the appropriation of bodies and minds by more powerful beings. I had my back turned to the cage at the time, and so it was once again for me to understand what lack of vigilance can mean for one's longevity here on the earth and what I can expect in the next, where bars and other protections may not be in play.

Second, Mia dissolved into a fit of tears after I laid down the law and forbade her to carry her container of sticky orange crush into the car. She would simply have to finish it before we drove off, I said. I was protecting the integrity of the rental vehicle, as I saw the matter. And when we left her sweet drink behind, crushed ice and all, outside the store and pulled away, there is nothing to report but the ear-piercing wail that came from little Mia, such was her heartbreak. The things that Mia held dear she held dear, Isabel. Her little heart was full of love for things lost to her. Bereft is bereft, regardless of one's age.

And yes, somewhere in San Luis Obispo, I came upon some railroad tracks, in fact a sprawling rail yard, a sanctuary where the trucks of America had not yet reached. My nose filled with the thick smell of diesel fumes and who knows what. Do not ask me what I cannot answer as to the ache in my heart seeing the silver and red twin diesel engines of the Santa Fe line. Some longing for California, for childhood scenes of railroad tracks I myself had once known. Some longing for a world that had vanished but now had reappeared. How hard it was to come back from that sight. How strong its pull.

One more thing to note, Isabel. Just one more. The matter of driving. It would be more than I can bear to say that I waged a campaign to undermine your confidence behind the wheel, but there is no denying my mutterings and even cries at those times when I felt the end was near. That time, for example, you passed tandem trailers on a rain-slick interstate while chatting with Mia, so desperate not to be forgotten in the back seat. Can it truly be said that your vigilance quotient was high at that particular moment, that every cell in your body was screaming to seal the deal and pass that marauding vehicle of death? Is it possible that you were there in the realm of the dawdler, the one who can neither pass nor fall behind, but must maintain an unbearable tension with the sixteen-wheeler ready at a whim to apply its weight and extinguish our presence on this earth?

Where do we go from here? Do we go to the country, that little house on a hill on seven acres, a piece of property Philip sought to appropriate for himself after the dissolution of your marriage? Though you showed strength by not giving in to his demand, the question needs to be asked: why should a man who left his wife and daughter to live with his newfound lover have the right to ask for, let alone demand, financial consideration? But it is of no use to reason with you in this way. You did not bring the same black and white thinking to the situation. You would look at me as if I lacked understanding, and such an attitude on your part could only be based on what you perceived in me. I had found the one man I didn't regard as a threat to take you away, and I played that card too often. In a sense you had given me an assignment, and it was only this—love and accept Philip exactly as he is. Relinquish judgment, Johan, relinquish it. These unspoken words of yours are clear in my ears. Is that not what you were saying?

For you, marriage had no great value. A man who didn't crowd you was greatly appreciated, and Philip met this need exceptionally well. No man had a right to come too close to you. No man. They had lost that right long, long ago. A man of my description, so in need of a woman's attention, could not be easily countenanced. You tried. You gave it your best shot, but I was simply too much. And too little as well.

Philip's influence on the country place was everywhere, from the wainscoting to the pale green color of the walls and the old Oriental rug in the living room with a tear in it. The house had been his idea, not yours, a second home outside Manhattan and yet within reach. He was not a city person, you had explained, but was born in a small town near one of Michigan's many lakes.

Throughout the house two-inch nails had been driven into the walls, as if Philip was staking a claim to the spaces he had so marked. When he got an idea, he drove a nail. Later, only later, would he get around to building on the idea. His ideas were big, of-the-moment things, that dissolved into nothing he could revive with the passage of time. Only the nails remained to remind him he had had a thought at all.

The Henry Hudson Parkway across the 225th Street Bridge; the Saw Mill River Parkway; the Taconic State Parkway; Bull's Head Road onto Milan Hollow Road and then onto Round Lake Road. Do towns like Chappaqua and Pleasant Valley and Millbrook and Hawthorne and Pound Ridge mean anything to you?

April 1984 to August 1990. Those would have been the years.

As a boy and ever since I have dreamed of the realm of trees and grass and wildlife and picturesque homes beyond the city limits. The dream was nothing more than that, of course, until Sarah came along and introduced me to Camp and her family. Evidently, I did not have the power to get to nature on my own. In my twenties I had bought a book on backpacking, with the idea that I might hike in the Catskills and even pitch a tent. But I was drinking, Isabel, and the more I drank the less I was able to do. In my fantasies I would set out on a trail, but when night fell in those same fantasies, loneliness would drive me back to civilization in the vicinity of the Vassar College campus, where I would hook up with girls and take them back to my campsite with a load of liquor for a night of endless pleasure. And so I would never get out of the Chinatown loft where Sarah and I were then living or the local bars, my fantasies having shown me the futility of any endeavor that required me to set out on my own.

But now here I was in a world I could not have created for myself, a ready-made world fashioned by you and Philip. The two of you had given me the form in which I could operate, since it was never for me to break the mold and create my own existence.

What kind of life can this be, of such extreme separation?

You had a car. You called it Abe, not because of the Biblical character or our Civil War president, but because those were the first three letters on the license plate. It was a cherry red two-door Ford Futura, which you had purchased as a demonstration model. You did no agonizing, Isabel. You simply put your money down. No need for exhaustive comparison shopping. You just got the job done.

And you bought American at a time when the Japanese were perceived to be outstripping us in the marketplace given the superiority of their Nissan Sentras and Toyota Corollas and Nikon and Olympus photographic gear and their Sony Walkmans, then all the rage. You held your ground. You affirmed the value of American products when others were abandoning them. It was your way to have a conscience and to think about the consequences of your actions.

You also showed the same exemplary thoughtfulness regarding taxes in this time, voicing concern about a society that did not care enough about its poor. You let it be known that you were not a fan of Ronald Reagan, given the political direction he was trying to take the country. You worried out loud about inequity even as his tax policies worked in your favor. "The rich are getting richer and the poor are struggling. What can such a thing mean?" you said.

In later years you were to say to me, "You came to me without so much as a credit card. You had nothing, nothing." You spoke in a tone of reproach designed to put me in my place, and your assertion was true. I came to you with a paltry publishing salary and the little money I kept as my share from the sale of the Bowery loft.

As I recall, there was some question as to whether we should file separately or together the first year of our marriage. The matter came up in a visit we paid to your accountant, Mr. Alexander Simonides, then in the employ of the firm Goucher, Grabnotti, and Fling, their main office being a glass and steel tower on Park Avenue. Let it be said that Mr. Simonides was powerful in his build and in his mind and only at the beginning of what would surely be a rapid rise to the top. He had a grasp of personal finances that needs no description. Strange to say, but the square shape of his face and the spacing of his eyes and teeth put me in mind of Ernie Borgnine, the actor, as he must have been as a young man. Alexander Simonides was a mesomorphic entity, power-packed and full of the energy and joy of life. But this was no Ernie Borgnine of the unshaven face and T-shirt. This was a young man in his uniform of power, an expensive pinstriped suit and a tie of golden silk that spoke of Armani or some other legend of the fashion world.

Mr. Simonides was required to interview me about my personal assets. No, there were no stocks and bonds or retirement accounts, I informed him. Such allocations were not even on the horizon. There it was, laid out in black and white in the office of Mr. Simonides. Your financial assets dwarfed my small salary.

We were in a time now when the human touch had been introduced into the work world. Mr. Simonides felt the need to inquire about my work life and my interests. Did I have any hobbies? I told him I liked to read and to walk. I told him I was especially drawn to park benches in the shade on warm, sunny days. There was no reason for me to dislike the young man. He was just doing his job. He was like those physicians whose training requires immersion in the hard sciences and who then take sensitivity training courses to develop a bedside manner. Should any of the patients be like me, this contrived human touch will produce an odd feeling of discomfort, for such personal concern seems out of keeping with who these task-driven doctors really are. In this culture I can feel that we are trying to limit intelligence and make those who have more appear to have only as much as the rest of us. We seek to restrain them from their own quite natural excesses in regard to arrogance and coldness, which they are inevitably driven to by their manifest gifts and the inability to suffer fools gladly.

Even as I was experiencing great humiliation, this wellspring of shame rising up and flooding my being that I had, in dollars and cents, no standing whatsoever in this world, there was a desire to help young Mr. Simonides, with his baby bull physique and temperament, through this excruciating personal touch format that our fatuous culture had imposed on him. And the only way I knew was to be extremely amiable and obliging, and to reassure him that all his efforts on my behalf were greatly appreciated. You could almost say, Isabel, that I feminized myself, if such a word is any longer permissible, by my deferential and ingratiating manner.

It is all right for people to be pleased with themselves. If Mr. Simonides derived much self-regard from his achievements, so be it. He was clearly going somewhere in this world. He already had his wife and a daughter and doubtless he was a homeowner, driven as he must have been by the need for equity.

The world is full of such men and women, with their bulging portfolios and the path ahead so clear and sunny. Let us not make a virtue of poverty and darkness, and let us not rise on a note of spiritual conceit that would dismiss the treasures of the world as opposed to those of the heart and smugly offer in their place a life of prayer and meditation and the holy truth of the moment and the moment alone. Love is painfully won. It cannot be achieved by rising above or sinking below those in our path.

But can we let go of Mr. Simonides for now and perhaps all time? Can we say we have given him his day and move on?

In late March we drove to the country in Honest Abe to open the house, which was small and of white clapboard, and set on a hill above a small lake. It had a screen door, and when it snapped shut, it did so with authority. Let it be said that decisive action is commendable in the inanimate as well as those who have the freedom to walk this earth.

There was a lilac bush that would burst forth with flowers both purple and white. There was a shad tree that bloomed with whiteness to herald the spring. There was a hawthorn bush that had its own song of whiteness and a forsythia to offer the clarion call of yellow to emphatically herald spring. There was a tree line at which we could enter the darkness of woodland and a meadow that lay as an open space for wind and sun and moon and rain and all elements seeking interaction with the earth. A shed that spoke its history through its weathered wood. An oak tree, thick and massive, that sang its own steady song of praise. And pine trees showing too much trunk. These too were features of this property.

A man came calling that first night. You had forewarned me of his likely and surely unwelcome arrival. More than once he had threatened to destroy Philip and his friends in both their bodies and their minds, you had said. His name was Thor; he was a local contractor whom Philip had hired to modernize the kitchen, where we stood when he appeared with glass in hand and a malicious grin on his handsome face. This was a man with muscles under his flannel shirt and an aggressive, jeering manner. Without so much as asking, he appropriated from the table the half of Mia's sandwich she hadn't eaten in the car and demanded that we refresh his drink.

Clearly, this was a contractor who, in the course of work for you and Philip, came to see that he could take liberties, but there is no great mystery here. He had probably been on the bottle for a good part of the evening, and sought us out because the loneliness that afflicts all drunks had brought him to the place of being ravenous not only for food but also craving company, saying I must have a living, breathing thing in my midst. I cannot sit here with my bottle and my glass and only my music and the images on the TV. He wanted people to be hurrying toward him but knew they weren't, and so he came to us. Because the trees were not talking and the rocks had no songs to sing that he could hear, and he knew the animals to be uncaring whether he lived or died.

Isabel, whether in the bottle or in God, we all arrive at the place of being alone, with no one entering the room on our command, but it is only God who will render us whole and relieve us of the ache of loneliness so we can fly the flag of oneness with Him and all that is around us, and with no sense of separation to keep us in the fractured state. It is imperative that we understand the dimensions of the spiritual life, and the lack that afflicts us without it.

There was no defense to erect against Thor, no state of high indignation to reach. Our safety was in our defenselessness. Sufficient it was to say to Thor, "We have no alcohol in the house. Could we offer you a cup of herbal tea? We have soothing chamomile and a more vigorous raspberry and an orange delight that will surely prove itself a taste sensation," I said, sensing all the while that his need for another drink would get him on his way. He drew close so I would smell his boozy breath even more than I had. "I could smash your face. I could make it uglier than it already is. You're a gargoyle. DO YOU HEAR WHAT I AM SAYING?" Yes, Isabel, he went up the ladder with his rage, but then he came back down and was soon on his way.

Did I pray for Thor on that cold March night, with rawness in the air? Did I ask for healing for this tortured soul? Pray I did, as I always do, to be taught how to love, but I did not pray specifically that Thor's wounds be healed so displays of physical power would cease to be the only mode in which he lived his life.

Thor's disappointment that night was understandable. Philip had brought a party to the property, and had made Thor, a local boy, feel like he could belong. But now Philip was gone and I, with my gargoyle features and abstemious ways, had arrived, and so it was necessary for Thor to declare that I looked as unlovable as he felt.

Isabel, it is a dangerous thing for a human being to lose touch with himself so he cannot say, I feel this or I feel that. What is it to be part of a community for years and years, to cultivate and farm the land and then see city folk arrive with their big checkbooks and buy the very property where you were born and raised? Can we not surmise that Thor, having grown up in that house, might have felt displaced and resentful to be working on the property his family had once owned? Not to mention his brother Knut, who owned the farm across the meadow. Their father, a contractor, was now in the earth, and their mother had been displaced to a smaller house on the other side of the road. People come and people go. But these were folks who had stuck their hands in the fertile soil of this land. They had their history here. There was tension in the air that the rich should be arriving from New York City to appropriate the land that once had been theirs, and for nothing more than a weekender's part-time purpose.

What, in the light of day, was that white clapboard house with a pale green trim in a previous time and place but a motel down on Route 9? Thor's father had transported it on a flatbed truck to its present site back in the 1930s. One can only wonder what went on within its walls. I see bottles of bootleg gin being quaffed by trysting lovers, their roadsters parked outside. I hear the crackle of a staticky old radio and the cricket chorus in two-syllable chant all through the night.

Things happened in that house, Isabel, both illicit and familial. It was a house that knew things it wasn't telling.

Is it surprising that, just as Thor had come calling, his mother should follow the next day, or that she might be bringing something darker than her genial smile as she made her slow way up the rutted dirt driveway? An old woman who shows up at the front door of her former home and asks for permission to pick some flowers. Can we not say that her presence was a statement, even if we don't know of what, and say the same of the visit made by her volatile son? And can we not ask what the influence is of a mother on an errant son, that even as he rages, she comes forth with a meek request? Why is there not one voice and one face to humanity? What are these different voices, this cacophony of sound, and where are the interpretive devices that are required to understand them?

Secretly I longed for a railroad to be close by. My affinity for the rails is a lifelong thing. You could say it had something to do with a need for isolation that would, at the same time, place me close to throbbing power. A train, after all, is a long and extended thing, and penetrates the darkest tunnels as well as highballing along in the open air.

Father,
What is the past? Is it not an affliction of the mind? Why does a person not simply sit and stare, or walk about sufficient that he grows tired and can go home to the sleep that calls to him? What is the need to witness to episodes that contain no crime or sin except that of living? Why can my mind not permanently merge with yours so I can know only your peace?

Isabel,
Here's a story to make of what we will.

Recently, I saw a man and woman on Broadway with a child that could not have been of their own flesh and blood, as they were Caucasian and the girl looked decidedly Chinese. So you would have to assume that they were adoptive parents who had navigated a difficult process and perhaps had their hopes dashed several times before striking gold. They seemed to me prodigies of giving in this earthly paradise they had created, and that this romping child, for whom a New York City sidewalk was still a playground delight, was the source of their joy. At one point the man went racing off down the street with his daughter, seeking to endear himself to her with the silly noises and the strange faces he made and the energy he displayed. I had no call to be harsh with him with the administration of a hard slap, and in fact I didn't. No element of the confrontational, if you discount the look of disdain, did I impose on the man. The truth is that I looked away because I could not bear the spectacle he was making of himself. No man has the right to act like such a fool in coming down to the level of a child. Because in fact he couldn't come down to her level. Nakedly, on this busy boulevard, was he showing his absolute need for acceptance by this little girl, and if it took playing the buffoon, then so be it. The French have a term, *amour propre,* for what this man so clearly lacked.

And so it was with me in relation to Mia. I was afraid of her. I felt she had a rejecting heart even if I also held that it was only a matter of time before she came around to accepting me. Like that unfortunate man, I too displayed my foolish ways, exclaiming "Mia mamma Mia," in the spontaneous eruption of joy I would experience on sight of her. There are natural inclinations of the heart; the desire to form a bond with a child is basic. Thus was I intent on winning her over.

A sadness comes over me as I touch on the life of this child in print. You have no right, the voice says, forming as a dark cloud in my psyche. But the past is long gone, long gone. All that remains is memory, calling me back to that loft and the narrow entranceway inside the door where Mia and I would toss a ball back and forth. Such a feeling of sweetness attaches. What is that to assign an emotion to a physical space, that white floor and the slats of the tall closet door that opened outward and the photographs I hung on the nearby wall as my contribution to our life together?

All the while I couldn't help but feel that she was seeing things about me with her penetrating brown eyes, seeing, for sure, my need for her love but also, in relation to you, that I was something of a child myself, with my clownish ways at the dinner table that elicited your consternation. For me to be in your doghouse gave little Mia great satisfaction, as if I were a preposterously older brother in rivalry for your affection.

What do I know about any of this? Why even bother to stumble forward?

Poor Mia. She had so much to overcome. The heartbreak of a parent leaving is something I can't measure, as my own parents stayed together, but surely it is a seismic shock that one who brought you into the world is no longer there. And though she was too young to know the meaning of one man living with another in love, as Philip was to do, she surely felt his absence keenly as incompleteness in herself and had to wonder what she had done to cause such a rift. As the child of two artists, she wanted nothing to do with art and the world of narcissistic egotism that went with it, on her father's side, for was he not famous for crowing about his creative accomplishments on the streets and in the bars of SoHo even as he was committing himself to ruin? It was in Mia's disposition to want a family that was intact, from her childhood years on. How hard it is for us to reconcile ourselves to loss. And yet that was the challenge for her young heart. Her father gone and now this new man—tall, lanky, silly, and also prone to anger—on the scene.

Do you remember those drives, Isabel, do you? Your poodle, Cleo, in the front seat. Such a pooch with a coat crying out for coiffing and breath that made you recoil. And little Mia in the back, desperate not to be forgotten by you.

A child knows when she is rendering another insignificant and invisible, as Mia would at the dinner table, choosing to speak exclusively to you. It was for me to accept that she was only wishing me to feel the same exclusion she experienced in the back seat of Abe while I was there in the front seat with you. It was less about hurting me than it was about securing you, who were her absolute lifeline.

Accompanying us on one of our country weekends was Agnes, a chubby girl for whom Mia often expressed dislike owing to Agnes's habit of tagging along after her during the school day. Agnes was a girl without a father, having been born to a woman who had no use for men other than to select one with a gene pool worthy of being tapped. Just as Mia had no great love for Agnes, you had no particular regard for her mother, Kenda Klainor (a name that had the clank of her own calculating hardness). The premeditation that led to her brief affair with a professor back in graduate school for the sole purpose of pregnancy did not sit well with you. You saw such deviousness as a kind of theft.

One night I drove back from nearby Red Hook with Mia and Agnes. We had gone to one of those old small-town theaters that smell throughout of buttered popcorn and have rows of small, hard seats and run ads for local businesses—Phil's Pizza and Jeff's Car Wash and the like—before the main attraction. After parking outside the woodshed, I was seized with the notion to hide from Mia and her friend in the dark. Crouched in front of the car, I could see them moving away toward the light from the house. Without looking back, and in a loud, clear voice, Agnes called out, "We don't care where you are. You're not funny and you don't interest us." Harsh and cutting words, regardless of my foolishness, and yet I had placed myself in a position to be hurt by reverting to childishness at an inopportune time and making a foolish bid for their attention. It is a pathetic thing for a man to show such need for inclusion by young children, and yet it may also be reasonable to ask what eight-year-old child says such a thing to an adult? But Agnes was not your average child. She had the genes of her absent and brilliant father, and showed a proprietary hold on Mia. The pain of her rebuff stayed with me for the rest of that miserable weekend.

We need God to buck us up. There is nowhere else to go when we are in the emotional wilderness of pain and hurt. It is simply the function of every slight, infraction, rejection, humiliation, loss, etc. to drive us more deeply into his arms. Where else is one to turn? The body blows and the head shots we deal each other are simply too great to withstand without his help. These things I understood in the year I'm talking about, but I did not fully utilize the tools available. I too often let resentment have its way with me. I had not found the solace of a daily journal as the healing friend I needed to the extent that I now have. Words have power. We must learn to mitigate their potentially toxic effect by leaching any poison from our person through the pen and onto paper. We must also choose to speak with care or not speak at all.

I had time for myself but not enough for Mia. She had a child's need to explore the world around her and develop her abilities, but I held back from such participation in her life. I did not spend quality time with her, annoying as that term is. Seldom in those first years did she and I do anything on our own. It was you who read to her—a mother's domain—and taught her how to drive, an undertaking I could not begin to approach, given the safety factors I felt would be in play. There you were each weekend going up and down the driveway with little Mia at the wheel and you in the passenger seat of Honest Abe with your foot ready to press on the gas or step on the brake.

And where was I when this intensely bonding activity, so meaningful to Mia's growth, was going on? Sequestered, Isabel, the way I have been ever since the idea of becoming a writer began to afflict me in my early twenties. And where exactly was I holed up but in the apartment over the garage. What more perfect space could one imagine than this, with a view out over the property and the environs from several windows and ample space for me to pace back and forth.

Paper captured me, Isabel. It had me under house arrest. Still, a man has a right to further himself and honor this incarnation. What sort of life would it be to lack all ambition? But from the start I was hamstrung by the fact that I could only write about what I had experienced. There is nothing inherently wrong with that—people should write from what they have lived through. But I was the most extreme example of the autobiographical writer, bound and fettered by the past and lacking the power of invention that could begin to take the reader into consideration. Let us face up to it, Isabel—the word "writer" as it applies to me is true only in the literal sense—I wrote. Over thirty years sitting by myself in a room accumulating texts that no one will ever read and that I might be mortally horrified should they read.

And what was going on in my mind as you and little Mia drove back and forth in the driveway? Was it anything positive? You could not say so. I was angry, and driving that anger was fear that you and she would lose control of the car and an accident of horrible proportions would ensue. Is that not my nature to be Sammy Safety? At all times must things be in place, nailed down and secure. There can be no boldly venturing forth in my world. The gods are simply too injurious.

Despite your activities with Mia, you were not sold on our country life. Many times you were heard to wonder as to the purpose of a second home. "I just don't get it," you said. What you didn't get was why people would enslave themselves to the ritual of packing up their car for a two-hour trip from the city on narrow and dangerous parkways so they could arrive late on a Friday night in darkness at their property only to turn around and make the return trip on a Sunday afternoon. It was never a property where you could feel centered in your work. Never. The sudden arrival of a cedar waxwing on a tree branch outside the kitchen window might delight you for an instant, but could not dissolve the sadness and frustration that would inevitably return.

And let's face it, Isabel. I selfishly pooh poohed your concerns because I had everything I wanted at my fingertips—you, Mia, the country in all its glory, and the free time to sit in that apartment above the garage and pretend to write. Not so with you. You have always maintained a professional attitude toward your artwork. You are not the kind to jump up every half hour for a cup of coffee or a *snack*. Sarah had the same boundless energy as you, but within a few years of my regime she was dawdling over the kettle, having my example as a guide. Is the word I am looking for *pernicious,* or will *corrupting* suffice, and what does it matter? The point is to ask only this: what kind of man is it who infects healthy and aspiring women with his torpor, his malaise, his general and pronounced feebleness? Is there no one who will put an end to such an absence of vigor? Must I tell you, Isabel, how many times I have wept at the sight of you standing by the stove in the middle of the day instead of dealing with the task at hand, namely, your extraordinary artwork, knowing that I have no choice but to take full responsibility for this shameful contribution to your life?

And where was Luke in this time?
Had he gone north or south, east or west?
Disappearance a kind of death,
dissolving the ties that are meant to bind.
"Let the dead bury their dead."
Only Jesus could make sense of it,
But what did he truly know?

In this time a physician reported that the motility count of my sperm was lagging. My boys did not swim too tough or in sufficient numbers. So the physician said, with her figures at hand. She was a woman who got the job done, the kind who sets goals with measurable outcomes, and met my lack of concern with puzzlement. If a man and woman come together, then inevitably baby makes three. Such was her assumption. She did not know about Sarah, who mocked the idea of pregnant women. She did not know where I might be coming from. And then, because her intelligence was mammoth, she did, although the experience was new to her, perceive my essential nature—the dilly dallier, the shilly shallier, he who cannot make up his mind and so stays in the dawdle lane of life, and whose only accomplishment is to keep breathing.

Oh, life that is centered in reality, that cares about accurate testing. Such was Ernestine Gloss, M.D. Isabel, you were serious about pregnancy; it was to be your gift to me, as if you needed to give anything more. I felt ashamed, of course, before the clinical gaze of Dr. Gloss. My records right in front of her, she recommended that I choose showers over hot baths and boxer shorts over tight briefs.

She did not want scalding water to touch my testicles or tight-fitting fabric confining my stuff. What she could not bring herself to say was that perhaps I had been born feeble and that the best care in the world would not turn me into a breeder.

What was to mind in such a report, Isabel? What, I ask you? Who, with my disposition, would be saddened at such news? Should it be a day of national mourning that Johan M. could not cut the mustard in the potency department, making fatherhood out of reach? Had I ever said I wanted to be a father? Not at all. How could a man like me possibly make such a transition? Do I have to tell you the relief I would experience when your period came each month, the feeling of having received a reprieve from something terrible and possibly calamitous?

Suppose, just suppose, though it is a dark road to go down, I turned out to be an abuser of my own child? Suppose my father's hand was my hand and Hannah's pulverizing smacks *her tongue clamped between fat lips* mine as well? Suppose I burned with a fury that sanity could get no traction on and struck a defenseless one? Suppose I was so tormented by the sight of my own flesh and blood that I had to attack and destroy? Suppose, in fathering a child, I had to face the possibility that he would look as grotesque as I had as an infant, with my misshapen head completely bald? Suppose I couldn't sit, hour after hour, alone in a room with my teacup and the word processor I had recently purchased? Oh, Isabel, what is it to have a fear-mongering mind that would block me off from the reality of love and keep me within the mold where fetid waters gather?

Furthermore, when I look at children, even today, I am led to ask why have they been brought into this world on the edge of extinction. Do their parents not know that the end is near? And yet, I use the existence of these same children to help me, Isabel. They are an aid in restoring me to sanity, as are their parents who, God bless them, are saying that life exists in and around us. They are saying yes not only to life but to the future. And in so doing they are saying no, no, jamais jamais, to those who shrouded my mind in darkness so that I can foresee only doom and disaster, those like the Bible-slapping Pastor Horvath at the Pentecostal tabernacle with his sentences that lacked a beginning or an end, so drunk on his own words was he, or my mother, yes my mother, saying, when I was still a child, "Do you know we are living in the last days, Johan? Are you ready for the Judgment Day? Do you know he will come as a thief in the night?" Oh, Isabel, what is it to go against my own mother with words, to say to her, "You have had your life. Can you not allow me to have mine?" and then to see the smile on her face grow in proportion to my distress, as if it comforted her to see me so undone. Oh, Isabel, an entire childhood waking with relief that the clouds had not parted and that the roll call had not yet been called up yonder. What is the lunacy that infests the minds of the afflicted that they should be so off the mark in the matter of sin *blood pouring from the lamb the gnashing of teeth the fires of hell burning hot hot hot—in perpetuity, young man, perpetuity.*

Isabel, I have not entirely thrown off that darkness, but there was something more than the warped viewpoint from my childhood that prevented me from being of one mind about pregnancy. The primary obstacle was not fear of God's wrath upon the world but simply yours upon me. I was afraid you would reprimand me to the end of my days and beyond if you were pregnant; a baby would have been a gift to me more than to yourself. What need had you of additional offspring? After all, Mia, with her beauty and her intelligence, could only be seen as the crowning achievement of any parent. She was a child who drew other children to her as you drew the world to yourself. If your gift to me was to be the birth of a child, then my gift to you was to ensure that such a child was never born. You may well ask what sort of gift such a non-offering could be, but it was a caring and considerate gift nonetheless. Why? Because it prevented you from destroying yourself and the marriage as well, as you surely would have if you had been a party to misguided procreation. How you would have loathed yourself and me. How you would have poured out your bile upon me before banishing me from your presence forever for the crime of committing you to another eighteen years of selfless service to a child malformed owing to my genes?

Surely I've told you many times how astonished I would be by little Mia's indifference to the kids from her class who would call, and to whom she would say, when she had been virtually dragged to the phone, "Yeah, what do you want?" So entrenched in her world was she, so unhampered by the need for social approval. What can such indifference mean but that a child knows deep within her that she has the goods that her friends are seeking? A child with the right genetic makeup knows he or she has the necessities and requires no validation, unlike any progeny of mine would likely be.

And there was, for consideration, the work you put in as a single mother, Philip having vacated the premises to abide with his lover, with whom, because of your astonishing capacity, you became best friends, at least in his mind. And yet a hostile vibe emanated from him the night he came for dinner, the unexpressed but deeply felt wish that I simply vanish from the earth. He had no room in his being for a man of my kind. All he saw was an interloper, someone who could potentially threaten his and Philip's access to you. And yet I didn't go away. I stood my ground, holding firm in the face of his unspoken fury. This was a man with skills beyond those he brought to his job as a lab technician. He could read and speak five languages, each of which he had taught himself. There was also his legendary flatulence, sufficient, I was told, to empty out entire subway cars when he broke wind.

It is not fully clear to me where the breakdown in our communications began. Was it my eruptions? My erring tongue? Was it the time in the country I trashed your offering to me with a bitter rant that if I couldn't have success as a writer, at the very least you could give me a baby? How repulsed you must have been. How horrified.

"We could have a baby if you would only stop pushing," you said. Do you know the chill that went through me when you spoke those words—the distance that instantly loomed between us? Though you were right there beside me, it was as if you were speaking from a parallel universe that kept us close and yet ensured our separation. Your words did not have the right *sound* to them. You were saying, If you are good, Johan, and only if you are good, will I give you what it is normal to expect in a marriage. But if you are bad, Johan—if you are bad—then I will have no choice but to punish you. In this way you seized control. All power now emanated from you. You were judge and jury as to my performance. But is it not fair to say that a bias was obtaining in the judge and jury? Is it not fair to say that the proceeding was rigged? Was it not a foregone conclusion that I would fail to win acquittal? And would it not be accurate to say that the time was coming when, just as you had once seen me as wonderful, fantastic, and all the superlatives you employed, you would need to paint me in a progressively darker light, to mock me, saying "Yes, lord and master. Whatever you say, lord and master," thus articulating the hierarchy which had been established in childhood with your true lord and master?

Oh Isabel, your rage and weeping are made clear by all that went before in your trespassed-upon life. I am not without understanding, for life is only about that at the end.

Our love nest, our little one-room rabbit warren. Let us simply say that the slightest touch in the night could provoke instant escalation. Oh, the fire that burned in that space so small we could not fully stand but wide enough for our lying-down pleasure. Yes, Isabel, I had found Mrs. Kindelberger, so faithful to her easel back in that building of my childhood, but I had also found the hosiery shop owner's daughter of dark and dangerous beauty.

Down below, and at the other end, lay little Mia, now with her own room of sheet-rocked walls. You would come to me after reading to her. How hard it was for her to let you go. "I love you, Mommy." Every five minutes or less her desperate lifeline words.

The stairs leading up were wide-planked. A staircase without a banister. It was for you to maintain your balance without support.

Mia's ears would monitor for sounds of life. She had had you, and now that you had left her room, she didn't have you. But she had *had* you. For her first few years she had had you, and exclusively. Only now I had entered the scene, and you had come to me as your final destination of the day after leaving her, and so her young heart filled with hurt. *Stepfather.* What a word. Not a real father but not a non-father either. A title deserving of an asterisk.

Have you seen that film, *A Boy's Life,* starring the great Robert De Niro and young Leonardo DiCaprio? Years later, I had the misfortune to see it with Mia. Oh the pain, the discomfort, to see De Niro cast in the role of a stepfather who tortures the boy and his mother with anger and physical intimidation and in whose face is writ large his smallness and the wretchedness of his life. Do you suppose for a minute that little Mia did not make the connection between me and this abusive lout? Though she has always loved Robert De Niro and has watched *Mean Streets* and *GoodFellas* and *Raging Bull* countless times, we cannot assume anything but her full-fledged rejection of him in this odious role and her total embrace of young and battered Leonardo. How awful to make eye contact with her on the street afterward. How strong the impulse to simply run away, the full nature of my crimes having been shown on the movie screen.

Isabel, matters took a bad turn, the alleged impasse over pregnancy only the beginning. How frightening it was to feel you moving away. Oh, that I should have to be awakened to my primary fear of abandonment in this way. And yet, what parity. Just as you had your issue with your stepfather to contend with, so too did I have mine with my mother. Yes, I crossed a line in going to you. Yes, I could have and should have heeded the warning signs. Yes, I went where I didn't belong. But who is to say that God doesn't create opportunity where most see only disaster? Who is to say that he didn't bring us together for this very work? We talk of the success of this marriage or the failure of that one, but must we believe that such assessments even apply? A marriage is successful if it lasts and the two people are miserable together, but a failure if it ends in divorce and two parties grow in increasing oneness, their physical apartness notwithstanding?

You declared your liberation from me in small stages. "You're sucking my blood. You make it so I can't even breathe." This you would say to me when I came home from work, and decided you would no longer be spending weekends at our little second home. You had friends in the city you needed to see—Maude in particular—but another, Rhona, who had the manner of a rampaging rhino in clearing a direct path to you. Your ally in your developing war for independence she became, supporting your postponement of pregnancy and your break from the country.

Your college boyfriend you spoke of in a dismissive way. You had no choice but to hurt him with severe rebukes when he would confess his infidelities, which could never be the source of pain to you that his burdensome confessions, so contritely delivered, were. You had no choice but to disappear him, no choice whatsoever. Enter Philip. As a boy in Minnesota, he stole other children's toys and as he grew older, plundered his family's assets, starting with household possessions, before devising ingenious ways to raid their bank assets so he could stroll the streets of his small town as an elegant dandy. When his parents confronted him, he merely held a mirror to their faces. "The world is ruled by les chiens, les chiens," he asserted, hardly knowing what he was saying but grasping for profundity in a language not his own. How they reviled him. And how he, with the full power of his life force, held fast against their invective-laden blasts. "I am leaving here," he said to his parents when, exhausted and hoarse, they slumped to the floor. "I go to the far country to make a name for myself. The Midwest is not my home. Not for me the unrelenting ice of winter and the bugs of summer and the monotonous tick-tock tick-tock of the grandfather clocks that sit at the foot of the stairs in all these houses. And one too many pointed steeple."

Oh, Isabel, I am as alienated from Philip as he was from those he exploited, that I should write in such a fashion about your ex-husband. When will we melt down in love? When will the thaw truly occur and the mind erect more stellar defenses against the virus of judgment that it dares to call *observation?* When I ask myself where and how I gave myself the right to speak in such a way, the answer that comes to me is this: *"The incompetence that defines you is truly fathomless. And so you have no choice but, in perpetuity, to bring people down to the level on which you operate."* Is this any way for the universe to speak to me, Isabel? Without a measure of kindness?

As Philip had fixed upon his family's possessions, so too did he fix upon you, installing himself in the apartment next door to where you and your beau, Leonard, were living, and worked his strange and mesmerizing wiles. Philip was not without appreciation of your beauty. He doubtless placed you in the hall of fame in that regard, but would it be a stretch to say that your financial assets interested him as much or more? Quite simply, he had to have you, and quite simply as well, you had to have him because your freedom was worth any price you had to bear in the purchase of it. Leonard, or the conventions he represented, was the mold you had to break free of if your art was ever to flourish. People who professed to be in the know—gallery owners, fellow artists—were telling you as much.

While Leonard was tending to his books—books that he collected more than read—Philip was wooing you. He said he possessed more talent in one finger than Van Gogh, that the advertising agencies of New York City all bowed down to him, and that all the companies of America made pilgrimages to his door to plead for his artist's touch on their products. He was the oedipal man for you. Having slain his father, he now set about slaying poor Leonard.

When Leonard came home from one of his trysts to find you gone, he determined your whereabouts through all points bulletins, and soon tracked you to Block Island. Trapped at the edge of Mohegan Bluffs, you threatened to plunge to your certain death if he took a step closer, the white cap water far below in a foaming frenzy to claim you. Leonard had a core of stability as well as decency. Instead of taking that fateful step forward, he walked away, though over the next several weeks, he was to come back many times on bended knee. He understood that you were America itself and that to give you up would be to surrender his dream. He had been to Israel, but the Promised Land was nothing more than arid soil next to the gifts you offered.

Leonard's howling did not escape your ears, of course; your pain meter recorded an all-time high for his wailing. But there were no practical considerations that could entice you back to him. He was simply, like me, a man who had gone where he did not belong, and so he had earned everything that was now coming to him.

And so you left Leonard to his own devices. You were not unjust. Once again, is it not clear that men and women come together for one reason, and one reason only, that being to cause each other such pain and inflict such grievous wounds that they have no choice but to reach out to God? What greater shock can a human being receive than to realize at depth that people are not who we think they are and *never can be*. People disappoint, Isabel. They fall short of the mark.

And so you disposed of Leonard. You gave him the thrashing he deserved for threatening your freedom. And in so doing, you put all men on notice that they would be dispensed with in similar fashion should they dare to crowd you with their needs. And you have never looked back. Life had presented you with your perfect mate—a gay man who didn't need you more than you needed him. Or if he needed you, it was for the means to run wild and naked and drunk through the streets of lower Manhattan and to satisfy his buying frenzies.

You may say I have no business wandering in this wretched field where vanished are the flowers of yesteryear. But something takes me back there. Something. This is my life, too, and marriage has had a part to play in it. *Here in my aloneness I make this claim.*

Let me say this one thing further, Isabel. Let me say it. You knew, as all oppressed women who are struggling for their freedom must know, that essential weakness lay hidden in Philip's pose of greatness. You knew that he had the goods for success but not the true desire to access it. You knew that he was programmed for failure, that truly, as D. H. Lawrence wrote, "Men can suck the heady juice of exalted self-importance from the bitter weed of failure -- failures are usually the most conceited of men." Subconsciously Philip was eventually headed for the ruin ditch that claims all those who dither and stall at maximizing their gift.

And had you yourself not come to esteem failure in the same degree that your stepfather championed success? *You want success? I will be reckless upon the surface and the darker regions of the earth. I will show you the same love you showed me by ruining my life.*

Because you could not have a man who was strong in your midst. You had to work hard, if slowly, to dispatch him to the disintegrating place. But I was a man who was of even more meager substance than Philip. Who was I, after all? A man who had failed academically. A man who had been rejected by the U.S. Army on both physical and psychological grounds. A man such as this, who cannot pass muster in his physique or his mentality, has but one choice, to retreat into the sanctuary of art and pray that something worthwhile in himself will express itself.

Though your assessment was harsh, you were right in later years to say I had come to you with nothing. I came to you with strength of spirit, a revitalized core, but my will was still intact for success in the world, which was not in the cards. I had been spared from death as a sot, but that did not mean I would now garner awards.

"You want me to be a real person, but I can't be," you said early on. Your smile was what you showed the world, beyond which no one could go into the world of buried trauma that held you.

As you lived in your hidden terror, so did I live in my anger, whose sole purpose was to bring about that which I most feared, your abandonment of me, so I could find all that I was looking for within. I attacked Rhona, the rampaging one. I maligned her as trying to sweep me out of the way so she could have all of you. But you were looking for female strength wherever you could find it, a woman who would align with you against the patriarchal reign of terror and not succumb to it as your mother had done with your stepfather's power. Rhona seemed to fill that bill. She had given birth. She had vanquished husbands. And now she was applying the force of her own will to the dance world she insisted on being a part of, not allowing her squat muscular body to be a barrier to realizing her dream. You had your reservations about her, Isabel. Of course you did. You found her coarse and insensitive. You shared as much with me. But she offered you a place to go as a haven from all that I was and represented.

And yet you had enough trust to place little Mia in my care. Alone with her on those country weekends, a different dynamic took hold and all my joking dropped away. I lacked the latitude to lapse into the kind of infantilism your presence permitted, if not encouraged. I became fearful, tentative, desperate to please and win her over. Sadness would come over me when I saw that she was *seeing* me—seeing my limitation, my inadequacy—and with unsympathetic eyes. Mia would give herself to me only so far as she had to and no more. Children always see the truth from their vantage point below. Little Mia quickly learned that when we were alone she had me under her control.

The horse farm was several miles from the house. On those riding weekends the lot was crowded with BMWs and Volvos and Audis, cars owned by men who wore khaki and tweed and women with tight smiles. From the start Mia was passionate about horses. They were the power she sought to harness. She wore jodhpurs and a riding helmet and entered the world of dressage. She could spend an entire day just hanging around the stable. Pastern. Fetlock. Withers. She didn't wish simply to ride. There were things she had to know.

I was the man who could apply the coat of paint to the house that had already been built, but not the man who could build the house. Thus, I escorted the daughter Philip and you had brought into the world and made modest improvements to the property he and you had purchased, but what structures had I put in place, unless they are ones that are invisible to the eye?

There is a man I have not spoken to you about, Isabel. His name was Wilmer Abernathy, and he lived in room 11C4 of my family's building. He was in retirement and had a smile that could no more hide his anger than his thinning hair could hide his scalp. He went about in a vinyl slicker, dark blue and with the Columbia name and logo on it so one and all would know the quality of his being, because if he had attended Columbia, that said it all. In his walks around the neighborhood, he kept one hand in his pocket in the way men of importance did in those days, and wherever he walked you can be sure he did his walking alone, because he was a man unencumbered and unto himself, solitary in his cast of mind. His primary purpose in life was to pay his bills on time and to ensure that his bank account remained ample.

There is only this to say, Isabel, only this—Wilmer Abernathy represented the absolute horror that conventionality imposes on us. For whom was this man being good? For whom was he parading himself in the garb of the normal, the successful, the respectable? What is a life that is not turned inside out? What is a life that does not encourage challenge and in which turbulence and even blind hatred is not given expression? Are we to cover our pain with the thinnest of smiles? Is that what we are to do?

Isabel, let us be clear. If anyone was moving in the direction of Wilmer Abernathy, it was me. Like him, I have not waded deep into the waters of life. But while you had none of his pathetic quality and I had all of it, you did have that smile and also that anger, and perhaps it was my function in life to bring your anger to the fore so it burned away your smile as a roaring fire consumes a flimsy sheet of paper. And would that be such a bad thing if a man's number one function in life was to lead women to discover their rage at perpetrators who would seal away their culpability in the locked box compartments of their steel trap minds? I have always been mother's little helper, Isabel. That was the role assigned to me from childhood on.

I have more or less omitted so far the protracted periods of domestic disharmony in which I would find cause to be angry at you. It could be your tardiness in wrapping up your bedtime reading session with little Mia, the thought that *you were stalling me stalling me the whole world stalling me.* Or the trigger could have been the happy conversation you were in with Mia as I entered the loft after a day at work, all those loving feelings I had been experiencing as I mounted the stairs now driven out by rage that you should have the privilege of staying home all day devoted to your artwork while I had to toil away at the office and settle for the few crumbs of the evening.

Let us be candid, Isabel. Your success frightened me. It could lead to abandonment. Yes, there was this small voice for sanity within me that said, Come now, Johan, accept that you don't have the same necessities Isabel possesses. You don't have her intelligence or her ability.

Surely you could see through to my envy as I arrived home in my cheap suit and tie. I thought you were silently laughing at me in my Steady Freddy office attire. Your unspoken awareness was the flashpoint for my anger. It wasn't simply that you had won and I had lost but that you had seen you had won and I had lost.

How you must have felt hearing my footsteps on the stairs in anticipation of my face blazing with anger and the snappish response I might give to your tentative and fearful greeting, if I responded at all. How many hours and days did I spend in that state, punishing myself as I sought to punish you? At such times the home of yours I had returned to, the love of you and Mia in whatever degree it was there, the dinner you had prepared—all of this was as nothing to me.

Some families contribute success and happiness to the world. Not so with the Manootdjians. Our contribution has been our anger. A "condition," my mother called it, a term she applied to those of us unable to handle life's vicissitudes. My father had a condition and so too did Hannah. All my life I have run from them, Isabel; all my life I have lived in judgment only to find myself so like those from whom I fled.

Our battle over pregnancy was a twofold wound. For one thing, I was cast as wanting and pushing for something I was truly ambivalent about, for the reasons I have described. But my ambivalence was not sufficient to protect me when the realization finally came, two years later, that I would never father a child of my own. By that time, being alone in the country had become the norm, and it was on one such weekend, while painting the woodshed, that I suddenly, on a bright, beautiful day, let go of my brush and walked back to the apartment over the garage. Out there by the shed I experienced a sense of loss like none I had ever known. It was like feeling a part of me die. I had lost my calling as a man. What bigger rejection could there be than to be married to a woman who didn't want to have your child? And so I went to the only place I could. I fell on my knees and I prayed as I had never prayed before that God would give me the strength to live through the day and the days to come and to provide me with any new perspective that he could. I prayed as if my life depended on it, and it did.

Isabel, mystery began to attach to our nights together. I would be woken by your sobs and find you trembling. You would then grab hold of me as if for dear life. "I feel like I'm going to die," you would say. The violence of your shaking summoned fear in me that you would suffer a heart attack or stroke. For many months these nights continued. I would hold you and try to comfort you and eventually we would both return to sleep. To be honest, it was something of a relief to sense that I wasn't the primary cause of your distress, even if, at the time, I didn't know what was.

Nothing delighted me more as a newcomer to recovery than to reject a man sober many years who reached out his hand to help. There was a definite need to put such creatures in their place, as homicidal fury toward the father was not entirely absent from me as yet. Such was my treatment of Zed at the RoR Saturday night meeting in Greenwich Village. I rebuffed this frail, slow-moving man when he approached me with his phone number on a scrap of paper and suggested I call him. And yet, on returning to the meeting after weeks of hospitalization owing to being struck by a car from behind while riding my bicycle, I blurted the news of my misfortune to Zed. He didn't respond, as others had, with words of sympathy. "Maybe this will hasten your spiritual development," he simply said. Yes, my feelings were bruised, and yet his response was bracing and instructive. I was to learn that he had extensive experience with suffering that allowed him to speak in this manner. He understood that sympathy, in some cases, could be an accelerant for self-pity. Later, when I expressed the desire to flee from all creatures big and small, he said what I was running from was what I was running toward. I found it hard to resist a man who also said, "The truth without love is an attack." And so he entered my life in an increasing way.

And when, some years later, in despair, I spoke with him of your nocturnal terror, he suggested that I purchase a certain book and that I read a chapter for partners of those who were suffering before giving it to you. I found the book at Barnes and Noble and kept it in its bag as I left the store, as it was not the kind of book I wanted to be seen with in public. If the section Zed assigned me was revealing, the book in its totality was for you revolutionary. You had only to see the title to recoil and for all color to drain from your face. "No. No," you said, and slid the book under the sofa. But hourly you kept coming back to it. You'd read a bit before hiding it away once more. A door was opening.

For some years now you had been seeing a therapist, Madame DuPrey, a Frenchwoman who, while proficient in the plusque parfait and securing and holding a good man, nevertheless lacked the necessary resolve to do battle with the patriarch or even understand the cataclysmic effect of his oppression. Madame DuPrey was France of the ancien régime, not the sans culottes. She had no bloodthirsty swagger and no sword, and definitely no guillotine. When you said to her, "My stepfather is not who you think he is," she responded with affirmations of his worth, based on the position of eminence he had held.

If Madame DuPrey was an advocate of the status quo, Fay Blitzer was a warrior with little regard for the male sex. She had slain fathers and stepfathers all up and down the East Coast. She had their number, and their number was not a good one. She won your confidence from the moment you entered her office by not getting up to greet you, as she knew any movement in your direction might cause distress. It takes one to know one, her gesture of understanding was meant to suggest.

The manual, which had led you to Fay Blitzer as a pioneer in the field of healing from abuse, didn't add that she was also somewhat daft. If she supported you as you came out of denial, she also offered far-out theories that did not quite fit.

By this time the Oiseau had entered our lives. She had an office in a tall luxury building on the East Side. "Marriage is hard; the single life is hard," she said. The emphatic force of her words suggested she was speaking from experience. It was possible that her tall, blond beauty had taken her far and that a man of power and means had been in the picture before taking flight. I pictured foreign capitals and dignitaries and ambassador's balls, VIP lounges, expensive sunglasses, and perhaps the Riviera. She may have thought she was younger than her years, if the short skirts she favored were any indication. Seeing my attention to her bare legs, she would futilely seek to pull the hem closer to her knees.

There was a time when I would hear about married couples seeking out counselors and shake my head at the sadness and futility of such sessions. In my jaundiced view, the sole purpose of these intermediaries was to pull people apart. As I saw it, all the modern world wanted was for people to be alone, and these professionals were agents for that aloneness.But that was then. Now, I would leave work early to ensure that I would arrive on time for my appointment. If the train stalled in the subway tunnel en route, a feeling of terror would come over me, as if I were a child threatened with permanent separation from Mommy. Trust me when I say that every second of these fifty-minutes sessions with the Oiseau was precious to me.

But let's leave all this for now. We can return.

Chapter 22

While Miss Carmelli (never Ms., for a reason she felt no need to explain) has gone away from the org, let it never be said that she is forgotten. The truth is that Johan has been in touch with Miss Carmelli. In fact, Johan has spoken with her just this very day, and though he would not wish Lurleen Lulabella to know, for she is wrathful toward those who so much as mention Miss Carmelli's name and threatens to fine them beyond the limits of their purse for such a transgression, Johan is actually en route for a visit with his former boss.

The streets have taken on a quiet, residential look, a departure from bustling Northern Boulevard, where he had transferred from the train to the bus. He has left behind that congested strip with its masses full of immigrant energy—men in turbans and sari-clad women with those red dots centered on their foreheads. What he sees from the bus are not stores spreading their wares out onto the sidewalk but well-maintained, hedge-fronted buildings. And yet, he is in a residential desert, as a professor once described the borough, not one where you can fall out of bed and buy a bagel or where you can easily overcome the sense of displacement from the energy center that Manhattan is. Queens is a borough where deadness settles into your bones—where you shout from your grave hoping the bright lights across the water will hear.

Those Korean delis with their flower stands, ubiquitous in his borough, are hard to find here. This is not Broadway. Block after block he trudges before he can purchase a bouquet of tulips. He remembers that Miss Carmelli's office was often enlivened with bright arrangements of flowers—pink peonies or luminously white chrysanthemums. She had a developed aesthetic sense. You saw it in the outfits she wore and in the museum prints that hung on her office walls—the Van Goghs and the Monets. She attended art lectures and poetry readings. One such reading, by W. S. Merwin at the 92nd Street Y, sent her into a state of rapture.

The past tense. He realizes he has been eulogizing her. Oh love that cannot show itself face to face but must reveal itself only from a distance and through the distortions of memory. Oh, love that never was. Oh, lonely man on a pilgrimage to your former boss.

And now, his bladder bursting after an hour spent on mass transit, he must find a restroom, as it would be so embarrassing to enter his ex-boss's home with the urgent need to relieve himself. On the corner is a White Castle, a relic he thought swept away by Burger King and McDonalds and other fast food champs. He hears the usual revulsion in his head: patrons eating diseased flesh with their dirty hands.

The restroom is locked. A plaque on the door with those firm, forearm jab words, "For paying customers only." As if there are nonpaying customers, swine who steal the glorious burgers and fries of the great White Castle.

Behind a Plexiglas shield a young woman in a polyester uniform cracks gum. She is attractive. He wants to say a foolish thing. He wants to tell her he will be her slave, that he will weep for her for days on a rain-soaked street. Instead he hears himself say, "Do you suppose I can use your restroom?"

"Do you suppose you can read the sign?" Like shavings of dry ice stinging his face they are.

It is all right. The world is without promise for some, that they should feel relegated by life to service industry jobs like these.

And so he orders a hamburger, and only after she has taken his money does she slide him the restroom key. And when he has finished his business in the restroom he leaves without his hamburger and without looking back. Maybe she will eat the thing herself, or give it to someone who will.

It is a postwar building, recessed from the street, with glass doors and an intercom. The lack of a doorman induces insecurity. Memories of Kitty Genovese. Nineteen sixty-five? Stabbed repeatedly on a Queens street as her neighbors stayed behind drawn curtains, not even calling the police. How unsafe he can suddenly feel in this city. Why are there no people out and about and children playing? It's a Saturday, for Christ's sake. And that sense of danger doesn't entirely leave him even after Miss Carmelli has buzzed him in. A pokey elevator takes him to the third floor, where he enters a long and desolate corridor you could drive a truck through. A dimly lit space, the floor covered with chocolate brown linoleum. From an apartment he passes comes the smell of cooking. Comforting to know there is life on the other side of those doors. People who care for themselves and others. Community. What a brave thing Miss Carmelli has done, uprooting herself from Manhattan to create a life for herself in this urban wilderness. But then, that is Miss Carmelli's way. He thinks of her as a secular nun who treated her job as a religious vocation, and it is no surprise that her one sister is in fact with the Carmelite order out on Long Island.

Miss Carmelli comes to the door wearing a wig, a salt-and-pepper thing made of coarse fibers. Like a lacquered helmet of hair one size too big it sits on her head. Is it possible she is wearing it more for him than for herself? He imagines her sweltering and itchy under the synthetic mass.

"Good to see you," he says, hiding his astonishment and handing her the paper-wrapped flowers.

"They're gorgeous, just gorgeous," Miss Carmelli says of the yellow tulips, ushering him in. "Forgive the clutter. I've been so busy I haven't had a chance to tidy up," But nothing that amounts to clutter is in view. Just a small stack of books on the coffee table and some unopened mail on the soft beige carpet that covers the living room floor. He follows her into the kitchen and cuts the stems of the flowers as Miss Carmelli chooses a vase.

I could live here, he thinks that afternoon, settled comfortably in an upholstered chair in the living room. There might be some bittersweet emotion, some feeling of having been put out to pasture for the twilight years, but he could do it. It occurs to him that Miss Carmelli is showing him something, not only how to live but how to die. Not that she sounds like a woman approaching the end.

"Her writing is just exquisite. Every word inlaid into the sentence like a precious jewel. Nothing extraneous, not like most writers… And the Van Gogh show coming up at the Met. It's on my must-see list….And Mary Parsons, you remember her, from Finance, wants me to take a trip to Paris with her. We'll see." And then there is that class at the Met on the art of the Near East she is eager to take. And in the fall a new opera season at Lincoln Center—what a treat that will be.

But how? She is in treatment for cancer and has lost her hair.

Miss Carmelli sets out chocolate chip cookies and serves him a cup of herbal tea. The cookies are the kind of store-bought treats she would provide once a week for the staff.

"These cookies are great. Where did you get them?"

"At PriceRite. Where else? You see people today spending megabucks on fancy-schmanzy organic products. It's all a bunch of bologna. The problem with young people today is that they only think of themselves. All these gyms, all this exercise, all this attention to every little thing they eat. What kind of life is that, to invest in your figure but nothing else? The whole continent of Africa being decimated by AIDS, the homeless everywhere until that jerk of a mayor took a broom and swept them God knows where, and they're worrying about their waistlines. Give me a break," she says.

The cookies are a reminder that Miss Carmelli shops more for value than for quality. Purchasing supermarket goodies is an affirmation of her confidence that our food system is not poisoned but can truly nourish. In this and other ways is Miss Carmelli faithful to her working class roots and never a party to fads, bogus or otherwise.

And can he not say, with hindsight, that Ms. Carmelli, a St. John's graduate, took him to her for this very same reason, that he is not Mayflower American, not Harvard American, but City College of New York American. Witnessing the gleam in her omniscient eye, he sinks into sadness. Even with a potentially fatal illness, she projects a certain knowledge about him, a look that says she knows the gap between his ambition and his reality. She knows that he has failed, that he has not, since coming to her at a still relatively young age, gone on to become the published novelist and short story writer he had hoped to be. Excellence is her domain and *he is outside its gates in a way that Blanche Givenchy never was*, by virtue of falling short in his avocation and the mediocrity of his work at the org. As when he was a child and awoke in his parents' bed, having wet his own in the night, to find his father staring down with amusement, his arm like an iron bar strongly against Johan's chest, Johan seeking to hide his terror that he would never rise above his supine position, so too did Miss Carmelli have an iron bar against his chest, precluding the possibility of rising to a greater stature. He sees once again that, whatever the merits of Miss Carmelli's regime, he can be grateful she is gone from his daily life. There were reasons to have been unhappy during her time as the department director.

The phone rings an hour or so into his visit. Miss Carmelli excuses herself to take the call. "I will have to get back to you. I have company," he hears her say, from another room. Her voice conveys her frantic need to get off the line. *I have company.*

"I hope I'm not keeping you from something," he says.

"Oh, no. That was Mary Parsons. We talk enough," Miss Carmelli says.

Her return to the living room drives home the point that Miss Carmelli is a woman of exceptional quality, for she has been making a statement to the caller as well as to Johan that company is important and not to be kept waiting. Where many people would have allowed selfishness to have its day in staying on the line, Miss Carmelli adheres to the strict etiquette of being present for her guest, and this attitude is entirely consistent with her general need to put sly anti-socialism in its place, frowning as she does on those who wear headphones in buses and elevators and other public places. Miss Carmelli is simply not in favor of this earbuds generation setting themselves apart in such a rudely self-absorbed way, as if they have no connection with the people around them. A person should be able to expect undivided attention.

On the coffee table a glass paperweight he gave her some years ago. She herself had gifts for everyone at Christmas and on their birthdays. In her organized and efficient way, she bought well in advance. And those superb wrappings, all the corners neatly folded in a way that he never could. The paperweight an object. A trinket. Go out and buy someone something. What did any of that really mean?

Sunlight has begun to stream through the white lace curtains of the window behind him. The sun in the west means dinner will at some point have to enter the picture. Suppose Miss Carmelli has no quit in her? Suppose all concept of time has vanished from her mind? Suppose the call of death, which now she is doubtless beginning to hear, has given her a newfound and endless need for communication with people? Suppose age has left her on an island all her own that he has now rowed himself onto? Something has changed. The silences have become longer, the medium for communication more than any words, which only get in the way. She is waiting for him to see something, something that has been there all along; he is in some dreamscape in which he is being moved closer and closer to her until he is in her. Not in that way. No, no, God forbid. But in some way.

On the other hand, suppose she has been enduring this now marathon visit for his sake? Suppose she is thinking that he, for some reason, needs it more than him. Either way, it does not matter. He is now desperate to end the visit. *I have had enough of old age and dying. I must be among those more in life.* No that he has any social plans. Another Saturday night is looming, and yet he has no one but no one to be with.

"I should go. I have to be back in the city," he says, and hears his own Manhattan chauvinism that he would refer to his borough as the city.

"Do you?" she says.

That smile on her face. It has been there throughout, so oddly detached from anything he or she says. It is the kind of smile a person flashes but doesn't wear continually. It is more than a smile. She is beaming. A light has come on that she cannot seem to turn off. Is it the cancer cells causing her to burn incandescent? Maybe. But then, maybe it is the light of love. Why not think so?

"Well, yes, I'm afraid so."

As he retraces his steps down the long corridor he turns back. There she is, looking after him, the intensity of her smile causing her face to glow in the dull light—a smile that not even sleep may be able to extinguish.

Chapter 23

"I want a divorce. I want you to leave." You spoke those words calmly on a hot July day.

"You want a divorce? Fine? We'll get a divorce." That was my reply, pride seeking a cover for the hurt and shock I felt.

The prior two weeks I had spent in the country, trying to give you space. I had the car and would drive into town for groceries and for recovery meetings. I had taken to sleeping in the apartment above the garage. I even bought a few items for the apartment, including a night table and a lamp, trying to find some way to remain in the marriage and yet have my own separate space.

My hope had been that you would begin to miss me while I was away, but day after day the phone remained silent. I returned to the loft to find you in animated phone conversation with Nathan Sbar, whom I had taken a dislike to for asking if your parents knew you were living with me, and came to dislike as well for his need to boast about his daughter's high IQ. After being gone for two weeks and anxiously alone, I was starved for your attention, but you continued to stay on the line, chatting away in a loud voice. Something about you standing with one foot on a chair as you spoke on the phone drew my attention as well. The posture seemed one of confidence, decisiveness.

"You have to consider the common welfare," Zed said, when I shared with him later that week my plan to retain a lawyer and fight what I regarded as your unjust request. Zed was reminding me that Mia had been an unfortunate witness to my verbal tirades. His words elevated me, if only briefly. In this light, my departure from the loft could be seen as a gift to both you and Mia. I began to cry, and cried for many days thereafter.

I took a sublet on the East Side. In the morning I would wake and there would be a grace period of a few seconds before the pain found me. "Why me, God? Why me?" And of course the voice would respond, "Why not you, Johan? Why not you?"

A stranger stopped me on the street. "A reconciliation has to be reflective, not reflexive," he said, displaying a nuanced command of language before moving on.

And there was Leah, offering me her love in the way that she could. Saying that, with my permission, she would call Isabel and tell her what a wonderful man I was. But then there was my horror at the very thought of her interacting with you, the fear that you two would bond and that Leah would take you away from me, as she had appropriated my father.

Isabel, there were the East Side movie theaters I would stand outside, unable to purchase a ticket, as it would be a betrayal of you to step inside the darkened theater and be distracted for a couple of hours. The temporary abandonment of my pain would have meant an abandonment of you.

Love. Why did it have to hurt so much? Why did there have to be cars on the street that reminded me of Honest Abe, your Ford Futura, the sight of which would trigger associations and a stabbing pain in my heart?

Zed saying to me in this time, "Is love possession or is love unconditional? If you practice spiritual principles, you won't care if the marriage survives. All you will care about is the relationship."

Zed saying this, Zed saying that, in the emphatic way he spoke.

Eating now in pizza shops and relying on the salad bar at Korean delis for takeout.

Not knowing what I might do. As if what you might do was all that mattered. As if my fate were in your hands.

The time the phone in my sublet went dead and I panicked, thinking you might be trying to call at that very moment.

The Swedish porn magazines I bought at newsstands. The thin ones with short hair the ones who interested me most in those pages.

The teddy bear I slept with. Yes, the one you gave me.

Sundays the worst. A day without any movement to it.

And then getting together with you in that early phase. A Friday night. You wore a tight skirt and black stockings and a short, tight fitting jacket. I saw you only to have to let you go. What was that but a reopening of the wound?

Walking lifted my spirits. A bronze statue caught my eye, that of a World War I doughboy with rifle in hand, a bayonet attached. Such a heroic pose. Such a world. Fifth Avenue, where the rich lived and doormen stood guard.

So too, of course, did meditation and prayer summon a brief measure of peace and serenity. And self-examination in the form of a dialogue between higher and lower self. Zed saying, "Take a look at that," this in regard to judgments I voiced as to what you were doing to me. Zed saying, "Find some identification with her. Understand that it is more painful for her to be with you than it is for you to not be with her. She's not doing to you. She's just *doing*."

Me: "She said I was sucking her blood. She said she couldn't breathe."

Zed: "A chicken crosses the road and the house on the other side falls down. Don't take this personally."

Prostitutes were said to live in the East Side building where I stayed. One woman of the night jumped to her death, plunging through the awning to the pavement below. There was no long-lasting shock. This was New York City, where lights burned bright in the night and freighters waited in the harbor to unload.

And those spiritual texts I read, that told me love never had to die, that true love was not wanting or expecting things from others but coming from a place of giving. I read those texts as if my life depended upon them, not wanting my love for you to perish. That could not happen. It simply couldn't, even if I could not say why.

Isabel, in my mind the Upper West Side was boulevards with old buildings and old people—a retirement community, a place for dying—elderly Jewish men like Isaac Bashevis Singer sitting on benches and feeding the pigeons on those traffic islands in the middle of Broadway in a time when the city felt unsafe and an exodus was in fact occurring, well before the West Side became the prime real estate area in the city. And yet, six months into the separation, I took a sublet in that part of the city. In all the world there is only one home fire burning, and that is in New York City.

Placing my signature on a lease would be committing myself to a permanent separation. Emotionally, a sublet was all I could handle. The prime tenant, Melanctha Mellon, spoke about growing up in the South and of her coming out at a debutante's ball. Her ambition was to be a singer; she had been told her vocal range and expressive power were beyond those of the luminaries on the stage at the Metropolitan Opera House. But she was struggling. There had been a string of setbacks. The beau she was counting on had left, and then there were those mystifying maladies—the cancer scares that resulted in biopsies, the bout with pneumonia, the ovarian cyst that had to be removed.

The broker, Enzo Giovanni, ran a credit check on me.

"Johan, what is this? Your credit rating is through the roof." The credit report, of course, reflected your financial status and not my own.

It was clear, in our further discussions, that Melanctha had taken note of Enzo's comment. The hand she placed on the small of my back in showing me her bedroom, a boudoir really, with her queen-sized bed and satin sheets and satin fabric hanging from the walls, would not have been placed there without the credit information presented by Enzo, nor the light and feathery hand she placed on my leg as we sat on the sofa, where she reviewed with me the care her plants would need. I was a prospect. I suddenly understood what it was to be sought after for your money. It made me feel like a dollar sign, not a human being. It was the way you often felt.

I stayed on as a subtenant for a year, with Melanctha's things, her dying air conditioners and tangerine-colored curtains and worn carpets, her stained sofa and cheap wicker chairs. Stayed there too with her drawer full of racy underwear, more put off than excited by her thongs and panties and brassieres. And when, by the following year, Melanctha realized that she would not be coming back to New York City, or at least not to stay—because she could not come back, not to the past that she had left—I was strong enough to sign my name to the lease. First, however, there was the matter of negotiating the fixtures fee, and for this she flew back to New York City. "I could sleep on the sofa. I wouldn't be in your way," she said. But I couldn't acquiesce. The thought of having to cross the living room to get to the kitchen or using the bathroom as she lay on the sofa was too much. Melanctha understood. She arranged to stay next door with the Flessers. Their A-line apartment could easily accommodate her as an overnight guest. Like her, they were both singers, she said. Was she placing herself in the same league with the Flessers? The thought made me sad, as she was jobless and alone, whereas the Flessers had the whole schmear— children attending exclusive private schools, agents, bookings, powerful friends.

One afternoon I came home and found Melanctha and Riva Flesser standing in the living room—Melanctha had retained a key, as she still had her name on the lease. I heard flirtatiousness in their voices and could not engage them in a relaxed way. I was also ill with fever and chills and had been thinking of bed all through the day while at work. But my illness was not a factor in their judgment. Riva Flesser and Melanctha had seen something about me in that moment, that I was not a real man but someone who could, at times, behave ungraciously toward women. Perhaps they saw, in that moment, the hint of the abusiveness that both Sarah and you had experienced, my capacity for unbridled anger. And so I had to live with the shame this encounter brought on until the spell of it, like the fever, broke. Still, a fixtures fee was agreed upon and the lease placed in my name.

In the second year of our separation, I took off my wedding band and placed it under the base of the lamp on my bedroom dresser. I was free to see other women, according to the Oiseau and to Zed. That right had been mine since you asked me to leave, as it was yours to see whomever you chose.

There was Betty, an attractive woman who embarrassed me by singing along, and loudly, with the soundtrack of *Carlito's Way* in a crowded movie theater. And there was Janet, who nearly choked on her swordfish when she learned that I was still married, even though living separately from you. There were a number of such women, one thing or another about them sapping my interest after a single get-together. And then there were the women who wouldn't go out with me. But even with the unsatisfying experiences and the rejections, there was still the sense of possibility that came with my new life.

But you remained my orientation point. Every weekend, or every other weekend, we would meet for dinner, generally on a Friday night. And on those evenings when we had our session with the Oiseau, we would often spend time afterward in a coffee shop nearby. "We have to start over. We have to," you said to me, as if you had some conception in your mind that I wasn't privy to.

The summer following our separation, I flew to Italy. In the cab en route to JFK, I saw myself as a child. Not the desperately homesick child I had been in those summers at the Bible camp run by the Ukrainians my mother had sent me to in the Catskill Mountains, where punishment was routinely meted out, but a loved and cared for child, as if I were revisiting childhood in an adult body and being given a second chance.

The first day in Rome was difficult. Jet-lagged, I sat in my room at the budget pensione experiencing all those feelings of pain and terror as I had at sleep away camp, when time stopped and my every waking moment was an excruciating longing for Mommy. I had made a huge mistake. The trip would be unbearable. But I focused on my breath for twenty minutes and the pain fell away. The rediscovery of my center was huge. It allowed me to be where my feet were and to go out and explore the city with strength and confidence, in spite of the jet lag. Seeing the huge Victor Emmanuel Monument and its soiled white marble stirred an ache of longing, as if I had been here before on some sunny afternoon after a rain-soaked morning. It was a feeling neither the Colisseum nor Hadrian's Tomb could summon.

At the end of an English speaking recovery meeting on Via Napoli, a woman invited me for coffee. She had the power to place me in her thrall. Instantly my concern became how to get her free of others who came along so we could be alone together. Maybe she thought I was brighter than I was, and came to see I had nothing more to offer than the message I had shared with the group, having been asked to lead the meeting. Whatever regard she had for me was quickly fading. There is something in me that wants things fast, Isabel, as Luke once said, some deficiency in cultivating relationships. My experience of the nineteen sixties, when instant sexual gratification seemed to be the norm, only reinforced that impulse. It was for me to understand that I had emerged from the cocoon of marriage into a different time, one influenced by AIDS and perhaps the excesses of my generation. After all, young Republicans were to be seen out and about upon the land. There were high school students saving for their retirement. In place of Janis Joplin driving off the cliff, there was Madonna, Inc.

And yet I did wind up alone with her. She had an apartment on a narrow street near Piazza del Popolo. Down below Vespas tore along the cobblestones. Shortly after we arrived she went to call her therapist from another room, saying she would return shortly, but when the minutes grew to an hour and I could still hear, through the wall, the murmur of conversation, I thought to leave. But could she be so rude as to keep me on hold or did every minute and now hour that passed mean that she expected me to spend the night? Finally, the need for sleep led me to the door. As I headed out, she gave a brief wave without so much as looking directly at me through the half-open door of the room where she sat, the phone still to her ear.

Torn up I was, Isabel, torn up. Many times in the days to come I called this woman, only to get her machine. How far I had fallen from being the imagined *object of her desire*. How much, in short order, I had given myself over, making her the source of my happiness. How little enthusiasm I had for focusing on my breath, though my well-being required it.

And yet, a few days later, I once again sat at a café with a young woman named Jill and others after a recovery meeting. A man from the group was with us who, I sensed, had an interest in Jill, even though he was married and wore a wedding band. As I chatted with Jill, I felt his jealousy. Though she offered to drive me back to my pension, perversely I left with the man and some others. I say perversely, for I wanted nothing more than to be with her. Somehow I allowed the man's perceived anger to stand between me and her. From such self-betrayals can big pain come, Isabel. On the state of agony I returned to my room in I will not dwell. Evidently, I was only slowly being led from the life I had known.

With a second-class ticket, I traveled by rail from Rome to Florence, and then on to Venice, and took along this ache of longing that the Italian countryside could not dull. Oh, Isabel, what a life this is, that we must be burned and burned by attachment. A new opportunity for pain found me among the canals of Venice, where, as I was entering my room for the night at the pensione, I glimpsed another young woman entering her room down the hallway. The red sash she wore around her slender waist almost drove me to knock on her door. Mercifully, I went to my room and fell asleep. The next morning she darted past the table where I sat in the garden of the pensione, as if fate had determined to keep her beyond my reach.

And yet, alone now after years of enmeshment with women, a new line of thinking had begun to emerge. I would see a couple walking arm in arm or holding hands and be silently dismissive, choosing to regard them as too crippled and needy to be apart. If I had once scorned as feeble those souls who couldn't connect with another human being for more than a week or two, those who related to their cats but not to human beings and slept alone, now I silently mocked those who couldn't be out of each other's sight for five minutes, like the beautiful woman standing alone admiring Bellini's *Madonna Enthroned* in one of the rooms at the Galleria dell'Accademia. Within two minutes I heard "Honey, honey" as a man, surely her mate or husband, rushed to her side. Has Little Johnny come back for Mommy? Has little Johnny some exciting news he is bursting to tell her? Did little Johnny get scared being off on his own for a brief time?

In such a state of spiritual deformity did I find myself, with scorn for those who shared their lives and bodies but also bitterness that the women of beauty should open themselves to the grotesques of the world while spurning me. *Do you not understand that he is the very best person in the world for you? The Oiseau had said this to you, Isabel. In a state of exasperation did she say this thing.*

And then, in the next room, there she was, the woman from the pensione, a water bottle in hand and the red sash serving as a beacon. In reverent appreciation of a portrait by Titian she stood, with no Tom, Dick, or Harry streaking in to claim her for his own.

I waited outside the museum and prayed for the right words. When she finally emerged, I introduced myself and explained that I had seen her back at the pensione, leaving out the fever of longing the sight of her had triggered. The day was a glorious one, warm and sunny, and maybe the fair weather inclined her toward me. Who can say? We set off together for a boat ride to a nearby island; there was an old church she wanted to see.

And then it was back to the mainland, and Piazza San Marco. How unbearably sad to see professional waiters standing idle outside their elegant restaurants, the linen-covered tables empty behind them. Helplessly they watched as the tourists opted to give their lira to the outdoor vendors and eat on the fly. In some way the human drama would always have more resonance for me than what I saw on the walls of the palaces and museums.

Isabel, she established the agenda for the day. For the next three hours we wandered through the doge's palace, with its enormous tapestries, at her deliberate pace. She had credentials and a mind that could create structures. A graduate of Yale's School of Architecture, she had found herself mired in drudge work for some big design firm. Neither in terms of salary or satisfaction was it the path she wished to pursue. These things I discovered about her in our time together.

On the boat ride back to the mainland, I had said to Lena, for that was her name, "We should spend the whole day together. I'm a nice person." "Nice you are not," she replied. There was something playful in her response, an interpretation her smile seemed to support, as if she was saying, "You're actually quite dangerous, and dangerous I sort of like." And so I let her words ride. They held out the possibility of later intimacy. But when, on my return to New York City, I related the exchange to Dr. Tobin, a therapist the Oiseau recommended to me, his response took me by surprise. "She had no right to speak with you in this way. We must work on that here." Dr. Tobin had a theory that I gave women permission to behave poorly toward me by communicating a sort of destabilizing guilt. The conviction with which he expressed himself took me back to childhood and the treatment I had received from my older sisters, not only the physical abuse but the ridicule as well.

Lena would disappear in the slow-moving tourist throng. But then there she would be again, that red sash a marker. Altogether, the hard marble floors and the endless art-gazing and my anxiety about the tentative nature of my connection with Lena led me to believe I might be crowding her, and so I decided to wait outside on the piazza. My thinking was that she would appreciate me more if I stepped away for a while. Does this kind of reasoning sound familiar to you? Do you remember the Oiseau's cardinal rule that a pursuer in a relationship should allow the distancing one to come to him?

After standing for a while in front of the palace I grew anxious. What had I been thinking? Suppose I lost her in the crowd? Or she might be in there for hours, studying tapestries and paintings with her aesthete's gaze. And a single woman with her looks would inevitably draw men to her. But a short time later there she was, actually seeking me out, only what she told me next was completely deflating. She was already checked out of the pensione and hadn't the money to spend another night in Venice. She would be catching the train to Udine, where a friend would put her up. I proposed that we go for dinner. I would be back at the pensione if she changed her mind. Then I left her. I had no choice. I had to be alone for a brief while. There was no gas left in the tank.

Back in my room I sat quietly for twenty minutes. The brief period of meditation was restorative, but the hook was still in. It would be days, weeks, before I could recover from this encounter if she didn't show.

The shower was outside the room. I stared at the phone. Should I call down to the front desk and alert the concierge that I would be stepping out my room, in the event that she did appear? But no, no need for that. That would just be trying to will the situation to happen. Just let the whole thing unfold. Just stick to the orderly process of my day. Amor fati and all that.

An hour later, the concierge called to me as I passed through the lobby. There had been a visitor. The concierge had rung me but there was no answer, and so the visitor went away. Stricken, I read the note the concierge handed me. "That was great. Sorry we couldn't continue our evening. Ciao. Lena."

I ran with a mad energy in the direction of the train station. If the brief engagement with the two women in Rome had brought me pain, it was as nothing to the acute turmoil now unleashed in me. Was it simply life calling to life and the pain of a lonely man in a near miss with true happiness? Or was it a hole in me no woman could ever fill? Was it, in some way, a manifestation of my alcoholism? She was broke. She had spent the day with an amiable and interesting man. I had stretched myself to my emotional limit, had placed all my energy and intelligence into ensuring a connection that made her return to the pensione inevitable, and then placed this connection at serious risk by stepping out of my room to take a shower.

Back and forth through the Venice train station I ran. There were many young women, but none in the black skirt and white blouse and red sash that Isabel had worn. Nor could I find her on the 7:05 to Udine or the 8:05 either, though I did see two blond and jeering young men, perhaps Austrians, hanging out the window of that later train as it left the station. In the stricken state I was in, I found it easy to believe that they were laughing at my very visible pain.

The possibility never occurred to me that she had left her bags at the front desk when she checked out that morning and while retrieving them wrote that brief note. Nor did it occur to me that her interest in me was insufficient to leave her contact information back in New York. But then why, why, the call from the concierge?

By this time, Isabel, your stepfather was beginning to feel your wrath. Not that you went against him with words. Not that you said, "You wrecked my life. Do you have any idea?" You had too much fear and perhaps filial circumspection to make such a direct accusation. But you broke off communication. Week after week, and month after month, you refused to return his phone calls. Did he know that the past was alive in you? Or was all such memory sealed away in the recesses of his consciousness?

I had broken bread with this man. I had heard him give his blessing to my "regime," as he called it.

You were in a building phase, Isabel, constructing artisan furnishings. For my bathroom you made a small set of shelves and for my kitchen a spice rack, both painted in colors that had an unearthly vitality to them—a bright red and yellow such as I expected only to see in a Van Gogh canvas—and added your tiny signature lines. On your visits you lay down on the sofa, the same beige corduroy Sears sofa you had sent down from the country to help me furnish the apartment.

Our outings evoked in me a sweet sadness, as when we visited the Brooklyn Botanical Gardens and stopped off at Katz's, the landmark Jewish deli, on East Houston Street. Was it the lower East Side, there on the periphery of SoHo, where we had lived, that made me delirious? The sight of the Bowery, where I had spent those years of drunkenness? All I knew was that a new relationship was emerging from the ashes of the old.

One evening we saw a film about a man who, with the support of a powerful female patron, becomes a world-famous photographer. Afterward, we stopped off for a cup of coffee at a diner on Broadway, as it was not yet time to say goodbye. "I don't want you to leap across the table, but I've been thinking…" My inward reaction was not quite to leap across the table. The resumption of our physical relationship would mean relinquishing my freedom for the discipline of monogamy once again.

The Oiseau allayed my fears. She affirmed that intimacy with you would not mean the forfeiture of my freedom. Isabel, you came to visit. Friday was our night. There was weeping that first night.

Zed's wife Banja had left him, unable to endure his anger. They did not resume living together, but neither did they divorce. Even so, Zed made the frequent claim that their love for each other only grew and there was nothing they would not do for each other. The statement troubled me. A husband and wife who had split up had unconditional love for each other? What made Zed's claim even more dubious was the fact that Banja was living with her lover, a woman. Was Zed in denial that Banja had moved on with her life? Had his pride blinded him to this reality?

The truth lay somewhere else. A new perception about his relationship with Banja had come to Zed. He had taken full responsibility for his part in their marital difficulties and was not denying that the marriage was dead. He was simply saying that a new relationship predicated on giving, not getting, had arisen from the ashes of that marriage.

Isabel, you must understand that Zed held my heart; I could place no man before him as I could place no woman before you. And so, the modeling of unconditional love for Banja, about which I had harbored so much doubt, became my source of hope that you and I could achieve the same transformation following our separation.

"I can help you with this," Zed had said to me, when I came to him with my pain. Identification would be key, he said. I would have to find a way to understand and relate to your emotional reality. Was it hard for me to be apart from you? Then let me contemplate how hard it was for you to have me under the same roof. It was for me to understand that when you mockingly addressed me as lord and master, it was not me you were really addressing.

I would call Zed daily and turn the conversation to the future, prompting Zed to say, "What you really want is a guarantee of the outcome, and that is not very spiritual, is it? Bring everything back to the now. 'In this moment I have everything I need. In this moment I am being taken care of. In this moment I am being held.'"

In this way did Zed speak to me.

Over a two-year period, you would visit me at my apartment on Friday evenings. Toward the end of this period, you began a collaboration with a man named Jim Boulee. The name elicited great fear the first time you spoke it. It may have been the way Jim Boulee entered your life, casually and confidently joining you and Maude at the table where you sat in a downtown café. From that chance meeting a working partnership developed, as Jim Boulee had a book idea and asked you to provide the illustrations. Jim Boulee had certifiable intellectual assets, being a Dartmouth graduate. He had been a sailor and a gourmet chef, a rodeo stunt man, and an investment banker. There was little he could not do, but his career path was an erratic one. What had started out as bold experimentalism now came to be seen, in his forties, as dilettantism.

If you and I were chatting on the phone or having dinner, sooner or later you would speak his name. You were not of one mind about this new man in your life. Suppose Jim Boulee turned out to be shallow and untrustworthy? you asked. My fear was such that I could not see you were simply seeking my support. All I could imagine, hearing that this man had invited you to his apartment to review your drawings, was that he would have you in his bed as soon as the door was closed. There was little comfort in reminding myself that you were hardly likely to talk openly about a man you were planning an affair with. The basis of my fear was that, willingly or not, you had no choice but to acquiesce to a man acting on his desire. Was not your fear of men's advances the reason that you had stayed out of the workplace?

Isabel, it is all too tragic that men are born of women only to oppress them in the way that we do. It has come to my understanding that this is so, and for redemption to be earned I must pray for the willingness to accept that you have the same freedom that I seek for myself. While I said nothing in the way of a protest about your growing connection with this man, the emotional turmoil was substantial. I felt helpless against the threat that Jim Boulee posed and was brought to the breaking point when you told me of a party that he would be throwing to celebrate the completion of the book project. Even though Jim Boulee had invited me, all I could feel was that he had effectively swept me out of the way and would now be claiming you for his very own.

Isabel, that party represented everything I had been excluded from or excluded myself from. There would be found the life that had not been mine, whether the school parties I had not been invited to or the high school prom I was too phobic to attend. What would it mean for me, the husband you had asked to leave, to be present at an event in your honor hosted by a man with unknown intentions toward you? Seeing me in my stricken condition among the gathered would only draw you closer to Jim Boulee, whom you would see by contrast as strong and vibrant. Because the time of truth would have arrived, and what was that truth but that I was a weakling, a stripling, a pathetic soul who could not measure up. No man of such shameful quality can go unpunished by a woman.

And so I said to you, in the presence of the Oiseau, "Actions have consequences," hardly knowing what I meant beyond that I was feeling pushed beyond my limit. First it had been those hammer blows, figuratively speaking, to the head that you had inflicted in those last couple of years of living together, followed by your demand for a separation, and now you were replacing me with another man?

Thoughts came to me, Isabel. Was I such a criminal that I should have to live my life making an ongoing amend to you? Did I not have some rights of my own, some obligation to myself to not give my heart over so completely to a woman who showed so little caring about me?

Driven by a fear of imminent replacement, I resolved to find someone to connect with, that is, to really capitalize on the option of exploring other possibilities. I had been living in the no-man's land of ambivalence too long. The thing I didn't ask myself was whether I was seeking the hair of the dog that had bit me.

The night of the party I was alone in my apartment. Perhaps I should have gone to a movie or found a friend to be with, but there I was, on my knees, praying for release from the considerable pain I was experiencing. Sometimes our prayers are fairly rote, and sometimes we pray from a place of desperation, driven there by our inner turmoil. Such was the case on this night. It seemed to me that my annihilation was nigh, imagining you, my wife, surrounded by friends and admirers in Jim Boulee's apartment. And yet there is a way through. Not out but through. On this night my prayer shifted and I found myself praying that you and Jim Boulee have all the love and joy and peace and happiness and success and prosperity that I could wish for myself. Over and over did I pray for this, Isabel, and came to a place of peace. Always there is that, if only we seek it.

By now, it was three years since we had separated. In addition to our biweekly session with the Oiseau, I had continued with my twice weekly individual therapy sessions with Dr. Tobin, who was especially insightful during the emotional crisis I experienced regarding the party. He offered a theory that as a child I had become, in my mind, my mother's "little husband." According to Dr. Tobin, the universe I inhabited was to the exclusion of my father, and yet, with his nightly reappearance, he was a reality I could not ignore and posed an ever-recurring threat. After all, whatever my fantasy, his size and strength made it inevitable that he would displace me and occupy my mother's bed. In essence, Dr. Tobin was saying, I had been going through life as the "little husband," living in fear of Daddy's return. Such a theory had never been presented to me before, and it seemed to fit. More than that, it gave me some understanding of my pain and brought home that harm had been done to me as well as to you, if of a lesser magnitude. I had been as dominated by my mother as you had by your stepfather. What a terrifying prospect for a child whose whole world was his mother, his father being virtually absent except as an annihilating threat.

We have to understand where we have come from if we are to be free. And you and I, in our floundering way, were helping each other to that freedom. It doesn't matter if the world understands so long as we are sure of our purpose and our goal. But if I state to you the spiritual inevitability of our increasing oneness, is it a threat to my existence or to yours to also say there were times, not only on a moonlit night, when our relationship, so fragile and strange in its new incarnation, seemed not entirely adequate to my needs, that from the remote personal island I stood upon within the larger one of Manhattan an attractive woman's stare would trigger debilitating pain as I then watched her race into the arms of another. Particularly did the threat of Jim Boulee serve as an impetus for change, but day after day I would return alone to my apartment in the jacket and tie I daily wore to work, clothes forming a kind of plumage with which I sought to inflate my value in the eyes of women. Would I be lying if I said I didn't long for the touch of others as well, the sweet consolation of some new woman's breath upon my face, the feel of her lips and thighs on mine? Would it be a crime deserving of death to say I felt there were seeming deficiencies in the arrangement that life had brought us to?

I met Maura the week following Jim Boulee's party. She was new to one of the recovery groups that I attended, and though I didn't know it, fairly new to recovery as well. We went for dinner, where I spoke about my continuing closeness to you, though stopping short of saying that we were physically intimate. "The cardinal rule of sisterhood is do not steal another woman's husband," Maura said that night, and yet the die was cast. Separated from her husband, she had her own problematic enmeshment with some man she had been seeing for the previous year—a CIA agent, of all things. Mr. Right was turning out to not be so Mr. Right after all. Or maybe she was developing cold feet. She did have distancing tendencies, having once told men who pursued her that her only real interest was in the bottle.

That first night I walked with her to Grand Central Terminal. She lived in Irvington, on the Hudson River, just outside the city. At the gate to her train, she stared at my personal card and said, "It has nothing in the center." There was no disputing her observation. The center was indeed empty. Just my name at the left top and my address in the bottom left corner and my phone number in the bottom right corner.

"I am filling in all the time. A work in progress is what I am," I said, feeling this momentary dread that she was putting the kibosh on our relationship before it could even begin.

But neither scruples about sisterhood nor the hole in the middle of my card served to keep us apart. From that first chance meeting, she was on my mind, and on it constantly, even as you and I continued with our Friday night routine. Maura was the corn grown high in Kansas, she was the harvest moon, she was the Chevrolet sign on the old West Side Highway in my childhood beckoning me into the bright and open spaces of America. I lived for the days when I could see her and worried over every possible misstep. I lavished her with praise, accommodated myself to her schedule, and listened with great patience to everything she said. Her ex-husband was wealthy. There had been homes in four different states, a boat, two cars, the works. She saw me in his image owing to the brown wool overcoat I wore along with my suits and ties. This image was not in line with the desk job I held, and I came to dread the day she would visit my place of work and see my little cubicle and Miss Carmelli, my diminutive boss, and suss me out as an office minion.

I cleared the decks so I could be with her whenever she could find the time. She worked downtown as a publicist for a publisher and would call me during the work week.

"Just checking in," she would say, or "I'm wide open," the latter a startling statement given its sexual suggestiveness. To understand our emerging relationship, it was only necessary to note that I had been sober for a long time and she, Maura, only briefly. The initial advantage was with me.

And yes, I kept Zed fully informed of this new development. "Don't run from it. Let it teach you something," he said. "We pursue pleasure and receive pain. When the pain substantially outweighs the pleasure, then we let go of the rope." So too did Zed say. Sometimes I wished that Zed would die so I could live. So I could think even as I surrendered to the truth of all that Zed said to me.

We had met in the cold of winter, but now we were in May. Maura proposed that we get together on a Saturday afternoon, as she had to be in the city that morning. Surely this was a step forward, as we had only, to this point, seen each other on weekday evenings. However, the pain in my lower back made it a challenge to get out of bed. By the time I left the house some hours later, things were no better. I had read somewhere that tension and stress often get stored in the back, and now I was a believer, as I was in great fear that my meeting with Maura would have repercussions for my relationship with you.

My skinny legs lost in my white Banana Republic chinos, I walked with the tentative, struggling steps of an old man. After a few blocks I crossed to the middle of Broadway, where I sat on a bench on one of the many islands along the boulevard. What is this pain? I asked myself on paper.

> You are afraid of leaving Mommy. It is nothing more than that. You are afraid Isabel will die of a broken heart as you were afraid of the same thing regarding your mother. This is not real, Johan. This is the past, a past that doesn't exist and never did. Go on with your life, dear Johan. Go on with it. Love never dies. It never dies.

And with that little cathartic exercise did the demon leave my back, Isabel.

The day was warm and gloriously sunny. We met by the fountains on Grand Army Plaza on Fifth Avenue and entered Central Park, amid the tourists and sketch artists and vendors bringing vitality to the scene; altogether, a joyous celebration of renewal was before me. At the zoo we stared at the sea lions, the polar bears with their white coats dirty as week-old snow, the capuchin monkeys, the twittering birds in the humid aviary. And when she was tired, we rested on a bench, where she sat slumped and with her legs spread, as if inviting me to touch her. But fear kept my hand in place. A beautiful woman was giving herself to me and I was paralyzed.

When we had exhausted the park, I took her to a café with an outdoor garden over on First Avenue, a place you and I had patronized many times. Old New York was right there around us, clotheslines slung between tenement buildings, their bricks faded by age. In the park I had been talking incessantly, sharing with Maura the back pain I had been experiencing that morning and the release from it I had found through writing. I spoke with great energy and conviction, as if I were charting new territory. All my life I had lived in the extremes of black and white, but now my situation with her was leading me to an understanding and appreciation of those gray areas. "You talk so much," Maura replied, listening as a woman beset with weariness over my endless chatter, for she was from the Midwest, where perhaps verbosity was not the norm. If she was leading me on, then I was leading her on as well, as some kind of exhorter. And why not? There was no going back. In Maura's presence, any ambivalence had been burned away as the sun burns away the morning fog.

But there in the café a dullness came over me. My words were fewer, and shame came calling. Maura was right. I was a talker, not a doer. A genuine gasbag afraid to take her to my apartment. A man afraid all I could offer was flaccidity. The sun was well over in the west by the time we left the café. It would be setting over Manhattan in a few short hours and setting also on my dream of connection. There was nothing to do but see her to the train. From one block to the next, as we headed south on Park Avenue toward the looming MetLife Building over Grand Central Terminal, I felt her slipping away. How glorious the promise of the day; how abysmal and suicide-inducing would be the night. And yet, maybe it was the motion itself that summoned in me the necessary courage; on a block mercifully free of pedestrians, I gently guided her into the recessed entranceway to a building. Inside the gilded lobby I could see a maintenance man mopping the floor, but that was no concern of mine.

"Can we kiss?" I said. Her back was turned to me, which made the question easier.

"Good idea," she replied, as she turned and raised up on her toes. A long kiss, broken only when the maintenance man rapped on the inside of the locked door with the handle of his mop.

As we walked to the terminal, we held hands. Now the silence was brought on not by exhaustion but by a stunned understanding that something new had entered our lives. Once upon a time and forever, there had been Cary Grant and Eve Marie Sainte on the Twentieth Century Limited in *North by Northwest,* and now there was Johan Manootdjian and Maura Kilroy even if it was only the Metro-North commuter train that she was boarding at gate 28 and I was heading for the shuttle to Times Square. As I walked across the peaceful concourse, a song from my past played in my mind. Faintly and plaintively did I hear Dion and the Belmonts singing "Why Must I Be a Teenager in Love?"

The next morning Maura called me at home. I wasn't surprised. All through the night she had felt so close as to be living in my skin. She had a dream to share with me in which hundreds of frogs were covering the wall of her bedroom. "Ribbit," I said, causing her to laugh.

But she wasn't laughing the next day, Monday, when I brought flowers down to her office at the end of the workday. "They're so beautiful," she said, of the dozen roses, which I had to remind her to place in a vase before we left. In nearby Union Square Park we sat on a bench. "We can't do this. It's crazy, totally crazy," she said, between kisses. All around us the office buildings of the city rose, lights burning in only a few windows. I had pushed the visit on her. Better if I had waited for her to come to me. In place of elation there was now anxiety, but with it a sense that she would inevitably fall toward, not away, from me.

Maura's beef with her CIA agent beau was his reluctance to set a date for their wedding. "Tick tock," Maura said to me. "Tick tock?" I replied. "Do you not hear the tick tock, tick tock, of my little biological clock? Is time a-wasting or what?" Then there was the CIA agent's mother, a practicing Catholic who viewed Maura with suspicion not simply because Maura was a divorcee but also because of her religion, or her absence of one. The CIA agent's mother saw disappointment and unhappiness for her son down the road if he took Maura as his wife. The advice she gave him was to stay true to his clandestine ways. "Stealth equals health, my son," she advised.

About a month after our afternoon in the park, she went away with the CIA agent to a small island off the coast of Maine. It was no sudden getaway. They had planned this summit meeting for some time, and much was riding on it, as befits a meeting of such moment, she told me between kisses on a bench in Madison Square Park, another of our rendezvous sites. The matter of her biological clock would be on the agenda, she said. The CIA agent would come through for her or suffer the consequence.

Isabel, a summit meeting is no small matter. The consequence would be real and severe for me if the CIA agent renounced his vacillating ways for the forthrightness that Maura was demanding. But can I be accused of false confidence if I held to the conviction that time was on my side and that Maura was thinking of me every second of every minute while she was away, just as I was thinking of her? Nor was I in any way jealous about her time with the man. If anything, I had great regard for the CIA agent and his dedication to the defense of our nation. I seemed to see them from the vantage point of my years, as children for whom one feels a genuine fondness. In spite of his formidable gifts, I could not, at the time, see him as a significant threat.

Oh Isabel, how far I had come from the emotional battering inflicted by even your mention of Jim Boulee. And was I not in some way the interloper I had regarded that man as being? How the wheel does turn, constantly and forever.

And so, the following week, when I received a call from Maura, there was pure elation but no great surprise. "So many times I wanted to call you," she said. How easy it was when a woman leaned on me as a source of strength. And how strange, at the same time, that a man with my little job and minimal responsibilities in life should be seen in this light and not the CIA agent, who had guardianship of America's vital interests in his job description.

Now, Isabel, a relationship has to move forward or dissolve, and though it may do the latter regardless, Maura returned from her summit meeting primed for action. The CIA agent had been up to his old equivocating ways, casting the blame for his dithering on his rejectionist mother. "Mothers count," the CIA agent said. "And girlfriends? Do they not count too, Buster?" Maura shot back. Her resentment fueled her libido, compelling her over to my apartment for the first time, where, as I sat in an armchair and tried to show the proper restraint, she plopped herself on my lap, the full weight of her one hundred ten pounds somewhat burdensome, and declared herself "a horny chickster." *Horny.* A triggering word when spoken by a woman. She followed by shedding her skirt and blouse. "Like what you see?" she whispered.

It wasn't only her enormous breasts that astonished me but those thin, shapely legs and incredibly slender waist. And that golden tan and those sparkling white teeth and that head of blond hair. And yet the experience wasn't entirely a ball in bed. There was reticence unlike any I experienced with you, some sense that my performance would be no match for my desire and leave me unable to consummate. Maura, on the other hand, was a sexual athlete with only one all-out speed.

"I'm sorry. I must be nervous," I said.

"You're not attracted to me?"

"No, no. I just need time to get comfortable."

"Comfortable? You're not comfortable?"

"I mean, it's new. That's all."

"New isn't good?"

Overcome by shame, I buried my face in the pillow. The old days, when I could take an erection for granted, were gone. And there was fear. How could I possibly hope to keep a woman I couldn't sexually satisfy, especially a woman who spoke so passionately of *schwinging* and doing *the nasty*. I lay in that abysmal state for what seemed the longest time, but light slowly encroached on the darkness and my hand found the small of her back. Shame or no shame, failure or no failure, the desire for connection would go on.

Isabel, know only this. I was on fire now. I had drunk deeply from the bottle and wanted more. And it was the same with Maura. She found a way to live with my continuing performance problem. We did other things; our bodies grew more and more in tune with each other's. We talked dirty. I stuck my finger in her small hole and it drove her wild.

I am not a psychopath. I do not have airtight chambers in my mind where I can seal off heinousness or lesser levels of offense. I must do you no harm—in word or thought or action. This is a dictate from above, a guiding imperative of my life. Pain began to find me. My secret became a barrier that threatened our oneness—no, not threatened, obscured it. Innocently you called and said you had been given two tickets to a concert recital at Carnegie Hall. I barked at you, as a dog might bark at another threatening its food supply. I had left open every weekday night but Friday, when you and I had our several hours together, on the possibility that Maura might find time for me. The thought was simply unbearable that I might have to miss seeing her. One night a week later, after lashing out at you over another conflict, I called Zed. "I don't know what to do. I just can't bear the thought of hurting Isabel. But I can't go on snapping at her and deceiving her." I began to cry. "You'll be guided as to what to do," Zed said simply.

And so, the following week, at a session with the Oiseau, I approached the subject tentatively, feeling, as I did, the attention of the Oiseau drawn intensely to me, as if she sensed, before you did, the nature of what I was about to say. As you and I both agreed, she was not the Oiseau for nothing, so highly alert was she. "I didn't mean for it to happen, but I got involved with someone," I said, avoiding eye contact with both of you. And then I said more. I didn't see how I could continue with counseling given what was happening in my life. When I could bring myself to look at you, I saw that you had not fallen to the floor and died. What I also saw was a tentative smile on your face, as if you were struggling to assimilate this new piece of information.

But Isabel, if you smiled and said the right things at our last session with the Oiseau, your hurt found you later. It wasn't of no account to you that I had found another. Some repair work would need to be done, only it would have to wait.

Summer came, and Maura gave herself to me increasingly. Things had not been the same between her and her beau since their summit meeting, and now duty had called him to far points of the globe. Maura and I saw each other on weekends as well as weekday nights, but I could only offer her things that a man who owns neither car nor boat nor country house can provide. We rode the subways and buses of New York City and walked its hot streets, and sought our refuge from concrete with a lovely afternoon at the Brooklyn Botanical Garden and walks in Central Park.

Our lovemaking was unlike any I had ever known in its intensity and its duration. Entire weekends would pass and we would still be between the sheets. And when the day came that I was finally able to enter her, we were in a new dimension altogether.

But the day also came when she visited me at my workplace and discovered my cubicle guy existence. She saw I didn't have the right stuff to qualify for a door. A look of peeve was showing as she did a mental calculation of the meager square footage of my space. That she should have hitched herself to someone such as me. "Well, you look important, and I guess that counts for something," she said.

And then she found further cause for soreness. "Who is that woman?" She gasped, her arm outstretched and her finger pointing at the photo in the plastic frame.

"That is Isabel." I had thought, no, let me just present things as they are. Let me not hide you from Maura. It seemed a disservice to you and to me as well. Besides, didn't Maura have photos of the CIA agent all over her apartment, and didn't she carry in her wallet one of them together on some beach in Florida?

The truth was that if Maura had consigned me briefly to the doghouse, by summer's end she had let him back out. Maura was still seeing the CIA agent, whenever he could break free from his derring-do. She had a gift for clandestine activity of her own, never having revealed anything of her life with me to her man.

These developments being what they were, Maura called me up to Irvington for a summit meeting of our own. She had given our relationship a lot of thought, she said, and now she had a need to sit me down to present the reality of the situation. She remarked upon my many good qualities and the strong connection she felt with me, but the sad truth, she said, was that I lacked the necessities required for her to move to the next level and beat her biological clock. She had placed my assets next to the CIA agent's in the nuptials sweepstakes, pitting low-earning me with my desk job and frequent erectile dysfunction against a man with earning power commensurate with his global reach and sexual potency, and he had been the hands-down winner. "In your twenties you marry for love. When you are a woman approaching forty, you marry for security," Maura said. I did feel sad that she should describe me in such terms, but I had to accept that she was also speaking truth.

"Don't feel hurt, Johan. That's all I am, too. A girl with a little desk job. It's just that two of us in the same niche wouldn't make for a happy life. But that's not the same thing as saying you won't be in my life. You'll always be in my life, and I'll be in yours, too. You'll always be down the road from where I live, and I'll come visit you and you'll come visit me. Does that cheer you up?" She had seated me on the sofa with her, and now unbuttoned her blouse and unclasped her bra. Holding her right breast as an offering, she said to me, "Now come to Mama. Just come to Mama."

And so, Isabel, in spite of the summit our schwinging continued. In fact, that very afternoon she had me take her from behind right there on the sofa, even though our position placed us right in front of an enlarged photo of the CIA agent, shirtless on a beach and a fine specimen of American manhood with his blond good looks and fit, tanned body. And that same quality of brazenness became more apparent with the broadening of our theater of operations, as now she was calling me up to Irvington regularly as well as visiting me at my Manhattan apartment, as if in defiance of the CIA' agent's vaunted reputation for covert operations.

Was heaven anything more than the phone ringing on a Sunday afternoon and for Maura to be on the line inviting me to come to her? There would follow the exhilarated rush down to Grand Central Station and the short ride on the Metro-North up the Hudson to find her waiting outside the station in her red Saab, a remnant of her marriage, as was the vast apartment. And then to rent a video and sit with her knowing the time would come for making love and that, because of the hour and the certainty that the CIA agent was destabilizing some left-leaning government on some other continent, we were safe from his power.

The important thing was that I be perfect for Maura by never showing anger or expressing impatience. And that was easy so long as she was coming toward me. But with the arrival of September, things took another turn. Entire weeks went by without a call from her. I began to feel cut loose. And something else. The CIA agent grew bigger, more solid, in my mind. Now there was none of this easily dispensed fondness for Maura's beau, who suddenly seemed like a formidable force of inevitability. Why hadn't I seen it all along? The CIA agent was not someone to dismiss. The CIA agent was a man of substance, just as his title suggested, and he would marry Maura, and he would seed her womb, and they would beget not one but many children. And I would be discarded as a parasite exploiting the complexities of the relationship impasse that Maura had arrived at. As if she was subtly attuned to the shift going on in my mind and sensed my vulnerability, she said, "I used to think you were Seinfeld. Now I'm picturing you more as Kramer." Yes. Of course. Kramer, the doofus with the head of strange hair.

With the beginning of fall came my birthday. Maura had accumulated an astonishing abundance of small gifts: a dish towel, a scrub brush, oil and vinegar bottles, a calculator, and on and on. Whole afternoons she must have spent in some ninety-nine cents store. She presented at least thirty of them to me over a dinner she insisted on paying for, taking the carefully wrapped gifts one by one from an enormous shopping bag. The ritual was wearisome and made me greatly uncomfortable, but when I protested, saying, " You didn't have to go to such trouble," she snapped, "Get over it," as if to blast away any trace of self-pity in me with her loud sound, leaving me no choice but to laugh helplessly at her ferociously expressed perception. But there was a method to her excess, Isabel. It is possible she was seeking to pay off an imagined debt or assuage her guilt over the choice she had made. There was an underlying sadness to the event, as if she were saying goodbye.

You know my habits, Isabel. You know that fall became a time for me to step out of my narrow world and numbing routines and declare to one and all, without so much as a word spoken, I am out of here. Travel for me was a leave taking of all that I had come to call my own in this life, a rehearsal for the final departure from this life, when no luggage would be called for. That said, with my hard shell Samsonite suitcase in tow, I waited for Maura in Bryant Park on a cold afternoon, the sky overcast and darkness moving in. The rendezvous was my idea. I wanted a chance to say goodbye to her before catching the airport bus near Grand Central Station for the ride out to JFK.

She came slowly toward me along the walkway behind the big public library. She was wrapped in a buckled beige raincoat, a boxy item that didn't suit her. The clothes of summer—her shorts and sleeveless tops and the blue gingham dress she looked so electrifying in—had long since been put away.

It was an awkward meeting. We had little to say to each other. And the physical spark was gone as well. We had moved on from the heat of July to the rawness of October. A perfunctory kiss was all we could manage.

On the plane a Rumanian man in the next seat preached the virtues of Ceausescu and said the fallen dictator was the victim of Western lies and conspiracies. "We had light bulbs. We had things." At some point I closed my eyes, and when I woke the plane was landing at Orly Airport in Paris.

My accommodation was the top floor of a budget hotel in Le Marais. My needs were simple: a room of my own in which to sleep and meditate, a bit of food, water, boulevards to wander along and sights to see, and pens and paper. I was living in an intrepid state of mind that let me go at my own chosen speed with love as my guide. Oh yes, Isabel, the mind can be an assailing thing, seeking to shame me into a more muscular trip like a hike in the French Alps or an exploration of the south of France, and told me it was only fear that was conspiring to keep me in the routine I had established of being a flaneur. But though I wept and was bent down by the judgment storm that said I could only hang in the gray mass of an old city, still did I persist in my course. Was travel about Les Halles, Notre Dame, the Louvre, L'Arc de Triomphe, the Luxembourg Gardens, Versailles, or was it about finding a bench along the banks of the Seine on which to meditate when I felt my old irritable and discontented self emerging?

And yet, regarding the Eiffel Tower, how abruptly the massive and surprisingly brown structure appeared, looming over the residential neighborhood and putting me in mind of the time, as a teenager, I traveled by bus to Philadelphia to see my then beloved Dodgers go strong against the Philadelphia Phillies. As I turned a corner in a rundown neighborhood with weedy sidewalks, Connie Mack Stadium similarly appeared. Such memory traces of heaven these structures can trigger in us that the excitement is virtually unbearable.

Isabel, sometimes we have to endure and accept the grayness of our lives. That can be hard when we feel the disappointment of another that we are not more than we are. And yet the torment brought on by Maura's reassessment led me to try to regain her former regard. I called her from a Paris pay phone, but my inflated description of my trip failed to impress. "What are you doing over there anyway?" So she spoke, as if such travel were an oddity beyond her reckoning. One thing about her, Isabel, is that she embraced the things of America—DisneyWorld and the like.

"I'm wandering about. Right now I'm looking at the Eiffel Tower."

"Great," she said, as if it weren't.

Crossness was in her bones. There was no use denying that it wasn't. "Have you had your cup of joe yet?" I said, realizing the morning hour that it was back in Irvington and how cranky, by her own admission, she could be, without her brew. "Because, if I were stateside, I would hand-deliver it to your door."

"I don't know if I want you at my door anymore." And with that she hung up, leaving me in ruins. But there is no victory like victory over oneself, Isabel. Is it for me to live in the sissified state of victimhood and in perpetual bondage by holding the mirror up to her face or am I to walk free and proud on this earth by placing the mirror squarely before my own? It was for me to accept that I had invited her ill-temper by calling while in a state of neediness that thousands of miles could not hide from her awareness and further accepting that in the wake of great pleasure comes great pain.

When I returned stateside, it was another two weeks before she could fit me into her schedule. The CIA agent had some down time and was in need of her, having partially destabilized one regime while bringing a second to complete collapse. The effort had been herculean, and he had need of her warmth, but before there could be any tender loving care, there was the small matter of her tick tock, on which, after tense negotiations, she could report some new progress, and the same held true in the matter of the CIA agent's heretofore inflexible mother.

How long does this continue, I asked myself, staring at the phone which didn't ring.

In the GoAN cafeteria, I met a woman. In desperation I went out with her, happy to have a companion on a Friday night. She was forthcoming, surprisingly so. I had never heard a woman admit, least of all on her first date, to participating in orgies, but Penny did so in a matter-of-fact way. Such lustful activity did not go with my image of her.

She spoke of the cruelty of her businessman ex-husband, and of the difficulties of reestablishing herself in the work world after a lengthy absence. How far she said she had fallen that she would have to learn software systems and be a lowly secretary when she had been an investment banker in her single years.

In the back seat of the cab following dinner, I tried to kiss Penny, an effort that elicited a clear look of surprise. But by the time the cab pulled curbside at Grand Central Terminal, and we had crossed the concourse and arrived at her gate, my mortification had fallen away sufficient that I could say, in handing her my strange card (yes, the one with no center), "We should make love. Call me when you can." The words sent a thrill through me, the directness a sexual act in itself.

"Well," she said, seeming to recoil. And so I waved goodbye, assuming that her libertine ways were a thing of the past or never truly existed or that I just wasn't her particular idea of a mate.

And yet, the next morning she was on the line.

"Do you have plans for this evening?" she asked.

"Nothing firm," I said. Some vague notion to take advantage of the Metropolitan Museum of Art's late closing on a Saturday and wander about its Asian wing did not seem worth mentioning.

"Well, firm or otherwise, scrap them. I want you to come up here so we can have a ball in bed. I want you to give me a good thumping. I have a train schedule right in front of me."

Isabel, The ride to Larchmont was a long one, about an hour, and summoned none of the exhilaration I had experienced when journeying up the Hudson to meet with Maura. Despite my sexual impulsiveness, there had been no love-at-first-sight, electric shock response to Penny, as there had been with Maura. She was not waiting for me with a car at the train station. She had one, but it was in the repair shop. From the back of the cab I saw Lexuses and BMWs and other luxury vehicles in the driveways of well-cared for houses, wreaths and colored lights serving as a reminder that the holiday season was here. The scenes of warm domesticity served as a shocking reminder of the hugeness of life beyond my little world in New York City.

From the darkness at the bottom of a narrow set of winding stairs, I saw a light burning in the window of the house where the cab had left me, and then saw Penny pass by the living room window. I stood there a while, debating whether to flee, before trudging up the steps, tiny footlights illuminating the way.

Everyone has a story. Penny's husband Hal had dumped her after twelve years of marriage. Their assets had been considerable: their own home, two cars, European vacations, summers in the Hamptons, an exciting nightlife. But one day he simply said to her that he wouldn't be her meal ticket anymore. "So now I have to rent," she said, as if it were a humiliation not to have equity in her own home.

Isabel, all the familiar signs of aloneness were there. A computer occupied the table in the spacious kitchen, and a film of dust coated the copper pots and pans that hung from hooks above the stove. The red light on the answering machine was steady and unblinking, as if resistant to any changes she might will in her life of increasing solitude. I thought of what it is like to go around as if in a plastic bubble beyond the range of intimacy after a marital rupture.

"Well, are we ready for the tour?" Penny asked. There was a gleam in her eyes.

"The tour?" Johan asked.

"The ascent to pleasure?"

She led me upstairs to her bedroom, where a four-poster bed awaited us. As if she were shedding garments for an athletic contest, she pulled her top over her head and slipped out of her slacks. Beneath lay the disappointment of a stained, dull-white body suit instead of the more feminine attire Maura favored.

Isabel, nothing about her was like Maura in the course of our evening in bed, not her pointy tongue or breasts or salt-and-pepper hair. Being with Penny had the effect of intensifying, not curing, my longing for Maura.

She lived with a virtual menagerie—three cats and an aggressive poodle she called The General, whom she included in the message on her answering machine: "The General and I are unable to take your call right now." Her pooch lay curled on the floor, but the cats were everywhere on the bed. An allergic reaction caused my skin to itch and my breathing to become wheezy. Meanwhile Penny was sleeping the sleep of the just.

When I could take it no more, I eased out of bed and fumbled for my glasses on the night table, then felt my way out of the room in the darkness and down the stairs. I dialed my number and punched in the answering machine code. The double beep was as satisfying as the tug of a fish on a line. And there it was, gathered as if from some far corner of the universe just for me, Maura saying that she missed me and would I call and was there any chance that we could have the following night together?

I returned to the bedroom and felt around in the dark for my things until I remembered a flashlight on the table by the bed. I kept the beam low to the floor and located the piles of clothes and also my wallet and keys, which I lifted off the dresser with great stealth.

"Penny, are you awake?" I whispered. There was no snoring now, light or otherwise. I felt the weight of her consciousness bearing down on me.

"I am now."

"I've got to go back to New York," I said.

"You left the oven on, maybe?"

"No, it's not that."

"Should I try to guess?'

"It's just me."

"You have to go back to New York because it's just you?"

"Penny, are you angry with me?"

"I am astonished by your weirdness."

"All I can ask is that you not be angry with me."

"Thinking you're odd is not the same as being angry. Do as you wish."

The General began to bark in an unfriendly way from his place at the head of the bed. "The General has a fine sense about lapses of character, I assure you," Penny said.

"Yes, he is in a state of justifiable high dudgeon," I said, falling into the odd elegance of Penny's speech.

The trip home was dreary, the world seen as ugly through sleepless eyes. A depressing article about the spread of AIDS in some back issue of *Utne Reader;* the spectacle of homeless men sleeping upright on subway benches or curled up on the platforms. The world in a state of insanity that turns people into refuse as the Christmas carols play. And then, as an act of subterfuge, forcing myself to stay up until 9 a.m. so I could return Maura's call and confirm to her that I would be up to visit her that night. To my relief she accepted my excuse that I had been in bed when she phoned, feeling no need to add that the bed had not been my own. Even so, the evasive half-truth did not sit well with me.

"You have a lot of balls in the air. Sooner or later those balls will have to fall to the ground," Zed said, offering me one of his Zed-isms. Zed often talked of God not being a God of punishments and rewards, but here Zed seemed to be saying that I would get mine and I would get it plenty good, for if you must know, Zed was a man with a love of his own, and she had done him wrong by not doing him at all. He had fallen under her spell and spoke of her in the exorbitant terms that were characteristic of him. I am not talking here of Banja but of Venutia, thirtyish and blond and model-thin and all the rest. Her depth, the scope of their intellectual discussions—these things he cited while acknowledging his unrequited hunger for her. "She's not attracted to me," he said, with helplessness in his voice. "And why would she be? I'm an old man. Jesus, I see myself in the barber shop mirror and I can't believe it." Is that a good love when an old man whose powers have faded sits by the phone waiting in vain for a young woman's call? Is that a good love when such a man dotes on the young woman, lending her money and offering her gifts and living for her next visit, only to die and die when it does not come? When I shared with Zed that Maura and I had started down the road of physical intimacy, he had lashed out at me. The spiritual life is not an easy one, Isabel. We have human hearts. Zed found it too painful in that one moment to see me realizing with Maura the dream he had for him and Venutia, who had made it clear that lovemaking would not be part of their relationship.

Now Isabel, happiness was once again disproportionately mine as I left the house that evening, fully rested. And though a winter darkness obscured the Hudson from my sight, a wonderland of adventure awaited me at my stop on the Metro-North.

A man knows when he is being received and when he is not, and on this night, Maura's gates were open. She drove us from the station to the video store, a lonely outpost of brightness on an otherwise dark street, where I acquiesced in her selection of "The Age of Innocence" before we stopped off for Chinese takeout.

I did not come empty-handed. I had bought for her a box of Godiva chocolates and primo Colombian joe, and, my feature presentation, a white T-shirt with a cartoon panel on the front showing a blond woman holding a cuppa joe and her face registering full distress. The balloon caption read: "They *lied*. This is decaf." Now Isabel, this made Maura's night, for the shirt spoke to her about what was nearest and dearest to her heart, her beloved brew, and with a humor in line with her own. So you could say on this night that I could do no wrong. And don't believe for a minute that she was not bearing gifts herself, or one, to be exact, for had she not shown herself to be the woman of a thousand gifts on my birthday? A green chamois shirt from the folks at L.L. Bean she handed me, signifying further that I was in her mind if not her heart, and would be less than honest if I failed to admit to imagining the bigger gifts she had reserved for the CIA agent.

We were sitting on the sofa watching the video in what had been her husband's den when the phone rang. Isabel, that phone had a loud, probing sound, which only the CIA agent could instill in it, as if he were reaching right out to us through the wire. But in the matter of cunning Maura was every bit his match. "That's good" and "Great, great," I heard her say, in her flat, Midwestern accent. "No, no. Yes. Of course." So she continued with her monosyllabic responses, handling the CIA agent effortlessly and moving him off the line quickly.

The simple truth was that her performance on the phone was more engrossing than the movie. I understood something in that moment more deeply than I had. I was with a woman who could lie, and lie effortlessly.

In the powerful silence that followed she lightly touched my thigh with two fingers and then withdrew her hand only to return with those same fingers, once again lightly touching and withdrawing. "You could bounce a quarter off those thighs," she said, as she moved her fingers farther along, and then we kissed and her legs opened. "I'm all wet," she whispered in my ear.

As later she whispered, after positioning us so we were facing the photo of the CIA agent, "I want you to put it there. There, where your finger now is." And so I did, entering her in the smaller place.

But Isabel, there was no momentum that carried over into the New Year. Once again the CIA agent assumed pride of place in her life and I was left to languish by the phone. Spring came, blue skies and mild temperatures and the screams of children at play in the parks and in schoolyards, but I was mired in depression. When I told Maura that I couldn't go on this way and might have to make some changes in my life, she became angry and pressed me.

"Are you threatening to see other women? Is that what you are doing?"

"Only if I have to."

"What do you mean, 'If you have to?' Someone is holding a gun to your head?"

"Can't you understand that seeing you once a month is hard for me?"

"Have you been seeing other women? Is that what you have been doing behind my back?" Maura said, ignoring my question.

"Look, I don't see anyone. I go to work and wait for you to call me. What kind of life is that?" And then I thought of Penny. "Twice I saw somebody. Twice."

"You slept with another woman and then you dared to sleep with me?"

"I was lonely. You hadn't called in weeks."

"You creep. Was it unprotected sex?"

"No. "

"You'll pay for this, Johan. You really will."

A few weeks later Maura called for another sit-down. She said to meet her in Madison Square Park, not far from where she worked, at the lunch hour. I had no appointments to cancel. I had a desk to sit at and a few papers to mark up, but that was about it. Interaction with others wasn't anything I had to be too much a part of at the org, as you know.

It was one of those mild and sunny spring days with a gentle breeze when you are just so glad to be alive and share the glory of existence with all of Manhattan pouring out of the office buildings, shed of their winter clothes. The park was packed, the benches and the lawns filled with workers eating their takeout lunches and I thought of the restaurants and delis that provided the food and trucks that delivered it to the city and how we are all interconnected. I was having those kinds of thoughts, the kind I'm sometimes ashamed to admit, where I go all weepy with love for something or other on the inside even as I look like whomever I look like on the outside. What joy there is in love, all depression and crossness and all that stuff dissolved.

Maura had her serious face on, and it was fitting, as she had a late-breaking development—so she called it—to discuss with me, but first she wanted me to get settled on the park bench. "I'm ready. Shoot," I said, holding the container of hummus I had brought along.

"I've broken off my engagement with the CIA agent." If I haven't told you, she was sworn to secrecy about his name so as to not jeopardize his life. She said there were more than a few thoroughly bad people seeking vengeance for stuff he was alleged to have done.

"Why do you want to do that?" I asked, feeling, if anything, some discomfort that this triangle would be falling away. "The CIA agent has done me dirty, and now he will have to pay and pay," Maura said. "And you're not off the hook either. I will be placing myself back on the market."

"What can you possibly be talking about?"

"I will be seeing other men. That is what I am talking about. You have been dating, and so now it is for me to do the same."

"Dating? Dating? I wait for you to call. That is my dating."

"He has invited me to the Hamptons."

"Who invited you to the Hamptons?"

"Sean."

I trembled inwardly, hearing her announcement. It was one thing for me to share Maura with a man who was in her life previously, but the prospect of her stepping out with other men was terrifying, especially men from RoR, like the hound of all hounds Sean Seanohan, whom I knew from RoR. A satyr if ever there was one.

"Actions have consequences," I said.

"Yes, they do," she replied firmly.

That night I called Zed and got his answering machine. My message was a brief one. "I want out of this hellish thing," I shouted, and hung up. Then I went to my bedroom and prayed with the same intensity as I had the night of Jim Boulee's party, only now I was praying that Maura be removed from my life. "I don't want this anymore. I don't want it, I tell you." Over and over did I say this same thing, and yes, after a while I knew I was being heard and that the power had been given me to break away from the recovery meeting Maura and I both attended and to stop taking her calls, infrequent as they had become.

How hard could it be to sidestep annihilation, Isabel? If not the hound, there would be Joe or Fred or Alex. I could suffer the humiliation of seeing her go out with this guy or that or just take it on the lam. One day led to two, and then one week became two. For several days I left work with an impulse to head over to the RoR meeting we shared, and yet my feet took me in the opposite direction, to other meetings where I could take my pain and anger and hurt. Many years ago, when I was starting out on this sober journey, I would get dressed in the Bowery loft where I then lived with Sarah with the full intention of calling on you, only my feet would guide me instead to the rooms where the sober men and women of New York City could be found, and now once again my feet were working for me, for Maura had become the bottle from which it was imperative that I withdraw.

I felt tired, like a man who had held on to the tail of a wild animal and been dragged through thick and prickly brush. And now I had finally let go and was lying there on the good earth and recuperating. I had been returned to myself. I could sit calmly in my living room chair and read a book. Oh, what a sweet place to have found.

Isabel, today the banner of liberation is flying high and flapping and snapping in the breeze. We come to a place of knowing what we are seeing isn't real, even that which is radiant and beautiful, as we experience those invisible rays of enduring light in a more and more intense way. You could say of me in this time that I was less pained than impatient for this process of release to complete itself so I could truly be on the other side.

That summer, I took my daily stroll in either Riverside or Central Park but one Saturday evening did it up right, taking myself to the theater and beforehand, to a world-class deli. All that afternoon I had been hungering for a hot pastrami on rye, slathered with mustard, and not one but two pickles and a plateful of fries topped with half a bottle of ketchup. My body was talking to me big time. Every few weeks there would be that same yen for meat. Never mind the burdock root and bean sprouts and red kidney beans and all the rest. I could only be grateful that the craving wasn't for a drink. A waiter as old and weary as the restaurant itself (you could tell it was dying, Isabel, as a lot of things always are in New York City) took my order and I asked him to hit me as well with the special brand of root beer only this establishment seemed to serve.

Now, Isabel, having some concern that I might find myself in the sorrow acre with all the attendant tears, it being a Saturday night and I being alone, I fortified myself, not on the hour or the half-hour but minute by minute with the mantra "God, I am whole and complete as I am." Over and over did I tell myself that I was not alone but all one. We must not let shame keep us behind the locked door. Unlock that door and step on out. Do as Flip Wilson's persona Georgette did. Show ourselves, if you will, in those hot pants and be willing to say, "What you see is what you get." Life is calling and we are missing it, cowering in our thoughts that blind and bind. Imagine that, Isabel, a mind that says you're not fit to breathe or not fit to be in this room or that or go to this or that party or even attend your high school prom. A mind telling you all the things you don't have and none of the things you do have. If I am late in life to be saying these things, even with the light so very clearly waning, should I not say them anyway?

Now about the play, Isabel. Do you remember those TV quiz shows from the 1950s, in particular *Twenty-One,* and Charles Van Doren, the brilliant intellectual with the Columbia affiliation? Well, the play revisited that time and the life of this fallen hero. What a painful thing to witness, the corruption of someone so gifted. The world should leave such people alone rather than bring them low. But what grabbed me even more than his ruin was a giant prop suspended over the stage, a photograph of a residential building. The sporadic use of bricks of a different color from the rest and the casement windows gave it an art deco look, as did the entrance with its geometric patterns, and stirred in me a longing for that earlier time. But what stirred me even more and in truth became a torment was an image superimposed on the building of Maura, as in a double exposure, wearing that blue gingham dress from our time together. I tried to look away but I couldn't, and even when I finally did, the image had burned itself into my brain. "No," I shouted, an involuntary utterance, and others seated around me began to make shushing sounds.

Fortunately, I was seated at the end of the aisle, and so did not have to disturb the other theatergoers in making my early exit. Outside I ran through the streets as if my clothes were on fire.

Paper has a purpose in my life, Isabel, and I must use it if ever I am to be free of the tyranny of others. If I keep calling your name, it is in wonder that such glorious opportunities for our own liberation are given to us. That night it was to go behind the veil. The building, though in appearance very different from the one in which I myself had grown up, represented my childhood and the family I had been born into and the limitations, through lack of ability and circumstance, that life had imposed. And Maura, in all her tanned summer glory, represented the bounty of America, which, because of my lack of endowment, was only available to me through her. Is it anything less than a miracle that, in turning to my journal, the ache of emotion began to ease.

Isabel, you were not gone from my life nor I from yours in this time, though there was now a distance between us that made me uncomfortable. Some shoring up of our connection was required.

And in thinking this way, something became clear. Inevitably I would be drawn back to you.

For some time you didn't answer my calls. You were private about your sorrow. I couldn't stay too long in such thoughts, or I would have had to die. Better to see you as strong, as that was the quality we were both in need of recognizing in ourselves and in each other, so we could encourage and inspire each other in this life.

In any case, even before she gave the heave-ho to the CIA agent, you and I had resumed our get-togethers. They were different now, as the physical dimension had been removed. I talked with you about Maura. I told you how she was doing me wrong, and you listened.

Now Isabel, a man named Jergens said that it was his full intention to get married, and that I should be present at his wedding. Jergens stood apart from others with his sensitivity and wavy blond hair as well as his intellect and accomplishment: he had several advanced degrees in engineering and had built no less than four major bridges. Blessed with three-dimensional visual power, he could put things together to last. Now he wanted to put his life together by taking Jane Swainly to be his lawful, wedded wife.

I didn't tell Jergens that I had never been to a wedding, other than my own. It was information Jergens didn't need to know. The poverty of my life might be illuminated by this stark fact in such a way as to make Jergens recoil.

Jergens and Jane Swainly had researched and extensively planned their wedding, from the design of the announcement to the food for the reception and the musicians for the party that would follow. They had high standards that required them to leave little to chance. The site they chose was a church in Scarsdale, New York.

I rode the Metro-North to the wedding and on the way imagined purchasing a medallion and starting a one-person taxi service. Expansion would follow as I bought a second car and hired a driver. And then there would be a third and fourth car and driver, and probably I would need a bookkeeper and possibly a manager as well. A change came over me, a feeling of empowerment, as I got deeper into the fantasy. And then a colossal sadness broke over me, for I saw that the taxi service would become my life, a burden that would bring me great unhappiness. I saw in that moment the trap ownership could be, and why I found relative contentment in a modest position at the org.

The wedding ceremony in the old stone church brought tears to my eyes. How handsome Jergens looked in his tuxedo, and how goddess-like Jane Swainly looked in her wedding gown. The event was a major milestone in their lives, for they had had other, darker lives before this one. Jergens had been a barroom brawler and a stiletto slasher whom only those with a death wish approached when he was in his cups. And Jane Swainly had left her exclusive Scarsdale home to become a teenage prostitute on the tough streets of Detroit under the tutelage of Homero Frye, full of his bad self in his denim duds and wearing all that gold around his neck and in his teeth. But redemption was the theme of the world that Jergens and Jane Swainly lived in. It was the only way they cared to go, into the unending light. And when I heard the words "in sickness and in health…till death do you part…" I thought, well, yes, even as I also thought, why must they call death a parting?

A reception followed at a nearby center where a tuxedo-attired man with hair turned gray sang "Have I told You Lately That I Loved You?" as waiters maneuvered among the guests with silver platters of hors d'oeuvres. What a voice. How heavenly his sweet sad sound. Where did music come from that it could evoke such feeling? For a while I could contemplate something other than my obdurate aloneness. And then I thought of all I would tell you of this marvelous evening.

I felt conspicuous in my gray suit—yes, the same Brooks Brothers suit I had worn to our City Hall wedding and the reception that followed—but loosened up when the DJ got his sounds together and the lights were turned down low. I danced with a stranger, a woman with a mesmerizing cleavage. She was with me on my every move, and had some of her own. There seemed to be a definite groove that we had accomplished. And then the music broke and she moved past me to one who had clearly claimed her for his own—maybe even her husband. It was confusing. Who could know for sure on such a night with the tinkle of elegant crystal and so many sober drunks drinking expensive mineral water?

Suddenly, as if to cap the night, there came an unearthly howl. Alone, in the middle of the dance floor, stood Jane Swainly. "I don't want this night to ever end. I want my life back." In that moment did I see where her heart's treasure was, and it was not poor, sincere Jergens. From her depths I heard the howling of the insatiable drunk for more and more and more.

Isabel, it was not my nature to keep secrets from you but to share what I had experienced. And so I called you with my report of the wedding, as it was rare for me to be part of such a social occasion. But my words were no match for the feelings I was trying to convey. In fact, I couldn't be sure I even knew what it was I wanted to express. Maybe the event had sparked in me some of that ineffable longing Jane Swainly had been expressing, some longing summoned by the ceremony and the music and the women in those beautiful evening gowns, sort of like when I was a child in Riverside Park on a summer night and the Chevrolet billboard I've mentioned over the railroad tracks up near One Hundred Twenty-Fifth Street and the meatpacking plants suddenly made me delirious with the vision of all that life could offer. When I said I was sorry that I had not asked you to come along, you responded with steel in your voice. "I want a divorce. Do you hear me? This has to end, and it has to end now. I will be calling my lawyer."

I was hurt and humiliated. "Well, yes, OK." They were the only words I could muster. It was as if I were speaking into a ferocious wind.

And Isabel, you were true to your word. Within a week I found, there in my mailbox, a letter from your family's lawyer bearing a Park Avenue return address, written on letterhead that contained many names, including some that were famous. I opened the envelope and read the cold notice of a legal separation leading to divorce, with both parties relinquishing any claims to the other's estate, property, pension, etc. It felt like a hard fist had sprung out of the mailbox to administer socko plenty.

That same evening I walked uptown, beyond Ninety-sixth Street. Gone were the Riviera and Riverside movie theaters, with their jutting marquees. An apartment high-rise stood on the site, a forbidding kind of building, with its sealed windows and recycled air and complex engineering. A building for the rich, for those with elaborate finances. Not for the dispossessed, the disenfranchised. Oh there I was, so in love with the old, so unadapted to the new, in emotional turmoil that you should do such a thing, sic lawyers, *lawyers,* with their lawyerly lingo on me. When did a lawyer ever follow love as his guide? Did you know what you had done in placing our love in the maw of the law?

The sidewalks and the facades of the old buildings on Broadway looked dirty. Maybe all of Broadway, down to the Battery, was dirty. Maybe the city was dirty, hopelessly dirty, its filth abounding and nothing to save it.

At One Hundred Tenth Street, I paused. A few blocks north stood the building where I was born and raised, with its rotted window sashes and leaky pipes and hordes of roaches. I had spent my whole life seeking to prove that I wasn't a Manootdjian. Wasn't my marriage first to Sarah and then to you all about proving how different I was from them? Hadn't I been running from my family and standing in judgment of the whole crew my whole life? And now there was nowhere to run and no one to judge, unless I wanted to stand there and judge myself. What you're running from you're running toward, I could hear Zed saying.

Visitors from my past began arriving. "Hey, Johan, it's me, Jerry Jones-Nobleonian. Don't you remember how we called you Flathead and Squarehead and Box Head? And don't you remember how we used to sound on your mother because of those funny men's shoes she used to wear?"

"I remember," I said, recoiling.

"And don't you remember how we were close back in grade school and then you pretended that you didn't know me as we got older?"

"I'm sorry about that."

"Don't be sorry, motherfucking white boy. Don't be sorry for nothing you did to this Black man."

We had gone into Riverside Park with a six-pack of beer when I was fourteen. I was giddy because I had walked a girl home and kissed her the night before. I hadn't known that twenty years later Jerry-Jones Nobleonian would die in a Bowery flophouse with gangrene in both legs.

My dead sister Naomi appeared. "You were so scornful. Do you remember being that way as a child, little Flathead Svenska pojka? Do you remember telling my husband Chuck and me that we should get out of the lobby and out of the building?"

"You were both drunk and I felt embarrassed by your behavior."

"And do you remember what Mother said to you, little Flathead?"

"She said I didn't know what it was to have children."

"That's right, little Flathead. You lacked Mother's compassion."

I didn't tell Naomi that maybe it wasn't a good thing that our mother had allowed her to have a room rent-free in the building the family managed and that Naomi might have been helped by a push toward more independence. Nor did I tell her it wasn't so nice that I should have had to witness her threatened suicide leap from a ledge eight or nine stories up or that I had to absorb her numerous unwarranted slaps to my face.

And I saw my dead sister Rachel but she just sailed past me the way she always did when she was still in this life. Not even death could remove the smirk from her face, though maybe I was wrong about that.

And I saw my father struggling along with his walker, a truck narrowly missing him as he crossed Broadway and took his seat on a traffic island, where he sat contentedly waiting to die.

I saw their hopelessness, their helplessness, their fear, their warped personalities, their abysmal failures, their sad dull eyes infected with self-pity. I saw the stained bathroom sink and toilet and the sour-smelling towels. I saw dustballs and clutter and heard my classmate Johnny Joe spreading the word that Johan Manootdjian lived in a pigsty. I saw and heard all that and a peace came over me, as if, right there in life, I had come home to this family I had run from. There was no one or no thing to shun anymore.

I turned east up One Hundred Tenth Street and headed for the synod of St. John the Divine Cathedral. Oh, such names they gave to people in this world, assigning a mortal the moniker "The Divine." Well, never mind, Isabel. The need to exalt and live in the land of hype infects everyone. No one wants to be right size and normal, and yet there is freedom in finding such a zone.

The man selling tickets inside the door had a face that had molded, over time, into a mask of anger; to relinquish that look would be to let people in, which, for reasons of colossal fear and injury, he could not do. Isabel, I saw myself, not so much as I was but as I had been, in the unfortunate man. When younger, I too had known the torture of being unable to approach a woman. I saw now how the man, whose name was Fredo, would seek to comfort himself with the notion that he was doing a service selling tickets while others in the farther reaches of the synod were responding to the boogie-down beat. Whatever the man told himself, he would not be able to assuage the longing in his heart for a life more than the one he had.

Down in the big basement, a space that had known mostly the quiet of men and women seeking God in the shadows of life, a singer with an enormous head topped with dyed blond hair had the mike and was offering a raspy rendition of some old Creedence Clearwater thing. Soon the DJ sound master, who went by the name

Grand Master Funk, got his stuff together so we didn't have to listen to Big Head anymore.

Isabel, there were reformed murderers and thieves and all manner of creatures who had once reveled in unbridled immorality and licentiousness. A man named Feral said, "I'm just here to kick out the jams. I just need to air it out." Pushing sixty, he had the smile of a happy warrior and it was known throughout the community that his twin passions were making love and making war. In bar fights had he bitten off opponent's ears and noses and split their skulls with noggin-crushing blows. His heavyweight head was packed with scientific formulae and equations longer than a Conrail freight, but his attire was licorice-black: spandex tights, a body-hugging shirt, short black cape, and thin leather gloves. Soon he was primed to go, goony-grooving on the dance floor in some solo rhythm to the sounds.

Isabel, I found a woman to dance with, the two of us using each other as cover for our loneliness. No touching. Just a lot of gyration and waving of arms and crazy spins. And the sad horror when our eyes chanced to meet—the fear, the shame.

When the midnight hour arrived and "Auld Lang Syne" was played and I pulled her close, she did not resist. Her body felt good next to mine, and the smell of her freshly washed hair dizzying. But at the end of the New Year's anthem, she sprinted for a girlfriend, letting me know what was done was done. Soon I was back walking down Broadway, a corridor I had passed through thousands of times in my forty-nine years. Feral and Fredo were straggling along somewhere behind me. I tried not to look at the couples I passed. I tried not to look at anyone.

"Just let the situation evolve. If there is to be a divorce, let Isabel propose it. An accord will follow that will be mutually satisfactory." So Zed had assured me. But the terms of the divorce, as laid out by your lawyer, were satisfactory only to you. The coldness of the legal communication was a continuing shock. *A divorce on the grounds of abandonment…each of you waives maintenance (alimony), all pension and estate rights, and all rights to a division of property.* It was as if you had cast a blind eye, through your formidable proxy, upon me.

Generally, Isabel, I could count on Zed to provide some comfort when I came to him in pain over our situation, but now he could only say, "That's rough. I don't know what to tell you. I can understand how you feel."

Isabel, the fault was mine for relying too heavily on Zed's experience with Banja as a way of understanding my relationship with you. After all, no two marriages are alike. Just because Zed would never have divorced Banja and left her without any kind of settlement did not mean you would do the same.

As if I were doing something wrong, I brought up the matter of a lawyer to represent me. More than once Zed had expressed his disdain for the legal profession. In his opinion, lawyers as a breed were dishonest.

"Is that what you want? A pitched legal battle that could destroy the relationship you two have with each other?"

What I heard Zed saying was that it was somehow more spiritual not to retain a lawyer, though if I didn't, that left me in the position of advocating for myself, and wasn't there that adage about a man who advocates for himself in a court of law having a fool for a client? But if I didn't retain a lawyer, there would be no court of law, and so, how could I then be called a fool?

The barrier between you and me was the painful thing, Isabel. But in my morning meditation the answer came, dissolving the barrier. Love was back. We were one once again. I could hardly wait to call you with my joyful solution.

My proposal was simply this: we would divide up the balance in the checking account, money which came from your investment dividends. There would be no erosion of your capital. The one time I had brought up putting aside some money for retirement from my modest salary, you had adamantly vetoed the idea. "I have no savings." You quickly agreed.

Isabel, on my big day, I left the org at 11:30 a.m. From Sixth Avenue I could see the number "666" glowing at the top of the Paine-Webber building ten blocks away. The mark of the beast, the Antichrist, and all that, but why be weighed down by such superstitious foolishness? How modern the building looked, the glass and steel shimmering in the distance. For a moment I grew concerned. After all, Sixth Avenue was nouveau riche relative to Park Avenue, the erstwhile headquarters of Marks Denner Crush and Shive. And so I became aware of the workings of my mind, that it should preoccupy me with the fortunes of a powerful law firm when it was my own less robust fortunes that I might better be considering.

My stomach fell as the elevator zoomed with powerful ease to the thirty-ninth floor and opened onto an ultramodern waiting area. I was seated for only a minute before a tall, thin man strode quickly past the receptionist's desk to greet me with an outstretched hand. The man's dark blue silk suit and canary yellow tie were in contrast with the ashen color of his face and metallic gray hair.

"Mr. Manootdjian? I'm Orrin Hinckle. Good to meet you." Mr. Hinckle gave my hand a vigorous shake. "We look to be about the same age, wouldn't you say?"

Now Isabel, Mr. Hinckle had interaction strategies, as all good lawyers must, for he was in a league of the powerful and the wealthy, and here he was seeking to establish our common ground to gloss over the fact that we had divergent interests. It would take more than his opening words for me to live in our commonality and not our differences—the fact that he was a partner in a law firm that had a former high-ranking government official on its letterhead whereas I was a functionary in a not-for-profit org who hadn't even reached the level of director and insufficiently important to rate a listing in the lobby directory. But in truth I could more easily concede to Mr.

Hinckle a bigger brain and greater status than I could that this gray-haired man and I were the same age.

Papers were piled high on all the surfaces of Mr. Hinckle's spacious office, and now and then a secretary would enter seeking clarification of a hand-written correction he had made on some legal document. As you know, it had been a dream of mine, in my youth, to be a lawyer, and I thought now of the second-tier law schools that had accepted me while staring at the framed juris doctor degree from Harvard Law School behind Orrin Hinckle's desk, though more on my mind than discarded legal ambition was the simple fact that I was a signature away from removing myself from this powerful world I was still legally connected to through marriage.

But material distinctions and the dissolution of the marriage were not, emotionally speaking, where I was living, Isabel. Since making the appointment with Mr. Hinckle, I had begun to feel an overwhelming and uncontrollable urge which, throughout my life, had surfaced at times to dominate all others. It was simply this: the desire to be good. Specifically, the need was there to prove that I was not in the category of your previous husband who, through his lawyer, had extracted a sizable financial settlement before the divorce could be finalized. However, it would not be sufficient for me to place my signature on the agreement without in some way creating the opening whereby I could tell Mr. Hinckle the full story. Was it not too much to ask of a man to sacrifice not only money but reputation?

Quite remarkably, Isabel, for someone I would have thought quite buttoned down, Mr. Hinckle had his own truth to lay bare. "The firm assigns other colleagues to courtroom proceedings. It's been decided that they are better able to handle those pressures. I guess I have to accept my diminished role, but it is difficult." Even more jarring than his verbal attempt to see himself as more than chopped liver was what he said next. "I've been taking medication—Prozac—for depression. It seems to be working." Was I a priest? A psychiatrist? What on earth was prompting Mr. Hinckle to adopt this confessional nature? Weren't lawyers trained to utter not one extraneous word? Was this a further attempt by Mr. Hinckle to camouflage his power, or was he reaching out in a woefully insecure moment?

Mr. Hinckle was telling me that every org has a grid, and he had fallen on the Marks Denner Crush and Shive one, whereas he had previously known only ascendancy. The office was completely quiet. Outside his office the floor was empty except for a secretary. A clear-out had taken place. Power lunches were being consumed at four-star restaurants or partners had fanned out to do their power lawyering in the highest courts of the land, and here Mr. Hinckle was relegated to the relatively petty stuff of estates and trusts and divorce settlements and the likes of me.

If Mr. Hinckle initiated this uncensored communication, I followed with a long narrative of our marital history and its disintegration. I confessed to some rough edges, to silent scorn and bouts of unbridled anger that amounted to verbal abuse. But my heart had been in the right place; my shortcomings, glaring as they were, couldn't have been the major reason for the separation.

And Mr. Hinckle had a love supreme story of his own.

The woman in question, Lisbeth, had come into his life as a client. She was young, attractive, and the recipient of a large inheritance, which required the estate planning expertise of a lawyer such as Mr. Hinckle, who stressed that their first meetings were entirely on the plane of business. But as time passed he sensed a warming on her part toward him, which led to their having dinner together. And it went from there. Though she lived in a different state, weekends in her company became routine.

Mr. Hinckle had married right after graduation from law school. Blessed with a superior intellect, he also had the physical endowment for breeding. The joys of marriage, of family life, of a career with a high-powered firm, a country house—from humble origins had he risen to great heights. His children were bright and his wife socially adept and warm. She was, he said, a treasure the years could not deplete.

But they did. He lost his attraction to her. From separate beds they went to separate bedrooms and then the unthinkable, separate addresses. Now the house was in her name and his own name was on the lease of a luxury rental on the East Side of Manhattan.

Lisbeth was the catalyst for the rupture. Active in the pursuit of a fulfilling life, she rode horses and hiked trails and swam bravely and far in mighty rivers and storm-tossed oceans, and sailed the coastal waters in nautical white. He had none of her athletic prowess, but in the open air, away from the fluorescent wash of corporate interiors, he noted with pleasure that the sun began to make inroads on his prison pallor.

Sexually Lisbeth was Southern fire. There were weekends in bed, her only apparel a visor that read "Pleasure Palace Below." When they were apart, her face appeared on his codicils and torts and memoranda. Her phone calls gave him a happy glow and more. In middle age he had met a woman who had mastered the art of making love through the air. Once more he was a teenager in love, only now he would do it right.

And then his bright light turned to night, and it did not take a full season either. On short notice, and without explanation, she canceled their weekend plan to go sailing, and it was for him to call the following week when he didn't hear from her. But she had plans for that weekend, too. Her voice had winter in it. She was farther away than the many miles between them. When he reached for her through the line, she pulled back even more. He packed a bag, booked a flight, and drove from the airport in a rental car to her country house. Her car was right there in the driveway, content with its own idleness.

A vigil was not the thing. He took it upon himself to ring her bell; it was not lawyerly, but it was well within the realm of the human. The bell had summoning power. The door was flung open and there she stood, in T-shirt and jeans.

"Did you want something, mister?"

Her folded arms and spread legs supported her hostile vibe. On the next property a gardener was trimming the bougainvillea with his shears. Mr. Hinckle heard the snip, snip. He imagined the peaceful, puttering pace of the gardener's day and other tools of his trade— the spade, the trowel he plunged into the rich soil— with a sudden longing for the same, as if the gardener were the uncorrupted antithesis of all he had become. I have been seeing this gardener my entire life, Mr. Hinckle thought.

"You don't know my name?" Mr. Hinckle said quietly, withering in the face of her cold stare.

"I know I do not want you on my property," she said, with unrelenting firmness.

"Why are you acting in this way?" A note of plaintiveness entered his voice even as he sought to preserve his quiet dignity, but he could not check the onslaught of her negation.

"My father was an excellent horseman. In the saddle you are a comical sight. And to not know a jib from a mainsail? Do you wish to present yourself as serious?" The questions, which he understood to be fully rhetorical, were followed by a ferocious slamming of the heavy white door that rattled the glass in the fantail above.

And there, basically, Mr. Hinckle's tale ended. At the elevator he pressed on me his card. "Do stay in touch. We could meet for dinner perhaps," Mr. Hinckle said. But however close this mutual exchange had brought us, there was no chance we would ever continue the connection. A great revulsion would forbid it. We had shared the only common ground we had, and it would surely prove too narrow for us to stand on it again. Everything else was about difference—income, status, education, intelligence. Anyway, Mr. Hinckle had completed his mission; he had extracted from me empathy as well as my signature.

It was one of those freakish January days, the temperature in the sixties. But the weather wasn't the only thing out of whack. It was like a thousand things were flying around inside me, some crazy emotion I had no name for other than to call it shame or longing or both. Orrin Hinckle. That was my emotion. Not the marriage. Not the signing away of my marriage. It was him. The audacity of having spoken of intimate things with my better for a couple of hours. And now I was infected, polluted—something. His card felt like a torment in my pocket. I kept heading south, bound for the org, back toward my own league, the one where mediocrity was the norm.

Chapter 24

The past. It is tempting to go there, but what does any of it mean? The dead are forgotten before they are even buried. What is his goal? To make himself immortal through a written record of where he has been? Asinine. In the beginning there was the word? What can that possibly mean? In the beginning there was the silence, the void. The word was where the trouble began.

The Noddermans. He hears them now on the other side of the wall. The sound of metal hangers in collision after a blouse or shirt has been removed. And that crazy shouting Mr. and Mrs. N. find release in, a lifetime of bickering that never escalates beyond words.

Once upon a time there was Lucas Brown in that same apartment. He was Black and old and lay dying of the virus, entirely dependent on Meals on Wheels and God's Love, We Deliver and the kindness of Mr. Edgaron Smith in Apt. 9A, also Black, also aged. Johan imagined him unmoving in that apartment in his excruciatingly slow slide into death. Edgaron Smith being a story unto himself, aggressively badgering Johan to visit with him and his partner, as he called the man he lived with.

Saying, a while back, "Tell me. How long you been here in this building?"

"How long?" Johan says.

"You heard me. How long? Five years? Ten years?"

"Since the last century," Johan says.

"What kind of answer is that? I ask you a question and you tell me since the last century. Is that friendly?"

"Are you asking for friendship or or you asking for information?"

"Look. Don't be fucking with me. You fuck with me, I fuck with you. I fuck you up. That's how I fuck with you."

The Flessers' decorated door opens and Marty Flesser steps out onto the landing. "Hey, buddy, how's it going? Saw you on TV last night. What a great episode," Ned Nodderman says, having emerged from his apartment across the landing. Ass wiper and boot licker supreme.

"Just glad to be working."

The elevator comes and the three of them ride down.

"Maybe we can all get together soon," Nodderman says to Marty, cravenly seeking a place in the star's universe.

"Let's do that," Marty says, not a hint of hesitation in that clear, strong voice, so in line with the power-driving force of his personality. In the confined space Johan's self-consciousness grows. That familiar feeling of being the odd person out, of being suspect and outside the circle of community, attaches to him now.

As if Johan's thoughts are accessible to him, Ned says, "How about this guy? You think he'd ever have a friend over for dinner? You'd think he'd have a friend over at all? You think he has any friends to begin with?"

"Sure he has friends. Leave my buddy alone. We go back a long time."

And so it goes.

After Lucas Brown was expired from this earth, then did the Noddermans, Ned and Marsha, arrive. Ned is tall and thin and virtually bald, an idiot savant in the neckwear business, a boastful sort of man.

"What are you, some kind of professor?" Ned Nodderman says, on another occasion.

"Do I go and call you names?"

"What name? I asked if you were a professor. That's all."

"Are you a professor?"

"I'm a high school dropout. But I know plenty. Believe me."

"Now we're getting somewhere."

"You I don't wish to know."

The Noddermans drive a SUV and own a second home in the Hamptons. They sold their Greenwich Village coop because they couldn't pass up its incredible market value. Ned in particular has an attitude of prosperity. It is not only the SUV or the property, or even the exotic whippet he walks three times a day, a dog whose sleek slenderness is in line with its owner's. Something in the way he carries himself, some air of confidence and happy cheer, tells you his business is booming.

"That dog. Is it a relation of yours?" Johan says, seeing Ned with his pooch on the landing.

"Harry? Harry's my pet."

"There's a resemblance."

"Don't be calling me a dog."

"I mean that as a compliment. I'm only pointing out the similarities. You both have an admirable sleekness."

"Oh, OK. I thought maybe you were starting with me again."

The Noddermans represent change. They are a new type of tenant the building is drawing, people with far larger incomes than those they are replacing, like Lucious Brown. Ned Nodderman is all about securing what is rightfully his. He leaves no doors open to the past. That it is just the way the world turns, one group triumphing over another, one group evicting another, one group wanting another to go away. It is understood that war, not peace, is the essence of civilization. It is where winners and losers are established, if not for all time, at least until the next conflict.

When Johan arrived there were many Black tenants. Real estate in this part of town was not dear then. Some of them were elderly; some were middle aged; a few were young. Johan secretly wanted those who made him feel unsafe to go away, like the scary crack addict with the dreadlocks.

"I fuck you up in your sleep, white boy. I bust down your triple lock door so I can get mines. You know what I'm saying?" Demanding from Johan a receipt for his less than comforting words.

"I'm trying to hear where you're coming from," Johan said, fear ruling out any possibility of empathy.

Yes, I was afraid. The racial violence in Crown Heights. The stories of wilding incidents, the frequent intimidation on the streets and subways. And then I was held up by two young Blacks in front of my building, one armed with a gun, the other in possession of a knife. All I wanted was to feel safe in a city where I didn't feel safe. "White" came to mean "safe." "Black' came to mean unsafe. A blight seemed to be on the city, it occurred to me that New York might go the way of Newark.

But now it is not the young Black males of New York City whom he fears. Now it is Ned Nodderman, with his abundant financial resources, and the influx of similarly wealthy types that Johan is noticing throughout the building with their whippets and golden retrievers and Irish setters and beaming new babies and high-powered careers and aggressively white teeth. He has lost the momentum and the courage that the money of the marriage gave him. If once the retail spaces with whitewash on their windows and the rundown neighborhoods depressed him, now the spit shine that the city is receiving—witness antiseptic, Disney-fied Times Square—is cause for distress.

"Jesus, a padded cell once again," he says to Ned Nodderman in another elevator conversation. The movers have thrown up those quilted mats to protect the baked enamel walls. The elevator stops at seven and a couple of plaster-dusted Poles, speaking in their native tongue, enter. Workers already gutting the vacated apartment. Rewiring. Replastering. Repainting. A shiver goes through Johan seeing these tough, burly men with their hard-edged competence bought by the building owner at a cheap immigrant wage, no doubt, upgrading another unit and moving it out of rent stabilization in the process.

"It's all about change. You've got to go with the flow. I learned that a long time ago," Ned Nodderman says.

"Is that right?" By now they have passed through the lobby and onto the sidewalk. An enormous van is parked curbside. Into the back of it movers are loading boxes and furniture.

"What some people don't understand is that the market has to be allowed to operate. If it doesn't, you get these artificial price controls. That's what happened with rent control and rent stabilization. Assigning these low rents to one-third of the city's housing stock makes no sense. It drives everyone else's rent up even more. For years you have these losers living in a classic A-line apartments with three bedrooms and three bathrooms for nothing—nothing—when on the open market that apartment would go for five thou a month. And now that's exactly what the owner will be getting, you can be sure. People like you cower in your subsidized apartments because you're afraid to test yourselves in the world."

"Thanks for the information. Though what about you and Marty Flesser? You don't live in subsidized apartments even though you can afford a lot more?"

"The difference is that we don't need these rents. We're just taking advantage of the system. We've proved ourselves in the world. We've raised families, raised children, had big careers. We've proven ourselves to be mensches."

"Really, Nodderman? You sell apparel nobody wants anymore." And doesn't add that Marty Flesser sings like a man on the potty trying to squeeze out an obstinate turd. Cancel. Cancel. Cancel. So he says to himself that he should have such a mean thought about someone who clearly possesses great gifts that he shares with the world.

And if it's not Nodderman, then it's the media. That mean old bastard who chews barbed wire in his sleep, the upstate politico. George Mosconi. His Botox, septuagenarian, mob boss face all over the front page of a daily rag that calls itself a newspaper. NO

MORE FREE LUNCH, STATE SENATE REPUBLICAN LEADER DECLARES." "Rent Stabilization: The Beginning of the End?" "Freeloaders on notice!"

Now it is the ongoing gentrification of New York City. Now it is the daily, gnawing concern, a waking nightmare, that he will lose his apartment and have to leave this island where he was born and raised and wishes to die. Now it is the Blacks he cherishes and whom he wishes to stay and stay while desiring the affluent whites to move out. Now it is the Blacks he associates with safety and not these Wall Street and dot-com whites with their giant salaries.

Is this a shameful, self-serving way to arrive at identification? Should he discredit this change simply because it is driven, in part, by financial insecurity?

It is one thing for Nodderman to talk poorly about him to his face and even to Marty Flesser, but it is another for Johan to pass Nodderman chatting with the doorman Levan outside the building and to feel their eyes on him as he heads down the block toward Broadway. Looking back over his shoulder, he is confirmed in his intuition. There the two of them are, Nodderman with a mocking grin on his narrow face in that faux bonding act with Levan. What can Johan do but accept his powerlessness over his neighbor's viciousness while asking himself what kind of man is it who stands downstairs with the doorman and gossips, yes *gossips*, about his neighbors as they enter or leave? Johan, with the tall buildings of New York City as his audience, saying, Nodderman, are you a man or a yenta that you come from such a place? Oh the dinky dimensions that men possess that they should act in the way they do. What kind of respect for your neighbors is it that you seek to poison the building staff against them?

And that wife of his, Marsha Nodderman, screaming at Johan because her cat has darted out of the Nodderman's apartment and tries to get into his as he is unlocking the door.

"Didn't I tell you before that if she ever gets inside your door, it will be hell to get her back out? Didn't I?"

"But your cat didn't get in my door. Besides, shouldn't you concentrate on keeping her inside your door? That way I could be free to come and go as I need to."

"Just do as I say. I don't want my cat in your apartment. Do you understand?" It is for Marsha to take the liberty of reproaching him when all he has done is let himself in his apartment. But then, it's only a matter of time before a woman like that adopts such a tone.

"Are you saying that I do want your cat in my apartment?"

"I'm not saying anything, mister. Just do as I say or there will be big trouble. You don't know Schnubsy. She gets into your apartment it will be hell for us to get her out. We'll have to tear your whole place apart."

"You're just going to come in and tear my apartment apart?"

"We're going to do whatever needs to be done. Don't argue with me."

"Why would I not argue with you?"

"You watch it."

"Just find a way to keep your cat inside your apartment. Then you won't need to concern yourself with my apartment or anyone else's."

Maybe it would just end there, but then Ned Nodderman has to get involved. "Is he bothering you, Marsha? Are you messing with my wife, mister whatever your name is?"

"I'm not messing with anyone. I'm just trying to have my own evening."

"Was he being smart with you, Marsha? Tell me."

"Don't get started, Ned. I was just warning him about Schnubsy, but he gave me an argument. He's intent on getting Schnubsy into his apartment, and that's just what we don't want."

"You lure our Schnubsy into your apartment, I'll ring your scrawny neck," Ned Nodderman says.

"Lure?"

"You sex-offend our cat you're in deep shit, my friend," Ned Nodderman says.

"We've had our eye on you for some time," Marsha says. "Don't think we don't have your number. Keeping us up all night with your Internet porn."

"I'll bet he has one of those inflatable women in his closet," he hears Ned Nodderman say as Johan closes the door on the neighborly twosome.

Riva Flesser, with the singing husband, doesn't see him as sex-offending. She talks to him in the way that empty nester women with too frequently absent husbands —women living in the pall of semi-abandonment—can talk when another man they are familiar and comfortable with is around. Says to Johan, "Love your coat. It's beautiful," as he stands one morning in his long wool belted brown coat, the collar turned up and his hair still wet from the shower. It's the coat that attracted Maura to him, the coat he bought on sale with the money of the marriage (that phrase again) when he was still dressing to be seen. A vibration has begun. He has to be careful, not because he wants Riva but because he doesn't. Not even his oedipal impulses and chafing at the perceived condescension of Marty Flesser allow him to entertain the thought of bedding down with her. Less a principled stand against getting involved with a married woman or fear that the singing hubby will knock his door down and kill him but some physical aversion to this middle-aged woman who smells of the analyst's couch. He is also wary of that ranting and raving temperament. Today it is not fury about the latest outrages and shenanigans of that creep of a landlord. Today that regime in Washington, D.C. is the focus of her ire. Whales, peregrine falcons, the whole wondrous shebang perishing except for pigeons and rats and cockroaches as those evangelical crazies pursue their politics of deprivation. And that weight she has gained can only mean she has been doing some serious gnoshing.

"They're fucking us. Every day they fuck us. Excuse my French," Riva says, the two of them alone in the elevator. She touches his arm. "I couldn't sleep last night. It's killing me."

Her anger—transferable, he suspects, from heartless Republicans to him.

"I hate when that happens to me. It makes the whole day such a struggle. Can you take a nap later?"

"Who can nap? I have rehearsals all day for my play."

Riva is a player, too. Powerful, like her husband. Johan is desperate to be at his best for her. That is how her power manifests. What he wants from her is not sex but her good opinion because she is in the winner's circle. To bask in her light, as friends of Bill and Hillary seek to do.

And just as well that he doesn't explore new territories with her, as the next week he steps off the elevator clutching his bag of OrganicOnly groceries and nearly collides with Marty and Riva Flesser. Marty is back on the premises, and he and the Mrs. are now confronting Johan in their power garb—he in a tux and she in a black gown and pearl necklace. Bonded, the two of them are, and not acknowledging of him beyond the merry scorn he elicits in their eyes. Poor lost soul, destined to eat your thrown-together meal alone at your kitchen table while we are received and feted by the world. Riva knows where her bread is buttered and where power is to be found. She has been pulled back into Marty's orbit by his crumb of attention to her, and as she does so, her aversion to Johan grows and grows.

"If you will excuse me," Johan says, when Marty does not move.

"Dear, he needs to get by," Riva says.

"Oh, I'm so sorry. Is someone there?" Marty says.

Johan enters his apartment enraged.

Isabel, and supreme power of the universe,
To you I say the following: I showed restraint. I did not go too far. The forces for my annihilation have not gathered. But know also this: I do not have to adopt the sissy stance of the perennial victim, buttonholing this person and that and bending their ear as to my

sad tale. I can look into my human heart and see the murderous rage and the jealousy and envy and pettiness. I can see the judgments that form. I can say, as I couldn't in all my drinking years, Where are you in all this, Johan? What is your part in this impasse? Yes, Marty Flesser has made me feel small, with his negation of my existence, but have I truly worked to create the space that can accommodate someone of his outsize talent? Do I not then say, *they* get everything and I get nothing? Do I not then say, Everywhere the holocaust but nowhere the genocide of the Armenians? Oh, is it not the same defect that caused me to walk off the basketball court at halftime in my junior year of high school? Is it not simply a case of comparing myself with someone who is doing better than me in the game of life as in the game of basketball? Isabel, Marty Flesser is my teacher. I must pray for all good things for him. This I can and must do. I am on it right now. The lag time between the impulse and the action held and I did not act rashly, and so I have no need to review my procedural processes.

"Are you Jewish?" The usual morning rush hour. As the human wave flows past, a bearded young man in the Times Square subway station proffers a Jews for Jesus pamphlet.

"I am not a Jew, but I am Jesus," Johan replies.

"You are what?"

"Jesus. Jee-suss. Christ Jee-suss. And you. You are Jesus too, if only you did know it." To look into another person's eyes and see confusion, outrage.

The man gathers himself and moves on. "Are you Jewish?" he says to another man, who pushes past him.

He makes it a point never to play Marty Flesser's music. It would strike him as weird to listen to his neighbor's tortured tenor voice as the master himself is standing outside on the landing waiting for the elevator. Two neighbors who converse only minimally, let alone socialize, and yet, Johan is a secret admirer? Could he ever return to his aloofness from Marty Flesser once such covert connection had been revealed? Would their lack of conversational ease with each other increase? Would it not appear that he, Johan, was stealing something from Marty Flesser?

That morning he listens to Bach's *Brandenburg Concerto*. What a joyful sound the choirmaster created. How pleasant to shower and shave to the harpsichord, and not the miserable stream of news that flows from NPR, particularly that deadly time between 7:35 a.m. and 8 a.m. when you are likely to get some wrenching human interest story—a mentally ill woman living on food stamps in some Bayou backwater or cardboard boxes serving as a home for a family of six after their Bronx apartment building burned down. This morning he woke to the BBC reporting on a beheading in Afghanistan. How is that for a cheery start to the day? It occurs to him that Marty Flesser, and Ned Nodderman as well, might hear the concerto as they wait for the elevator and ascribe a hostile intent to Johan's playing it, given that these composers are German and they are Jewish. It is not, God forbid, Wagner, but it is still the music of the Hun. Verdi's *Requiem* is another concern. He is afraid of offending his neighbors with the monstrousness of Christianity as seen through their Jewish eyes. Johan has to remind himself that world-class Jewish conductors lead orchestras that include the classical music of Germany and other countries in their repertoire, and if these conductors are not reviled, then why should he be either?

He manages to get out of the building without incident that morning, but when he returns in the evening a rack crammed with coats stands on the landing and partygoers seeking breathing room are chatting outside the open door to the Flessers' apartment.

"Have you seen Riva's new play? It's magical. And that divine CD that Marty just released. Oh, what gifts they give us," an elderly, white-haired woman is saying to a younger woman. Seeing Johan struggling toward his door, she says, "Say, you're a nice-looking man. What is it like for you living next door to such a mensch as Marty? Tell me, if you don't mind, the richness he adds to your life. Are you made to pay extra just so you can live next to the great man? No, I'm just joking, of course. Say, aren't you coming to the party? Go inside. Raise a glass. Sing. Dance. Don't look so serious. I haven't asked you for your IQ. Anyone can see you're an intelligent man."

"If you will excuse me," Johan says, pushing closer to his door.

"Excuse. Excuse. What kind of life does that give you, excuse? Excuse what? Excuse you for breathing? Stop being such a sonny boy. Come up in the world, like Marty. Show your mensch-ness."

"I will see what I can do."

"What kind of way is that for you to talk? Why is there quiet but no strength in your vocabulary?"

"Yes, I see what you mean," Johan says,

From the other side of the door he hears the woman's parting shot. "Like a wounded animal wanting only to return to his lair."

But oh happy day. With all the lights out and only a candle burning, he lies down by the door on an old foam exercise mat he has taken from the closet. Yes, the woman has seen his retreat, yet how sweet that l'chaim is on one side of the door and he is on the other, safe now from her pain-inducing inquisition. Tonight is such a night that even the candlelight has to be snuffed. Oh, hidden away child, yearning for the deepest darkness.

In the morning he wakes stiff and sore. "Have we had a good night, Johan? Have we slept the sleep of the just? Have we exceeded even our wildest adventure? Was it scrumptious to have slept far away from our bed and yet within the confines of this wonderful apartment? Do we want to go potty now?" In this way does he talk to himself so he can get started on his morning of meditation and journaling.

It is Wednesday, or Wed-nes-day, as his mother pronounced it. It is the bright day of the week, the red rectangle of gummy sugar in the Chuckles pack. Oh, happy hump day. Put aside Bach and Beethoven and Mozart and the serenity they give him for the exuberance of *Hair*. Yes, *Hair*. *Hair* thrills him to the core—"Aquarius," "Three-Five-Zero-Zero," "Good Morning Starshine," "Easy to Be Hard," the works. But the laughing thing. If he turns up the volume will Marty Flesser out there on the landing assume that he is stuck in the sixties? And yet Marty Flesser hears him playing the symphonies of Beethoven. Does that mean Johan is stuck in the nineteenth century?

"Would you like to play *Hair* so it is detectable to your ears as you shower and shave, Johan?"

"Yes, I really would."

"Well, let us do just that, Johan. Let us do that."

Oh happy, happy day when he and the country can be young again.

And on the floor below the Hoykmans.

"Are you seeing someone? Because if you are not, I have just the woman for you," Helena Hoykman, who waits with him in the lobby for the elevator, once said, standing close. Attractive. A woman he would have liked to reach out and touch. A woman straining on the marital leash, wed as she is to a man whose tirades carry through the walls and the ceiling to Johan's ears. Strange how much you know about a couple when you hear them fight, or when one rages and the other cries, which is how it would be with Helena and her hubby.

But now she can barely say hello to him. There is just the dull and numbing predictability of him. Johan alone with his OrganicOnly bag. Johan alone without it. He is a disappointment to her. That is all.

"How's the family?" Johan says, flipping through his mail.

"Everyone's well. How's your family?" she says drily. A second child has come along to go with their seven-year-old daughter, a chubby two-year-old who has his father's unfortunate features.

"Well, unless I'm forgetting something, I don't have a family." It is not for him to explain about Isabel and Mia, not to a woman like Helena. He does not need to see any more dubiousness in her eyes. And that husband of hers. As tubby as she is slender, with his big belly obscuring his belt. Another Johan doesn't like, as he is a man who will talk with Marty Flesser in the elevator about their kids while studiously ignoring him, the goy putz without the wife or offspring.

"That's too bad," she says, as they step into the elevator.

"I don't see it that way," he says.

"You don't see very much."

"Am I missing something?"

"The thing in front of you?"

"Would you like to come over?" Her eyes are big, and seem to grow even bigger as she takes in his words. A woman with a quiver of tension showing in her face, there is even more of it now.When she says nothing, he adds, "12D, as in domani."

That night Johan has a powwow with himself, a high-level summit the likes of which he had not experienced since his days with Maura. Self, he says, what have you done that you would, through directness, gain dominion over a married woman so that now, in her family domicile, her thoughts can only be of you, as yours are of her? Admit the thrill you are experiencing over this development, this new and potent image of yourself that you would now embrace, and pray that love be your guide should she come knocking on your door.

As surely she does the next night.

"Is this your hovel?"

"It is where I live. Yes."

"Do I get a tour?"

He leads her into the bedroom. "This is not a torture apparatus, but my NordicTrack cross-country ski machine, which I am faithful to four times a week so I can keep my weight right where it is and possibly extend my life on this planet."

"And what is that?"

"What is what?"

"That teddy bear."

"Schnell is my constant companion during nocturnal journeys, though the truth is we rarely talk anymore."

"Men don't normally sleep with teddy bears."

"Normally I don't know. Schnell I would have to look for if he went missing. It is that way with my boxer shorts as well. If, once settled into bed, I realize that I have not brought them along for the journey, then must I get up, even on the coldest night, and fetch them."

"Is this something you should be telling me?"

"You I can tell anything. Because you have the look of anger on your face, but what it really is is hurt. You feel that you are not where you belong, that you have gifts that outstrip those of some others, but you are fettered."

"I have a happy life. I have children."

"Yes, of course."

"What do you have? You have this contraption and your boxer shorts."

"This is true. And I am looking forward to the day when I shall buy new ones that will satisfy my idea of the perfect rotation—Wednesday a certain color, Friday a certain color. That sort of thing."

"Are you really such a simpleton, going on about your underwear?"

"The things that excite us we must seize upon, no matter how seemingly small."

"We?"

"Forgive me for flying into the plural. It is only happiness that leads me there, like the girl discovering the 'we of me' in Carson McCullers' play."

"What do you want me to do?"

"What do you want to do?"

"I want to leave."

And so she does.

The next day he rides down in the elevator with Riva Flesser. It stops at eight.

"Hi, Ellen," Riva says, to the woman of similar age who has just stepped in.

"Hi, Riva."

"Do you know—I'm sorry, I keep forgetting your name."

"Johan, " Johan says.

"We've met," Ellen Quell says.

"How are you, Ellen?" Riva asks.

"You and I will do lunch, and I will fill you in." Ellen Quell says, and darts off through the lobby.

"I used to think, and still do, that you and Ellen are like two ships passing in the night and that you just might be Mr. and Mrs. Right for each other."

"It's better ships pass in the night rather than collide, leaving everybody to drown in frigid ocean waters. Wouldn't you rather that we survive to sleep alone in our own warm beds?"

"I don't know about you, mister. You have a brain wired for aloneness."

"Actually, I had dinner with Ellen."

"She didn't tell me that."

"It was only once, and long ago." And she has resented him ever since, or so he used to think, seeing that wounded look on her face, as if she had just been slapped. Her anger is reserved for all men now, he suspects, noting the way she did her speed-walk thing in bolting from the elevator, her elbows high and out, like someone in urgent need of a bathroom break. And saying, with her fast exit, "You don't want me, baby? Well, I doubly don't want you."

"Did you follow up?"

"I just wasn't able to."

"What do you want?"

"Clean underwear."

"Excuse me?"

"Clean underwear."

"I worry about you. I really do."

Or there is Agnes Marshall, who lives with her son, an angry teenager, and her teenage daughter, who may be angry but doesn't show it.

"Hey, Johan, how's it going?" she says to him that same day. A woman with the sparkle of intelligence in her eyes, she has processed abandonment by her husband for the bottle and a woman born two decades before her.

"I'm doing OK. Holding my own against the elements."

"That doesn't sound so great there. What's going on?"

One of those women like water, always exploring a crack. She's got that action engine going, that need to get in there and clean up other people's messes. That's what the drunkenness of her ex-hubby left her with.

"No real problems. Everything is good," he says.

Those searching eyes. That fox's face. "We should continue this. Let's get together soon. What do you say?"

"That sounds good. We'll do that," he says, the way they say the same thing every time, because in the long ago he went out with Agnes Marshall too, if only once. Couldn't extend beyond that with her either.

"Should we set a date?"

"I'll get back to you. I don't have my calendar with me," he says, feeling like now he has done it. Now he has really done it. Now he has made a promise he can't keep and even Agnes Marshall will be angry with him for not giving her what it seems she wants.

Althena Jefferson is singing sweetly in the lobby that she has her love to keep her warm. A sophisticated lady wrapped in her winter coat. A coquettish smile she offers.

"Have we met before, my handsome man?" Althena Jefferson says. Her eyes watery.

"Oh yes, in pleasant dreams have we been together," Johan says.

"How you do talk. You men with your sweet nothings," she laughs, her voice softly Southern. "Will I see you again?"

"You will see me forever and forever, on halcyon days and in times of tumult."

Beauty attached to her face as well as her name when she was young, she would have you know, when she was the queen of Manhattan, the dazzling bride of the famous light heavyweight Roscoe Jefferson, he with the takeout power in both fists and the dancing feet *slams him with a right a left another right a thunderous left hook Basilio is down, down.* But now it is Roscoe Jefferson who is down, down, long since down, and the count has long since ceased.

"Miss Jefferson, I have need of you," Levan says, in that strong East European voice of his.

"Is someone calling me?" she says, cupping her ear.

"I am calling to you. Your good friend Levan," Levan says, from ten feet away.

"What is that name again?" she asks.

"Levan is my name. You come to me now, Miss Jefferson."

"Come to a stranger? A man I do not know? Who do you take me for, mister? Do you know who I am? I must get away from this atmosphere of deceit and betrayal." She wanders past Levan and toward the front door.

"She doesn't remember. She is lonely. She has no one upstairs," Levan says, escorting Johan to the elevator and pressing the button. "Do you understand?"

"Yes, of course," Johan says.

"Everyone here impatient with her. No one in America wants death near. She you someday. One day you stand in lobby, too. She showing you your future."

"Levan, you are a prophet."

"What is prophet? No prophet. Just Levan, who tells the truth," he says, as the elevator door closes.

Chapter 25

Isabel,

The thread of even the most meager narrative must be continued. And if I do not represent you well, if I am deficient in sagacity and skill, your story has become intertwined with my own and must be recorded for me to be part of this earth when I am gone, absurd as that may seem. Or it must be spoken for me to feel there is any semblance of purpose to my day; this is what I am led to by everything that is within me.

We had gone to the French Alps. Denuded of trees, a sad grayness, like that of an elephant's hide, attached to them. You had been there as a child with your family, and when your stepfather suddenly disappeared down a crevasse, you had no regret and offered no fervent prayer for his return. It was one of a number of stories that you told, which caused sorrow and horror and the perception of your violated holiness to take hold in me, like the time two men led you away by the arm outside a movie theater before other adults could intercede. Oh, lost, all those with their innocent openness on display for the world to do with as it will.

Some strange mentality afflicted you on this trip we took as a family. You showed no patience for the laggards in your midst, and went on ahead of little Mia and me on these alpine trails. Is it possible you arranged this vacation to cast me more deeply in the role of the violating stepfather and yourself as the trembling child in the night? And yet, from a slow beginning, I shrugged off an ailing knee, found a higher gear, and with this newfound power proclaimed myself a number one American doing backflips over the highest mountain peak. Such braggadocio did not sit well with you, as there was one, your stepfather, who came before me, with chest-thumping tendencies of his own.

The next year we traveled to Ireland for a trip from Limerick down to the Dingle Peninsula by horse-drawn carriage. Rain came and went—sun showers, without the gloom of cloud cover. And there were flareups—my own—that Mia was witness to. There was also the happiness you showed when I threatened to leave.

The following year Mia was sent to sleep away camp, where she launched a campaign by mail to win her quick return. An unrelenting wail could be heard from way up in the Adirondacks. And yet, by the time we visited, she had made a friend and her pain had eased. You and I then headed out on the Northway for Montreal and the Gaspé Peninsula, where my mother grew large in my consciousness when I saw her virtual double serving as a waiter in a Quebec restaurant. A patriarchal mentality still flourished in this old city sufficient that she appeared downtrodden and sad and meek. My heart opened to her, this proxy for my mother. While driving alone into a Canadian sunset, the Bible hymns of my childhood came back to me and I began to cry. Seeing a roadside phone, I pulled over and called her. My call was timely, she said. She had been knocked down by the continuing heat. Yes, I thought, the heat you and I fled and which I left her in with only a portable fan to cool herself with.

At times I have felt I have only ever belonged to my mother, Isabel. This you should know. She had a circle that radiated outward to envelop me.

Much has fallen away from that trip, but I do recall the acid rain that scarred the hills and mountains, like severe ringworm afflicting a child's scalp. The heavens returning our toxins to us. And the coin-operated batting range where I longed to spend the rest of my days. It stood there alone, with no context but the desolate straightaway it was situated on. A site like that has meaning, Isabel. It takes us back to childhood and a place beyond conscious recall—the warmth of summer nights and *everyone together in love*. Team sports can foster that sense. They surely can. Some sense of family as it's meant to be—parents admiring of their energy-filled children running free on a field.

There was Mount Royal Park in Montreal. The time of day was afternoon. We were climbing a hill. In an open field a child raced along with his kite. Clouds had gathered, obscuring the sun. You were ahead of me, walking at a brisk pace I couldn't keep up with until I broke into a jog. We had been walking for several hours and the dinner hour was approaching. To my surprise you wanted to keep going. Though we were in a city, there was woodland nearby. Behind the thick trunk of a tree I spotted a man loitering, a stray sort in bondage to a desire he felt in his groin but which was really loneliness brought on by disconnection. A man without a woman's love such as yours, which had spared me his fate. From that nourishing space of union, with all its warmth I looked at this rootless soul. When I called your attention to this voyeur, you said, "Why don't you go back to the hotel?" In that moment everything changed. A smile was on your face as you spoke, but your words had a wintry coldness.

This trip, like the one to the Alps, was a recreation of a childhood vacation you had taken with your parents, only now you had a chance to liberate yourself from your oppressor, if only by proxy. You had been buried alive, and now you were scratching your way to freedom, and providing illumination to those who think the answer is to cling rather than let go.

It was some tormenting hours before you returned to the hotel.

"I'm so full," you said, when I commented at a restaurant that night on your untouched dinner.

"How can that be? You've nibbled on only a piece of lettuce," I said.

"I've been eating all day."

"Eating what? Thin air?" And, of course, my clumsy refutation helped nothing. If anything, you perceived me as a bully.

(Why should I visit this place again? We have vacated those premises and moved on. It is like hovering over a rotting corpse rather than recognizing the shining light of a new day.)

"You look like a concentration camp survivor," I said that night, speaking from a place of desperation. Your arms like sticks, your hair falling out, the flesh receding from your face and your cheekbones growing more prominent. But you were not in Dachau or Buchenwald. You were on the Gaspé Peninsula. That was not a false alarm sounding in my head. I was not imagining your emaciated state. You were making a very serious statement here. You had announced yourself as a hunger artist, to be sure.

We took a ferry from somewhere to somewhere. When we lost sight of land I became frightened. The cold, choppy water was waiting for us. Always my safety has been of paramount concern to me.

There was a man on this ferry, Isabel. He had the character of that stray I pointed out behind the tree some days before and all those who in their anomie-driven lewdness give over their days to spying on lovers lying in grassy meadows from behind trees or bushes. Only now he had eyes for me and not for you, a look that could mean only one thing, taking me back to a world I had escaped from and never wanted to be a part of again. I am referring now to my childhood, when the men with big things made themselves known to me. Forgive me for stylizing them in this way; it is not for me here to go beyond this description. But that was then. Now, and for many years, any such interest has stirred a negative reaction in me, as I was now feeling toward the man on the boat, whom I glared at with such obvious hostility that he turned his attention elsewhere.

If there were other things from that trip, I feel we have no need to talk about them. Perhaps, after all, memories needn't live on but fade into the past, as we are destined to do?

My mother passed on the following year. I was at work when I received the call from Leah that she had suffered a stroke and an ambulance would soon arrive to take her to the hospital.

Things were not great with my boss, Miss Carmelli. She had given me a written reprimand for a production oversight—the contents page was missing from a manual that went to press. The reprimand had become part of my file up in Human Resources.

"Do what you have to do," Miss Carmelli said when I asked to leave early. There was coldness in her voice, as can happen when you underperform for your boss and go against her with angry words, as I had done. The sun was shining on New York City that spring afternoon as I debated whether to hail a cab or take the subway. Do not conclude that I was being ruled by frugality. To hail a cab might suggest to the universe that my mother was in true peril of extinction and that I needed to race to her side. Thus would anxiety have been injected, whereas a ride on the subway would suggest that time was not of the essence and that no great haste was required.

With death, or the shadow of it, comes that private space that those of my kind cannot put into words. And if, in fact, I did flag a cab on Third Avenue, heavy with the impersonality of its modern high rises, I did so with a casual gesture less likely than a frantic wave to summon the beast of anxiety so mercifully at bay.

The driver took the route through Central Park. Oh, the heaven that exposure to greenery restored me to, with memories of the fields of childhood I would play in, when dungarees and a T-shirt and sneakers were all one needed. There would be merriment in the park that afternoon—the whirl of the carousel, those stationary horses rising and lowering to Strauss waltzes; the wonder of children at the zoo gazing at sea lions and polar bears and capuchin monkeys and all the rest and birds with dazzling plumage in the aviary. There would be lovers on the Great Lawn and manicured diamonds awaiting the company softball teams that would take the field in friendly competition that evening.

At Seventieth Street I looked east to the Frick Museum and the private school down the block that I had attended. I thought of those years of social paralysis, when I could not so much as tell the other kids where it was I lived, and of my failure on the SAT, but more than that, of my mother, and how, in her orthotic shoes and support stockings, she would show up for parents' meetings with the East Side swells, for the school was abundant with the children of doctors, lawyers, CEOs and others of great means with Park Avenue and Fifth Avenue addresses. And I thought how, in return, how little I had showed up for her.

Though the sun above was constant, a shadow came over the park as the cab continued north. Yes, there were landscapes and walkways of breathtaking perfection, but a sense of danger attached that left the area desolate and unexplored, at least by me. Such was my fear of the other, the young gunmen who lacked the capacity to hold life dear. I am only telling you what was true of me, as random capping was driving the murder rate up and up. This was 1988, before the Italian American mayor, for better or worse, was elected.

"I am here for my mother. She would have arrived by ambulance a short time ago," I said to the receptionist in the emergency room.

"Does your mother have a name?"

I gave it.

"Don't have nobody with that name here," she said.

"But—"

"But what?" she said. If I heard unkindness in her voice, it may simply be that she wanted me to eat a reality sandwich, Isabel, of the kind that she had had to eat herself more than once, being a heavyset woman with possibly an attitude of grievance over all she had not been given in this life. Besides, she had a function to perform that required some toughness. Despite the bright lights, this was a dark environment. People sat moaning in the pastel-colored chairs awaiting the healing touch of the young residents.

My mother was no more. That is what the woman at the desk was telling me.

I walked the long block between Amsterdam Avenue and Broadway slowly, my childhood and youth right in front of me: the field at St. John the Divine where I had played softball; the pharmacy on the corner of Amsterdam Avenue where I had gone to fill a prescription for my mother ("Run on your long legs," she would say) only to be tossed out by the owner, who had caught me trying to boost a Parker T-Ball Jotter. But it was different, too. The tenements along Amsterdam Avenue and One Hundred Thirteenth Street had been razed; in their place stood a residence for physicians. Gone were my friends and not entirely friends from those tenements: Fatso Scully and Jimmy Jone and Sean McConnell. I was a ghost upon this scene.

The sound of dogs relentlessly barking came to my ears as I approached Broadway. It was an unwelcome sound, one that summoned a feeling of anger and the desire for a crushing reprimand. But the dogs were nowhere in sight. Across the avenue stood the building. The exterior had been sand-blasted free of that dark grime and the crumbling cornices that had imperiled passersby had been removed. Gone too were those rotting wood window frames, replaced by metal frames. The stamp of order was on this building my aunt had once owned, a predictable development given that Columbia University, which was known for imposing stability on the neighborhood with ruthless evictions, was the new owner.

The rooms may have been chock full of Columbia students, but the family apartment remained, the front door half open.

"She's gone," Hannah said, as I stepped into the vestibule. She sounded neither bereft nor relieved.

"Gone where?" I said.

"What do you mean, Gone where? Gone is gone," Hannah said.

"Gone is gone?" I repeated.

"That's what I said."

"Yes, of course." It was good to draw her crossness to the fore, where I could keep an eye on it.

Rachel was there as well. She was fifty-two by then, with a pale face in which remained vestiges of her youth. Her clothes were from a Goodwill bag: a loose-fitting dress that hung shapeless on her thickening frame and a pair of low-cut sneakers almost comically large for her feet. Depression emanated from her. The years, and mental instability, had brought her to this place.

My mother didn't worry about Hannah or Luke or Leah or me, but she did worry about the effect her passing would have on Rachel. Rachel was alone. She had no one and nothing, apart from the vigil she maintained at the window of her room for signs of Jesus returning in the night and solitary walks in the park and a visit to Chock Full O' Nuts for a sugar doughnut and cup of coffee. That was her life. And there was my mother's fear that she would wind up back in a mental institution and suffer the same fate as Naomi, my deceased older sister.

Sisters so beyond me in years are an elusive thing, but that doesn't mean they haven't had an impact.

There you would go with another meaningless flight into history, you escape artist, you. So do I hear a voice, not your own, Isabel, saying. What is this colossal absorption with the past? So my interrogator demands, bringing with him his cohort to commence their laughing thing. I must raise them from the dust of oblivion. I must atone. I must say to Naomi in her room and Rachel in hers and my vanished brother and my beloved, beleaguered mother and my disappearing father and all of them, Come out and come out now. We, the Manootdjians, whom I have collectively and individually renounced, are going for a stroll down Broadway.

Isabel, I brought an attitude of superiority into my mother's apartment. I had come not to comfort these sisters but to feel proudly apart from them in my ability to be happy for my mother that she had found release. Even as I stood in their presence did I hear these words: "Will your selfishness, your clinging (the force of that onomatopoeic word) never cease. You with your death. You with your bodies that merely serve as an encasement for the soul. When will you ever be free?" Oh, the opportunities for love I have squandered in my spiritual haughtiness.

The crackle of a walkie-talkie could be heard in the next room.

"Who's in there?" I asked.

"A police officer. She has to be here until the mortician arrives," Leah said, with some coldness, perhaps picking up on my attitude.

"Where is Mother?" I asked.

"She's in the hallway just outside her room," Hannah said. "I found her lying on the floor by her bed. It was horrible. A sheet was twisted around her and her head was partly under the bed. How could she have wound up in such a position? That's what I would like to know."

Hannah was looking for mystery, that perhaps our mother's death involved foul play. All day long Hannah watched these courtroom dramas on TV. Husbands suspected of murdering their wives. That sort of thing. She couldn't contemplate our mother falling from her bed while in her death throes.

Just as Leah said, a police officer was sitting in our dining room. She wore a dark blue uniform and a cap and her belt was laden with a holstered gun, a flashlight, handcuffs, and other accessories. Her presence placed a heavy burden on my mind, for I could only see the apartment and our family through her eyes so long as she remained seated in that chair. The words she spoke had a metallic edge.

"Afraid to see your own mother? She's right in there behind that door," the officer said, her teeth flashing white and working hard to crack that gum and crack it some more in that tight and churning mouth of hers.

"Did I say I was afraid?" I said to Officer Lucs, gaining her identity from the nameplate over her left breast.

"Yeah, you said it. You said it just the way you stand there."

"What way do I stand here?' I said.

"Don't talk sass to me now, boy. I'm an officer of the law. I can determine your fate. Don't make me have to do that on such a fateful day. Now get on in there and do your business so I don't have to do mine and regulate your life for you."

Isabel, she carried extra pounds from too many doughnuts. But no, I surely had no need for the cuffs she was seeking to slap on my wrists for impertinence toward her authority. It is the way of the police, as of all of us, to be separated from the mentality of service. It was for me to understand that and to walk on by with the understanding that she had her function and I had mine. We are always to gauge the spirit of the persons we engage with and move away from those afflicted with soreness or corruption or outright vileness, but in the case of Officer Lucs, I cannot with 100 percent certainty know her intent. Though my mind told me that she was seeking to rule supreme over me with her case-hardened words, was it possible that she was speaking only as she had been spoken to for her whole life? This strategy for living comes from dire necessity, as I must quell the beast of anger, simply remove the god of umbrage from his throne if I am to live in peace in this world. What is the point of entering the murky labyrinth of motive? Am I God that I should fathom the workings of Officer Lucs's mind? Why not *just answer the question she had asked, on the assumption that it might lead me somewhere?*

And so I had to acknowledge that not just anyone lay a short distance away. This was my mother of whom we speak. And this was the dining room where I had sat with her and just ahead was the kitchen where, as a boy, I would spread my legs against both sides of the door-less frame and rise to the very top and call to my mother, busy at the stove, to look, so in need was I of her love and attention, which to me were one and the same.

My mother lay beyond the hallway door, as Officer Lucs had said. She lay covered by a sheet up to her neck. On her face was a quizzical expression, as if she were processing information that required her full concentration. Or maybe it was instruction, as a dutiful child receives from a directive parent. In any case, she had simply vacated the premises of her body and gone elsewhere. How happy I was for her in that moment.

Chapter 26

Whispering. Always with the whispering. Just bits and pieces of conversation Johan hears in the next cubicle, where Hank Farquist has gone to visit with Alice Piccoli. Loathsome whispering, unfriendly and even conspiratorial.

"Yes," Johan himself whispers, and claps his hands when Alice begins to choke on the food she gobbles even as she tries to speak, a commotion that lasts for a minute or so before Hank can resume. Resolved, that he will fix their asses:

Rule 1: Lower your eyes whenever you stand up in your cubicle. Never look out over its walls to the floor beyond. Remain self-contained within your world and remove the risk of inadvertent eye contact with anyone beyond those walls. In this way people might be looking at you, but you will never be seen looking at them. They will have to present themselves to you for their existence to take place. No more anxious lunging for people with your eyes or with sudden turns.

Rule 2: Whenever possible, avoid entering the cubicles of others with whom you are at odds, the goal being to minimize their power or influence. The one downside: you are deprived of the perverse pleasure of actually witnessing Alice Piccoli devouring her swill and trying to talk at the same time, or seeing her bring that mug down on her desktop with a thud. Option: remove her food from the refrigerator in the cafeteria and throw it in the garbage and then have the pleasure of hearing her go all to pieces when she discovers that she has been denied the ritual of clogging her throat with the contents she has been driven to consume in a gluttonous frenzy.

"Do you have a minute?" Hank Farquist says, later that day, working some chewy morsel around in his mouth.

"What's up?" Johan says, pulling his face from the computer screen.

"I think I may be striking it rich."

"You expect to win the lottery?"

"Not exactly. But my landlord wants me out of my rent-stabilized apartment."

"Why?"

"It's a small building and he wants it for his own personal use."

"So he would give you money to leave?"

"That's what I am hoping."

"Suppose he doesn't?"

"I gave his lawyer a figure and now am waiting to hear back."

"You deserve it. You're the best," Johan says, feeling the stirrings of envy that a windfall is coming to his nemesis. A kindred soul, with no one but himself, the sort who stares at a TV screen at night in a dark room as he spoons peanut butter out of the jar.

Hank ignores the blandishment. "The only thing I'll regret is having to leave New York."

"Why would you leave?" Some ray of light has entered, and yet everything depends on concealment. Otherwise Hank just might change his mind. This won't be over until it is over, until Hank is out of the org and out of the city and even then, if Hank senses that Johan is smiling at his good fortune, he might simply, from perversity, return.

"I can't afford it," Hank says. His tone is suddenly brusque, as if Johan has asked a question to which he already knows the answer.

"But where would you go?"

"Wilmington. It's where I grew up. I have a couple of nephews there. And it's more affordable."

Wilmington, Delaware? Did anyone really live there?

"That's right."

Johan avoids looking at the calendar, lest someone notice. Then he gets up and walks about the floor to further throw off the trail those who have nothing better to do than rob him of all joy by taking away what little he has. Hank Farquist has come too close. While standing at the urinal in the men's room, Johan taps a tile on the wall five times. Five times. No more. No less. Tap tap tap tap tap with his index finger. Oh such happiness. A little tap for you, he whispers. And now a little tap for you. Then he five-taps another tile and another and another. Five tiles does he five-tap. Five. And then he taps still another. Six.

But now Hank Farquist has entered to stand over the urinal Johan has just left.

"By the way, how are you doing with that novel I typed onto a disk for you? Find a publisher yet? Have you become world-famous?"

"Which novel would that be?" How good to wash his hands in warm water.

"That novel about the men with big things in those subway bathrooms. Don't you remember that novel? The one in which the boy had gross feelings of inferiority about his intelligence? The one you asked me to transfer to a disk?"

"Sure. I remember."

"I kept a backup file of your novel for myself."

"What?"

"No what? You remember. You gave me the manuscript of your novel to place on a disk. You're an intelligent man. Your SAT scores are proof of that."

Hank has infected him with his venom. Hurtful, very hurtful. And the shame. A violation has taken place. Johan will have to deal with the emotional turmoil and his resentment with writing and prayer and meditation and sleep. So much can be left behind in sleep. Still, Hank arrived too late to witness him tapping the tiles, and even if Hank suspected that he had been tapping them, Hank wouldn't know *which* tiles he had tapped, or the number of taps or the order in which he tapped them. That is something, isn't it?

"Believe me, I've done everything in my power to induce him to stay, but he says his mind is made up. And I have to tell you that it makes me very sad that we should be losing him." Lurleen looks genuinely sad. She is not beyond human affection. Far from it. She recognizes her loneliness and her need for connection. In that moment her feelings for Hank are apparent.

"There are two reasons for me to leave. One, I simply can't afford to live here anymore, not in an apartment that goes at the market rate. The second is an absolute horror of growing old alone in New York City, where I have no family."

There, Hank has spoken, forcefully and with complete lucidity, in the resource room, where the farewell party is being held. And if he has been emphatic, it is clearly because he doesn't want staff to override his resolve.

But here comes Rhoda Bahr anyway. "Maybe there are cheap apartments available. Maybe you'll get lucky. Have you checked around and seen what's out there?" Always with the questions, this Rhoda Bahr.

Melvin Kleiner agrees. "Rhoda's right. You're too good a person for us to lose, and for New York City to lose. You should inquire," Melvin Kleiner says, so bright, so alert, so affirmative.

"What possesses you two to want to hold on? Stop with the snagging already. Hank is on the runway and taxiing for takeoff. Why not wish him safe travels?" Johan can't restrain himself, even after his resolve the day before to conceal his good fortune in learning that Hank Farquist is leaving.

"What is your problem? Why can't we say what we want to say?" Rhoda Bahr says.

"Go ahead. Say whatever comes into your head," Johan replies.

"I would say you're the one who says whatever comes into your head," Rhoda answers back.

"You've got to get off the tarmac. That's all. You've got to stop trying to bind him with your dinky ribbons of false affection. These office relationships can't really stand the light of day, at least the natural light of day. Don't you see? In here we're a phony-bologna family, exhibiting all its manifest dysfunction. But out on the street we're perfect strangers to each other, or just about. Everyone should be given the right to go off and die, if that's that they want to do."

"Rhoda's right. You're too sharp-edged," Melvin says.

"Just let people go," Johan says. "Just let them go. Let freedom ring."

"You're just jealous. Hank is a good man. That is a fact. He has real integrity, with qualities of character that simply shine forth. He is hardworking, helpful to a fault, quick to praise others, a model of tact and sensitivity. He always gives his best. There is a reason why so many people in the company like him. And he's intelligent, too. You just want him to leave because you are afraid he will get your job," Rhoda Bahr says.

"Ms. Tooth has spoken," Johan mumbles.

"What did you say to me? I have had it up to here with your abuse," Rhoda says, holding her hand at neck level.

"Oh, the passion that spring unleashes, even when spring it is not."

"That's what I mean about you, Johan. *Spring it is not.* You try to sound more intelligent than you are. The only phony-bologna around here is you. Again, stop with your abuse."

"Was I being abusive? I was just noting one of your best features."

"Stop it, I said. Just stop it."

"But why do you buy such shiny new teeth if you don't want people to notice them? That's like telling someone not to notice a gaudy imitation pearl necklace."

"Lurleen, make him go away. Just make him go away."

"I am working on it. Believe me, I am working on it," Lurleen says, her eyes like beads.

A windowless room with a big conference table and clunky chairs on rollers and on three walls, shelves to the ceiling stocked with books, brochures, pamphlets, all the printed materials the org has published through the years. Books on property management, strategic planning (with tactical planning always to follow), council performance assessment, outcomes measurement, corporate planning, diversity and pluralism, communications. Books for girls of all age levels. A history of the org, from its visionary founder Minerva Rowe to the present. And on the free wall a bar graph tracking all the projects that come into the department, Lurleen intent on showing how busy Publishing is. Resources for the dead and dying.

Stinky food, from some hovel in midtown Manhattan. Greasy egg rolls, MSG-saturated pork, chicken, and shrimp dishes. Peking duck. Vegetables bathed in cheap cooking oils. Glistening fare, all of it, cooked in haste by subsistence-wage men in soiled white garb with feces under their fingernails and now on offer on the conference room table in aluminum trays.

"Oh, heaven," Lurleen says.

"I'll say," Rhoda Bahr says.

"Good stuff," Alice Piccoli manages to say, catching the partially masticated food that drops from her mouth as she speaks.

Oh joy, that no cube is there to shield her from his vision as she continues her devouring. Her eyes fixed solely on the food now. Periodic breaks to wipe her mouth with a napkin and brush crumbs from her clothing. A few signature airings of her ghastly tongue, like a drop-down window on the computer. Then some further tongue action as she tries to dislodge particles stuck in her yellow teeth.

"What's the matter, Johan? Not hungry," Rhoda says.

"He eats like a bird, like that Philip Roth character in *Goodbye Columbus*," Melvin Kleiner says. "Actually, he eats like the abstemious soul that he is. He lives on hummus and pita bread and oranges."

"Rice cakes, actually. No more pita bread," Johan says. Once again he can only marvel at the garbage people place in their mouths.

"Yeah. I hear him," Alice says.

"How terrible for you," Johan replies.

"It's the only sound he ever makes."

"You make enough noise for the two of us."

"You and your smart mouth. You'll get yours," Alice Piccoli says.

"It's for sure you're going to get yours. You'll be fleeing the building this afternoon with shopping bags full of leftovers."

"I won't have this fighting. I won't. I want us to be one big happy family," Lurleen says, visibly upset. A reminder of the distress his mother would express over family conflicts.

The gathering is about the food. Simply a ritual to foster the illusion of closeness. All the gushy effusions notwithstanding, Hank seems to grow smaller as the hour moves on.

Rhoda hands Hank a gift from the department. He opens the envelope and extracts a card. "Oh, wonderful. A gift certificate. This is great. Wal-Mart is one of the first places I had been planning to head for," Hank says, manufacturing an enthusiasm that is not genuinely there.

"Melvin wanted to get you a subscription to *The Copyeditor's Corner,* but we talked him out of it. The thought of you suffering through a harsh winter sitting all alone in your apartment and reading about the series comma was unbearably depressing. Sort of like giving a plumber a set of wrenches on his retirement," Johan says. What he doesn't say is that union-busting, slave wages Wal-Mart, a big box in the middle of nowhere, is even more depressing.

But it isn't depressing to Lurleen. "My favorite store," she says. "Can't wait till we have one here in New York City. Not too long before we will." Whatever desecrates she can be counted on to embrace.

Not wanting to be present at Hank's departure, he has taken refuge in the Mid-Manhattan Library, where he has pulled from the shelf a tired-looking copy of the novel *Affliction,* by Russell Banks. A real writer. A writer who can compose a decent sentence and whose vast reserves of intellectual power allow him to construct complex fictional structures. One of the heavyweights, Russell Banks, like Philip Roth and Don DeLillo. He opens the book and the first paragraph is enough to pull him in. It sparks a sense of hope that he too can go forward with his own work, that he can put on the page all that is in his heart in a way that people will want to read. What folly, what foolish pride, to pursue a dream when you don't have the means to succeed and never will have. But what can he do with this life? No one wants him, and he wants no one. So at least let him have the consolation of words. Can he not have even that before he leaves the scene?

He is not back in his cube five minutes before Lurleen arrives.

"Why?" she says.

"Why what?"

"I said *why?*"

"And I said, *Why what?*"

"Why do you destroy everything? Why are you so dark as to not allow love to flourish?"

"Love?" he says.

"You drove Hank off. You made it impossible here for him with your intimidating ways. Always the sharp, nasty comment."

"I drove Mr. Chow Down, Mr. Twizzlers, out of here?"

"You see. Nasty, nasty, nasty."

"What's so nasty about the truth? It's just like you to try to get everyone on your side and then try to make me feel guilty when I stand up for myself. "

"You're so twisted."

"Right. And you're as straight as they come."

"I just came here to say I feel sad. This is a big loss for me. Can you never be kind?"

"You have opted for loneliness and prayed that God would convert it to aloneness in the best sense of the word. You are a train running on another track from that of others. Parallel yes, but apart. Recognize the consequences of your decision and where you are at with it."

"You are insane."

"Blunt, maybe, not insane. There are enough histrionics in the world. We don't have to add ours."

"You…." She begins to weep openly.

Dear God,

I have been gored by a bull and a bitch, Sir Flatulence and Ms. Tooth, and have no place to go but unto death. Last night I slept on the floor by the front door of my apartment, thinking I could capture the deliciousness of privacy in that spot. And those times I awoke, I tapped repeatedly—on the wall, on the floor, on books, on a nearby shelf. I have even begun tapping on myself, dear God. Five-tap on my left knee, five-tap on the back of my head. Even so, the world is putting me in my place. The socko plenty I received is well deserved. There is high-level odiousness in my nature that certain others inevitably discern. Ms. Tooth had it right: I try to be more intelligent than I am. My pride is endless. And as for Sir Flatulence, he has my number as well. I am on my way out. I am done.

Dear Hank,

Forgiveness will always be the key, of ourselves for sure and inevitably of others as well. Life is a battleground as well as a lover's lane. Fighting you does not mean I don't love you, and I'm sure that love will be restored in the sweet bye and bye. It had occurred to me that I should show my appreciation of our relationship over the years by taking you for lunch or even dinner. This would have been in addition to the party at the org. After all, you would be leaving not only the org but the city. How callous and heartless it would be not to. But when I tried to visualize the two of us breaking bread in a restaurant, all I could imagine was the mutual discomfort of two people who don't belong together. Frankly, it gave me a sense of satisfaction, as the days passed, not to act from this impulse to make more of our connection than it truly is and not to try to smooth over differences as if they didn't exist. My life has been about excess in ways I can't even explain, some misplaced sense of responsibility leading me to do more than the situation required, or at least to feel that I should. But now I have looked to the actions of others for guidance. Did Lurleen take you to a private lunch? Did The Vulture? Fat chance of her scavenger self ever doing that. But how painful not to reach out past the divide and share my love with you.

Late on a Saturday night on a stretch of Broadway in delicious darkness owing to the failure of a street light. An Indian vendor at the illuminated corner newsstand.

"Do you know you are holy?" Johan says.

"Holy, sir?"

"Holy, sir. Holy."

"What I can do for you, sir?"

"How many times I have seen you without seeing you, as now I do. You are like Edward Hopper's painting of the gas station and the attendant circa 1941. You glow with the purity of a quiet time gone by. The tree over there speaks to that and the old building. Don't leave, sir. Please do not leave. Please."

"I understand, sir, but please, sir, step aside. You are all right, sir? You want newspaper? Magazine? Candy?"

"No newspaper. No nothing. Just tap tap tap tap tap. That is all. Five taps."

"Taps, sir?"

"Tap, sir. Do you ever tap tap tap tap tap?"

"Do you want hospital, sir? Is that what you want?"

"Tap," Johan says. "Just tap."

"You heard the man. Step aside." It is Hank Farquist, with the Sunday *New York Times* under his arm.

"Why, Hank, you are heavy laden," Johan says.

"Not as heavy laden as you," Hank says, pushing past, with dollar bills in hand, and then speeds off.

A gallon bottle of water and a bag full of hastily purchased groceries at OrganicOnly. These are he toting. Some years before Hank had seen Johan in virtually this same location and Johan had not been alone but in the company of a beautiful woman. Never mind that at the movie theater she had confessed to being a coke addict struggling with her addiction and that a trip to the ladies' room had set off the most powerful urge to do a line or that two weeks later she left Johan for a man half his age. It is the thing of being seen with a beautiful woman, the cachet that attaches to you. But times have changed for Johan. Times have changed.

Isabel,

Tonight I saw *West Side Story*. In living color, as we used to say. I sat alone in my bedroom, with only the glow of the TV in the darkness, and wept—for my youth, for the passion I had known. I was fifteen and in love at the time of its release. I cried, seemingly from the depths of my soul, as Maria sang "When Love Comes So Strong." I suppose I was crying for the idea of love, the purity of it. I had it then, with Jane Thayer, and with Sarah Van Dine, and now with you. But for Lurleen I show no love. I show only a lacerating harshness. It appalls me to say this, but I believe she is in my heart, as I believe that I am in hers. But she is also a hole I must not fall into, a past I must not succumb to. I must not once again be a victim of my own kindness. The journey must continue. There is no turning back.

"Melvin, did I ever tell you about my ballroom dancing days? I could do it all. The foxtrot, the rumba, the cha cha, salsa. But what I really

took a shine to was the waltz. My box step was in a class by itself."
It is the afternoon of the next week, and any worries Johan might
have had about Lurleen are evidently unfounded. She is surviving
without Hank Farquist just fine.

"Poetry in motion, were you?"

"Oh, I was that, all right. Even won a lot of contests."

"You're full of surprises."

"I've got another one for you."

"What's that?"

"You're fired." Gale force laughter follows as she throws back
her head and continues as tears fill her eyes. "Your face, Melvin. It
turned white. You are priceless, my little joystick."

"Glad to be of service," Melvin says, causing another eruption
of laughter.

"Melvin, you are killing me. You're just too, too much."

"Whatever I can do to help."

"Stop, please. Have mercy. Oh, Lord."

"Knock knock," Margo Breeder-Fullsley says, in that little girl
voice as she stands at the door to Lurleen's office. "You wanted to
see me, but I could come back." In her arms she cradles two big
loose-leaf binders.

"No. You come on in, Margo. We have stuff to go over. I will see
you two boys later," Lurleen says.

"She's all yours," Melvin says to Margo, who responds by closing
the door to Lurleen's office with authority.

"Why don't you sit in on those meetings? You're important
here," Melvin says.

"Why does Lurleen call you joystick?" Johan replies.

"What's that supposed to mean?"

"What is calling us boys supposed to mean?" Melvin Kleiner
should watch his step, coming into the org. with his head back and
his chest out, as if he is a prince upon this earth.

"She's not entirely PC. So what? She's been good to me. Real
good. She gave me a job."

"Right."

"And she likes me. I can tell. You see, you and that woman who left, I keep forgetting her name…"

"Blanche. Blanche Givenchy."

"Right. The thing is, according to Lurleen, you weren't getting in there and challenging the writers, if that's what they can be called, to produce lapidary work. In fact, Alice told me that before Rhoda and I arrived, the editors here were really copy editors. They didn't really have the wherewithal to do the heavy lifting in order to create meaningful content. "

Melvin leans back in his orthopedic chair, his feet up on the cantilevered desk. The soles of his shoes are scuffed. He is not a careful dresser. Baggy pants. A wrinkled shirt. The lenses of his glasses need cleaning. And his face is poorly shaven. His mouth draws Johan's attention. It is unusually wide—a mouth designed for consumption.

"Well, if Lurleen says so, then it must be so."

"You seem to have a personal issue with Lurleen. Why is that?"

"Are we playing psychoanalyst?"

"Not at all. I'm just curious."

"What is that poster?" Johan asks. It shows a familiar face with an X through it.

"Our imbecilic president. That's who it is."

"Why imbecilic?"

"Because that's what he is. He's a silver spoon-fed rich boy mucking up this country."

"You don't care for him?"

"I detest him."

"Do you have a personal issue with him?"

"Insofar as he is ruining the country, yes, I have a personal issue with him."

"Insofar as Lurleen is ruining the department, yes, I have a personal issue with her."

"How is Lurleen ruining the department? Is she advancing the wealthy over the poor? Is she infringing on our constitutional liberties? Is she disfiguring the land with strip-mining practices that blow the tops off mountains?"

Johan's assertion sounds extravagant, now that he has stated it to someone else, even someone with the liberal or radical stripes of Melvin Kleiner, judging from the "Impeach Bush" poster on the cubicle wall.

"She leaves a degraded environment wherever she goes. She has the heart and soul of a strip miner." Does he not know who he is talking to? What can he hope to accomplish with such extravagant statements but a quick exit from the org? And yet a kind of helplessness has led him to this place.

"So she's blowing the top off mountains, plundering the treasure within, and then moving on?"

"Who's blowing the top off what mountain?" Lurleen has appeared at the entrance to Melvin's cubicle. Her sweaty face shows a mischievous smile.

"Johan and I have taken a break from the demands of the workday to discuss energy issues and the environment, including the disfiguring scar on the land that strip mining leaves. In fact, he was just comparing you with such folks," Melvin says.

"Strip mining companies do not disfigure the land. They provide an efficient means to meet the country's energy needs. And their operating procedures, when completed, are such that the natural beauty of the sites are preserved. Everybody in the country knows that. You just have a pocket of ignorance here on the East Coast fostered by a campaign of disinformation."

Lurleen's dismissal triggers a feeling of pain in Johan that is almost too much to bear. It is not right to demonize. He is aware of that tendency in himself, but her assertion is further proof of her destructive bent. She belongs to a movement of deformers who now control the levers of power. People with a format. People who meet in some secret place and whose lives are informed by a fixed need for repression and revenge. It is a fear rooted in his childhood and that Pentecostal church he was made to attend. It is as if they have come back, only now they have power, and the words "Jesus" and "hate" exist side by side. People who would ban the sun if they only could and drain the oceans.

"Well, that takes care of that. Thank you for setting the record straight," Johan says.

As if she hasn't heard him, she says, "Melvin, I have need of you. Come with me to my office." Her smile is now gone.

I have need of you, Johan says to himself. *I have need of you.*

"Oh, here's Johan, Let's ask him. After all, he has only been here a gazillion years. Right, Johan?" Rhoda Bahr says. He has entered the resource room seeking an old annual report for a project he is working on.

"Only a gazillion?" Johan asks.

"Well, you have to admit, Johan, you have been here an abnormally long time."

"Abnormally?" Pulling words from her sentences like dead fish to hold under her nose.

"How many years have you been here, Johan? Twenty?"

"You have something against longevity?"

"Who stays in a job twenty years?"

"Maybe people who like their jobs or need their jobs?"

"Or maybe people who are just afraid to move on?" Has this anger that informs her barbed words always been there? Is there a deficiency in the love department? No one to touch or hold her? What possesses a woman to come to a new place and decide that a longtime staffer should depart? People are ugly, deformed, insane. He includes himself at times.

"I have to say I don't enjoy working with you on the style guide committee," Melvin says.

"There are some in this building who would say the same about you."

"You shouldn't say things like that," Melvin says quietly.

"You shouldn't either."

Johan has hurt Melvin. He did show himself in a bad light in the style guide meeting, getting all exercised about what? Abbreviations of states. Is it N.Mex or NM? Ariz. or AZ? Calif. or CA? Holding the line against the newer arrivals Melvin and Rhoda, and their supporters, Alice Piccoli and Hank Farquist, and resenting Mary Terezzi for her neutrality. Advocating as if his life depends on it, as if they will drive him into the sea if he doesn't take a stand. Do they not see the ugliness of these all caps abbreviations. Sure, they have their place—on letters and packages and mailing lists and tabular matter, but for God's sake, not in text copy. Do they not read the style guides? Melvin saying, "The style guide is not the final word. We are."

"Ignorance is the final word?"

Ultimately there was a grudging agreement to conform with accepted usage, but feelings were bruised by Johan's vehement defense.

Melvin accepts Johan's apology for speaking as he did. Even so, he cannot talk to Johan. Not for a while at least. He is not used to this level of exchange and cannot easily come back from such an assault. He is not everything you would think, even with his chest sticking out and his head back and that powerful body moving as it does with seeming effortlessness on a cushion of air. He has his vulnerabilities.

So, when Johan, after spending the lunch hour in Bryant Park on a gloriously sunny day, sees Melvin Kleiner coming out of the Taste Sensation Deli on Fortieth Street, he runs up to him. Like a big, sloppy, but affectionate dog he comes to Melvin, only he is not a dog that Melvin can be next to now, not to speak to or to pet.

"I'm still not ready to talk to you. I'm sorry," says Melvin, and walks away.

Isabel,

This is not the crime of the century. Melvin Kleiner and Rhoda Bahr may be Lurleen's darlings, but to see Melvin kissing Lurleen's butt every day. Oh, the level of cravenness a man can descend to when he is of woman born and to woman he remains umbilically tied. Did Melvin Kleiner ever think to apologize for the lack of respect they have shown me? Is that what I should do, spend my work life cowering in my cubicle as the Obese One and the Prince of Chutzpah and Fang, she who drips venom from her snazzy teeth, have their way with me? I have been weaned from that world into what? The strength to walk alone and sleep alone and love alone and be connected to the universe alone. Is this not strength? And is it not bearing witness to deformity to see the crippled ones such as Melvin Kleiner who live their lives as tiny satellites orbiting the consuming sun that such as Lurleen surely are?

"Don't do that again," Zed says. To the farthest corners of Johan's universe do Zed's words travel. His every pore and cell do they saturate with their laconic power. He has reported to Zed his abuse of Melvin Kleiner. And though Johan wants to say, in response, Don't make it more than it is, don't make a peccadillo into a federal offense, don't drop me deeper in the hole I'm already in, don't punish me for not being perfect, he holds his tongue. It's that way when Zed has spoken, as if Zed has an understanding, an empathic range, that he, Johan, lacks.

Melvin,

We are often, unfortunately, leaning to our own understanding. This came to me as I was walking and sounding a low, mournful *whoo whoo* train whistle, for imagine the deliciousness of trains where now only vehicular traffic flows. We have to understand what the org is, and our relationship to it. Though we are not working with professional writers, that is no cause to disrespect them. They have, after all, built the house. All you can do is decorate and tidy it up a bit. You are assisting them, not vice versa. You must remember to leave your own aspiration at the door when you enter the org. Long ago I worked for a man named Marg. It was my first job in publishing. He was a senior editor and had a writer under contract, a reviewer for the *New York Times* with a prolix style. The author lived in his words, fashioning long, complex sentences, as if he were Faulkner in a critic's guise. So one day Marg says to me, 'Shorten those sentences.' And I did as he commanded, chopping the sentences apart. Some weeks later the writer called. He spoke with the voice of a heartsick old man. Who was the perpetrator of this assault on his manuscript? he inquired. I feigned ignorance and said Mr. Marg would get back to him. In fact, I learned everything in that brief exchange— respect was due an author, and it is for an editor to tread carefully. Do not rampage, Melvin Kleiner. Do not be the bull in the china shop.

"Is that your wife?" Johan says to Melvin some weeks later, when Melvin's hurt has eased sufficient that he can once again engage with Johan. An 8 x 10 photo of a woman who appears to be close in age to Melvin is tacked to the partition.

"My one and only. We met at the ashram."

"What ashram would that be?"

"Acres of Bliss. I was Guru Mahabata's right-hand man for over twenty years. I helped him build the place."

"Guru Mahabata?"

"I was in graduate school and floundering. One day a roommate invited me to a lecture being given by a spiritual master. Immediately I felt some desire within me to break from the academic mold in which I had lived my whole life. At the gathering were bearded poets; hippies; wife-beaters; drug addicts and alcoholics; women seeking safe passage out of lives that karmic forces had made for them. Only the guru was missing. And when he finally arrived, he changed my life."

"How was that?"

"He lightly trailed a peacock feather up my spine and I experienced this surge of energy through what I now know are my chakras. For days afterward, I was in another world. His world."

"What did he look like, this guru?"

"Dark, powerful, barefoot. He often dressed only in a loincloth."

"What happened after that?"

"He said I had come for a reason, and told me to work with him to build a spiritual community. And so I did, for the next twenty years. I left graduate school and physically helped to build the ashram here in New York City and the center up in Wappinger Falls, New York."

"And why aren't you still there?"

"Her," he said, nodding toward the photo.

Isabel,

There are trips I have never taken. Even now the railroad tracks down in Riverside Park call to me, as they have the capacity to spark my greatest joy. They are some kind of default setting in my mind, though no sensible person would think that there is any future in riding the rails, if in fact you still could, with so many flatbed cars carrying containerized cargo and a dwindling stock of boxcars or gondola cars in which to seek refuge. And now Amtrak passenger trains fly over the Hudson River line. But if I were to be my own train, my journey along the rails would be a statement of departure from the world. The world has its trains, and I am my very own train. Where I go, my train goes also, and vice versa. And once out of the dangerous environment of the tunnel underneath Riverside Park and into the open, I could expand my life beyond the city lim-its. I could sit with my deceased brother, Luke, on that hill sloping down to the tracks along a nice stretch of straightaway. And if contemplation of the eternity of that realm he has crossed into becomes too much to bear while physically present at his burial site and the weight of my aloneness is driven home to me, eliciting a cry of pain from the depth of my being, I could nevertheless rally and hang tough all the way up to Rhinecliff and then head east along all the roads I have left behind and see who now lives in the house I shared with you but which I left on the eve of the first Gulf War. A family would be there now. They would be happy. I would have no part to play in their lives. I would be just another creature of displacement forced by my fatigue to lie down in the dewy grass. Would I tell them that, only the week before my departure, I was applying a coat of cardinal red paint to the trim of the door of the apartment above the garage while the drums of war were beating, the president of the United States of America preparing to spank the ruler of Iraq and spank him hard? Our president had drawn a line in Arabian sand and said the men of Iraq must not cross it, and then, when they did cross it, that they would have to pull back. Our president was saying that Operation Crush and Compact was coming and coming hard. Yes, I could tell them that, and that I fell into the habit of listening to the radio incessantly and that the station I turned to offered not mellow jazz or the thrill of hard rock but 1010 WINS, yes 1010 WINS, all news all the time. I would explain to the startled owners that I relied on these radio broadcasters to provide comfort even as they inspired fear. How is a man to get better who feasts on the insanity sandwiches of the world? I would ask. And this family would have no answer for me, of course, for I would appear sad in their eyes, as is anyone who has only his past to offer because there is no present ground to stand on. And I would say, no no no, you don't understand, love was here, love stood on this ground, the love that I felt requires that this place become a shrine. And still would they stare, and maybe they would invite me to sit down for a cup of tea, though just as likely they might call the police, for they had children whose laughter filled the air as they romped about in a nearby field. Or could I tell them that I had gone around back and climbed a twelve-foot ladder to paint the trim around the windows in an attempt to preserve the weathered wood? Could I tell them that I did these chores slowly, tentatively, unsure of myself as I always was when it came to the manly task of maintaining the property, that in some sense, I was still looking to my older brother to set up the Lionel trains so I could watch them? Sure I could. And I could tell them about the chainsaw that I purchased and the hours I spent with its whine in my ears as I cut the trunks and branches of fallen trees for firewood and of my dream of a sufficient supply for the oncoming winter. I could share my plan for energy efficiency to keep down the high cost of the electric baseboard heat and how I would pitch every last scrap of wood into the fire, except for that ugly treated wood, and watch as the flames reduced even the thickest log to ash. How satisfying to see the wood burn and burn. A man could spend his whole life there by the fire, just watching. A man needed nothing more than the flames quietly licking the logs, and then the fire's roar when it began more and more to have its way, disappearing the things it touched. Fire was pure, much purer than anything else in this world. Everyone has a time of hope and promise, and I could tell them of the one year when doors that had been closed suddenly opened—how out of the blue an editor called and told you, while I was at work, that her magazine would be publishing my story, the one I thought was no good when months passed without hearing from the magazine, the way all of them were no good, a realization that led me to begin carving up the story before the editor reached out, because I was so sure it was just another failure, the way everything I wrote turned out to be. A forty-page story, and she changed not a word. And then there were the other magazines that returned not my stories in those manila self-addressed stamped envelopes but who wrote me letters saying my stories had been accepted for publication, the one editor saying my writing was good and more than good, it was extraordinary. And then there was the established author who took a liking to my novel at the workshop I enrolled in, saying to me that I didn't belong there, that I had to understand that no workshop would ever be able to help me, given the point to which I had developed, and that I would have to go off and do my own work. But before I would tell them all that or somewhere in the middle of telling them all that or after telling them all that I would say that this author who had taken me under her wing sat me down with my novel and marked the pages that needed changes and gave me pointers for shaping it and then sent me off to do the rest, and with the names of several agents. And I would tell them how, in this time, I gained some insight into the demon that the will could be and what the need for *more* could do to a human being, how a letter came from one of these editors saying that my story had been entered in a literary competition and that it won, hands down. And I would say how I read between the lines that the editors had wanted someone else to win the prize, some woman they had been cultivating and grooming and whom they conferred with over every one of her precious little words, only to have this goof who knew no one awarded the prize by the judge, an outsider (they would not make that mistake again) because my story had more power and immediacy than all the others combined. But I would only tell them that by way of saying something else, that within a half hour of the good news a fire was burning in my belly and melting down my mind that this piddling amount of recognition should come to me when the great work, the work that sang its way off the pages and into the universe, should be ignored so that my happiness was as nothing, it was trampled in the agony of needing more, more than I presently had or ever could have. I saw in that moment the nature of the insatiable demon within. I saw that the success I did not have was simply another illusion if I thought it would bring me any peace. It was an insight I tried to hold onto, I would tell them, but the will was ferocious. I would tell them that I wanted and needed the things of this life, mainly a professional identity, like a good suit of clothes, so I could say to the world, This is who I am. I am a writer,—yes, a writer. I would no longer have to mumble that I worked for GoAN and witness their stares of incomprehension and misunderstanding and disappointment that a man who looked important should fall so short of their expectations. And when they asked, "Do you publish?" I could say yes, and doors would instantly open to me. Isabel, by then I was gone from the loft, following your ejection of me. I would tell these homeowners how I packed up my novel with a cover letter listing my handful of publishing credits and sent it off to agents, who responded that the work would be a tough sell, didn't have the needed commercial appeal, was too literary. And I would tell them that when I had exhausted the possibilities of mainstream publishing, I then turned to the small publishers and that one wrote me a long, glowing letter extolling the virtues of the novel and how there was a definite and necessary place for it in American literature, but there were financial constraints, he was sorry to report, that compelled him to make the hard decision to forego publishing the work. Still, he was sure the work would find its place in the end; I was too good a writer not to find an audience. Like a knife to my heart the letter was, I would say to them. Better a boilerplate rejection. And tell them too of an editor at one of the small press magazines who had felt the need to say to me that he alone of the editorial staff voted against taking one of my stories, as if he delighted in thwarting me. And, maybe I would tell them that a few years later that same editor who declined my novel with great apologies came to town on a book tour. There it was, an announcement in one of the local newspapers. Bartley Brine would be reading at the Barnes and Noble on east Eighty-sixth Street from his radiant first book of poems, *Methusaleh's Hoary Children*. I wasn't obliged to show up; no one in his right mind could say I was. And yet my inner guide said it was the dharmic thing to do. A failure to attend would mean surrender to my resentment and competitiveness. And though I would be responding to the situation from my higher self, it might also be an opportunity to introduce myself to Bartley Brine face to face. Maybe we could sit down over a cup of joe and develop a friendship. Maybe, just maybe, Bartley Brine remembered my novel and the effusive letter he had written in praise of it. I hadn't knocked on Bartley Brine's door since. I had not been an importuning pest. No, I had taken Bartley Brine's "close but no cigar letter" for what it was, and Bartley Brine's respect for me would only have grown for not having pursued him. But Isabel, you and I both know I would have to tell these occupants of the house that nothing of the kind happened. Yes, Bartley Brine was there, a chunky fellow staring out through formidable horn-rimmed glasses at his audience. He came across as disappointingly cold when I introduced myself and tried to refresh his memory. A forced smile appeared on his face and he hurriedly said, "Well, best of luck to you," before moving away with a pretty blond woman half his age. Was it not clear now that, in a moment of generosity, Bartley Brine had composed the letter to me and likely wrote many such letters to would-be authors? Still, Isabel, showing up and introducing myself to Bartley Brine and receiving his response now allowed me to bring some closure to that episode. I would tell these homeowners how I walked out into the street alone as I was always walking out into the street alone, believing that my relationships with people were more than they were. The point is that I would try to confer some respectability on myself with this offering to these people. They would come to see that I was the literary equivalent of Marlon Brando in the back of that car, telling his older brother that he could have been a contender instead of a chump with a one-way ticket to Palookaville. Not that my brother should have looked after me but that the world should have done just that and how life offered cruel blows—something like that would I say. I would tell them of the literary novel competition that I had entered when I had exhausted the commercial publishers. The contest was sponsored by a publishing company in the Midwest devoted to mid-list books, the kind that publishers might support in years past before the advent of the mega-book. A mid-list might include, for example, a first novel with a modest print run that would gain for the new author a growing following with each succeeding novel. And if I won the competition, the company would sign me to a standard contract with a royalty clause and publish my novel and I would be on my way. And I would tell this family occupying the house where we had lived part-time of the letter I received weeks later, informing me that my novel was one of four selected from over one thousand submissions as a finalist for the prize. And I would tell them that as soon as I read the contents of the letter, I sensed that I would not be the one and that the sole purpose of the letter was to raise my hopes only to thwart me. There was rain coming down the day I received the letter, rain strafing the pavement and streaking the dirty window of the apartment I had sublet and telling me no good could come from this letter. Because it was a cold rain, the kind that got into your bones and laughed at you and all your attempts at shelter, saying that sooner or later it would wash away your home and give you such a soaking that your teeth would chatter and your knees would knock and rheumatic fever would bring you close to death. And it rained for all the days that passed, and when the follow-up letter came, it had the dampness from the rain on it and was cold and soggy to the touch. The letter didn't say, "Ha ha, we fooled you." It didn't say that at all. It said, "We regret to inform you, you with such meager bones…."

Melvin Kleiner saying, a week later, "My father was a professional boxer turned labor organizer. He gained a reputation as a thumper, and maybe he needed that physical dimension to survive and rise to the top in the rough world of union labor. That wasn't the library crowd he was rubbing shoulders with. A lot of the guys he dealt with carried guns. Everybody in Camden knew my father—the shop stewards and trolley drivers, the butchers and the truckers and the railroad workers. Either workers organized or they fell prey to the bosses, who would simply use and discard them; that was his simple philosophy. And the weapon they had was the strike, with which they could bring management low."

"Thumper. I like that word. Sounds just like what it is."

"Onomatopoeia."

"Yes."

"Was your father a thumper?"

"Not in the ring he wasn't."

They are seated on wire chairs on the plaza outside the building, away from the quarantined smokers by the revolving door.

Two honks of a car horn draw their attention to a four-door sedan parked curbside.

"That's Eliana," Melvin says, hurrying toward the car with the broom and mop and bucket and other domestic items he has purchased at the Odd Lot discount store on a stretch of increasingly tacky Fifth Avenue, right next door to the tourist shop with "I Love New York" T-shirts and nearby stores with laptops and other electronic doodads owned by urban banditos who prey on the gullible and whose only real purpose is to suction big bills from your wallet.

Johan pauses, startled and annoyed by the abrupt abandonment, then trails slowly after Melvin, who by now is loading up the back seat of the car, a shiny new red Nissan. The woman behind the wheel is somber, tense, with Brillo hair and a turned down mouth. She remains rigid in her seat as Melvin deposits the goods.

"You've got Melvin well trained," Johan says, leaning down. What surprise can there be that Melvin is an uxorious husband, given his tendencies with Lurleen?

Sphinx-like, Eliana continues to look straight ahead.

He has come to her from a laughing place that says, "Oh yes, I was there. I too played that little game of man and wife, but now I am too strong, too advanced, too *ambitious,* for that." And yet his assertion has a suspicious sound, as if he is speaking from a place of weird aloneness while men and women go about their lives hand in hand and sharing the same bed. What kind of truth is it that keeps a person alone?

"This is my friend Johan," Melvin says, after slamming the trunk of the car.

"I'm late," she says, and drives off.

"We just bought this house upstate. Eliana's nervous about it."

"Where upstate?" Johan hears himself say.

"Dutchess County. Eliana is uptight about living in the city. Something bad is going to happen here, she says."

"Bad how?"

"Dirty bombs. An uninhabitable wasteland."

"In a real hurry to get out of Dodge and leave the rest of us saps behind, is she?"

"I didn't say that."

Johan imagines her in panicky flight from the madness, maneuvering the long, tight street, past the trucks and vans, the office workers streaming from the boxy towers and others making their shopping pilgrimage to Macy's and the other retail venues down at Herald Square. He sees her cutting west on once seedy Forty-second Street, banked with high rises where decrepit movie theaters once stood with marquees overhanging the sidewalk. Onto the West Side Highway she eases, the GW Bridge far in the distance a talisman her eye can focus on, the promise of green coming closer as she speeds over the 225th Street Bridge and onto the Saw Mill and Taconic Parkways, with their tight curves.

"What she's running from she's running toward?" Johan asks.

"What?"

"It's something I heard."

"I like that. "

"Rural areas are not free of danger. There's such a thing as country crime. We've known that since the Clutter family."

"Who is the Clutter family?'

"You never read *In Cold Blood?*"

"The Truman Capote book?"

"Yeah. The family slaughtered by those drifters. Anyway, there's been terrorism in this city going way back. Like the subway back in the 1950s. You had to duck if you were tall not to get your head taken off by those overhead fans. But the fans were nothing next to the possibility of a bomb silently ticking under a rattan seat and the fear of having your legs blown off at the knees. Don't you remember the Mad Bomber?"

"Not really."

"George Metesky? The disgruntled Con Ed worker? It took sixteen years for the police to catch the guy. And in the 1970s, there was the FALN. And then the Weather Underground."

"Not my thing," Melvin says.

"I can relate to your wife. Back in my second marriage, we had a place upstate. This feeling of panic would come over me that racial violence would break out all over the city. I would picture myself racing to escape from Manhattan to a community of whiteness, and that a mob of tough young Blacks would intercept me, drag me from my car, and beat me close to death."

"A community of whiteness?"

"Well, the city wasn't safe. That was the general perception. Not like it is now. But probably the fear went back to childhood and things I saw."

"What things?"

"Racial fights. Beatings. The uncontrollable rage some seemed to have. It created an unreasoning fear in me. Probably it blended with the threat of annihilation by my father. Those bicycle caravans of Black kids from Harlem. The way they brought terror to the neighborhood with their violence."

"That's too bad."

"Does it work, trying to overcome fear by running away?"

"Sometimes. Flight is a primal instinct for survival. Animals flee from a burning forest. Human beings flee a burning building."

"But the city is not on fire."

"This is true."

"I try to be where my feet are."

"Are you suggesting that my wife isn't?"

"I guess it sounds like that." He feels older than Eliana and older than Melvin. He has been in that married life of intimate sharing and country homes and the empowerment and privilege of money. He remembers when the org was just a place to hang out for the day but his real life was elsewhere. But the elsewhere has fallen away, as everything is falling away, except for the fact that he is where his feet are and he must love the life he has and dispel that sense of separation.

"Actually, it's not only fear with Eliana. We have a co-op apartment on East Eighty-sixth Street, but it's not enough for us. We need both worlds. Or at least Eliana says she does."

"How do you afford two homes and a car? Except for the upper echelon, the org pays modest salaries."

"Eliana's amazing. She knows how to construct deals and see them through. Her mind is really something."

"What exactly does she do?"

"She's an investment counselor."

"You remind me of myself."

"How's that?"

"The way you sing the praises of women."

"There's something wrong with singing the praises of women?"

"There doesn't have to be."

As they head back inside, they get out their wallets, which contain the ID cards they must swipe. One after another, several women flop their huge bags onto the scanner. One has to reposition hers when the light won't flash green. She sighs, begins an excavation. Finds her wallet, in which the pass is buried. Gets the green light. Jeanine Juddster doesn't have a bag. She doesn't have a wallet either. No scan. No nothing. Just walks on through only to be called back by Denagthon Diapagore, the security guard, who sits on a stool by the scanner at the entrance to the bank of elevators.

Jeanine Juddster returns, one hand in her pants suit pocket, her trademark pose.

"Do you know who I am?"

"Don't matter none if I do, ma'am. You still need to show your card."

"I left my card upstairs."

"Then you got to go to the concierge desk and get yourself a pass."

"Do you know what I do?"

"No, ma'am. I can't say that I do."

"I am an important person in the org."

"If you say so, then it must be true."

"What is your name?"

"What you want my name for, ma'am?"

"I will ask the questions here."

"So you say. Now you just go to that concierge desk and tell them who you are and then you can come back here with a pass so I can know who you are."

She turns silently, because words are not to be wasted on those she considers the ignorant and obtuse and, yes, walks with one hand in her pocket the way that in another time the fathers of Billy Baines and Johnny Joe, walked with their hand in their pocket, the way all the powerful—in their minds—walk with one hand in their pocket. And returns a minute later with her pass, holding it gingerly between two fingers away from her as if it is something contaminating she doesn't want too close to her person.

Isabel,

I just witnessed a spat involving the security guard Denagthon Diapagore, who may have been led to create a new identity so he could be free of the hands of whiteness seeking to appropriate him. Denagthon was simply at his station, perched on his stool, and reading his Bible on the slant surface of the high table at the entrance to the elevators. He had no mind to hurt anyone or anything when Jeanine Juddster happened by to demonstrate the true nature of the org, for is this not a place for women to feel important and for men to feel less important? Not that there is anything wrong with that. Where is it written that men have to have power over women? Would the world be worse off if women ruled and men were placed in a position of subservience? In fact, what higher function can a man have than to serve a woman of full integrity? But Jeanine Juddster falls short of that standard. She shows that deficiency by walking with that hand in her pocket. And the words she uttered were a match for the face she wears.

Turning to Johan and Melvin, Jeanine Juddster says, "I guess this is how people spend their time who don't have anything to do."

Johan cannot contain himself. "Maybe it is you who has nothing to do. Leave the man alone. Just leave him alone."

"I will deal with you," Jeanine Juddster says.

When they arrive at their floor, Johan says to Melvin, "Now do you understand what is going on? Well, do you?"

"What I see is your anger in response to an arrogant woman."

"And do you know what the telltale sign of true arrogance is?"

"Tell me."

"Have you not seen that Jeanine Juddster walks with one hand in her pocket, thinking she is number one in the entire universe?"

"The things you say."

Chapter 27

Isabel,

A word about the Oiseau. Yes, her, the woman I could never call by her given name. And well you might ask why I couldn't and was I being disrespectful? The answer is no. The mere thought of her summoned a rush of affection that I could not directly inflict on the woman. Perhaps I should have called her The Sun, as she was the bright light in that time. In her had I invested my hope for us. And so I call her the Oiseau, though never to her face, and that is no hanging crime. And what a big, big bird she is, and all-seeing, and yes, with that weight that has tested the limbs on many a tree. In any case, I have gone back to her, some years after we saw her together. And what I find is a woman worn down by the daily round.

I am losing track of time. The years have begun to blur. It is no longer the months flying off the calendar, as in those old movies, but the calendar itself flying away.

Apropos the Oiseau, I read a book recently, and though I have forgotten the title and the author's name, he recounts a profound malaise he experienced as a young man. Confronted with what he perceived to be the unappealing choices this society offered him on his graduation from an excellent college, he traveled to the Far East, where he apprenticed among Buddhist monks in Thailand. When he reappeared in America some years later, he wore the saffron robe that had become the staple of his wardrobe before the incongruity of his garb in the big cities and small towns of America became apparent to him. He came to understand that he would have to adapt not only the dress code of the spiritual East to the materialistic West but also the teachings themselves. And so, through the years, he has sought to fuse the practices of Buddhism with psychotherapy, the inexact science of the mind. Most instructive for me was the author saying that people who have been practicing meditation for a long time inevitably turn to psychotherapy, as they find that they need to talk. The image came to me of William Shawn, in *My Dinner with Andre,* conversing intensely with his friend as if his life depended on it—because it did. Whether Shawn himself is or was a meditator, I have no idea.

Isabel, I have begun to feel that too much is eluding me and the lights are not turned fully on. I sit in my cube, where my phone does not ring the entire day, and then I go home, where the phone messages, if any, are few. Other than you, there are no dinner companions. I am recognizing my own aloneness. Am I too proud to admit to loneliness as well?

But there is the matter of Zed, who is not partial to psychotherapy. He thinks these practitioners have some of the sickest egos in the Western world. Zed has the capacity to figure things out on his own. His lights are always turned on. Not that Zed is only one way. Zed goes one way, and then he goes another way. But whatever way Zed goes—whether he zigs or he zags—I inevitably follow. And that is the point. On this matter I did not want to go with Zed. I wanted to go with myself. Like William Shawn in *My Dinner with Andre,* I want to talk and talk. I want to get to the bottom of something that I can't see on my own.

I see my older sister Rachel in those mismatched clothes from the Goodwill bag walking alone in Riverside Park or sitting by herself or eating powdered doughnuts with her coffee in the old Chock Full O' Nuts on One Hundred Sixteenth Street and Broadway. I see the severity of her mind, a mind that allowed room for God but not for people, and that led her into that place of solitude. And I see myself as somewhat similar to her.

But it is not really about Zed or about Rachel. It is you, as it has always been you, Isabel. It is what Dr. Tobin meant when he said my internal wiring leads back to you. And yet, recently, I feel that you are not quite seeing me. Is some slow withdrawal underway? Operation Separation? Years ago, when I came back into your life you were still drinking, although in a measured way I had never achieved. Two vodka and tonics and you were done. The personality change was subtle and yet there. You would become animated. Alcohol clearly lifted your spirits. Nothing wrong with that. But I would become afraid. Alcohol had taken you away from me, if only temporarily. You were there without being there.

It is only this. You forgot my birthday. And if I had not reminded you, you would never have known that you forgot. We had always made a point of paying attention to my natal day and yours. I tried to let the oversight go, which Zed encouraged me to do. "So she forgot your birthday. What's the big deal?" He himself gave his own no special attention. But I had not reached the place where Zed was. It meant nothing to me if others didn't fuss over me on this day, but it was painful to see that it was not in your consciousness either. And yet it wasn't as if there were no extenuating circumstances. You had gone away, something you rarely do, and only returned from Cuba the week before the actual day. You had visited the island of the bearded patriarch in his drab fatigues, a man in love with the sound of his own voice, the whole island held captive by a mad father sitting at the head of the table and unable to zip it. The trip was organized by Maude and some of her friends, and you were invited along. A person has to be packing the goods to be part of some circles, and you certainly are. You could easily hold your own with the gifted professionals in the group. You were only in Havana a few days when word came to you that the planes had flown into the towers, and so, how can I fault you if my birthday was lost in the trauma of the inferno that resulted.

When I was still a child, a burly man in the service of evil took a room in my family's building. What I remember about this dark soul was his unsmiling face and eyes that stared at you menacingly through thick lenses. The day following his arrival did the fires begin, the alarm bells sending waves of fear through all the tenants. Rags were set ablaze outside the door of a tenant who, it turned out, had spurned his request for a dinner date. It took a firetruck ladder raised to her fourth floor window to rescue her from the smoke and flames. When we are turned away from love, Isabel, we are turned away from life. Mr. Arthur Morrell, from north of the border, was never arrested for his crimes, arson being exceedingly difficult to prove, and yet when he left the building, the fires ceased.

Within a year or two, there were more fires, only now it was not Mr. Arthur Morrell setting them, nor were they of the life-threatening kind. No, a match would be set to a shower curtain or newspapers would be set ablaze in the tub in the public bathroom, only this time the perpetrator did not go free. Ms. Lydia Gawaltney, in room 6D4, was taken into custody and quickly confessed, through her sobs and tears, that she had in fact been the one, but did anyone on God's green earth know how lonely she was, with no one to talk to and no family to turn to? Could no one understand what it meant to her to have the big, brave firemen on the premises and all the tenants out on the landing in a buzz of speculation and excitement, of which she could be a part and not have to be so shut off by herself? Could they not understand?

Isabel, there is no use saying Osama Bin Laden was lonely and that he had a crying need in his heart for attention, not when a man has reached such a level of detachment from the value of human life. What can we say of him but that he was Charles Manson with a trust fund. Is there anything else to know?

Which brings us to September 11. Is it possible that I, like Ms. Lydia Gawaltney, had been lonely too long? Here I tread on dangerous ground in saying that if I am not to dwell in the domain of the dinky, then honesty must prevail, even at the risk of extermination by the posse of the self-righteous. When I heard that morning from the concierge at my place of work of a plane slamming into the World Trade Center, I assumed it was a small aircraft. My mind was unable to conceive of it being anything more. And yet some part of me, like Lydia Gawaltney, wanted a heightened drama that would create a community all around me.

Jane Fallows, our CEO, was on the scene. We turned to her, as ducklings to their mother. She had been the head of counterintelligence in her military career and knew a formidable amount about how terrorists think. So she informed us. GoAN was not on their radar, she went on to say.

"What about the Empire State Building? Won't that be on the agenda of these maniacs," Blanche Givenchy said, imagining, along with the rest of us, that nearby colossus of steel and concrete crashing down in a huge pile of smoldering rubble. Blanche Givenchy was a lover of life. She knew when insanity had been unleashed upon the land. But Jane Fallows held her ground. She said the safest place in New York City was right where we were and that we should stay there in the building for the day. People come and go, Isabel, their heroics unrecorded, and that's how it was with Jane Fallows. She had a soundtrack going in her head. She wanted to save us as she wanted to save the org. It was all understandable. It was clear that she was seeking to come out of her coldness, and she had the idea, as many did, that the inferno the terrorists had precipitated could be her moment to shine and wear the hero's mantle.

The TV was going in the resource room. All that dark smoke pouring out of the massive structure and the orange flames amid all that blackness. From the street the constant wail of the fire engines and the police emergency vehicles. Surely an exercise in futility.

Fiona Beasley stood by the TV, and gasped as a section of one tower gave way, like a chunk of a burning log breaking off and settling with a soft thud. Only now were we realizing the magnitude of the disaster. My pride was at work. I would not be a captive of the media, as Fiona and the rest of them were. I understood its game: infect us with fear with its reportage and make us reliant on further newscasts as the answer. She would do it all that day—go to CNN and the *New York Times* online—and listen for more and more *late-breaking developments.* And so I sat at my computer, feigning concentration on my work. Better that than staring in a trance at the inferno two miles south.

Recognizing my absurd posturing, I would return to the resource room. "God, my investment firm is in that building," I heard Fiona exclaim, but you must not think that Fiona was a callous soul. When the Bosnian Serbs were being heinous toward their Muslim population, Fiona was outraged that no intervention was launched to stop the massacres. And she was no less livid when O. J. Simpson was acquitted for the crimes he was alleged to have committed.

At the same time, Fiona's money was her life's blood. She had an accountant. She had her figures. She had a certain level to reach before she could secure a coop and say to the org, "I Fugazy Motor Lodge all of you. No more will you instill terror in me that I could be out of a job. No longer do I have to kiss your royal asses." For Fiona Beasley had her finish line, just as I did. A man was seen on the screen fleeing the remaining tower. Long lines of traumatized office workers streaming up the West Side Highway as those trapped inside jumped to their deaths, and I go on about Fiona Beasley, perversely forsaking her talent for mathematics and art appreciation and instead devoting herself to the org newsletters when writing was not her forte. Isabel, Fiona fathomed the mysteries of pi more than 98 percent of the people on this planet, and yet the proper function of the colon and semicolon eluded her. About the restrictive *that* and the nonrestrictive *which* there is ample evidence for concluding that she was hopelessly confused. And yet language was where she chose to focus. The org reports became her world, and she protected her hegemony over them with a fierce pride. Poor Hank Farquist, that he should have been the object of her desire.

Right then and there did lust fester, in the sterile confines of the office. She suddenly saw his powerful haunches and all he could do with his driving power if he only would. And Hank Farquist saw her seeing him in this light and grew sore afraid, for she had placed him in her power by assigning him the proofreading of the names of 15,000 girl members with the longest, most complex names. Names with four consecutive consonants. Names that started with "X" and ended with "q." Names that used dots and other symbols in place of letters. Names that contained numbers and even the Pythagorean theorem. And in berating him was she berating all those men who had wanted her and no longer did and all those who, when she was but a child, had gone where adults were not supposed to go. The point was that Hank Farquist became the recipient of her ire and then her fire. Because there were times, in the grayness of her life, that lust called her from her tennis matches and her 24/7 *Law and Order*. Hank Farquist received her unwanted attention to the extent that he came to me and said he could not have such a thing anymore.

So, yes, Isabel, Fiona's heart was lonely for love when she wasn't settled into her figures and the comfort they afforded as she sat with her salads from the Korean deli before her TV set. But is not the purpose of life to exhaust our judgments and to see, in the end, that we are just as those we observe in some degree? Was Fiona Beasley not simply the precursor to Alice Piccoli on my list of women to both fear and loathe and ultimately recognize as mirroring myself? We must talk plainly, Isabel. We must exhaust this ire so a new spirit can enter. We are a discharging species. From both ends it flies out of us.

So I returned to the Oiseau, though she would not have been my first choice. Dr. Tobin had left town. His phone was no longer in service, and the operator's message contained no forwarding number. The Oiseau had referred me to him initially. With her help, I was able to contact Dr. Tobin. He was living in Massachusetts and sounded as far away as he in fact was. He had moved on from me and I from him. That's what I heard and felt, Isabel. Time had dissolved the thin thread of connection. The Oiseau stepped in and bent me to her will, saying "Come to me." My hope had been that she would refer me to a competent and available therapist. I didn't want just anyone, having been down that road before. There was the doctor whose hand trembled as he lifted a glass of water to his lips, a shake induced not by Parkinson's Disease but by withdrawal from alcohol. Picture a waiting room covered in dust and once-white curtains now yellowed and dead plants and old magazines. Or the one I went to for a consultation and withdrew from inwardly when he came on too strong. The next day he called and pleaded with me to see him. He would give me a reduced rate. When I said no, he began questioning me aggressively as to the identity of the creep who had turned me against him, when there had been no such person to guide me, only my own common sense. It is safe to say there is some quackery about in the land, Isabel.

But about the Oiseau. "I'm the one. I know your history. I have a feel for who you are and where you need to go," she said. Eight years had passed since our time with her. In her sharp-featured face that paleness of the senior years had set in. And yet you could see that she was clinging. No Buddhist mentality evident. She was of the body, Isabel. There was that first session when she wore a short skirt which, years before, would have had men kneeling at her feet. She had been heartbreaker material, of this we can be sure. She had had the juice, the voltage, coursing through her. She had known what it was to be voracious in bed. And that the skirt was of black leather only accentuated the delusional nature of her quest to extend her time beyond its limits. But there are those of all descriptions frolicking in such fields of folly—geriatric rockers throwing out their hips and snapping their spines while doing the herky-jerk or funky chicken or the Icky Woods shuffle. Or the convict lover, fat and pasty white and bald, modeling women's lingerie at the age of seventy. Oh, Isabel. Let us die and die and die some more so we can live and live. Let the song of love abound. Let us not get snagged.

The Oiseau was Botox nation. She had traded her ability to smile for the erasure of a few wrinkles. Her skin taut as a drumhead when she tried to relax her facial muscles. And that same small stack of books— an unfinished biography of Edith Wharton and another on an examination of the Arab mind—on that large wooden table that served as a divider between her living room and her "office," the vestibule where we would sit with her in those straight-back chairs. And that tired-looking and frayed oriental rug. Oh, the things of life, Isabel, that in themselves are nothing, but when seen in a certain light can bring such sorrow.

The name Yorkville is no longer applied to this area of the east eighties, nor is Germantown. No more bratwurst. And Luigi's shop is long since gone, and Luigi himself is buried somewhere in the earth. What is this past that calls to me when I visit this section of town, compelling me to think of that store he rented on First Avenue for his furniture repair business? Luigi is a man who befriended Luke and me when we were kids ("Oh what a bunch of bums you a gonna be," he would say, tears of laughter welling up in his eyes as he spoke in his Sicilian accent). To Coney Island would he take us— the Whip, the Tornado, the Cyclone, the hot sands, the Nathan's franks heavy on the mustard and sauerkraut. At that time he had a basement shop in our building. What a blow when he moved across town. What fear it caused, as if my world was collapsing. And what a thing it was to remember how, when we came to him as teenagers in his store, he didn't want us anymore, from the look of peeve on his face.

So what? you say, and have every right to say. What is the point of this rambling reminiscence? What does it possibly achieve? Why can I not stay with one thing? And the answer, of course, is that everything is one thing. This world is of my own invention. I go where I can in it, knocking about here and there.

Isabel, it was not a betrayal of you, or of Zed, to talk with the Oiseau. This I declare emphatically. At the same time, we must do as Fleetwood Mac instructed and go our own way, or else it is for naught that I listened to them all those years while draining bottles of cheap wine. But with this difference. We are calling it not quite another lonely day but a resurrection of the light. The decision to see the Oiseau was simply an acknowledgment of my need for connection. Did the Oiseau not note that writing and meditation are introspective activities? Did she not question the adequacy of standing on the street observing passersby as an antidote to existential despair—those moments when I have been known to fall down weeping at the perception that I am alone in this universe? Did she not suggest allowing more people in?

None of the above means I considered the Oiseau to be the proper choice, even though she claimed the advantage of knowing my history. Was it progress or regression to seek out the marriage counselor who had served us? I was looking for something new, Isabel, and settled for something old.

As you may remember, the Oiseau's policy was pay first and talk later. She would acknowledge the check I placed on the side table with a distracted thank you. Next there was scheduling the next appointment in her little book. I felt put off by this ritual. Could it not wait till the end of the session? Would a more skilled therapist not choose to create a space of attentive silence in which the patient could unburden himself of all that had been stored up and fermenting? But the Oiseau needed certain things nailed down and secure before her patient could begin. And let's not pretend she was as distracted as she appeared to be when I placed the check on the table. Let us say instead that her preoccupation with her appointment book was feigned lest I see how rapt her focus was on having that check in hand. First the money, then the talk. No element of trust there.

You have probably never been to a hockey game, Isabel, as your interests run toward the arts and theater and music. A lot of forechecking goes on, players slamming each other into the boards to impede forward progress. And it was often that way with the Oiseau. Asking what I meant by this or that before I could even finish my thought, as you see a leashed but unruly dog lunging at passersby. She lacked the meditative discipline. Her synapses were firing too rapidly.

One evening I noticed a vacancy sign outside her building. One- and two-bedroom apartments, not for sale but for rent. No co-op boards here. No one with the income for that kind of investment. When you and I first began seeing her, she had lived and worked out of an apartment in a glitzy high-rise, probably a leftover from her marriage which she could no longer afford. She was like me, Isabel. She was alone. She had been left, a bright piece of cloth out in the sun too long and now bleached of all color. Fading away, as I was.

Zed was fairly contemptuous of my reconnection with the Oiseau, as the strong and the self-sufficient can be when presented with the weak and the fumbling. I could feel his disgust that he had dispensed years of wisdom on a dunce. He may even have seen my delusion as a kind of betrayal. You have to understand the man's independence and originality, Isabel. He walked out of a high school for the gifted, lied about his age, and shipped out on a merchant marine vessel. He knew even then that there was no truth to be found in school. Sure, you could learn a few facts, but there was no instruction as to how to think. And what good were facts unless a person knew how to apply them?

Genius ultimately seeks guidance from within. It was that way with Zed. These were not idyllic times to be bobbing about in the Atlantic on a little merchant ship. Though German U-boats were on the prowl, Zed showed no fear. I think of his life's experience, and then of my own, and understand his disgust that I would seek the comfort of a woman I could talk to for a forty-five minute hour, provided I first produce a check.

Time accelerates, Isabel. People vanish. That is what I see now. I was trying to keep the door closed against the void. I went to her for something I no longer wanted—a woman, flesh, perishable goods.

I had gone someplace else. Life had taken me there. Zed had taken me there. God had taken me there. You had taken me there.

I had seen this woman. I had seen that woman. This woman said this to me. That woman said that to me. I said this to that woman. I said that to some other woman. Such would be a fair summary of the five years I spent with her. The Oiseau seemed to listen raptly to all this reportage. This is a conscientious woman of whom I speak. She could not help but give full value for the forty-five minute hour she allotted me, the two of us moving toward dust before each other's very eyes.

The Oiseau examined me closely as to where I met these women. I responded with the truth. I mentioned the anorexics who flocked to OrganicOnly, and the many cards I had given out by the produce area. I told her that women became soft when they were fondling arugula and broccoli rabe and endive and bean sprouts. It reminded them of the familial aspect of their lives that they were missing and that not everyone went home with a bag of popcorn for dinner but actually sat down at a table with another human being and conversed while eating a savory stew. I told her that I met women on the subways of New York City, although not so much anymore. I told her I met women where I could, which meant increasingly in my dreams.

The Oiseau had a suggestion. Why not join a hiking club or take ballroom dancing or find another activity that would bring me in contact with women? Ballroom dancing? I imagined elderly folk learning the foxtrot and the waltz, a lonely hearts club for people who couldn't make friends and build a life on their own.

"Why don't I dance with you?" I said. "Isn't that where this is leading?"

"Isn't this where what is leading?"

"Your bedroom. Your boudoir. Your theater of action, or inaction?"

"That is what you want?"

"That is what you want me to want."

"I want you to want to dance with me and then enter my bedroom?"

"Isn't that what this is about, you and me here in perpetuity, talking and talking while the meter runs?"

"Let's try to understand more at our next session," the Oiseau said.

But there was no continuity, Isabel. Two weeks between sessions was a lifetime.

"My dilemma is that I am not really attracted to women in my age range. My attraction is to younger women." So I said at our next session.

"Age isn't just a number?"

"Many things are numbers. That doesn't negate their importance," I said.

"Are you sure you are not just using age as a barrier to intimacy?"

"I can't reason myself into an interest in women I don't find myself drawn to." I felt uncomfortable for saying what perhaps men should leave unspoken. On the other hand, the Oiseau was my therapist, and so it was reasonable to expect that she could process whatever I presented. When she held her silence, I went on, my words now in the service of self-justification. "It may be that I am beyond sex altogether."

I then told her of that afternoon browsing the shelves of the Mid-Manhattan Library, where I opened a novel and read an epigraph that startled me as few written words have. Ernest Becker was the philosopher's name. In a few words he articulated my experience and legitimized my path with his assertion that once a man *sees* his creaturely nature, he can never not see it and cited Buddha's epiphany in his father's palace, when, after an evening of festivities, he came upon the sight of sleeping courtesans. Here were these creatures gifted with loveliness, who were only hours before radiant, now in a drooling state of unconsciousness, their faces contorted into masks of anguish. I must have a way out of this nightmare of the flesh; life is otherwise a meaningless slide into decay and death.

So the Buddha's thoughts were said to have been. The Buddha had reached a true turning point in his young life.

Isabel, with great conviction I related this experience to the Oiseau. How deflating, then, that she should receive this shaping experience of mine with an amused smile, as if to say, "Little boy, I hear what you say, but I also know what you really want. You aren't fooling me with this spiritual make-believe." An excuse-maker afraid of life. By her lights I had merely pressed the play button on some old and predictable tape to the effect that essentially my life with women was over and had been over for some time, given the wounds that had been inflicted.

A sequestered life, Zed called it, the life I began to lead when I turned fifty. What kind of man is it who passes this milestone birthdate without so much as receiving a phone call or a card, Isabel? And yet sometimes we have to stand and receive our aloneness, absorb it deep into our bones. The hunger for God is an enormous thing. Do not believe that the howl within for the ear and the touch of a beautiful woman is the answer, once a certain stage is reached. This hunger is real, and morsels will not do. Nor will it do to mince words on this matter. *The road narrows.*

Chapter 28

Isabel,

The following must be said as well. Comprehensiveness is everything, even when low behavior conspicuously reigns.

Just prior to my fiftieth birthday, while dining with you at Taku, I noticed a woman at a nearby table. She inhabited that self-consciously solitary space I have been in many times amid the happy buzz of couples with their adorable young children. She looked solemn. She also looked available.

After walking you to your car, I made a beeline back to the restaurant, where I saw her still inside. I couldn't enter, as our waiter, who had us bound in his mind in matrimony, was still present and alert. In fact, I had to stand to the side of the restaurant when he looked out and saw me. His careworn face registered a certain perplexity at my lurking presence.

Yes, the laws of karma are ironclad; we will definitely reap what we sow. But our conjugal bliss waiter notwithstanding, the reality was that I was divorced. Even so am I shadowed by guilt.

"Are you surprised to see me?" I asked, when finally she stepped out. The fact that I had been with you would only boost my value in her mind. Such is the calculus of some women.

"Should I be?" She asked, as she handed me her card.

Dinner, a movie, the mating rituals that do not try the limited imagination or budget of a person such as me. She had spent ten years in Benares, living in submission to various masters while learning Sanskrit, and was now back in New York City to formalize the education she had received with a PhD at Columbia University. Store windows exercised a magnetic pull, making walking with her a tedious process. "Oh, I'd love to have that dress…That sofa would go great in my apartment." In her late forties, she had spent many years out of the mainstream work world and was now trying to squeeze by on a stipend and whatever she could earn through tutoring. She lived in a drug-infested area of upper Manhattan. "There is an abundance of violence and noise and hardness in the eyes of many of the young. They need daya."

"Daya?"

"Compassion. Care and support. They have lost the maternal kiss of their sun-splashed island paradises and the tranquilizing effect of large bodies of water."

She was impressed with my humbly furnished apartment.

"A real adult place," she said, with genuine surprise.

"Aren't all apartments rented or owned by adults?" I asked, seeking more in the way of her approval.

"You know better than to ask. Not all apartments have upholstered chairs and nice rugs and a comfortable, attractive sofa and good artwork on the walls." Her words caused an inner glow. I have told you many times of the living circumstances of my childhood, and the shame I felt over splotchy linoleum on the living room floor and cast-off furniture.

We had one good night in bed, and it was all downhill from there. The reality of AIDS was a problem, as it required the use of a condom if we were to practice safe sex. Even without a condom it was hard for me, and that latex sheath sank any hopes I might have of performing. I felt like a child with the hat of a grownup covering his head, and Natalia was too life-affirming to let me go forward without wearing one.

Depression comes with nonperformance. It's an unpleasant place to be with a woman, lying there on the bed with your face down in the pillow. But unlike Maura, who fell into a sulk, Natalia was forgiving. In fact, she didn't see why I should be so apologetic in the first place. "You do so much for me," she said, "and, whatever you may say, you're not impotent."

I didn't ask her to elaborate. I didn't go there.

Though Natalia was struggling, she brought more to the table than I did, as would have become apparent if we had continued. Her natural curiosity and intelligence would have led her to a more critical look at me somewhere down the road. What woman wants a man who sits in meditation two hours a day and lives frugally, fixated on securing his future through savings, and who thinks a good weekend activity is a walk through Central Park with some rest time on its many benches? Or a man who, to blot out painful memories, will suddenly exclaim, "Honduran national economy," startling Natalia, as it had Maura.

"Why did you go, and why did you return?" I said to her as we lay in bed, her brown hair freed of the bun she normally wore it in.

"I suffered a wound. I failed my College Boards."

"What do you mean, you failed them?"

"You know exactly what I mean. I failed them, just as you did."

"And how do you know I failed my College Boards."

"You said so in the story you showed me."

"That was fiction," I said, of the story in the small press magazine I had given her to read.

"That was your life," she replied.

"This is true. Sort of," I said.

"We're bottom-dwellers," she said.

"Happy to hear that," I said.

"Flush us down the toilet."

"If you insist."

"Giant turds."

"You bet."

"In India I witnessed disease, famine and abject surrender to various spiritual masters. And then one day, awareness came that I had buried myself alive, which sparked a longing to return. I saw my exile as a form of self-abuse, a prolonged tantrum in which I was hurting mostly me. And you are the same way. Without leaving home you have created a distorted self."

"How so?"

"You seek to appear more intelligent than you are. Now I must go."

"It's 9:30 p.m.," I said.

But her spiritual practice required her to rise at 4:30 each morning, A bandaid does not suffice for a gaping wound. "The energy is pure before dawn and perfect for meditation," she said.

She had given herself to the celebrity guru Bagamaya, a spiritual prima donna whose ego was gratified by the adoration committees set up by her devotees, lost souls who were trying to find their bearings in this world. Every month, as part of a yearly subscription, Natalia would receive in the mail a Bagamaya lesson, two or three pages of writings by one of the more evolved members. I kept my doubts to myself. Natalia was on life support. You don't want to be messing with someone's belief system.

Things went well enough that Natalia scheduled us for a visit with her elderly mother in Forest Hills, a community whose Tudor buildings I have only seen in transit on a Long Island Railroad train. What a lack in her life that she would haul me out there as some sort of trophy. Twice divorced Johan Manootdjian, Manhattan boulevardier, loyal customer at OrganicOnly, a daily presence at its salad bar. Oh, Lord, it made me want to fall down weeping, the very thought of that. The old meeting the older. The dying meeting the soon to be dead.

But it was more than my perceived shabbiness, Isabel. There was an internal affront. A line was drawn in my mind that I must not cross, and now Natalia was asking me to do just that. An introduction meant a step forward in my relationship with her, and that I could not do, without the risk of unbearable sorrow. The romance with Natalia was a charade in itself, but to build on the charade would have triggered sharp conflict within me bearing on my relationship with you. I could be with Natalia, if just barely, but I could not belong to her, and there must be no rituals to suggest that I did. And so I took a raincheck.

Some evening thereafter, we attended the ballet with tickets courtesy of Natalia's mother. It seemed that if the woman couldn't meet with me face to face, she would reach me through her largesse. Lincoln Center brought back memories of our nights at the opera, Isabel, those marathon weekday performances at which I would doze off, as during *Der Rosenkavalier,* your personal favorite, and yet marvel at the wonder of the life you had provided me with. But other memories also came, the more strife-torn evenings, after you had begun to withdraw from me and I reacted with fear-driven fury, verbally slashing at you right there at the Met, knowing even as I did that I was wrecking something wonderful and yet unable to stop. What was Natalia supposed to be after you, lacking as she did your style, your culture, your beauty?

"Aren't they great?" Natalia whispered feverishly. Lithe dancers, a whole company of them, performing on slippered feet criss-crossing patterns punctuated by contorted poses. Evidently, dancing had been Natalia's passion in her younger years.

"The women are mesmerizing," I whispered back.

At the intermission we headed for the bar. She looked perturbed.

"Is something wrong?"

"You bastard," she said, just about snorting her espresso out her nose, and drawing the attention of the aesthetes with her fire.

"What have I done?" I asked, as the bell rang, signaling the end of intermission. Back in our seats her frostiness was palpable, and afterward, she hauled me across the street to a café, where she continued. "You're only interested in anorexic younger women, is that it? You don't even *see* older women, do you?"

My little remark had been like a depth charge. All those years in India. All that slavish devotion to the mega guru, all that meditation before the sun came up over Manhattan, and there it was, her vanity, her pride, call it what you will, rising to the surface.

"I don't know what to say." The restaurant was done for the day, the tables cluttered with dirty dishes. A bleary-eyed waiter took our order.

"You can say yes or no."

"It's not as simple as that," I replied, feeling she had no right to put me in the docket.

"It is as simple as that. I repel you. You don't want to sleep with me. You don't even want to touch me."

"Sex has become problematic for me," I said.

"That's it," she said, and tore off.

Our relationship didn't end on a dime, but drift set in. I wouldn't be saving her from her life of graduate school poverty. Now and then I would run into her at OrganicOnly, where she was doing her weekly shopping. At first I felt a perverse happiness at the sight of her wounded face, but why even call it perverse when I was acting for a supreme good, the removal of that slyness that afflicts all those who purport to live in God's realm while scheming to hold onto each other?

Isabel, we must do the good we can in this life in the way that we can. Or maybe the world is right and I am a sadistic and vengeful creep, toying with this poor woman the way that so many women have toyed with me.

But no, the world is not right, for what should I see on the great *Seinfeld* the other night but an act of unapologetic cruelty. Did I not hear the not so great George Costanza break up with a woman to her face? Did he not denigrate her with the word *pretentious*? And did she not, as a result of his attack—because the truth without love is nothing less than an attack, as Zed often said—wind up in a mental institution? And did George not further, aided and abetted by Seinfeld himself, visit the afflicted woman seeking not to make an amend but to retrieve the tax papers George had persuaded Seinfeld to turn over to her, as she was an accountant?

Can it be said that I attacked Natalia in a comparable way, Isabel? Did I barrage her with insults? Did I so much as say anything of a personal nature about her? No, nothing. I made a single comment about the attractiveness of the young dancers.

And yet. And yet. Tear down this dinky, Johan. Tear it down. Admit that your lust lights were shining for those ballerinas. Admit it.

Natalia's legacy was not insubstantial. Her routine of rising early, which I had feared would plunge me into suicidal depression, within a few months I too embraced. Some recognition had come that time was running out. I needed to prepare, in a more disciplined way, for my departure. Memories came to me of my father sitting in that wicker chair in his little corner of the dining room where he had his shelf of religious literature. He was a tired man by the time I came into this world. He was done. My scorn for him had long since gone. I felt the need for deeper surrender. I would not be able to save myself by reading a book or writing a book. I would have to throw myself upon the mercy of the infinite.

From a place of inner darkness that mirrored the predawn blackness I would, in the course of that hour, enter a place of light and love. as if I was passing through one door after another into some deep inner chamber. A feeling of great happiness would come over me. We can talk of spiritual beliefs, but a spiritual experience is of another order. It changes us. All the discrete forms, all the worry, all the cares dissolve before this intense light of love that radiates itself through every cell and extremity of our being. We know, in this experience, that we have found the thing we have been looking for and that we need look no further.

When the timer rang, I would walk to the bedroom and pray, my forehead touching the floor, to be kept safe from alcohol and drugs. And I would give myself to God as I could, telling him what he already knew, that my life was not my own because on my own I had almost lost my life. Certainly I had drank a good portion of it away, and the years before the onset of active alcoholism had proved to me the truth of the saying that a mind can be a terrible thing to have. And so I knew I needed God's help and that I was lost without him. Though I had found God by a different route, I came to understand my mother's experience in that church of my childhood and how she drew on the power she received to live a positive life.

Isabel, in this period I took down from my shelf the manuscript of a novel that had been collecting dust. I called it *In My Garden Are to Be Found Many Treasures.* At the time the title had a sound and length that appealed to me. Had Kierkegaard not written a book titled *Purity of Heart Is to Will One Thing,* showing no regard for those who insisted on anorexic titles? In any case, the title did capture the theme. It featured a young man in his college years who should perhaps have been devoting his energies to his studies but whose true major was Mona, she of the wealthy and cultured family. (How often, sadly, have I used that very phrase "wealthy and cultured," so that it should by now be one word. We get lazy in our minds. We let our tired thoughts and solutions and phrases take us where they will.) Luther is in the grip of an obsession that removes everything but her as the thing of value in his life. It was the novel I could write, and it followed the worn tracks of my own journey. Abusive and a thief, he shows a strong antisocial streak and lives under a dark cloud. He is not the abysmal failure who can wink over his feigned ineptness because he has a ton of intelligence and other capital with which to inevitably distinguish himself. No, he is simply a failure. And he is an Armenian failure, on his father's side. Can there be anything worse, in Luther's troubled mind?

Back in third grade, our class had been given an assignment by Sister Mary Claire. She had a formidable face, so white and severe and scrubbed free of any of the cosmetics that the world so values. Her headdress and her habit only added to her stark visage. The assignment was simply this, to sketch a design on the stiff squares of construction paper given us. But no pattern appeared in my mind.

All I experienced was terror as I plunged into the abyss. Desperate to brake the fall, I copied the graceful circles and diamond shapes that Carola Madrid, a girl who sat next to me, drew so effortlessly (she lived at 610 West 116th Street—this I know, Isabel, as it was a building that stared out at the eternity of Claremont Avenue, where all those blessed with Columbia University and the Ivy League did live). And in copying Carola Madrid's drawing, I can only suspect that the poverty of my imagination was established for all time in my consciousness. We learn our place early. We learn who is chosen and who is not, and then seek confirmation of this fact for the rest of our days.

But Sarah erased all that thinking from my mind, at least temporarily. She said she wanted me. Seeing me in that dingy little room half a block from where my family lived, she said I reminded her of a Russian poet. Is it possible she fell in love with me because I used a Pepsi bottle with beveled glass for an ashtray?

In any case, it was in this time after Natalia that I began to revise the novel. With my meditation behind me, I would sit down to write, and from the start, a feeling of exhilaration overcame me. All the frustration and pain of having given birth to a deformed child lifted. A surge of great energy moved me forward. The tone of the novel was jubilant. From the start the words just flowed.

You must understand. Alcoholism, for me, was a magic carpet ride, as I have said. The illusion persisted that I had found the easier, softer way, and inevitably wound me up dashed on the rocks like every other sot. I had listened to no one, only the dictates of my own foolish ego. Was it really so very different with this writing project? Did I not feel here that I had found a painless path as well? And was not that path simply to write a spontaneous prose, to use phrases like "the recrudescence of homeopathic dawn" without, in some instances, a full understanding of their meaning, the phrase having first come to me from the jubilation center of my young mind on a halcyon spring day on a Manhattan street? Isabel, I was flying down a road easy to navigate, as it had no guardrails, seeking to throw a lasso around the past and to bind it tight while also seeking to invigorate every sentence with the shakti of my newfound self.

I showed the work to neither you nor anyone, although later I gave you the entire novel. And yet I had great faith in the quality of what was unfolding. When I reread portions, my heart leapt up. The work was infused with an intensity and self-honesty and uniqueness of expression that pulled me along. Yes, the character was strange, self-destructive, at times offensive, but why on earth was it necessary to strut characters in their perfumed finery? Why not tell a certain kind of truth, and allow it to have its day? Such was my mindset—at times exhilarated, at others not quite sure.

Then came a time when it was necessary to come forward with what I had wrought, and that time arrived four years later. A friend put me in touch with an agent from the Acton Lord firm. They represented the home run hitters, Isabel. All their authors had the downtown swing. Many, many were the fences they had cleared.

A word about this friend. He stood tall and had a massive brow and the stamp of the Stanford University writing program upon him. A poet of no small accomplishment, he was married to an author of several novels whose stories appeared regularly in the pages of the *The New Yorker*, yes, *The New Yorker*. His name was Gumbo, and he was good to his very bones. But I did not belong with him, Isabel. I did not have the necessities, and so he had moved away from me.

Why, then, did I go to him, when a strong wind was blowing against such a contact? I will not answer that question. I have had enough, for the moment, of the humiliations life deals out whenever I lose sight of my true function.

By this time, Isabel, my manuscript had grown to 1,500 pages. My strategy had been to leave a portion of the novel with the agent, Camilla Quest, but I simply couldn't decide on *which* portion. If she read one part, then she would be missing another that might grab her more. It was all very problematic and anguishing.

Isabel, count those as among the happiest days of my life, knowing, as I did, that something wondrous and extraordinary was about to happen, for now the world would be seeing what I had been seeing for those four years. I solved the selection problem by packing the entire novel into three boxes. Paper is heavy, Isabel. I was not in a position to lift those three boxes, each of them the thickness of the Manhattan yellow pages, without strain, owing to my back injury.

With the boxes in a small suitcase on castors, I boarded the M104 bus, and as it passed OrganicOnly and yummy yum Zabar's and Fairway heaven (the price is always right for their organic table grapes, Isabel, both seedless and seeded), and then the Ansonia with its ornate façade and the newly constructed subway kiosks at Seventy-second Street and Lincoln Center, less than spectacular in the plaza set out for it, and finally arrived at Columbus Circle, where the New York Coliseum was soon to be no more, God's light was bright in my being. Now and then in my childhood had I been exposed to the world beyond the close air of the church and the weeping and Christ rapture of the worshipers, such as the time the uncle of a friend took us to the annual boat show at the Coliseum. Oh, material world of promise that opened to me on that day— shiny yachts soon to be navigating the deep waters of America and beyond. And now I too would be venturing forth, powered by my newfound stature. I would be seen and heard by millions walking tall and talking loud on the avenues of this earth.

The agent's building was old and under renovation. Some new energy and entrepreneurial spirit was sweeping the island. Scaffolding had been erected to repair its cornices and sand-blast it free of grime, and now its neglected spaces were filled with those who had drive in their hearts and minds and cleverness informing their tongues. In the vast lobby a concierge had been installed where none had been. Though he had a job to do and surely did it well, let it also be said that he may have been overwhelmed by the human traffic sufficient that, on this day, he became lax about the protocol for packages, for when I announced myself to him as being on the march to universal renown, he simply waved me on. He had the apparatus at hand to call upstairs for verification, or he could have had me leave the manuscript at his desk. (These are the small spaces where my mind goes, Isabel. These are the contingencies it dwells on. There is no hurry in my words, as there is none in my feet. Not anymore, Isabel. Not anymore. The time for rushing is done.)

It was just as well that the concierge failed to hard-check me, as so much can happen in this life and not everyone has my vigilance quotient. For example, a careless building worker could have diverted the package to the wrong party or even discarded it accidentally. Is there any tragedy more unbearable to contemplate than uniqueness on the threshold of discovery only to be denied by the hand of man or God? Such was my thought as I ascended in the elevator to the fifteenth floor.

Let me stop here and say I was not reckless. Prudence dictated that it would be in my best interest to avoid a face-to-face with the agent Camilla Quest before she had set eyes on the manuscript not because I feared she might have had a dragon's breath and temperament. It was only this. I was asking the woman to do something for me, and anytime you place yourself in a position of need, contempt is waiting in the wings. And her contempt would be withering. Of that I was sure. A woman can never be expected to love a man endlessly. Sometimes he must disappear before he has even been seen in order to remain in her good graces. Such is the understanding I have been brought to by the years that I have been on this planet and experiencing the state of affairs between the sexes. When I stepped off that elevator, it was my intention to leave the parcel with the secretary and simply flee. Then, and only then, could my sense of delicious anticipation be preserved. Anything less would mean that the work and I had been disposed of.

Oh, Isabel, life unfolds in the way that it can. There was no secretary, for it was the lunch hour, and she had doubtless fled to Burger on the Bun while Camilla Quest, like all high-powered agents, was off at Le Cirque or Twenty-One doing her deals.

A young man was present to open the frosted glass door. He had the look of American royalty, with brown wavy hair and deep-set eyes in his handsome face, and stood tall and thin and self-possessed in khaki slacks and a blazer and a pin-striped oxford shirt with an open collar. You could be sure, from his gravitas and steely gaze, that someday he would be counted in the ranks of those who had done their deals and vanished unheralded. Or maybe he would succumb to a calling that would require him to put words on paper in a hopeless bid for immortality.

Nearby, at the south end of Central Park, was a traffic circle. Cars get oriented as they go around it. They have a choice, and it is all theirs: do they zip along Central Park West and, as they proceed, enter the realm of Stanford White and the regal apartment buildings that he designed, or do they opt for the slant of Broadway. And there is the choice they are compelled to make farther up, at Seventy-second Street, as to whether they deal with the staggered traffic lights of Amsterdam Avenue or stay with the stop and go system of Broadway. Photos of trolley cars rounding the circle and a scene from a 1950s movie I saw sometime ago of a man and woman in an open convertible driving around the circle come to mind. All those people dead and gone, of course. Life will do that to you, remove you from the scene.

Gone too was the Chemical Bank that had stood on the opposite corner, where I opened my first checking account in my early twenties. Pastel-colored checks that gave a sense of order to my life. The money, of course, came from the renting office of my family's building. What need there was for me to give my life such a turn I may never be able to say, but they were years of consequence, as any activity that involves stealing must be. What insanity, what fear, what greed, that I should act in my own perceived self-interest with so little regard for the well-being of others, mainly my family, or myself.

But imagine that, Isabel. A checking account with my name on the checks. And a savings account at the same bank and others, my thinking being that small piles of unreported money were somehow less conspicuous than big ones to the IRS.

I had been a foolish young man, Isabel. Rather than shoulder the responsibilities that others were assuming, I had sought an easier route, dropping tenth grade biology because I found lab work too demanding and later picking up the bottle in response to the daily stresses of life and embezzling money out of the family business rather than make my way in the world. Now I was back here in the vicinity, not daring to ask myself if I were involved in another kind of theft—not of money, but of the experiences of others. Really, I am talking about Sarah and her family, who had taken me in as virtually a member back in those years. Oh, Isabel, to seek to bask in the reflected glory of others. I ran from my heritage, thinking I was running toward the bright lights of America. Such was my folly that I chose a garden now weeded over. All of this dementia was in the novel, Isabel. All of it.

The walls of the suite of the Lord Acton Agency were covered with deep, ceiling-high shelves that held multiple copies of works by writers the agency represented: the complete oeuvre of Fred Limestar, whose prize-winning novels created an inimitable and moving portrait of the Old West. And Franz Mobile, whose detailed reconstruction of European Jewry pre-World War II had brought him lasting fame. And Sage Cursor, whose sharp-eyed depictions of contemporary Hollywood resulted in cinematic as well as literary success for her novels. And Madge Bulwar's monumental study of the Iron Lady, Margaret Thatcher, which spawned an entire month-long docudrama on PBS. A sinking feeling came over me as I surveyed the suite. I was an interloper, an ill man in an environment of health and success. The young man intently peering at his computer screen through his designer glasses, his hair falling over his ample brow, had to be wondering, with each passing second, how big a mistake he had made in letting me in the door. Like an avalanche did this idea break over me, burying me under its oppressive weight. My eyes averted, I fled the premises.

Isabel, I would have taken the stairs, did I not need a security pass for access. So I was forced to wait for the elevator. But we develop strategies for survival. After pressing the down button, I stood with my back to the elevator, feigning absorption in the small square tiles on the landing, so I would know where to keep my eyes should Camilla Quest herself stride boldly forth when the door opened and, our eyes having locked, recognize me instantly as the unprepossessing soul who had imposed with a request for her services. But no one emerged. No one.

In the privacy of the elevator did I pray, and an answer came, should the formidable one be waiting in the lobby. I took out my small notepad and pen and began to scribble words, an activity that would engross me sufficient that my eyes, so betraying of my fearful and seeking self, would not instantly be drawn to those of the fierce and vengeful Camilla Quest when the elevator reached the lobby.

Isabel, never mind for the moment Camilla Quest and the power of life and death I gave her the right to assume and to reduce me to the dimensions of an importuning child. The world has its ways, and I have my own, and they do not always conform, and we will have to wait and see where past and present meet and what the contours of eternity are for each of us.

In days gone by there was a newsstand on the northwest corner of Fifty-seventh and Eighth, the hot air of the subway rising through the grates. The A, the B, the C, all letters of the IND singing and on the next level up, the IRT checking in as well. This is New York City of which we speak, with its millions and the joyous madness of anonymity on the busy streets. A man with ink-blackened hands and a soiled apron heavy with coins in its pouch owned that stand, and around it his life revolved. Nightly the trucks of New York City pulled up and dropped wire-bound bales of newspapers right there at the curb. With a powerful "Yo" did the drivers announce themselves, men of grit who made the daily round of cafeterias and hot dog stands and all-night diners where the solitaries eased their loneliness with cups of coffee and lemon meringue pie. Those bales hit the pavement with a thud but did not rest there on their lonesome. With a wire cutter in his hand did the man do here a snip, there a snip giving them the freedom they were seeking. Every day a feast of boxscore ephemera for delicious devouring: the stats of Charlie Hustle and his cohort on the Big Red Machine, who had abandoned Crosley Field for a cookie cutter park that featured the contemptible concrete hardness of Astroturf, as if man could make a credible substitute for what nature had wrought.

It was to this stand that I would come on the BMW R-60 motorcycle I rode in those days as an emblem of my solitariness and my power before heading to the tiny diner next door, where I would eat eggs over easy and nitrite-rich bacon, ravenous hunger coming over me after a night of drinking in the bars I had discovered, in particular one down on Broadway near Houston Street. In its cavernous space I would spend hours, drinking glass after glass of wine, as if trying to stay close to shore and not voyage farther into the alcoholic deep but with no understanding of the waters I had already entered or the power of the current. There from the jukebox would come Carole King singing "It's Too Late" and "So Far Away" and "I Hear the Earth Move" while I stood alone, dependent for refills on the abstemious bartender behind his altar of mahogany. I wanted a woman. I wanted to feel the texture of her lingerie, to unclasp her bra and peel off her panties. I wanted her physical avowal that she was as hungry as I was.

One night I saw my double in terms of his stark desire, though surely a man of greater intellect and further gifted with a round head. A solitary and sad soul like me, and also, like me, a drunk and a hunter. I was relieved on those nights he wasn't there and I could immerse myself in those three-minute bursts of song that would summon pathos or jubilation. Words and phrases and story fragments and opening lines of novels would come to me, which I would jot on scraps of paper.

"Don't go with him. He has only himself," a woman cautioned her girlfriend, who had taken a shine to me. And then there was the one with an urgent need to inform me that I was not who I wanted to be. She had intuited what I couldn't, with any consistency, grasp, that I had been simply a thief: the money for the alcohol, for the eggs and bacon, for the daily *New York Post* I rubbed my face in, for the motorcycle I rode, for the apartment I rented, for the clothes on my back—all of it from the renting office where I purported to work three evenings a week captive to the fantasy of a blossoming writing career.

A week after dropping off my novel, I almost aborted my trip to Portugal by walking off the check-in line at JFK. I could not, in that moment, summon any good reason why I should leave my apartment and my life on the Upper West Side of Manhattan for the same sort of solitary trek I had been taking since our separation. These journeys seemed more about scrimping and saving than embracing the Old World. Once again I was struck by how alone I was, a man without substantial connection to family and with no real friends. Once again it came to me that a partial motivation for travel had been the belief that my absence would cause people to miss me; I saw how peripheral to the lives of others, including yours, I was. Only my Samsonite hard-shell suitcase, having already gone through the check-in, held me in place. I imagined it abandoned and weeping in the baggage compartment as the plane streaked over the Atlantic, and this I could not bear, or imagined it unclaimed and circling endlessly on the carousel at the Lisbon airport. At some point in this life, Isabel, a man must embrace the principle of fidelity. Heartbreak may be the inevitable outcome of a world dead set on change, but we needn't inflict needless trauma either on the inanimate or those of us privileged to walk about.

My memories of Lisbon are slight: the peeling facades of buildings in the square crying out for a fresh coat of paint; the menacing Angolan who bird-dogged me on a dark street; a waiter lifting a piece of grilled chicken with his bare hand onto a plate; and a young German couple of exceptional beauty awaiting a ride back to Lisbon from an outlying tourist site. From my room at night I would hear, in the distance, the mournful sound of a woman singing fado, and sometime before dawn the colossal racket of glass bottles being dumped into a garbage truck.

Within a few days I traveled south to the Algarve, a once remote area ideal for camping and known for its beaches. On the train an immobilizing nausea overcame me, perhaps owing to the figs I had eaten. A woman shared the compartment with me. She spoke in English and with pride in her native country. Did I know that some of the best doctors in the world were right here in Portugal and that its universities would soon be on a par with those of England? Her eyes searched mine as she spoke, as if from my expression, not my verbal response, would she receive her answer. Her insistence was no cover for her insecurity and doubt. In that moment did I know that Portugal itself was sitting beside me, a country that strove to measure up to others but feared that it didn't. She heard her nation weeping and wanted it to stand proud as an equal partner among the Western democracies. There is much passion in Portugal, Isabel. Many are the women and men who sing fado long into the night. Such inexplicable loss and longing. The problem of inferiority is widespread in this world, and causes much suffering and many tears. Oh Portugal, now I knew why I had found you, for you were me and I was you.

Here is the thing. Without a word she placed her hand on my stomach, near the area of discomfort. She then closed her eyes and mumbled an incomprehensible prayer with her head lowered and her eyes closed. This went on for some time. I had a strong sense it was not for me to interfere but to allow her mysterious power to unfold. The art of concealment I was in need of summoning to hide my dubiousness. My nausea and the fact that we were alone in the compartment lessened my self-consciousness. At one point the conductor looked in while passing through the corridor. Our eyes met, but if his registered any surprise, I couldn't say.

Alas, no miracle of faith healing occurred, not for the next three days, at least. That night I was laid up in a hostel, a budget accommodation I took to hold the line on spending. We often think that joy comes from indulging ourselves, but restraint has its place, with its promise that thrift might yield a brighter future than I might otherwise expect to have. And if there was a price to pay, if I had to share a space with generally far younger folk than myself, well, so be it. There was no law saying Johan M. could not take a bed in this or most hostels for fear that he would be ostracized or mocked. Even so, a sort of ghetto effect derives from staying in such an establishment. It lowers your status in your mind to be always sharing a room and a bath with an assortment of backpackers. On the other hand, you are with people in whatever oneness you can achieve with those of a younger generation. You surrender to the fact of where you are and embrace them with love, thus removing all the walls that would separate.

That first night I was roused from sleep by a loud crash. There followed, in the dark, the most astonishing torrent. I turned on my flashlight to find a young man hosing down the floor with his penis. Oh, the sounds and disturbances and the smell of a drunk, on whatever continent. A foul odor he spread with his liquor breath in the airless room. The man was straight up blotto. I flung open the window and took care of his mess after guiding him to his bed. Blissfully unaware of the chaos that he had caused, he immediately passed out and serenaded me with snoring as disturbing as a porcupine ravaging the bark of a tree.

The young man was from Lund, in southern Sweden, and though his Christian name was Peder and the Swedes are noted for their reserve, he set aside the national character and went by the name Main Event and bragged the next afternoon, after finally coming to, that he had women on every continent, though a number one in his hometown who, while she cared for him, was expressing increasing concern about his drunken ways. Isabel, he had a handsome face and a natural endowment that did lend credibility to his boastfulness.

How strange, I thought, that the imperious American culture should manifest not only in the marketplace—a McDonalds not far from the Uffizi in Florence and a Seven-Eleven selling Kraft Philadelphia Cream Cheese in Copenhagen—but also in the psyches of foreign nationals such as Main Event, with his braggadocio.

For the next couple of nights I sought to sleep in a state of heightened alertness and a bucket by my bed to catch his emissions, should he once again mistake the floor for a urinal. I was fully determined to reestablish the reign of order and was successful in my effort, so noisy were his entrances.

On the fourth day, Main Event held his head in his hands on waking, having slept away the morning. He still had his good looks and his strength, but blows were clearly being delivered by King Alcohol. While sipping from a can of beer and gobbling a bag of salty chips, he confided to me his fear that he would lose his job (he was a social worker, of all things) and that his girlfriend would inevitably write him off. I shared with him my own experience with alcohol and where it had wound me up. I told him further that I had stayed in Lund while traveling in Sweden, and where he could go for help. Being a social worker, he was familiar with such resources, he said, but not in dire need of them for himself. Even so, my encounter with Main Event had the noticeable benefit of rousing me from my sickbed and lifting my spirits. Connection will do that, Isabel. It surely will.

You could say these trips thrust me into life, and that would be true, but they were also retreats. When abroad, with the midday sun beating down, we can easily become frazzled. There is the bewilderment of strange streets. There are those pockets of fear when it strikes us that we may lose all of our necessities—our money, our credit cards, our passport—and be stranded in a strange land. There are those times when you feel so conspicuously alone and must endure the pitying stares of the wait staff or their contempt that you have so little to show for yourself in this life. At such times there is regret that you are without a life partner and have no progeny among the creatures of this earth. The inevitably assailing sense comes over you that your life is utterly futile because you lack the tangible proof of having loved. At such times do you see yourself as you imagine the world perceives you.

As I have said before and will say again, God has an augmenting power, Isabel. When we sit for an hour, we rise above those gray clouds and all the toxicity of life even as we descend deeper and deeper into ourselves, down down into the fundament of our being, and there we find him, our fear dissolving as he spreads his joy throughout us. We are home, Isabel. We are one at such times with the source of life, and when we kneel afterward and pray, Oh, Father, of myself I am nothing, but with you I am everything, we are transformed. What then is there to do but wander about and do the things we do in a state of constant detachment, for it is not that the world has something we need so much as it is we have something we need to give to the world, and that is the message of hope.

There is a collection of stories by the very fine writer Leonard Michaels called *I Would Save Them If I Could.* I felt that way about the Swede, as I did about Luke and my deceased sister Rachel. You cannot be born into a family such as mine without such solicitude being part of your makeup, and all kinds of derision can be heaped on those so conditioned, as by calling them do-gooders and the like, But there are worse things than to live by the precept "Do good' or at least "Do no harm," so many worse things that it becomes safe to say there is nothing better.

These hostels I would stay at were truly enclaves of the young and adventurous. If I was lucky, I would find a room for myself. But in the dorms there would often be four or five and sometimes even six to a room. Numbers of them struck me as compulsive travelers. That is the mentality of the young—to see six countries in seven days. As we get older, the journey becomes a more interior one.

I am grateful for those hostels. They free us from the isolation that a hotel room can impose, and the staff are generally friendly and eager to share their knowledge. Because my vigilance was soaring, illuminating necessities others might not see, I had brought along a portable alarm clock, which I had sleep with me in my bed. I had only to press a button for its little face to glow in the ongoing dark. Before the dawn it would call me to wakefulness, fetching me from my dreams with its insistent sound. Being the first to rise, I had the use of a clean shower stall in the common bathroom and could generally stand, in privacy, at the sink and perform my morning rituals, with the purpose of making myself right with myself and presentable to the world. And if I groaned at the sight of my thinning hair and my pale face, as reflected to me in the mirror over the sink, a kind of survivor's will took over that said I was as I was and that had to be all right. We have a guide within us who will take us where we need to go. Of that we can be sure.

And so I saw to it that I had clothes to cover my nakedness and shoes on my feet and my hair had been brought to a state of reasonableness—I had brought along a hand mirror to check that, after the morning brushing, my hair was fluffed out in the back so as to hide the flatness of that part of my head, the mind having a long memory for the taunts of childhood. And I also saw to it that my teeth had been rid of the detritus of the day before with careful flossing and then the insertion of the efficient little interdental brush to ensure that plaque-building gunk had been ushered from the premises, and followed with stimulation of my gums with a little rubber tip attached to a handle. My dental hygiene completed, I could go to the common area and sit, just sit, in peaceful meditation and be given the power I needed for that day, for while I had been performing my ablutions, I knew that all such preparation would be for naught if my focus were to be solely on the body with no attention to the spirit.

Isabel, as I have said, I went away in part so people would miss me, but now I had come to the understanding that no one would miss me in the least. We become slowly invisible as we grow older, and freedom to live or die comes with that awareness. I entered a depressive state where I understood how people come to a place where they do not care if they pass on and perhaps hope that they will. Years before, I had spent some days in the town of Gythion far down on the Peloponnese, and while there had fallen into a state of darkness that I could only attribute to isolation brought on by an inability to speak the native language and the unavailability of English-speaking people. Even incidental conversation by and large eluded me. In the hills were these worrisome brush fires giving off an acrid smoke that stung my eyes. During my stay I resolved that I would never take people for granted again. I saw that they were as necessary as food and air and water. But here I was, eleven years later, stricken by my sense of social poverty. How many restaurants can we sit in alone eating our evening meals, Isabel? How many?

Portugal didn't go on forever. Nor did the suspense while waiting for a response from Camilla Quest. I was home a few days when the e-mail came. I said a silent prayer before opening her message. She was a woman of few words where I was concerned. She thanked me for the opportunity to read the novel, but couldn't summon the necessary enthusiasm to commit to it. And, as if to address my unspoken concern that I had been an intruder in the premises of her office, she gave me a specific day and time for the pickup of the manuscript. This time I would not be getting past the concierge desk, as it was there where she would be depositing the novel.

Chapter 29

The unspeakable in full pursuit of the unavailable? It can seem so.

A ray of sunshine she is, the willowy woman in jeans and a black top at the other end of the floor. Their eyes meet, and distance only magnifies their unspoken communication—his a charged longing and hers revulsion that prompts a retreat into the warren of cubicles from which she had emerged.

All that day she lives in his mind. And when he does finally see her again, not that day but the next, she is in the company of Mary Terezzi, the two of them standing by the photocopier. The glance she gives him before turning back to Mary is full of that same animus. Clearly, she is warning him away. And then it is another painful day of not seeing her, of not meeting the challenge he has set himself to win her over.

The following morning he steps into the elevator at work and lets out an audible groan when the only other person to join him is Jeanine Juddster.

"Johan," she says.

"Jeanine," he replies.

"Happy to see me?"

"Always."

That smile/smirk, as if she can toy with him. He is just like her, stuck in this place, grown old in this place.

"Someone told me you're a writer. Is that true?"

"Is your source for attribution?"

"What's that mean, attribution?"

"Can you name your source?"

"Why didn't you just say so? You see. You writers. Always having to trot out the big words."

"Is that such a big word?"

"For little people like me it is. But you haven't answered my question."

"And you haven't answered mine."

"Touché."

"What's that mean? Touché."

"Very funny. Hah hah hah."

The elevator stops at his floor. On the landing he turns in time to see her staring at him between the closing doors. The conversation has put him in a bad mood, that he should have to start his workday with Jeanine when what he wants to see is beauty. And now the gray mass of women that follows. All of these he sees, but he doesn't see *her*. He doesn't see Heather.

Something wrong with him for such judgment. And yet, and yet.

Rita O'Rourke sits alone in the cafeteria with her cup of joe and her blueberry muffin. She looks despondent.

"Are you OK?"

"I guess so," she says, attempting to smile. "Tell me about yourself."

"I always tell you about myself."

"It's just Ellen. She's so cold and mean. Since last month there's been this feeling of estrangement. We used to get on so well, but now work is being routed away from me. I have nothing to do anymore, or virtually nothing. I get these little scraps of assignments."

Yes, she has been a star, living in Ellen Deutsch's love. But now mother has passed her love onto someone else. It is a mother's prerogative. What can he say that won't offend her? "I struggle with emotional dependency. I see the power I give people and how afraid I can become when their approval appears to be withdrawn."

"But I like Ellen. I love her."

"Yes," he says, seeing the futility of telling her that converting your boss into your mother and working for love are foolish. He won't tell her how bracing it can feel to survive the absence of that approval, what a hard won but worthwhile struggle it is not to fly here, there, and everywhere asking of people their love.

"I do. She means the world to me. We've always gotten along great. Doesn't she know how painful it is to be dismissed like this?"

"Did anything happen between you?"

"Ellen said something about my lateness last month. She's never done that before."

"Are you late?"

"I was getting in at 10:30. And sometimes I leave an hour early. But so what? I do the work."

She wants things to be nice. She wants to have fun. Johan sees what he sees, that she is sliding toward the exit.

"Is it possible to get to work on time?"

"I just had a bad night. Actually, it was kind of scary. I came to in the Sheep Meadow in Central Park with no idea how I had gotten there."

"You don't remember anything?"

"I just remember being in a bar and drinking. That's the last thing I remember."

"You had a blackout."

"What's that?"

"It's when a person drinks a lot and doesn't remember what he or she has done."

"How would you know about such a thing?"

"Because I've had them."

"You don't even drink. All you ever have is herbal tea."

"When I was younger—your age—I drank."

"What happened in these blackouts?"

"I don't really know. That's the scary thing about them—what I might have done."

"Is that why you stopped?"

"That was one reason."

"What were the others?"

"Alcohol was ruining my life. I was unable to get through a day without a drink, and when I drank, I was unable to control how much I drank."

"Gee, that's awful."

"Actually, it was a good thing, a really pivotal time in my life."

"How so?"

"I feel like I have had the chance to live two lives in one. There was my drinking life, and there has been the one that has followed."

"You don't drink at all?"

"No."

"Not even one glass of beer? Gee, that's too bad."

"It's the first drink. That's the one I have to stay away from. I attend Rooms of Recovery meetings. If ever you should want to go, let me know."

That same morning he hears the power sweep before he sees it. "We're number one. Preeminent. On the move. On the go." A phalanx of blue-uniformed women, striding three abreast, turn the corner and head down the long corridor. With incredible speed do they close the distance. To avoid a collision, he flattens himself against the wall as, with intense commitment to their purpose and full awareness of their chosen status, the cohort speeds past. No need for acknowledgment, no need for an excuse me, no need for anything but recognition of their eminence. In that moment do they scream his invisibility, his nothingness.

Make way for the Leadership Team.

Make way indeed.

Make way for Jane Fallows.

Make way for Whitney McNair.

Make way for Jeanine McQuaid.

Make way for Maeve Muldoon.

Make way for Pensiva Gwalt.

Make way for Snook Pomelly.

Make way, I say. Make way.

Isabel, it was like being in the tunnel of my childhood. Oh, the power of that train moseying around the bend and picking up steam on the straightaway. I saw it. I saw it again just now. We should all be trains all the time. Whoo! Whoo!

In an atmosphere of hush the administrative secretaries at their open work stations carry out their tasks for the women of power who occupy the offices behind them—big, well-appointed offices, with top-of-the-line executive desks and even sofas, as he sees through the open doors.

To the other side of the floor he heads. Again those old cedar-shingled water towers sitting atop the smaller buildings. Again the startling view, the reminder that he is here behind sealed windows in an insulated world of recycled air, separated from his life, from his aspiration. Where has it gone, the passion and the intensity? All he has ever wanted to do was to record the past, preserve it, love it. That is all. He should be out there photographing those water towers. He should be the twenty-four-year-old he once was, wandering the city with his camera. Boxes and boxes of photos in the back of his closet he has from those years of intensity, boxes that he can't bear to open lest they kill him. He ran away from his intensity. And now what? He cools his engine collecting a paycheck. He allocates the maximum to his 401(k). He plays it safe waiting on his female superiors. He is their little boy.

In spite of his warning call to her that he would be right up, Marie Crain sits with her back to the door in her small office dozing, her head on the desk.

"Good morning, Marie. It's me, Johan," he calls out to her, and she comes to.

"Hey, there, Johan. Got something for me? Whatcha working on?"

Groundhog Day, for sure.

Age has shrunk her. How small she looks in her smock dress.

"Have you heard from Human Resources about the forms for the appendix? I believe they were supposed to provide us with samples of a new system they are putting in place for review and evaluation of staff." Johan can only hope that she hasn't. The manuscript is an ever growing monstrosity, a chaotic merger of three smaller volumes. Its essential purpose is to keep CEOs and board chairs from killing each other in savage power grabs out there in council land, where he himself has never been. The connecting threads are thin and frayed, and the resource remains top-heavy with charts unsupported by accompanying text.

"We'll have to get onto that," she says. "I'll get my assistant to help me. She's new and really good. I've trained her well. She'll get everything straightened out right away. What else do you have for me?"

Marie stares vacantly at the text. Surely the end is coming for her here at GoAN. But where will she go? To her sister across the country in Portland, Oregon, with whom she jointly owns a home? Just the two of them in that grayness, the constant fine drizzle that almost drove him mad the three sunless weeks he was out there in the Pacific Northwest some years ago? No, neither her apartment nor the house in Portland will do. She will stay here as long as she can, until they carry her out in a box. This is her retirement home.

"All right. We're making progress," he says, collecting his papers, squaring the edges as those camera-worthy newscasters do on the evening news that he never watches anymore.

By the elevator a woman waits, petite, sparkling, her skirt short and tight-fitting, as is her blouse, her hair gloriously thick and full of curls. She smiles, confident in her manner. Without looking, she sees him noticing her, sees and feels his hunger.

"Who are you?" he hears himself say, as they step into the elevator.

"Who I am? I am Zofia. Who you are?" Her words come with a foreign accent.

"Me? I am Johan," he says.

"Hello, Mr. Johan," she says, as the door opens and she steps onto the landing.

"Hello, Ms. Zofia," he says, as she turns left toward the cafeteria, her purse in hand.

Oh dear, he thinks, watching her perfect form. Just oh dear.

The snideness of Ms. Tooth, Rhoda Bahr, and the obsequious ways of Melvin Kleiner when he performs like a trained seal for Lurleen Lulabella may incense him, as do some of the tendencies of tongue-exposing Alice Piccoli, but now there are new and happier dimensions to his org life—Zofia Kozlowski, from Kraków, Poland, and Heather Redleaf, from Knoxville, Tennessee—to contemplate.

All he is looking for from Heather is a sign, some melting of that permafrost demeanor she displays with him. And oh, happy day it is when she does emerge from seclusion and, unattended by Mary Terezzi, breaks into peals of girlish laughter, doubling over as he passes her in the hallway. Oh, delicious laughter of teenage cheerleaders swept up in boy talk, pompoms in hand, on the sidelines of the Knoxville High football field awaiting their young gods in helmets and shoulder pads. Girls at that stage of attraction/ assessment, coming from behind their mother's skirts toward the fire that warms, then burns, and removes all laughter once the passion of the thing itself begins. Because you do not laugh in the act, only before. Drawn to the fire because it is inevitable; because what else, ultimately, is there in this life, if not that, even as the caution flags remain?

His bold stare, his simple and direct expression of interest, has caused her laughter. Because it calls her from her aloofness, calls her to a recognition of him. He needs for this desire to be seen. It is the flag he waves to assert that he is a human being and that he is not lost to the things of the flesh any more than she is. It is because he hasn't had this in a long, long time at the org. All he has had is bear-like Lurleen Lulabella and devouring Alice Piccoli.

So that, on another occasion, he says to her, as she stands by the photocopier, "Maybe we can go to lunch some time," and she says to him, her mane of strawberry blond hair shimmering under the fluorescent wash of light, "But I'm married."

"I didn't ask you if you were married. I asked you to go for lunch." Because she has said everything, implicitly raising the matter of his interest in her—his sexual, not platonic interest, unstated as it might be—as a barrier. What he also hears is not a wintry blast of outrage but her girlish laughter to go with the girlish smile on her freckled face, a reaction that suggests she is flattered and has left the door open, as if she is saying, not simply that she is married— end of sentence—but that she is married, and what is he willing to do about it? This is a woman who knows the dark path and has contemplated the downward journey on it.

The husband as protector, as human shield, to keep the wolves at bay.

"I think of you all the time, and always with the pain of longing. It must be that I knew you in another life."

"Yes? You were in Kraków maybe?" Zofia Kozlowski, replies to him as he stands behind her on the cafeteria line.

"It could be. I have an affinity with things Polish."

"What that means, affinity?"

"Come. Sit with me. I will tell you all about affinity, and infinity, the moon, the stars. All of life's mysteries we will discuss."

She can only laugh. "Understood," she says.

He falls out of the line and waits at a table with his cup of ersatz coffee.

"I stay only a minute. My Milly will be waiting for me."

"Your Milly?"

"Milly Degenber? You do not know her?"

Yes, he knows Milly Degenber. Formerly the head of Business Services. Now the director of the Records Department. One of those women who says suggestive things to him, causing him to recoil. In working with her on a project a while back, she made reference to French lingerie, her voice teasing and seductive.

"So, Mr. Johan, what you want?"

"That is a big question."

"You are big man."

"Is your boyfriend a big man?"

"Do I tell you I have boyfriend?"

"All women who look like you have a boyfriend."

"So, yes, I have boyfriend and he is big," she says, elongating the last word.

"But you are not so big."

"No I am small. I am small Zofia in big world."

"I am small too."

"You? You are not small."

"In my mind's eye, I am five feet six inches tall. That was my height when I was fourteen, before I grew like a weed."

"What you do here, Mr. Johan?" She has had enough of big and small.

"I work with words."

"What means?"

"I am an editor."

"Editor?"

"I take a manuscript and make it into a book."

"Redactor. You are redactor."

The life of an immigrant. What is that? He is with a creature from a foreign land, an alien, struggling with every fiber of her being to comprehend her new environment.

"Yes, I am a redactor." Redactor. It sounds like a prehistoric bird.

"I go now. My Milly wait for me."

And he must go, too. Mindy Jacobs, in Executive Search, is waiting for him to share his expertise. There are résumés he must review. Add his commas, his semicolons. Take out this and refine that. Be sure the bulleted lists are parallel, that is, that they all start with a verb or a subject; that restrictive clauses receive no comma while nonrestrictive (those that start with *which,* though not always) are left open; all done with his old tools of the trade, his red pencils and his art gum eraser, before this new electronic tracking thing that Lurleen brought in.

She is waiting for him, a middle-aged woman with big, heavily made up eyes. Tons of mascara and eyeliner and some sort of blush she applies to her face to rouge her cheeks. He thinks of Mlle. Gallimard, his septuagenarian high school French teacher, her powdered cheeks quivering as she walked down the aisle grilling the class, and of all those bright girls with their copies of *Paris Match* and Camus's *Etranger.* But he is not in the tortured and yet, in memory, halcyon days of adolescence, staring out the window of an exclusive private school at Central Park across the street. He is with Mindy Jacobs, from Queens, New York, who kvetches and connives and pulls him this way and that with her stuff.

"Hello, you handsome man. Have you come calling on me? He's all mine, girls."

"No, he isn't, Mindy. I saw him first," says merry Jane Cranshaw, with a disability that requires the aid of a cane. Women he has known around the org for some years. Women who, like him, are afraid, now that the winds of change are blowing.

Their words tear at him. He hears acute mockery. He is back in that ramshackle apartment of his childhood, with the taunts of those troubled older sisters. Women setting him up as a prelude to tearing him down. Because he is not a man. He is not handsome. He wants to run away. He doesn't want to have to handle these people anymore.

"Did you hear?" she says, her voice suggesting that whatever it is is big news.

"Hear what?" he says.

"Human Resources is considering outsourcing our department."

"You're kidding."

"I should kid about being put out on the street?"

"How do you know?"

"I have my sources in HR."

"Wow! That is big news," he says, feeling the weight of her eyes on him.

By now they are in the conference room and she has closed the door. The truth he dare not speak being why not outsource the Executive Search Committee? What kind of service is that which requires six staff members and a secretary to recruit candidates for executive level positions with councils and help them with their résumés? At most, they send him about three résumés a month, all of them a couple of single-spaced pages in length. A temp could handle such a minimal workload.

Mindy has awakened his own fear; she has passed it along like a communicable illness. Not for the first time does he think of the long ago, and that building in which he was raised, with all those solitary men and women in their rooms, and of his impractical aunt, alive in the spirit but with her feet off the ground, and of his mother, so dependent on his aunt; the whole family dependent on his aunt, given the low wages that his father earned. The unreality of that operation is the unreality of this one as well. He is in a building full of dreamers incapable, in spite of their strategy sessions and tactical planning sessions and those corporate titles they now walk around with—senior vice president of this, senior vice president of that—of making a buck.

"Why? Is that happening to your department, too?" she asks, her words coming slowly, with a hint of doubt. She will give him a chance to explain himself.

"Not yet. But you never know."

"No one's said anything to you? No rumors?"

"No. Nothing like that. But it's not like the old days."

"What old days? Not all of us have been here since the year of the flood. I'm still a young woman. Don't I look like a young woman?"

"Sure. Sure you do."

"What have you got for me?" Her tone is brusque now, signaling the end of chitchat. And so, for fifteen minutes, he goes over the three résumés, line by line. Explains why he has replaced "which" with "that" and vice versa here and there, the difference between a restrictive and a nonrestrictive clause.

"Yes, I keep forgetting that," Mindy says, when they come to a typo correction: "capital" for "capitol." People become insecure. They are returned to their childhoods during these editorial reviews. Old shame about classroom lapses surface. He knows something that many people don't—that there is no necessary correlation between writing skills and intelligence. Time and again he sees clearly bright people, people who can speak in balanced sentences with not a word out of place rendered helpless when they put words on paper. They aren't taught properly in grade school the rules of grammar, or maybe they have undiagnosed dyslexia. And so they give up or try to compensate by excelling in other areas. Defeat comes early in life for many. It's at times like these that he sees his mediocrity, that he should know what a predicate nominative is or a gerund or how to form a possessive with a name such as Dickens. He is grateful for some skill by which he can earn his daily bread. But there is also sadness and even more that this is all he has to give the world. Or maybe not. It should be all right if he does his best with what he has been given, if he can't reach the stature of those with a larger endowment. He will be good for this woman, Mindy Jacobs, as he will be good for all the women of the org. He will clean up their clutter, scrape away their excess. He will tidy up, as he was born to do, the boy with the broom in his hand. He is, after all, a servant, born to please and to receive approval for his efforts to restore order where it had been lacking.

All is not lost with Mindy Jacobs. He is as peripheral to her life as she is to his. He is but a half-hour distraction.

"Good job, Johan. Good job. Come see us any time. You hear?" she says, in earshot of Jane Cranshaw, as they are leaving the conference room.

Yes, any time, he thinks, as he stands waiting for the elevator.

Chapter 30

Isabel,

Do you remember that room in the loft that the contractor Creighton Mueller built for us? You suggested this addition so as to ensure my privacy with a room of my very own. I have been thinking of that room recently, especially the calendar on the wall and the month of August that it was turned to when I left for good. Actually, two rooms were created, a bedroom for Mia and a study for myself. Suddenly the loft had a different shape. No longer was it that beautiful open space. Instead it had this ballooning whiteness, the sheet-rocked walls violating the space's integrity.

I liked that room, however much it compromised the purity of the loft. In it I would sit for hours after work. It had a small casement window with opaque colored glass. Sometimes I would peek out from the crack at the bottom of the window between the base and the sill to the dining area. I was not spying but was like a child hiding from the adult world. I suppose I was looking for the safe spot, the place where no harm could come to me. The womb. In the silence of that room, surely there was joy at all that had been given me, and all I might become in this new beginning. But there was also fear and apprehension. How had I come to be here? Revulsion would overcome me that I had dared to impose myself on you and Mia, and only my complete disappearance would serve as atonement. At such times I saw myself as an ape wandering about in your delicate garden.

You had a visceral connection with the suffering in the world, and acutely so when it came to animals. For this reason did you choose to be an agent of mercy and rescue a pooch from the pound so it would not be destroyed, as those that aren't adopted inevitably are. Put down. Imagine that, having the power to put down. You fell in love with Bonkers on seeing those soulful eyes staring back at you there in the cage. A coon hound, a black and tan creature who vomited in the car and put on his brakes at the doorway, as he was to do at virtually every entranceway for the rest of his days. This dog knew from abuse. This dog was trauma central. God only knows what had been inflicted on him. Tossed from a speeding car? Starved and tortured by a brutal owner? Creighton Mueller called him Yikes, given Bonkers' penchant on the street for being all into everybody else's business. Dog owners saw us coming and crossed to the other side, dragging their pooches with them, or picked up their smaller ones to keep them safe. You could not say that Bonkers was violent or bad-intentioned. A reckless enthusiasm, easily misunderstood as aggression, is what generated concern among the neighbors.

In those years I wore a jacket and tie to work, and sometimes a suit. I rode the Number Six train from Spring Street up to Thirty-third Street. Imagine that, Spring only one below Bleecker, where I used to board the train, and Bleecker only one below Astor, where I would get off after work for my supply at the wines and spirits supermarket back when I was living with Sarah. I was not meeting with clients and doing business over lunch. But I had that need to look and feel important, just as my father did in those Robert Hall suits he showed up for work in at Jack Dempsey's Restaurant down on Forty-ninth Street and Broadway.

To be honest, that need for a secret place pursued me at work as well. There was a stall in the often unused men's room, given the few men on the floor. On the metal partition I made a faint mark with my ballpoint pen, thrilled to know that it would be discernible to no one'e eye but my own. And in my cubicle, I could see through, where the ends were joined by hinges, to the carpeted floor outside, noting the legs and feet of the passersby. What a delicious feeling of safety derived from knowing that they could not possibly, from the height at which they stood, see me. Oh, the joy, the sheer joy. And sometimes, I would close one eye and virtually close the other, so it appeared as if I were staring out at the world from the slightest crack. I could create this window on the street, in a crowded elevator, anywhere.

To pass the time, I watch old movies, which I borrow from the Mid-Manhattan Library. *High Sierra,* with Humphrey Bogart and Ida Lupino, is my latest find. Bogart plays an ex-con named Roy Earle. Recently released from prison, he returns to a different world from the one he knew during Prohibition. He is a man whom time has passed by, and who lives and dies by the gun while keeping the love of a woman. And then, right there on top of my TV, next to the gladiolus you gave me, I have two other films, *The Awful Truth,* a romantic comedy starring Irene Dunne and Cary Grant, and the great Arthur Penn film *Bonnie and Clyde,* with Faye Dunaway and Warren Beatty.

Once, long ago, Sarah and I were walking along Broadway when suddenly she said, "That's Faye Dunaway." I looked around but there was no beautiful blond movie star within my range of vision. So I said, "Where?" and Sarah pointed to a woman in an oversized raincoat walking into a Merit Farms store. (You could find them in many neighborhoods back then, the rotisserie chickens in the window turning on those spits. All gone now. All gone.) I gave pursuit, so in need was I of confirmation. But Faye Dunaway was ready for me. She really was. Truth to tell, she didn't look like a woman who ate Merit Farms chickens, or maybe it was that I just couldn't imagine her taking a rotisserie chicken home in one of those silver foil bags with maybe a side of slaw or fries to go with it. Licking her fingers if she was alone and didn't have a paper towel handy. She had a face verging on anarchy, the prominent cheekbones somehow contributing to a visage of fragile beauty, and eyes that fixed you with a cool, flat stare.

"Are you Faye Dunaway?" I said. "The Faye Dunaway from *Bonnie and Clyde?*"

"Yes," she said, undoing me with her one-word answer, just throwing me back on myself. With the affect she was presenting did she create a wall I had no way through or over or around, a wall that bounced you hard off its surface and left you crumpled on the ground. Because I had come to her as the legions of the stupid came to her, when what she was really needing was to see if there was something more that I could show her. And so she returned me to the ordinariness of my life with the understanding that I could not be a part of the world she inhabited even as she was presenting herself as plain folk out on a neighborhood errand among the populace of New York City.

Isabel, Faye Dunaway was a going and a coming woman in that time. She was on movie sets in different countries and different states. She had men pursuing her and admiration societies on every continent. Many, many were the times that she flew on jet planes. It was not so with me. I walked the streets of Manhattan as my father had. My world was small and security-driven.

In this time, as I am often telling you, I was much in favor of the railroads of America, though the writing was on the wall for them, given the macadamizing and vulcanizing thrust of America, which had a plan for cars to pollute your dreams as well as your waking state. I ask you this question. I ask it. What sort of culture is it that makes man and woman and child subordinate to a gas-powered vehicle, that says, "You have exactly thirty seconds to get your sweet self from one side of the street to the other, and God help you if you dilly-dally or shilly-shally, because you will pay for your dawdle-acious ways with your life"? A culture that says, "Go on, you cars and trucks and buses, maraud up and down the streets of Manhattan and bear but briefly these fool pedestrians and their plebeian mode of mobility"?

So no, those roadways did not interest me. They did not hold my passion. I went in this time to the railroad yards of New York City, over toward the Hudson River alongside the elevated portion of the West Side Highway, to the sprawling freight yard from the glory days of the New York Central Railroad, though now the tracks had been thinned out and you would see only the occasional switcher shunting cars from one siding to another. I came by night with my pint bottle of Old Mr. Boston Blackberry Flavored brandy. Sarah was back in the Chinatown loft doing her artwork. I have told you, have I not, how it was arranged? That money from the till of the renting office in the lobby of the building my family managed funded this purchase of the loft? Oh, life built on corruption and deluded thinking, that had me committing experience on the play sites of my childhood.

There was a spiral staircase, a caged-in structure, that led down to the yards below. The diesel smoke floating up from the muck and ordure was an intoxicant in itself. It conjured gruff, stolid men in flannel shirts and lumber jackets or the striped denim overalls of the train conductor, and summoned the forlorn whistles of the night to my ears. To be a drunk is not to be a finite soul but to reach beyond the sun and stars for some point beyond. It is going back in time as a way of going forward. It is about nestling in the good and the bad and calling them neither.

If Hemingway ran with the bulls in Pamplona, I was running with the trains in New York City. Boosted by the brandy, I crouched breathless before a new world unfolding. There was an element of potentially imprisoning fear in all of this, the least of it being the faux hobo ride itself. What challenge was there, after all, in hoisting oneself onto a slow-moving freight? The fear, of course, was of the criminal element, the vagabond demon, the psychopath, the creature who dwelt in darkness and had been lurking there my entire life. But my drunken state and the confidence that motion can bring held this otherwise paralyzing dread at bay.

I waited while the shunting switcher did its work, pulling cars from one siding or another and coupling them to the midnight train, the engine signaling its intent with a high-beam that brought me to a state of delirium. In full pursuit I ran into the tunnel, gripping the ladder of a gondola car, its hold full of old and creosote-soaked railroad ties. Looming, like a lodestar, was the tunnel's end, and as we drew near, the roar of highway traffic, the rapid revolutions of rubber on the roadway, began to sound in my ears. We soon approached another golden marker of my past, the old meatpacking plants, where huge sides of beef were once offloaded from those boxcar freezers by burly men in soiled white aprons. From below I could now look up at the single spire of the Riverside Church and the low-slung, heavy weight of Grant's Tomb, all of it summoning childhood and cherry Cokes and cherry cheese danishes and the tune from the Good Humor truck that called you to it, the white-uniformed driver reaching in through that small square door at the back of the truck for the raspberry and orange sherbet popsicles I favored. All of that came back to me, the curbside position of the truck outside the entrance to the Columbia University mall at One Hundred Sixteenth Street and the Chock Full O'Nuts on the southwest corner and the intricacies of alleyways and basements I had explored as a child. But now there was no longer the delirium that had quickened my pulse. The train had eased into a steadier, faster pace, now passing the northbound cars on the highway. Up ahead the great span of the George Washington Bridge spread a glittering trail of lights across the burdened waters of the Hudson. I was in a growing panic that the speed of the train would keep me bound to it. From the routines of my regular life was I being moved into a cold and inhospitable space, and with fear as the impetus for action, I flung myself free of the gondola car and fell forward into a weedy patch of earth. As the train roared past, the boxcars and all the rolling stock, I watched on hands and knees, stunned by the rapid evaporation of my dream and the train's cold indifference.

Now at liberty to pursue another course, I headed not for isolation in the northern wilds but human connection, and within a half hour, courtesy of the IRT, was down at The Muse on West Broadway and Spring, a bar I had been patronizing since moving to Chinatown with Sarah. In browns and tans, and with a sleek design, it was softly lit and drew in the sots, the wannabes, and the occasional SoHo star.

I started with Courvoisier. Cognac seemed the way to go to build on the brandy that I had consumed. Soon the promise of the night was alive in me again. There was a partitioned table area raised above the bar floor, and there I joined two women about my age, one of whom soon left with a man she had met that evening. I told the remaining woman of the endless novel on which I was underway, and, when she asked if I always went around with such dirty hands, I explained to her my adventure on the train. But she was not of the world of reckless adventure and so didn't respond. The designer boutique black top with the small gold star in the middle suggested she was a woman who knew how to present herself, as did her boldly short black hair. Maybe the fact that her friend had departed with a companion for the night inclined her to consider doing the same.

We walked west. It was one of those warm New York nights, with strollers out in the warren of narrow streets of the West Village. On Christopher Street, past the newsstand and the all-night diner, we saw gays living their truth in tight, rolled up denim and black leather vests and white T-shirts and those motorcycle caps favored by Marlon Brando in *The Wild Ones*. Some had key rings attached to their belt loops and kerchiefs hanging jauntily from the back pockets of their Levi's and other insignia familiar only to the initiated. On the corner of one such street, with the river in view, stood a bar, sharp points of red light in its otherwise dark recess beckoning you to enter. There were men of stud proportions milling outside. A commotion-hungry crowd had gathered nearby, drawn to some drama I could sense, with a pounding in my chest, but not see. And suddenly there it was, two men faced off against each other. One stood bare-chested, a stiletto in his hand. The open blade, silver and of fatal length, was an object of wonder and horror at the same time. The other man, about ten feet away, held no weapon at all. It was like some dream of childhood, in which the inevitable flash of knives predominated. Even more than a shooting, the prospect of witnessing a knife penetrate flesh was too gruesome to witness.

I turned my newfound friend—her name was Debbie Berg—down another street, this one dominated by a gloomy former armory. For a while the dread summoned by the scene of conflict was overwhelming, and I could only hope that it had been a kind of posturing. But Debbie's thoughts were elsewhere, and soon we were climbing the stairs to her walkup, past the disapproving stare of her Italian landlady. Below we could hear the roar of truck traffic entering and exiting the Holland Tunnel, a sound she had gotten used to, as Sarah and I had to the N trains rumbling over the Manhattan Bridge just down from our Chinatown loft.

I began visiting with her weekly. It was not long before she guessed I was living with someone. "You're a bastard," she said, with some gentleness. I don't suppose I meant enough for her to really care.

That first night I walked home along Canal Street, the trailer trucks speaking to the loneliness of their long journeys as they roared past the closed and shuttered shops. The stairs of my building were steep and brightly lit, a pitiless fluorescent wash in contrast to the darkness of our top-floor loft. My socks balled in the pockets of my Levis, I heard with relief Sarah turn and moan in her sleep on the boxspring mattress we used for a bed. That night, or what was left of it, she murmured my name as I lay beside her. I felt her warmth, her beautiful breasts against my back. I was in bed with blond and pretty Sarah. I had just come from dark and pretty Debbie. I was twenty-four.

"Where were you?" Sarah said the next morning. She was raised up on one elbow, her head tilted and resting on her hand.

"The train took me farther than I wanted it to."

"How far did you go?"

"A ways."

We made love that morning. It felt like something untended to unless we did. She was my anchor, my orientation point. Without her fear found me.

Even as I write this, Isabel, in this removed phase where life has delivered me, the wonder of human touch comes back to me. And some fear grows in me that I am as deluded today as when I drank. Is it possible that I am as isolated in God as I was by the bottle? Will I spend my eternity longing for the human touch whose memory I have just summoned? Is it a dangerous stance to be dismissive of the physical realm?

Chapter 31

"Where do you live?"

"Why you want to know? You have some urgent business?"

"Because without you I fear I might fall down and die."

"Everybody die."

"So I'm not to know where you live?"

"Brooklyn." Like "brew" she pronounces it, taking a long ride on the double "o."

"'Only the dead know Brooklyn.' Thomas Wolfe said that."

"I do not know your Thomas Wolfe, but maybe true."

"You don't look so dead, Zofia. We need to do something."

"We are not doing something now?"

"We are doing plenty. We are laying the basis for profound happiness. But when can we, as we Americans say, take it to the next level?"

"What level?"

"Let's step out of the box."

"I don't know your box. Besides, I have boyfriend."

"Gangster boyfriend?"

"Just boyfriend."

"This boyfriend. He kill me for saying hello to you?"

"Is possible."

"And what does he do to you?"

"Doesn't do nothing."

"Exactly. He doesn't do nothing. Or maybe he does something, and then he does nothing for a long time? Here is what I think."

"Tell it to me what you think."

"I think woman with man who does nothing most of the time needs man who does something some of the time."

"I like what you think, Mr. Johan. And now I must return to my Milly."

Heather keeps off hours. Her feeding time is 3 p.m., most of the workforce having left the cafeteria by now after devouring their heaping portions of stinky food—fatty sausages and trichinosis-inducing pork and whatnot. There Heather is now with her plastic tubs of lentils and rice and curried vegetables. He arrives as she is removing her supply from the giant steel gray refrigerator, the tubs held against her chest. Even beautiful women are diminished by leftovers in plastic enclosures. The portions are tiny; a certain amount of deprivation is required to have a body such as hers.

"I guess I should leave you alone."

"What's that supposed to mean?" Her voice is like iron, as it often is.

"Only that eating is probably a private matter for you."

"Not if I'm in a public space," she says. Triumphant. Needing to have the last word.

He moves forward toward the urn and pours hot water for his tea. When he returns she is gone, vanished, leaving her cruel laughter to linger in the air. *I blew him off.*

But then there she is again at the end of the day at the photocopier. She has her face against the glass as the light bar flashes across it. Again and again the same thing—full frontal, one side, then the other side.

"You could damage your eyes. You know that, don't you?"

She has a hard smile for him. "An artist has to be willing to sacrifice everything. Everything."

"You are an artist?"

"Of course. I do the man's work by day and then I stay late and do my own and then I go home and feed my boy and then I work some more and…"

"When do you sleep?"

"The problem with you is that you are in a comfort zone. That means you sleep all the time. The point is not sleep but awakening. An artist is not an artist unless she is pushing the limits."

"Yes?" he says. He cannot afford to say "Is it?" to Heather. That would sound challenging and harsh and cause her to break off the conversation, which has a twig-like fragility. But in that moment he is embarrassed by the poverty of her idea. She is a little old to be preaching the virtues of self-abuse. That would seem to him to be a young person's fallacy. But he also sees, his heart softening, that she is a young person, a young thirty-five-year-old only now leaving the safety of her home to come out in the world, a waif-like creature spouting important-sounding but ultimately nonsensical maxims, like one of those doomed characters in those Godard movies from the sixties.

And there are other thoughts as he stands there staring at the bizarre photocopies of her face and anatomy: that she is a younger Audrey Eastbrook, Sarah's old friend, an Audrey Eastbrook who has given birth and maintains a life, till now at least, with a husband; that if she is full of folly, it is because the South is not so much a state of mind as a religion. To be a Southerner means only one thing— you will fight to the death, and then you will fight some more, and that she, no matter the featheriness of her name, is a fighter who puts her elbows in your eye and her fist to your mouth.

"So you live for your art. Is that it?"

"I told you. Art is an awakening. You have to feel your breath. You have to live your breath." So emphatic. So tight.

She has no curiosity about him. If there is to be anything here, it will be of his creation.

"She has good ideas and a lot on the ball. She's a real change-maker. And I can tell she really likes me. She laughs at all my jokes," Melvin Kleiner is saying. The barrier created between them by the style guide spat has gone into the past. They sit in Bryant Park on those green folding chairs paid for by the business district or whatever it is that supports the maintenance of the park. All those down-on-their-luck men, and even a few women, wandering about in green uniforms, like prison garb. And maybe that's where a lot of these folks have been—Riker's Island or upstate even—like the lanky African American man now emptying the overflow garbage can five feet away, yanking from the receptacle the black plastic bag filled with Styrofoam cups and containers deposited by the lunch hour crowd and loading it into his wheelbarrow. The burden of guilt for being white and privileged.

"You haven't been here long enough."

"What do you mean?

"You'll find out."

"Are you being purposely mysterious?"

Even without the goad, Johan would not be able to restrain himself, so tied is Lurleen with a national trend in his mind. "She is like a member of the Daughters of the American Revolution or some other mean and crackpot right-wing organization. There is something repressive about her."

"That sounds like a serious judgment."

"Weren't you there when Lurleen said she would ban all teenagers from reading *Vogue* or *Cosmopolitan?* And didn't you hear her say that strip mining is a good thing?"

"She was probably having a bad day."

"We'll see." Soreness has been rising in him. Best to let go. He can't win Melvin over with this sort of argument. With his inner ear,

Melvin is hearing the complaint about Lurleen as simple jealousy that he, Melvin, has his boss's love and Johan doesn't.

Melvin has bought a complicated salad and a chicken kebab on a skewer at the Hez over on Fortieth Street, a deli that features big tureens of soup and glistening meats and cheeses and pastries under glass. The fare is served by rough-looking men with stubble on their faces and outfitted in crisp white uniforms. Their sandwiches start at $8.00, probably more than the workers' hourly wage, and go from there. What are people thinking paying out such money when they could bring a container of hummus and a couple of oranges to work? That and a few slices of spelt bread should be enough to get them through the day.

"What did you get?" Melvin asks, seeing the small white bag that Johan carries.

"Tomato soup." Thin and watery soup. If he is lucky, some disgruntled and underpaid employee hasn't spit into it, as a chef did in the soup of a complaining customer in George Orwell's *Down and Out in Paris and London.*

The deli is next to some fancy hotel, the Park Bryant, a red runner extending off the sidewalk, as if the shoes of the residents should not touch the city's sidewalks. The bellboys in their tight burgundy livery and white socks and black shoes, the doorman in tails and a top hat. Something alienating about all this striving for refinement and class, as if anyone who used such a word as the latter could have any.

"This is nice," Melvin says. "I'm glad we got out. It's a strange life, staring into a computer screen all day. Easy to get disconnected. And we're fortunate to have this park. Green grass and trees are a tonic."

"It wasn't a pleasant place to be some years back. It was overrun with junkies and drug dealers. Now it's sparkling."

On the west side of the park workers are erecting a stage for the summer entertainment program, stars of Broadway shows singing and dancing, their voices projected to the far reaches by the powerful microphones in this park that changes its appearance as frequently as some girls change the color of their hair. For a while the park goers will forget their workday lives, emotions stirred by the songfest, and Johan will have a glimmer of understanding of what it means to be warehoused in some home for seniors with card parties and other entertainment. The sense that he is in the waiting, the observing phase, of his life as it slowly winds down.

"Yes, so I remember," Melvin says. He looks old in the natural light, his skin pale and dull, his hairline rapidly receding, what remains on top in need of tamping down. Not that he has anything to fear from the exposure that hair loss brings, not with the power and substantiality his well-shaped head projects. A not entirely fastidious sort, Melvin. His worn and scuffed shoes in need of a shine, his pants shapeless, and his white shirt wrinkled and missing a button. Well, it's often a few months before new male arrivals to the org doff their ties and retire their suits for more casual wear. Sooner or later the org works its dulling magic on everyone.

"That's it? That's all you eat?" Melvin asks, between mouthfuls. It is an omnivore's mouth, wide and devouring.

"I would have bought more, but I wasn't feeling well." Meaning that he wasn't feeling well while standing in the stinky food deli, a phrasing that protects him from telling an outright lie.

"You deprive yourself. You're like Kafka's hunger artist," Melvin says.

"Kafka minus the 'k' spells 'kaka.'"

But Melvin won't be deterred. "You've been with the organization so long. You must be doing quite well. But you don't seem to go out and do things."

"I'm here in the park with you. That's something, wouldn't you say? And you see that stage the workers are constructing? The shows will be coming to us this summer, at least snippets of them in song. And I go to the library and get my movie videocassettes. This weekend I'll be watching *Out of the Past,* with Robert Mitchum.

Classic film noir. You can't get much better than that on a Friday night."

"You're happy with your life as it is?"

"There's contentment, and then sometimes there's longing."

"Longing for what?"

"Well, sometimes I could wish I had a woman in my life."

"Don't you have someone you see?"

"I see my ex-wife."

"On what basis?"

"We're the best of friends."

"That's why you don't have a woman in your life. You have to let go of your ex-wife for that to happen."

"Really?"

"There may be an energy leak. Energy is finite. There's a quantum of it and no more."

"I see." An opinion he has heard before. And generally the people who make such assertions fade from his life while Isabel remains. It will be good for him to sit through the emotional turmoil he is feeling and not reach out for reassurance, just let the waves of pain and discomfort break over him.

Isabel,

I had to hold myself last night and slept with my underwear tucked right under me. Melvin Kleiner lifted the roof off my house and removed the walls, and now all the elements were pouring in on me—rain followed by big balls of hail and lightning bolts like jagged and brilliant white spears. Oh, what a purgative aloneness truly is, that when everything, *everything,* is taken away we can still, on our knees, say, "Father, help me, just help me. Hold me, just hold me. If the premise of my life, that love never dies, is itself a lie, then tell me, just tell me, and if not, let me be silent in the groves of peace and contentment where you have delivered me."

There is heavy lifting going on. Like a war room Melvin's spacious cubicle is. Pinned to the wall is a large diagram with color-coded boxes and those map markers, pins with little round heads.

"Melvin is a genius, an absolute genius. There is nothing that he can't do. He is the cat's meow," Lurleen Lulabella says.

"Is that better than the dog's bark or the cow's moo?" Melvin asks.

Lurleen throws back her head and gives the gathered her one-minute laugh special, tears pooling in her eyes. "You are the one," she says, when she can continue. "You get *it*. You can take us where we need to go. The national organization and the councils will soon be one."

The org has committed to an intranet that will link the councils with headquarters and advance the communications possibilities.

"The technology is great, but what will we have to say to each other that we aren't saying already?" Johan asks.

"The problem with you, Johan, is that you are not an agent of change. You are not a vision person," Lurleen says.

"We have to ride the waves of change," says Mary Terezzi.

"Well, I hope it doesn't carry us out to sea and drown us," Johan says.

"You don't know how to break the mold. You don't know how to move on," Rhoda Bahr says. "That's why you're still here."

"Maybe so, but you seem to have a mold of your own, the way you go on and on about change."

"I will not be talked to this way."

"That's what you always say. Maybe that's a mold you need to break."

"Why don't you leave? Why don't you just get out of here?"

"Because you love me too much and it would break your heart should I go."

"Fat chance of that," Rhoda says.

"Are you sure?" Johan says, and laughs.

"I'm not talking to you anymore," Rhoda says.

"Another thing you always say," Johan replies.

"Children, must we fight? Can we not be one?" Lurleen says.

Isabel,

Something big is happening here. I can feel it. Melvin is my teacher. He is leading me from the illness where I have lived, the demon of competition that led me to walk off the basketball court in the eleventh grade because a teammate was excelling and I wasn't. I must not go out the window or under the ground. I must stay and see where all of this is leading. I must stayed tuned to my own life.

"Were you there?"

"Was I where?"

"Columbia, in 1968. Where you there?"

"During the demonstrations? Sure. We occupied Hamilton Hall, as I recall, for a couple of days."

"You weren't among those out there on One Hundred Fourteenth Street between Broadway and Riverside protesting unfair landlord practices by Columbia?"

"No, I missed that one. Why do you ask?"

"Just curious."

"Out of the blue you're curious about 1968?"

"I was there."

"Where? Hamilton Hall?"

"No. Outside the building. I was arrested that night, along with others. I didn't want to be. I didn't belong. I had just come from my part-time job at the post office and started talking with one of the girls who was protesting. I knew her from City College. She was with her boyfriend, a Columbia student. Once I made contact with her, I couldn't leave, especially when the police captain gave an ultimatum to disperse or face arrest. No one got up. And so my self-consciousness guaranteed my arrest and a miserable night in the Tombs."

"You just happened to be there. The accidental agitator." Melvin laughed.

"Something like that. The cell was packed with all these bright Columbia students. The one I remember most had this powerful build and kept rattling the bars and yelling, 'Yadda yadda, warden.' Maybe it was a line from some old prison movie. But he could also quote Yeats about the center not holding. Was that you?"

"I have never been in the Tombs, so I don't see how it could have been."

"You're sure?"

"Yes."

"Right. It wasn't you. But that's not the same thing as saying it couldn't have been you."

"It could have been me?"

"Right. It could have been."

"You're saying something. I just don't know what it is."

"You could be my brother, my smart older brother."

"Not so smart. I have no savings, no pension, and I gave away all my inheritance."

"To whom?"

"My guru."

Alice Piccoli stands outside Melvin's cube in her men's shoes and shapeless gray corduroys worn bald of their threads in the seat and a blue work shirt. Before an open bank of filing cabinets she has pulled out a small shelf on which to rest flat one of those hanging files and has gotten her tongue into action, wetting the index finger of her right hand to more easily turn the pages.

"What's that about saving?" Alice treats them to a dropdown of her tongue, a piece of raw, glistening meat.

"Actually, we were just having our little satsang. Would you like to join us?"

"Satsang? Is that like dim sung?"

"Just a little meditational break in the middle of the workday," Melvin says.

"A little bit of goofing off, eh? No thanks. Back to work for me," Alice says.

"She's an interesting person. A good copyeditor." Such is Melvin's dispassionate assessment.

Interesting she may be, but a good copyeditor she isn't, though Johan offers no contradiction. How naïve Melvin is and how ready he is to think well of people. In that moment Johan sees Melvin's natural endowment of goodness, which probably goes with the higher plane of thought on which he operates, a plane that doesn't allow for what lesser intellects gravitate toward, the pettiness of personality, as they do toward, say, the sports page.

"Be careful what you say around Alice. She runs right to Lurleen with negative information."

"Really." That word again. And then Melvin picks up the ringing phone. "Oh. OK. Sorry. I'll be right there," he says into the receiver.

"That was Lurleen. I forgot. I'm expected in a meeting. To be continued."

Like a knife to the heart that is, Melvin being called away because Lurleen has need of him but she doesn't have need of him, Johan.

The heavy lifters, the wave of the future, have arrived. Here now are Jody Murchison, by way of Abilene, Kansas, and MIT, and Sigourney Judd, by way of Worcester, Mass., and CalTech, architects of the org intranet, carrying looseleaf binders chock full of diagrams into Lurleen's office, where Melvin is already seated. Johan sees the future, and once more he is afraid. He is the boy weeping because he can't do the multiplication or long division problems in the pop quiz that Sister Mary Christabel has sprung back in third grade. He is Mr. Flathead impostor, here among the real deal.

He hears the door close with loud authority.

"Wish you were in there? Wish you were a player?" Alice Piccoli appears in his cubicle.

"Go away," he says.

"Don't think I don't know what your looks mean. Don't think I don't know."

"Am I in the business of caring what you know and don't know?"

"You care, mister."

"OK, I care."

"You treat this place as if it is your private fiefdom, and everything should conform to your wishes. And when it doesn't, you're full of hate. You don't deserve to be in that room with Melvin. You don't have the brainpower and you don't know how to work with people."

"Go find your feeding bag, Alice, if you would."

"It's not a crime to be hungry. It's not a crime to be a human being."

"And someone said it was?"

"You. You said it was, with all the contempt you show."

"And you. What is behind what you show? Do you imagine your tongue is the eighth wonder of the world that you let it hang out of your mouth like a panting dog?"

"You're an abusive bastard and you're going to die alone."

"Is there another way to die, Alice?"

"Fuck you, mister, just fuck you. And here, take this." Out came the tongue, Alice pointing at it fiercely, maniacally, with the index fingers of each hand.

Yes, Johan, thought. Just yes. Life is nothing if not about this.

I will lie low, he says. I will nurse my wounds, calm my roiled waters. I will see where endurance has its place in the daily scheme of things. I will reconnoiter for open spaces when I can. I will let intuition run wild within me. I will be a sage in the wild of my own bewilderment. I will let poetry spring from the dead flowers around the grave. I will run amok amid plenty. I will do what I have to do.

All this while Alice Piccoli is having a hall of fame chow-down one cubicle away.

And then the procession out of Lurleen's office, but not before the laugh storm. Like a great and powerful train does the Intranet team rumble past his cubicle. Down, Johan, down. Into your smallness go. Hang back in the outlying bush, away from the danger zone.

That afternoon Melvin comes back to him. "Sorry. I got called away."

"No problem."

"That was a difficult meeting."

"How so?" A look of concern has wrinkled Melvin's brow.

"It's only this. Lurleen was abrasive. It was like she was trying to undercut Jody and Sigourney. Those two are cyberspace architects. They can make platforms out of thin air."

"But what did Lurleen do?"

"She insisted that all communications regarding the online network we're building go through her, or that she at least be cc'd."

"And there's something wrong with that?"

"It was her manner. She suddenly seemed controlling."

"Stay here and find out just how controlling."

A male friend is not an often thing in his life, and he must apply great energy and thoughtfulness to preserve what he has found. All those years at the org when he had only women to run to with his wounds: Mary Terezzi and Blanche Givenchy and Ms. Carmelli herself. A woman's man. A toady. A man with nothing better to do than to try to please women.

Melvin will come to see what he is up against. The light will soon turn on, even if, on his way out, Lurleen waylays Melvin again and he enters her office to perform like her little monkey and have her great peals of laughter wash over him.

Isabel,

Though only a few days, it feels like a month since we last connected. You know I will always come back to you, across mountains and rivers and all the artifacts of humankind that would seek to divide us.

A fantasy has been recurring frequently and has my mother outside the luncheonette on Broadway, owned and operated, as you know, by Sol and Iggy, who sold the commodities of America in their store: Action Comics featuring Spider Man and Superman and Batman and the Green Lantern, panel after panel of colorful wonder, for a child's eye and imagination; and all the adult books for the men of America, paperbacks that featured those like Eddie, whose lust had him wander all the day long until he met Babs, who was more than willing to accommodate his insatiable desire. My mother is an enraged woman in these fantasies, Isabel. "Don't you touch my children. Don't you ever touch my children," she screams, as she confronts a man who has been free with his hands in striking her and now would do the same to us, as we huddle behind her. And in my mind I must stay with this outrage and build and build upon it. And there is Dwight David Eisenhower, who twice defeated egghead Adlai Stevenson, as he was then characterized. Eisenhower is bearing witness to this deplorable scene and on the verge of stepping forward, and it is for me to take pleasure of a kind in this manly man's disgust, his contempt for the cowardly ways of this attacker. Oh Isabel, that is what it is to live in America, to have the endless spectacle of the good guys and the bad guys, those embracing the highroad passing judgment on the lowlifes. At some point these poses, these dualities, must cease; we must step out from behind the masks we have been wearing, or be consigned to the folly of our own assumed virtue.

Chapter 32

Omertà had a hold on Hannah. A code that cherished silence she could easily live by. So many are the parental attitudes that an oldest daughter must absorb. For release she would head down to Little Italy, a shrinking section of the city bordered roughly by Houston and Canal Street. On Mulberry and Mott Streets would she sing doo wop with Sal and Vinnie and Angela and the other hard-nosed remnant of the greaser gangs she had come to secretly idealize even as they terrorized the city.

It was no surprise to Johan that this sister should embrace Richard Milhous Nixon throughout the Watergate years, and stand by her man even as he waved goodbye for the cameras after resigning from the office of the presidency of the United States of America.

Hannah was an *oldest* sister. She knew the things that could rile a very much younger brother, as when she said, "So have you heard what they're saying in the papers about President Nixon?"

Only she didn't rile him. Not outwardly.

"I'm not sure. What exactly are they saying? And who is 'they'?"

"Don't get smart with me. You know who 'they' is. 'They' is all the media who want to drive him out."

"Why would *they* want to do that?"

"Don't play stupid."

"But I am stupid."

They sat in silence this way for a few minutes. It wasn't anything terribly uncomfortable. They often coexisted this way now. Her power over him had waned, now that he was in his twenties. He danced around the bait she offered. By not biting, she had no way to hook him. Because the purpose of the conversation, he suspected, and not even suspected but knew, was to achieve polarity. Hannah lived for and thrived on conflict, it being the antithesis of unbearable intimacy.

"They are picking on him," she said, resuming as if they had never left off.

"Picking on him how?"

"They hate him because they don't like what he stands for."

"What does he stand for?"

"Righteousness."

"Nixon stands for righteousness?"

"That's right. Righteousness."

It was hard for him to be balanced about his sister. He didn't struggle with his perception of her as a figure of darkness. She had struck him often when he was a child, and it was not her way to apologize. Now, when she grinned and tried to hook him in useless argument, it was all too clear that detachment was the only course to chart.

He left the word out there on its own and took the elevator to the penthouse. It was in darkness except for the small candle burning on the dining table. The air smelled stale, the way it often did, like a bedroom with sealed windows in which people have been sleeping for days on end. His brother was drinking wine from a chipped mug. Chianti, in one of those wicker-covered bottles, rested on the floor, within reach of his arm.

"I mean, she just flipped out the other night and split. She's a goddamn nincompoop. Her father must have screwed with her head real bad." Luke gulped the wine. His Adam's apple bobbed when he swallowed.

Johan understood his brother's pain, his insides screaming for Brenda to come back and make everything all right. The primal scream of Stanley Kowalski in *A Streetcar Named Desire.* Johan shared the same emotional wiring with his brother.

There was a luncheonette below street level up on One Hundred Nineteenth Street, just off Amsterdam. To get there Johan walked through the Columbia University mall. There was Columbia and not-Columbia. His whole life it had been that way, he thought, seeing the massive dome of Low Library and Butler Library facing it on the south end of the campus. America itself was like that—the powerful rubbing shoulders with those who lacked all power, those with qualities of mind that made them radiant and the unfortunates whose bulbs were of a low wattage. The pain of living outside the gates of paradise.

And not-Columbia was where he was headed, a pocket of the Upper West Side where he would find Luke's girlfriend Brenda sharing a booth with Conor Quinn in the luncheonette. Lest Conor inflict his violence upon him, Johan would offer a testimonial to Conor's legendary street fighting prowess and his numerous KO's but also his love prowess. Johan would say how he recalled Conor, where Claremont ran into LaSalle Street, sitting on a stoop with his back against the wall and his legs spread singing "Oh, Carol" because Conor knew a girl named Carol and he wanted her to come out into the night. Smoking and spitting, making little white islands, when he wasn't singing. Would say he remembered that wavy black hair falling over his forehead and what it meant to him, Johan, to see a boy with the necessities to do the things he did with his fists.

Brenda came to him. She was with her own kind now. Catholicism. It created a bond, like Jews had among themselves. That essential communication forged by the religion and the race. All that incense they had breathed, and the Catechism they had recited. And the punishment inflicted on them by the nuns and brothers and inflicted on each other. Abused children made crazy by the concept of sin.

"I'm not going back, if that's what you're here for. Your brother's insane."

Her freedom excited him. Suddenly she excited him. He said nothing.

Conor got up and put his scarred face close to Johan. There was killer coldness in his blue eyes, the pupils down to pinpricks.

"Do I know you, man?" Conor finally said. Johan had his opportunity and took it.

"You remember all that?"

"Oh yes," Johan said.

Conor put him in a powerful, if brief, embrace. "This guy's all right," he said to Brenda. "He's all right." Because remembering him was a form of love. It wasn't everyone who would be remembering Conor Quinn, not with the direction he was going.

"I'm seeing this doctor. They're trying to keep my anger under control. It got me thrown out of the army. I punched out a drill sergeant. Not good, man, the beating they threw on me." Conor put his arm around Brenda in a way that said much.

Then Johan went away. He couldn't stay long with his past, not the way Conor Quinn looked now, a primitive walking about in a changing world. Roughnecks grew old quickly, met violent ends. The world, as it was evolving, meant for more cowardly, less direct types.

Isabel,

A young man was standing on the sundial on the Columbia mall on my return trip. I did not want to stop for him, but he called to me, as all the past was calling to me in that campus environment—the south lawn, where I had downed the beers of New York City (Rheingold and Schaefer and Knickerbocker, in cans that required church keys) with the Irish boys from the tenements along Amsterdam Avenue, and the hedges on the lawn's perimeter I would throw up in; and Hamilton Hall, where, as a fear-filled adolescent I had shown up wholly unprepared for my college entrance exams and failed them, or did not score as someone with my education might be expected to, and suffered the wound ineradicable by everything but God's love, and not even that entirely doing the job.

The young man's steel wool hair had grown out like an untamed shrub and his front teeth were chipped and yellowed. Beyond his deteriorated physical condition, lunacy had come to visit and decided to stay.

"Whenever I want a woman I have only to open my fly and they come running."

"How are you, Roberto?"

"No. How are you, Gargoyle? You're still a gargoyle. You know that, don't you?"

Several years before he had been my roommate, both of us students at the City College of New York. I had moved into the apartment where he had grown up with his mother. He had demanded that she move out with her boyfriend, whom he would not acknowledge as his stepfather. And so she did, taking an apartment on another floor in the same building. What can this mean, in retrospect, but that the poor young man had some unsatisfied grievance against his mother and her companion that he should make such a strange request.

It was not for me now to caution him about exposure by saying it went against civilized conduct, let alone the law, or by reminding him of the penalty for such lewdness. It was only for me to accept that a decline had set in, which I somewhat ascribed to drugs. For a time we had been dropping a lot of acid. Standing now with Roberto on this Ivy League campus, amid kids ensuring themselves of a bright future with a primo education, I shuddered, fearful that one day I could, in my own way, fall to a similar level.

As I continued along the angled red bricks of the footpath on that mall, I saw a tall young woman in a tan trench coat, her arms cradling a stack of books against her chest. The sight of my sister Leah brought no more happiness than my encounters with Luke and Roberto. I neither called out to her nor took any steps in her direction. Oh Isabel, you might think that the prospect of a sibling's success, for my sister was now an instructor at the university, might bring happiness and a ray of hope, given the failure I was witnessing on that day, but it was not so. As I stood in the recess of a doorway and watched her slowly climb the wide steps of the plaza up toward the statue of Alma Mater, her ascent was a greater source of pain than the wayward path Luke and Roberto were trodding, and so I headed home with the reality of all she was and I wasn't.

There's a kind of man who can't easily take responsibility for his life. Did I not maneuver and manipulate my way into the renting office for the purpose of having my hand in the till? Did I not rationalize this behavior, saying to myself that I was only making a claim to money that would otherwise go to the building owner, Simon Weill, whom my mother repeatedly accused of exploiting and oppressing us? Did I not intrude myself into your life as well? And am I now not challenging the legitimacy of my boss, Lurleen Lulabella, to be my boss? Is it not clear that I am dependently independent? Am I not, like my father, a man ill-equipped to take on large responsibilities? Oh Roberto, you lost soul from my past, you awaken these thoughts in me.

Chapter 33

At the monthly breakfast, which Lurleen has initiated so staff can leave their cubicles and socialize with one another, there is only one rule—no talk about work-related matters. And so Melvin Kleiner tells a story about his wedding, and how the yogi who was present said, "Don't do anything I wouldn't do," causing an eruption of laughter.

"Oh, Melvin, you are too much," says Rhoda Bahr. Even Johan laughs, surrendering to Melvin's magic.

Sugary treats are spread out on the conference table: cheese danishes, blueberry muffins, apple tarts and linzer tarts, sticky buns and cinnamon rolls, pear- and chocolate-filled croissants. There is even a small cheesecake from Junior's. It is Sweet Tooth Heaven.

"How about you, Johan? Aren't you going to partake?" This is Rhoda Bahr. That poison tongue, expressing itself so gently.

"Remarkable," Johan says.

"What, may we ask, are you referring to?" Rhoda asks.

"The spread. But the thing is this: you have to understand that sugar is a drug."

"We have to understand that sugar is a drug?" He watches her upper lip curl, the better to show him some *tooth*. Is this some exquisite Southern thing?

"Oh yes," he says, declaring himself emphatically. "And now, I will tell you a story, if I may."

"We're all ears," Lurleen says, cupping hers.

Johan has stepped into something, and now there is nothing for him to do but finish. To lessen his self-consciousness, he must become the one who sees, not the seen, as he has read in some spiritual text on a day gone by. "It is simply this. For some time now I have been seeing a healer. Her name is Maria, though it could be Glorious as well. A person must suspend disbelief, for she works with crystals and other unconventional diagnostic tools to divine the nature of your ailments, as well as to intuit their remedy. If she has won my heart and mind, it is because she is full of conviction. She is no house divided against herself. There is no double mind. And this I find compelling. And so I say to her at one such session, 'Maria, it is like this. Come the afternoon at my place of work, if I so much as think of a peppermint patty, then I must soon thereafter leave my cube and descend in the elevator to the lobby and from the prickly Indian man at the concession stand purchase not one or two but three, yes three, of these bite-sized patties, wrapped in silver foil. And then it is for me, in what has become a ritual in the quasi-privacy of my cube, to open first one and then the others lovingly and nibble each chocolate covered patty to prolong the ecstasy as long as possible. But because the hour was running late and my description was too long, Maria cut me short and said, as I say to you now, 'You must understand that sugar is a drug.' Now it is possible that I have heard the same from countless others, but this time I *heard* it and I have been free of the not ruinous but definitely harmful sugar fix ever since. Like a laser penetrating the thickest and most resistant metal, she penetrated me with her simple truth. And if you ask me why I repeat her words to you, it is simply this: we are what we say. When I tell you that sugar is a drug, then I magnify the message within myself." Words—the effort of them—have left him spent.

"Well, I think I need a chocolate croissant after hearing all that," Melvin says, and once again there is an eruption of laughter.

"Now we've gone and hurt Johan's feelings, when all he wanted to do was establish that he was better than the rest of us," says Rhoda Bahr, giving the room some more of her inimitable intonation.

Seeking to change the conversation, Mary Terezzi says, "My daughter just got accepted to Cornell and the younger one is at the top of her class." So confident and centered is Mary. Johan hears her words with his third ear, the pride in her voice as she says, I have something you don't have. I have multiplied myself upon this earth. I have children who will warm me in my old age and who provide a context for my life in the right now. I am slow and steady and complete. I have given myself the means to fulfill myself in body, mind, and spirit. I am not destined for the poverty of your barren lives. I have been spared nothingness by creation. I will not die all alone in some vast metropolitan hospital or lie rotting on an unshared bed in an unvisited apartment, if you're lucky enough to have one, or some dilapidated senior center. I will have family to bury me and to visit my grave.

And, of course, sees as well as hears: the furious action of Alice Piccoli's mouth, her free hand hovering over the spread before reaching down to snatch a tart even as she devours the croissant in her free hand. And then that further action of her tongue after the devouring has been done, that restless exploration of every nook and cranny to free her mouth of any residue.

Well, yes.

Heather does not flourish in this kind of gathering. Shyness holds her in its grip. Her edginess has no place amid all this chatter. Johan would tell Heather that her allure does not lessen when he sees this social vulnerability if ever she would allow him near, but that would be a lie. It does.

He is a part of them as they are of him, in that brightly lit room, he is obliged to concede, even as he prays for the day he will have sufficient means to free himself of GoAN and organize his papers and revise his will so he can leave this life behind.

Isabel,

You yourself would have to agree, if only begrudgingly, that there was revolutionary significance that day in our marriage when I declared my renunciation of meat. Yes, we had been having a fine time with those pork sausages you purchased and which I slathered with ketchup, but the time came when I could no longer abide the consumption of flesh. And though you expressed exasperation and even disdain for what you clearly regarded as my pretentious foolishness, even threatening to never cook another meal, a shift had occurred, spurred not by faddishness but some force moving me onto another path. And something similar occurred when I sought to part ways with refined sugar. I did not invoke my father's diabetes to the mocking Rhoda Bahr. I did not tell her and Lurleen and the rest of the crew of the insulin sterilizer he left in the bathroom each morning, a metal contraption like a miniature sarcophagus that gave me the chills just to look at it. Did you hear me saying a word about the the sight of my father injecting himself in his meager and hairy thigh? Or the wheedling tone of voice in which he said to my mother, at the breakfast table, "Just a little. Just a tiny bit," reaching for the sugar bowl over her strong protest. And those diabetic comas, and later the gangrene that set in on his foot and how it soon spread up his calf like a disfiguring stain and the resulting amputation at the knee, as if my father were saying, take me in bits or take me whole. I'm tired. I don't want to be here anymore. Because he didn't, Isabel. The last days were the last days. That is what religion, at least the religion I was raised in, comes down to, a longing for one's maker. And it is the way that I can feel sometimes, just walking around doing the same thing day after day. But did I impose any of this on the group? Not at all. I was saying to them, Care for your bodies. Do not be as children, believing you can eat with impunity.

And as for Heather, I did not go down memory lane with her either, as I will with you now. That look she displayed I have seen before. In 1967, to be exact. There was an Adonis of a boy whom Lenore, Sarah's sister, had taken up with, and who broke her sixteen-year-old heart sufficient that the next year she took her life. A wild youth with a relish for LSD and for speed, he was vulnerable without these aids. I refer you to the Hotel Endicott, near Lincoln Center, where a party was held in the late summer of that year and at which Adonis stood fearfully alone, his insecurity exposed, in a corner.

I have thoughts about people, Isabel, and connections to them, at least in my own mind.

Heather has a husband and she is walking the floor with him. "This is Johan. I don't know how to pronounce his last name and so I don't try," Heather says.

"Manootdjian?" the man says, reading from the nameplate.

"Perfect. Nice to meet you."

The man appears to be Indian, with coal-black eyes. A man who looks good in his dungarees and blue Oxford shirt unbuttoned at the top and his rich black hair swept back.

"I'm just giving him the tour," Heather says.

"Yes," Johan says.

"I will remember your name," the man says.

A powerful man. A man who may soon find out where his power ends.

A month passes and the next departmental get-together is approaching. Johan has been paired with Heather as the co-host.

"I will stop by the local Sweet and Deadly for the goodies tomorrow morning. Not to worry. A sugar fest bonanza will I provide." It is something he feels obliged to say, a sort of preemptive statement, lest she grow visibly upset that she has to be alone with him. He will ask nothing of her, expect nothing of her. He simply must be good and prove that he is good by being alone. It is the only hope he has of making her want him. He is up against his nothingness, his worthlessness. Go run to the train tracks, Johan. Run. Run now.

"Don't be silly. We'll go together first thing in the morning to Chez Raoul. How about 9:15? Is it a deal?"

Isabel, I had been made to understand I had to be away from you for long periods of time so you would possibly be with me for brief periods of time.

"Your husband has been made nervous by your job."

"It is a man's nature to try to control women. Look at what you have done to the earth. But he is a good egg. He has provided for me, and now, when times are tough, it is for me to provide for him."

"Provide for him?"

"His business is in the toilet."

'What kind of business might that be?"

"He does online speculative training."

"I see. Then he is in the Major Leagues with full command of all his pitches."

"I am an artist. I do not indulge in vicarious pleasures, such as baseball."

"And your husband is the house you have moved into so you can live a life free of trepidation. Because the world is a giant noise in your head, and everywhere there is the threat of violation. And because he has dark skin and gentle ways, you can love him. He is not the white man who has imposed his power on you. He is not that at all."

"Buzz off."

Chez Raoul could easily be Chez Alexei. Yes, there are piercing, darting eyes full of ingrained Gallic disdain, but there is also the rougher Russian sound, so incongruous with her beauty, of the woman who takes their order. "What you want?" she says.

"Je voudrais quatre petite fours, deux éclair au chocolate, trois croissants, deux tarte au fraises—yummy yum yum in any language—and deux mille-feuille."

"In English, please."

"You have a voice shaped by centuries of autocratic rule and brutal temperatures," Johan says.

"And you have voice of dead fish on Brighton Beach."

"Thank you for planking me. Thank you so much," Johan says.

Heather has been fumbling in her bag for money.

"Have no fear. I have brought the necessities," Johan says, handing the cashier his charge card. "I will recoup the expense from petty cash."

"What else do you put on that card?" Heather says.

"Lots of things."

"I'll remember that," she says. signifying that communication of a sort has been established at the depth charge level where words have meaning beyond their meaning, exploding to the farthest reaches.

Isabel,

Heather has the poverty of her afflicted mind, and Appalachia is beginning to show beneath the fashionista front. Yes, she is still styling, in the way that office workers will, in her tight black slacks and colorful tops, and with her hair sparkling like honey dew heaven. But there are off-days too, when her hair is matted and dull and her denim duds are but a drab sheathing. For her daily bread she toils on the org mag *Girls Rule!* and holds herself up as an authority on type. If the mag is a graveyard for her talent, virtually unread by the vast majority of those who receive a subscription with their membership, it is not because of her lack of effort. "I'm being slammed by this impossible deadline," she will say, but truth must sometimes live beyond and around the words that are spoken.

What one hears in her assertion is love of this type she "lays down" and love of being loved, of being needed.

What should move me, if only I were more attuned to her humanity, is her desire to break free of the mold that her beauty would bind her to. An aspiration to immortality and all the urgency of the artist which comes with that *are* manifesting in her. There are her art books, *her truth*, as she calls them, clumsily bound volumes of Xeroxes and some out-of -focus photographs of her and Allen Neverby in org interiors, for she has bonded with the insinuating one, who poses no threat to her territorial integrity. Everyone needs to be seen for who they are and not for what their bodies can provide. In these books are a John and a Jane, and Jane has done a service for this John who, for reasons not entirely clear, is stiffing her. "Give me my money," she shouts, more than once, working herself into a rage at the withholding one.

Many times, and in all seasons, have I seen our secretary, Allen Neverby, in the realm of smoke heaven as he stands in the recessed entranceway of the org building. Huddled with him are the young and the beautiful, the old and the haggard, quarantined souls all. Increasingly, Heather is there as well, not to light up but simply to be with her office mate. Trust me when I say that they are unto themselves when together and regard me neither with their eyes nor hold me in their minds. In fact, with a hardness that is formidable have they both sealed themselves from any awareness of my existence. And yet, there she is one day, in spite of her bias toward health, sucking on a lighted weed herself. The sight of her degrading her lungs is not a happy one. When I had the occasion to ask about this new habit, she replied that it was merely an occasional indulgence when in the company of Allen.

And it is not entirely true that she always snubs me when in the company of Allen. One afternoon, as I return to the org with a Lord and Taylor bag, she calls out, "Are you bringing me something? Are you delivering the goods?" Yes, those very words does she speak, before being carried away by peals of laughter. And there is more the next day. "I don't take credit cards. My policy is cash on the barrelhead. And by the way, no refunds or exchanges. Got it?" she says. There, in this environment of women where my purpose, at least some of the time, is to please, does a feeling of my power surface. If I could not draw Heather to me with my physical appearance or manner, then could I do so with my wallet? It is then that I understand a possible benefit of my scrimping and saving.

And lest you think this is all a concoction of a sad soul desperate to make connections where none are to be found, know only this: within an hour Heather makes a rare visit to my cubicle, where she says to me, "You should have seen the look on your face when I said that." But Isabel, I do not go down the road of exploration by saying to her, "Here is my address. Can I assume you make house calls?" Nothing comes from nothing, and then there are times when something comes from nothing.

But if I have experienced the power of illusion in my past life, does that mean I have to do so now by engaging with a woman willing to hire herself out, especially a woman who works in the same department and who has a husband and child at home and who shows attitude in her prickly speech? No no, jamais, jamais. There are barriers to progress that call for the fullest vigilance.

Some nights in my sober yesteryear, fever would come upon me for a woman of a certain kind. A Japanese woman. Never had I been with one. Escort services advertising Asian beauties abounded in the directory. I would stare and stare at these ads for twenty-four hour service. At some point I would even occasionally summon the nerve to call, and the women who answered all gave the same quote—$200 dollars per hour. I would promise to call back, unable to confess that it was not in my budget to pay out $200 per hour and it was not my way of life to have escort women to my apartment. What would the doormen or my neighbors think if a young woman came calling at 11 p.m. on a Saturday night? Would their moral concerns be brought to bear? And there were other considerations. Would these women bring disease into my apartment? Would I be careless and contract HIV/AIDS? Would they import drugs—amyl nitrate and cocaine—and lead me down the disaster path? Would the escorts themselves become habit forming? The clinching deterrent was simply this: Was I really about to engage with women who, by choice or coercion, had become human receptacles, women who had been with perhaps a handful of other clients that very day?

There was a time, back in the day, when I visited with my mother and she would talk about my father. Some years before I was born, he had taken her to a Times Square burlesque hall. It was not for me to know what kinds of dances or routines the women were performing, or what garments they wore. She did not describe the vulgarity of the men or the smell of booze and cigarettes. None of these things did she touch upon. She only told me that she approached the stage and said to the dancers, "You poor women. Do you not know you don't have to do this?" for her heart was aching for them. Even as she spoke to me she relived her pain. No, my mother did not tell me how the women responded. She did not say if they took issue with her or even hissed at her for imposing her sorrow for them on their lives. She only showed herself to have some recognition of what perdition means.

And there was this one year that I flew to Vancouver, in the great Pacific Northwest, where I stayed in a youth hostel near a park and spent an afternoon watching schoolboys in a soccer match. I was in a world of trolleys and old Victorian buildings faced off against the high rises funded by Hong Kong emigrés. The Asian invasion, it was called by some. And there were those afternoons I spent in Stanley Park, weeping on the nature trails and falling down virtually dead of joy at the sight, in an open meadow, of a baseball field and a lanky Canuck, yes a Canuck, into his southpaw windup and dishing heat to the helmeted batter in his coiled crouch. And yes did the hurler bust him out of his crouch with his hard stuff and send him back to the bench, as he did all others who came after.

And then there was a different scene, the madness of East Hastings Street, where, amid the ruins, the abused and drug-addled children of Canada swarmed over me like flies. Their young faces and bodies marked with lesions, they bird-dogged me for money, so that I had no choice but to flail my arms in seeking to fend them off.

I next found myself in Victoria, where I stared at an elegant old hotel. Some oppressive air of the past hung over the time-warped city, making it hard to breathe and compelling me to cry out in desperation for the present. There was no life here, only the repression wrought by buttoned down souls on quiet, tidy streets. Such was my feeling on my short stay.

One morning I attended a RoR meeting, where, among others present, a young woman who had led the life of the streets was now trying to get sober. She had a chipped front tooth and bruises on her face; a battered being she was, like that East Hastings Street flock back in Vancouver. With all my heart and soul I wanted her to make it, Isabel. After the meeting, I went out into the street, and as I did a woman with Brigitte Bardot lips and her approximate figure crossed my path. Her gait was slow and her smile inviting and when she turned and saw that I was staring at her, there being no power in me not to, she turned and said, "Are you looking for something? I have an office. It is down the way." Her pupils were pinpricks. She seemed possessed with an animal's morality, feeding herself being her only concern. Not everyone is human simply because they show themselves in human form. I felt her grabbing at me.

"What kind of office?"

"An outdoor office. We go down some stairs."

Her condition gave me pause. This was a drugged out girl in a downward spiral, yes, a human receptacle. And AIDS gave me pause, as did the prospect of some squalid outdoor site and possible arrest.

"Do you know where I have just come from?" I said.

"From hell, where all white men come from," she shot back.

"I've just come from a meeting of the likeminded, those trying to stay sober."

"Didn't I just say that? Didn't I just say you came from hell?"

Because it is that way. The mind that is sick will embrace every lie, every illusion, every distortion. It will serve as a chronic magnet for the bad idea. But let the truth be presented and the guns of war appear and fire in a deafening roar. Such is the nature of the will of man and woman to fashion folly.

Across the street I came to notice a man richly Black. He stood long and lean wearing at a jaunty angle a Borsalino fedora with a large red feather prominent in the band; a flowery and billowing shirt half unbuttoned to expose his powerful chest; a chain of gold around his thick neck; and dark shades that obscured his eyes. Isabel, make no mistake. He was presenting himself as a man of menace with preternatural psychic strength down for taking on all of white Victoria with his adamant will. He had an understanding about his life beyond the ken of commonplace philosophers. It was simply this: his life could leave him at any moment since he would not back down, no matter who or how many sought to go against him with the whiteness of their skins. He further knew that any show of weakness would bring on his death far faster than going strong to the rim on every shot and throwing down with maximum authority.

I did not linger, as by now her man was crossing the street, the nature of his mission heralded by his powerful affect. It was for me to note this pimp and his meal ticket among the infinity of forms this earth features and be on my way. Only this did I further say: "Up there in that meeting will you find the love you have not found. The young. The old. White. Black. It will not matter. Come when you can."

Chapter 34

The odor of gas permeated the Chinatown loft, a smell Johan and Sarah became as accustomed to as the roar of the N train passing over the Manhattan Bridge some blocks away, causing a tremor in the windows and the floorboards of the old building. An eight-foot length of green garden hose ran from the gas fixture to the water heater; at each end a mass of duct tape served as a joint. The primitive plumbing they had inherited from the previous tenant, a wiry and wily Hungarian emigré artist named Grosz, who couldn't be bothered paying Con Ed a utility bill. And though Johan had wondered out loud about the safety of cheap plastic piping as a conduit, Grosz had merely shrugged and said, "Tell me, please. Where is safe?"

The question, of course, was rhetorical. Safety, for Grosz, was in himself. Within a few years of his arrival in America, he was living in a 4,000-foot loft on Crosby Street, in SoHo, far west of Chinatown; the plumbing and wiring, the tiling and sheet-rocking, was done by him and him alone. Though he was but a fleeting presence in Johan's life, he nevertheless made an impact, as when he said, "You are not so bright, are you?"

Because Grosz had seen what Johan hadn't wanted him to see. He couldn't break the mold; he could only live within it. The mold that Grosz had shaped and left behind became Johan's living reality. And the building in which Johan was raised, that too had become a mold, and he couldn't break that either. He could only wait for it to fall down. Or help it to fall down, as he did with the sums of money he extracted from the rent till.

Shaken by Naomi's death and the uncertain circumstances surrounding it, Johan made an appointment with Edgar Wilnatchi, MSW, to whom he confessed, "I'm concerned about my drinking. My sister was found drowned in the East River and she drank and took drugs, and now the waters are roiled and threatening and greedy for more, the two rivers of New York City not being what they appear to be."

"Tell me about your drinking." Dr. Wilnatchi said. The pipe he smoked went well with the tweed jacket he wore with patches on the elbow.

"I am a writer. I am exploding with the voice that is great within me when I walk along the streets of New York City. It is only when I sit down that it disappears. Alcohol fuels my creative impulses. Did not F. Scott Fitzgerald drink?"

"F. Scott Fitzgerald dissipated his talents through drinking. Tell me briefly about your family," Dr. Wilnatchi said.

And so he told Dr. Wilnatchi that his parents went to church, though his father was now dead, and that his brother Luke liked his wine with breakfast and lived with a woman with a passion for lingerie and how Naomi would drink and abuse pills and how Rachel used to drink before she found God and how Leah couldn't drink very much because alcohol often brought on painful headaches. He left out Hannah, because her thing was to park herself at the refrigerator for nocturnal gnoshing.

"So how far does the apple fall from the tree?" Dr. Wilnatchi said.

The doctor wasn't being kind or unkind, he was just striving for a dispassionate stance. All Johan heard was dread and doom, for Dr. Wilnatchi was saying he could wind up dead in the East River like his sister Naomi or in a church pew like his mother. And because he knew what God would do to him and what the bottle could do for him, he had only one pathway forward to follow.

Isabel,

When the building fell away, when the owner Simon Weill came with his strongmen and closed us out, I sought a doctor for the pills that I took in my Chinatown time with Sarah, and which I have spoken of before. Though amphetamines had been a problem for my sister Naomi and contributed to her demise, I felt that I needed them if I was to live. I was feeling the burden of my own ambition, which was to write a novel about the building and the family I had been born into. Understanding had come to me that I lacked the necessities for accomplishing such a thing with my own resources. The doctor's name was Ernesto Samm. I told him there had been several deaths in the family—my aunt, my father, and now Naomi. I said the deaths had made me sad and that I lacked energy. Would he be able to provide me with a pill to lift my mood? I left his office with a prescription for a month's supply of Fastin, a capsule for the suppression of appetite for those with a weight problem. One of its side effects was to induce euphoria. Dr. Samm could not let me go without putting the laughing thing on me, of course, remarking that because of my thinness it was possible that I would simply vanish from the earth.

That summer, I boarded an Amtrak train for Miami. By this time it was an unhappy fact in my consciousness that the old Penn Station, with its exquisite concourse, was forever gone, demolished by the wrecking ball of those with no regard for the city's treasures. Even so, a surge of joy gripped me as I entered the pedestrian mall, one element being the romantic allure of train travel, with the promise of adventures to come on the beaches of Key West, my ultimate destination. More than that, it was the sense of myself as free. Had I not walked that same mall as a child, seen with my own eye the explosive redness of a candied apple at the concession stand, and devoured countless Nedick's franks on their trademark toasted buns topped with a coating of pickle relish? Had I not passed the Doubleday bookstore, the flower vendors, the magazine stands, the deli with live lobsters displayed in the window, and the Savarin Bar with its frosted glass windows? Had I not seen all these signs of life as my mother's rough hand gripped mine through her white linen glove with the ribbed backing for it not to be a scene of holiness? Had our destination not been the church and an afternoon of the disappearing words of Pastor Horvath, when what I aspired to was the world beyond that the trains of Penn Station seemed to promise? And was I not now leaving all that behind, not only the church but the building we had been in bondage to? And did I not, as the departure track was being announced, bolt for a liquor store, where I bought two pint bottles of blackberry-flavored brandy for the twenty-six hour trip ahead?

Sarah had accompanied me to the station. Her breakdown and hospitalization were behind her. Under the guidance of Dr. Frodkey, she was on the mend and assimilating to the world beyond our Chinatown loft, working part-time as a waitress at Hamburger Heaven, up on Thirty-third and Lexington.

At the Newark station, an elderly Black woman requested my help in placing her one suitcase in the luggage rack. "You're a fine young man. I can see that you are," she said, in gratitude for the task I quickly performed. Some uneasiness came over me. Her words were kind, but was appropriation her intent? Was this a woman who knew how to move men around and make them hers through flattery?

I had a book in my possession. *Pale Fire,* by the great Vladimir Nabokov. But it was too much for me. A feeling of Siberian coldness came from the pages. Conceivably it was the cleverness, the artifice. You understood in reading the text that you were entering an imaginary world wrought by a higher intellect, a space where feelings could not have much play. Footnotes, a poem in heroic couplets. My mind resisted, yearning for the dark pain of *Laughter in the Dark* or the stunning brilliance of *Lolita*.

Staring out the clouded Plexiglas window, I succumbed to the newfound rhythm of the train. As night fell, cars shone their brights on lonely roads and houses appeared like luminous specks in the vast darkness of America. From the engine came a long, mournful whistle. I heard it as a summons to head down the aisle to the bathroom, where I broke the seal on the first pint, and took two good belts of the syrupy sweet stuff. The time for action, for interaction, was nigh.

Isabel, let us speak plain. Alcohol was truly the wild nights calling. It was shedding clothes and structures and strictures and running bare-ass through streets and villages and even coach cars. Deprivation or misfortune do not explain creatures of excess.

In the dining car were a gaggle of teenagers, identifiable as a group by the Christians for Nixon T-shirts they wore. Though there was an age gap, I seemed to assume that the words "Nixon" and "Christians" gave me some entrée to their world, as both had been part of my past. But my brandy breath and the fact that I was older may have put them off. As one, they stared at me, their silence part of their resistance. I needed to be received. I am not built for wearing people down and winning them over.

The film *American Graffiti* was playing in the club car. The rock and roll soundtrack, with Wolfman Jack delivering the goods, put me under its spell.

Trenton and Philadelphia and Baltimore and Richmond were on our southward route, and by the time we had pulled out of Rocky Point, North Carolina, the confines of the coach car were insufficient for the expression of my liquor-fueled joy and longing. I tore through the aisles of one car after another until I came to the baggage car, where I had a notion to express myself, though with no clear idea how. Before entering I pulled an ax from its clamp on the wall and, once inside, stood among the parcels and suitcases and slid open the loading/unloading door in the middle of the car, then flung the ax toward the red clay earth beyond the rails. I closed the door and returned to my seat with no thought for the potential consequences of what I had done. Only the crescent moon had been my witness. But then, how could I be sure lovers were not mating out there in the field, and what had given me the confidence that I wouldn't be seen by someone in the train and possibly arrested for vandalism? And maybe there would have been further trouble with the law owing to the Fastin I was carrying in my bag.

My behavior was not that of a normal man, so it is perhaps best that the rest of the night is lost to memory. Suffering from dry mouth and feeling like my head had been concussed by a polo mallet, I came to in my seat the next morning with the sun pouring through the dulled window as the train sat in the Jacksonville, Florida, station. As I staggered toward the bathroom, the elderly Black woman who had boarded in Newark recoiled in her seat, her eyes wide with horror, and one of the Christians for Nixon, a teenage girl with her blond hair in pigtails, cowered in her seat as well. Not good, Isabel. Not good.

I had no credit card, but the rental company was willing to accept cash. It was a different time in the life of the country, and one that is not coming back in that regard. Hungry and without the nutritional awareness I now possess, I chowed down at a Kentucky Fried Chicken, pulled in by the colonel's big friendly face. By myself at a formica table I sat weeping, just weeping, over Sarah, while munching on a mostly bones chicken breast. The sadness at the beginning of the train trip had now returned.

On the drive from Miami to Key West, I was held captive by the Loggins and Messina song "Please Come to Boston." Yes, it was strong in my mind and emotions more than manatees or wild palms or the causeway itself, the narrow road shimmering in the noonday sun. Such a plaintive voice the song was sung in, that of a man who sounds as if he has been left when in fact he has done the leaving. There was this sweet pain, nurtured by the one diet pill I had already swallowed and sustained by the next one I soon took. Loggins and

Messina were doing for me what *Pale Fire* could not. They were giving me the kind of emotional experience I was seeking. We all want to take a bath in love, and when we start, it is so hard to come out into the cold.

Mama Herrero was waiting in her nightgown on the steps of the screened in porch of the rooming house down on Duval Street, at the other end from the marina. A pelting rain met me as I sprinted for refuge from my parked rental car.

"You are late," she said.

"I was delayed by traffic." In truth, I was delayed by the beer I stopped off for on the other side of town, and then the two more that followed.

"You are a good man. I can see that." Her pale skin said she was not a woman who bothered with the sun anymore. It was where she was with her life.

Behind her a white-haired man was bent over the cane he leaned on with both hands. "My uncle Pedro. He is my second pair of eyes and ears. He know people. Have good smell. He smell the bad one and all he need is make a face and the bad one is gone," she said, tapping her nose.

I was in the guest home of this Cuban woman who had put me on notice that my goodness rating was at stake. Like the Newark woman of color, she was saying she would start me out high with the implicit threat of bringing me low. She gave me my room key and said I could pay the next day.

When I opened the louvered shutters in the morning and saw down to the street that the sun had broken through and that plastic pennants above a car lot on the corner were snapping in the breeze, it was everything not to fall down right there at the wonder of this gift that I had been given—three weeks on my own, with no one to answer to but the landlord below. The wild palms. Houses painted with pastel colors. And the circumference of the ocean to bind it all together.

I set up my days to write in the morning and early afternoon, and only ventured onto the beach after 3 pm, when the sun had lost some of its intensity. It was a routine I stayed faithful to. I would type out, on the Remington portable I had brought along, a few pages, not of the novel I was attempting to write but an account of the trip itself. At least let me do that. What writing I did was in a state of Fastin bliss. Instead of concentrating on the task at hand, sweet thoughts would ensnare me. Whole hours would pass in such a state of mind. Or I would count and recount my money or rearrange the few items of clothing I had brought along. And yet, somehow, some way, I would tap out my necessary quantum of words—500 minimum—so I had pages to show for my day's effort. For many years has this pattern been going on, Isabel, for many years.

There were bars along Duval Street, and some of them had jukeboxes that played "Please Come to Boston." And there were women in these bars, like the one with bare feet who said she had come down from Brooklyn on vacation seven years before and never returned. She just walked out of a business and into a new life, and lived in a tent and drove a cab to make ends meet. Her hair was frizzy; her teeth were white. Nature looked to be making her skin darker than it could possibly stand.

"You're not here. You've gone away from me even as I speak." She was hearing my attachment to the world, my incapacity for letting go as she had done. I did not have to tell her that I needed modern plumbing. Her words articulated a divide that would grow still greater, I sensed.

That same night I met a nurse. Would it be safe to say she saw enough of dying in hospital wards to give her a healthy appetite for life? We drove in her car to a dock where, by day, men fished. A skinny barefoot Black kid in a T-shirt down to his knees said the silver ring I wore would draw barracuda, and they would remove my finger and maybe my calves, as they were known to do. He laughed, his teeth as white as a bleached sheet in the moonlight, and walked away. Though his words reverberated, we shed our clothes and lowered ourselves down the ladder. She was petite, with red hair and a sunny disposition. We were there in the warm water a brief while before we returned to the dock, where we made love, using our clothes to pad the hardness of the wooden slats on which she lay.

But this was not an entirely secluded paradise, Isabel. A powerful beam of light washed over us, generated by a police car parked at the foot of the dock. The girl did not panic, nor did I. We were done by then. Who this officer was I cannot say, but of his desire I can speak when I say the beam followed her as she climbed back into her clothes. He harangued us with amplified words over the loudspeaker apparatus of his vehicle. He may have had some shame at his own interest that caused him to stay in the darkness of that car. Or maybe he simply had a good heart and was showing a degree of kindness for two young people connecting in the way that they could. Maybe he was remembering a time when he had done the same, before the wife and kids had come along. Living near the water, closer to the equator, can pacify and soften us. I'd like to think that this is so, Isabel. I really would.

I did not see the girl again. She went on her way. But maybe there will come a time when I will. Maybe time will circle back on itself. Maybe it has been doing that all along. Maybe there is further sweetness in the bye and bye.

And there was another, Isabel, just one other, a girl who came back with me to Mama Herrero's. She was not in a helping profession. It is conceivable she had no job at all but was young and lost and trying to find her way. I remember her as thin and with features of face and body that would pull most men to her. I remember that her hair was brown and fell straight down to her shoulders. I have some memory of us climbing the rooming house stairs and the pleasure of my contact with her in bed. But I remember too the aftermath and how she recoiled, saying "You're the remotest man I ever met," before she fled.

More than anything, I suppose, it is those parting words of hers that stay with me. *Remotest.* There is a place you came to when you were on Fastin where even to speak was to compromise the happiness you were feeling and there was no need to smile because you were lit up within. People were telling me something, Isabel: the woman of color who boarded in Newark, the Christian girl for Nixon cowering in the coach car, and now this girl down in Key West had put words to what she was feeling. And that is to say nothing of Mama Herrero and her uncle with the gifted nose, for they had a gauntlet of disapproval for me to run as well before I could leave town.

Chapter 35

"You want to do what?"

"Go out. Into the night. You know. The darkness. Where we can be alone with only the moonlight."

"But I have boyfriend. I not tell you?"

"You have boyfriend in your head. That is what you tell me."

"When do you want we go out?"

"Now. Now is the only time for going out."

"Why you talk like that?"

"Why you look like that?"

"You are dangerous man. Very dangerous."

"Danger is what you like."

"Maybe."

Bensonhurst. Formerly Italian, now mainly Asian. An hour each way on the N train. And the predatory landlord who made it necessary for her to move to a lesser apartment where she lives in one room with her teenage daughter. And the ex-husband against whom she has an order of protection. She can't be sure he hasn't found a way to tap her phone line.

"Two years we divorce and still he say we get back together. He is crazy, yes, but I even more crazy to stay with him all these years, and more crazy still that I ever marry him."

Him. As in *heem*.

A woman who likes attention. "This doctor person. He say to me, Why you dress like that? This he say. Why I not dress like this? I say to him. I am woman, not man. I dress like real woman dress."

There is a play for which he has bought discount tickets at the Ticketron right there where Broadway and Seventh Avenue converge, an area of the city that frightens him, as if he has entered the nadir of civilization. Too many people crowded together under the neon glare of movie marquees for the pursuit of pleasure for pain not to occur. The heedless one who steps off the curb looking the wrong way and is crushed by the M104 bus or the one all intelligence and no brains, as Joseph Heller wrote, who does not understand there is a permanent underclass for whom prison is not a penalty but a sanctuary, this one a tourist standing on his rights in some confrontation and trying to reason with the ruffian plowing ahead, reminding him to mind his manners. Manners? He will give him manners, slicing his cheek with a switchblade. Those childhood prohibitions against worldliness rising to his consciousness.

A play about the murder of an abducted child in which, inexorably, an encounter between the murderer and the child's mother draws closer. From their side balcony seats a view down at the actors profile to them, close enough that he can see sprays of spit in the footlights as they emote. The reviews have been lavish in their praise of the production, but he feels nothing—neither criticism or appreciation—as the scenes unfold. The world increasingly made up of these personal dramas in which he has no strong investment. Some half-forgotten quote from Godard about the childishness of actors. So earnest in their passion as they mouth lines they themselves have not created. And the sense too that he has lost track of time, a big chunk of it, owing to the sameness of days since—since Isabel. The theater and the opera had been frequent occurrences in their lives. She was kind to him, never made him feel ignorant that he couldn't remember *Rigoletto* from *Carmen*. A time before all this scrimping and saving.

Afterward they walk across Broadway down toward Sixth Avenue. One recessed glass and steel office tower after another. A hard bench fixed to the pavement set out in front of one of them, where they sit. A blur of lights in the night.

"So what did you think?"

"What I think of play? I like it. And you?"

"It was OK."

"Only OK?"

"Yes."

"But the ending I do not know about. What is this forgiveness? The man has killed her child."

Zeese for this, her tongue sliding along the word.

"You are a creature of your environment," he says. "You laugh at us here in the West. All you immigrants do. You believe you are stronger and tougher than we are, and perhaps this is true."

"Of what you speak? I say to you about forgiveness and you say to me about environment."

"This is true," he says, speaking the words as he imagines hearing them from her mouth. He stares down at her shoes. They look to be made of black plastic. And the front of the shoes have this exceedingly long thin taper, like Pinocchio's nose.

"So what about this forgiveness."

"It is nothing. It is something Jesus Christ dreamed up as a means of removing barriers of hate. Jesus Christ had some idea that love is the only reality."

"A baby is reality."

In the vertical city they continue their walk. There, ahead, with the happy lights of its huge marquee, is Radio City Music Hall. Behind it, cast into darkness, would be the towers of Rockefeller Center. Ahead, on the avenue, he can see a line of yellow cabs, their taillights glowing red, waiting for fares in front of a luxury hotel. He remembers those hackie days. The life of a small man who should have died to the dream that he was special a long time ago.

Does he have to spring for cab fare back to Brooklyn? Expensive. Twenty bucks, at least. He has been looking for signs of unspoken anger in her, but so far has detected none. No sullenness, no sharp words. Of course, he could simply ask her, but no, why go down that road that wouldn't be so simple after all, since even if she says no, she might mean yes? A set of stairs takes them into the vast IND station unfamiliar to him despite his status as a lifelong New Yorker. A surprise to see shops—a shoe repair shop, a florist, even a photocopying service—animating the dull concrete and tile décor. Signs everywhere—B, C, D, F—that he has extended to new dimensions of this city?

Isabel,
Do you see? Do you? I had only to let things take their course. No need to spring for a cab. There she was, with her metro card in hand. To swipe or not to swipe was not the question, for swipe she did, and quite emphatically. And so now it was time for me to swipe too, and with the sense of joy that the twenty could stay in my wallet and my frugal ways not suffer a setback. I headed down the stairs to the northbound B train, while Zofia was bound for Brooklyn on the D. And I could hide behind a column so she couldn't see me from across the tracks, in this way avoiding the kind of hideous prolonging that occurs when there is a failure to recognize that the night is over and done with. Within a few minutes, I was staring out the window of the rear door of the northbound B train and thrilling to the darkness of the tunnel. Only the occasional blue light, deep under Manhattan. Oh, Lord, Isabel, to be there soaking in that luscious blackness as a promised land far more enticing than the footlights of Broadway.

At the concession stand in the lobby, the stars are out in force, their glamorous faces adorning magazine covers on the wall racks. A queue of org workers with their sugar- and sodium-filled snacks in hand. But they are really there for their main course, the winning ticket in the weekly lotto drawing. "I want 423899," one says to the slight Indian man behind the counter. "Got that? 423899." And another wants 330872. The man takes their bills and in exchange gives them colorful tickets hanging in strips over the cash register. A form of prayer, this activity, though what would they would do if they won? Buy gold watches and sit in their newly purchased condos watching *Oprah* all afternoon? Some he recognizes from the quarantined crew that stand outside in the blazing heat or numbing cold getting their nicotine fix. The ones who say, "Oh, my God. It's only Wednesday," canceling out today for some better tomorrow. As if he is not the same.

He must have the space he craves, and so he pushes through the revolving door and heads toward his refuge, Bryant Park. He walks slowly, hardly knowing the season or the year. Such a good activity walking is, moving one's thoughts onto a higher plane. Workers are re-sodding the lawn in the park section by section. Backbreaking toil that leaves them sore and dirty from head to toe at the end of the day, and for what? A few bucks an hour? No health benefits. Uncared for. He sees the same thing out on the street. A construction crew throwing up those ubiquitous scaffolds that he tries his best to avoid walking under, for fear that they will collapse, as some now and then do. A man unsteady on a beam on the unfinished platform receives another beam from workers hoisting it from the sidewalk below. A sense of relaxed safety standards, of corners being cut. The foreman barking orders at the scared rabbits in his charge. Some new current of energy and revitalization in the land. It's not that they are all bad, these Republicans. There is joy in work and opportunity. Maybe too great a preoccupation with a social safety net makes one feeble and tentative in the face of life. Bullshit.

"Where have you been?" Melvin Kleiner says.

"I went out walking to give my mind a break from all that is contained within these walls."

"The walls of your mind or the walls of the org?"

"Both."

"I just thought I would sit with you. Have a little satsang."

"What's that, a satsang?"

"It's about sitting in the presence of truth."

"And where do you expect to find it here?"

"I've been homing in on it."

"Did you find truth at the ashram?"

"I found truth and an evasion of the truth as well."

"Do you miss it?"

"No. It asked too much of me and gave too little."

"How so?"

"The food was less than plentiful. I often felt hungry and would go down the road to a diner for a break from seitan and tofu and sprouts. I'd order a big greasy cheeseburger and fries and a malted."

"Croak food."

"Fun food often is."

"Did the world seem strange to you, given all your time at the ashram?"

"The ashram was a world too, only there was an element of spiritual make-believe. You can't live your life chanting mantras. Reading the Veda won't pay for your dental bills. The ashram had no benefits program. They gave you a dormitory room and food and a very modest stipend, but after that you were on your own."

"It must be scary to invest so much in a guru. I mean, it's one person."

"I began to see things."

"What things?"

"That my life couldn't be their lives. And then I would deny it, until I had the same feeling again and knew I had to get away."

"Get away from what?"

"Illusion."

"What was the illusion?"

"That the real world was make-believe and the life on the ashram was real. I saw that I had run away and was using the guru as a drug."

"Did something happen?"

"They wanted me to act as a spy."

"A spy?"

"At some event here in Manhattan. They wanted me to report on some of the ashram members. Who they talked to. That sort of thing."

"Why?"

"They didn't say. I guess they were suspicious. And then it occurred to me that they might be asking some others to spy on me. It started to become something sinister and paranoid. Money can do that."

"You should write about that."

"No. I couldn't."

"Why not?"

"Just not a good idea."

"They would come after you?"

"It's nothing to think about," Melvin said.

"I'm part of something, too."

"You're part of something."

"Not an ashram. I go to meetings. I'm in recovery."

"Recovery from what?"

"From alcoholism. I drank too much. Now I don't drink at all."

"Why are you telling me this?"

"You show me yours; I'll show you mine?"

"What a disgusting idea."

"Triumphalism. Don't underestimate it."

"What about triumphalism?"

"I'm better than you. That's what I'm saying. The ego invading and pervading God's realm. Only once I've given you that as my motive, I can move beyond it. I have to."

"Why is it ego to tell me that you are a recovering alcoholic?"

"Doesn't have to be. Only if I'm seeking praise for staying alive."

"What are the meetings like?"

"Like a New York City subway car. Folks of every stripe sharing what we call experience, strength, and hope."

"You cheer each other up?"

"What we can do together we can't do alone."

"So it's group reinforcement?"

"Sort of. But something more, too. We lay hold of a source of power otherwise not our own."

"God?"

"The rooms are God, if you believe that God is unconditional love. There is no love like the love of one drunk for another. We accept each other without judgment. Collectively, this is so. Individuals are individuals."

"You're making me miss the ashram. Is it a cult?"

"No. No cult. No spiritual ghetto either. We seek to carry the message to others who have our illness, but we also practice these principles in our relationships, seeking the best possible relations with everyone, even our so-called enemies. Not that I do such a good job of that here. Drinking is a cult. Drinking is bondage. Booze enslaves; God frees. It is as simple as that."

"You have a good thing going," Melvin says.

"I was a peripheral part of the guru's community for a couple of years. I received a new lesson every month through the mail as part of a correspondence course and would read the lesson through religiously at least twice a day, just as I was asked to do. I even attended the meditation center here in the city and considered it a holy place, in spite of all the icons of Guru Gaia and the slavish devotion of those who prostrated themselves before her image. The desire for surrender is a powerful thing, and they are not to be faulted. What I really want to say is that I'm so glad you broke free."

"It was time to leave."

"How it's going with the council network."

"It's moving along. Sigourney is exceptional. She is able to think conceptually."

Sigourney. He has seen her fleetingly—in the corridors, in the elevator, coming as she is going, a new and pretty face at the org— and then one afternoon browsing among the stands of brightly colored books for children on sale in the lobby of the org building. Her back to him, he says, "Excuse me."

She turns, training eyes that know what he wants without any need for words. He is barely able to introduce himself.

"OK," she says. He hears unfriendliness, coldness, in her terse response.

"Sorry to bother you." And with that he walks off.

Because it is what he often does, goes wild over someone new who rejects his overture and then has to live with his discomfort every time he sees her as she settles into her new environment. The outsider reaching for the outsider before she becomes an insider. The humiliation of third grade repeated over and over again, springing on the girl as she emerges from the girls' coat room with a kiss on the cheek only to be called upon that same day to explain to the class why he has done such a thing.

"You want things fast. Too fast," Luke said to him, one day in the long ago, Johan having met a girl at a party and slept with her right there in an unused room. The need for instant gratification— the euphoria alcohol could bring him with a few drinks and the release quick sex could bring as well. The ability to integrate socially lacking.

Isabel,
I am hearing in Melvin Kleiner the unmistakable sound and substance of my brother, that same blindness in assessing women for the sole purpose of placing them above him. And though it is a loathsome word reeking of pomposity, as used by some, I must seek to *educate* Melvin as to the pitfalls of this emotional tendency. Melvin Kleiner must not remain Lurleen's little boy, or a boy at all. Obviously, this change cannot be effected with harshness. Patience

and intelligence, neither of which I have in abundance, will be required. For as Melvin is to Lurleen, so have I been to women too numerous to name. Or is it that women are holy and men must fall down in love at their feet if we are to be whole and complete? I will get back to you on this matter. I will try, though distraction has been my ruin, to give it my full attention.

And later, this from Melvin:

"My mother had a cold and scolding manner. She said that I was a mistake and that her marriage to my father was a mistake and that she really had been in love with another man. My father was a community leader speaking truth to power. He would take me with him on his rounds. Everyone in the neighborhood loved him. Every material comfort he provided me with. At my lavish bar mitzvah I passed out in the middle of the rabbi's spiel, as if, down deep, I had to repudiate manhood and Judaism and my father at the same time. I dropped out of graduate school when Baba came along. I gave him all the money in my trust fund, to the consternation of my parents, and lived in a dorm room with five other male devotees, surviving on the skimpy stipend the ashram provided. On the other hand, I flew first-class to mega-events all over the world as Baba's fame grew."

"Your life was unmanageable. Baba came along and organized it for you." Johan shudders, imagining the tight quarters in those dormitory rooms, like the hostels he has stayed in when budget traveling in Europe and parts of the U.S.

"In one sense, it was a way for me to stay a child, with grownups to arrange my life for me."

"You were Trotsky in another lifetime. Is that possible? I read about him, you know, in the Isaac Deutscher trilogy. He sprinkled salt on his bread and referred to his tendency to get lost as topographical cretinism. A man with no sense of direction was determined to social engineer an entire country, and possibly the world."

"Trotsky?"

"I meant it as a compliment. A man of vigorous thought and action. Actually, how do you know you are not Leon Trotsky?"

"Do I need to count the ways?" Melvin says.

"Do you not have a little épater the bourgeoisie in you? Do you not, like your father, make it a life's work to go against the captains of industry who would treat working stiffs as little more than serfs?"

"You are an odd man, with your notions."

"I am an odd man without my notions."

"Eliana didn't have the same attachment to the ashram as I did. She was not the flighty, ethereal kind of creature you were likely to find in that community but someone with a solid career, a woman with a car, bank account, credit cards, professional contacts. I had empty pockets and a dormitory room and holes in my teeth. I had Eliana to organize my life as Baba had organized my life and books had done before that. Because Baba was gone. He had passed on. Gaia, his successor, did not have the same hold on me. I saw through to her vanity and coldness. I saw my forbidding mother."

And so Melvin Kleiner came to the org. He did not arrive with a blank résumé. He had taken outside work when the stipend was insufficient for his material needs, including the occasional succulent steak he craved in place of seitan and tofu. Brochures and catalogs he had put together for companies that did their calculations to a fine decimal point, gave their employees one day off a year and fined them prohibitively if they took more. Melvin Kleiner knew what the hardball of American business was, and could stand the pressure sufficient to deliver the goods in those arenas. Both Lurleen and Eliana saw that he was someone who could do more than stand by the Xerox machine.

"It's off the subject, but listen to this. Down below, at the bottom of the escalator in Grand Central Station, stands a man. He is unkempt, his hair uncombed and his face unshaven. A big man with a gut that hides his belt. He wears unflattering clothes—those cheap Dickey pants and a flannel shirt too warm for the season. In a threatening voice he is promising retribution for all the worldly ones who stream past him, sinners who just want to get home and out of their work clothes and maybe have a bit of dinner and watch some TV before going to bed so they can start the whole thing over the next day…"

"Wait. Where are you going with this?" Melvin says this coolly, so Johan can know he isn't to throw out just any kind of slop when they meet.

"Nothing, I guess." His confidence has been shaken.

"No, tell me."

"It's just that I saw something dark there for a moment. A threat to our cosmopolitan way of life. I saw that angry white man as one of millions slouching toward this city that they loathe from their rural communities, crazed men who want to roll back the clock to a time when their supremacy was assured. I see them as an extension of the president's will. You have to understand where I come from, what the childhood influence of the Pentecostal religion was on me. I wasn't allowed to enter a movie theater as a child. Something about moving images on the screen being idolatrous. That's what frightens me, that my freedom could be taken away."

"Some people assume that their religious convictions are the truth and not simply an unprovable belief. It's the Taliban mindset here in America. Take this guy in Membership I'm helping with a project. He belongs to a fundamentalist church, near where he lives. Before we can actually get any work done, he reads a verse from the New Testament and asks me if I know that I am a sinner and eternal damnation awaits me unless I repent. And so I tell him I know no such thing and that he doesn't know any such thing either. At this point he becomes furious. His eyes bulge. I have dared to thwart his will for me. Our man Bush has done a serious thing in letting the religion genie out of the bottle. It's very, very dangerous. Who knows what kind of homicidal fury lurks behind the religious posture of some of these zealous men."

"Not only men," Johan says, staring at the door to Lurleen's office.

"To be continued," Melvin Kleiner says.

Yes, indeed.

But then Melvin Kleiner, in league with Rhoda Bahr, must put on the mask of mockery again. Publishing is to make a presentation to promote its services to the org. But who can abide such a thing? Rules of capitalization? Series commas? When and when not to use the subjunctive? Who or whom? Is this the stuff that will make people happy or make them mad? This is what they need to do, make the rest of the org feel they are back in grade school having their grammar corrected?

"You're the senior man here. You know more than God. We thought to have you on a kind of throne with coworkers importuning you for answers, as if you were the oracle at Delphi. So is it OK if we dress you up in a robe and create a paper crown for your head and have you seated on a throne-like chair, your hand resting on a giant volume like Webster's Third International Dictionary?" So Melvin says.

"Do what you need to do," Johan says. "But do it without me."

In Bryant Park with Melvin, Johan says, "Our relationship is a miracle, plain and simple. It took two marriages and two divorces for me to live on a plane of equality with another human being, not above Isabel and not below her." He is emphatic in his delivery in seeking validation from Melvin where none was previously given.

"Maybe you need to examine this."

"Examine what?"

"Why you are always alone, and if it has something to do with Isabel. Haven't I already discussed this with you?"

"You would move me to the cold and separated place where pain replaces the constant of love I need in order to live."

"Pain is a prelude to growth."

"Peut-être."

While Melvin's truth bomb about Johan's relationship with Isabel has an initial disturbing effect, it soon fades, as does the impulse to respond to Melvin or seek out anyone else for reassurance. Melvin has shared his point of view, obnoxious as the certainty is with which he presented it and the fact that he presented it at all.

"Eliana and I butt heads about money. It's one area where we don't merge."

"You don't pool your resources?"

"No. Eliana won't go for that. She has all kinds of investments that she is private and even evasive about."

"Isabel and I had what a friend called the money of the marriage. We did pool our resources." Johan likes the sound of that term, *money of the marriage.* It is nothing he himself could have thought up. It had to come from someone with the mind and the understanding of Zed. And Melvin agrees.

"The money of the marriage. That's good. That's really good."

"Maybe Eliana will come around."

"She may not trust me when it comes to money. She knows my history. Great natural resources but poor stewardship of those resources."

"Great natural resources. That's what I have wanted my entire life."

"You seem to be OK in that department."

"Consumer society."

'What about it?"

"Say it. Say those words."

"What words?"

"Consumer society."

"Consumer society."

"Now say them again."

"Consumer society."

"Take them with you and say them again and again and again in your own private space. Meditate on them for hour after hour until the horror is almost too much."

"Is that why you brown-bag it every day?"

"Happiness comes from not taking the first drink. A similar happiness can be derived from surrendering the impulse to make unnecessary purchases. It gives your life a feeling of manageability."

"Two old hippies sitting in the sun in Bryant Park on a glorious spring day," Melvin Kleiner says. He scrapes up the last of his store-bought Niçoise salad. Twelve dollars he has shelled out for raw vegetables, a scoop of mercury-saturated tunafish, a slice of egg from a tightly caged chicken. A man with the omnivorous appetite of a python.

Isabel,

There was Robin Dell, on Broadway and One Hundred Thirteenth Street. It featured a porky waiter who wore a bowtie and on every table was set down a tomato-shaped ketchup dispenser. Only once did I eat there, served by the very waiter I had seen as I passed by so many times. A hamburger on a bun, with a slice of raw onion and lettuce, and thick-cut French fries. Both the burger and the French fries got a heavy dousing of ketchup and a fair sprinkling of salt and pepper. This was the kind of food I wanted in my life back then. Robin Dell. The image of nature was strong in those two words. Sherwood Forest and hill and dale and dell. Oh happy day, that I could sit there peacefully and have such a meal.

My mother had given me the money. "Go get yourself some normal food," she had said, as she tended to the business of the building.

And let us not forget Prexie's, "The hamburger with a college education," on One Hundred Fourteenth Street, with a big sign out front in the shape of a mortarboard. Or Riker's, on One Hundred Fifteenth Street, where food was delivered from the kitchen on a conveyor belt and it was for the waiters to recognize their orders. At Prexies and Riker's, I sat at the counter and ate the food of America, down to the sprig of parsley the burgers came with. Even then I wondered that I was eating alone with the grownups and not at home, and that my mother had the means to hand me a ten-dollar bill. Not that I wanted to be at home. Home was not the place for my peace of mind. It did not have the clean surfaces of these restaurants. It had the burden of its grime and disorder to yoke me to and so I kept apart, in the public spaces, where America and the hope it provided was more likely to express itself.

Something permanently distracted about my mother, unable to sit down and come to grips with what she had brought into the world. My mother as a child herself—stunned, in disbelief, but here, amid America's bounty. She had only to reach into her bag to prove it.

Isabel,
The parking lot runs from Fortieth Street to Thirty-ninth Street, where it narrows to a driveway between two buildings. When I am here, I am in an older New York, back in my childhood days of alley-climbing and neighborhood exploration. Once again I am roaming the city with Jerry Jones-Nobleonian. How I wish I could stay here, off the beaten path.

Something concerning to report is that there has been trouble in these streets. Right down on Fifth Avenue. Shoppers, tourists, everyone scattering as a gun-wielding man chases down a couple desperately fleeing into a parking lot, where he shoots them dead.

Yes, Isabel. You guessed it. The very lot where I took my strolls so I could be more alone with myself than in other environments.

Here are the comments of a witness:

"The scariest thing I ever saw. The man ran right past me with a loaded gun."

"But how do you know it was loaded?" the other woman says.

"Because five seconds later he started firing. That's how I know."

Two lovers dead, emphatically so, unable to avoid the cuckolded husband's wrath. There in all the papers for everyone to read the next day.

Harm's way can call to anyone, Isabel. Anyone, those who have done harm and the holy innocents. We must focus on the breath. We must. We must live our lives as if on the runway taxiing for takeoff.

"What you doing down here, Mr. Johan?"

"Loitering."

'What does mean? Loitering?"

"Just hanging around."

"Hanging around?"

"I just came down for a snack."

"A snack, Mr. Johan?"

"It's dangerous out there."

"Talk to me, Mr. Johan. What means dangerous?"

"That gunfire earlier. Two people were killed. Shot to death."

"Where?"

"Across the street. In a parking lot."

"Life is not a picnic. Is that how you say?"

"Sure. That's how we say."

"Tell me what you think, Mr. Johan."

"You could have been in harm's way. I could have been in harm's way."

"In harm's way now, Mr. Johan, is what you say to me?"

Isabel,

I am a man of the middle ground, taking from both poles. Today I do not go to my medical doctor, Dr. Cohen. Today I go on the A train to Cortlandt Street, under the World Trade Center, at the lower end of Manhattan, where the island narrows, east and west converging. The weight of the structure presses down, prompting me to hurry anxiously along the main floor, where a dazzling number of brightly lit stores call to the foot traffic passing by. It's not only the height of the building but its width; the earth cannot possibly support such a massive load. A building monstrous yet bland that inspires nothing but dread.

Those late-night walks with Sarah, wandering west from our Chinatown loft on the other side of Manhattan to gaze at what was then only an enormous hole in the ground. Sarah hadn't liked the new development either. She too was wedded to the old. After the WTC's construction, we had gone to the Windows of the World Restaurant at the very top. I hadn't wanted to stay. No one should be dining that high off the ground, and not in a building that swayed, I thought. There was a punishment for hubris. The Greeks had said so. One of them, anyway, though I didn't know who. The restaurant had been her parents' idea. It wasn't the sort of place either Sarah or I went to on our own.

Maria greets me in a white lab coat. A painfully thin and pale woman is leaving as I arrive, the kind of woman I often see at OrganicOnly, determinedly alone and painstakingly assembling her dinner at the salad bar—a few shreds of carrots, a smidgen of seitan, a tiny mound of beansprouts, some dripping hijiki. One of the wounded of the earth maintaining the illusion of control as her means of dealing with mammoth trauma, some invasion too painful to get near.

It crosses my mind that maybe this is no place for me to be. I could just walk back out the door. But Maria's words remain as a kind of goad. "Don't you want radiant health?" That one word, *radiant.* Not good health but a health that glows.

She sits with me on the sofa.

"I don't do well with women. I fail to perform most of the time."

"I can help you to be young." Young, as in *gh-yung.*

She is from Spain and famous, rightly so, for her healing powers. So Natalia, the woman who spent time in India, has told me.

"Young?"

"Don't you want to be young?"

"Yes. I suppose I do. But I'm not young."

"I can make you very young. Tell me, do I not look young?"

She thrusts her face forward so we are virtually nose to nose.

"Young?" To give myself a reprieve from answering, I repeat the word stupidly as I ease back and stare at her face, as if to soberly assess the quality of youngness I am seeing. Though she is no sweet bird of youth, there is a glassy smoothness to her skin; it does not go with her wrinkled neck. "Yes. Of course. Very young," I lie.

The apartment is spacious, with a spectacular view down from the twenty-ninth floor to the Hudson River. Ferry boats shuttle back and forth between Manhattan and the Jersey shore. The immensity of life and the energy that drives it forward are before me. And from the north exposure, a view of the gray WTC monster rising, rising.

Once, when I was a child, a handyman employed by my aunt took Luke and me fishing. We weren't five minutes out of Sheepshead Bay, down at the tip of Brooklyn, before I became seasick. While the men and Luke cast their lines and reeled in fluke and flounder and sea bass, I sat propped on a soda cooler, where the men had deposited me so I didn't fall overboard while heaving into the Atlantic Ocean. The day was gray and a thick mist set in. At some point the ringing of a bell came to our ears as through that mist the outlines of a behemoth appeared, an aircraft carrier of a size beyond my ability to comprehend even now without terror flooding my entire being. I am told that the frantic men on board our little boat manually lifted the anchor while the captain gunned the engine to avoid being sunk by the massive beast heading out to sea from the Brooklyn Navy Yard. As it was, the waves in the carrier's wake were almost enough to sink us.

And now the behemoth is on land, seeking to assault the sky.

"Fill this halfway with your saliva, so I can do my work." Maria hands me a tiny cup, of the kind the hot bar man at OrganicOnly gives demanding customers who request to sample the soup before committing to buying it.

It takes a little effort to provide the saliva, as my mouth is dry. I have made a decision to suspend disbelief and place myself in her hands. If she wants me to spit in a cup, and if she then takes that cup and with her back to me, stands at a long counter on which she has spread out some crude chart of the body, and if she holds a pendant over different parts of the chart and mutters to herself, "Neck all right, chest all right, kidneys all right…" and makes notes as she goes along, that is OK by me.

Before starting in with the pendant, she has me sit quietly with my eyes closed.

"Is very important to get centered in the light," Maria says. And she does the same. Her full conviction, the certitude with which she approaches her work, doubt anathema to her, is attractive. No self-mockery, no self-contempt, no irony. She is completely one with what she does, and isn't that what all brilliant people must have to drive them forward into the winner's circle?

I feel at home with her. This is no American Medical Association doctor, no body mechanic with blood tests and more diagnostic tests and invasive surgeries. This is a woman who understands the life of the spirit, who lives near water and light because she draws on it for her work, and so is a fellow traveler on the journey. Anyway, I am in a part of town I would normally not travel to. Now I have a place I can add to the daily cycle of work, meetings, OrganicOnly, home.

And one thing more. I am not in a medical office or a restaurant or some other commercial space. I am in a woman's home and I am being received by her. It feels *nurturing*. When was the last time I had such an experience? In that moment my mind turns to Isabel, across the water. In some way my life has not been complete since the rupture occurred. Or is it just different?

When I leave, an hour and a half later, it is with a list of things to purchase, from the hormone DHEA to specific vitamins and minerals and flaxseed oil, and instructions as to when to take them in the course of the day.

"You will come back in three months younger. This I can tell you," Maria says, in showing me to the door.

"Am I bad?"

"Tell me what is bad, Mr. Johan."

"Nothing is bad."

"Why you ask what you already know."

"Maybe you think I am bad."

"How I can think what is good is bad?"

They are in his apartment. She excuses herself and goes into the bathroom. When she returns, some minutes later, she is wearing only a gray bath towel.

"Good or bad, Mr. Johan?" she says, standing before him, and allowing the towel to drop at her feet.

"Good. So very good."

Later she says, "He is crazy man. Yells and yells. Afraid to even use telephone at home. I take calls only on cell phone."

"But he doesn't live with you anymore. How could he hear your conversation?"

"Crazy not same as stupid. He is electronics expert. He do wiretapping for secret police."

"Is he violent?"

"What you think? I have police order of protection because he send me flowers?"

"You have an order of protection?"

"Where I live before is OK for man to beat wife. Not OK here. Not OK for man to kill wife either."

"He has threatened to kill you?"

"He says we be together forever and is only man for me."

"Wow."

"What is this wow, Mr. Johan?"

"Just—I didn't know."

"Do not be so worried. You are big man. He cannot kill you if you do not let him. Yes?"

Isabel,

This afternoon I passed the conference room. Among those around the table was Julie Morrow. Some years ago we worked together on a maddeningly thorough research report she had written. Her style was relentless, weaving around and around like a Bach fugue. The text was too intricate and had a specific density too great for substantial alteration. How do you edit a writer's sensibility? Possibly she, as all of them in that department, was writing for two audiences: the org, for sure, but also for the academic community, from which she was seeking approval. Hyperbole is the org style, and the Research Department is no exception, identifying itself as the premier authority on girls, as if Robert Coles, at Harvard University, and other experts had never existed. Julie is slender, has penetrating eyes, and cultivates an aura of deer-like fragility, as if men have universally recognized her beauty and are desperate to possess her, I being one of those who succumbed to her power sufficient that I asked her for lunch. Our collaboration had created a false sense of closeness, or perhaps it was a genuine closeness that our real-life differences could not bridge. I found her intimidating. It was her academic pedigree. She had gone to Cornell on a full scholarship and was, within a few years at the org, higher on the grid than I was. Something in the way she looked at me one day as I made my meager and hesitant contribution to her text suggested an awareness that I was her inferior. And perhaps this attitude of superiority was a goad. She excited me more than most women at the org ever could. She ordered a gloppy egg salad sandwich, supremely trustful of the establishment, and bit into it. Clumps of egg fell onto her plate and excess ringed her lovely mouth. My pathology, if that's what it is, was no match for her beauty. Even witnessing her in the act of defecation might have entranced me. I began to babble. Did she know that the restaurant had once been a Chock Full' O Nuts? Yes, I told her, I had sat with my mother in that same space, then owned by the legendary New York franchise. We were on our way to B. Altman, another New York legend, a department store with a sales force that were fully trained in the art of customer service. Some things I omitted—the new blazer and charcoal gray slacks and white oxford shirts my mother would purchase for me just before the beginning of the school year. Nor did I recount the unbearable shame the saleslady summoned in me, sensing as I did she was looking down on my mother and on me as well, having recognized that I was an impostor, just the squarehead son of immigrant parents seeking the appearance of a WASP.

The barrier that I was seeking to dissolve between us went up as she spoke of her childhood in Brooklyn and public school education and the change it made in her life to be accepted to Cornell, summoning in me heartbreak that the indelible stain of failure had been stamped on me at such a young age. She had won and I had lost, as my sister Leah had won and I had lost. Once again I was reliving the wound of my low board scores.

There had been a man in her life. They had lived together for three years. A week before the wedding, he informed her that he was in love with another woman. The woman was pregnant with their child and he would be marrying her instead. The pain and suffering in Julie's story comforted me. Adversity, rather than a smooth ride to relationship success, seemed to increase whatever remote possibility for connection there was.

From the beginning, I was imprisoned by self-consciousness. It had to do with the disparities in our ages. I was careful to avoid cultural references, like where I was when Kennedy was assassinated or Woodstock. But then she asked how long I had been with the org.

"Fifteen years," I said.

"Fifteen years?" she said, the surprise registering in her face as well as her voice. "Did you come here out of college?"

"Not exactly. I was thirty-seven."

"Fifty-two? You're fifty-two?"

"Guilty," I said.

She was now in a full state of smiling incredulity, and I was too paralyzed with shame to inquire what her amazement might mean. Left to my own interpretation, I concluded that she would not have consented to have lunch with me had she known my correct age and that the revelation exposed me, in her mind, as a freak of nature if not a fraud, a character worthy of inclusion in *Ripley's Believe It or Not.*

After another work session at the end of the week, I found myself back in my cubicle staring at the phone on my desk as if it were my connection with the universe and consignment to a hellish eternity of aloneness is what the weekend without her would be. Sensing the futility of the action I was about to take but unable to prevent it, I dialed her extension and got her voicemail. The message I left laid it completely on the line. I would like to see her that weekend if she was interested. *If she was interested.* With that phrase did I also present my insecurity and lack of self-regard. It's just little old me. Don't hold yourself to calling me back if you're not *interested.*

There was no call-back. She wasn't interested. There was no reason for her to be interested.

That weekend it was not loneliness but fear that found me. There seemed no limit to the torment my mind could inflict. Julie might be slender and trembling, but she was a strong feminist whose work was focused on helping girls achieve parity with boys in the classroom and in life. It was not beyond possibility that she would go to the HR people and accuse me of harassment. "I don't feel safe with him," I could imagine her saying to Jeanine Juddster.

I was in the docket, and the prosecuting attorney was relentless.

All this because I asked a woman at work to go out with me? I said to myself.

And so the following week I said I was sorry.

"Don't worry about it," she said.

"Don't worry about it?" I said.

"That's what I said."

"That's all?"

"You made a mistake. Just be sure not to do it again."

"Excuse me?"

"Look, I know you're attracted to me. Your body language says as much. But you can't have me. I don't want you."

"You don't want me?"

"Why would I want you? You're fifty-two. You could be my father. Do you imagine that I want my father?"

"I don't really know. Do you want your father?"

"You have no right to ask me such a question. No right at all."

"But why not? You just asked me."

"Yes, but whose father is he? Is he your father or my father?"

"Maybe he is both our fathers."

"Now you are going too far. Are you saying I am your sister?"

"I don't know what I am saying."

"I am not your sister and no one is my brother. No one."

"Did you ever have a brother?"

"That is not your business."

"What is my business?"

"This research project. That is your business. In fact, it should be your life."

"My life."

"You should bring more to it than you do. You should be helping in a bigger way."

"A bigger way."

"Stop repeating after me. Can't you understand? I don't want you."

Bill Romney, the org's alpha male, is also present in the conference room. Handsome. Gray haired. Married. Two children. A commute from somewhere upstate. A PhD in something or other. Head of the research department. Romney's Angels was someone's name for that department, after that popular TV show from years past, *Charlie's Angels.* And in truth the most attractive women in the org are members of his staff. Julie and her cohort with their crushes on their boss. Sitting there in the resource room in a complex emotional involvement not with a boyfriend but with Mr. Alpha. A way of remaining in perpetual adolescence. No ring on her finger. The kind of woman only available for the unavailable man.

If only Johan could say one thing to Julie and communicate it effectively, he would say, "Please, please. Don't be more interesting than you are."

And yet she is interesting—and talented. She has a point of view, a vision, which will carry her far. From a myriad of ideas pick one, just one, that is salient, and stand behind it. And Julie has done just that. The org has to change. The org has to allow girls to take the lead. Let them provide direction. Move aside, stodgy old troop leaders with your boring arts and crafts. Empower girls to believe they can be everything they want to be. Give them a diversity of ways they could become members. Accept that they are beyond your command. She has, with another young person in the org, created a proposal for a program. A reaction follows. Anarchy will result. The org is pandering to these kids, whose enthusiasms are as fickle as the wind. It would result in ruin to let go of the org's adult leadership model.

Sleepy, dull of mind, Johan watches the new direction take hold. Who cares? Where is his lunch? Why can't he just sit in his chair all day and contemplate the pension that will come to him?

And so there is a reason Julie is in that room and he isn't. She cares, and he doesn't care—or he doesn't care enough. He is saving himself for other things.

"It's like looking in on your parents. We're not supposed to. It's the adults' time," Melvin Kleiner says. Johan has come for a satsang.

"Yes, that's it. That's it exactly. So you feel it, too?"

"They want you to feel like a minor appendage."

"Three weeks ago you wouldn't have spoken this way."

"Three weeks ago I wouldn't have been in this tiny space."

If anyone is a poster child for what the org. can do to a man, it is Melvin Kleiner. Indeed his big cubicle is gone. Now he is in a cramped, windowless space, which has led him to distribute a haiku throughout the department:

Man in tiny space.
No chair for guest to sit in.
What can it all mean?

"I had this therapist years ago. It was at an intense period of my life. Isabel and I were separated and I was in pain. He said that with so much going on it would be a good time for me to lie down on the couch. A kind of psychoanalysis, only his unique brand of it, he said. It's possible he thought very highly of himself, and maybe he had good reason. One memorable thing he said was that it would never have been possible for me to win in a family such as mine. He said this in relation to my increasing conflict with my younger sister Leah in my twenties, when I felt that she was trying to isolate me from the family. 'The outcome could never have been anything else. Not in a family such as yours,' he said. And yet I never asked him what he meant. I suppose I didn't think I had to."

"So you've recreated the family here?"

"Yes, something like that."

"But how can you be so detached? Doesn't it make you unhappy?"

"Let's just say I'm disappointed. This is a place that reduces people."

He feels peaceful sitting with Melvin and wonders what his life would have been like had he stayed with Dr. Tobin. Dr. Tobin gave him so much attention. Attention of the right kind. Dr. Tobin was one of those special people. And then, after three years, he, Johan, up and left, just like that, left because Zed had said to him, what are you still doing there? That's all it took, that subtle nudge from Zed, for him to leave. Not that Dr. Tobin tried to hold him. Still, thinking about Dr. Tobin made him hungry for the journey all over again.

Isabel,

It may be that the war-afflicted provinces of the earth are spreading to the point where fractiousness is the norm and every man is pitted against every other man. Surely federalism is the way to go; man's tribal tendencies can only be fed by an excess of nationalism so that his instinct is to march en masse in the dark of night and burn down neighboring villages.

The intuition I had, well before 9/11, that America was vulnerable to attack from abroad, and that it could come with devastating finality, still haunts me, in spite of the ugly machinations and muscle flexing of the current regime. The fact is that there are those out there intent on cleaning our clock, their mass destruction malice driven by envy. My monitors are all on high alert, I can assure you.

All I know is that I took a break from the office and sat in Bryant Park today. The weather was cool and the sky gray, with the promise of rain by evening. Isabel, sometimes I need to take stock. Maybe it's the trees and the green grass, but I begin to get some perspective when I am out of the office in the early afternoon and the crowds have dispersed back to their offices. I see then that things are winding down. I say to you that life beyond a certain age is only about preparing to leave, whatever other activities we may be engaged in. I don't mean to suggest that these activities are negligible. They definitely press in on us. We are both people who fight for the time we need to devote to our work. But we are in a new place, a clearing. The midday crowds have dispersed, and the peace of the park has returned. Some eternal vista looms beyond the shadow of the library.

I have in fact been to the library and taken out two films, *Butterfield 8* and *Bang the Drum Slowly*. It is possible I saw *Butterfield 8* when it first came out, way back when, and maybe it is that time I am reaching back for more than the film itself. A veneer of malice shows on Laurence Harvey's face. Then there is his poison tongue poised to strike. And there is that neck, as reed-thin as mine. Lydia, my ex-mother-in-law, was the most nurturing of women, and yet, provoked by my excesses, was driven to say, "I prefer a man with a good thick neck. It tells me what I can expect of his more private parts." In this way did she speak to me from the back of the car one evening, Peter having driven me to the bus stop for the trip back to New York. Earlier she had mocked me as having bedroom eyes. It could be she was responding to what she perceived as my interest in her, though the idea of her as a partner in bed was beyond my ability to contemplate. And it is entirely possible that her words were not meant for my ears alone, that in fact they were words that would not have been spoken at all if Peter, whose neck had the requisite thickness, weren't present. So yes, she was putting me down to elevate herself as well as him, and it was for me to endure with a weak smile, as my stricken insides could manufacture nothing more. And would it be too much to suggest that Sarah herself heard it, since how could she not? A few years later did she not say to me, threat on her very breath, "I know something I could say that would get you out of here." So yes, the body, remorse, shame, the whole mishegoss the mind can manufacture, time-traveling as it does.

And about *Bang the Drum Slowly* does much need to be said? Slim pickings at the library caused me to select it. But really. To see the Italian-American city slicker Robert De Niro play a country simpleton headed for an early grave? One could meditate a long while on the term "tear-jerker," and only end with complete dissatisfaction and revulsion at the manipulation this term suggests, not to mention the brutality. Although the mind softens when we consider that it may be in the same family as "soda jerk." The point is there is too much manipulation going on in this world. All this emoting. And yet, to see things as they are can be dangerous, very dangerous.

If my mind goes to the Van Dines, Isabel, it may be because Sarah has been writing to me. It is my fault, of course, if "fault" is the word I should be using. What I mean is that I opened the door to this communication by not entirely closing it. For many years, I wanted her in my life without actually having her in my life. I wouldn't call it guilt so much as I would a sense of responsibility, though maybe there is a measure of ego that leads me to believe I am more important to her than I am. I could go through a year without speaking with her, but then the holidays would come and I could not bear the thought of not sending her a card. Such a cold dismissal that would be. And so, for years, things continued with this minimal contact. Within a week of my sending her a card would I receive one from her, no matter how close to Christmas Day I actually mailed my card. I could feel her isolation, virtually weigh it by the bulkiness of the envelope, which would invariably include not merely the card, on which all available space had been written in ballpoint ink, but also another two or three pages written on three-hole loose-leaf paper. Whereas I struggled to write a line or two, her words just flowed, I imagined. And then came the year when I added something more than a few pleasantries and a wish for health and happiness in the new year, and asked after her sister Claire and her brother Jeffrey, sensing even as I did that the door was being swung open. But curiosity, and more, led me down that road, as I have probably told you.

In the aftermath of 9/11, I scuttled my plans for a trip to Europe and chose instead to rent a car and tour western New York. Before setting out I found myself crying. I just cried and cried and cried. Those tears I shed were for Sarah's parents, Peter and Lydia, who by now were no more on this earth, and for that wonderful country estate, and for a whole chapter of my life that was gone forever, and for an America that was gone forever. A photo came to mind of Sarah as a small child reaching for a cookie on a table set out on their lawn. Deep down we all want to return to something we have no conscious memory of, and so we find these substitutes.

Following my inquiry, I received a long letter from Sarah about an ongoing dispute she and Claire were having with Jeffrey over inheritance matters. And there have been more letters since, and now there are phone calls.

Let's talk about this another time, Isabel. Another time.

Chapter 36

"I wash your hair today, Johan?"

"Not today, Toshiko. Just spray with water."

"Why you not want clean hair?"

"Tomorrow. Tomorrow I will have clean hair. You will see," Johan says, taking his seat in the chair by the window. Better for him, for his peace of mind, if the chair was toward the back, and away from the street, but Toshiko has only that one chair, looking out on Columbus Avenue. She puts the blue smock on him, the same one she used for the customer before. It feels cool around his neck. He tries not to think of the sweat and dirt the smock has absorbed.

"You take big trip, Johan? Where you go now? Russia? China? Tell me."

"I go to Japan. Kyoto. Nara. You want to come?"

"I born in Nara."

He has said the wrong thing. He has come too close to her past. He has stirred up something in her. "We'll go to a restaurant after this. OK?"

"How? You have date. What's her name?"

"Toshiko. Toshiko's her name. I'm going to sit with Toshiko and watch her eat chicken tempura."

Toshiko smiles. Gives him a light punch on the arm. She is a thin woman, in her fifties. Abstemious, careful. Guarded and circumspect once she leaves the salon. Whatever they might say, they will never get together, not outside the salon. Their time together is right there, while he is in that chair.

Once the snipping ceases and he is on his feet, the spell is broken. And it is a spell, Toshiko wetting what remains of his curly hair and pulling it straight before she cuts while leaning up against him, intentionally or not.

"I need the very best haircut you can give me, Toshiko." He likes saying her name. Cute. That wide open "O."

"Short? You like short?" She laughs. She is a geisha at heart, if to be a geisha means to live to please men. Once, just once, he was less than effusive about the haircut he received after appraising it with the mirror she always hands him to inspect her work. She had taken too much off, so he said, and she has not forgotten though it must have been over a year ago. Her smile does not fool him. He can see it still rankles.

"Everything you do is great. You're a genius with the scissors."

"Thank you," she says. She has received what he says. Levity and flirtation are OK, but he has to be perfectly clear and sincere about this communication. And he is.

"Toshiko, am I going bald?"

"Will not happen."

"Ever?"

"Ever."

"Remember to leave some extra in the back."

"I do not forget."

"No, of course."

Some men can handle baldness, men with powerful, well-shaped heads. Round heads. He is not one of them, not with the flat head he was born with. "We wish for him the rest of his head," some classmates wrote under his photo in his eighth-grade yearbook. "The only thing funny about you is the shape of your head," one of the girls in his ninth grade class had said. And the names the neighborhood kids called him—"Squarehead" and "Flathead" and "Boxhead." No, his hair should not be taken away from him. He might have to leave, go to another town. Someplace where no one knew him and could make no before-hair and after-hair-is-gone comparison. Somewhere like the northernmost reaches of Canada.

"Where are you going, Toshiko? Do you have a big trip?"

"I go home to Queens. That is my big trip."

"You don't want to go anywhere?"

"Maybe Flagstaff. Maybe I go there. I don't know." Her voice drops when she mentions Sedona. The smile goes from her face.

"You should come to me, Toshiko."

"No can do. I am married woman."

Her husband is in Sedona. He owns a restaurant. They have been living apart for years. Toshiko is in that place some people don't understand, of having a husband without having a husband, or having no more of a husband than she wants except for those times when a man sits in her chair and she can bring herself to think that maybe she wants something more. But she doesn't want that more than she wants the safety of her own bed and the TV shows she watches and the meals she eats alone in her little kitchen and the money she socks away for old age. It is a place Johan understands, not because he has been there, but because he is there.

"Even married women go out for dinner once in a while." He knows better than to dispute the fact of her marriage. Because it is a fact and will remain a fact until the day comes when it isn't, if that day is ever to come. He is not there to destabilize Toshiko; he only wants to bring her to the edge of her limits.

"You have date. You say so."

"I have a date with Fairway. That is my date tonight."

"Who is Fairway?"

"A grocery store. A big grocery store."

"I find you a woman. Very nice woman. Friend of mine. Journalist. Very smart."

"Yes. Send her my way." Now and then she sends him her friend, but her friend never arrives.

"She will love you real good."

"Yes. I will like that," Johan says.

He gives her a five dollar tip, believing it is is generous. Toshiko appears grateful. "Goodbye," Johan." She bows. He bows in return.

Isabel,

The problem may be that when healing occurs, there is less to say. We become stifled by our own "goodness." Where is the validity in writing about the one we love? Where is the honor? What is the spiritual damage incurred by such recordings? Is it unmanly to mine such a vein for one's writing? Think of someone like John Gregory Dunne. Did he put his wife, Joan Didion, in his novels? Of course not. John Gregory Dunne had a first-rate mind, and first-rate minds do not draw from the lives of those they profess to love. Frankly, I am tired of the whole business of mind. This one has this mind, and that one has that mind. And this one has achieved this preliminary to achieving that. Where is the life of the spirit, where is God, in all this striving?

Speaking of God, I went to Dr. Gold yesterday for a colonoscopy. The procedure was not as objectionable as was the fact that he would be administering it. Not that you would want such a procedure annually, as the preparation that we go through the previous day as well as the procedure itself can be an ordeal. You may recall that an issue developed between Dr. Gold and me some years ago when my healer Maria, whom I consider one of my great loves, was still in my life. (Maria will always be in my life, as far as that goes.) Dr. Gold is a gastroenterologist, and it was to him I was referred by my primary care physician, Dr. Silverman, when my liver enzymes soared some years ago. No, Isabel, the exact year is beyond my memory to recall, and it is not easy for me to reach into my files. I find that I have to emotionally gird myself for such a seemingly simple task. But about

Dr. Gold. "He is an old friend and colleague," Dr. Silverman assured me. (We could sing that song, of course: "Make new friends and keep the old—one is silver, the other is gold." It is a sadness in my life that people from my past are not more plentiful. But then, I also have to admit that sufficient interest in people or the expenditure of time necessary to keep them in my life has been lacking. What can we do about such a circumstance but resolve even more fully to embrace the present moment, and to make our connections there, as if to say, You, stranger, walking down the street so proud or forlorn, will you be my love this day, this moment?)

Dr. Silverman had asked me how much I drank. When I told him that I didn't drink at all, and hadn't for many years, he inquired about supplements I might be taking. Here I would have to say that I had not been forthcoming. There are many, like me, who place great faith in vitamins while knowing instinctively that to share that faith with AMA-certified doctors would be to expose ourselves to their doubt, disbelief, even objection. Faith is indispensable to some of us who choose to place ourselves beyond the reach of scientific skepticism.

And yet, Isabel, honesty is essential for healing. It is surely the sine qua non. And so I provided him in writing an exhaustive list, and as you may have guessed, the only reticence I had was regarding DHEA. Though I knew little about the substance other than it was a hormone, I could hope that Maria was correct in asserting it was the fountain of youth in capsule form and a possible boost to my flagging sexual powers. And Dr. Silverman confirmed my worst fear when I confessed to using this wonder supplement. "I think we have our culprit," he said, and placed me on a regimen of complete abstinence. No vitamin C, no multivitamin, no ginkgo biloba, and no DHEA. And it was here he did something more. He referred my case to Dr. Gold, whom, as I say, he presented as not only a friend but a colleague conveniently located on the very same floor, Dr. Silverman and Dr. Gold both being members of the same medical corporation. (Have you ever marveled at the ability of those who contribute to society in a meaningful way to tolerate stress and bring attention to bear on the detail work that complex operations require, those who don't have to run for breathing space into the parks or the wilderness each and every day or to alcohol or to illicit sex or any of the escapist ills of those like me, who, for one reason or another, cannot endure the thing-ness of life and simply want to have done with the uncertainty and unbearable responsibility success imposes and so never succeed at all?)

If I haven't told you, whereas I could sit with Dr. Silverman and relax knowing that I was in the presence of a man I could trust, I cannot say the same of Dr. Gold. When a man leads with a smile and is committed to showing off his winning ways, then we would be wise to sense danger. Dr. Gold's proposed course of action was for me to submit to a blood test every six weeks to determine whether my enzymes—the three of them with which he was concerned— were falling back into the normal range. When I gave him the same list of nutrients I had been taking that I had handed to Dr. Silverman, he made a face and said, "Why? Why would you do this? You don't need all this vitamin C. You don't need all this vitamin B." His voice was quiet and inquiring, as if to say he was open to an intelligent response. And he had a point, Isabel, if I am to be fair and balanced about the matter. There was no need for me to take both a multivitamin and a B-50 capsule daily. But apart from this, I could see no great excess. Well, maybe it wasn't necessary to take 800 IUs of vitamin E. Conceivably 400 IUs might have sufficed. But we are living in New York City, and the air has taken a turn for the worse. We are downwind of some noxious fumes and EPA standards are surely lax. A person would be wise to protect his or her lungs with antioxidants. Dr. Gold caught me at a vulnerable time. I had put great faith in Maria as a counterbalance to the diagnostic frenzy of the AMA and all their probing instruments, and yet those diagnostic tests don't lie, they simply don't. Furthermore, it wasn't Maria who detected that my enzymes had risen. It was for these medical tests to determine that. So what kind of argument could I make when

Dr. Gold said to me, apropos DHEA, the last item on the list, "We all want to be younger than we are, but you need to understand that killing yourself won't help you achieve your goal"?

Whatever suspension of disbelief I had needed to initially form a relationship with Maria, she had become a pillar of my faith over the years, and now that pillar was crumbling, and Dr. Gold was a witness to my emotional disarray. Though I loved Maria and would never say she came from the land of quackery, she had let me down, or if she hadn't, something had gone wrong. It was tantamount to being forced to believe there was no God, that all we had were these miserable bodies, and thus to elevate doctors to the status of God as they were the only ones who could, if not provide life everlasting, extend our journey on this planet.

Something you must understand about these doctors is that they eat at KFC and McDonald's, that they embrace the fast food culture that many of us try to avoid. Even my beloved Dr. Silverman sends out for the same fare as his receptionist and other office staff—burgers and fries and vats of Coca-Cola. They are pasty-faced, overweight, and old by age fifty. I suppose you could say they have seen one too many health-conscious types croak to believe in the efficacy of a more disciplined lifestyle than the one they practice, but I have also seen, if I may use Dr. Silverman as an example, their admiration bordering on envy for some of my past numbers. "Your triglycerides and LDL are unbelievably low. Your total cholesterol count is that of a well-conditioned athlete," Dr. Silverman remarked, at my last annual physical.

However, that was not the case now, where my liver was concerned. And so, Dr. Gold questioned me closely, as a doubter would, when the first test showed my liver enzymes had fallen only slightly. Was I sure I wasn't drinking? Not even a little alcohol here and there? I said no, frankly feeling sullied by his question. The power of his dubious mind housed in that massive head was almost too much for me, threatening what seemed suddenly my fragile hold on reality. And in that moment, let me say it, I felt his contempt, shared by many doctors for their patients, we who come to them with our anxious questions and vague complaints and virtual incoherence in matters of science and medicine. The simple fact that they triple-book, with no thought to the hour or two we will have to wait for the cursory visits they afford us, is revealing of their self-importance, never mind the regulations imposed by managed healthcare that they argue necessitates such strategies.

"And what about all that stuff you were taking? Are you 100 percent abstinent from those substances as well?" *Stuff*. In this way did he speak, as if to suggest that these life-enhancing nutrients were of a kind with street drugs procured from the local dealer.

"Well, I did take a multivitamin the other day, I have to admit."

Here I will tell you a story, Isabel. It is a brief one. Some years ago an Israeli man took two of my area rugs for cleaning. How did I know Shimon Bauer was Israeli? His heavy Middle Eastern accent and the yarmulke on his head. The price he set seemed to me high, but in a state of passivity, I gave in. What right did I have to reject the quote of a man who had spent the better part of an hour crawling on my floor inspecting the warp and woof of these very ordinary rugs and singing their praises as if they were treasures? And so he rolled them up and left. Only after the fact did I bother to comparison-shop, a testament to my laziness, and when the several quotes I received came in at one-tenth what the Israeli man was charging, I called him and sought to cancel the order. He said that was impossible. When I threatened not to pay, this ferocious noise came through the phone line, as if he were right there with me and breathing his fury into my face. Terror shot through me. I imagined the man breaking down my door. And so I went belly up.

Something happened during that word storm, Isabel. An image came to me of a Palestinian boy in the custody of the Mossad. In that moment I was that Palestinian boy. It was as if, for the very first time, I could actually imagine what had been previously unthinkable: the capacity for brutality on the part of some Israelis, and Jews in general. In that moment it occurred to me that I had been the prisoner of a myth, that of the gentle Jew, the nonviolent Jew. Jews were the source of all light, given the fact that Jesus was a Jew. And anyway, the Palestinians deserved what they got for their intransigence. Nothing counted over there but the state of Israel, its safety inextricably tied to my own.

But now it was Dr. Gold unloading on me on the phone, making the Israeli rug man sound like a gentle inquisitor. His fury penetrated my bones. "Did I not tell you…?" I can't say how long his display of protracted rage continued or easily describe its crushing weight, except to say I felt like a bug being blown about in a tornado.

So I learned what was behind Dr. Gold's big smile, as you, Isabel, learned what was behind mine, and many women the world over have learned what is behind the smiles of their men. It was not so hard for me to see that if he, a doctor and an accomplished professional man, could display such ire, and have it be triggered by something so small as a minor lapse regarding a regimen of abstinence on the part of his patient, then perhaps some more monstrous, even fatal, response might also be possible.

Chapter 37

It is time for the annual employee recognition luncheon. Johan has sent his e-RSVP to the Human Resources people, whose job it is to put on this all-staff affair. This year it will be held at the Roosevelt Hotel, within easy walking distance for most of the staff (not for Lurleen, who will cab it), and a happy choice for Johan, who, like most of the org, did not care for the last site, a former bank whose spacious rotunda featured bricked-up teller's windows and a peculiar echo chamber effect when you spoke.

Oh, happy day, when there is diversion from the norm. Plus, school will be getting out early. Everyone can go home afterward, or do whatever their hearts desire. Values. Excellence. Leadership. Vision. Categories of excellence have been established. Those who embody these qualities will receive awards. Johan never wins anything. He says he doesn't care. Every year he nominates someone, generally Lisa Benton. Never heard a peep about her from Johan? A worker bee for the department. She hums with a quiet sense of efficiency. Task-oriented. Gets the job done, and has inbred in her the modesty of the Great Plains, where she grew up. In life are gems now and then found among the detritus. He extols her virtues, which are multiple. Dedicated. Gives her very best. He sits down and interviews her each year, as he is doing now. Goes with pen and paper and asks her for the facets of her job. It's a generous impulse. He wants to do well by her. The woman is the salt of the earth. Survived a serious bout with cancer with impressive stoicism. A private person. She has some mysterious computer gift. Can solve any problem. Back in the day she input all his corrections—his en dashes and em dashes and series commas and other stuff. Things technophobic Miss Carmelli didn't want him doing on his own. Lisa Benton was the department's word processor person back when there was such a thing. He had some uneasy sense, even back then, that he was going to her for something he himself should learn for himself, that he was in some way not preparing himself for the future.

"I maintain the subscription database for the magazine, see to rights and permissions for photos, trouble-shoot where there are technical problems within the department, maintain a production schedule for the magazine…"

She is from a farming family. There are things she knows but does not say. Used to be he could make her laugh, as if they were on the same wavelength. One day Miss Carmelli was knocking on a locked door and they were on the other side and he whispered, "Let's not let her in," and she began to giggle uncontrollably. Like they were kids together, brother and sister, conspiring against a parent. The sense that she had a crush on him. Then she got sick. A bulge on her neck the size of a tennis ball. A long time away from the org. Over a year. Lucky to be alive, the doctors said. All the while Miss Carmelli kept the position open for her. Brought in Hank, he who assesses all situations, as a temp. Why a temp? Because Miss Carmelli had integrity and loyalty was part of that integrity. But the memory of Lisa Benton faded. Johan didn't want it to. He wanted love to last forever. He was like everyone that way. But she was gone. She was out of sight. And Hank was here. And Hank was doing good work. And maybe after a year of meritorious service and an exemplary attitude of helpfulness, Hank should be considered for Lisa Benton's position. Did the org not have an obligation to marry a temp after a certain point? Because over time Johan had come to feel that he just wanted Lisa Benton to stay away for good, and when she came back, with her American Gothic face, as Melvin Kleiner called it, he felt guilty, guilty for having such thoughts. Is it possible that she senses he has betrayed her? All he knows is that things haven't been the same between them since. Some subtle coolness, similar to the coolness Mary Terezzi now displays toward him.

Jane Fallows introduces the speaker. Wendy Wang is the national president of the org. A largely ceremonial post. A petite Asian woman who has made her fortune as the founder and CEO of a pharmaceutical firm in San Jose, California. Johan feels for her, this competent woman who now serves as the nominal head of this very visible org. He wonders whether, behind that placid façade, she must burn with fury at the waste and inefficiency. He reminds himself that he has no business going there, as he hears the hollow words her position requires of her. "You are the ones who make us proud and strong. You are the ones who provide direction for thousands and millions of girls…" But the liftoff is not there. The words do not soar. They simply fall to the floor. There is a disconnect between Wendy Wang and the words she speaks. He can feel it. Surely everyone can. But why? Because she does not know these people, and she doesn't want to know them. You don't value people because you say you do in a five-minute speech. It's not her fault, it's not anyone's fault. It's just a structure that remains in place year after year, an acceptable form of insincerity. It is what you expect to hear when you work for an institution.

He sits in his chair and eats his pasta—how badly can they mangle that—and avoids the rubber chicken and other glop these burned-out waiters are schlepping to the table. And it's OK to have a roll and smear it with a patty of butter. Oh yummy. He has not forgotten how good salted butter can taste. What must he look like stuffing his face with buttered bread? No matter. Feed the face. Why not have another? He'll adopt even more of an austerity regime in the aftermath. Hit the hummus hard. Besides, no impending cholesterol test. Plenty of time to correct this dietary lapse. And nix on the dessert as well, a delicious-looking piece of key lime pie with some sort of sauce on it. Passes it on to Lurleen.

Poor sad Lurleen. She looks sweaty and overweight and peeved. No point to asking her if she is having fun, when half the building has seen through to her aggrandizing ways. And no point to feeling too sorry for her either. Has it ever occurred to her to recommend one of her staff for an award? As Lisa Benton has subtly suggested, the committee is more likely to pay attention to a recommendation from a higher-up than from someone such as himself, right there in the low middle zone of the grid.

"Have I ever told you all that I entered ballroom dancing competitions right here in this ballroom, and that I was queen of the ball? Won first prize right here in this very room?"

No one appears to be listening. No one appears to care, although it is fascinating to imagine a younger Lurleen doing the foxtrot or whatever she did. Luther can see it. She probably did have some physical agility and grace before she blew out her knees, as she tells them.

In the reception area before the ballroom doors open those same waiters with hors d'oeuvres on silver trays. Toxic shrimp from the polluted ocean and other things he has no name for. And there, mingling with the hoi polloi, the senior leadership team, having been directed to do so. The peons being graced with their presence.

Dolores Klink. Gladiola Feingold. Ernesto Che. Dominick Aranado. All of them called to the dais to receive congratulations and a small envelope from Jane Fallows, with her forced smile, and to pose for a photograph with her that will be posted in the cafeteria the next week, a whole bulletin board full of them. Poor Jane Fallows, wondering what on the good earth she is doing here in the minor leagues while fantasizing about prime time Washington, D.C., and her someday seat in the United States Senate.

He has been here before, in what seems another lifetime. Those broad carpeted stairs to the main lobby. Above, a balcony sitting area with potted plants and comfortable chairs. A step back in time to the nineteen forties. *The Maltese Falcon.* Mary Astor. Peter Lorre. And of course Bogart and the fat man, Sidney Greenstreet. Intrigue. That tug of the past and the desire to be enfolded in it. The railroads too, of course. Only a stone's throw from Grand Central Terminal.

Was it really him, the boy who came to this same hotel with his friend Jerry Jones Nobleonian, the two of them going from door to door of this grand hotel seeking contributions for Nixon from the hotel's tenants, men and women coming from the shower or wherever to give him nickels or quarters or even dollar bills, while others slammed the door in their faces. That's nothing Luke would have done, he hears himself saying. Luke too good and innocent for such nickel and dime duplicity. Luke's sins, if they were to be called that, were those brought on by his libido. Imagine that. In blind thrall to the Republican Party was Johan. The alternative the anarchy of the Democrats. Somehow the GOP had gotten through to him with its messaging. Somehow they knew the way to his mind. Scary to contemplate such a thing. To live in America is to be sentenced to unreality, some poet wrote.

Zofia has a big smile for him. Together they can show off their connection and allow people to see that they are not alone in the universe, even if they are. They go off to a movie. Lincoln Center. A young people's movie. Italian kids. Privileged university students. Politically sincere. Headed for a bad end. A college demonstration goes wrong. A police officer badly hurt. Lost innocence. Crushing bureaucracy. Beautiful faces bruised and swollen from harsh beatings. Prison doors slamming. Not the kind of thing Johan can easily bear. Doesn't want to see harm come to others. That has never been his thing. Even when he was a child, he had to flee from scenes of violence. The reckless young with their passions, knowing nothing about the world and the consequences of their actions. With one dumb act forfeiting their middle class privileges. No protection, no mercy, once you're in the maw of the machine.

And the theater. So dark. All this playacting. Isn't that what it is? Pressing himself against Zofia on the escalator up to the Walter Reade Theater. Even as she thrusts her butt backward at him, a sense that he can go no further. His hand on her thigh there in the dark. Reduced to a tease game now that consummation is not possible.

"What do you want? Tell me. I will do it," she says afterward.

He has been generous with her. Paid for the movie. Now it is for her to repay him. This is how she thinks. She needs to be able to give. A generous heart. He could say no. He could just call it a day. But he can't. If he stops it there, she will see, in broad daylight, that he is a fraud, and a groping fraud at that. He cannot bear that look of recognition he will receive from her. He cannot bear to hurt her, not after building her up. What is it she says? "You feed me with your words," when he describes her physical assets to her.

And so they go back to his apartment, where once again he cannot perform and once more is led by shame to bury his head in the pillow, unable to tell her he has more than he needs with Internet porn.

Here she is again the next week, a group of girls in shorts and blue org T-shirts trailing behind her in the corridor. "This is where organization make their executive decisions," Zofia says, leading the girls past one cubicle after another. Slackers tear themselves from their computer screens to desperately scatter papers over their desks to show they have something more meaningful to do than check their e-mail ten times an hour. A tidal wave of paralyzing shame grips Johan. A colossal gyp, he wants to scream. Someone take them to the Empire State Building or the Central Park Zoo or for a ride on the Staten Island Ferry. What is that to come from South Carolina to pay for overpriced trinkets in the GoAN gift shop and eat bad food in the cafeteria?

Turning to the girls, Zofia says, "This is Mr. Johan Manootdjian. He is redactor."

"What is that?" one pudgy girl with freckles asks.

"Book editor."

An uncomfortable silence follows. He has nothing the girls want. The troop leader, a heavyset woman from the hinterland with small, suspicious eyes and perhaps some fixed opinion of city folk and books and the people involved with them, gives him a hard stare before Zofia mercifully leads them away.

Chapter 38

As if the org has come to recognize the carnal beast that lurks within the human heart, harassment in the workplace is the topic of the Human Resources meeting, and attendance is required. Refreshments are available on a side table: tea, coffee, pastries.

"Before I give you our special guest," Jeanine Juddster says, "let me be frank. Any staff who put their hands where they don't belong or say what shouldn't be said, they will be shown the door. Now, as to our guest, first you should all know that she is a great theatrical talent and had leading roles for many years in Broadway and off-Broadway shows and significant parts in some major motion pictures. But burning as her passion for stage and screen were, she had a deeper sense of herself and her mission that she couldn't postpone indefinitely, and that passion was for *justice*. This is a woman who wants to right wrongs and see that the aggrieved get their day in court. This is a woman who says to all the women of the world, Victim no more. Momma's tough. Momma's real tough. She walked away from a fabulous career to enter New York Law School, from which she graduated at the top of her class, and has become a nationally recognized authority on harassment in the workplace. With no further ado. I give you Justine Justice Jugeforte."

Such excess. "Praise to the face is open disgrace." Didn't Hemingway say something like that? Johan himself had been admitted to that law school, way back when. A law school for cops, someone once said—everyone walking around with a gun. However, Justine Jugeforte does not appear undone by the introduction. It may be that she takes it as her due. Or maybe she is only focused on the fat fee she will be paid for her services.

"Thank you, thank you, for that wonderful intro. It's a pleasure to be here, and let me say right off the bat that it's *necessary* for me to be here for one reason and one reason only, and that is to free you to thrive and achieve excellence in the workplace. For that to be achieved, each and every workplace must be contamination-free. No winks, no leers, no pinches, no kootchy-koo, no sidebar sub rosa activity here. Are you hearing me, women and men of the org?"

"We hear you," comes the response.

How easily she has won them over, Johan thinks, trying to understand the real story. A fading star, with fewer parts as she crossed the line to the other side of forty? Too many crappy temp jobs between gigs? Some longing for security, a steady paycheck so she can pay the rent? A desire to control her own destiny? An abusive husband that led to divorce?

"So you are hearing me and I am hearing you. This is major. *Major.* So what is harassment anyway? What does it mean when someone says she or he is being harassed? Anybody care to jump in here?"

"People be walking around with booty on their brain and giving you that look."

"They be trying to get in your pants when you don't want them to," another says.

"Ain't nobody getting in my pants if I don't want them to. You got to be something special to enter my house," still another says.

"Ain't nobody want to visit your sagging old house anyway," someone else says. Laughter ripples through the curtained space.

Suddenly the org is sounding like the Rikki Lake show.

"Whoa, whoa," Justine Jugeforte says, as if reining in wild horses. A pile of frizzy hair frames her small face. The stamp of dullness is on her features that the years bring to everyone and that no amount of makeup and treatments and affirmations can offset; regardless of the promises of the beauty industry, age is unstoppable, one pale, washed out puss after another. "This is one creative group. You guys bring *passion* to the workplace. And I love passion. I adore passion. But what do we need to do with passion? Anybody in the group have an idea?"

"I believe what we have to do is *channel* our passion so it is always at the service of the org." Johan's head turns involuntarily, and there to greet him is Lurleen Lulabella with a full-out glare, her mouth a thin line, to remind him of every bad thing he has ever done to her.

"A plus E superior. I had a teacher once who gave out such a grade, and now I give the same to you. Of course. Yes. *Channel your passion. Channel it.* But channel it where? Anybody know?"

"Into the work itself," Lurleen says.

"Of course. The work itself," Justine says, giving Lurleen a validating nod, though with less enthusiasm than initially.

"How many of you guys are good at performing?"

Some of the older men have nervous smiles on their faces; others are blank. There is another nervous ripple of laughter through the room.

"Not that kind of performing. That we can talk about off-line. I'm talking now about performing in the sense of acting. We're going to do a little role-playing here this morning. Which of you guys wants to step up to the plate?"

Hands stay down.

"None of you wants the chance to do a little acting with a warm, vivacious woman?" A fearful stillness hangs in the air, and grows as she slowly moves up the aisle casting an appraising eye on the men. Johan wears the blandest, blankest look he can summon. This is no actor coming closer; this is an executioner. He wants no part of this activity, to be fodder for the org's purposes. Surely she will go for one of the more extroverted types who have been shooting up their hands and cracking wise.

"How about we choose this gentleman sitting here quietly. What do you say, group?"

"Oh, man, he ain't got nothing. He ain't barely alive," says one of the rowdies, provoking a laugh storm from Lurleen.

"Come on, now. Let's give the man a chance. What do you say?" Justine is at the place where she can exercise crowd control. She has presented herself so openly that the group has no choice but to accept her.

The staff member's comment has seriously eroded whatever confidence Johan possesses. He is at that dangerous place now of acute self-consciousness as Justine Jugeforte leads him to the front of the room. His clothes are not quite right. The pair of Docker's khakis, the low-end slacks he buys for $29 at Macy's, are baggy in the seat and the legs. He chose them over the black slacks he normally wears because he wanted a summer look, but he should have known not to trust the full-length mirror on the back of his bedroom door. It's always far kinder to him than the full-length mirror in the bathroom at the org. And when will he ever learn that he can't judge his appearance in a pair of slacks until he has inspected his image in the shoes he has chosen? In an exercise in wishful thinking, he assumed that a pair of light brown slip-ons would blend well, but they don't. These are not sleek, thin-soled Italian designer shoes. They are clunky, thick-soled things made in China. And the shirt is too young for him. He picked it from a catalog. Some twenty-something on a sunlit beach modeling it with his Greek god figure. And he is wearing his shirt outside his pants, the new look favored by some, but not one of those dress shirts with the long tails that, untucked, cover virtually the man's entire ass. This shirt has an even hem that he figured would cover his belt and obscure that little Docker's label over his right back pocket so he too could have a kind of carefree, with-it image without looking sloppy.

But standing at the front of the room with Justine Jugeforte, he fears he looks like a python that has just swallowed a cow. He is a man in need of a serious tummy tuck.

Justine directs Johan to stand ten feet away from her. "Now your job, group, is to watch closely because I'm going to ask you some questions about this. Are you ready?"

"Yes," they roar back.

Slowly, she sashays toward Johan, her head tilted and one hand provocatively on the back of her neck. "Hi, you tall, cool glass of water. Momma's thirsty. Can Momma sip from your glass, pretty please?"

The group is looking for repartee, for something to make them howl.

"What do I look like, lady? Poland Spring?"

Justine Jugeforte's stage voice booms through the hand-held mike, easily dominating the ripple of laughter. "So what do you say, group? Harassment or not harassment? H or NH?"

"H," the group roars back.

Someone pipes up. "Why you be harassing a sad-looking man like that who wouldn't know what to do with a woman like you?"

"I will take that as a compliment," Justine Jugeforte says, and then huddles with Johan, their backs to the group. "Can you suck it up and just do it, like the commercial says? Are you a big game player, buster? Do you have the right stuff? Or are you a lousy dickhead like all the rest of them, all talk and no action?"

"Just bring it on," he says.

Justine Jugeforte takes three steps toward the audience. "Listen up, now. Mr. Honcho Head here is going to strut his stuff. And then there will be little old me. I will need all of you to be on the ball. Are you with me?"

"We're with you," they roar back.

"And remember—you need only determine this: Is it H, or is it NH? Got it?"

"Got it," they roar back again.

In the scene that follows, Justine Jugeforte is seated at her desk, where she simulates running her fingers over a keyboard and peering intently at a computer screen. Johan approaches, sits down beside her as she is typing, and says, "You look really great. Love your hair. Love the way you look in that tight blouse. Where have you been all my life?"

Justine Jugeforte jumps up, her hands in the air. "Whoa, Nelson. Time for a breather." Addressing the group, she says, "What about it, gang? Do I hear an H or a NH?" She then cups her ear and leans forward with a goofy, expectant grin as if straining to hear.

"Double H. Triple H. All the H's in the world." is the verdict of one rowdy.

"Damn, you never know what a person's got going on. Could be one foot in the grave and still wants to get into your business. Ain't that something? I be seeing that guy tottering around with his coffee mug. He always be drinking from that mug, like it's a part of his hand. And to think he's still got some life in that tired old bod. Damn." So says another.

"We've heard from two people now. What do you say, group? Is it an H or an NH?' Justine Jugeforte struts back and forth. She owns this space.

"H," they all shout.

"So we have this guy dead to rights, would you say?"

"He a dead man, all right. He be dead and gone. Don't need his kind around here." So speaks another rowdy.

"So what have we learned from this? Important to extrapolate. Important to message content. Important to thrust it into the consciousness. Otherwise, what is it good for? Get my drift?"

"With you, sister."

"Rule # 1—no touching. Rule #2. Watch what you say as well as what you do. Tone of voice *counts*. Let's get some fresh talent up here to show what I mean. You can go back to your seat now. I've forgotten your name."

"Mr. Stud. That be his name. Mr. Lecher Stud."

"Now, now, group. Be nice."

She beckons Bill Romney forward. He bounds out of his chair, drawing a laugh. "I'm liking your zip, Bill. If I say to you, 'Nice slacks, Bill,' do we call that H or NH, group?"

"NH."

"And if I say, 'Oh baby, nice slacks, Billy Boy, and I bet what's in them is even nicer'"?

"That definitely be H," someone says.

And so it goes for another half hour as Justine Jugeforte continues to take the group through the nuances of H/NH while Johan, mortified, stares at the wall. A wall can be such a refuge in a time of trouble. All you need to do is focus at a point slightly above the heads in the room.

Still, you can only look at a wall so long before you begin to wonder if people aren't beginning to notice. When he lowers his gaze, he sees a disturbing sight. Julie Morrow, from Research, is staring directly at him. A woman who makes it a point to avert her eyes from his. Not only is she now making eye contact: her eyes are burning into him. It is a face that says, "I know who you are, you creep. I know only too well."

Chapter 39

Dear Terminator and Future Boss of Mine,

You ask me about our department's relation to the org as if you truly wish to know. We are servants of the regime. So long as we understand that, we will be OK, but if we forget, then we place ourselves in peril. We exist to make them look good. Let us hope our department is not seduced by the quick fix of "ordering out," thus denying the org the "home-cooked meal" that we are capable of serving up. I like your idea for filtering projects through our department. In that way we get to touch everything. However, I am made nervous by your reference to our potential to reach "rock star" status. I have been there. I know what it is to start your day with Led Zeppelin's "Stairway to Heaven" or even Foreigner singing "I Want to Know What Love Is" or Donna Summer doing her "Bad Girl" thing and find yourself all revved up in that American space where you you hold your index finger in the air to signify that you are number one in all the universe.

"For the first time I understand why you say bad."

"Bad?"

"That you are bad person." Zofia smiles. "You are bad person. Maybe very bad person."

He feels unsure of himself, uncertain of his footing. Feels suddenly like her prey.

HR Notice

It is with much regret that we inform you of the passing of Marie Crain, senior governance specialist. Notes of condolence may be sent to her sister, Eudora Crain, at the Mercy Senior Citizens Center in Laramie, Wyoming. In lieu of flowers, Marie's sister asks that you send—potato chips. That's right, folks, potato chips. Eudora says the passing on of her sister has given her a yen for the salty things of life.

He steps off the elevator on the fourteenth floor. Through the glass door the formidable bronze bust of the founder on a marble pedestal confronts him. A woman cast off by her husband in the first decade of the last century. A woman with a dream, a vision, and the ability to turn it into a reality. This culture here. It molds you. Leads you on the path of some peculiar goodness. All these oversize framed photos on the walls of smiling girls. Girls. Girls. Girls. As if they are human bonbons. After a while you no longer see them, no longer want to see them. On the street the other day, in front of the stone lions outside the New York Public Library, a camera-laden man bearing down on a preadolescent girl with his priapic lens. The young as a drink, as a drug. Not so much wanting to help the young as to be the young? Saying, the only two real crimes in America are to be poor and to be old? Both confer on you invisibility?

Once again the trigger of the old cedar wood water towers on the rooftops of the buildings below with their distinctive beanie-shaped tops. The world out there, but he has been here, tethered, lulled into a half-sleep by the narcotic comfort of a twice-monthly paycheck.

"Johan. How good to see you," Belvedere Selwin exclaims, which can only mean that Belvedere has her ducks in a row and is feeling happy. "Are you here on business?"

"I am."

"How would we do without you?"

"Very well, I am sure," Johan says.

"No way. You are indispensable. The very best."

"In my dreams." The hype machine is going. It is his own fault if people take the liberty of elevating and setting him apart so he cannot be one with them. They are only giving him what they suspect he wants, and so the blandishments will only cease when something shifts in him, signaling that it is no longer required.

"I went birding in Central Park this morning before work. I saw two cedar waxwings and even a chicken hawk. It's amazing what you can find in this city."

"It's good to have interests that go beyond the workplace."

"Are you kidding? It's absolutely necessary. I mean, you have an interest in writing, don't you?" Belvedere says.

"Do I?"

"Oh, someone told me that is your passion."

She has come too close. "I have no passions."

"Everyone has passions."

"The living dead have passions?'

"Sure. They have a passion to be dead."

Belvedere looks like a bird, with her beaked nose and hard, observant eyes, but without the spectacular plumage of the Oiseau. A chicken hawk maybe, such as she sighted this morning with her binoculars. And here she sits, in her organized and spacious cubicle, with the kidney-shaped desk that befits her status as a director. The CEO down the hall. The office of the national president right next door. Big offices with wood-paneled walls and sofas and heavy, official-looking desks and spectacular views. And the senior vice president also down the hall. Best to be careful here and understand that Belvedere, despite her birding hobby, is one with her job and identified in her mind with the levers of power and that she could hurt him. She has in the past, the way she pulls rank by not seeking him out in his cubicle but going straight to Lurleen's office, one director speaking directly to another. Or the e-mails to Lurleen about projects he is responsible for, with only a cc to him. A woman who knows how to put people in their place. No, you don't want to get on Belvedere's bad side. That wouldn't do.

"I guess I'd better be careful what I say to people."

"You don't have to be careful with me, Johan. You never have to be careful with me."

Memory triggered by those water towers, taking him back, in a wounding way, to the old Penn Central rail yard in Riverside Park, where he places the sidelined boxcars in the viewfinder of his old Yashica 2 ¼-inch camera. The weight of impending loss too unbearable, he wants to capture on film this dying site before it vanishes. But it is too hard. No one can capture the whole world. And what would it get you even if you did?

The previous fall he had freed himself from the yoke of law school before the yoke could even be applied, though there was that one brief shining moment on the bus ride out to Newark for the orientation when a new self burst forth. He would break free from the renting office; no longer would he siphon a portion of the rent income he had been taking since starting his two-hour shifts several nights a week, an activity akin to stealing from his mother's pocketbook as a child, and move forward with his life. For the duration of the bus ride he was engulfed in joy. His mother would be proud of him, as would Sarah. But on disembarking from the bus and moving briskly through the scarred streets, the burnt-out shops a reminder of the days and nights of rage three years before, that euphoria, that new world he had briefly been lifted into, began to fade. That evening he was back in the renting office pocketing a portion of the rent income. In her early seventies, his mother was alone with the business now, his aunt, the one-time owner of the building, having died senile and withered, and his father gone as well.

He was seeing a psychoanalyst at an East Side clinic at the time. Three dollars a session three times a week. A German émigré to this country with the reality of war forever in her soul, Dr. Frieda Bauer wondered how he had gotten as far as he had when he first came to her. For a month he said repeatedly he wasn't fit to be in her presence. He wasn't fit to be anywhere. She told him she couldn't make him more intelligent but perhaps more moral on learning of his activity in the renting office and constant sexual activity, and suggested he try the "old-fashioned tranquilizer" when he asked for Valium to calm his anxiety that Sarah might leave him. And so he did.

Isabel,

Those three years I spent with Dr. Bauer were not meaningless. An intimacy developed, though she could never convince me to lie down on the couch. I had to sit up and face her at all times. Who can say why? It is possible that her black hair and thick frame reminded me vaguely of Hannah, though her personality and character were nothing like my oldest sister's. She would suck in her cheeks to show how gaunt I looked. How beautifully she dressed in bright, coordinated colors.

Some years later there she was walking south along Lexington Avenue as it slopes downward through Murray Hill. She had the slow gait of one who has experienced a full day, and that is the impression she always made, of a forty-something woman in right relationship with the world.

Once I expressed fear that I might go to prison for taking all that rent money that wasn't mine from the building my family managed.

"You already are in prison," she said. In such a way did she speak to me.

"This is your novel," she also said, holding up the spiral notebook in which she took notes during our sessions, after I had expressed an interest in writing fiction.

After getting sober I wrote a note of thanks for all her good help during those difficult years. She was still here on this earth and in the phone book. Some days later, to my surprise, Sarah called me to the phone. Dr. Bauer was on the line. She thanked me for my note and asked if I was still writing. Perhaps she picked up on my discomfort. I say this because she suddenly apologized for intruding on my evening and expressed some concern that Sarah might misunderstand the nature of her call. I wonder now if my reassurance was strong enough, and wonder too at the curiosity Dr. Bauer expressed about the recovery I was engaged in. Did the meetings really work? Was it absolutely necessary that I attend them? Is it possible that she was becoming increasingly reliant on the "old-fashioned tranquilizer" she had recommended to me those years before? Again, there is that hymn from my childhood, Isabel. "Rescue the perishing/Care for the dying." It truly is for me to be a fisher of men and women and to offer assistance should they cry out for help or ask for it in more subtle ways, and I did not answer her in the full way that I would now. If I had it to do over, I would have said, "Why not join me at a meeting? You can see for yourself." I have sisters who perished and a brother who perished. The unbearable pain. I have no choice but to count on the next life for a do-over, so Dr. Bauer can feel my love, for how often does love come calling? This you must understand, Isabel. You must.

"Something is on my mind, related to where I have just been. Can you bear to listen?" Johan asks, after Melvin has removed his headset. When he is not on the Web seeking to fill his time, now that he has been displaced, he has taken to reading the Vedas and expanding his meditations. Lurleen has done a terrific job bungling his brilliance.

"Sure. Go ahead. We'll have our little satsang."

"Have you seen *Saturday Night Fever?*"

"What is that?"

"Yes, what is that? It's a film about disco fever that came out in the late seventies. I didn't see it at the time for the simple reason that I couldn't. It was sheer hell for me to try to be without a drink in my hand for ten minutes let alone two hours, and so I stopped going to movie theaters and stayed home with the bottle. Anyway, as the film opens, Tony Manero is bopping along a Brooklyn street in his mod outfit. But the telling detail is the paint bucket he is carrying. Whatever fantasy life he has going on built around his Saturday night disco exploits, he is a day laborer with a dead-end job in the neighborhood hardware store. And just now, while upstairs visiting with the org power structure, I saw myself as Tony Manero, only I carry a pencil, not a paint bucket. There is pain in realizing I have spent my life tethered to this place."

"An interesting image but somewhat narcissistic," Melvin says. He has the ability to make Johan want to be better than he is. Those degrees of Melvin's. They count for something. They give him the stamp of authenticity. "To be continued," Melvin Kleiner says. "To be continued."

Chapter 40

Dear Shelly,

My mother would say, 'Do my words mean nothing?' when she felt she was not getting through to me or the other children. And now I say the same to you. You call me over and over about your son and the lack of respect he shows you. At some point it's necessary to not merely listen but to be willing to take the action suggested to heal the situation. And what I tell you over and over again is to write out your resentment against your son. 'I feel he is an ingrate. I feel he deliberately hurts my feelings when he doesn't return my phone calls,' etc., and then what it affects in you. And then to see your part. And to follow this up with a prayer of forgiveness. You will benefit from asking yourself, in writing, what you are contributing to the situation. I suspect the main issue is control. You are trying to pull your son closer to you. And why? Because you are afraid. Down deep you have made your son your retirement plan. It is in him that you have invested. And how do you secure your investment? By burdening him with guilt. You put him in the docket and fire away at him with prosecutorial zeal. Once a month you scorch him with your fire. You must begin to understand that inducing guilt in others is a form of attack. Take it from one who knows. Understand at depth that as we grow older we become sideshows in the lives of others, especially the young. No strings must be attached to love. None. Were you so wonderfully attentive as a young man to your father? By your own account, the answer would be no. You need to draw on your own experience in reshaping your attitude. It's for you and your partner to have a life and allow your son to have his. There is no other answer. The young are busy mating, acquiring, moving on. Those of us who are older exist but as signposts for them. Ultimately we must go to God with these difficulties. It is on him that we must depend increasingly, as people will never give us what we want to our specifications, and what are our specifications, but for more and more and more? And please remember the futility of comparison. If your son sees his mother more than he sees you, is it not possible that this is so because you walked out of the marriage when he was three? Listen to him when he says, "You are driving me crazy," because you are.

By the way, you have taken to calling me at work recently. It doesn't occur to you to ask if I am busy or to call me at home in the evening or on the weekend. You just start talking. And what do you talk about? How you pooped your pants on Sixth Avenue or did a mammoth dump within a block of your Bay Ridge apartment due to increasing incontinence. Or about some young store clerk you have the hots for. Leisurely, drawn-out anecdotes, as if my sole purpose in life is to listen to you. And should I say I have to go, or try to snap you to attention by asking what is really going on, you take an aggrieved tone. And that little laugh I have come to notice. It's your fuck you laugh, isn't it? I don't know what I can tell you more than I have.

Of course, you could be right. It may be that men like you get things done. Certainly it can be said that you are on the ground with the demands you place on life for satisfaction of your needs. And yet, you have a tenacity that is, I have to say, sometimes off-putting and even unbearable, as when we sit in a restaurant and you grill the poor waiter as to every last ingredient in the arroz con pollo you are thinking to order at your favorite Spanish restaurant.

Are you not concerned with offending or even angering the poor man? And then the way you tear into the flesh of the chicken, as if everything has fallen away from your consciousness other than the rapture of ravaging the roasted creature. You definitely have an appetite for life. You don't peck at it like a bird pecks at a crumb of bread, as Peter, my first ex-father-in-law, said of me some years back. It must be that, in that moment, I did something to irritate him. We were sitting on the terrace up at Camp, and Lydia had thrown together a lunch from the leftovers of the previous night's dinner. They were dealing with the recent death by suicide of their daughter Lenore. Peter would hover over the dishes of food with his fork—pieces of steak and asparagus and salad—before spearing a morsel, an irritant in and of itself, but what caused me to visibly shudder was the repeated scraping of his fork against his teeth. I do believe he took pleasure in my discomfort and in that context made his remark. And who is to say he was wrong? He saw my reticence, not merely about food, but life. The point I am making, Shelly, is that you have bitten into life and tried to shape it to your satisfaction. It is quite possible that, on the other hand, I have withdrawn too much. Maybe you do need to make demands on your son. Maybe that is the nature of true relationship, to ask things of others, to express our hurt, even our anger, when they disappoint us. Shelly, pester the waiters in all five boroughs, do whatever you feel you need to do to secure a better relationship with your son.

As for your concerns about money, what am I to say? You've been speaking about this approaching financial insolvency for the last seven years. Like a number of people I know, family members left you a substantial inheritance, which you have been living on without any thought to the future other than an acknowledgment that you will be in dire straits when the money is all gone. What I mean is that in these years you made no attempt to find suitable employment. You contented yourself with being a house husband, and by all accounts you have performed this service well. Not only did you not try to put aside for the future, but you also indulged in lavish spending—silk suits, expensive art, overseas travel. And always that little laugh, as if you were a naughty and self-indulgent boy.

How is it that I wind up with people like you in my life? Though I merely listened, I felt troubled the other night, listening to you go on and on about your looming poverty and the admission that you have been thinking of suicide. I see you as too much a lover of life to go that route, and was somewhat relieved at your assurance that you had not yet worked out a plan. However, my concern returned when you laughed and confided your plan is to jump off the Brooklyn Bridge.

You explain that the neckwear industry went kerflooey, that ties today are made in China and South Korea, that at most, Milan now does the design work. And you point out that as the service economy grows ever larger in America, department stores are staffed with kids who are paid little and know nothing. "They have no need for someone with my abilities and qualifications," you say. You tell me about those futile two years you spent at a career counseling agency polishing your résumé and sending out thousands of copies.

OrganicOnly is often looking for qualified people. On my way to work, I think of calling you to raise your flagging spirits. There is real urgency, as I walk through the garment center along what is now Fashion Avenue, with that outdoor sculpture of the giant button and the needle through one of the holes. I must call you and make everything all right. My pace quickens. Soon I am in my cubicle and the computer has come to life and awaits my password. The urgency is not there. Where have you gone, "Rescue the perishing. Care for the dying"? No matter. I call anyway. I tell you of this lead, saying what do you have to lose. Even as I do, I see that it could never work. It is simply not the place for you. What is more, you see it too, judging from your lukewarm response. I do not sing "Rescue the Perishing." I do not sing at all.

—An unsent letter in Johan Manootdjian's journal

Chapter 41

Isabel,

You ask me what I am feeling, and so I will tell you. It is that someone in particular has an eye right into my very soul and the pain from her witnessing is excruciating. I feel impaled by her penetrating vision, if you must know. I feel the eye says everything that needs to be said or that could be said. I am referring to the baby shower for Mia's firstborn. I had made up my mind to buy books as a gift, though I was doubtful about their appropriateness. For this reason I had to solicit the advice of several people, the consensus being that it was an unusual but generally appreciated sort of gift, as most young mothers want to build a library for their children. One I could not go wrong with was the picture book *Make Way for Ducklings,* by Robert McCloskey. The book is famous the world over for its humorous story and generous charcoal drawings. And maybe Maurice Sendak's *Nutshell Library,* a collection of tiny books that are practical as well as entertaining in introducing an infant to the alphabet as well as counting. Yes, I know Mia had registered online with Babies R Us, but somehow I could not go there. Was it too complicated? Did I wish to be different? Did I fear confusion? Was there something distasteful— too ephemeral—about items for a baby? Was I looking to make a contribution that could be more enduring? I really can't say. And when I finally did overcome my resistance and visited the Web site, I will have to admit to some sharp pain, for you, Isabel, were listed as the grandmother but the grandfather went unlisted. Right there Mia was telling me something—if not who I was, who I wasn't. Not that I should have been listed, as I have no blood tie with her. Even so, I felt cast, in that moment, as a complete stranger in her life, as if stepping into her home was transgressive, an invasion of her space. I felt it brought us close to the enduring problem of our relationship—who was I? How far in the way of acceptance of me would she be willing to go? And behind all that was the possibility that I was not good enough. Intelligence is important to those like Mia who have special gifts.

After her scintillating doctoral thesis presentation and the big hug I gave her, she did question me closely as to whether I had understood the material she presented. She was looking at me with great acuity, as if to say that if I didn't understand, then I could not be part of her world. And so, when I said yes, sort of, I was not telling the truth, the fact being that so much of her presentation had gone right past me. A more honest answer would have been to say that I had sat in mindless appreciation with Isabel and Anri, Mia's Georgian husband, simply in thrall to her youth and beauty and intelligence.

"While I did not understand her presentation in even a minimal way, except to say that it had something to do with dendritic cells, what I did understand was the dynamics of the situation and how I might be rightly perceived as not quite belonging, for when I arrived at the research center, where I was told to wait for you so we could be escorted into the building by Anri, you had not yet arrived. But Anri had. I knew it was him right away, though I could not read his name off the ID card dangling from his neck. A well-built man with graying hair, he stood leaning against the wall, his right foot raised and pressed against the wall as well. A man in his mid-forties smoking a cigarette and projecting an image of cool toughness.

When I went over and introduced myself, he asked me how I knew it was him. There was guardedness in his question. His tone was brusque and not quite friendly. 'Mia described you,' I replied. He merely grunted. All the while I was impatient for you to show up, and when you did, something significant occurred. You and Anri bolted down the corridor toward the auditorium and left me far behind. At that moment I saw that I was completely expendable. It was everything for me, in that moment of your disappearance around the corner, to not turn back and just leave the building. You were reminding me, in that moment, how close and not close we are.

"Mia's friends from the scientific community had gathered for the baby shower. They were women rendered gorgeous by their intellects. Fear gripped me that I could not control. I could feel myself contracting while watching others settle into conversations, and found myself wandering from group to group, with no access point available. At one point I went into the kitchen, seeking to dissolve my apartness by chatting with Anri and a couple of his Georgian buddies, but they were speaking in their native tongue and barely gave me a glance, as if I did not qualify for their high testosterone circle. And then there was a friend of Mia's who had brought her dog, a Chihuahua, and though I didn't mean to, I quickly sensed that I had offended her by remarking on the current fad in Manhattan for having small dogs as pets. The woman was unhealthily thin and so it also occurred to me that this dog was like her child. And so she turned away from me as well.

A further moment of truth arrived when the gifts were presented. A bassinet, even a baby carriage, rattles, and clothes for the baby, too. Anri was the master of ceremonies, calmly opening each gift, appraising it, and with a smile giving acknowledgment to the bearer. His equanimity was admirable. He clearly had a measure of self-esteem I did not possess. And so, as this ritual went on, I withdrew deeper into myself and began to tremble. My paltry gift was symbolic of the meagerness of my contribution to Mia's life.

I was there as a sort of friend to Mia, a something undefined to Mia, neither this nor that. And so, when Anri shed the wrapping and said, in a questioning voice, 'What is this? Book? Someone give book? Baby come from womb ready to read book?' in his article-less English, and people laughed, I shrank further within myself, fully separated from my betters, these high-achieving women and men from elite universities who had aced every standardized test they had taken.

"No one give gift? Gift given by person of mystery? Sorcerer make gift appear?"

A nervous silence ensued, in which I feigned an air of distraction, busying myself with an inspection of my shoe, as if possibly I hadn't heard the question or it didn't pertain to me. You, of course, knew very well the gift was mine, and so shared with me the uncomfortable moment I couldn't break free from with a simple confession, for that is what it would have been at that point. Others would have witnessed the reluctance and interpreted it as shame, as an admission that somehow neither the gift nor I were good enough. In that moment, too, Isabel, you understood anew why we are no longer married.

Dear Ellen Deutsch,
The problem is simply this. Despite all our posturing, our "We're number one in all the universe" stance, we don't believe in ourselves. As an organization we have an inferiority complex. If we're here, there must be something wrong with us. That is why we are continually going outside the org for new hires. And that is why, for the first six months, they are part of the solution and thereafter become part of the problem. You say you were not recognized. How painful that is to go unseen and have one's work be unappreciated. At the same time, there's something unwise about talking to a person like me. Some fundamental lack makes me a bad risk. I believe you began to see this, but even so, the momentum of your

lamentation kept you going. You were so hurt, your emotions so roiled, that your need to communicate overrode your inhibitions. And now you are thinking that, free of the org, you will thrive, that you will get to all those unfinished manuscripts going back to your twenties, as you say. You did talk movingly about the retreat you attended, where you grasped that your big investment was in the org but your heart lay with your unfinished projects. And I said the right things, of course. I said it was time to let go of the org, as you have done, in announcing your resignation. "You're a writer. You understand," you said at one point. I wish you hadn't gone there, hadn't introduced that aspect of my life into the conversation. Some things need to remain private if the dream is to be fulfilled.

People saying you have to be married, you have to have a relationship. Have a relationship with yourself. That is what I say. Some of the loneliest people I know are married. Some of the happiest people are single, as well as vice versa. Things aren't always as they seem. Conventions are falling away. We live in the time of AIDS. Stuff is happening. So he thinks as he approaches the Seventy-first Street Pier on the Hudson River. An act of desperation, a half-measure, when what he needs is a real trip? See the planes in the cloudless sky. See the Circle Line boat circling Manhattan. See the lovers and families walking about. See the doggies in the dog run run. See the flowers in the flower garden and the volunteers who make them grow. See the Trump Towers risen where once there was only open space. See the words forty thou and nine hundred thou and three mil written across the billboarded sky. See this island forever changing while remaining the same.

His real pleasure in life when he is not staring into a computer screen is lying down. Such a happy thing to spread out on his back on the queen-size bed, sunlight streaming in through the west window. Tranquility is what he lives for. This afternoon he has a special reason to be happy. The quarterly returns are in on his investments, and they are doing splendidly, just splendidly. They are up dramatically for the quarter and the year. Yes, the only thing to know is that the market goes up and the market goes down, but he can see them surpassing another level seemingly unattainable only a short time ago. Oh happy day. Oh happy happy day. Maybe he'll be able to pay for a lawyer to assist with his will. Maybe Feng shui his apartment. Maybe switch from the credit union to a bank, though the credit union seems more pure. Don't they have something to do with labor unions and better interest rates and a higher regard for the working people of America? He remembers the shame he felt on receiving a credit card from the credit union because it wasn't good enough—it wasn't a brand-name bank like Citi or Chase. But it would be a betrayal to give himself to a more commercial outfit. The country has had enough of rampant materialism and outright greed. And he doesn't have to get his CD player fixed that day either. Why bother with a tangle of wires and schlepping it ten blocks to the repair shop. No need to pull the unit from the wall and risk disorder. Nice, nice, just leave things nice. And the windows can wait a week for washing. That way he can come in under budget for the month. He can just have the day for himself. Do some writing. Have a bit of hummus and half a grapefruit and a cup of green tea. And send out a story or two. After all, he is fortified now, having recopied his favorite mantra and taped it to the computer—"One thing, not everything, in the course of the day. One thing." And he does it, he really does it. He goes into his pile of old manuscripts, dusts them off, checks his files to see where he has sent what, types up a cover letter and places it and the manuscript and the envelope on the bed. Tomorrow he will go to the post office for stamps. He will put himself out there in the world again. He will be somebody.

And now it is evening, a glorious cool summer evening, and people are heading into Central Park, in pairs and threes and fours, and he cannot get enough of them, their joy, as they head to the

Delacorte Theater, and he resolves to do the same someday soon. He too will stand on line for tickets and maybe get two and bring a friend, so he can be part of that joy that he is seeing, because he has been alone too long and it is no good to miss your life forever.

Zofia,

Drifting back toward the office along Fifth Avenue and thinking how many times do I have to see the Princeton Club, the Century Club, the vendor with his food cart on Forty-third and Fifth, or the tobacconist on Forty-second and Fifth (soon to be another icon deposited in the dustbin of history), the New York Public Library and its two stone lions, or the banner hanging from the facade advertising this show or that show I never go to, you entered my mind as a do I or don't I proposition. It would mean giving up my solitary walk in the evening through Central Park, but I also thought I might lose my mind if I kept myself apart and witnessed the doings on this earth without a modicum of communication.

On your visit to me in my cube the previous week I had become, as you remarked, passionate, not a word I like, as it invites mockery. You were wearing a light brown dress that excited me. That ex-husband of yours—he doubtless went half-mad trying to possess you who cannot be possessed. "More, more," you said to me there in the cube, beside yourself with glee as I confessed how painful it was to see but not be permitted to touch. You actually made a motion as if scooping my words into your being before making clear that yes, there could be dinner but no more "fooling around." "Why no fooling around?" I said, hurt, stricken, or pretending to be. "Because you do not need me for that," you replied, remembering that I had stopped you in the middle of a sexual favor in my bedroom when I grew self-conscious about my flaccid member. You didn't forget that experience, and why should you?

Over dinner you explained why you don't shop at Lord and Taylor anymore. You had been oppressed by the "Russian-ness" of the salesperson. She laid an authority trip on you when you asked her for a discount coupon because you had forgotten to bring your own. "No, no, you cannot do that," she said, firmly, on hearing your request. Always with the nyet, nyet. That is what Russia means to you. The eternal nyet, the eternal restriction on your being. And so you fled, as you have fled from Brighton Beach and other enclaves of Russian-ness. And yet, when I asked you about the current regime in Russia and the anti-democratic process that is underway, you said that Russians don't do well with democracy, that they need to be told what to do. "So you want your Russian salesperson after all?" I said, and you could only nod. At that moment I saw the effect, though you are a Pole, of Russia on your psyche. You are a truth seeker, Zofia. That is what I see about you. You do not pretend that what isn't so is so.

And then I told you a story of a time long ago, when courteous customer service was still to be found in a store called B. Altman on Thirty-fourth and Fifth Avenue. "Where CUNY University now is? That building?" you asked. "Oh, yes," I said. My reason for even mentioning B. Altman was simply to say that courteous staff were the norm at that excellent department store, and that I was sorry you had been deprived of the experience of shopping there. But I couldn't leave it at that. First you snare one pocket of experience, or so you think, and then another one pops up, somewhere else, with the same burning urgency for expression. Things push in on us, the seawall breaks, and soon the surging waters sweep us away. It was like this. I had come to the store for a pair of pants, and gave the salesperson my department store credit card. He looked from my card back at me, and said, with some curiosity, "Armenian?" Antipathy rose in me for what I perhaps unfairly considered his prying manner, though generally I am open and patiently explain that I am Armenian on my father's side and Swedish on my mother's. And so I merely nodded, or maybe I said nothing. Whatever I said or didn't say, he took my response to be in the affirmative. "You're rather tall for an Armenian, wouldn't you say?" And so I hadn't been wrong, after all, to be put off by his initial query, for in his follow-up question there was now what I perceived as a tone of insinuation. "How tall should an Armenian be?" I asked. "That is for Allah to determine, wouldn't you say? Allow me to introduce myself. My name is Ahmet Suleiman. I am, of course, Turkish, and we are great friends with the Armenian people."

"What is that you say? You are friends with your mother, the great whore of Istanbul?" I replied. His eyes narrowed. In this way did an uproar begin in the men's department of genteel B. Altman, the Turkish swine having to be separated from the patricidal son of an Armenian survivor of the Turks' genocidal fury. What I mean to say is that I, a son of America and loathing of all ethnic affiliation, within an instant had been taken over by an ancient enmity that left me understanding, for the first time, how people can be driven to homicidal rage. In that moment did I grasp the power of the blood tie and tribal identification. But then, Zofia, it occurred to me that I had assumed too much about your knowledge of history, as you had no idea what I was talking about.

I have seen this expression and action of your tongue before. Please understand that the image is now part of the file I keep on you.

I was ready to say goodnight, Zofia. But you wanted to extend the evening with a visit to the Strand Bookstore, down on University Place and Twelfth Street. Though those tables stacked high with fiction and nonfiction and the rows of shelves crammed with volumes on this and that were a treasure trove for you, they promised me little happiness, for what I saw there in the venerable Strand was a fruitless endeavor to stop time and preserve it forever. I was in the bastion of mind when where I really needed to be was in the expanse of spirit. Employee recommendations on hand-written signs were posted above copies of some of the books. *If you read only one novel in your life, let this be the one*—Jason; or *This novel changed my DNA*—Emily. They were the comments of young people who themselves dreamed of being published writers. You tried to interest me in a book on Jewish immigrants now living in

Brooklyn. You said you would buy the copy for me, but I declined your offer. Already I had begun the process of divestment. For every new thing that came into my apartment, two would have to go.

You left the Strand with one book, Richard Yates's *Revolutionary Road.* There it was, on the recommended pile. I felt I was coming back to something I had left behind in suggesting the novel to you, in spite of declining your recommendation. No, I didn't remember its contents in detail, only the skillful presentation of a marriage that reaches an impasse. I had some idea you would find out something about yourself in reading these pages.

What a scene of overdevelopment and rampant commerce the area has become. Those monstrous boxy condos, towers of opaque glass rising high into the sky. Five hundred thou, one mil. Five mil.

I said my goodbye and wandered west past the old Salvation Army building, gated like a fortress. The stench of human filth found me. A couple of homeless souls wearing tattered garments and grimed beyond description were sprawled on the stone steps, their possessions stuffed into bulging plastic bags. No cell phone yak yak coming from them. Time had not been kind to them; now their only ambition was for oblivion.

At Seventh Avenue I remembered to pull from my backpack a story I had written. There it was in a manila envelope, with a SASE enclosed. How many of these have I mailed from different mailboxes throughout the city, Zofia? How many have come back? No, it's not *Revolutionary Road,* Zofia. Not even close. But it is mine. And now it has a chance to say hello to the world. There is power in action, Zofia. This is who I am. This is what I do. I spend time with people and then try to find the words to describe where I have been. There are worse things in life.

Isabel,
Let me no longer be ruled by fear. Instead, let truth be aligned with love, bonding us as one. At the restaurant that same evening, a

woman named Alison approached the table where I sat with Zofia. "I had been thinking of you only hours before," she said. I had led a RoR meeting one night a month before. Alison came to me after the meeting and said I had, from an emotional standpoint, told her story. She seemed to be waiting for me to leave the meeting with her, but she was only six months sober, and so I felt I shouldn't. There it was, a young woman receiving me, placing me on a pedestal. Did I want to go through the inevitable torture of her slowly removing me from the pedestal, as Maura had done? Did I want to endure her seeing more and more how ordinary I truly am? Did I want to see her grow increasingly more unavailable as I gave myself more and more to her? Did I want to run the risk of possibly even getting drunk from the pain of losing her? In fact, only minutes before I had expressed my regret at not having been blessed with a bigger brain. Did I not ask Zofia if she wouldn't prefer to be sitting with Vladimir Nabokov rather than the likes of me? "What would a bigger brain do for you?" She said with a shrug. Alison was trouble. I couldn't expect her to have the same mature and accepting attitude as Zofia expressed. She would want me to be something huge. My last memory of her that evening of our first meeting was of her walking off alone and looking back toward me over her shoulder. Oh, God, the pain of ceaseless longing I felt for the next week. Is that kind of lovesickness appropriate for someone my age? To be honest, I was relieved to be sitting with Zofia when she approached our table. Zofia gave me a measure of protection from her. And then she went and sat at the next table, her back to us, with another woman. Nothing I talked about with Zofia meant anything after seeing her. My mind had gone elsewhere.

Chapter 42

She is there in Taku before him, seated at a table for two. He has something to tell her before he can go on to other things. He hopes it will be all right to say what he has to say. He doesn't mean to be self-centered. He just needs to say it.

"So tell me," she says.

He hears permission in her voice. Too often he comes to her and throws everything at her feet, like a little boy with his mother. He doesn't want to be that way. But things he doesn't think to tell others he tells Isabel, or maybe he does tell others, but not in the same way. With Isabel he can give expression to his vulnerabilities, his insecurities.

"It's this tiny thing on the inside of my ear. It doesn't hurt, and yet it stays in my mind. Many times during the day I reach my finger in and touch it. Then last week I actually picked it. Have you ever squeezed a big blackhead when you were a teenager? It was about that size, I would say. And yet there was none of the satisfaction that comes from squeezing a blackhead, no sense, that is, that something had been successfully removed. What I am saying is that I didn't feel that it was the end of the story."

"And was it?" Isabel asks, endlessly patient.

"No. It has come right back, like a kind of scab. And I have no sense that the scab will just fall away. Have you ever had anything like this?"

Because he is thinking cancer, pain, death.

"I've had what feels like a pimple in my ear for a few years. It goes away and comes back. Sometimes it itches and so I scratch it. Sometimes I pop it and there are little drops of blood. But I don't worry about it."

"That is exactly what I need to hear," Johan says.

She has a doctor out there in Tenafly, a Korean man. Dr. Sun Yun. But she doesn't put much faith in him. She doesn't have a great deal of faith in doctors in general. She lives with things, her aches and pains.

He tells her about the Fourth of July, and how, when he woke to the Declaration of Independence being read on National Public Radio, he turned off his clock radio, unable to listen, whereas in previous years he would be moved to tears hearing different people read portions of it. "I wanted to listen, but I couldn't. I just couldn't. Not with all that is being perpetrated by this administration."

"That is sad," Isabel says. "I used to read the Declaration of Independence to Mia when she was young."

It is something he doesn't remember but can well imagine her doing.

There are other things to tell her, such as the sculpture exhibit he saw at MoMA. Huge slabs of steel. Walking through the maze produced a disorienting and sometimes intoxicating effect on him. Isabel has already offered her opinion of the artist's show. One of those mega-events that she shrugs off, as if to say, what is the big deal? She is withholding toward some of the recognized greats of the art world. Picasso, for one. She doesn't call him a fraud, and yet she doesn't see what all the fuss is about either. Is resentment against her stepfather a factor in these judgments—small compact men with bald or balding heads who think that they're so great?

Even so, he must be free to express his opinion, while trying not to antagonize her.

"Do you ever hear people say, 'I need to put my affairs in order.'? That is the way I feel. I can't just leave behind this great mess of manuscripts. It is a growing concern of mine. I fantasize about leaving my job. I really do. I don't want to be a coward. I don't want to stay there just for security. And how much is enough in terms of savings? I wouldn't bet that I will live beyond seventy, not with my plumbing and my thin bones. As it is, it feels like plate tectonics going on in my chest some days. I'm just not put together from quality ingredients. Not built to last. I give my best energy to the workplace, and then I have these crumbs left over. Did I tell you about Ellen Deutsch? She was a guiding light in the Program Department for many years. A vice president. So she goes on this retreat, where she is asked to rate things in terms of their importance in her life. And so she places writing first. That is her passion. That is her life, she says. Then she is asked to determine how much time she gives to the things that are most important in her life and to the other things in her life, and she sees that there is this great discrepancy, that the huge investment of her time is in her job. And at this point she cries. She just starts crying. A brutal truth has been presented to her. And within a couple of weeks, she gives notice. Long story short, writing is very important to me."

""I know that your writing is important to you," Isabel says. "You've told me many times."

Nothing more need she say to send ripples of discomfort through him. She is reminding him of the days when he held sway with his anger, when his needs came first. It doesn't take much for him to see himself as a boorish oaf trampling all over her delicate garden. (Later, but only later, he will think to remind her how unhappy she can become when kept from her work. But that is not a path to go down. Isabel's life circumstances are not his, and he has no business commenting on the difference. And she has given him that reminder with her comments a reminder of all she had to put up with from him in their married life.)

The party at the next table has been listening in. Out-of-towners bringing their small-town judgments to the Big Apple? Their prune faces. Their pinched ways. People who go through their lives saying "Yep" or "Nope" and look with suspicion on anyone who bothers to talk in full sentences. Treating New York like some kind of freak show. Well, let them have their own damn conversation or find another table where they can't eavesdrop.

They walk in Riverside Park and come to a flower garden where a volunteer putters about with a trowel in hand.

"I hate to say it, but there's something to the ownership model. It's that old thing about no one washing a rented car," Johan says. "This flower garden wouldn't exist if these people weren't homeowners."

"You're probably right," Isabel says.

He cautions her about cyclists. Some are aggressive, maybe even mean. He is thinking of a couple of close calls. It's not only in the park but on sidewalks. Those kids who whiz past you on those small-wheeled bikes are the worst.

"What kinds of trees are those?" she asks.

"Honey locust trees, I'm pretty sure." They are all over the park. He sees a verifying nameplate on the trunk of one. He feels proud of this minimal store of knowledge about nature he can share with Isabel, whereas she is, in general, a fount of information about flora and fauna.

"The leaves look kind of fragile, but the tree is pretty rugged."

"It has to be to survive here," she says.

They head down the long, sloping path. Through the dark, smelly tunnel they can see the river and feel its peace. Across, on the Jersey horizon, the sun is dipping in an orange technological haze.

He needs to sit, and so they do, on a bench, the water and the horizon commanding their attention. A young couple stroll past. They stop to kiss. This is the place for it. This is where lovers come.

He talks about the baby shower, his embarrassment when Anri began to open the gifts. "Book? Book? Who give baby book? Baby come from womb a genius and read book?" Isabel laughs at his imitation of Anri, though probably he has taken it too far.

"Everyone feels that way. People feel self-conscious about giving gifts."

It's kind of her to say, though he isn't just everyone or anyone. Still, he sees where his mind can take him and the deep pain it can manufacture.

"How was your visit with Alf?"

Zed having passed on, he tells her how it went fine with his new mentor, though he was in turmoil afterward, how he couldn't think a reasonable thought, how hysterical distress had him filling the air with nonsense, including the old reliable, "Honduran national economy," in a futile attempt to keep the shame at bay. "There are people who don't understand that sort of reaction. They don't understand what it was to have a father like mine, that I began to shake every time he stepped through the door and so could never be close to him. They don't understand that a surrogate father, even though he is only a half year older than I am, can have this kind of powerful effect."

"I understand," Isabel says.

And he knows she does.

"I was thinking of renting a house on Block Island this fall. I'm not sure. Maybe you could come if I do?" He continues looking out at the water. He thinks of those fishermen out on the pier who cast their baited lines and then wait for a bite as he continues to look outward at the river and the Jersey shore. But no nibble on the line. It's as if she hasn't heard him. Some things rightfully belong in their past, like sharing a public space for more than a few hours. Slowly, subtly, occasionally forcefully, she is bringing him in line with the reality of their new relationship.

Chapter 43

Johan brings his own chair for his satsang with Melvin in his tiny and windowless cubicle. After all the heavy lifting he did in helping to create the OCN, Melvin assumed he was a cinch for the position of manager when it was posted. But now the org has reached outside the building, seeking someone who can *interface with the future*. Amanda Billingstock is the chosen one. Her words create an impenetrable grid of sound, like a train rumbling along the tracks only inches from your ear.

"What's with the Coke? Always with the can of Coke in her hand," Melvin Kleiner says.

And what's with the few org pretty boys all in a row whom she has assembled, their colorful shirts hanging out of their tight slacks and the sexy stubble on their chiseled young faces? He also asks. And the hot young women with workout-slim bodies. And the fact that she never returns e-mails and zips past you as if you smell bad when you run into her in the hallway? An expression of her longing for her lost youth? Or the bonding affairs she organizes like that afternoon down at the Mexican restaurant on Fourteenth Street, waiters plying everyone with margaritas, the atmosphere of false revelry fueled by nonstop games that the staff are obliged to play.

Melvin Kleiner does not fit Amanda Billingstock's image of who she wants reporting to her, for she has now taken the OCN unto herself, causing Lurleen Lulabella consternation. When the position is posted for internal as well as external applicants, Melvin Kleiner must go to Amanda, but finds his audience is with her young assistant Beatrice, who assesses his application, thanks him for his thoughtful comments, but goes ultimately with someone else. Melvin, though you possess serious intelligence, you are in older age and not into styling. And there will be other challenges, you who lived your life sequestered in the ashram before emerging to prostrate yourself as a devotee of Lurleen, ready to blindly do her bidding.

In fact, acceptance about the technology avenue denied you comes fairly easily. Your pride is in your writing, Melvin Kleiner, your muscular prose, even your adverbs flexing their biceps. You invest hours of research on this particular piece and write a moving and engaging opening, deploy your facts, and offer dazzling turns of phrase and one illuminating insight after another. You submit your well-crafted piece to Lurleen and bask in the glow of her approval and admiration. Weeks later do you open the new issue of the org magazine and go right to your article. But what are you seeing? Astounding. Surely a mistake. The elegant opening gone. Whole paragraphs missing. Other paragraphs rewritten, the graceful prose replaced by stringy, pedestrian sentences. The organic whole mutilated virtually beyond recognition. Wires are hanging loose from your precious construct; ornate fixtures have been savagely ripped from the walls, leaving gaping holes.

"Why?" you say to her, rendered virtually speechless by Lurleen's mauling of his copy.

"Why what?"

"My article. What have you done with it?"

"I have improved it."

"You have done what?"

"The article was too long. It needed pruning."

"Why didn't you tell me? I would have made the cuts."

"We had to move quickly."

And so you stare at her with pained incomprehension, only slowly coming to grasp that she is playing with you, or, to use the more contemporary term, playing you, that her strength is in her shamelessness, that there is no vile act of hers that she cannot spin to put herself in the right. How does it feel, Melvin Kleiner, to have your cojones cut off by the object of your affection? How does it feel when she bores in on you with that grin that says she has mauled you and knows she has mauled you, made you hers with the abuse that she has imposed on you, broken your will in spite of yourself so that you will come back to her and back to her, seeking, as the loved ones of drunks do, to get doughnuts from the hardware store or, as my mother used to say, blood from a stone? Do you understand, in that moment, what America itself is up against with this regime in Washington, and that in fact she is part of that regime that would gaslight the country and bend it to its implacable will? Not only has she disemboweled you. Now she torments you further, saying, "You keep up the good work, Melvin. You're one of my most valuable staff members," followed by more volcanic laughter. Tell us how you felt in that moment, little Melvin Kleiner, so we can help you. Tell us about the goodness in your heart and the beautiful gift you had come bearing, and the unspeakable hurt it caused you that Mommy threw your gift into the street. What was it to have been born to a mother who never wanted you in the first place, who said you were a mistake, who confided to you that your father was a poor third choice for a life's partner, who routinely mocked and abused you? Feel your pain, Melvin Kleiner. Feel it. Feel it, I said.

Zofia,

Yesterday, on my way back from the Mid-Manhattan Library, I saw you standing, with your back to me, at the curb outside the org trying to flag a cab. Zofia, it was not the closing hour. Far from it.

You looked worn out. And that black dress with white polka dots, so boldly loud.

"I go home now. Dizzy." Dee-zee, like a swarm of bees have flown from your mouth.

Days later we have arranged to meet at MoMA on a Friday afternoon when admission is free. But you are not there at the corner of Fifty-Third and Fifth, across from the old church. Only ten minutes later do you arrive, breathless and trembling and holding onto the wall of the building for support. You are not yourself, Zofia. You are not one to make scenes but something is terribly wrong. (Even now I pick up the phone and think I should call but I don't, even as I hear you crying upstairs as once I heard my mother cry and all the women in my life cry and cry, but I say no, enough, I must have refuge in these words, they are my lover, my womb, my sanity. They don't betray me. They don't waste my time with idle chatter. They flow, like a beer drunk's piss.) Among a sea of strangers I held your hand at MoMA as we sat there in those wire chairs by the wishing pond, pennies by the dozen at the bottom. You love art, Zofia. You love life. But there you were, bent over in pain. This hand holding a form of intimacy. Words left behind for the human touch.

Chapter 44

The Terminator is living up to her name. Alice Piccoli blows her homemade lasagna through her nose when Jane Fallows formally presents the Terminator and applauds her for her institutional knowledge. She makes the announcement in the assembly room at 11:30 a.m., a time Alice Piccoli rigidly reserves for her feeding frenzy. "Oh, no." Alice Piccoli's cry is audible and causes heads to turn and stare at her anguished face. Alice Piccoli has a history with the Terminator. In fact, Alice Piccoli worked for the Terminator. It is quite likely that Alice Piccoli senses she will get the can once again, unless Lurleen can do her trademark diabolical work and terminate the Terminator before the Terminator can terminate Alice. And, in fact, following that audible gasp, does Alice then stick out her tongue and point to it with her right index finger as a way of communicating to Lurleen that the time is coming when she will have to use her own tongue and wiles to slay this newly arrived nemesis.

Within a day of the Terminator's return, an org bigwig has gotten the can. Rumor is Amanda Billingstock got drunk and made a lewd request for hanky-panky with one of her young staff members. HR gathers us in the assembly room. There is Bigwig with her trademark Coke in hand, blubbering through her farewell speech. Her poor mother in critical condition out there in Boise, Idaho. Bigwig having to place family before personal aspiration. "A person has many jobs but only one mother," she says. Jeanine Juddster standing to one side of her and Jane Fallows to the other. Neither of them smiling. A serious bum's rush going on. Has she pleaded with them not to humiliate her? Those margaritas her downfall.

Now an off-site party for Bigwig at Where It's At, a dark, gloomy toilet down the block from the org. A blonde at the bar and a man leaning in toward her over drinks and there will be more drinks and bad food and desperate sex to loud music and then it will be morning until they get too old to do this anymore. Bigwig upstairs, above the bar, in a room she has reserved. A party she has thrown to which only a precious few have shown up. Her can of Coke ditched for a martini in a stem glass. Her job, her title, her salary, her status, her security—all gone. Magnanimity and warmth easy for Johan when people are down, even the powerful. He wishes her well, while knowing she probably would have outsourced half the org if she had had her way.

Isabel,

As you may recall, I had a history with the Terminator as well, back when Miss Carmelli was at the org, The Terminator was no friend of our department in those years. In fact she was, as head of Communications, our rival, and buried many hatchets in the head of poor Miss Carmelli who, while fond of saying ,"There's more than one way of skinning a cat," had no means of skinning this particular cat, for the Terminator was not only nimble but fierce. Let us be plain. Like Lurleen, she could machinate: bypassing and devaluing our department, creating alliances against us, the ultimate indignity being Miss Carmelli having to report directly to her. Even so, Miss Carmelli came to a place where she expressed grudging respect for the Terminator's intelligence and ruthlessness. "She knows how to bury the bodies," said Miss Carmelli, including bulldog Rebecca Masely, her assistant, who made the mistake of wanting more than the Terminator was willing to give. One day Rebecca Masely was there and the next she was gone, never to be seen again. No memo, no nothing—just vanished. The Terminator just worked her disappearing magic on you and moved on.

Johan is frightened enough of The Terminator to even behave in his mind toward her, as even unspoken apostasy could bring on her wrath. And, like Miss Carmelli, he has some admiration for her. There is a light emanating from her that mitigates against vilification.

The Terminator is not immune to the aging process. There are wrinkles and she is paler than he remembered her. So he sees, as Jane Fallows introduces her in the assembly room. The dust of time is upon her. He senses she has stepped back and that the fire within burns less hot. Time is moving her into the other world, as this one has done its work upon her. The weight of conscience shows in her sharp-featured face. She has come to set things right with the org, it strikes him, and with herself, for she herself is facing termination.

The Terminator had been a climber. She had aspiration written into her very soul. And she had the sharp claws that could give her traction. She too had been a member of the National Leadership Team but the pinnacle of the org she could not reach. She applied to become CEO back when, but the org looked elsewhere. It was not in her makeup to remain with an org that had bypassed her. The Terminator was a woman who needed room to grow. Glass ceilings, or ceilings of any description, she could not abide. To stay would mean living with the status of the shunned, the also-ran. And so she sought a higher level at another org, and then another.

All the while a drama was being played out at the org she had left behind. Selena Crackner, her friend of many years, was being hammered and traduced by a wily newcomer, whom she herself had let in the door, on the theory that a woman blessed like herself with a lively intelligence would be on the same page in bringing new life to the org. But the woman spoke with a forked tongue. She sent her armies crashing into long-respected org domains as agents of her imperious reach. She sought to oust Selena herself, claiming for herself a marketing expertise superior to hers. In such a fashion did she repay Selena for the confidence and trust Selena had placed in her. Duplicity, thy name is Lurleen Lulabella. And when Lurleen Lulabella succeeded in fully undermining and isolating Selena, then did Selena have no choice but to pack up and call it a day. "We're cracking the code. We're uprooting entrenched interests. Clearing away the deadwood." All this did Lurleen say, from behind her big desk.

The Terminator does not go to Lurleen and say, "You're history. You're toast." She doesn't offer Lurleen a baleful stare and run her hand flat across her throat. What the Terminator does is assess, and what she finds is dysfunction at every junction: writers who cannot write, secretaries who can't type or properly answer their telephones, executive-level staff who can't lead. What she finds are firebrands on fire for the brand. Everything is the brand, the brand. "Brandish the brand" the new mantra. Then there are those who play Solitaire on their computer screens all day. Sometimes it seems that the only person doing his job is the security guard down in the lobby.

And the Terminator sees other things. Americans are largely depressed and in need of cheering up, that Americans are always rallying their spirits with sudden, unprovoked chants of "We're number one" and that it would be hard for America to cede this ranking to another nation (nay-shun). And that the endless photos of young girls on the walls are confection for those wrinkled and withered and deflated by time.

Isabel,
Evidently Lurleen has badmouthed me to the Terminator. At least, so the Terminator said, without going into details. God knows

what Lurleen told her, but surely enough to place doubt in the Terminator's mind as to my worthiness.

Rhoda Bahr continues on the premises, though now with the newly created Oversight Department, after falling into disfavor with Lurleen, this to my relief. Alas, New Teeth has found new life in her new environment. Under the auspices of a powerful boss, Augusta de la Gusté, she is cherry-picking documents from other departments and placing them under her torturing gaze. One such project Alice Piccoli had been unleashed upon to do her Alice Piccoli "edits."New Teeth has concluded that Alice Piccoli has no business being near a manuscript with a colored pencil. And so, in the eyes of one and all, does New Teeth discredit the work of Alice Piccoli. I do not grieve for Alice Piccoli. Odious as New Teeth is, I am not surprised at the shoddiness of the work she has found. The department needs standards. If those standards are seen as compromised, the entire department is in danger of being discredited. But Lurleen herself has no standards. Not caring is an offense against Miss Carmelli.

But what is up with all this caring? By caring, do I mean that I should have the last word? Is the driving force behind editing to correct and subtly admonish, to place yourself above others on the basis of language? Why put all this energy into nothing, absolutely nothing? Who will remember? Who will care? Was the Preacher not right in declaring all under the sun to be vanity and vexation?

And yet people do remember Miss Carmelli. They absolutely do.They hold her in their hearts because of the purity of her dedication, in spite of Lurleen's warning to staff not to even mention Miss Carmelli's name on the org premises.

New Teeth has moved on to take issue with the quality of the copy produced by the Communications Department, for she finds arrogance is in their manner and their speech and their gait, parading as they do throughout the corridors of the org and chanting "Ratchet up our BRAND" and boasting that subliminal messaging is embedded in their meretricious copy. New Teeth has brought them out of their dream world, as a rope around the neck will do. It can't be said that the comedown is a bad thing. Let all fantasies end so the kingdom of truth may finally arrive.

Isabel,

An incident has occurred that has ramifications for my own survival. Trucks get hijacked on highways and byways. Planes get hijacked in the air and on the ground. And now my project got hijacked. Who was the masked terrorist, you ask? And I say to you, does a mask cover the entire face, or does it leave an opening for the eyes to see and the mouth to speak? And if that mouth shows the signature sparkle of NEW TEETH, then what are we to conclude but that a force of nefarious inevitability has descended upon us?

With Gestapo imperiousness does Ms. Tooth appear before me, acting on the authority of her new and powerful and seldom present boss, Augusta de la Gusté, demanding that I turn over the file of a manuscript I had edited, for her review. In the full flower of institutional power does she convey to me that I have been big-time busted.

Some days later I receive a call from alpha male Bill Romney, director of Research. I am not to take this matter personally; it is simply that the org is going in another direction. A stronger, more confident person would leave it right there, but I am slow to let the matter go. It is a struggle not to speculate, not to defend myself, not to disintegrate, not to say, Alice Piccoli, c'est moi.

Maybe New Teeth deserved to be projecting her power in this way. Now I was afraid. Her smug smile conveyed that she had won and I had lost. She had stripped me of my identity and any positive sense of myself with that one visit to my cube. You've got to know where you are in this life, I told myself. I thought of Orrin Hinckle, your divorce lawyer, and his tale of being passed over. Now I would be working on catalogs and internal newsletters, while others were being assigned to flagship publications. Whatever gifts I had, the org would no longer want them and maybe believe I had never possessed them.

Stricken, I went to Melvin Kleiner. He had taken to long meditations in the lotus position on the floor of his cube. "Teach us to care and not to care,' he said, quoting T. S. Eliot, before returning to his reading of the Vedas and his focus on the breath.

Now in this time the Terminator was aware of New Teeth's initiatives and brought her to Johan's attention for poaching Communications' properties. And Johan listened carefully while managing to say nothing about New Teeth that would place him in the position of a person biased against her, though yes, it was fully on his mind that he too had been one of her victims. Why burden the Terminator with this information? More bluntly, why risk self-destructing?

But some days later the Terminator showed up at Johan's cube for a sit-down.

"Your philodendron has a lot of dead leaves. It doesn't look good to have a shaggy plant anymore than it does to have a shaggy manuscript. Am I right that all dead leaves need to fall?"

"Right as rain," Johan replied, hardly knowing what he was saying with the Terminator putting her full knowingness upon him.

"I want to hear your side of the story in this Research Department matter." The Terminator said it just that way. A trial, of sorts, had begun. The Terminator would be the judge. Johan would have to choose his words carefully.

The Research people generally had a dual audience in mind, he explained. They were writing not only for the org but for the academic community as well. Thus, the text was rich in nuance, which might at first appear to be simply repetition. To support his point that Julie Morrow had an academic as well as GoAN audience in mind, Johan cited the documentation that Research employed, a notes/reference system generally used only in social science and science publications.

"Sounds like these people threw you under the bus," the Terminator said. "But we'll fix that."

The Terminator acted decisively with an email staunchly defending Johan's editorial approach, citing the fact that the document was intended for a dual audience. What might seem like repetition was in fact a nuanced variation on a point just made, and Research had shown itself adamant in its opposition to any changes that would have resulted in a trimmer narrative.

New Teeth wasn't having it. "That's a total crock," she said.

"Def," Julie Morrow echoed, finding brevity in her speech but not her prose. It was telling that neither of them entered into disputation with the Terminator, whose reputation for fearsomeness generated terror throughout the org, but did inject their low regard for Johan's editing skills deep into his being, where it would sit as poisonous as toxic waste. Many, many were the days and even months the toxin lived on, in the nighttime as well as in daylight hours Johan hearing the duo saying, "We've got your number and had it all along," and he with no defense against having been laid bare.

Isabel,
The Terminator may not know her own mind; on the other hand, she may know it quite well. Lately I have cause to wonder if she really is serving only as interim senior vice president. She has a business and says she is committed to making it work, but the salient fact appears to be that she is still here and no new senior vice president has been hired to replace her. Somehow they fall short in Jane Fallows' estimation. So long as the Terminator is present, I have a protector, and when she goes the sharks will circle around, smelling blood. One thing is for sure. The Terminator will countenance no sass. I cannot conduct myself with her as I do with Lurleen. The Terminator, as her name suggests, has the power of finality.

Chapter 45

Isabel,

There is no substitute for love. It is the only reality. But there are forces in the mind and heart that work against it, and such is the case today with my thought stream saying, Where is mine? Where is mine? Oh yes, I am back in the grievance mode, which you came to painfully experience in the course of our marriage. I am going to your show as graciously as my mind will permit. I misspoke, after saying a thousand times how important words are. I did not pause to listen to my own inner guide. God lives in the pause. God is the pause. I asked if any of the pieces had been sold, and when you said there was a potential buyer for one, then did envy take hold. In that moment I was led to glimpse the bigger picture and the ongoing amend I need make to you and the universe—to vanquish the dinky that would seek to rule my being and instead raise up and feel unadulterated happiness for your success.

That same day I saw a hardhat on a scaffold staring at the humanity below. Copping a smoke was he. The hardhat was working. America was working. And then I thought, who are you not to be among them, Johan? Who? Are you exempt from the demands of life? Are you entitled? And I would not have needed this surge of perception if I had not been drawn back into the snare of invidious comparison: the house you own, the artistic freedom your financial security provides. Let the war against the dinky be ongoing, Isabel. Let vigilance against it soar.

Lurleen is gone, terminated, finito. The Terminator has struck in Terminator fashion, that is, without warning. There are no words, I thought. This is beyond words, I thought. The words have all been spoken, I thought. Cruel, inhuman, to dispose of any employee in this way, especially this woman in the image (sort of) of my mother. The ushering out. The ejection. The hasta la vista. The hit the road, Jack or Jill, or whatever your name is. Why was it I ran right over her tears, her sorrow, and sought to scorch the earth free of her underlying sadness? Not a trace of her to be found except deeply embedded in my psyche.

It was blah blah this and blah blah that. A dense volume of monkey shit I had more than my share in spewing. There was one instance in particular I seized on. Lurleen held forth as if a certain project was hers, this in front of the Leadership Team. In an email to the Terminator, I cited this self-promotion as but an example of why the morale in the department was low, this to reinforce the message that the department was all about her, Lurleen. Out, you with your warped, pinched vision of America that we might begin anew. Changes. I will show you change. I will have you changed right out the door. Such was the real purpose of my note.

No posses rode hard in the night seeking to impose their imbecilic justice on me. Not a one. Out was out. Done was done.

I am a terminator, too.

Once again The Terminator has swung into action. Late-breaking developments everywhere. Alice Piccoli has been canned, just as she feared. No more aluminum foil unwrapping. No more cup thudding. No more frantic whispering, her throat clogged with food. No more tongue de la tongue. There was no place of sorrow to which I went at her looming departure. And why should there be? She came at me spitting sparks. Who was going to fill in for me when I was on vacation? Did I know I was getting the position before I was officially told? Why wasn't I required to apply for the position? In such a manner did she come at me.

Of course she could afford to retire, she said, when I asked. She could easily live on Social Security and her pension. But she had been working since she was a kid. Work and making money are what she loved best. No farewell party. Instead she took the money the org would otherwise have spent on catering it.

Strange, the things you remember about someone on their departure. There was the day she stood watching the Veterans Day parade down Fifth Avenue. The Second Gulf War was about to begin. "Those poor kids being shipped off to war," she said. Something about the scene she felt deeply. Was she relating it to her own experience as an orphan, of feeling expendable. Whatever, it shook me, for the moment, from my judgment of her. Like everyone else, she had a story, a wound.

Chapter 46

It has not brought happiness. These things never do. The "it," of course, is Lurleen's departure. That locution "of course" can be, of course, annoying. There are no "of courses" in this life. "Of course" burdens the listener with the idea that he or she knows something he or she may not know. So please, Johan, enough with "of course."

I am afraid. I want to slip away so my new life can begin. I want to leave this world with my papers in order. I don't want to be embarrassed. No one does. Such a thing must not happen. I must have the courage to let go of sloppily written manuscripts. There must be no Augean stable for others to deal with.

The Terminator says I must be more decisive. She says I must develop leadership qualities. She says I must lose some of my introversion. She is stronger than I am in the ways of the world. She doesn't know how I long to sit alone on a park bench and say little nothings to myself. "Are you comfortable, Johan? Do you want your peanut butter sandwich now or later?" "Oh, I will have it later, if you don't mind," I will say.

When nightfall comes I will sleep in different locations throughout the apartment. I will place a cot by the front door and sleep there. And the next night I will pull out the convertible sofa. Bunched in my hand will I have my underwear, a necessary sleep

"

aid. Yes, my underwear will stay close to me. And no, it will not matter if I roll over on this underwear and wrinkle it. It will not matter at all. It will just mean that the underwear is in relationship to me. It will be a relationship of touching, as I have ceased to have with those who walk about.

So will I live my life.

Isabel,

When I don't hear from you for three or four weeks, I feel I am in a bind. If I call or e-mail, would it be an imposition? If I don't, am I being irresponsible—suppose something has happened? What is your silence meant to say, that unless I reach out your natural inclination is to drift away?

The river of life is flowing and I have poor materials for a dam. Time cannot be contained and even special moments lose their significance. People and things fade away.

You say you are gardening. For myself, I bought a beefsteak tomato at OrganicOnly and ate it, lightly sprinkled with salt. Dr. Gruniari, my endocrinologist, says a pinch of salt can kill. I have the sense that he finds me peculiar. He is thickset, as if his life experience has been impacted within him. He dismisses the host of vitamins and herbs I take and also scoffs at my vegetarianism, even when I acknowledge a monthly craving for a ham sandwich. It may be that he is attached to the body to a degree that I am not. I have, in my way, been trying to cultivate a life of the spirit, though I can't imagine anything can fully prepare a person for the transition. We have been housed in these bodies for so long and cannot help but embrace this world as our home.

Dr. Gruniari grudgingly acknowledges the radiant good health my lab test numbers attest to except for my spinal issue. One day I saw on his shelf a statue of the Buddha, and so I asked him what for me was a logical question: was he a meditator? He answered no, that the statue was the gift of a "peculiar" student in one of his medical school courses. His tone was scornful, as if he had command of the hard facts and those of us who engaged in holistic remedies or sought to cultivate the life of the spirit were but New Age knuckleheads.

Yesterday, I donated to the thrift shop the silverware you had inherited from your parents and gave to me but which I have never used. They had darkened with age. A polish could have been applied, but I came to a place of wanting my own things, inferior though they might be. Somehow I didn't want the history that attached to these pieces. Not anymore. That darkness I saw in them—it was the darkness of the past.

If I have not told you, once I had a dream in which I was living not with oldness but in an apartment with modern furnishings. A blue light shone over the Smith-Corona Coronamatic typewriter I wrote on. The apartment, as I recall, was where Tom Smits, my old high school friend, had lived, only he had vacated the premises for the world at large. But his mother was there. She was a scientist and perhaps represented a secular and open-minded counterbalance to the strictures of the religion of my childhood. An overwhelming feeling of freedom came over me; all the encumbrances of the past I was free of. I was traveling light.

Now you have written to say that you are busy with gardening and that when a couple of weeks go by without contacting me, you become frightened that I am angry, which makes it hard for you to call. Always do you surprise me with the complexity and subtlety of your thinking.

The weekend was difficult. I felt very alone, conspicuously so. Unlike you, I have gone through life without a capacity to draw people to me. I am admiring of your social gift and happy when you share that this woman and that woman from the community garden has invited you for dinner. People recognize quality when they see it. Anyway, I did my shopping at OrganicOnly. Two beefsteak tomatoes, two avocados, two containers of organic hummus (one with olives), three containers of soy milk, a small tub of pre-washed baby spinach, a box of organic corn flakes (fruit juice sweetened), organic peanut butter (smooth and lightly salted). Several nights a week I give myself the OrganicOnly experience. The store has a communal vibe. I can feel I am part of humanity in a way that is not always so apparent to me when I am walking the streets. The beautiful women of Manhattan were in the store, of course, but I made a point of avoiding eye contact as we passed or trying to engage them in small talk as we stood in the checkout line. In this way did I endeavor to win their respect and appreciation if not their love.

Awareness has come to me that my time for physical intimacy is over, that age truly has rendered me invisible to the opposite sex. It is a whole new relationship to life and one which, owing to its its seeming finality, I was not quite ready for. I will never lie in bed with a woman again. A woman will never again seek out my company. All promise of that sort of interaction has disappeared. I do at times feel like a ghost in this life. It is at such times that we must have faith, we simply must. And what exactly does that mean? It means only this—help is on the way, but I must wait for its arrival. I must learn to live in the basement where these feelings of abject helplessness place me, and trust that sooner or later I will be led to higher ground.

It may be I am giving myself too much to do, setting the bar too high for someone with average abilities. And yet, I want to leave something behind, and am determined to do just that. Recently, I have been revising old stories and genuinely improving them. It would be an embarrassment if only badly written drafts were to be found in my apartment after I am gone. If memorializing the deceased has always been a galvanizing force with me, now the driving force is my own approaching departure. Maybe, as human beings, we desire survival above all else, like the women in the lifeboats indifferent to the cries of their men in the cold waters of the north Atlantic as the *Titanic* slowly sank. I sometimes feel the plates shifting within my chest and the arresting shock of pain that lightning-fast flashes through it. Those tremors, I imagine, are but a hint of the rupture to come.

But all of this talk postpones the stating of a simple fact: the arc of your orbit has widened so you pass over my place on the planet less frequently. If once it was every two weeks that we met for dinner, now it is every month. "I have to be careful to check in more regularly," you wrote in your e-mail. I am someone to report to? To pacify lest I become angry, as you suggested? Busy child at play with all your friends though you are, you must be mindful of your father?

Let me be careful here. I feel the old me spoiling for a showdown, some dramatic resolution to a crisis that in truth does not exist, as love is the only answer for a relationship such as ours, in which it is for me to continue to let you go. What meaning would it have to utter an ultimatum such as the following: "Let's just agree not to see each other anymore. Let's both just move on." Where would such a "proposal" leave me but with pain and regret and guilt? And what would drive such an utterance but self-will?

Heather is gone. We have a new graphic designer. Her name is Andrea. She is from Belgium and has a sober, European bearing. Married and with a young daughter, she is not a good prospect for love. Her wedding ring should serve as a deterrent. But she has been dropping hints. Her husband is a bit controlling. She could use a little more freedom. She speaks of her three-year-old far more than hubby. When she says "we," I have come to understand she means herself and her daughter. She is looking for a way out, as Heather was looking for a way out. I have been through this cycle before, and I should see it for what it is, and maybe, at times I do. I should say that Andrea possessed an entrancing beauty when she arrived but her physical allure has lessened, for reasons I will not specify, as it would be a terrible commentary on me as a human being should I note these deficits. Still, perceptions are powerful. Even so have we gone to lunch once. A game is being played here, and it is a dangerous one. A moral blindness attaches that does not allow me to see the potential harm not only to her and her family but to myself. I need to take the moral high ground. I certainly do. I can't go down a road of sin and corruption, no matter how straitlaced that may sound. If Andrea wants to venture out, let her get a separation or a divorce.

The fact is that Andrea came to me yesterday and asked if I would join her for lunch again. I do wonder if she felt my interest in her waning, as inevitably happens. After a time of working together, the newness wears off and a certain dullness settles on even the most glamorous. While I put her off—I did not want to give up the hour of writing at the lunch hour that I had planned while sitting at my desk—we did agree to reschedule for later in the week. It is hard to know what to do. It just is. Most women spurn me, treat me as invisible, and here Andrea comes along.

It was the same old story of attraction followed by a slow leak in the initial ardor, and so I will spare you the details and only say that within a few months she and her husband separated. Thereafter she found a beau of formidable physical strength about whom she developed growing reservations. We met for lunch one weekend and she put her head on my shoulder, but it was far too late. All vestiges of my initial attraction to her had vanished. I say this well aware that I achieved gargoyle status as a young man and have maintained it into middle age, so please, those of you riding hard for your nincompoop justice with your unspeakable posses, rein in your horses and your soreness, or better yet, don't even begin to saddle up.

Chapter 47

Isabel,

You are alpha and omega, as God is love and you are love and love never dies. And because the posse will continue to indulge its ceaseless and mindless riding hard in this and the next life and no one, not even the masochist supreme, wishes for an eternity of merciless flogging, it is for me to make what amends I can to New Teeth and Ms.Tongue and the whole sorry lot of them. No love is more true than misanthropy. This we must assert with full conviction, lest the treacle squadrons spread their sweet goo over everything. But some background, please, so order can maintain itself.

I was in my new position six months when I decided to leave. I was done. The title meant nothing to me, nor the office. A velvet prison. So it had been. A very good velvet prison. Unfit to be anywhere else, I had been taken in, given shelter from the storm. Who else would have a man such as me, one whose primary interest was the boxscores of baseball games, his "career" spent, for the most part, staring into space and tapping on bathroom tiles? A man who walks about with a backpack containing nothing more than *The New Yorker* and his lunch?

My mind was made up about departure but there was one snag. Did I dare to walk out the door without a retirement party, a la Alice Piccoli. Self-hatred seized me at the thought of inviting family and friends. What family? What friends? I had no one in my life, and what were they to see me retire from? A quarter century of loafing? I thought of that basketball game I had played in at Madison Square Garden in my last year of high school and how I had been too ashamed to invite my mother and father and brother and sisters. I had told no one, not even my girlfriend Jane Thayer, and afterward had been ashamed to show up at the party a classmate was throwing, the one party I had been invited to in the years I had been at that school. What had you done instead, Johan? You had walked alone up Eighth Avenue and all the way home. It was there I had died, at that school, having failed the SAT. Ever since I had been dead. Ever since I had been wearing the mask of the impostor, seeking to hide my inferiority.

Day by day I did not bail. Yes, I heard the very great Donne Warwick instructing me to do the walk on by, but I had the equally great Aretha Franklin exhorting me to be a do right man. We take our moral instruction from whence it comes. On the final day I came to the org in a wrinkled white linen jacket purchased at a thrift store. The Terminator made a face and sent me home for more appropriate attire, and so I returned in a black blazer and black slacks and blue button down shirt and rep tie so I might live for the day in the safety of convention. I do not know what possessed me to initially dress so drably, only that resistance was stirring.

"You're depriving me of great joy by heading for the exit ramp today." So the Terminator said.

"Yes. I know your way and have known it for a long time," I said.

"And what way is that?"

"Terminators terminate."

"Put that in the singular."

"This Terminator terminates."

Now these are the ones whom I invited, in addition to you and Mia, in no special order: Hannah, who was instructed to leave her smacking ways behind and never, ever, on org property to clamp her tongue between her thick lips, however riled she had become, or walk about with her hand in correct smacking position, or do the sulky sulk; my sister Leah, on condition she leave her academic bona fides at home; Melvin Kleiner, that the org might see the excellence it had lost with his recent departure; and for many, many, from the spirit world to present themselves, starting with my mother and father, but to startle no one with their presence. If there were others, I have forgotten. What is not forgotten was that I was less than fully centered in love, no matter how often I spoke of it. Vileness must run its course. Let us not indulge the dinky and say otherwise.

"I must be honest with you," I said to the gathered, including the power-sweeping ones exulting in dominion over their minions. All were there. "It has been hard to resist the water towers on neighboring rooftops and their insistent calling to me, finally reaching a crescendo of exhortation to leave the premises of the org in favor of the park bench, where I might sit in the sun with my camera and my notebook and give time to stopping time or, at the least, to arrest its flow, that the world might know that I had been here over and above languishing on the premises of the org."

Second, I was compelled to tell the gathered that shame is the dwelling place for the preposterous Manootdjians. We are well known for our big feet and other disturbing features. My older sister Naomi was called to high ledges and later the fouled waters of the East River. My older sister Rachel heard the call of her own aloneness and would share her solitary life only with her creator, whom, as I have said many times, she kept a faithful nightly vigil for. My older brother Luke bored into his arm with his nose, monitoring, always monitoring, the quality of his blood. My father, like his entire Armenian race, was covered in hair and blood. My mother was in perpetual retrieval of her drunken father, before he was frozen in the unforgiving snows of Sweden. To hide the reality of my misshapen head I have always felt to be a life or death matter. And yet does narcissism live on among the Manootdjians, in spite of all the evidence amassed as to its complete absurdity. Manootdjians will spend hours reflecting on and reinforcing this notion of their beauty. There is no stopping them. What choice do I have but to resist their embrace of delusion by waving the unwelcome banner of truth?

Love is seeking entry and my weight against the door means nothing to it. Where there has been scorn, there must be reparation. Must. Must. Must. Only my mother glowed white in the night, in daylight, all day and all night and all the time. To Mother was I born and to her do I owe allegiance. Of her there must be no betrayal in a life such as mine given to the continuing recrudescence of seemingly inevitable dawn.

Seek no refuge in the minds of greatness, dominion minions. Live within your own.

Isabel, eventually I came heavy with my truth and walked a straight line to it. Said you were soulmate number one in the entire universe and later edited out "number one" as there is no other. Even so, I felt a twinge of fear and doubt. Quite possibly I had stepped over the line by overstating the case. Sentiment has no place in your life. I have witnessed your hard-hearted realism. A man whose wife initiated the divorce now making an extravagant claim as to their oneness? Really? Well, Johan, at least you didn't blurt, "The devil made me say it" or your usual nonsense.

Smoke was coming from the gallery. Ire and Fire were at it again. The code of omertà violated. How I loved to see them dance in their own hot flames before deep diving into their individual lakes of shame.

That one should receive the gift of love and proceed to spew such bile, even as he claimed the gift for himself. And yet he makes no apology. Not a shred of contrition does he display. In a brazen attempt to distort reality, he posits that mockery itself is a form of love. What can be wrong with pushing the slugs beyond their self-imposed limits? In just this way does he respond to their fury. The avowal of love, the intimacy of it, so unbearable. The cudgel, the knout, the more comfortable alternative. But know in my heart I love you all. More he will not, cannot, say, as he bolts for the door.

On the crowded streets he could hear the tall buildings talking down to him, the way their haughtiness had them do, not one of them knowing they would one day be reduced to rubble and perished from the earth.

Isabel,

I was streaking for the park, not the one always putting on airs but the one centered in its own history, and claimed my seat on a bench and looked at the boats I would never step aboard and the river I would never test and the Jersey shore I would never explore and the planes aloft that would never again take me to distant lands and the railroad tunnel of my childhood behind me that I would no longer visit, a song coming to my ears as I sat. I've got my love to keep me warm. So Frankie sang. So warm. So wonderful. Oh yes, I whispered, lest passersby overhear and snatch my happiness from me. Oh yes!

www.ingramcontent.com/pod-product-compliance
Lightning Source LLC
Chambersburg PA
CBHW062057290726
48975CB00001B/10